W.i.t.c.h.

Will   Irma   Taranée   Cornelia   Hay Lin

Part II. Nerissa's Revenge
Volume 1

Will Irma Taranee Cornelia Hay Lin

Part II. Nerissa's Revenge
Volume I

CONTENTS

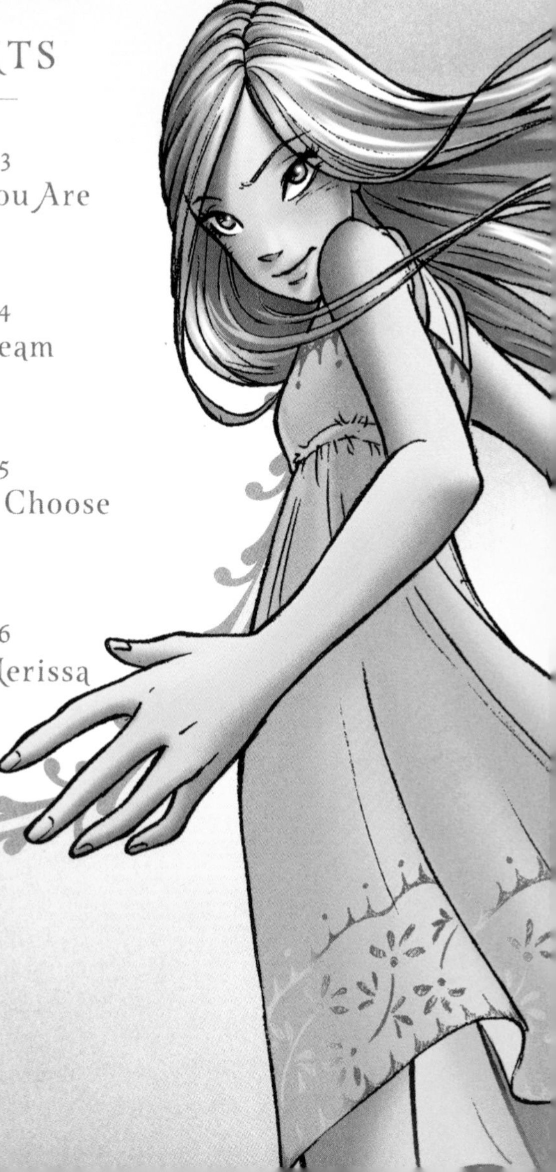

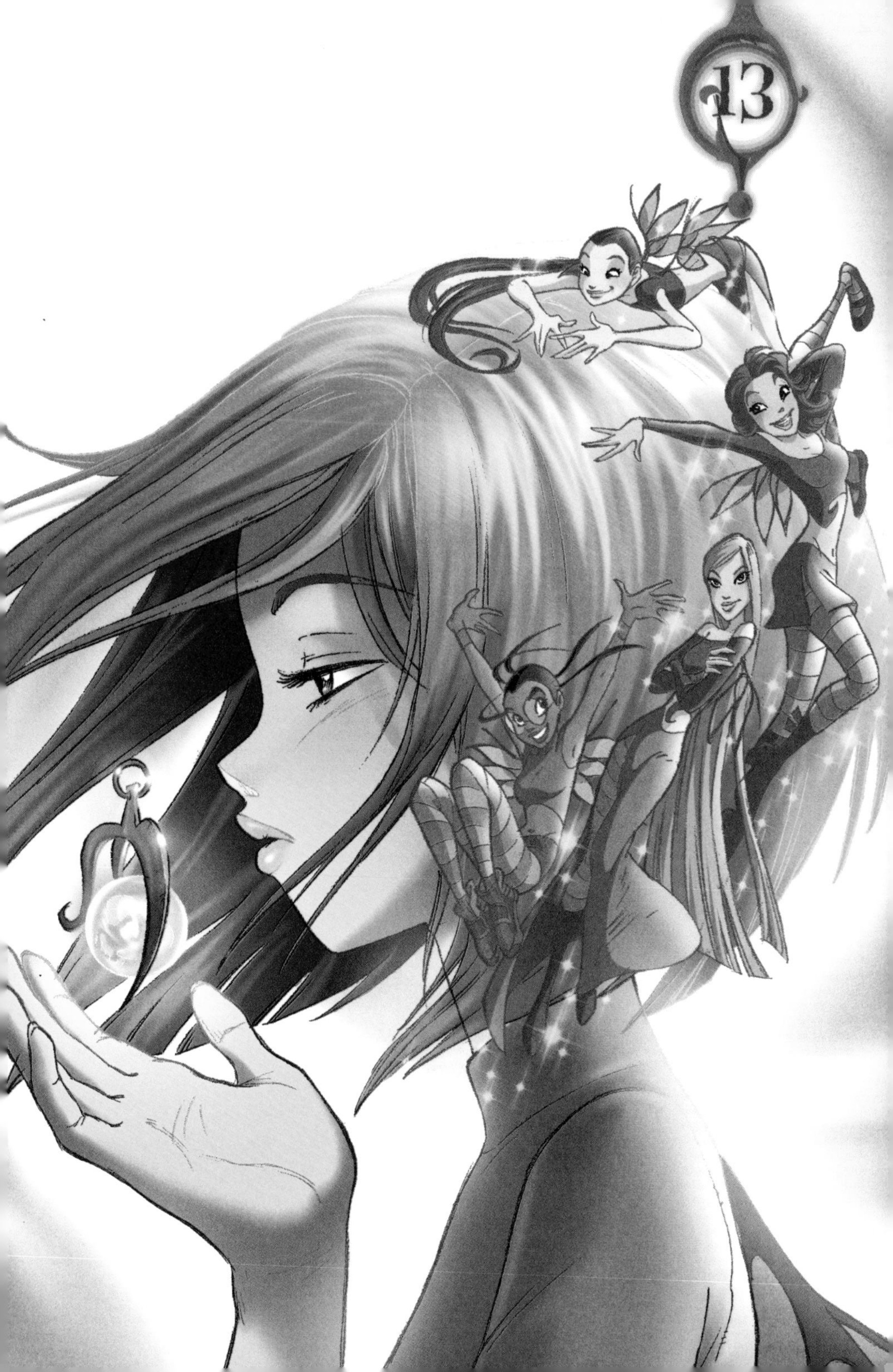
13

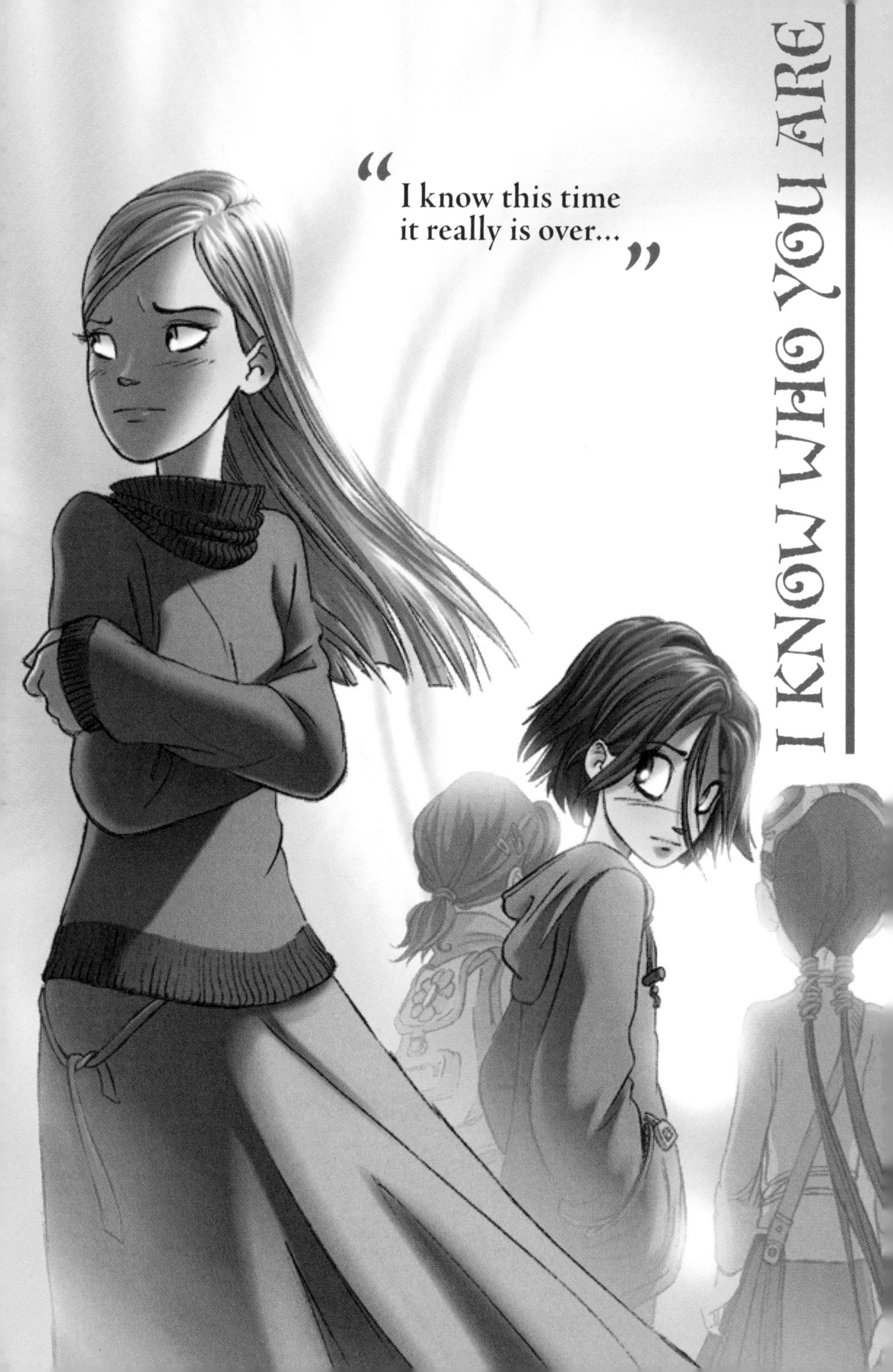
I KNOW WHO YOU ARE
"I know this time it really is over..."

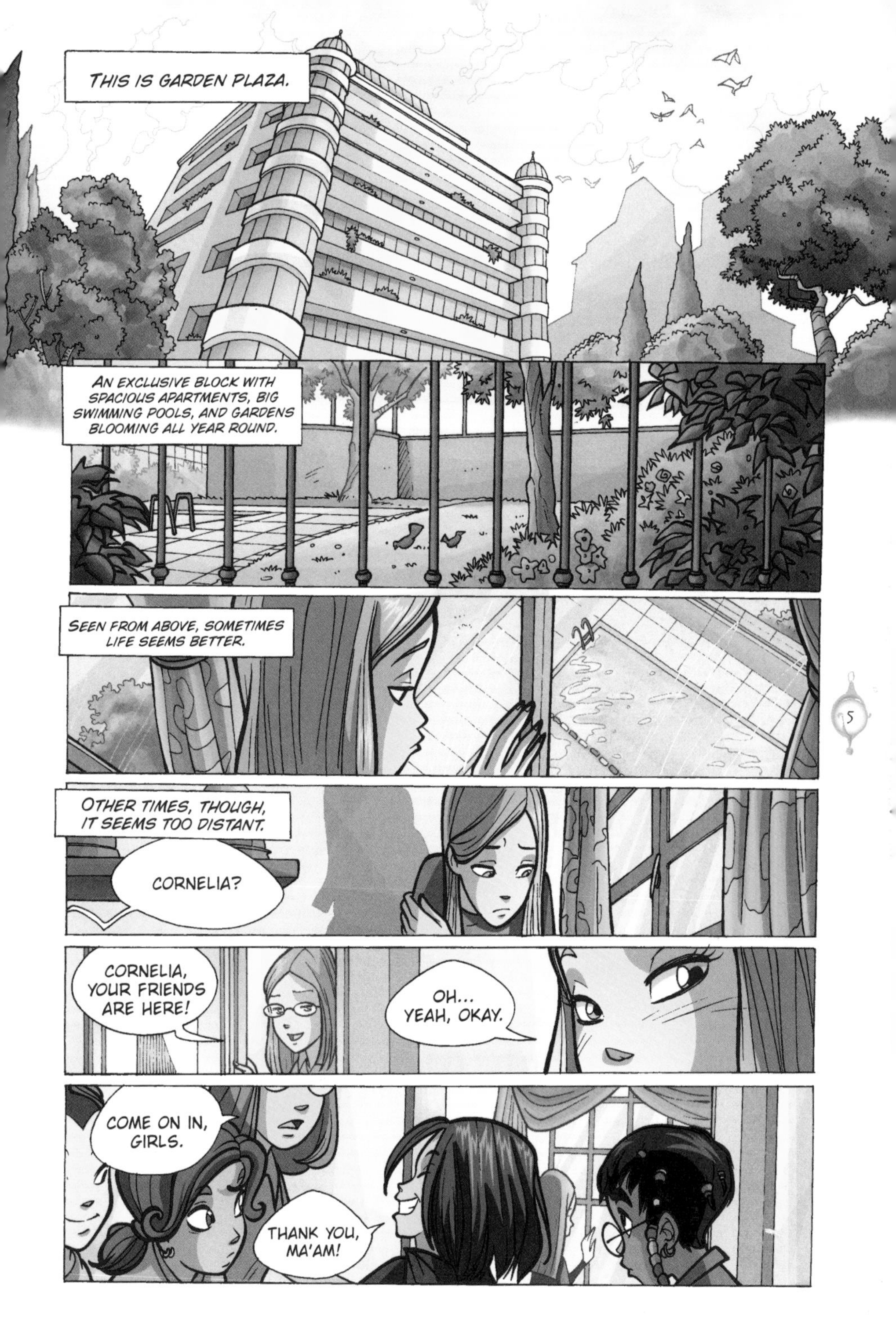
THIS IS GARDEN PLAZA.
AN EXCLUSIVE BLOCK WITH SPACIOUS APARTMENTS, BIG SWIMMING POOLS, AND GARDENS BLOOMING ALL YEAR ROUND.
SEEN FROM ABOVE, SOMETIMES LIFE SEEMS BETTER.
OTHER TIMES, THOUGH, IT SEEMS TOO DISTANT.
CORNELIA?
CORNELIA, YOUR FRIENDS ARE HERE!
OH... YEAH, OKAY.
COME ON IN, GIRLS.
THANK YOU, MA'AM!

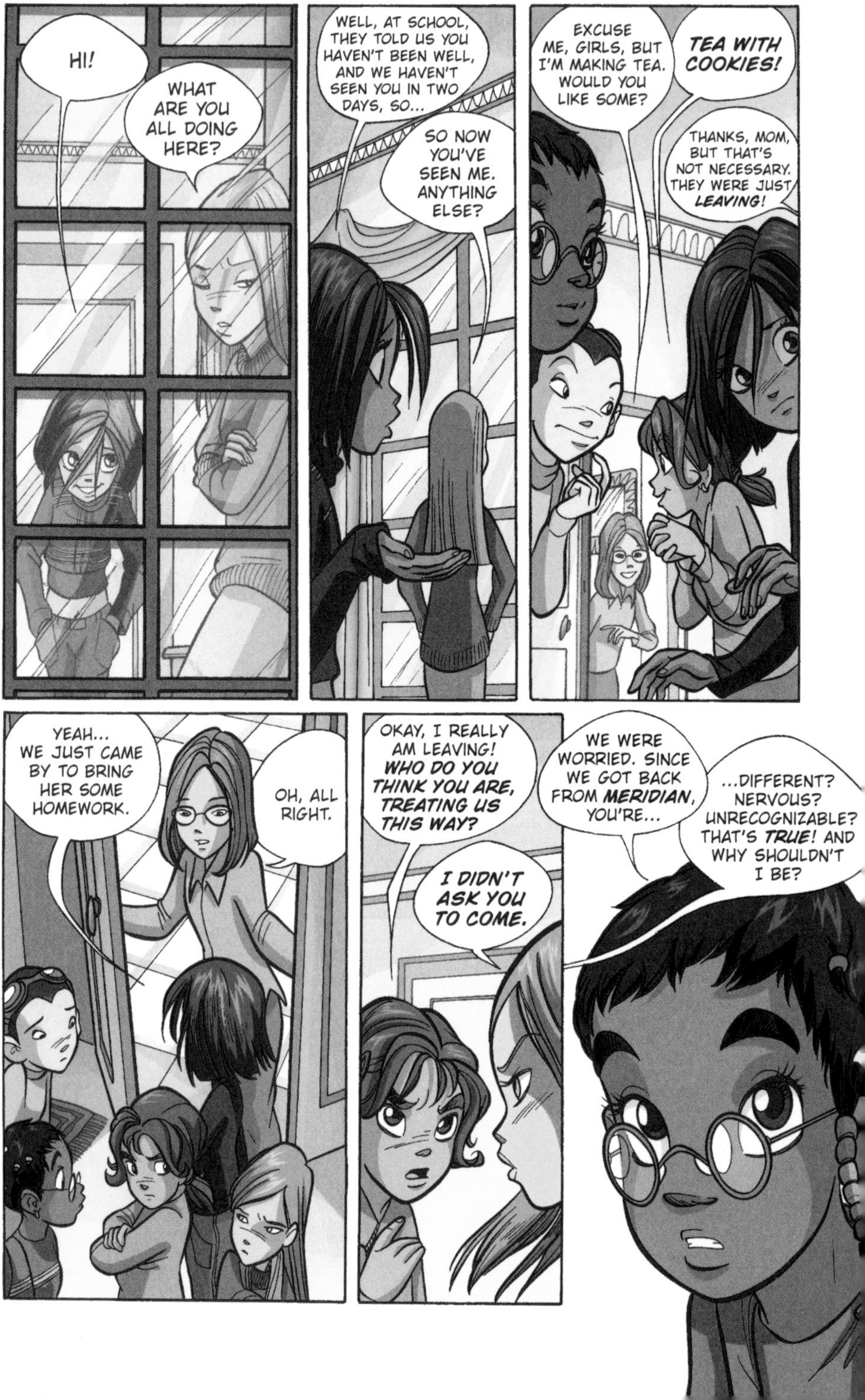
HI!
WHAT ARE YOU ALL DOING HERE?
WELL, AT SCHOOL, THEY TOLD US YOU HAVEN'T BEEN WELL, AND WE HAVEN'T SEEN YOU IN TWO DAYS, SO...
SO NOW YOU'VE SEEN ME. ANYTHING ELSE?
EXCUSE ME, GIRLS, BUT I'M MAKING TEA. WOULD YOU LIKE SOME?
TEA WITH COOKIES!
THANKS, MOM, BUT THAT'S NOT NECESSARY. THEY WERE JUST LEAVING!
YEAH... WE JUST CAME BY TO BRING HER SOME HOMEWORK.
OH, ALL RIGHT.
OKAY, I REALLY AM LEAVING! WHO DO YOU THINK YOU ARE, TREATING US THIS WAY?
I DIDN'T ASK YOU TO COME.
WE WERE WORRIED. SINCE WE GOT BACK FROM MERIDIAN, YOU'RE...
...DIFFERENT? NERVOUS? UNRECOGNIZABLE? THAT'S TRUE! AND WHY SHOULDN'T I BE?

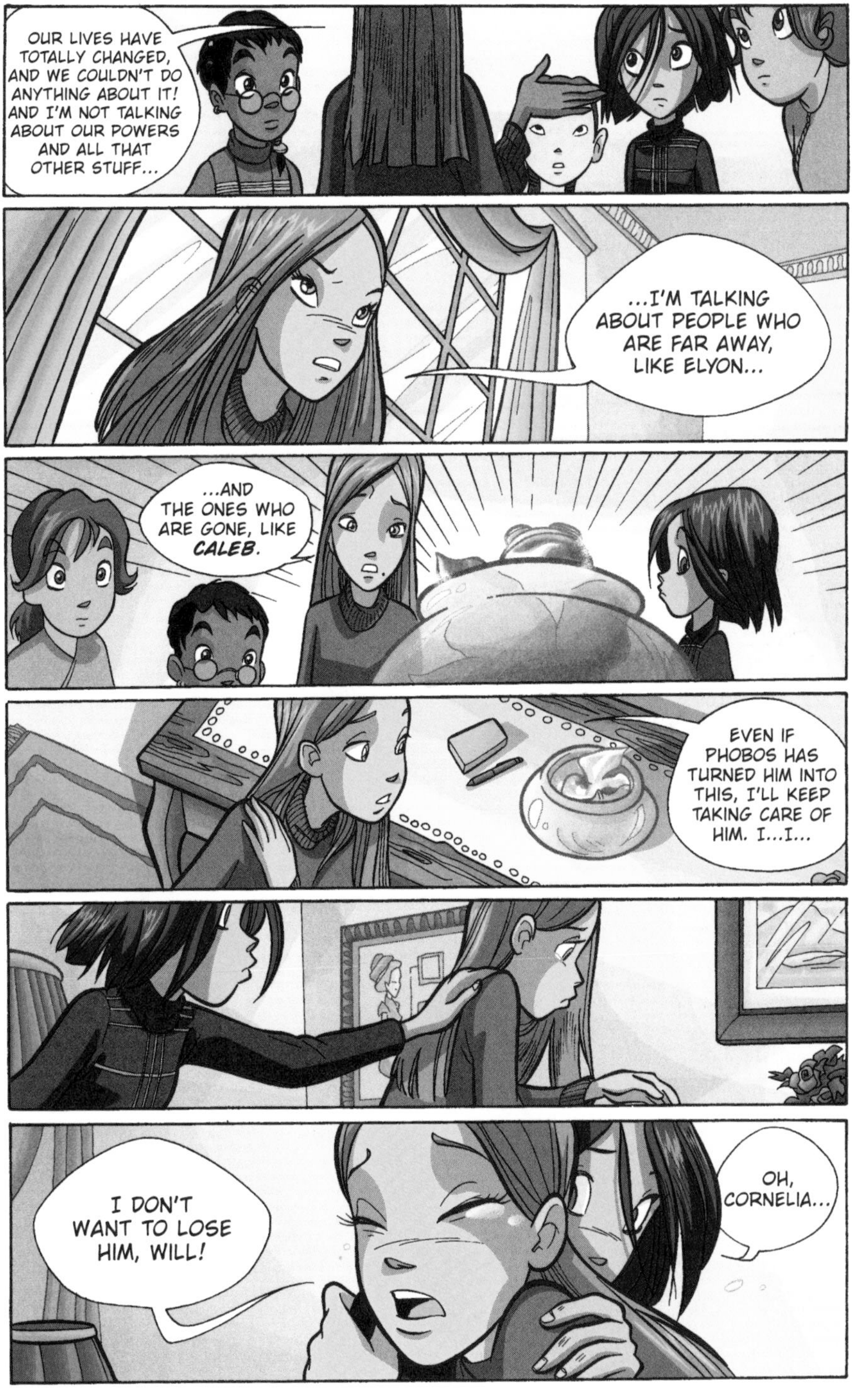
OUR LIVES HAVE TOTALLY CHANGED, AND WE COULDN'T DO ANYTHING ABOUT IT! AND I'M NOT TALKING ABOUT OUR POWERS AND ALL THAT OTHER STUFF...
...I'M TALKING ABOUT PEOPLE WHO ARE FAR AWAY, LIKE ELYON...
...AND THE ONES WHO ARE GONE, LIKE CALEB.
EVEN IF PHOBOS HAS TURNED HIM INTO THIS, I'LL KEEP TAKING CARE OF HIM. I...I...
I DON'T WANT TO LOSE HIM, WILL!
OH, CORNELIA...

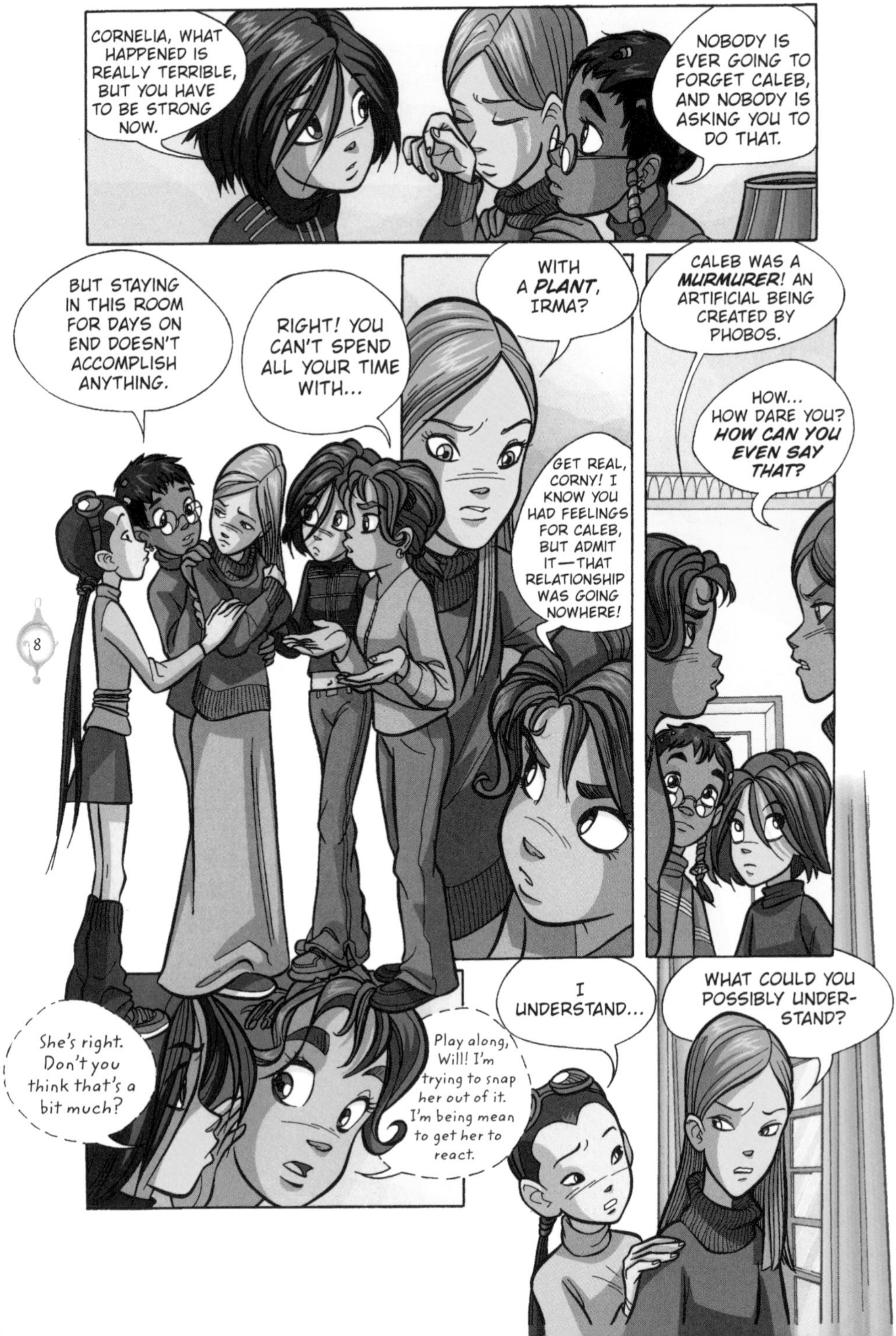
CORNELIA, WHAT HAPPENED IS REALLY TERRIBLE, BUT YOU HAVE TO BE STRONG NOW.
NOBODY IS EVER GOING TO FORGET CALEB, AND NOBODY IS ASKING YOU TO DO THAT.
BUT STAYING IN THIS ROOM FOR DAYS ON END DOESN'T ACCOMPLISH ANYTHING.
RIGHT! YOU CAN'T SPEND ALL YOUR TIME WITH...
WITH A *PLANT*, IRMA?
GET REAL, CORNY! I KNOW YOU HAD FEELINGS FOR CALEB, BUT ADMIT IT—THAT RELATIONSHIP WAS GOING NOWHERE!
CALEB WAS A ***MURMURER***! AN ARTIFICIAL BEING CREATED BY PHOBOS.
HOW... HOW DARE YOU? ***HOW CAN YOU EVEN SAY THAT?***
She's right. Don't you think that's a bit much?
Play along, Will! I'm trying to snap her out of it. I'm being mean to get her to react.
I UNDERSTAND...
WHAT COULD YOU POSSIBLY UNDERSTAND?

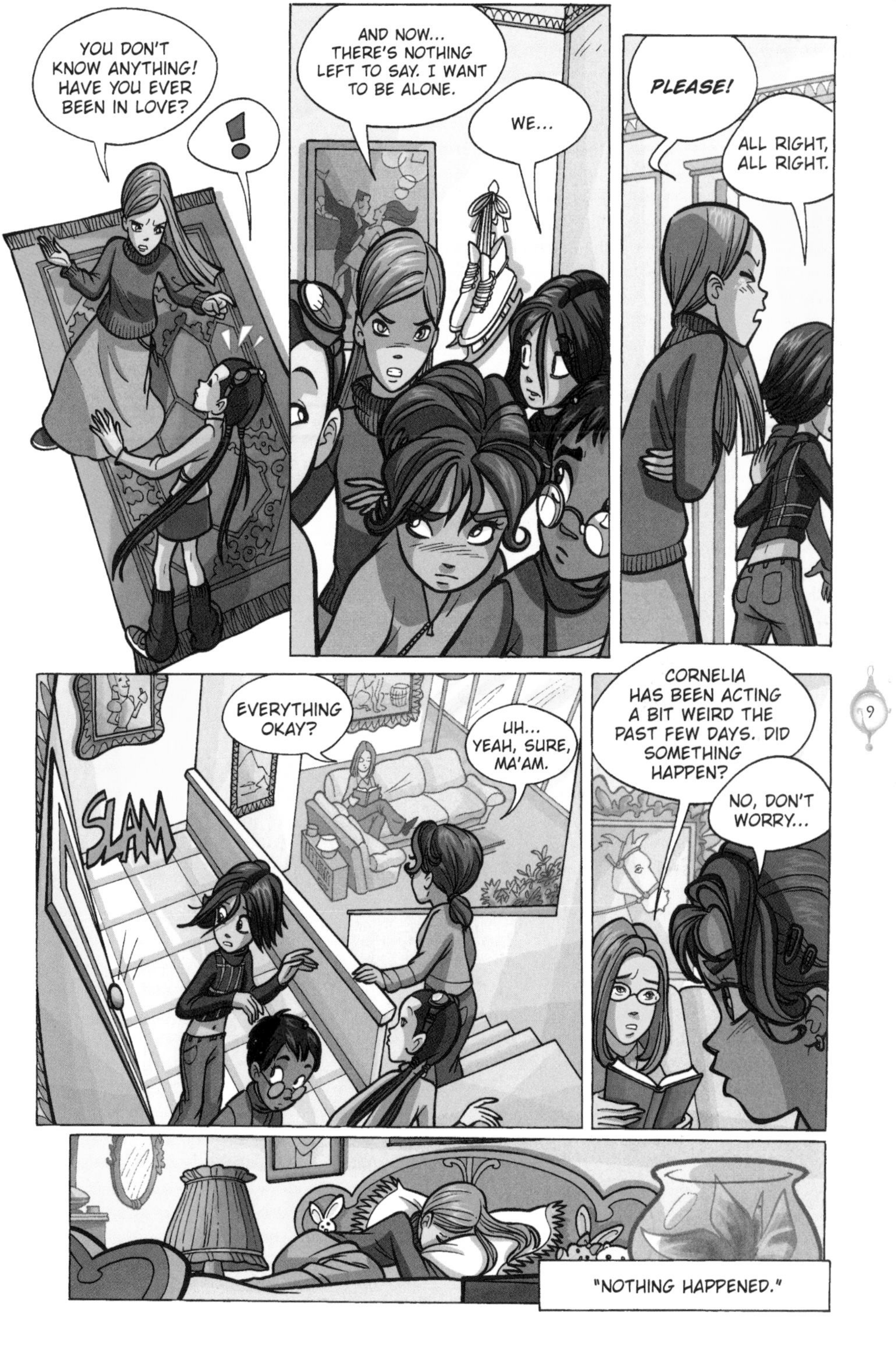
YOU DON'T KNOW ANYTHING! HAVE YOU EVER BEEN IN LOVE?
!
AND NOW... THERE'S NOTHING LEFT TO SAY. I WANT TO BE ALONE.
WE...
PLEASE!
ALL RIGHT, ALL RIGHT.
SLAM
EVERYTHING OKAY?
UH... YEAH, SURE, MA'AM.
CORNELIA HAS BEEN ACTING A BIT WEIRD THE PAST FEW DAYS. DID SOMETHING HAPPEN?
NO, DON'T WORRY...
"NOTHING HAPPENED."

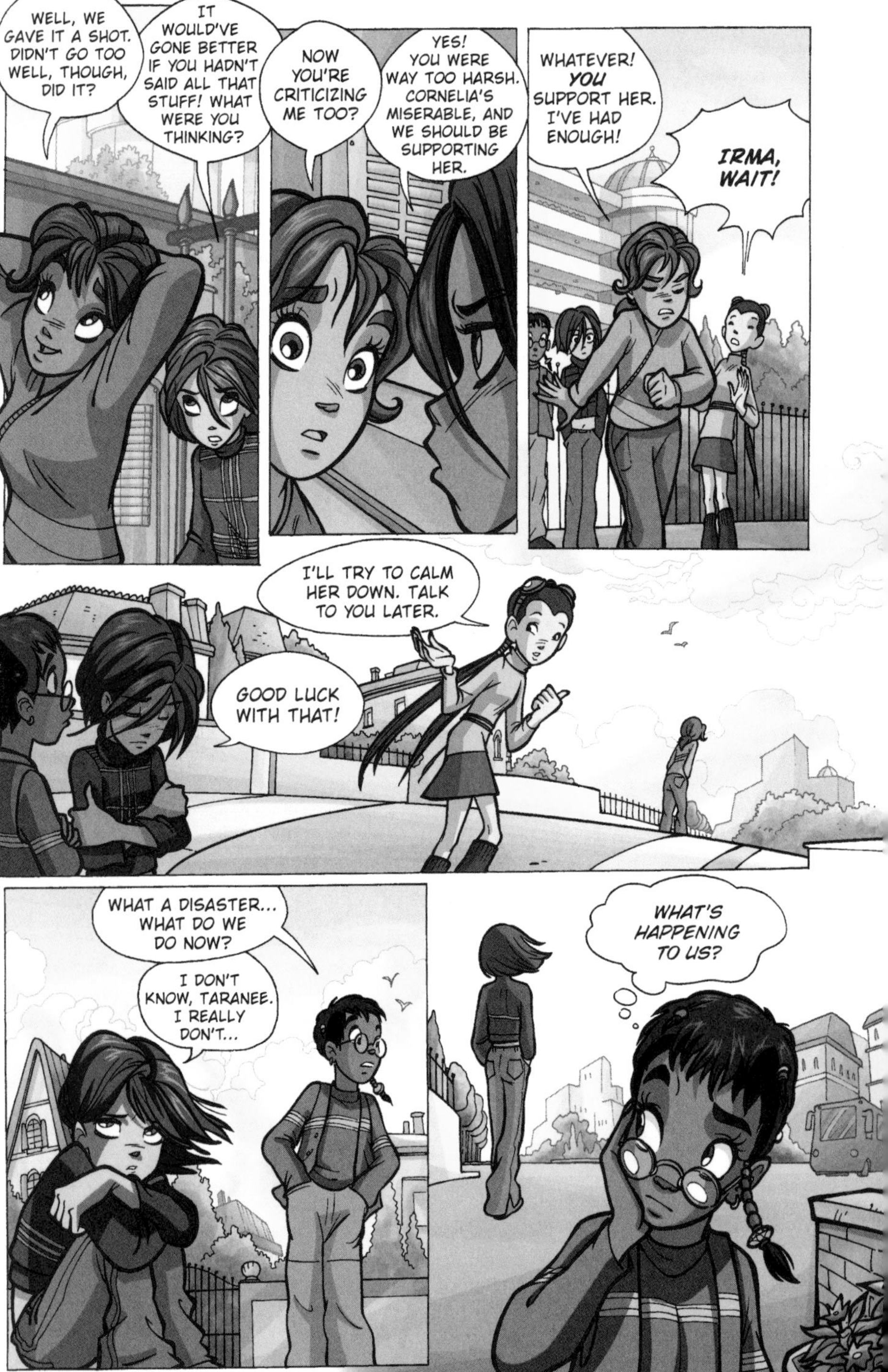
WELL, WE GAVE IT A SHOT. DIDN'T GO TOO WELL, THOUGH, DID IT?
IT WOULD'VE GONE BETTER IF YOU HADN'T SAID ALL THAT STUFF! WHAT WERE YOU THINKING?
NOW YOU'RE CRITICIZING ME TOO?
YES! YOU WERE WAY TOO HARSH. CORNELIA'S MISERABLE, AND WE SHOULD BE SUPPORTING HER.
WHATEVER! YOU SUPPORT HER. I'VE HAD ENOUGH!
IRMA, WAIT!
I'LL TRY TO CALM HER DOWN. TALK TO YOU LATER.
GOOD LUCK WITH THAT!
WHAT A DISASTER... WHAT DO WE DO NOW?
I DON'T KNOW, TARANEE. I REALLY DON'T...
WHAT'S HAPPENING TO US?

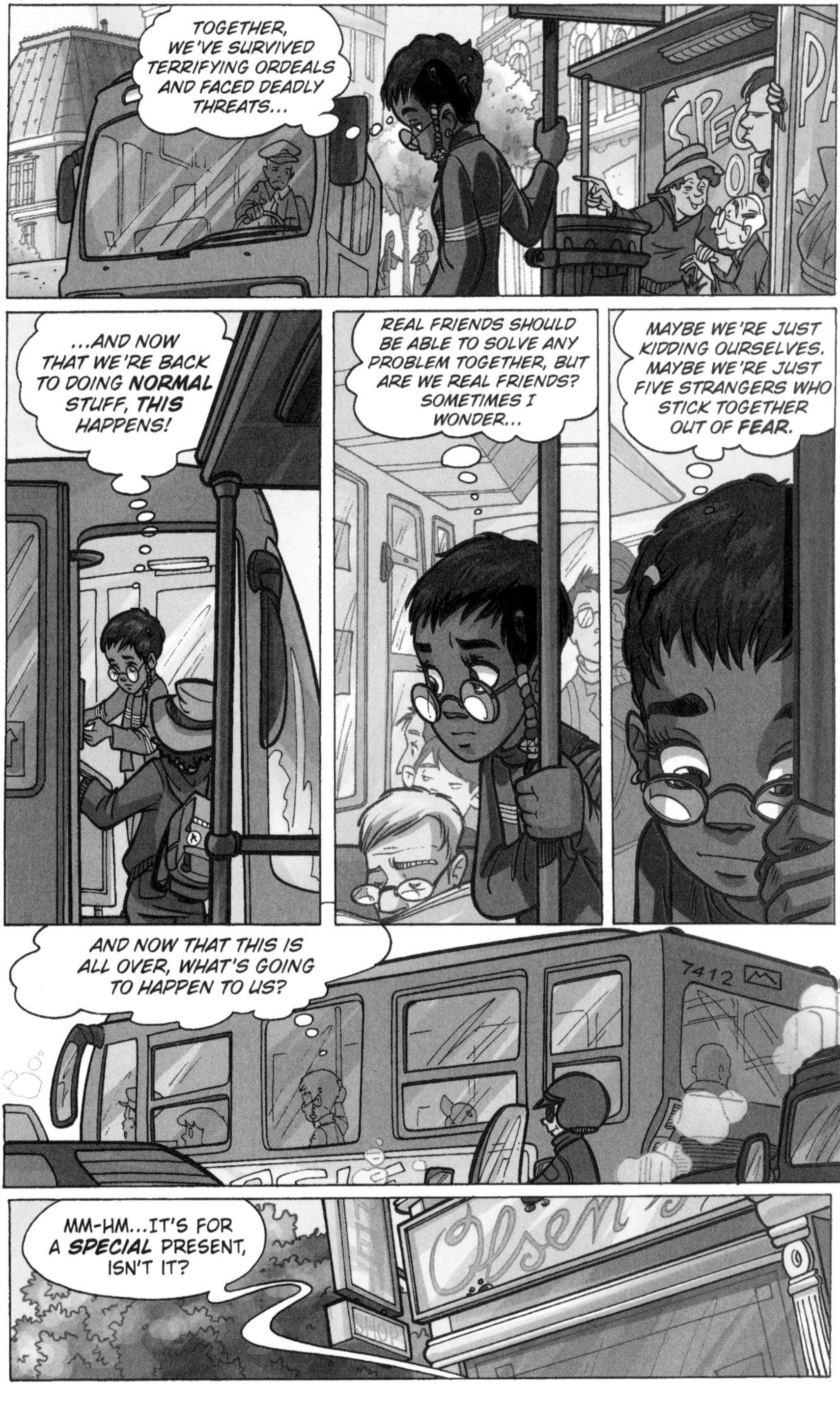

TOGETHER, WE'VE SURVIVED TERRIFYING ORDEALS AND FACED DEADLY THREATS...
...AND NOW THAT WE'RE BACK TO DOING NORMAL STUFF, THIS HAPPENS!
REAL FRIENDS SHOULD BE ABLE TO SOLVE ANY PROBLEM TOGETHER, BUT ARE WE REAL FRIENDS? SOMETIMES I WONDER...
MAYBE WE'RE JUST KIDDING OURSELVES. MAYBE WE'RE JUST FIVE STRANGERS WHO STICK TOGETHER OUT OF FEAR.
AND NOW THAT THIS IS ALL OVER, WHAT'S GOING TO HAPPEN TO US?
7412
MM-HM...IT'S FOR A SPECIAL PRESENT, ISN'T IT?
Olsen's
SHOP

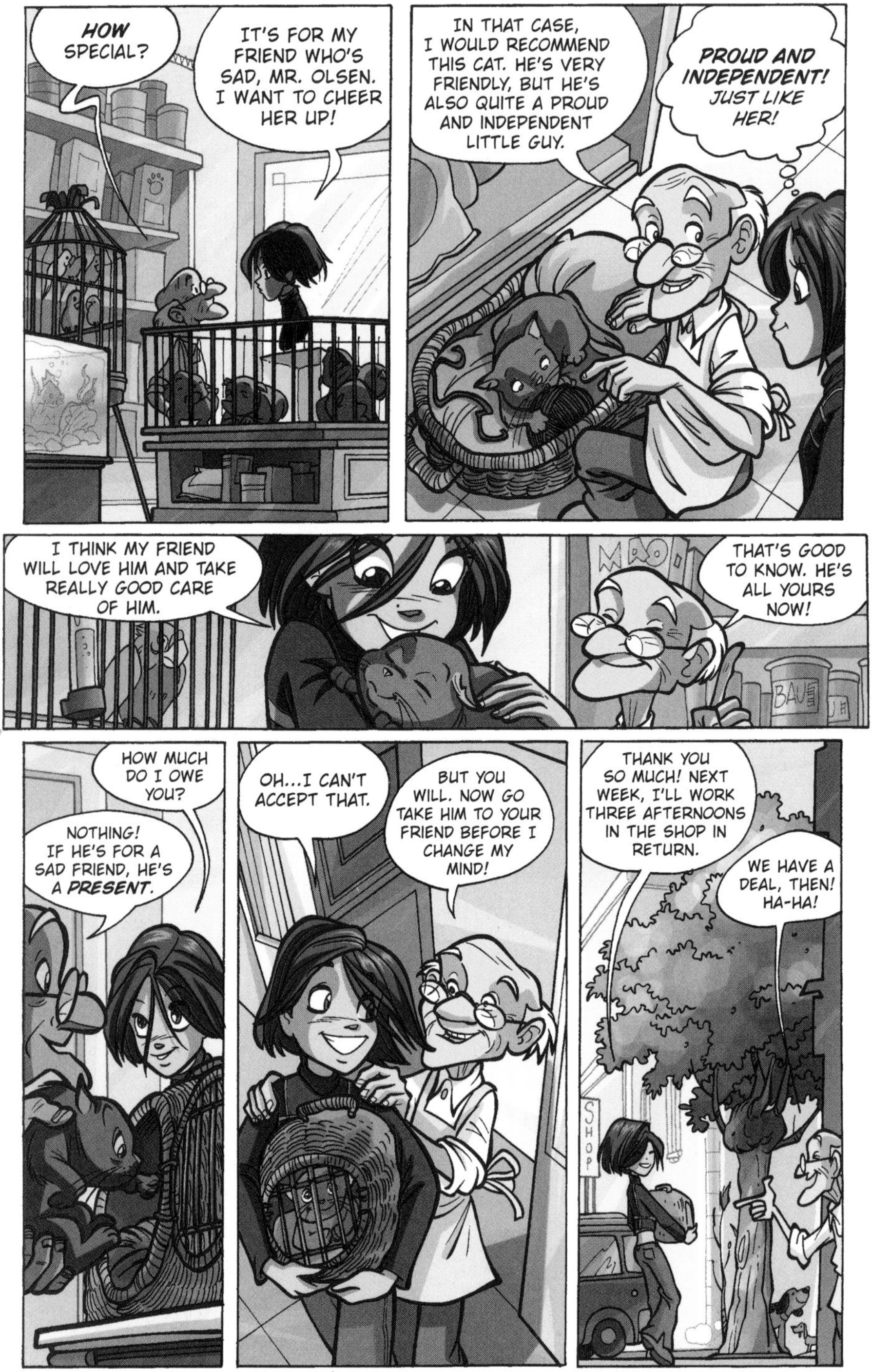
HOW SPECIAL?
IT'S FOR MY FRIEND WHO'S SAD, MR. OLSEN. I WANT TO CHEER HER UP!
IN THAT CASE, I WOULD RECOMMEND THIS CAT. HE'S VERY FRIENDLY, BUT HE'S ALSO QUITE A PROUD AND INDEPENDENT LITTLE GUY.
PROUD AND INDEPENDENT! JUST LIKE HER!
I THINK MY FRIEND WILL LOVE HIM AND TAKE REALLY GOOD CARE OF HIM.
THAT'S GOOD TO KNOW. HE'S ALL YOURS NOW!
HOW MUCH DO I OWE YOU?
NOTHING! IF HE'S FOR A SAD FRIEND, HE'S A PRESENT.
OH...I CAN'T ACCEPT THAT.
BUT YOU WILL. NOW GO TAKE HIM TO YOUR FRIEND BEFORE I CHANGE MY MIND!
THANK YOU SO MUCH! NEXT WEEK, I'LL WORK THREE AFTERNOONS IN THE SHOP IN RETURN.
WE HAVE A DEAL, THEN! HA-HA!

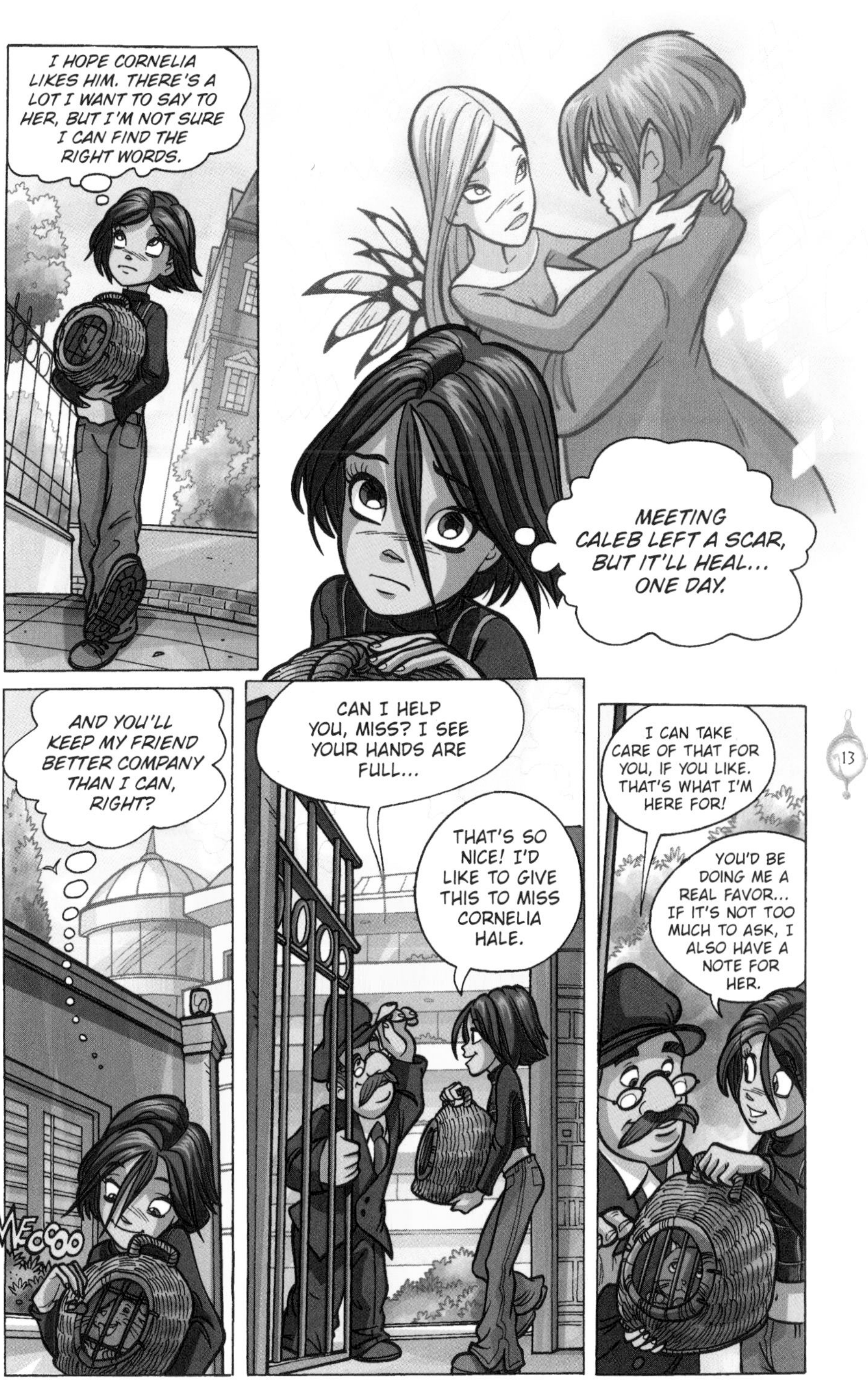
I HOPE CORNELIA LIKES HIM. THERE'S A LOT I WANT TO SAY TO HER, BUT I'M NOT SURE I CAN FIND THE RIGHT WORDS.
MEETING CALEB LEFT A SCAR, BUT IT'LL HEAL... ONE DAY.
AND YOU'LL KEEP MY FRIEND BETTER COMPANY THAN I CAN, RIGHT?
MEOOOO
CAN I HELP YOU, MISS? I SEE YOUR HANDS ARE FULL...
THAT'S SO NICE! I'D LIKE TO GIVE THIS TO MISS CORNELIA HALE.
I CAN TAKE CARE OF THAT FOR YOU, IF YOU LIKE. THAT'S WHAT I'M HERE FOR!
YOU'D BE DOING ME A REAL FAVOR... IF IT'S NOT TOO MUCH TO ASK, I ALSO HAVE A NOTE FOR HER.

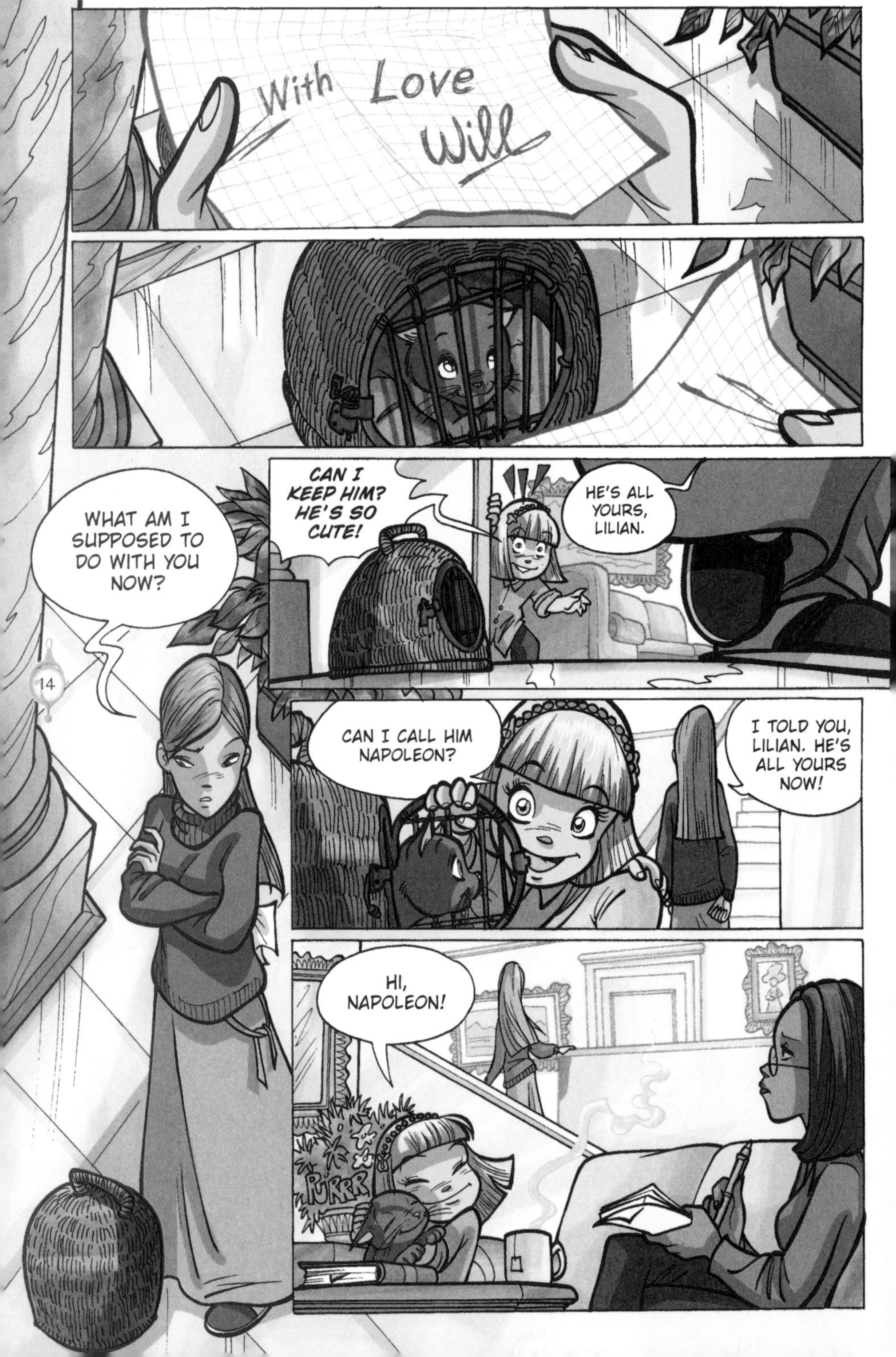

With Love
Will
WHAT AM I SUPPOSED TO DO WITH YOU NOW?
CAN I KEEP HIM? HE'S SO CUTE!
HE'S ALL YOURS, LILIAN.
CAN I CALL HIM NAPOLEON?
I TOLD YOU, LILIAN. HE'S ALL YOURS NOW!
HI, NAPOLEON!
PURRR

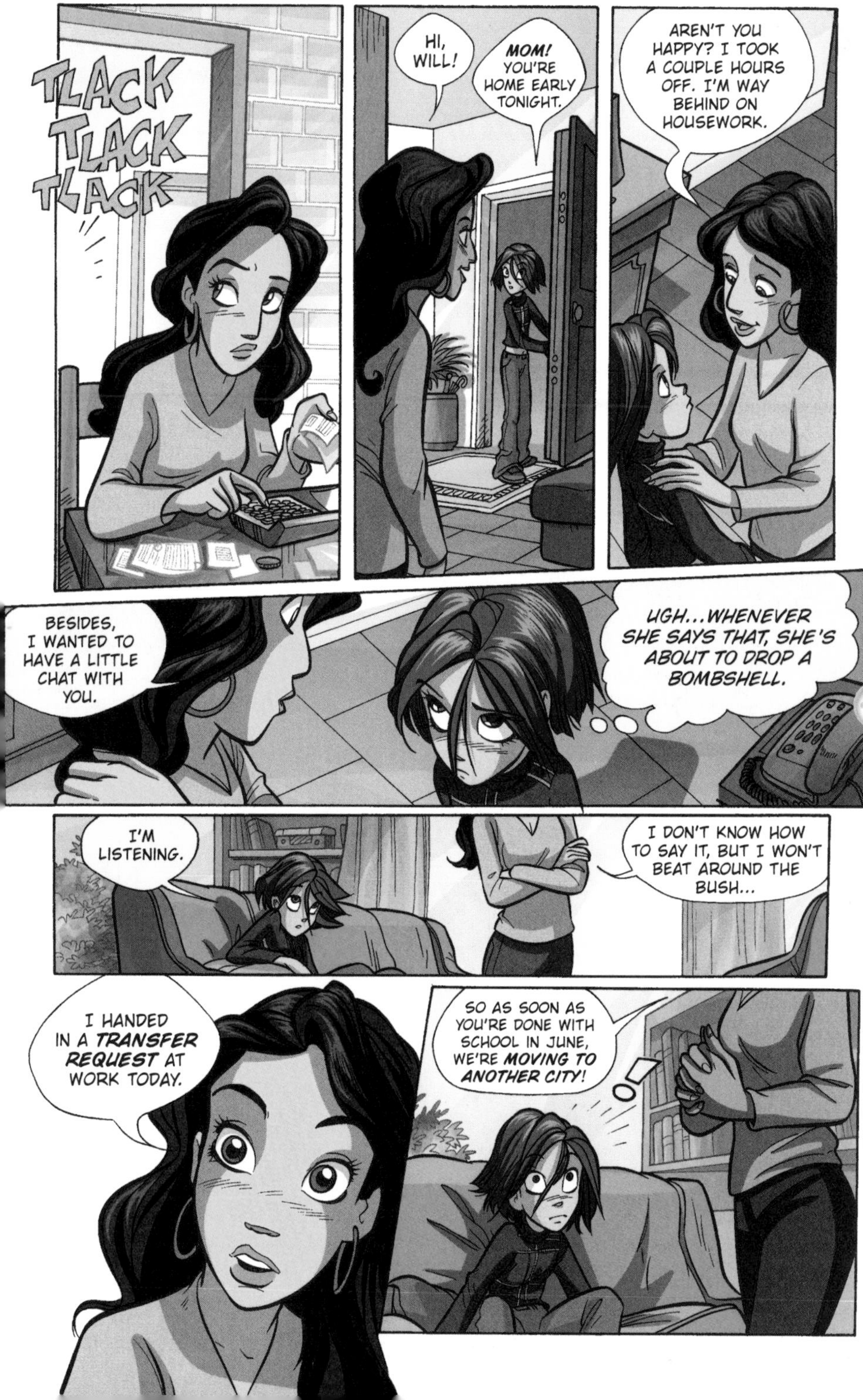
TLACK TLACK TLACK
HI, WILL!
MOM! YOU'RE HOME EARLY TONIGHT.
AREN'T YOU HAPPY? I TOOK A COUPLE HOURS OFF. I'M WAY BEHIND ON HOUSEWORK.
BESIDES, I WANTED TO HAVE A LITTLE CHAT WITH YOU.
UGH...WHENEVER SHE SAYS THAT, SHE'S ABOUT TO DROP A BOMBSHELL.
I'M LISTENING.
I DON'T KNOW HOW TO SAY IT, BUT I WON'T BEAT AROUND THE BUSH...
I HANDED IN A TRANSFER REQUEST AT WORK TODAY.
SO AS SOON AS YOU'RE DONE WITH SCHOOL IN JUNE, WE'RE MOVING TO ANOTHER CITY!
!

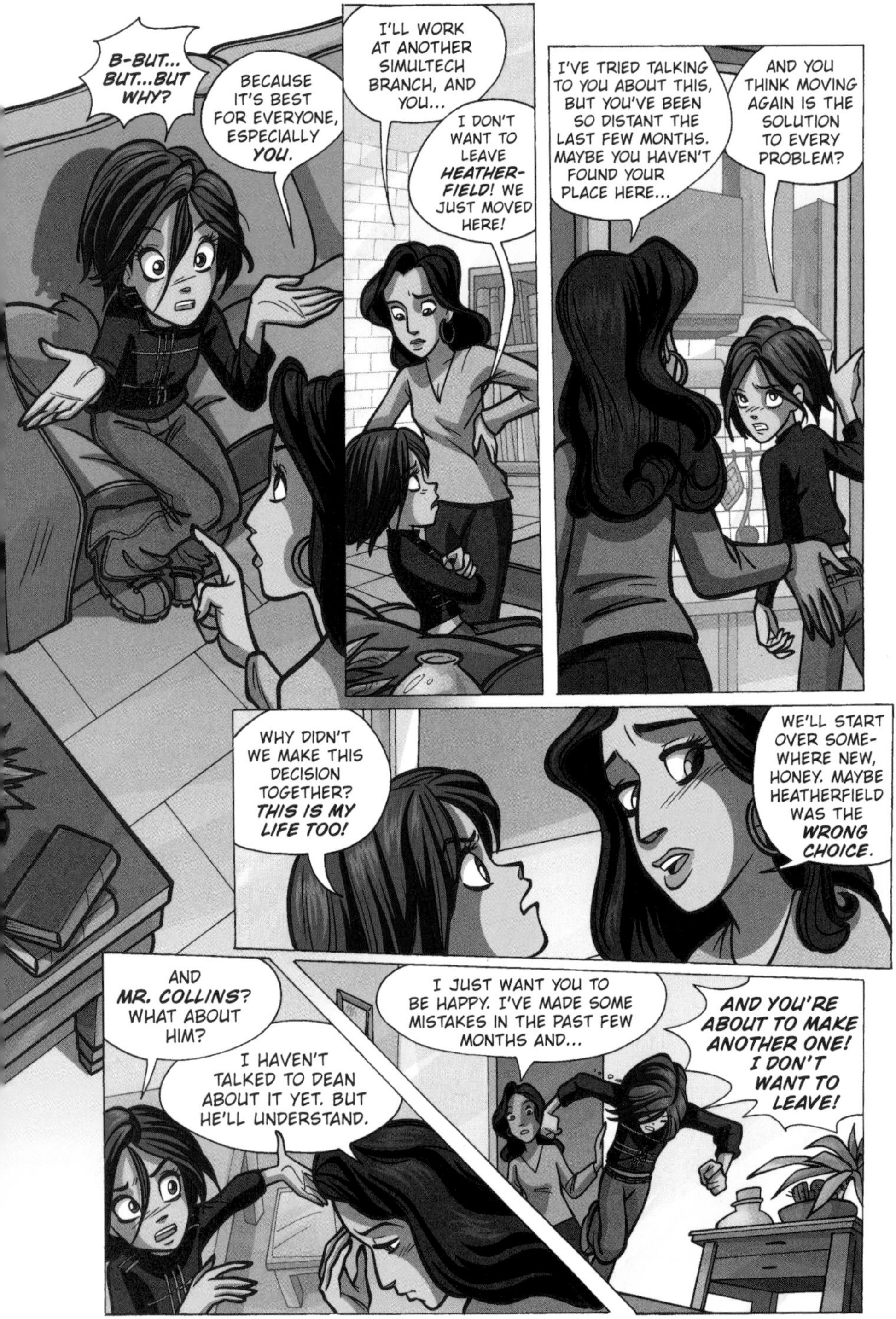

B-BUT... BUT...BUT WHY?
BECAUSE IT'S BEST FOR EVERYONE, ESPECIALLY *YOU*.
I'LL WORK AT ANOTHER SIMULTECH BRANCH, AND YOU...
I DON'T WANT TO LEAVE *HEATHERFIELD!* WE JUST MOVED HERE!
I'VE TRIED TALKING TO YOU ABOUT THIS, BUT YOU'VE BEEN SO DISTANT THE LAST FEW MONTHS. MAYBE YOU HAVEN'T FOUND YOUR PLACE HERE...
AND YOU THINK MOVING AGAIN IS THE SOLUTION TO EVERY PROBLEM?
WHY DIDN'T WE MAKE THIS DECISION TOGETHER? *THIS IS MY LIFE TOO!*
WE'LL START OVER SOMEWHERE NEW, HONEY. MAYBE HEATHERFIELD WAS THE *WRONG CHOICE*.
AND *MR. COLLINS*? WHAT ABOUT HIM?
I HAVEN'T TALKED TO DEAN ABOUT IT YET. BUT HE'LL UNDERSTAND.
I JUST WANT YOU TO BE HAPPY. I'VE MADE SOME MISTAKES IN THE PAST FEW MONTHS AND...
AND YOU'RE ABOUT TO MAKE ANOTHER ONE! I DON'T WANT TO LEAVE!

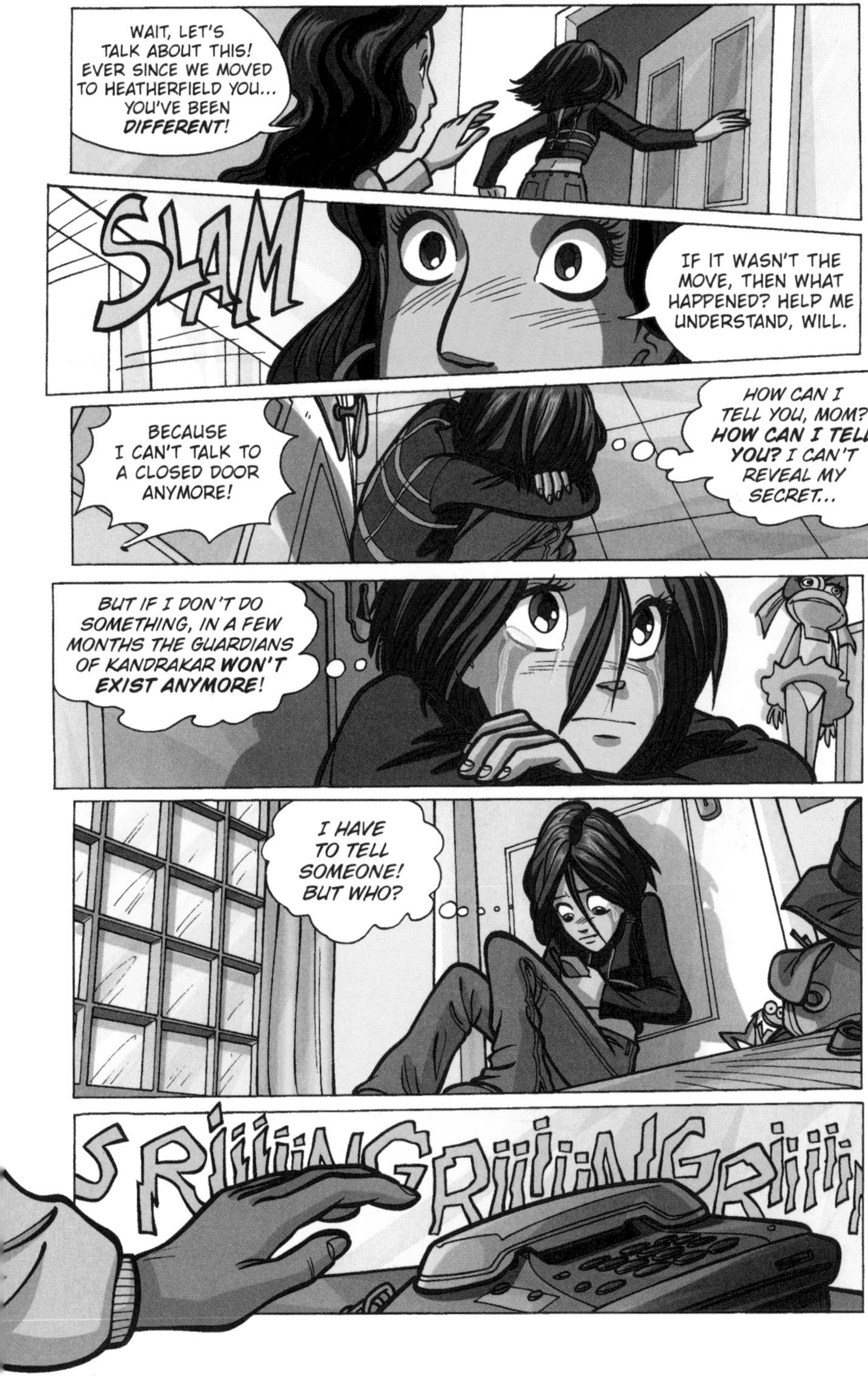
WAIT, LET'S TALK ABOUT THIS! EVER SINCE WE MOVED TO HEATHERFIELD YOU... YOU'VE BEEN DIFFERENT!
SLAM
IF IT WASN'T THE MOVE, THEN WHAT HAPPENED? HELP ME UNDERSTAND, WILL.
BECAUSE I CAN'T TALK TO A CLOSED DOOR ANYMORE!
HOW CAN I TELL YOU, MOM? HOW CAN I TELL YOU? I CAN'T REVEAL MY SECRET...
BUT IF I DON'T DO SOMETHING, IN A FEW MONTHS THE GUARDIANS OF KANDRAKAR WON'T EXIST ANYMORE!
I HAVE TO TELL SOMEONE! BUT WHO?
SRIIIING GRIIIING GRIIII

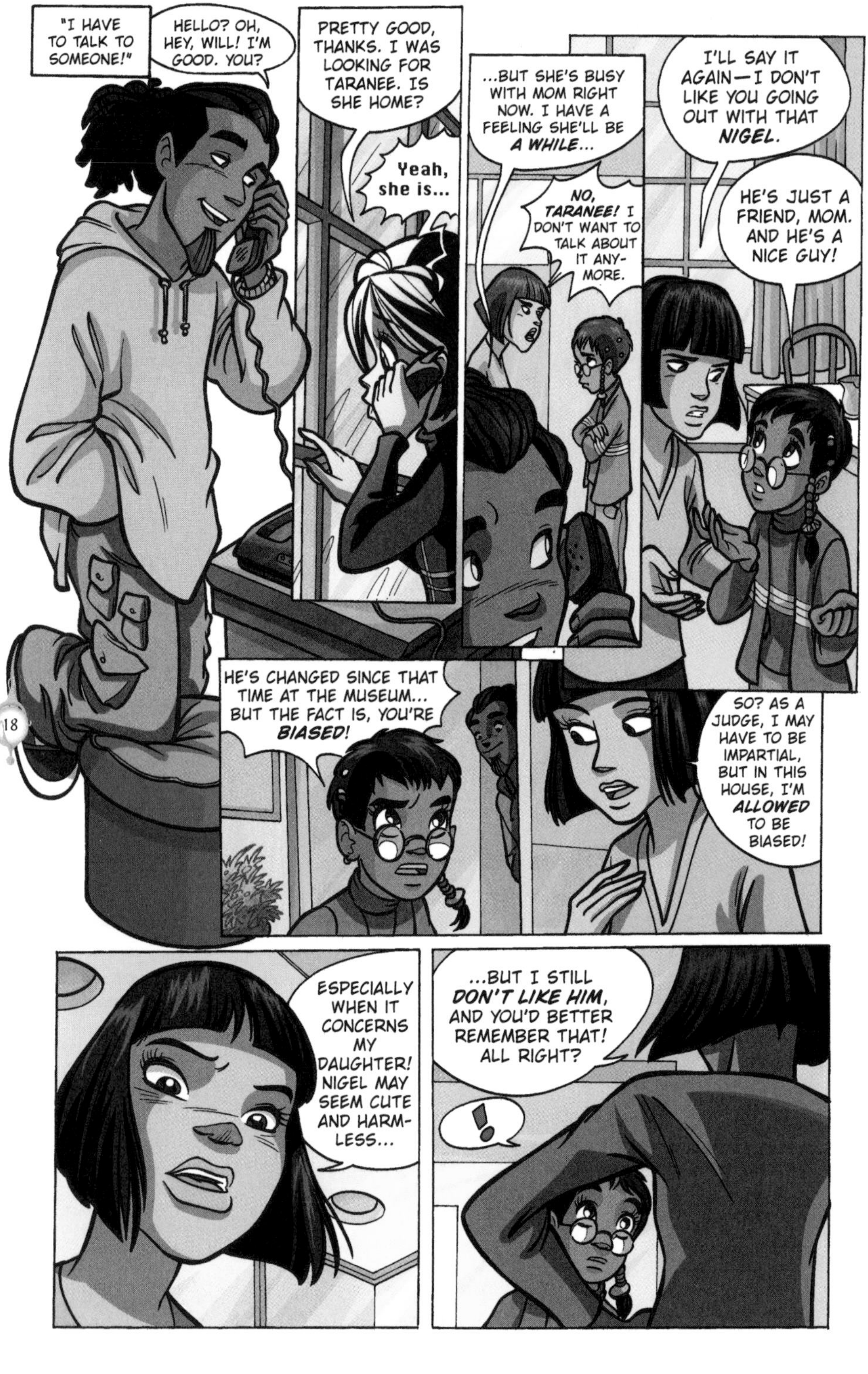
"I HAVE TO TALK TO SOMEONE!"
HELLO? OH, HEY, WILL! I'M GOOD. YOU?
PRETTY GOOD, THANKS. I WAS LOOKING FOR TARANEE. IS SHE HOME?
Yeah, she is...
...BUT SHE'S BUSY WITH MOM RIGHT NOW. I HAVE A FEELING SHE'LL BE *A WHILE*...
NO, TARANEE! I DON'T WANT TO TALK ABOUT IT ANY-MORE.
I'LL SAY IT AGAIN—I DON'T LIKE YOU GOING OUT WITH THAT *NIGEL*.
HE'S JUST A FRIEND, MOM. AND HE'S A NICE GUY!
HE'S CHANGED SINCE THAT TIME AT THE MUSEUM... BUT THE FACT IS, YOU'RE *BIASED*!
SO? AS A JUDGE, I MAY HAVE TO BE IMPARTIAL, BUT IN THIS HOUSE, I'M *ALLOWED* TO BE BIASED!
ESPECIALLY WHEN IT CONCERNS MY DAUGHTER! NIGEL MAY SEEM CUTE AND HARM-LESS...
...BUT I STILL *DON'T LIKE HIM*, AND YOU'D BETTER REMEMBER THAT! ALL RIGHT?
!

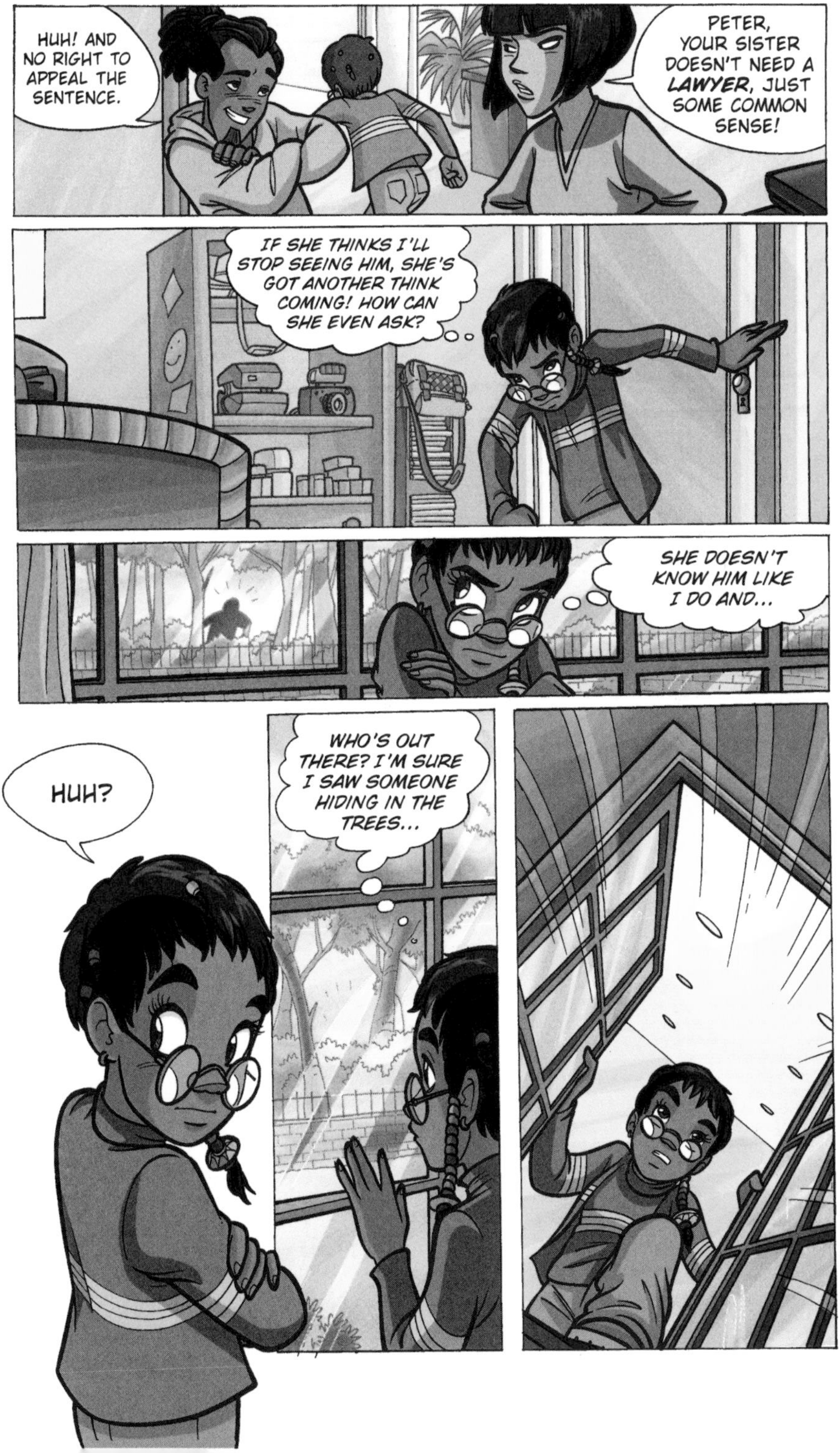
HUH! AND NO RIGHT TO APPEAL THE SENTENCE.
PETER, YOUR SISTER DOESN'T NEED A LAWYER, JUST SOME COMMON SENSE!
IF SHE THINKS I'LL STOP SEEING HIM, SHE'S GOT ANOTHER THINK COMING! HOW CAN SHE EVEN ASK?
SHE DOESN'T KNOW HIM LIKE I DO AND...
HUH?
WHO'S OUT THERE? I'M SURE I SAW SOMEONE HIDING IN THE TREES...

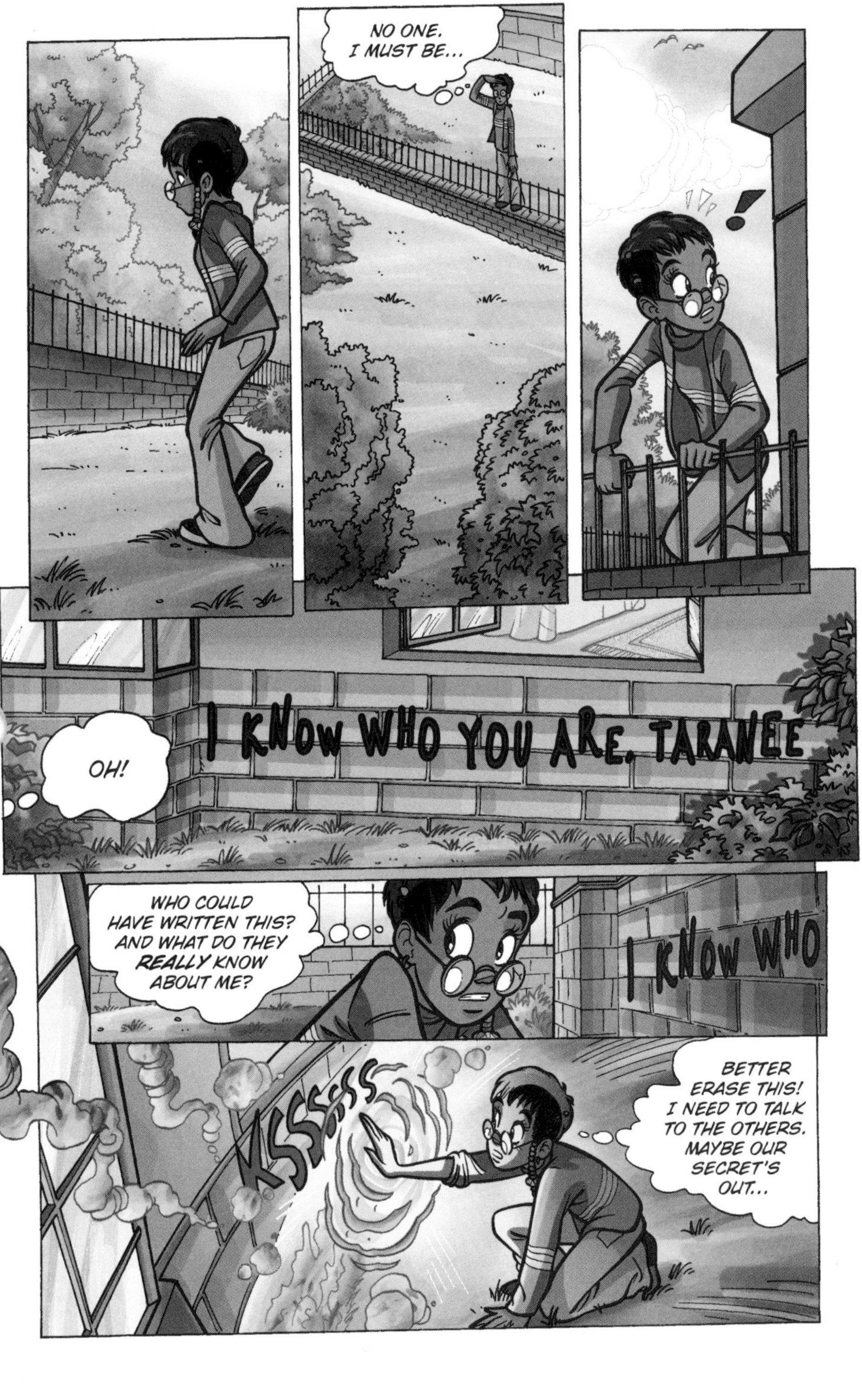
NO ONE.
I MUST BE...
I KNOW WHO YOU ARE, TARANEE
OH!
WHO COULD HAVE WRITTEN THIS? AND WHAT DO THEY REALLY KNOW ABOUT ME?
I KNOW WHO
KSSSSSS
BETTER ERASE THIS! I NEED TO TALK TO THE OTHERS. MAYBE OUR SECRET'S OUT...

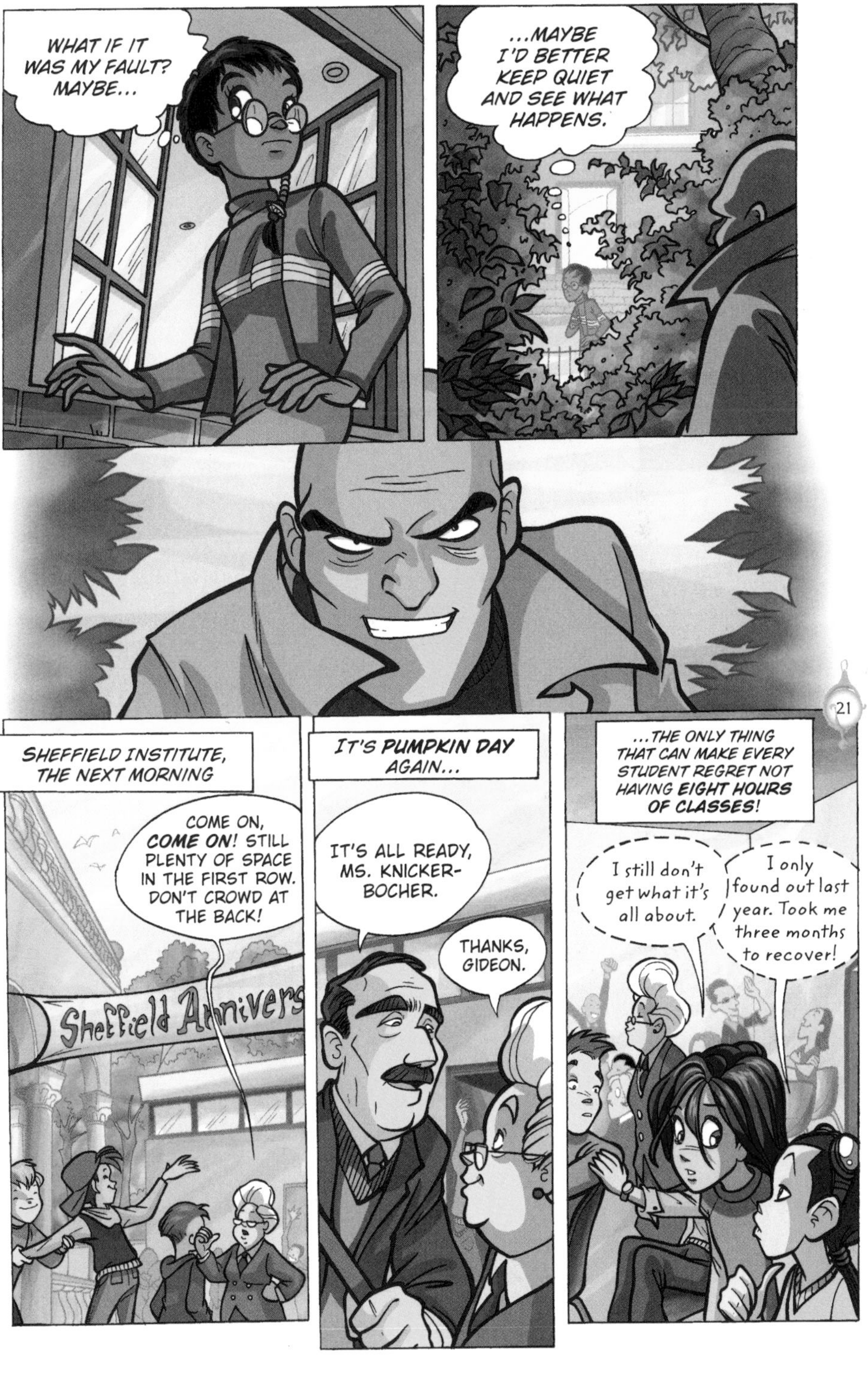
WHAT IF IT WAS MY FAULT? MAYBE...
...MAYBE I'D BETTER KEEP QUIET AND SEE WHAT HAPPENS.
SHEFFIELD INSTITUTE, THE NEXT MORNING
COME ON, COME ON! STILL PLENTY OF SPACE IN THE FIRST ROW. DON'T CROWD AT THE BACK!
Sheffield Annivers
IT'S PUMPKIN DAY AGAIN...
IT'S ALL READY, MS. KNICKER-BOCHER.
THANKS, GIDEON.
...THE ONLY THING THAT CAN MAKE EVERY STUDENT REGRET NOT HAVING EIGHT HOURS OF CLASSES!
I still don't get what it's all about.
I only found out last year. Took me three months to recover!

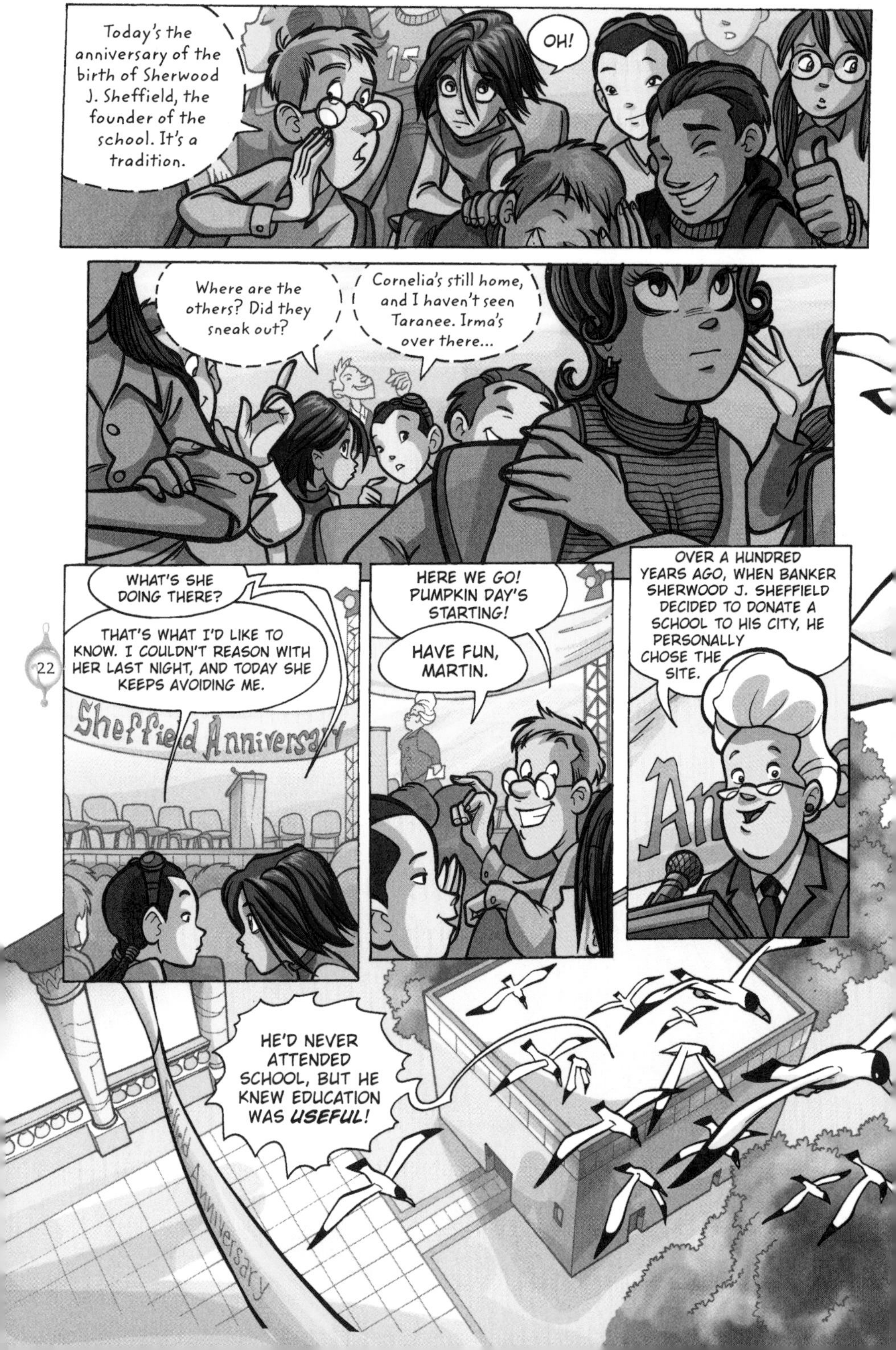

Today's the anniversary of the birth of Sherwood J. Sheffield, the founder of the school. It's a tradition.
OH!
Where are the others? Did they sneak out?
Cornelia's still home, and I haven't seen Taranee. Irma's over there...
WHAT'S SHE DOING THERE?
THAT'S WHAT I'D LIKE TO KNOW. I COULDN'T REASON WITH HER LAST NIGHT, AND TODAY SHE KEEPS AVOIDING ME.
Sheffield Anniversary
HERE WE GO! PUMPKIN DAY'S STARTING!
HAVE FUN, MARTIN.
OVER A HUNDRED YEARS AGO, WHEN BANKER SHERWOOD J. SHEFFIELD DECIDED TO DONATE A SCHOOL TO HIS CITY, HE PERSONALLY CHOSE THE SITE.
HE'D NEVER ATTENDED SCHOOL, BUT HE KNEW EDUCATION WAS ***USEFUL***!
Sheffield Anniversary

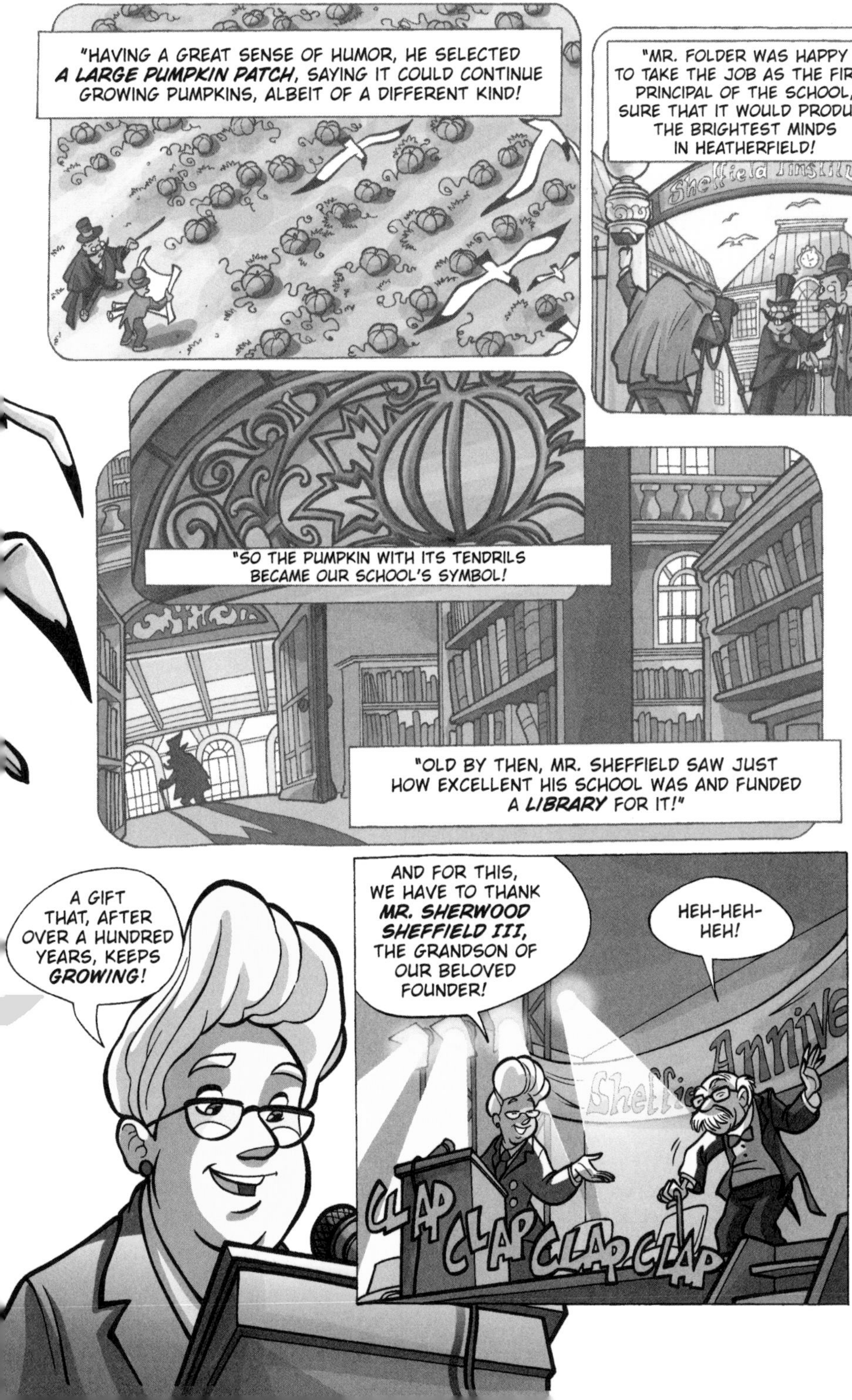
"HAVING A GREAT SENSE OF HUMOR, HE SELECTED A LARGE PUMPKIN PATCH, SAYING IT COULD CONTINUE GROWING PUMPKINS, ALBEIT OF A DIFFERENT KIND!
"MR. FOLDER WAS HAPPY TO TAKE THE JOB AS THE FIRST PRINCIPAL OF THE SCHOOL, SURE THAT IT WOULD PRODUCE THE BRIGHTEST MINDS IN HEATHERFIELD!
Sheffield Institute
"SO THE PUMPKIN WITH ITS TENDRILS BECAME OUR SCHOOL'S SYMBOL!
"OLD BY THEN, MR. SHEFFIELD SAW JUST HOW EXCELLENT HIS SCHOOL WAS AND FUNDED A LIBRARY FOR IT!"
A GIFT THAT, AFTER OVER A HUNDRED YEARS, KEEPS GROWING!
AND FOR THIS, WE HAVE TO THANK MR. SHERWOOD SHEFFIELD III, THE GRANDSON OF OUR BELOVED FOUNDER!
HEH-HEH-HEH!
CLAP CLAP CLAP CLAP

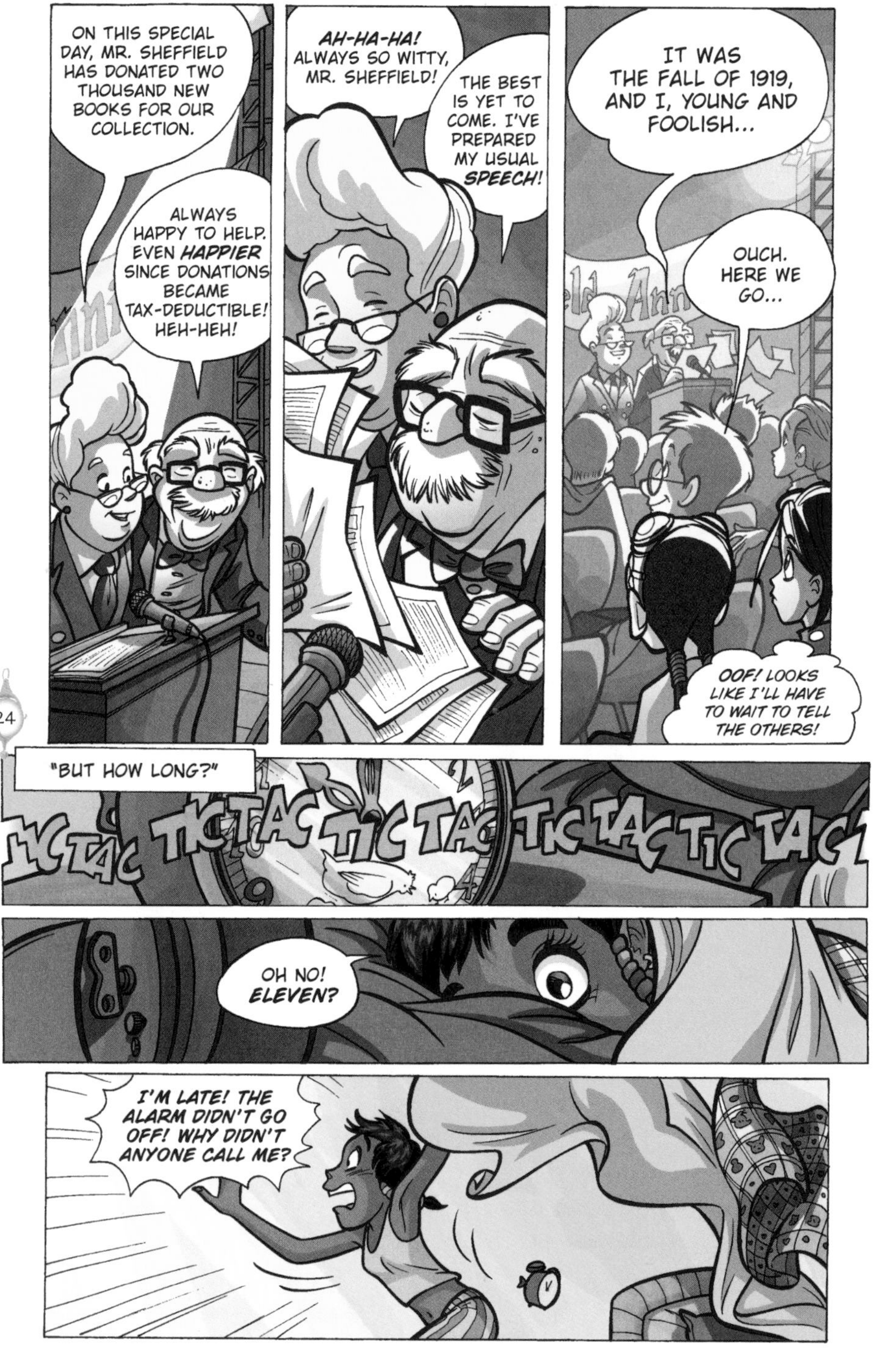
ON THIS SPECIAL DAY, MR. SHEFFIELD HAS DONATED TWO THOUSAND NEW BOOKS FOR OUR COLLECTION.
ALWAYS HAPPY TO HELP. EVEN HAPPIER SINCE DONATIONS BECAME TAX-DEDUCTIBLE! HEH-HEH!
AH-HA-HA! ALWAYS SO WITTY, MR. SHEFFIELD!
THE BEST IS YET TO COME. I'VE PREPARED MY USUAL SPEECH!
IT WAS THE FALL OF 1919, AND I, YOUNG AND FOOLISH...
OUCH. HERE WE GO...
OOF! LOOKS LIKE I'LL HAVE TO WAIT TO TELL THE OTHERS!
"BUT HOW LONG?"
TIC TAC TIC TAC TIC TAC TIC TAC TIC TAC
OH NO! ELEVEN?
I'M LATE! THE ALARM DIDN'T GO OFF! WHY DIDN'T ANYONE CALL ME?

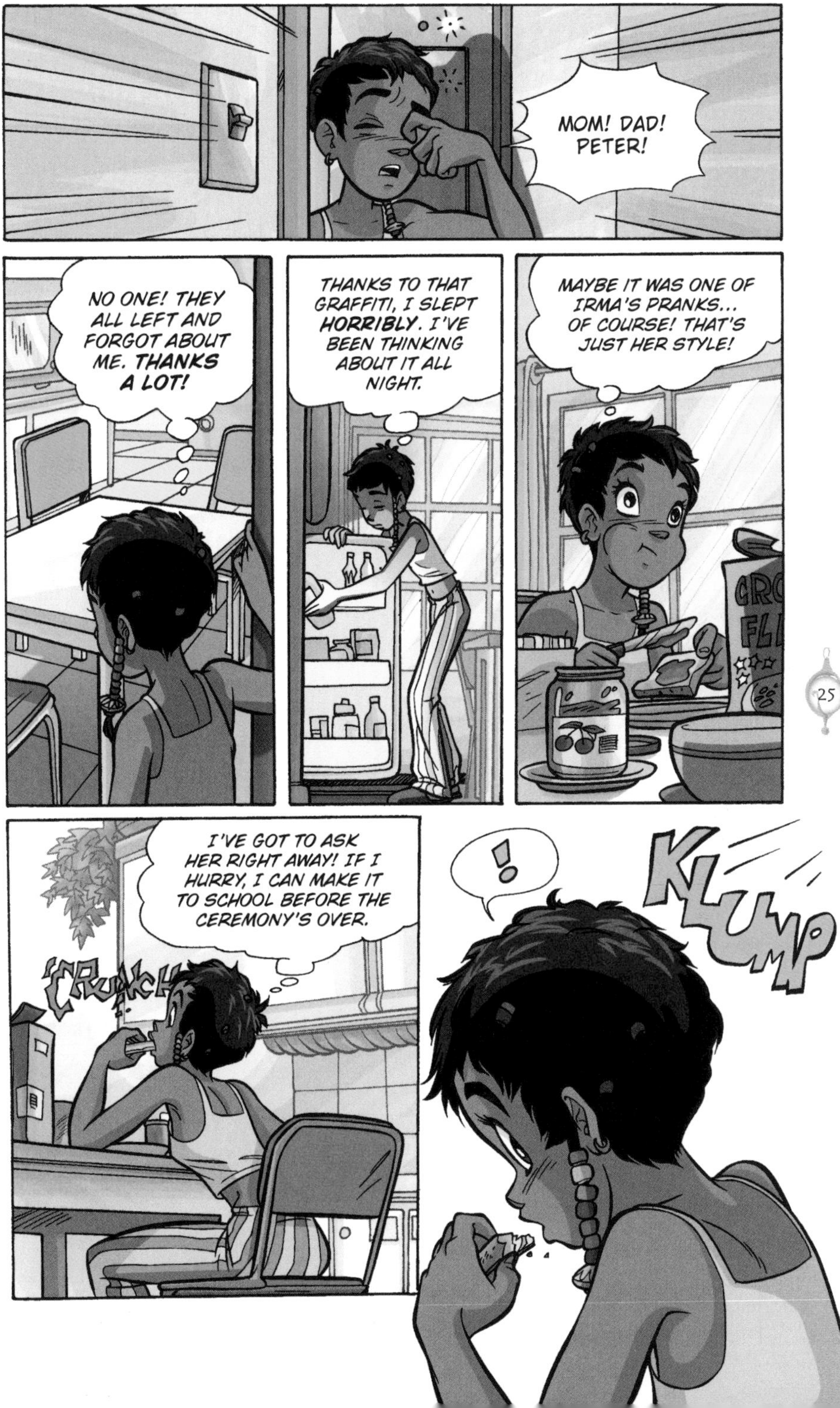
MOM! DAD! PETER!
NO ONE! THEY ALL LEFT AND FORGOT ABOUT ME. THANKS A LOT!
THANKS TO THAT GRAFFITI, I SLEPT HORRIBLY. I'VE BEEN THINKING ABOUT IT ALL NIGHT.
MAYBE IT WAS ONE OF IRMA'S PRANKS... OF COURSE! THAT'S JUST HER STYLE!
I'VE GOT TO ASK HER RIGHT AWAY! IF I HURRY, I CAN MAKE IT TO SCHOOL BEFORE THE CEREMONY'S OVER.
CRUNCH
!
KLUMP

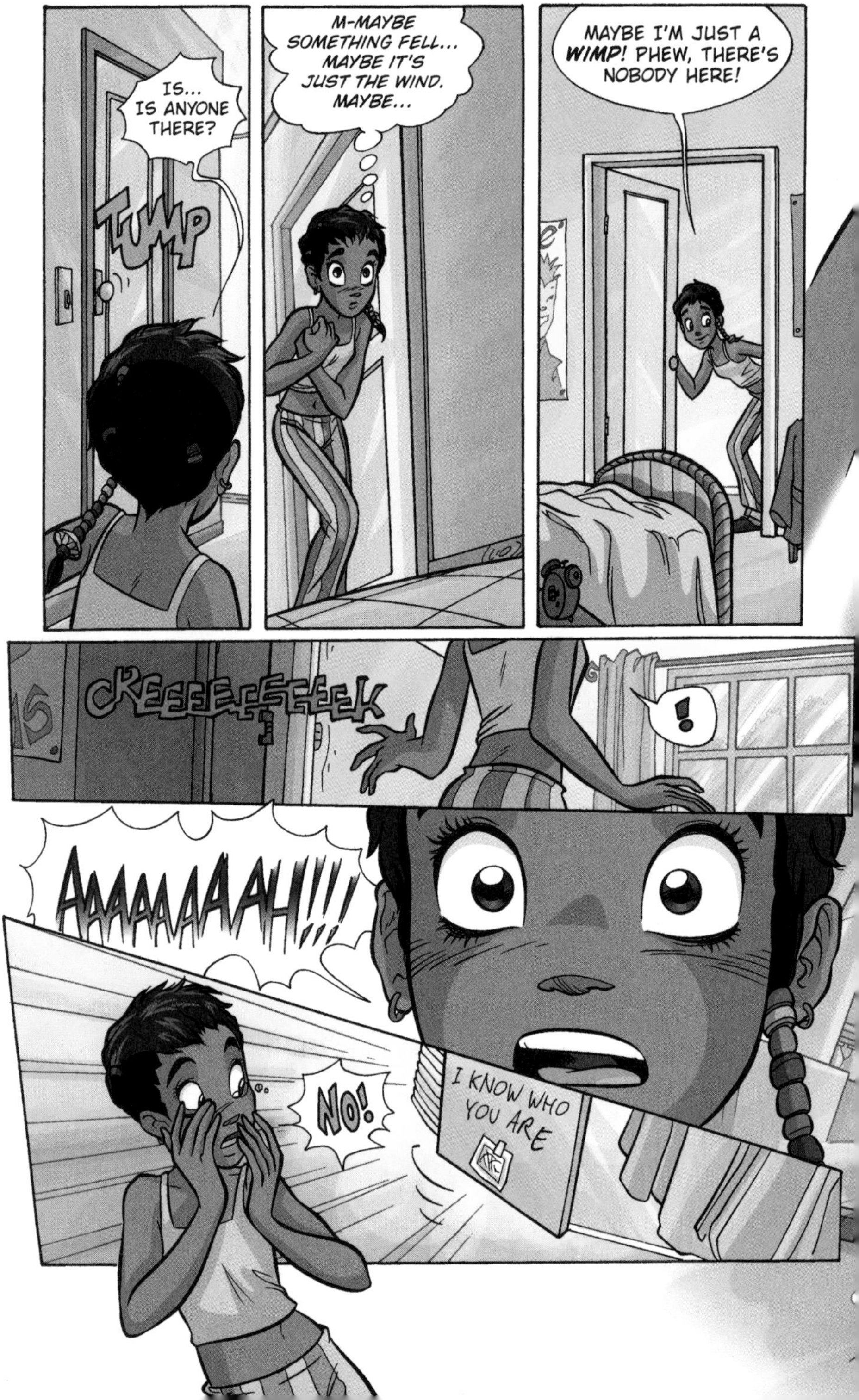
IS... IS ANYONE THERE?
TUMP
M-MAYBE SOMETHING FELL... MAYBE IT'S JUST THE WIND. MAYBE...
MAYBE I'M JUST A **WIMP**! PHEW, THERE'S NOBODY HERE!
CREEEEEEEEEK
!
AAAAAAAAH!!!
NO!
I KNOW WHO YOU ARE

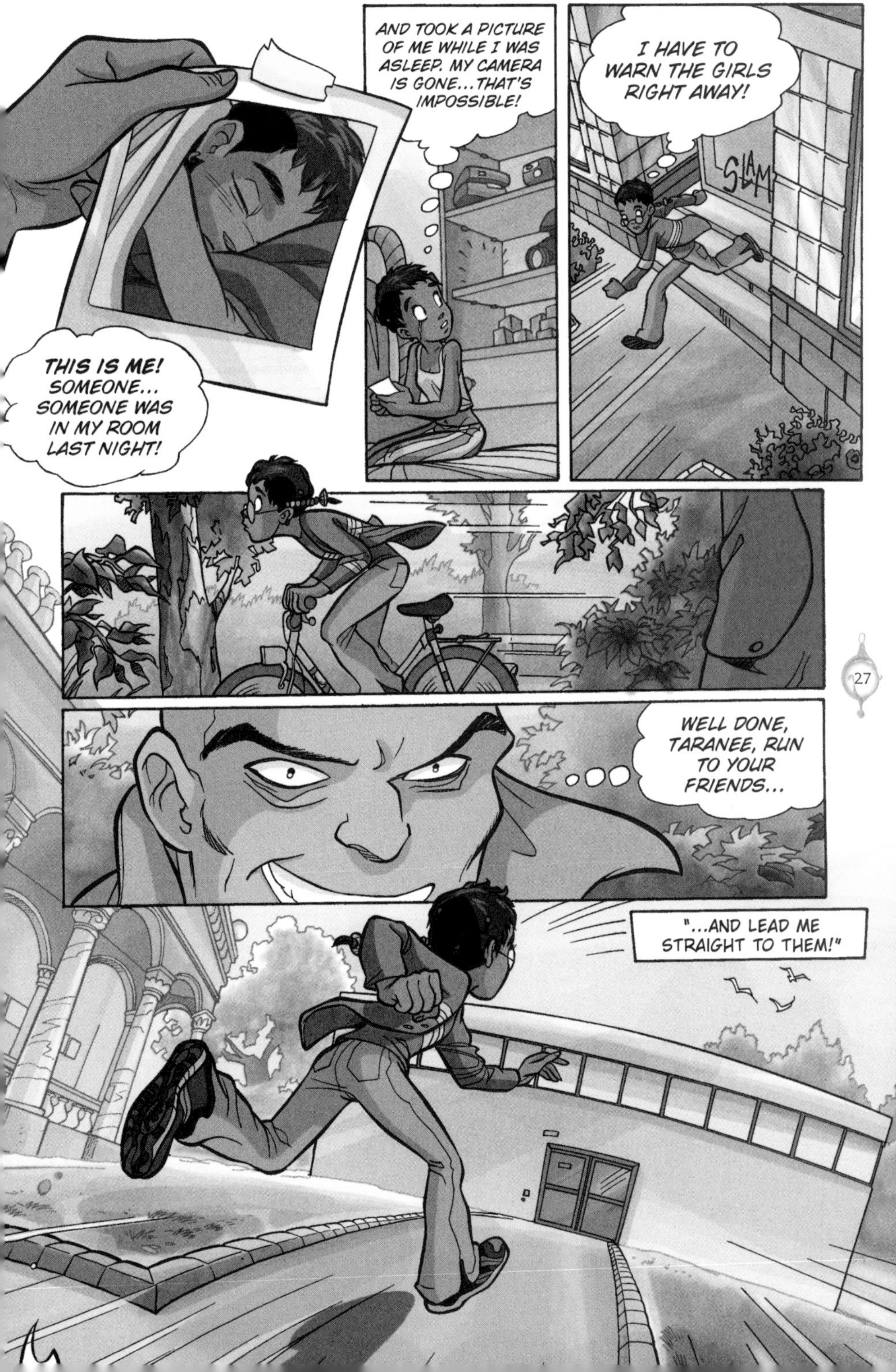
THIS IS ME! SOMEONE... SOMEONE WAS IN MY ROOM LAST NIGHT!
AND TOOK A PICTURE OF ME WHILE I WAS ASLEEP. MY CAMERA IS GONE...THAT'S IMPOSSIBLE!
I HAVE TO WARN THE GIRLS RIGHT AWAY!
SLAM
WELL DONE, TARANEE, RUN TO YOUR FRIENDS...
"...AND LEAD ME STRAIGHT TO THEM!"

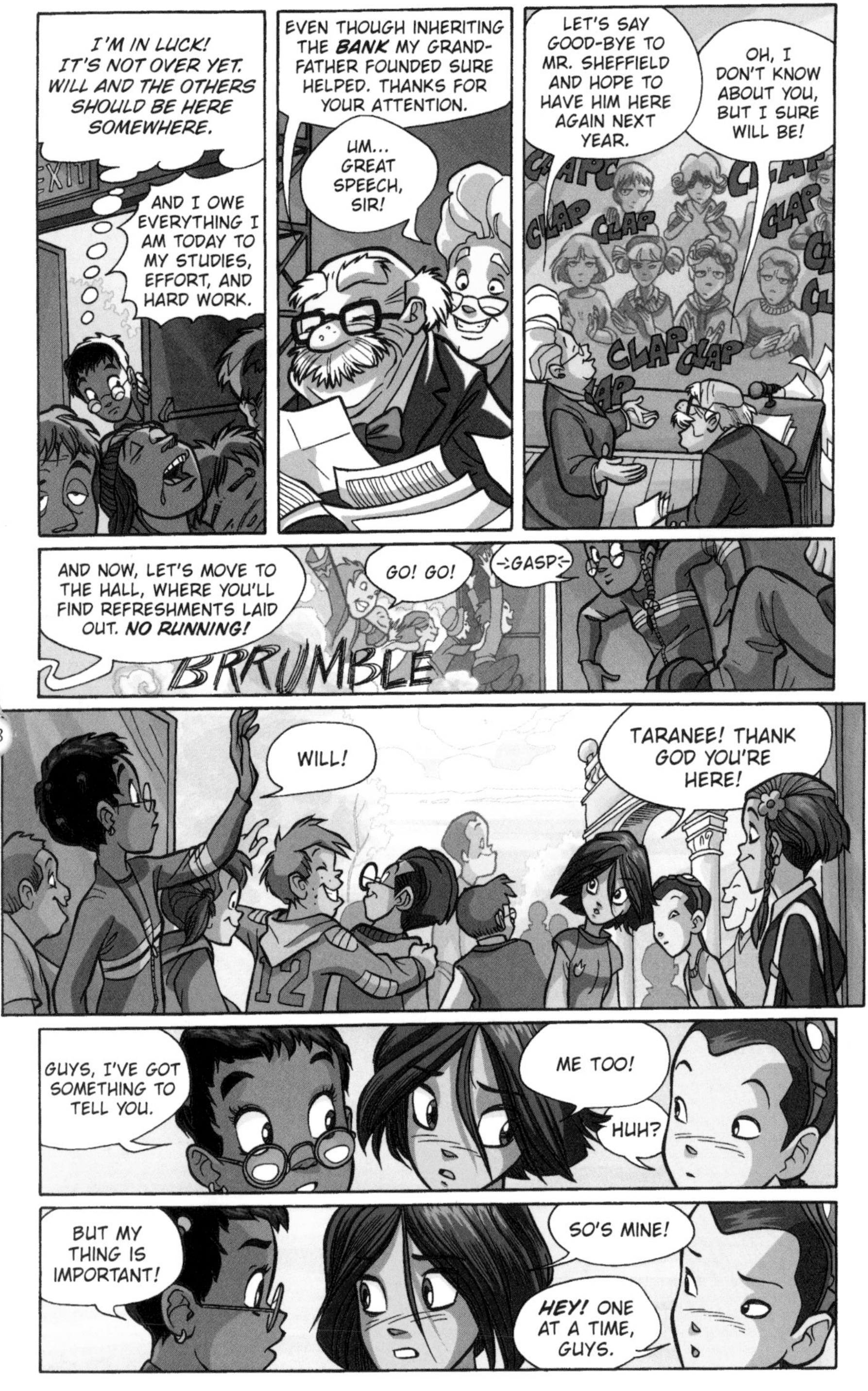
I'M IN LUCK! IT'S NOT OVER YET. WILL AND THE OTHERS SHOULD BE HERE SOMEWHERE.
AND I OWE EVERYTHING I AM TODAY TO MY STUDIES, EFFORT, AND HARD WORK.
EXIT
EVEN THOUGH INHERITING THE BANK MY GRANDFATHER FOUNDED SURE HELPED. THANKS FOR YOUR ATTENTION.
UM... GREAT SPEECH, SIR!
LET'S SAY GOOD-BYE TO MR. SHEFFIELD AND HOPE TO HAVE HIM HERE AGAIN NEXT YEAR.
OH, I DON'T KNOW ABOUT YOU, BUT I SURE WILL BE!
CLAP CLAP CLAP CLAP CLAP CLAP
AND NOW, LET'S MOVE TO THE HALL, WHERE YOU'LL FIND REFRESHMENTS LAID OUT. NO RUNNING!
GO! GO!
GASP
BRRUMBLE
WILL!
TARANEE! THANK GOD YOU'RE HERE!
GUYS, I'VE GOT SOMETHING TO TELL YOU.
ME TOO!
HUH?
BUT MY THING IS IMPORTANT!
SO'S MINE!
HEY! ONE AT A TIME, GUYS.

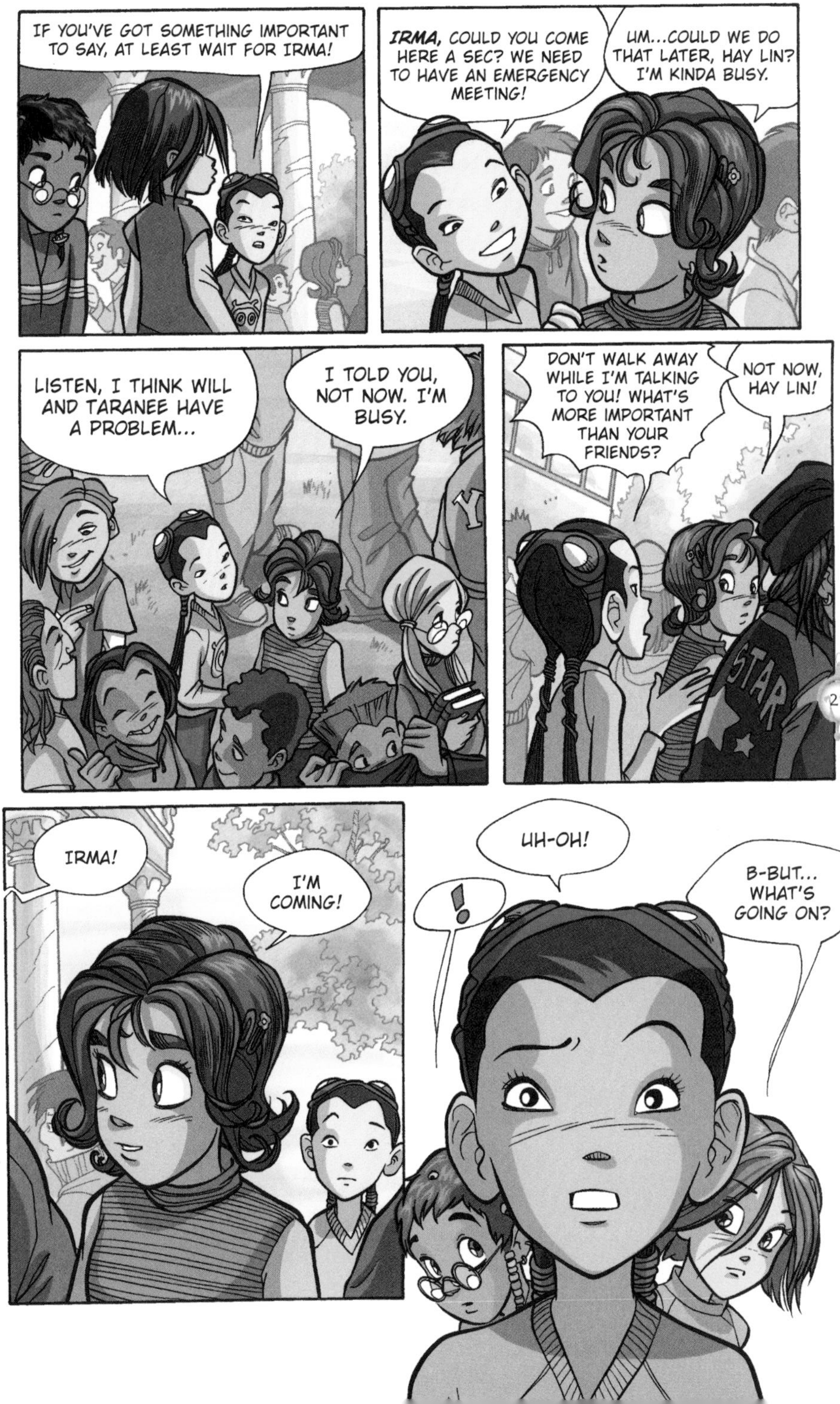

IF YOU'VE GOT SOMETHING IMPORTANT TO SAY, AT LEAST WAIT FOR IRMA!
IRMA, COULD YOU COME HERE A SEC? WE NEED TO HAVE AN EMERGENCY MEETING!
UM...COULD WE DO THAT LATER, HAY LIN? I'M KINDA BUSY.
LISTEN, I THINK WILL AND TARANEE HAVE A PROBLEM...
I TOLD YOU, NOT NOW. I'M BUSY.
DON'T WALK AWAY WHILE I'M TALKING TO YOU! WHAT'S MORE IMPORTANT THAN YOUR FRIENDS?
NOT NOW, HAY LIN!
STAR
IRMA!
I'M COMING!
UH-OH!
!
B-BUT... WHAT'S GOING ON?

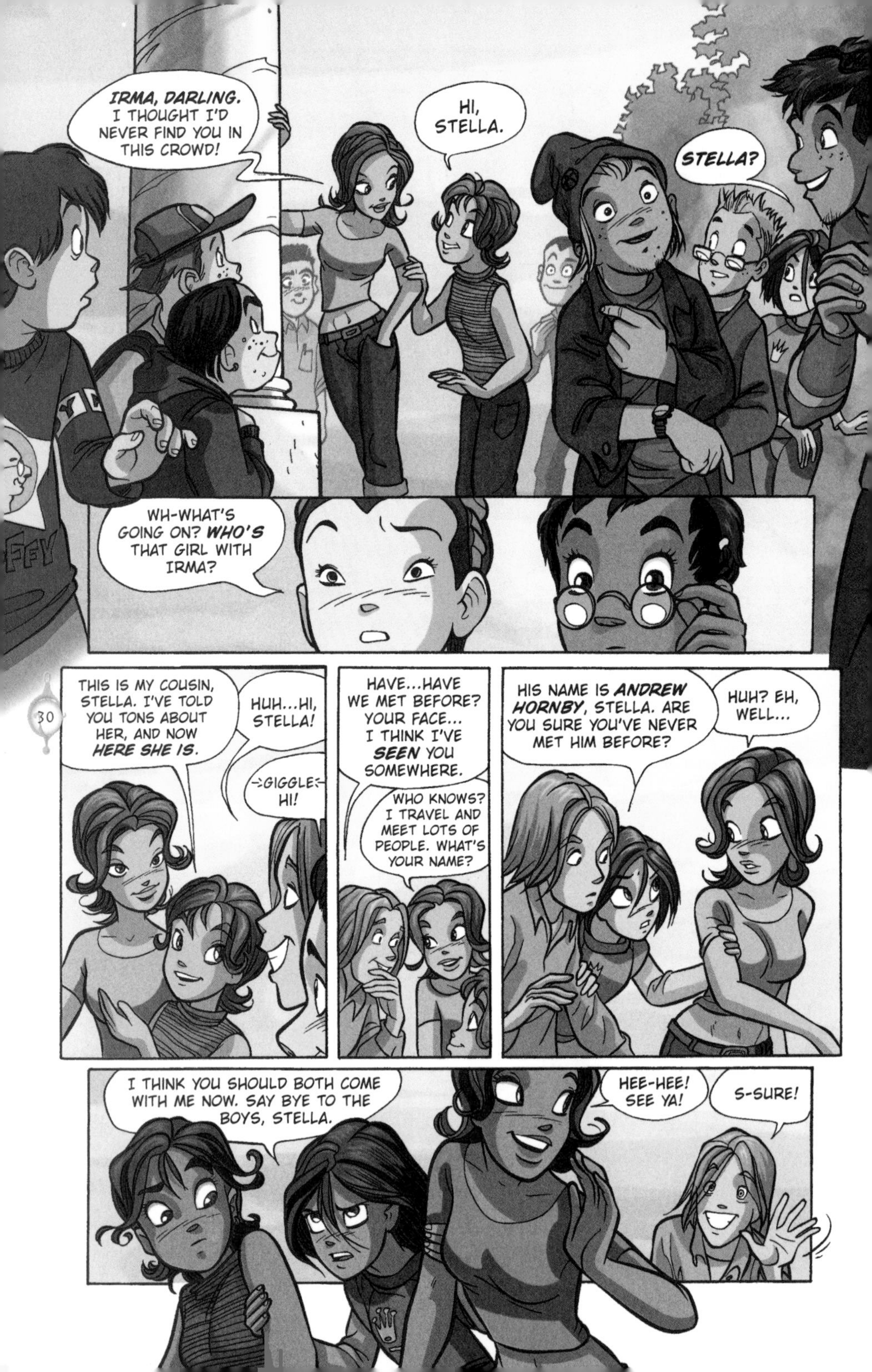
IRMA, DARLING. I THOUGHT I'D NEVER FIND YOU IN THIS CROWD!
HI, STELLA.
STELLA?
WH-WHAT'S GOING ON? WHO'S THAT GIRL WITH IRMA?
THIS IS MY COUSIN, STELLA. I'VE TOLD YOU TONS ABOUT HER, AND NOW HERE SHE IS.
HUH...HI, STELLA!
GIGGLE HI!
HAVE...HAVE WE MET BEFORE? YOUR FACE... I THINK I'VE SEEN YOU SOMEWHERE.
WHO KNOWS? I TRAVEL AND MEET LOTS OF PEOPLE. WHAT'S YOUR NAME?
HIS NAME IS ANDREW HORNBY, STELLA. ARE YOU SURE YOU'VE NEVER MET HIM BEFORE?
HUH? EH, WELL...
I THINK YOU SHOULD BOTH COME WITH ME NOW. SAY BYE TO THE BOYS, STELLA.
HEE-HEE! SEE YA!
S-SURE!

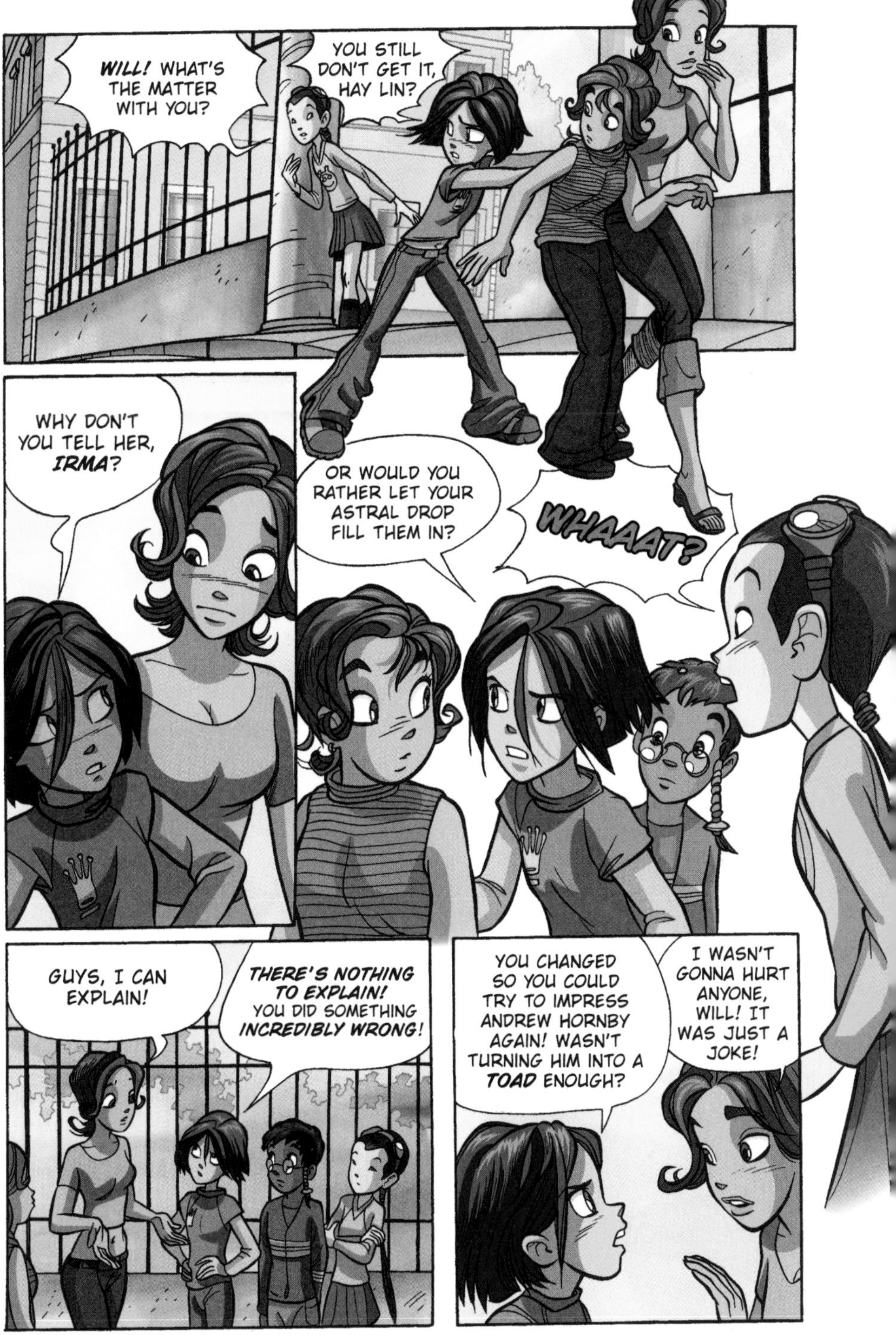
WILL! WHAT'S THE MATTER WITH YOU?
YOU STILL DON'T GET IT, HAY LIN?
WHY DON'T YOU TELL HER, IRMA?
OR WOULD YOU RATHER LET YOUR ASTRAL DROP FILL THEM IN?
WHAAAAT?
GUYS, I CAN EXPLAIN!
THERE'S NOTHING TO EXPLAIN! YOU DID SOMETHING INCREDIBLY WRONG!
YOU CHANGED SO YOU COULD TRY TO IMPRESS ANDREW HORNBY AGAIN! WASN'T TURNING HIM INTO A TOAD ENOUGH?
I WASN'T GONNA HURT ANYONE, WILL! IT WAS JUST A JOKE!

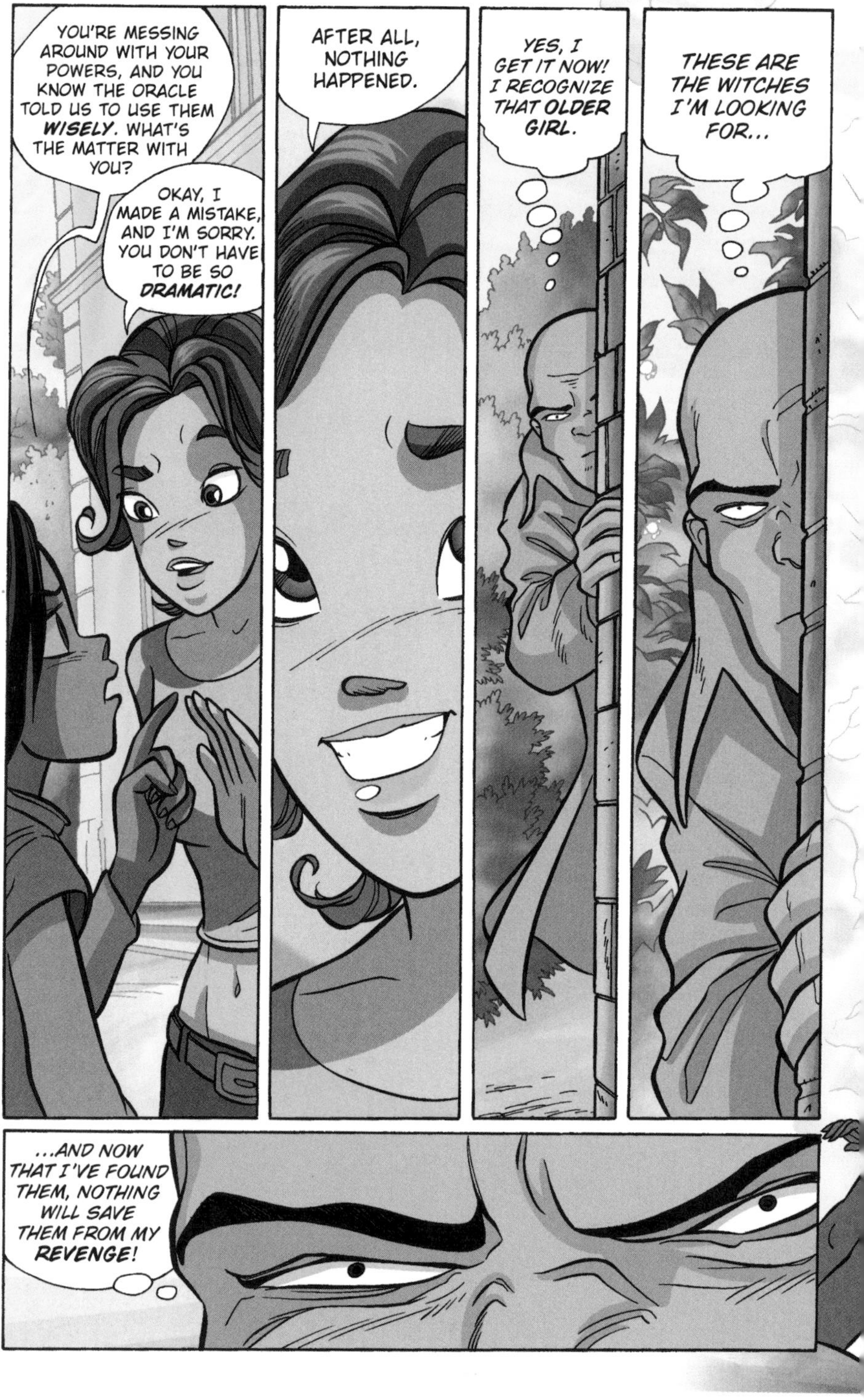
YOU'RE MESSING AROUND WITH YOUR POWERS, AND YOU KNOW THE ORACLE TOLD US TO USE THEM WISELY. WHAT'S THE MATTER WITH YOU?
OKAY, I MADE A MISTAKE, AND I'M SORRY. YOU DON'T HAVE TO BE SO DRAMATIC!
AFTER ALL, NOTHING HAPPENED.
YES, I GET IT NOW! I RECOGNIZE THAT OLDER GIRL.
THESE ARE THE WITCHES I'M LOOKING FOR...
...AND NOW THAT I'VE FOUND THEM, NOTHING WILL SAVE THEM FROM MY REVENGE!

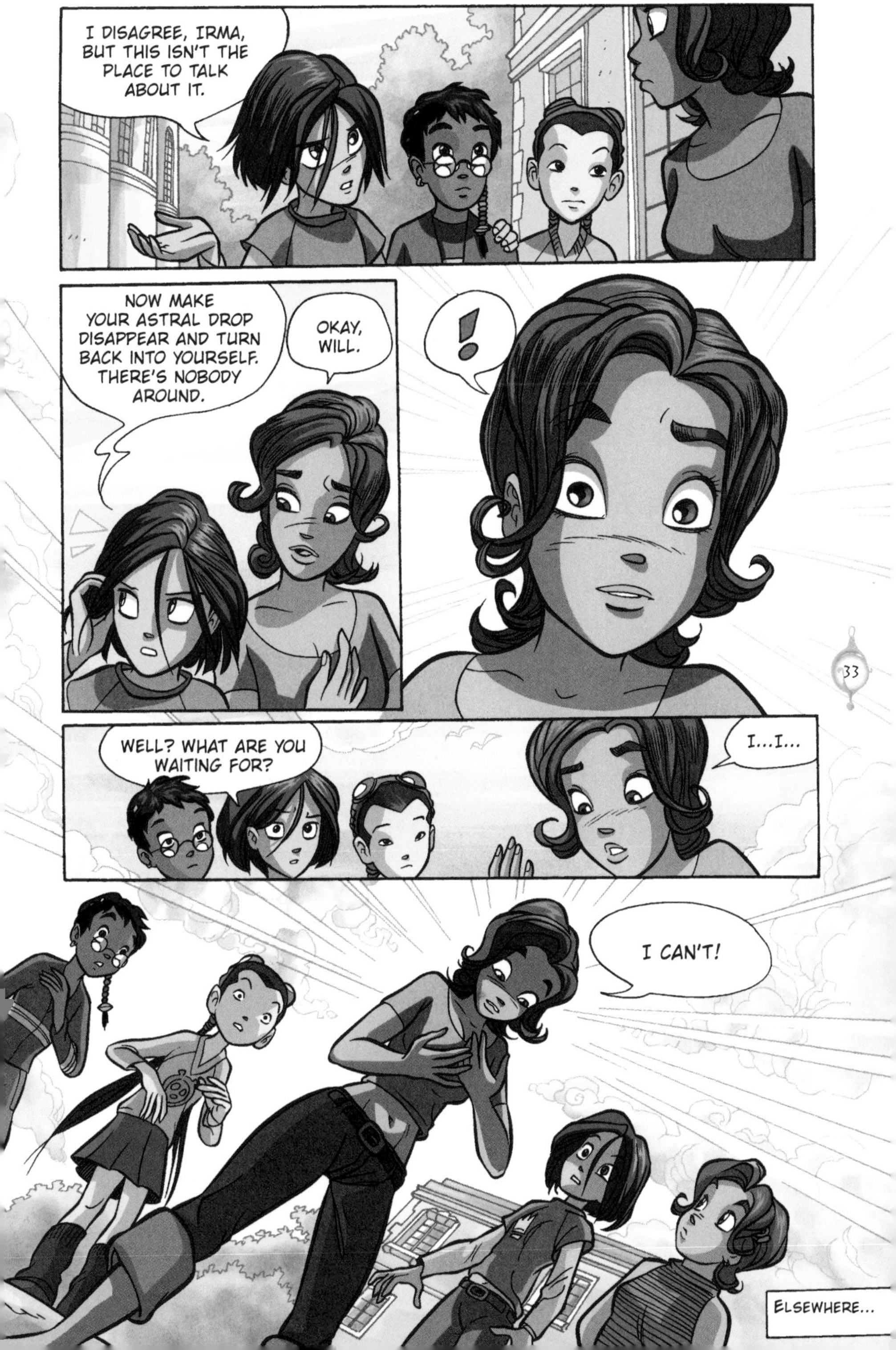
I DISAGREE, IRMA, BUT THIS ISN'T THE PLACE TO TALK ABOUT IT.
NOW MAKE YOUR ASTRAL DROP DISAPPEAR AND TURN BACK INTO YOURSELF. THERE'S NOBODY AROUND.
OKAY, WILL.
!
WELL? WHAT ARE YOU WAITING FOR?
I...I...
I CAN'T!
ELSEWHERE...

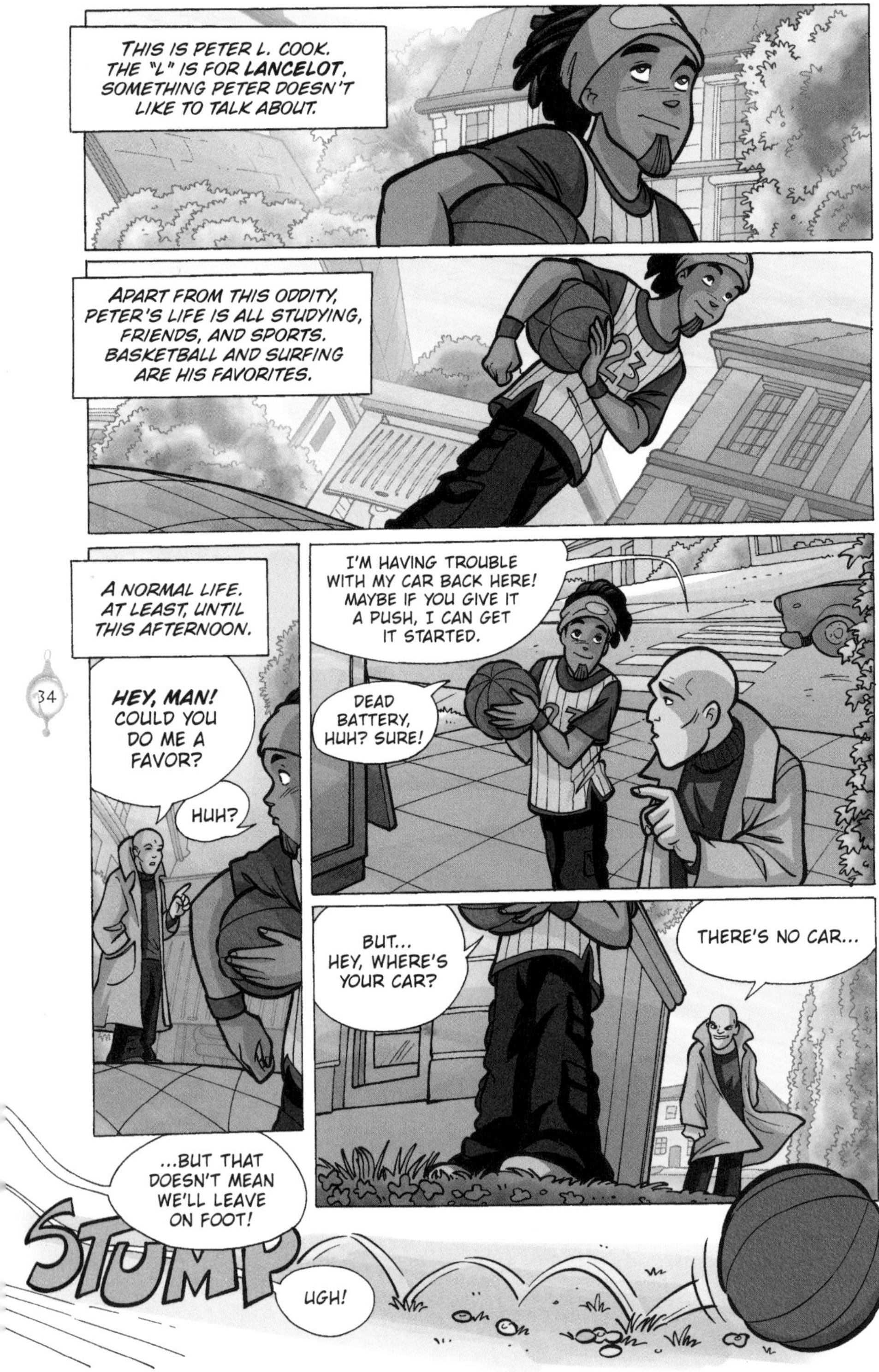
THIS IS PETER L. COOK. THE "L" IS FOR **LANCELOT**, SOMETHING PETER DOESN'T LIKE TO TALK ABOUT.
APART FROM THIS ODDITY, PETER'S LIFE IS ALL STUDYING, FRIENDS, AND SPORTS. BASKETBALL AND SURFING ARE HIS FAVORITES.
A NORMAL LIFE. AT LEAST, UNTIL THIS AFTERNOON.
HEY, MAN! COULD YOU DO ME A FAVOR?
HUH?
I'M HAVING TROUBLE WITH MY CAR BACK HERE! MAYBE IF YOU GIVE IT A PUSH, I CAN GET IT STARTED.
DEAD BATTERY, HUH? SURE!
BUT... HEY, WHERE'S YOUR CAR?
THERE'S NO CAR...
...BUT THAT DOESN'T MEAN WE'LL LEAVE ON FOOT!
STUMP
UGH!

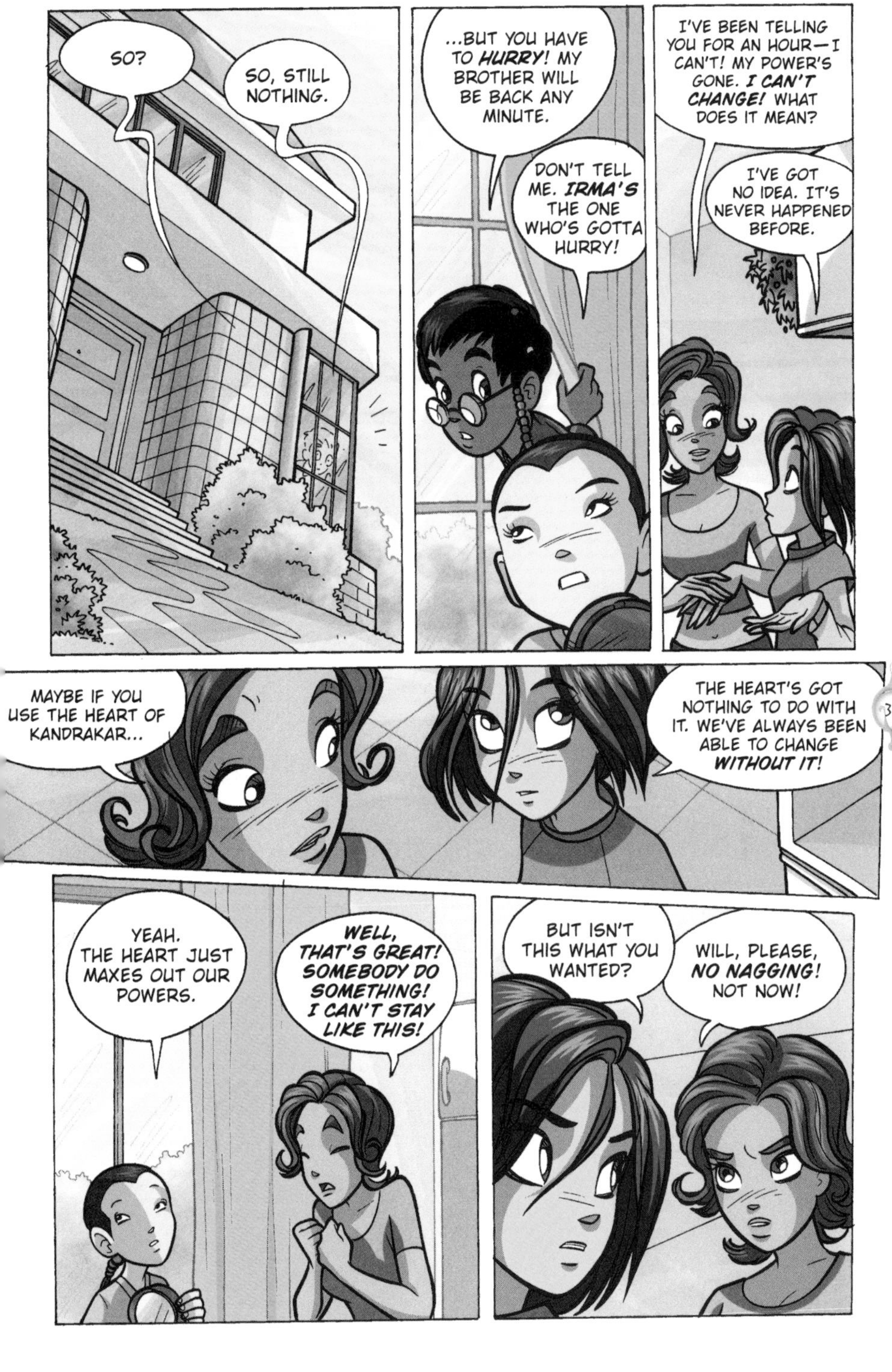
SO?
SO, STILL NOTHING.
...BUT YOU HAVE TO HURRY! MY BROTHER WILL BE BACK ANY MINUTE.
DON'T TELL ME. IRMA'S THE ONE WHO'S GOTTA HURRY!
I'VE BEEN TELLING YOU FOR AN HOUR—I CAN'T! MY POWER'S GONE. I CAN'T CHANGE! WHAT DOES IT MEAN?
I'VE GOT NO IDEA. IT'S NEVER HAPPENED BEFORE.
MAYBE IF YOU USE THE HEART OF KANDRAKAR...
THE HEART'S GOT NOTHING TO DO WITH IT. WE'VE ALWAYS BEEN ABLE TO CHANGE WITHOUT IT!
YEAH. THE HEART JUST MAXES OUT OUR POWERS.
WELL, THAT'S GREAT! SOMEBODY DO SOMETHING! I CAN'T STAY LIKE THIS!
BUT ISN'T THIS WHAT YOU WANTED?
WILL, PLEASE, NO NAGGING! NOT NOW!

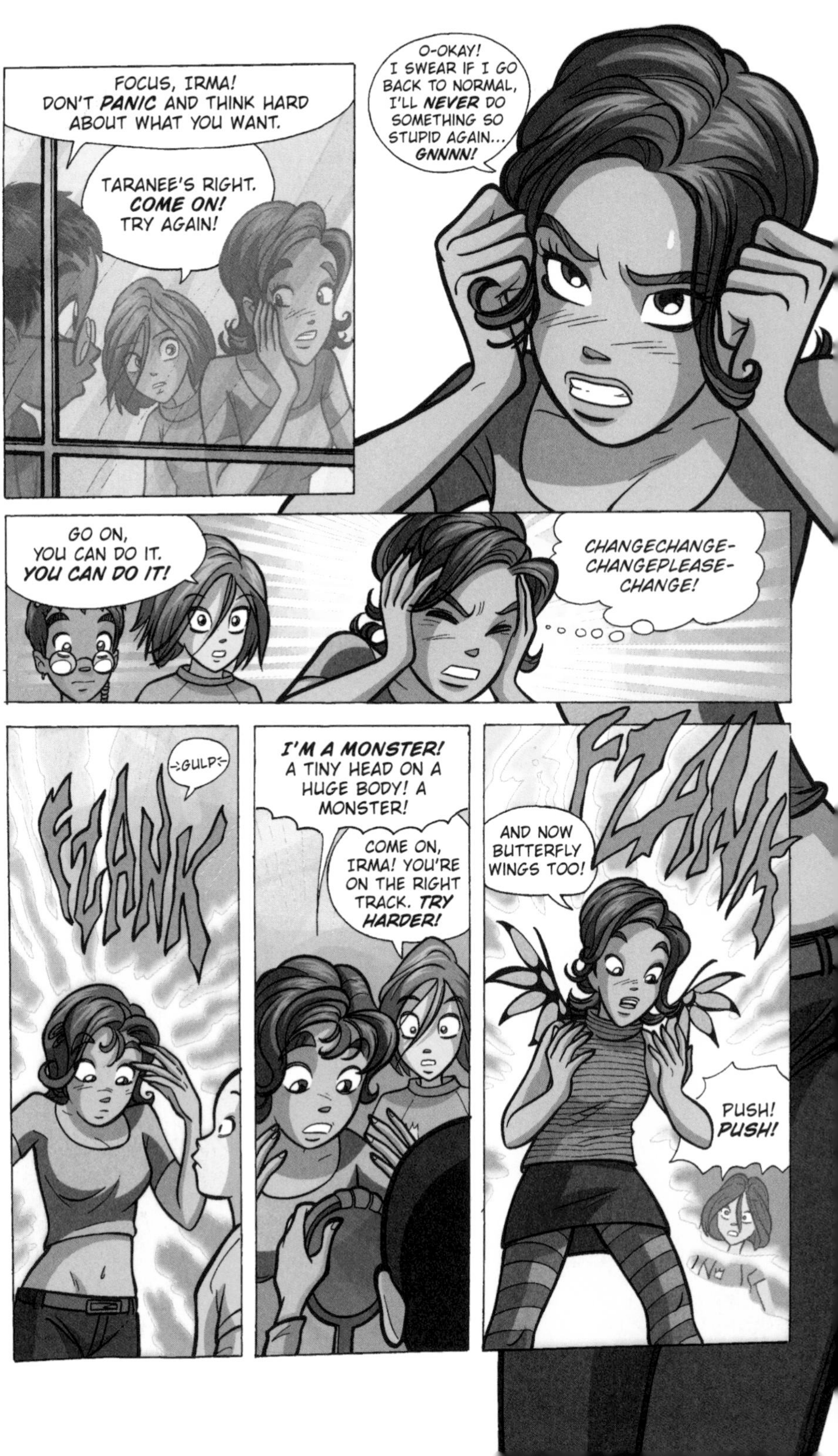

FOCUS, IRMA! DON'T *PANIC* AND THINK HARD ABOUT WHAT YOU WANT.
TARANEE'S RIGHT. ***COME ON!*** TRY AGAIN!
O-OKAY! I SWEAR IF I GO BACK TO NORMAL, I'LL ***NEVER*** DO SOMETHING SO STUPID AGAIN... ***GNNNN!***
GO ON, YOU CAN DO IT. ***YOU CAN DO IT!***
CHANGECHANGE-CHANGEPLEASE-CHANGE!
FZANK
GULP
I'M A MONSTER! A TINY HEAD ON A HUGE BODY! A MONSTER!
COME ON, IRMA! YOU'RE ON THE RIGHT TRACK. ***TRY HARDER!***
FZANK
AND NOW BUTTERFLY WINGS TOO!
PUSH! ***PUSH!***

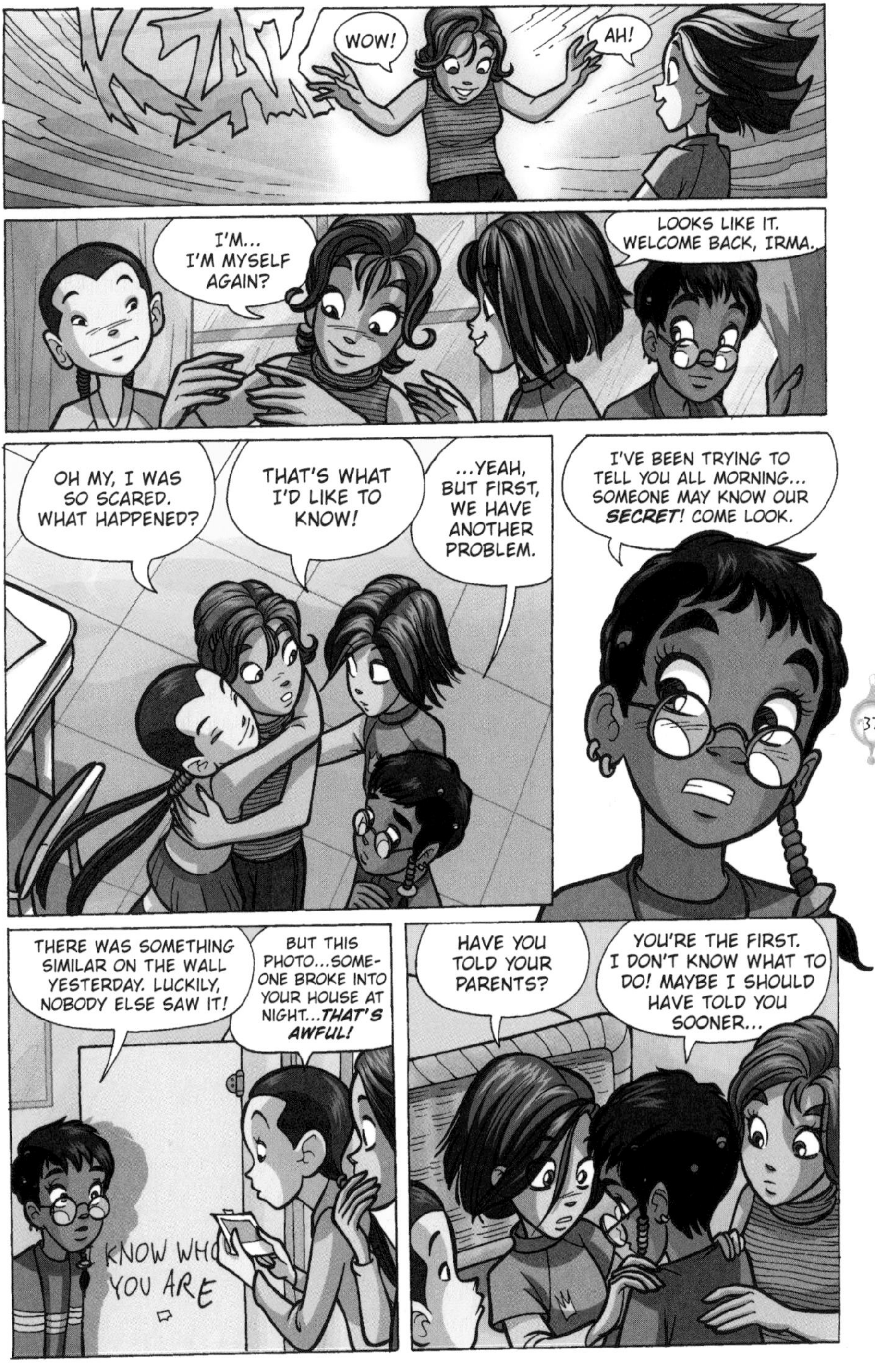
KZAK
WOW!
AH!
I'M... I'M MYSELF AGAIN?
LOOKS LIKE IT. WELCOME BACK, IRMA.
OH MY, I WAS SO SCARED. WHAT HAPPENED?
THAT'S WHAT I'D LIKE TO KNOW!
...YEAH, BUT FIRST, WE HAVE ANOTHER PROBLEM.
I'VE BEEN TRYING TO TELL YOU ALL MORNING... SOMEONE MAY KNOW OUR ***SECRET***! COME LOOK.
THERE WAS SOMETHING SIMILAR ON THE WALL YESTERDAY. LUCKILY, NOBODY ELSE SAW IT!
BUT THIS PHOTO...SOMEONE BROKE INTO YOUR HOUSE AT NIGHT...***THAT'S AWFUL!***
I KNOW WHO YOU ARE
HAVE YOU TOLD YOUR PARENTS?
YOU'RE THE FIRST. I DON'T KNOW WHAT TO DO! MAYBE I SHOULD HAVE TOLD YOU SOONER...

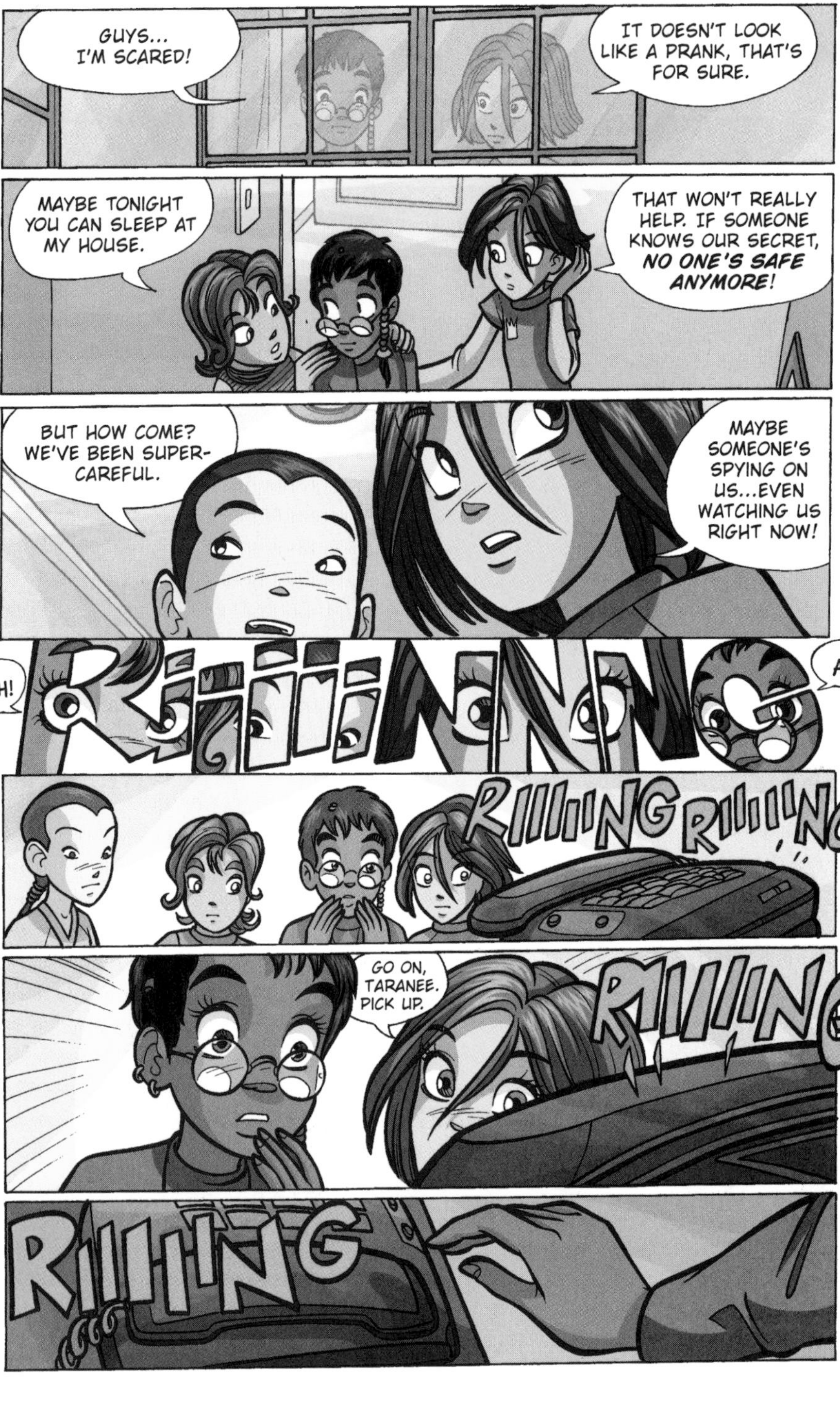
GUYS... I'M SCARED!
IT DOESN'T LOOK LIKE A PRANK, THAT'S FOR SURE.
MAYBE TONIGHT YOU CAN SLEEP AT MY HOUSE.
THAT WON'T REALLY HELP. IF SOMEONE KNOWS OUR SECRET, NO ONE'S SAFE ANYMORE!
BUT HOW COME? WE'VE BEEN SUPER-CAREFUL.
MAYBE SOMEONE'S SPYING ON US...EVEN WATCHING US RIGHT NOW!
GAH!
RIIIINNNG
AH!
RIIIING RIIIING
GO ON, TARANEE. PICK UP.
RIIIING
RIIIING

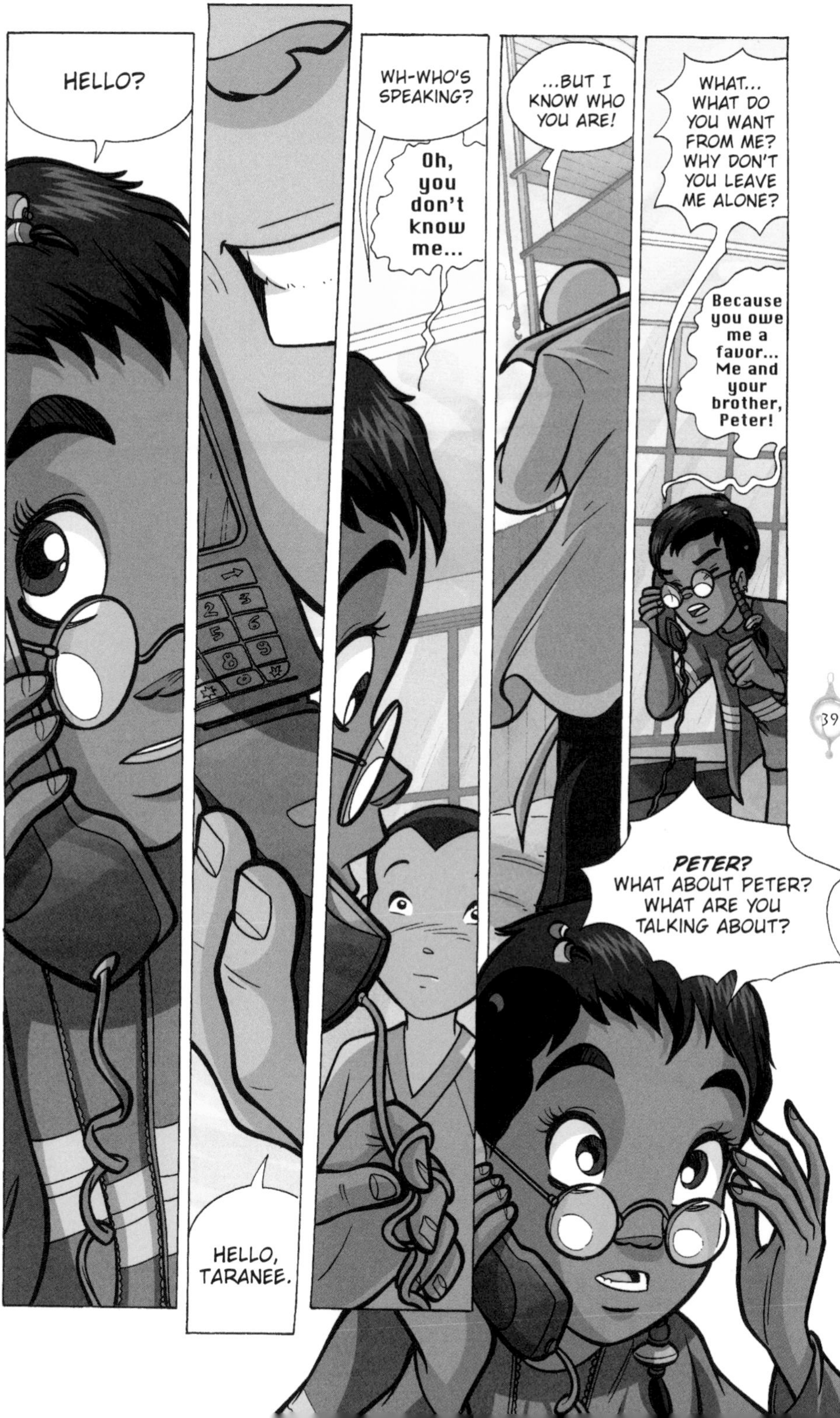
HELLO?
HELLO, TARANEE.
WH-WHO'S SPEAKING?
Oh, you don't know me...
...BUT I KNOW WHO YOU ARE!
WHAT... WHAT DO YOU WANT FROM ME? WHY DON'T YOU LEAVE ME ALONE?
Because you owe me a favor... Me and your brother, Peter!
PETER? WHAT ABOUT PETER? WHAT ARE YOU TALKING ABOUT?

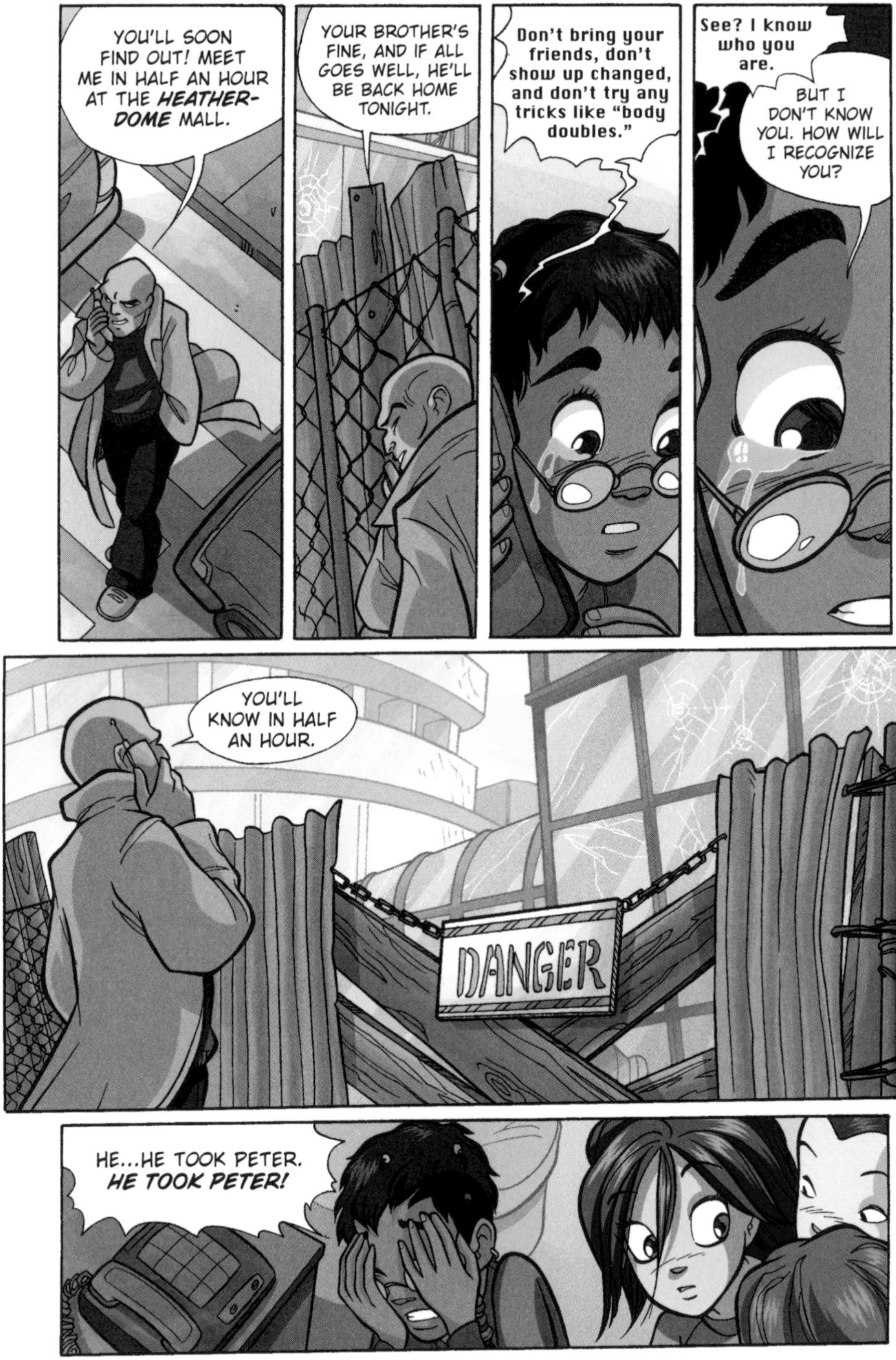
YOU'LL SOON FIND OUT! MEET ME IN HALF AN HOUR AT THE HEATHER-DOME MALL.
YOUR BROTHER'S FINE, AND IF ALL GOES WELL, HE'LL BE BACK HOME TONIGHT.
Don't bring your friends, don't show up changed, and don't try any tricks like "body doubles."
See? I know who you are.
BUT I DON'T KNOW YOU. HOW WILL I RECOGNIZE YOU?
YOU'LL KNOW IN HALF AN HOUR.
DANGER
HE...HE TOOK PETER. HE TOOK PETER!

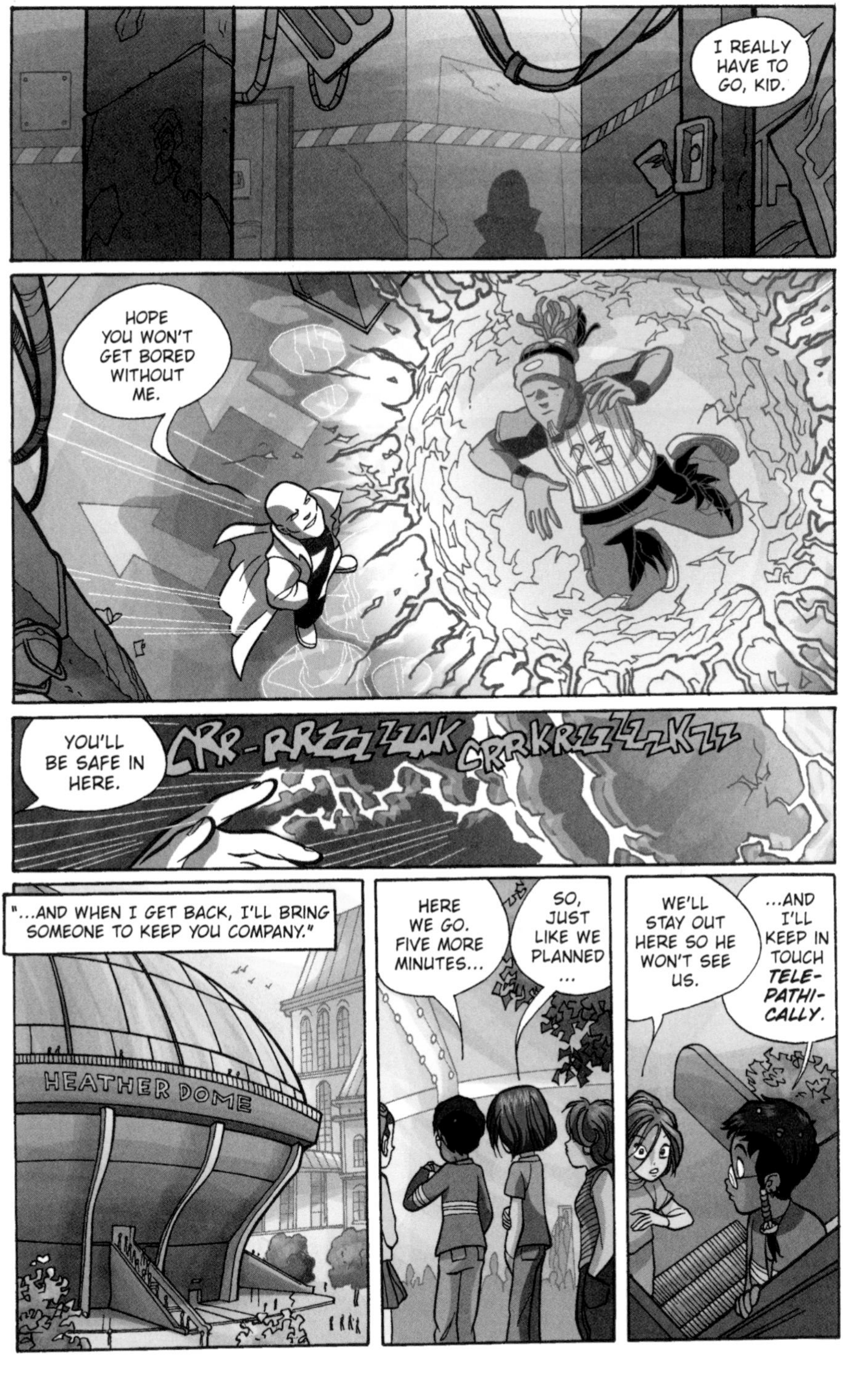

I REALLY HAVE TO GO, KID.
HOPE YOU WON'T GET BORED WITHOUT ME.
YOU'LL BE SAFE IN HERE.
CRR-RRZZZZZAK CRRKRZZZZZKZZ
"...AND WHEN I GET BACK, I'LL BRING SOMEONE TO KEEP YOU COMPANY."
HEATHER DOME
HERE WE GO. FIVE MORE MINUTES...
SO, JUST LIKE WE PLANNED ...
WE'LL STAY OUT HERE SO HE WON'T SEE US.
...AND I'LL KEEP IN TOUCH TELEPATHICALLY.

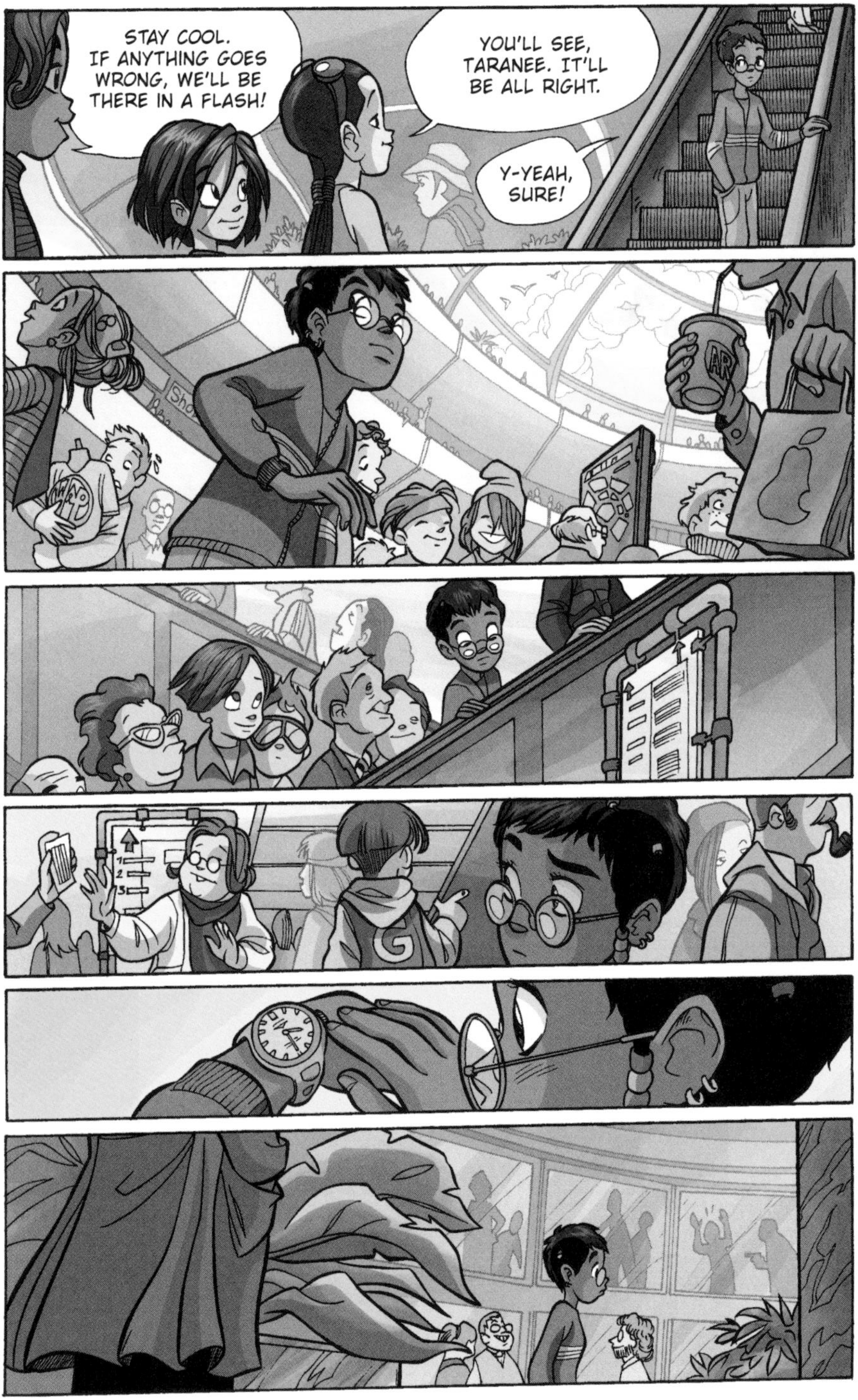
STAY COOL. IF ANYTHING GOES WRONG, WE'LL BE THERE IN A FLASH!
YOU'LL SEE, TARANEE. IT'LL BE ALL RIGHT.
Y-YEAH, SURE!

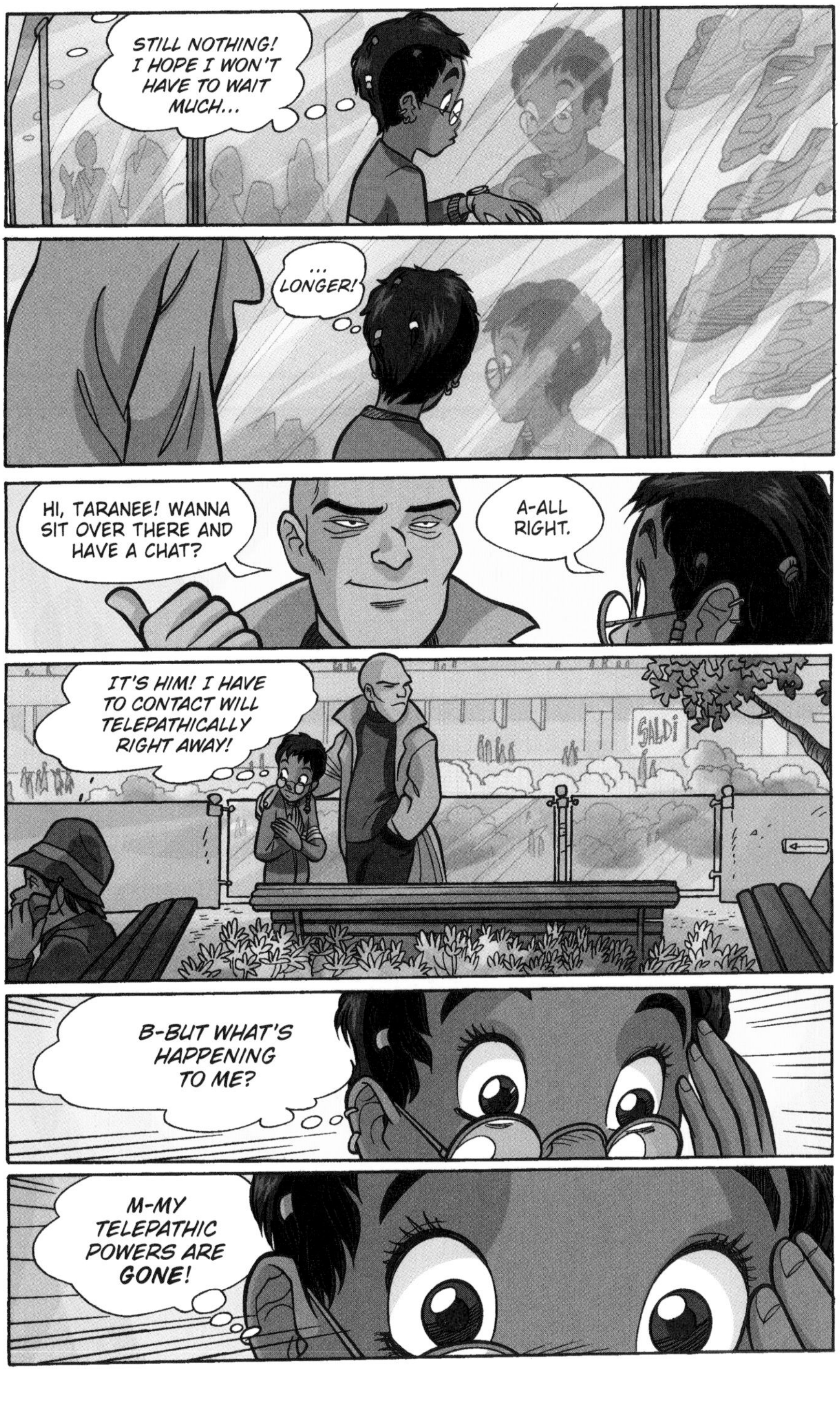
STILL NOTHING! I HOPE I WON'T HAVE TO WAIT MUCH...
... LONGER!
HI, TARANEE! WANNA SIT OVER THERE AND HAVE A CHAT?
A-ALL RIGHT.
IT'S HIM! I HAVE TO CONTACT WILL TELEPATHICALLY RIGHT AWAY!
SALDI
B-BUT WHAT'S HAPPENING TO ME?
M-MY TELEPATHIC POWERS ARE **GONE**!

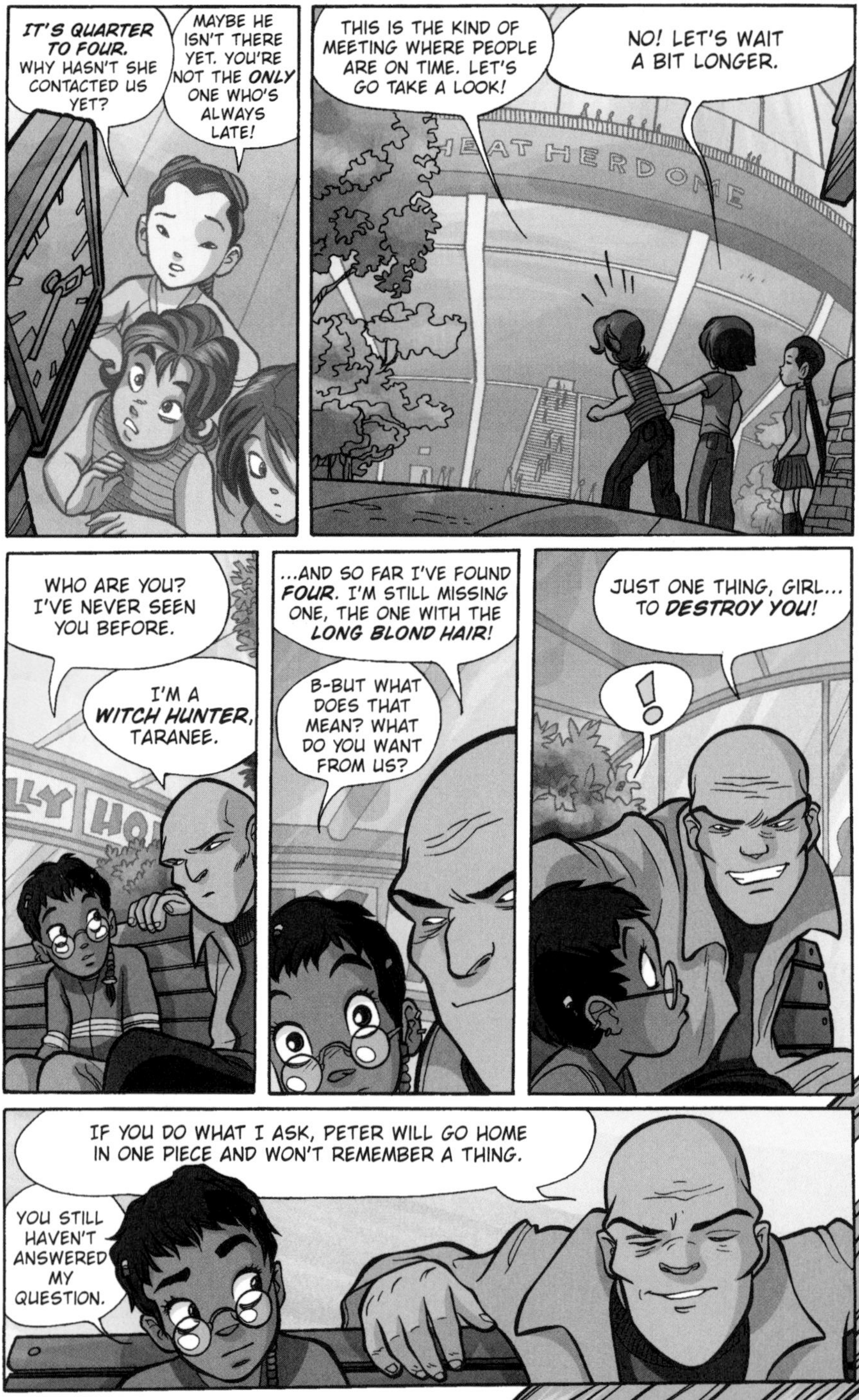
IT'S QUARTER TO FOUR. WHY HASN'T SHE CONTACTED US YET?
MAYBE HE ISN'T THERE YET. YOU'RE NOT THE ONLY ONE WHO'S ALWAYS LATE!
THIS IS THE KIND OF MEETING WHERE PEOPLE ARE ON TIME. LET'S GO TAKE A LOOK!
NO! LET'S WAIT A BIT LONGER.
HEATHERDOME
WHO ARE YOU? I'VE NEVER SEEN YOU BEFORE.
I'M A WITCH HUNTER, TARANEE.
...AND SO FAR I'VE FOUND FOUR. I'M STILL MISSING ONE, THE ONE WITH THE LONG BLOND HAIR!
B-BUT WHAT DOES THAT MEAN? WHAT DO YOU WANT FROM US?
JUST ONE THING, GIRL... TO DESTROY YOU!
!
IF YOU DO WHAT I ASK, PETER WILL GO HOME IN ONE PIECE AND WON'T REMEMBER A THING.
YOU STILL HAVEN'T ANSWERED MY QUESTION.

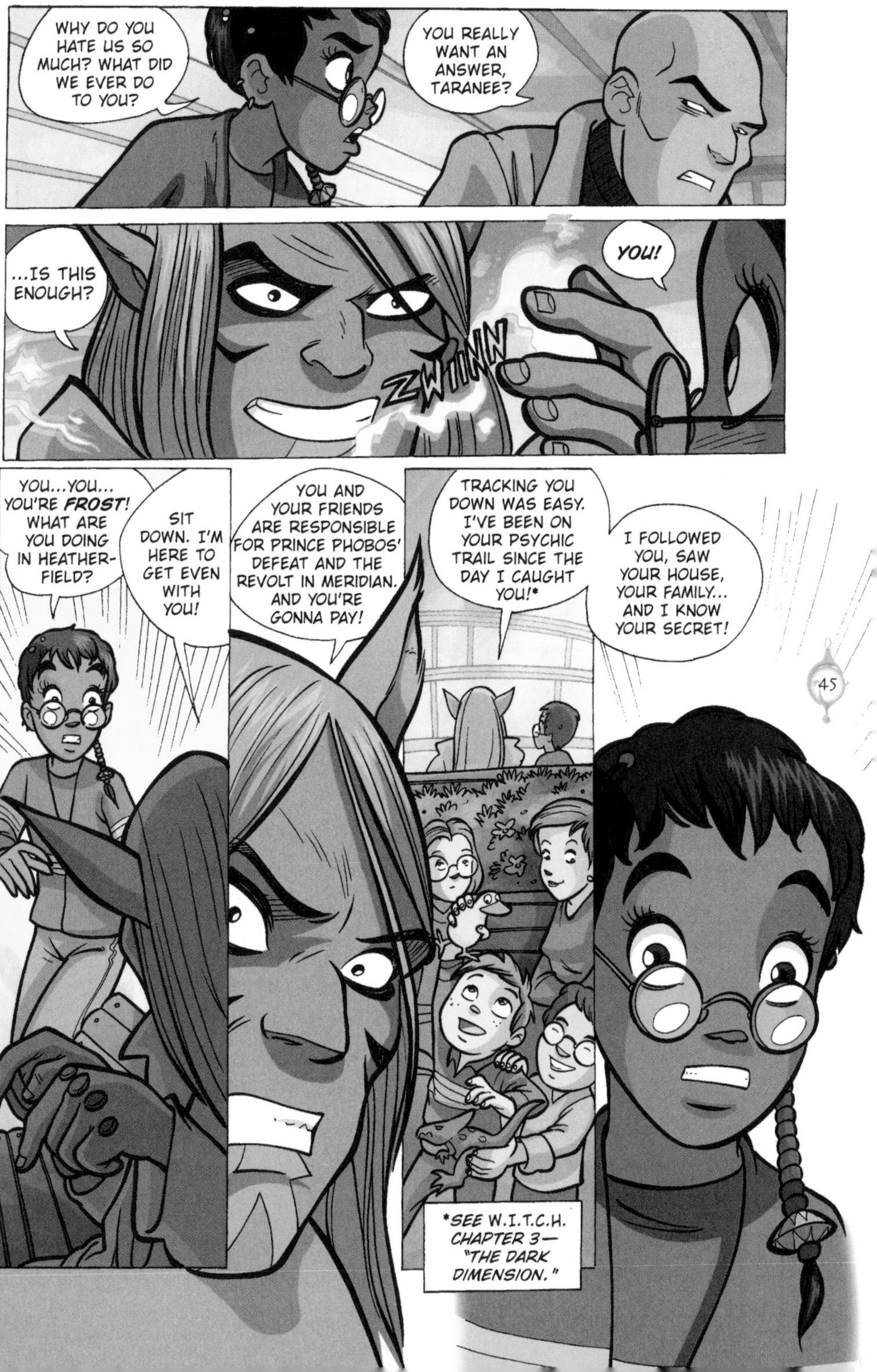

WHY DO YOU HATE US SO MUCH? WHAT DID WE EVER DO TO YOU?
YOU REALLY WANT AN ANSWER, TARANEE?
...IS THIS ENOUGH?
ZWINN
YOU!
YOU...YOU... YOU'RE *FROST*! WHAT ARE YOU DOING IN HEATHER-FIELD?
SIT DOWN. I'M HERE TO GET EVEN WITH YOU!
YOU AND YOUR FRIENDS ARE RESPONSIBLE FOR PRINCE PHOBOS' DEFEAT AND THE REVOLT IN MERIDIAN. AND YOU'RE GONNA PAY!
TRACKING YOU DOWN WAS EASY. I'VE BEEN ON YOUR PSYCHIC TRAIL SINCE THE DAY I CAUGHT YOU!*
I FOLLOWED YOU, SAW YOUR HOUSE, YOUR FAMILY... AND I KNOW YOUR SECRET!
*SEE W.I.T.C.H. CHAPTER 3— "THE DARK DIMENSION."

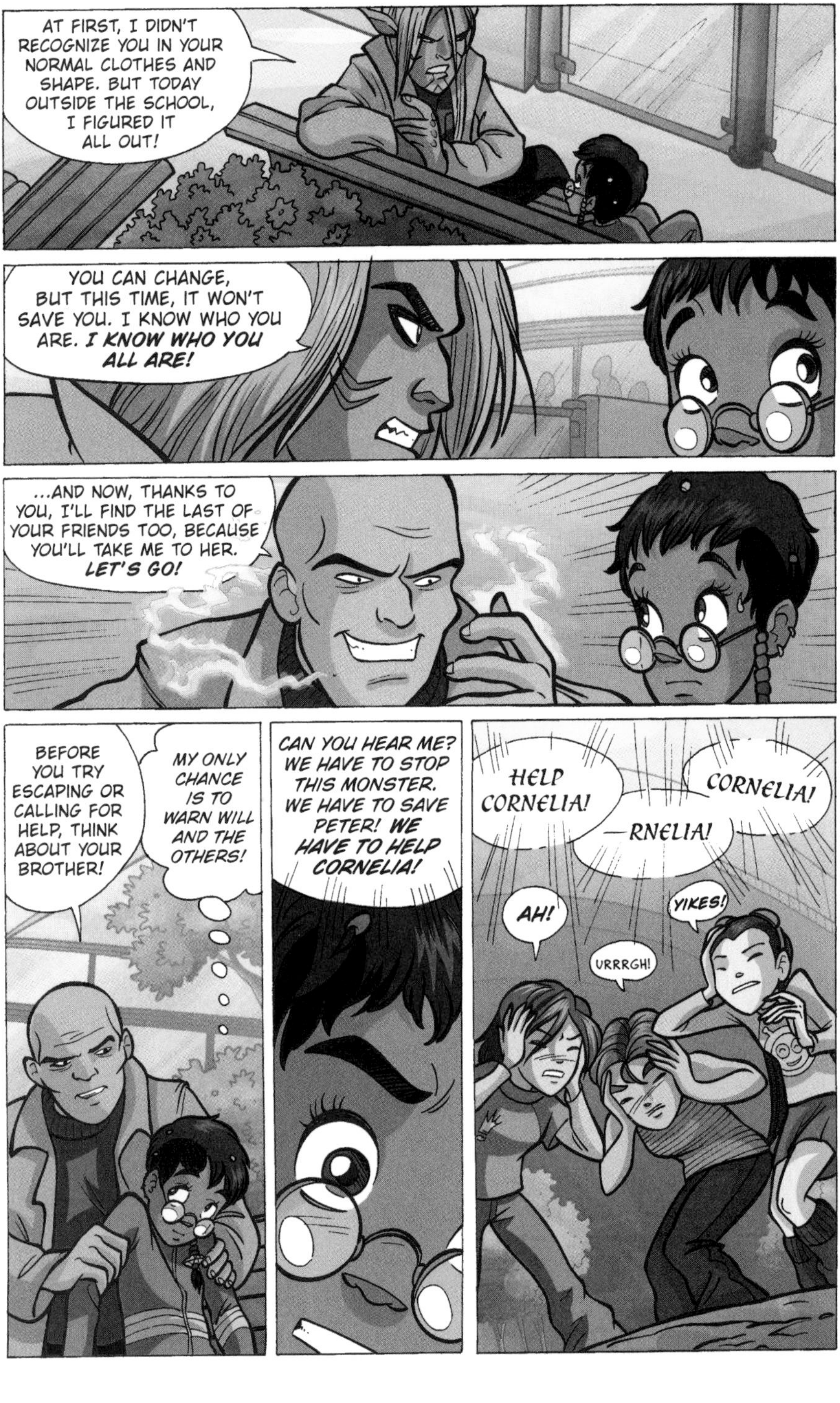

AT FIRST, I DIDN'T RECOGNIZE YOU IN YOUR NORMAL CLOTHES AND SHAPE. BUT TODAY OUTSIDE THE SCHOOL, I FIGURED IT ALL OUT!
YOU CAN CHANGE, BUT THIS TIME, IT WON'T SAVE YOU. I KNOW WHO YOU ARE. *I KNOW WHO YOU ALL ARE!*
...AND NOW, THANKS TO YOU, I'LL FIND THE LAST OF YOUR FRIENDS TOO, BECAUSE YOU'LL TAKE ME TO HER. *LET'S GO!*
BEFORE YOU TRY ESCAPING OR CALLING FOR HELP, THINK ABOUT YOUR BROTHER!
MY ONLY CHANCE IS TO WARN WILL AND THE OTHERS!
CAN YOU HEAR ME? WE HAVE TO STOP THIS MONSTER. WE HAVE TO SAVE PETER! *WE HAVE TO HELP CORNELIA!*
HELP CORNELIA!
CORNELIA!
—RNELIA!
AH!
YIKES!
URRRGH!

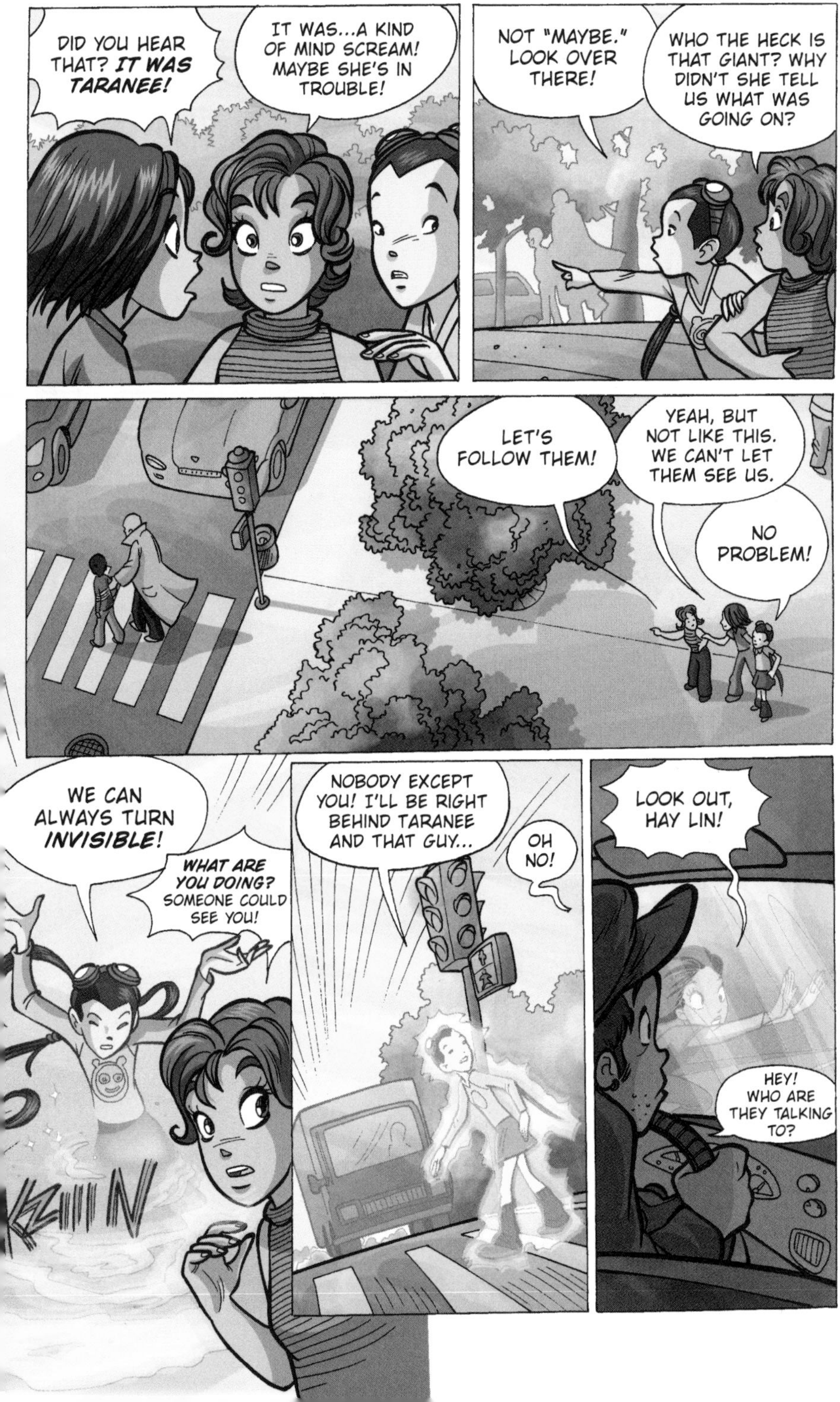

DID YOU HEAR THAT? IT WAS TARANEE!
IT WAS...A KIND OF MIND SCREAM! MAYBE SHE'S IN TROUBLE!
NOT "MAYBE." LOOK OVER THERE!
WHO THE HECK IS THAT GIANT? WHY DIDN'T SHE TELL US WHAT WAS GOING ON?
LET'S FOLLOW THEM!
YEAH, BUT NOT LIKE THIS. WE CAN'T LET THEM SEE US.
NO PROBLEM!
WE CAN ALWAYS TURN INVISIBLE!
WHAT ARE YOU DOING? SOMEONE COULD SEE YOU!
KZIIIN
NOBODY EXCEPT YOU! I'LL BE RIGHT BEHIND TARANEE AND THAT GUY...
OH NO!
LOOK OUT, HAY LIN!
HEY! WHO ARE THEY TALKING TO?

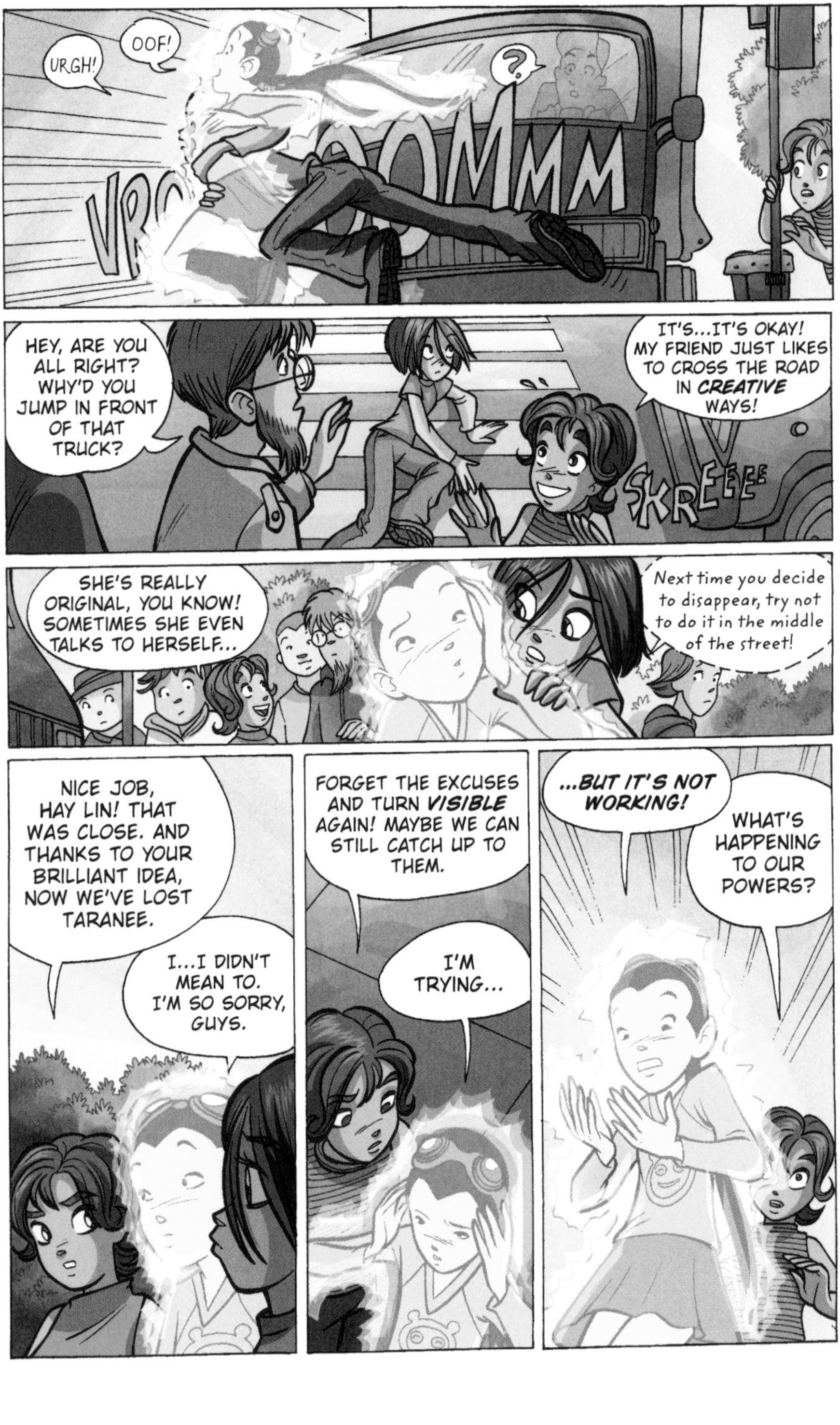
URGH!
OOF!
?
VROOOMMMM
HEY, ARE YOU ALL RIGHT? WHY'D YOU JUMP IN FRONT OF THAT TRUCK?
IT'S...IT'S OKAY! MY FRIEND JUST LIKES TO CROSS THE ROAD IN CREATIVE WAYS!
SKREEEE
SHE'S REALLY ORIGINAL, YOU KNOW! SOMETIMES SHE EVEN TALKS TO HERSELF...
Next time you decide to disappear, try not to do it in the middle of the street!
NICE JOB, HAY LIN! THAT WAS CLOSE. AND THANKS TO YOUR BRILLIANT IDEA, NOW WE'VE LOST TARANEE.
I...I DIDN'T MEAN TO. I'M SO SORRY, GUYS.
FORGET THE EXCUSES AND TURN VISIBLE AGAIN! MAYBE WE CAN STILL CATCH UP TO THEM.
I'M TRYING...
...BUT IT'S NOT WORKING!
WHAT'S HAPPENING TO OUR POWERS?

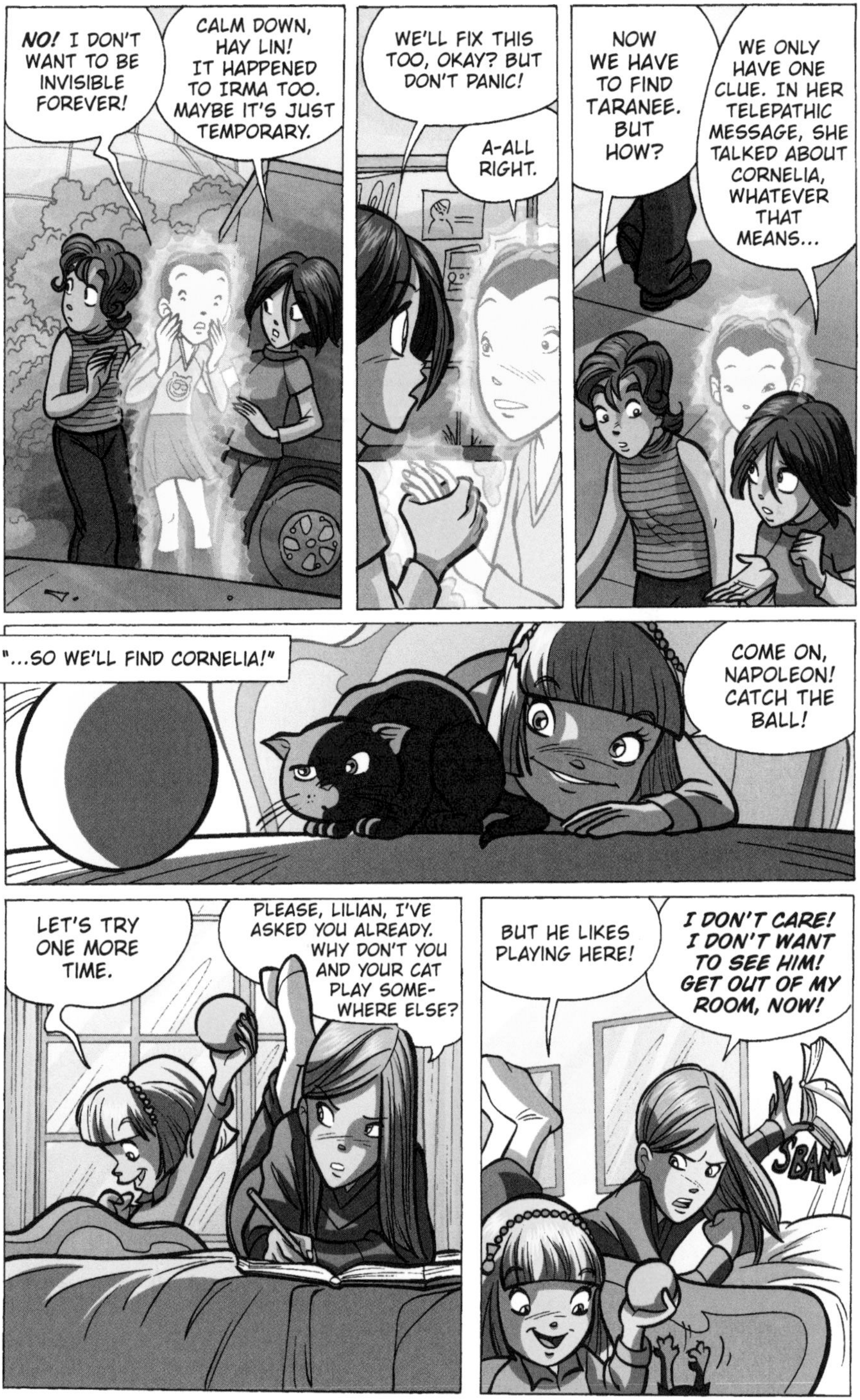
NO! I DON'T WANT TO BE INVISIBLE FOREVER!
CALM DOWN, HAY LIN! IT HAPPENED TO IRMA TOO. MAYBE IT'S JUST TEMPORARY.
WE'LL FIX THIS TOO, OKAY? BUT DON'T PANIC!
A-ALL RIGHT.
NOW WE HAVE TO FIND TARANEE. BUT HOW?
WE ONLY HAVE ONE CLUE. IN HER TELEPATHIC MESSAGE, SHE TALKED ABOUT CORNELIA, WHATEVER THAT MEANS...
"...SO WE'LL FIND CORNELIA!"
COME ON, NAPOLEON! CATCH THE BALL!
LET'S TRY ONE MORE TIME.
PLEASE, LILIAN, I'VE ASKED YOU ALREADY. WHY DON'T YOU AND YOUR CAT PLAY SOMEWHERE ELSE?
BUT HE LIKES PLAYING HERE!
I DON'T CARE! I DON'T WANT TO SEE HIM! GET OUT OF MY ROOM, NOW!
SBAM

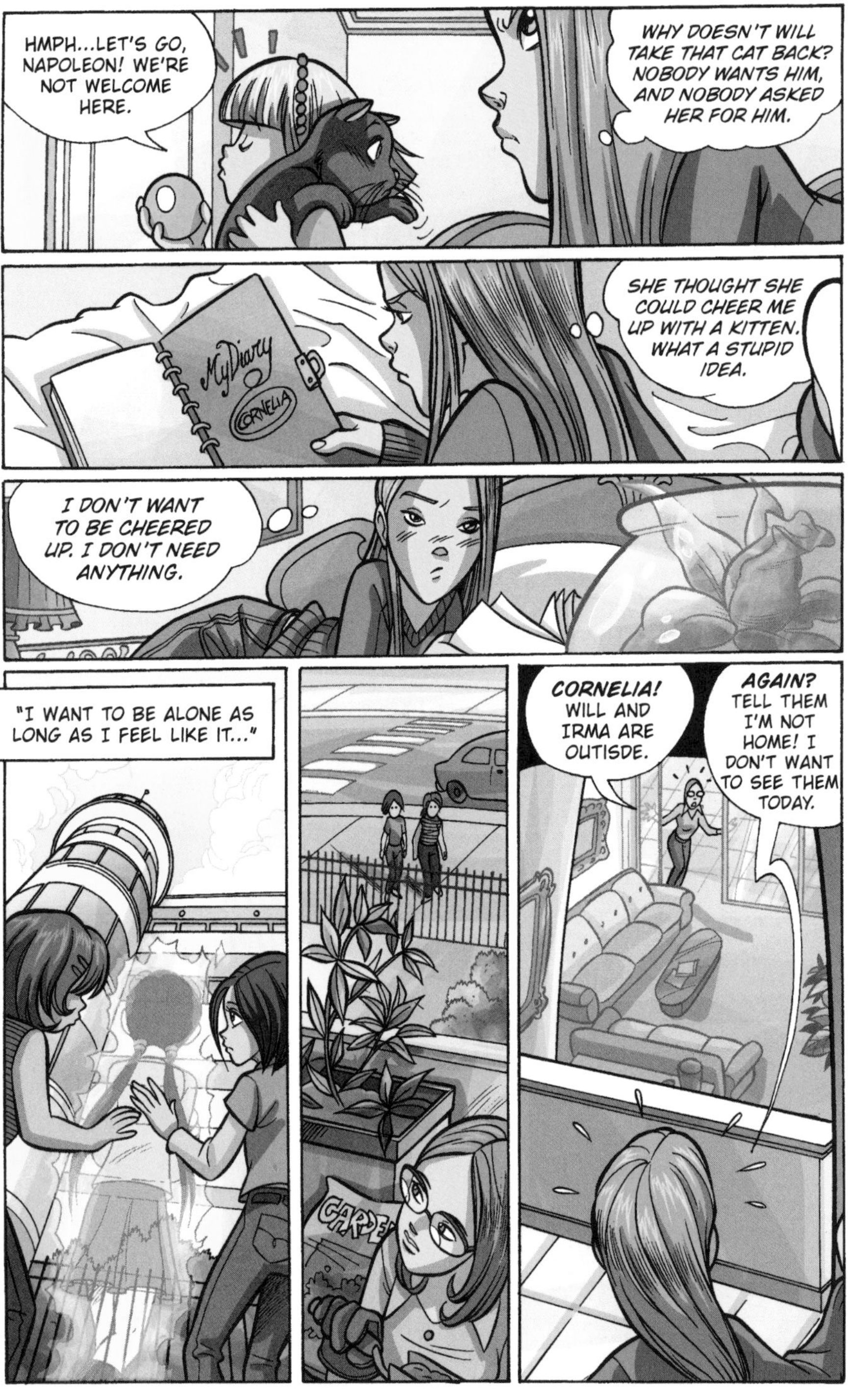
HMPH...LET'S GO, NAPOLEON! WE'RE NOT WELCOME HERE.
WHY DOESN'T WILL TAKE THAT CAT BACK? NOBODY WANTS HIM, AND NOBODY ASKED HER FOR HIM.
MyDiary
CORNELIA
SHE THOUGHT SHE COULD CHEER ME UP WITH A KITTEN. WHAT A STUPID IDEA.
I DON'T WANT TO BE CHEERED UP. I DON'T NEED ANYTHING.
"I WANT TO BE ALONE AS LONG AS I FEEL LIKE IT..."
CORNELIA! WILL AND IRMA ARE OUTISDE.
AGAIN? TELL THEM I'M NOT HOME! I DON'T WANT TO SEE THEM TODAY.

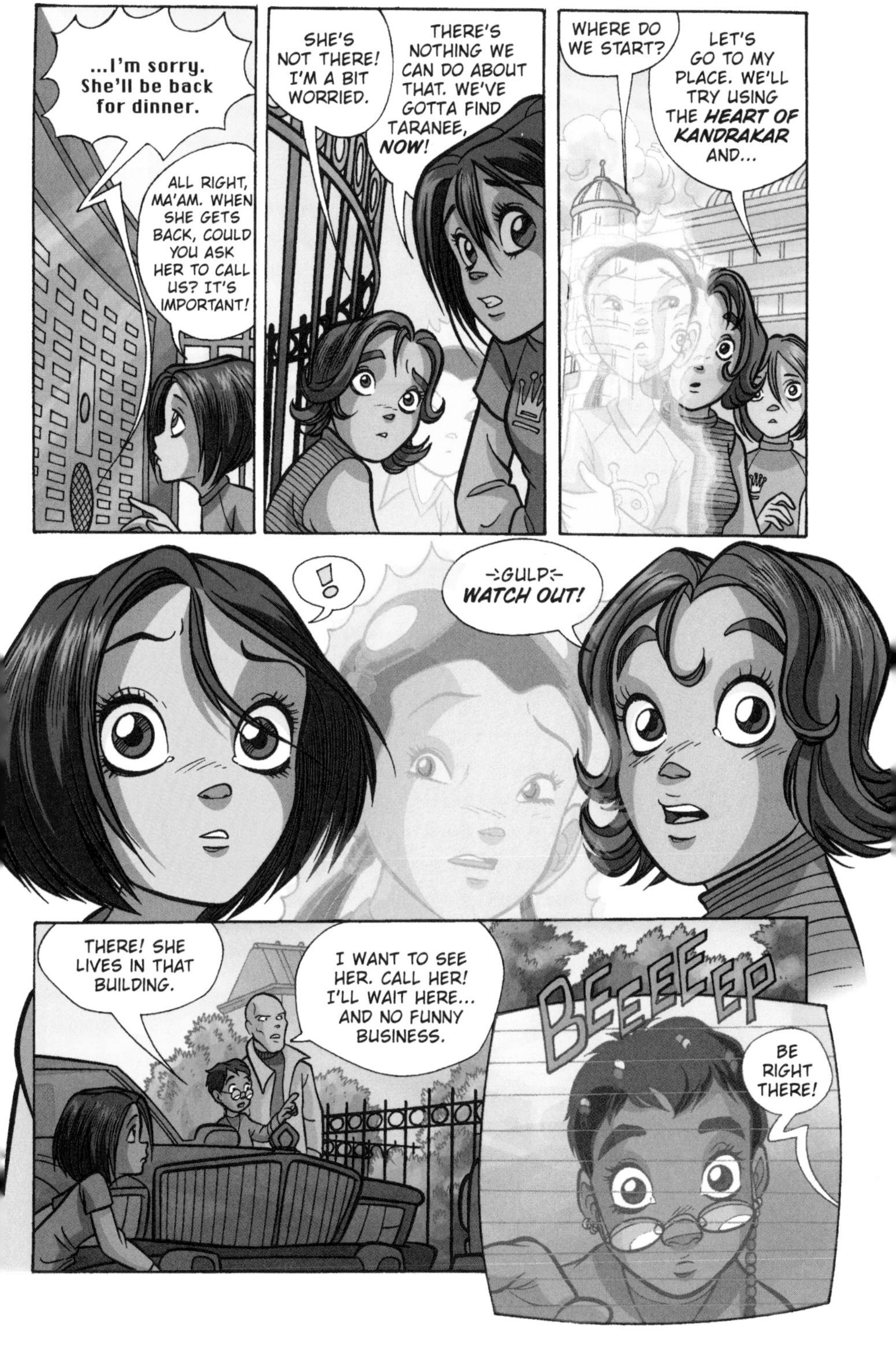
...I'm sorry. She'll be back for dinner.
ALL RIGHT, MA'AM. WHEN SHE GETS BACK, COULD YOU ASK HER TO CALL US? IT'S IMPORTANT!
SHE'S NOT THERE! I'M A BIT WORRIED.
THERE'S NOTHING WE CAN DO ABOUT THAT. WE'VE GOTTA FIND TARANEE, NOW!
WHERE DO WE START?
LET'S GO TO MY PLACE. WE'LL TRY USING THE HEART OF KANDRAKAR AND...
!
GULP
WATCH OUT!
THERE! SHE LIVES IN THAT BUILDING.
I WANT TO SEE HER. CALL HER! I'LL WAIT HERE... AND NO FUNNY BUSINESS.
BEEEEEP
BE RIGHT THERE!

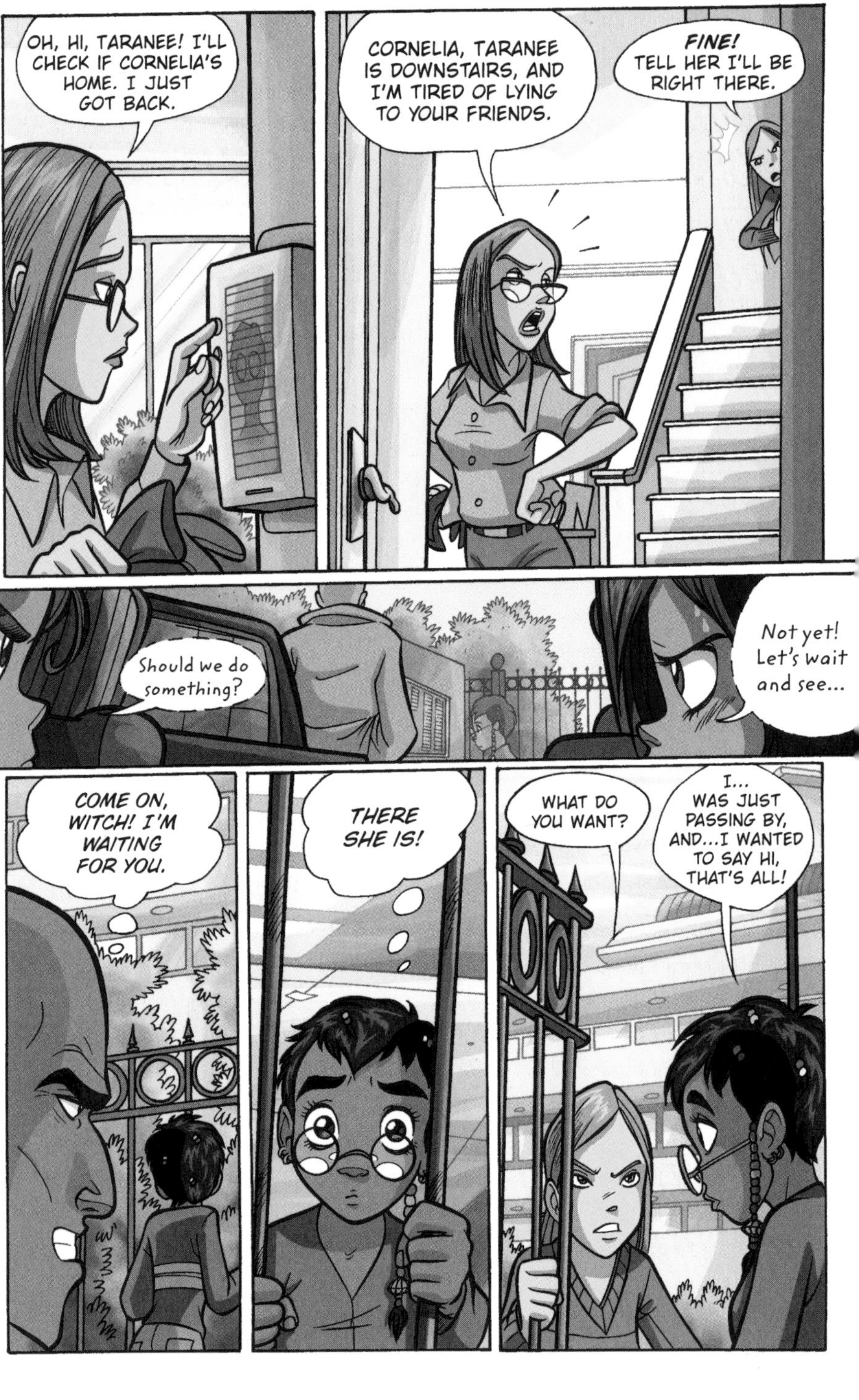
OH, HI, TARANEE! I'LL CHECK IF CORNELIA'S HOME. I JUST GOT BACK.
CORNELIA, TARANEE IS DOWNSTAIRS, AND I'M TIRED OF LYING TO YOUR FRIENDS.
FINE! TELL HER I'LL BE RIGHT THERE.
Should we do something?
Not yet! Let's wait and see...
COME ON, WITCH! I'M WAITING FOR YOU.
THERE SHE IS!
WHAT DO YOU WANT?
I... WAS JUST PASSING BY, AND...I WANTED TO SAY HI, THAT'S ALL!

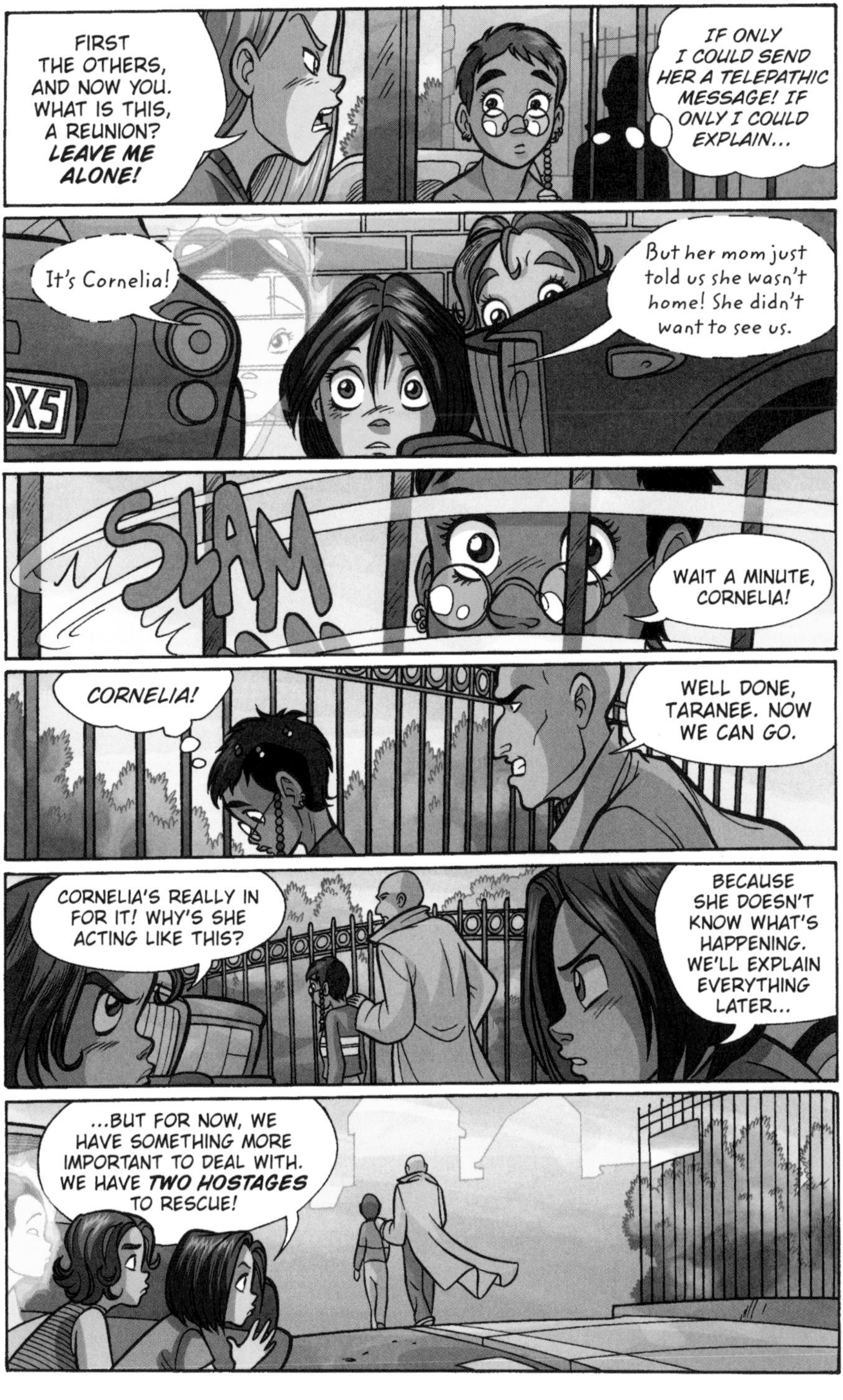
FIRST THE OTHERS, AND NOW YOU. WHAT IS THIS, A REUNION? LEAVE ME ALONE!
IF ONLY I COULD SEND HER A TELEPATHIC MESSAGE! IF ONLY I COULD EXPLAIN...
It's Cornelia!
DX5
But her mom just told us she wasn't home! She didn't want to see us.
SLAM
WAIT A MINUTE, CORNELIA!
CORNELIA!
WELL DONE, TARANEE. NOW WE CAN GO.
CORNELIA'S REALLY IN FOR IT! WHY'S SHE ACTING LIKE THIS?
BECAUSE SHE DOESN'T KNOW WHAT'S HAPPENING. WE'LL EXPLAIN EVERYTHING LATER...
...BUT FOR NOW, WE HAVE SOMETHING MORE IMPORTANT TO DEAL WITH. WE HAVE TWO HOSTAGES TO RESCUE!

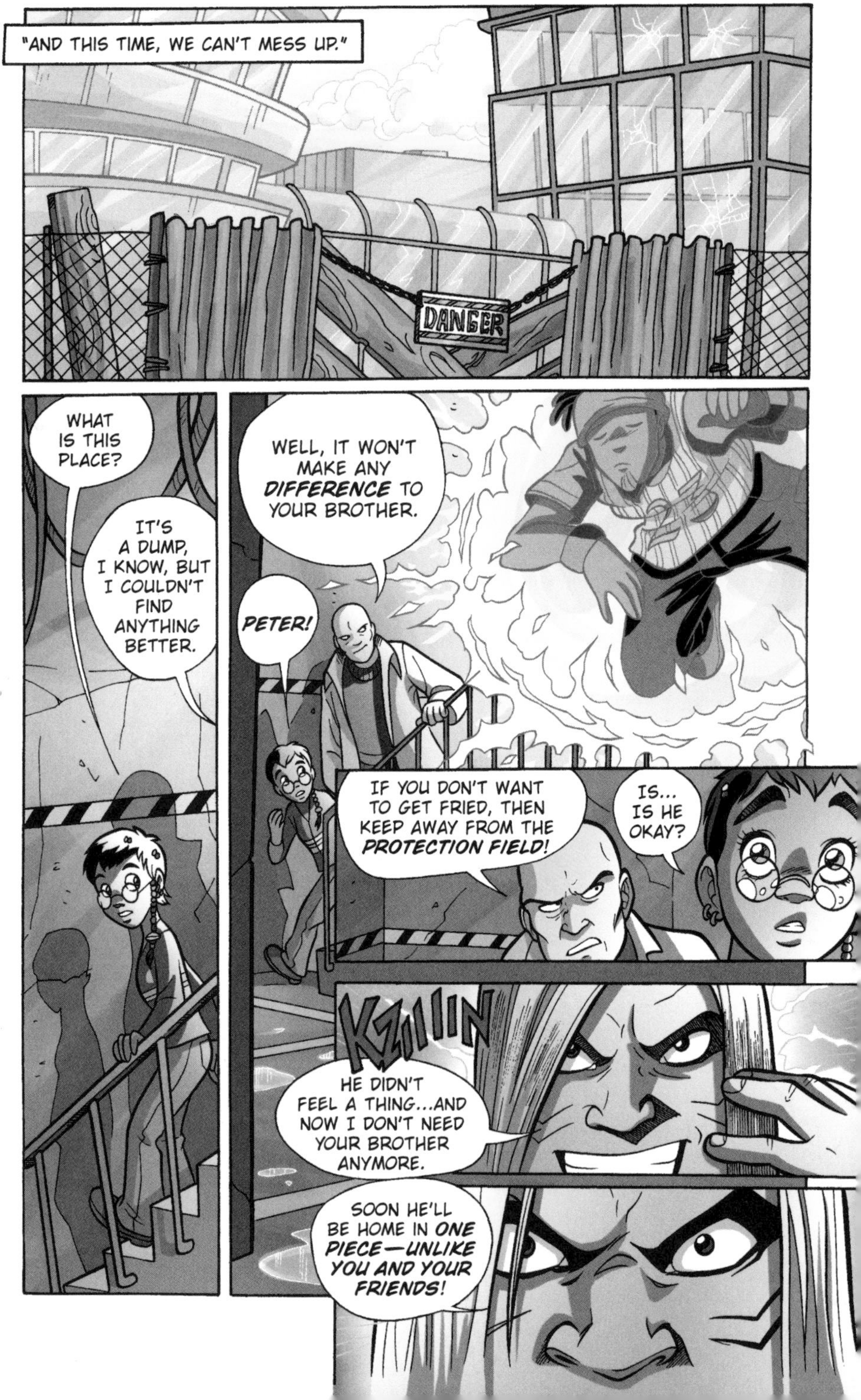
"AND THIS TIME, WE CAN'T MESS UP."
DANGER
WHAT IS THIS PLACE?
IT'S A DUMP, I KNOW, BUT I COULDN'T FIND ANYTHING BETTER.
WELL, IT WON'T MAKE ANY DIFFERENCE TO YOUR BROTHER.
PETER!
IF YOU DON'T WANT TO GET FRIED, THEN KEEP AWAY FROM THE PROTECTION FIELD!
IS... IS HE OKAY?
KZIIIIN
HE DIDN'T FEEL A THING...AND NOW I DON'T NEED YOUR BROTHER ANYMORE.
SOON HE'LL BE HOME IN ONE PIECE—UNLIKE YOU AND YOUR FRIENDS!

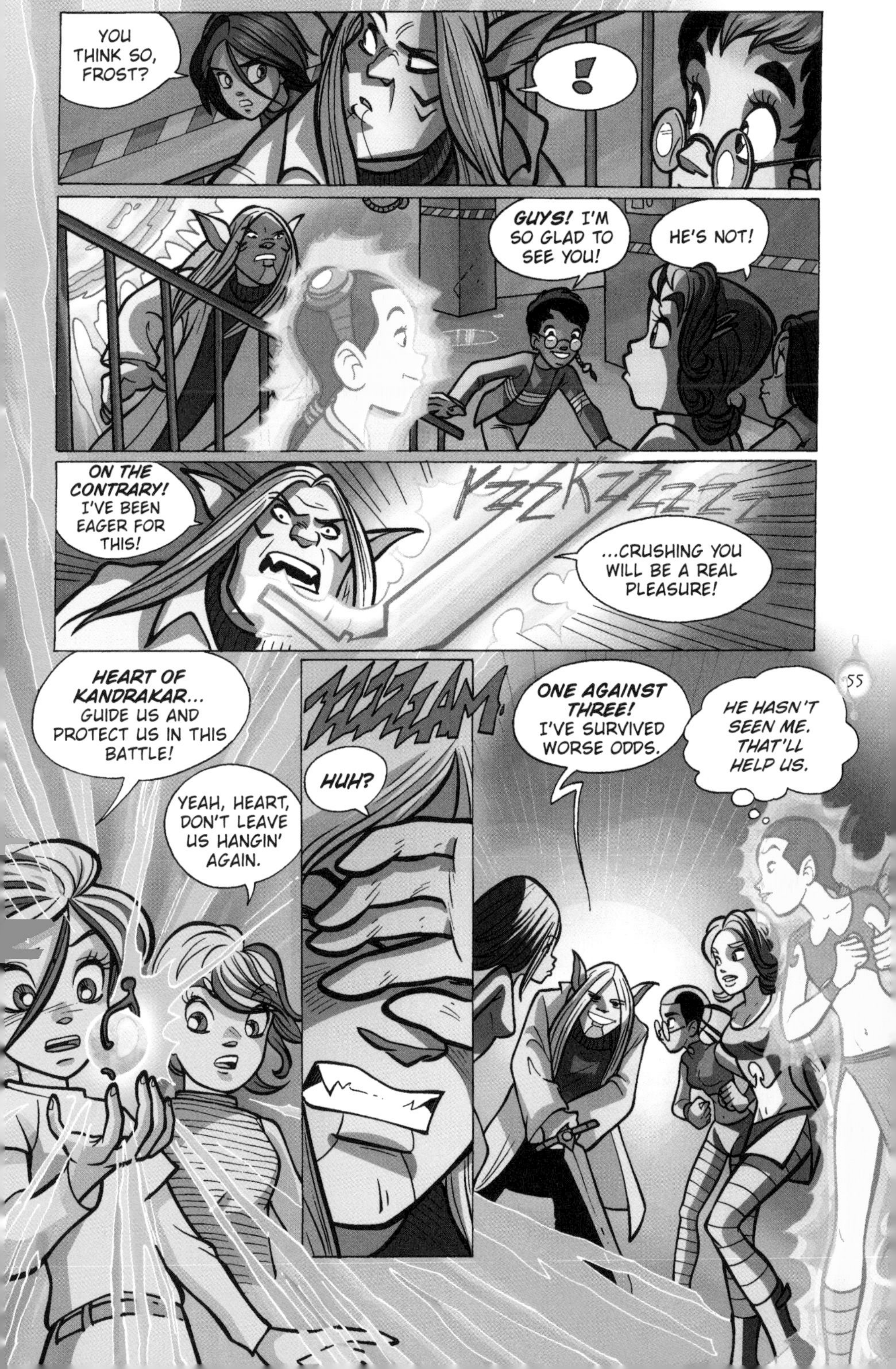

YOU THINK SO, FROST?
!
GUYS! I'M SO GLAD TO SEE YOU!
HE'S NOT!
ON THE CONTRARY! I'VE BEEN EAGER FOR THIS!
...CRUSHING YOU WILL BE A REAL PLEASURE!
HEART OF KANDRAKAR... GUIDE US AND PROTECT US IN THIS BATTLE!
YEAH, HEART, DON'T LEAVE US HANGIN' AGAIN.
HUH?
ONE AGAINST THREE! I'VE SURVIVED WORSE ODDS.
HE HASN'T SEEN ME. THAT'LL HELP US.

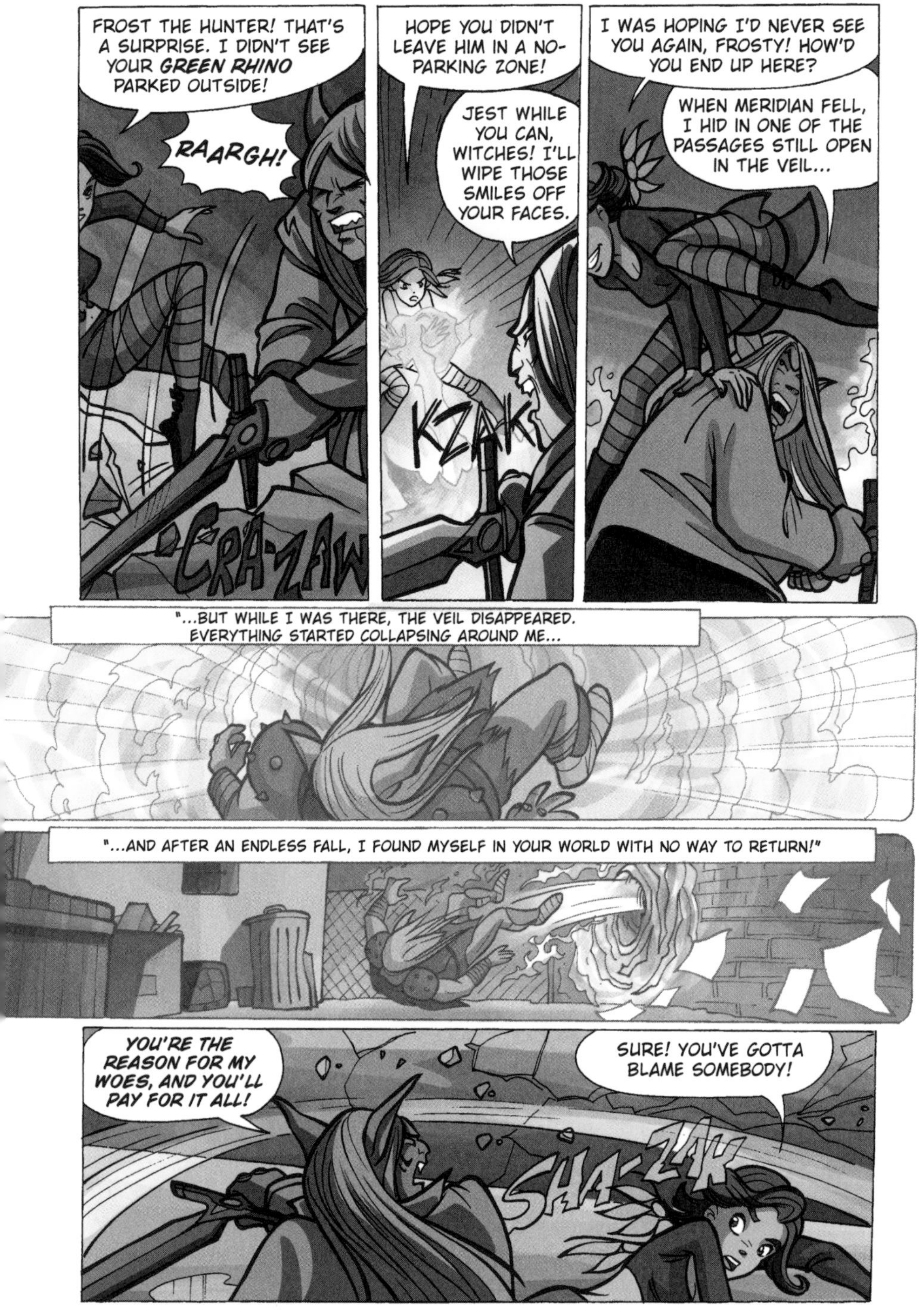
FROST THE HUNTER! THAT'S A SURPRISE. I DIDN'T SEE YOUR **GREEN RHINO** PARKED OUTSIDE!
RAARGH!
CRA-ZAW
HOPE YOU DIDN'T LEAVE HIM IN A NO-PARKING ZONE!
JEST WHILE YOU CAN, WITCHES! I'LL WIPE THOSE SMILES OFF YOUR FACES.
KZAK
I WAS HOPING I'D NEVER SEE YOU AGAIN, FROSTY! HOW'D YOU END UP HERE?
WHEN MERIDIAN FELL, I HID IN ONE OF THE PASSAGES STILL OPEN IN THE VEIL...
"...BUT WHILE I WAS THERE, THE VEIL DISAPPEARED. EVERYTHING STARTED COLLAPSING AROUND ME...
"...AND AFTER AN ENDLESS FALL, I FOUND MYSELF IN YOUR WORLD WITH NO WAY TO RETURN!"
YOU'RE THE REASON FOR MY WOES, AND YOU'LL PAY FOR IT ALL!
SURE! YOU'VE GOTTA BLAME SOMEBODY!
SHA-ZAK

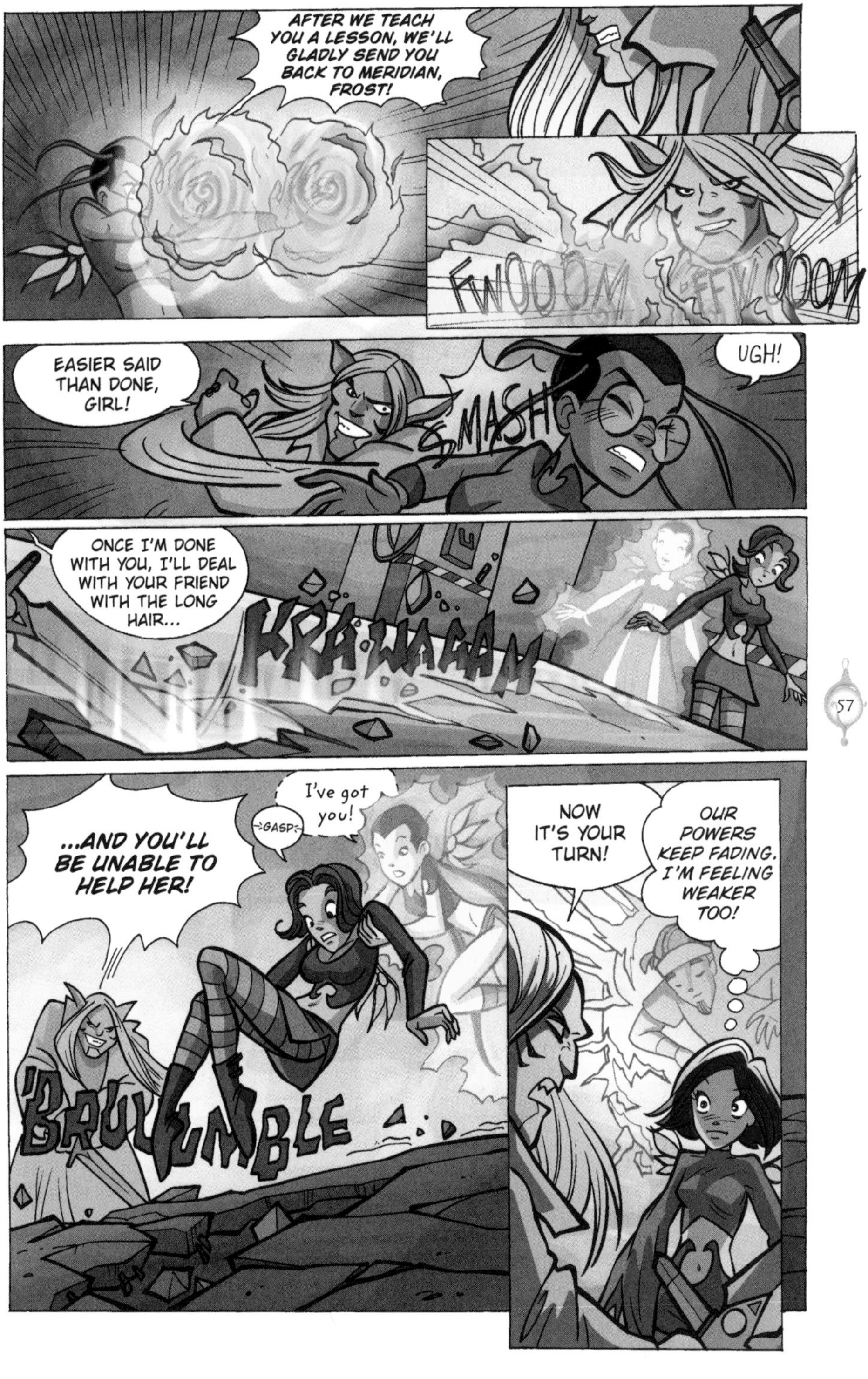
AFTER WE TEACH YOU A LESSON, WE'LL GLADLY SEND YOU BACK TO MERIDIAN, FROST!
FWOOOM
FWOOOM
EASIER SAID THAN DONE, GIRL!
SMASH
UGH!
ONCE I'M DONE WITH YOU, I'LL DEAL WITH YOUR FRIEND WITH THE LONG HAIR...
KRAWAAAM
...AND YOU'LL BE UNABLE TO HELP HER!
GASP
I've got you!
BRUUMBLE
NOW IT'S YOUR TURN!
OUR POWERS KEEP FADING. I'M FEELING WEAKER TOO!

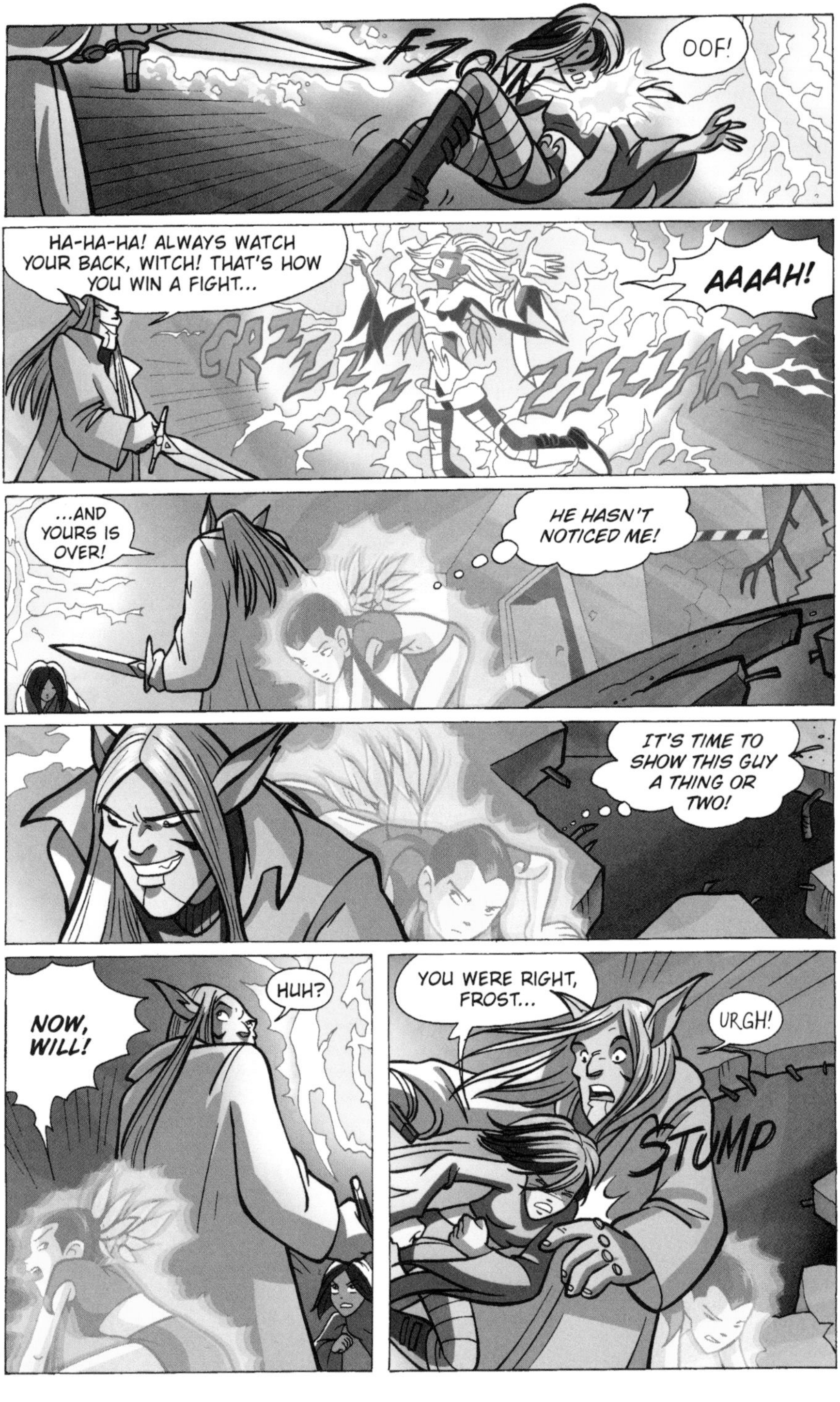
FZOOM
OOF!
HA-HA-HA! ALWAYS WATCH YOUR BACK, WITCH! THAT'S HOW YOU WIN A FIGHT...
AAAAH!
GRZZZZ
ZZZZZAK
...AND YOURS IS OVER!
HE HASN'T NOTICED ME!
IT'S TIME TO SHOW THIS GUY A THING OR TWO!
NOW, WILL!
HUH?
YOU WERE RIGHT, FROST...
URGH!
STUMP

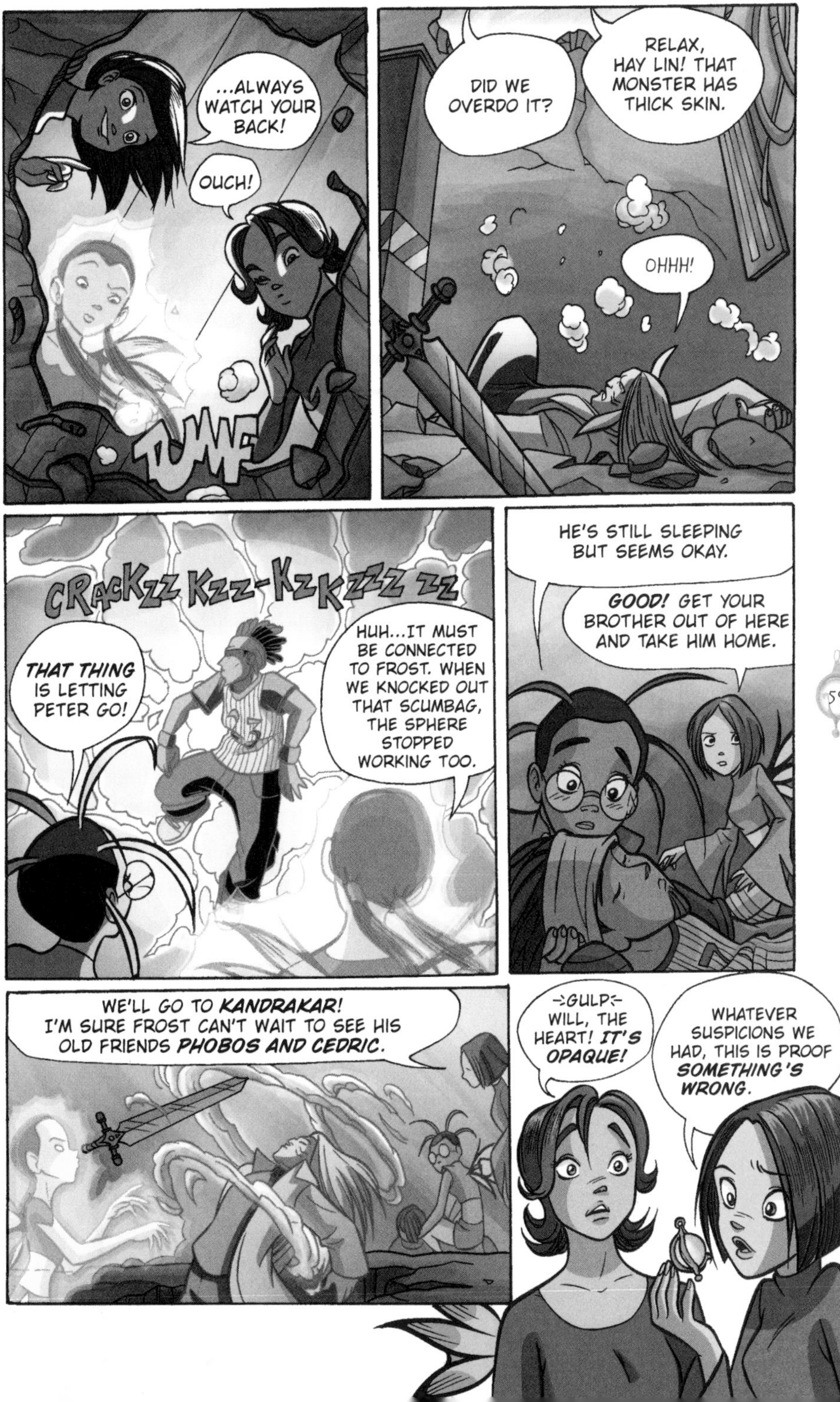
...ALWAYS WATCH YOUR BACK!
OUCH!
TUMF
DID WE OVERDO IT?
RELAX, HAY LIN! THAT MONSTER HAS THICK SKIN.
OHHH!
CRACKZZ KZZ-KZKZZZ ZZ
THAT THING IS LETTING PETER GO!
HUH...IT MUST BE CONNECTED TO FROST. WHEN WE KNOCKED OUT THAT SCUMBAG, THE SPHERE STOPPED WORKING TOO.
HE'S STILL SLEEPING BUT SEEMS OKAY.
GOOD! GET YOUR BROTHER OUT OF HERE AND TAKE HIM HOME.
WE'LL GO TO KANDRAKAR! I'M SURE FROST CAN'T WAIT TO SEE HIS OLD FRIENDS PHOBOS AND CEDRIC.
GULP WILL, THE HEART! IT'S OPAQUE!
WHATEVER SUSPICIONS WE HAD, THIS IS PROOF SOMETHING'S WRONG.

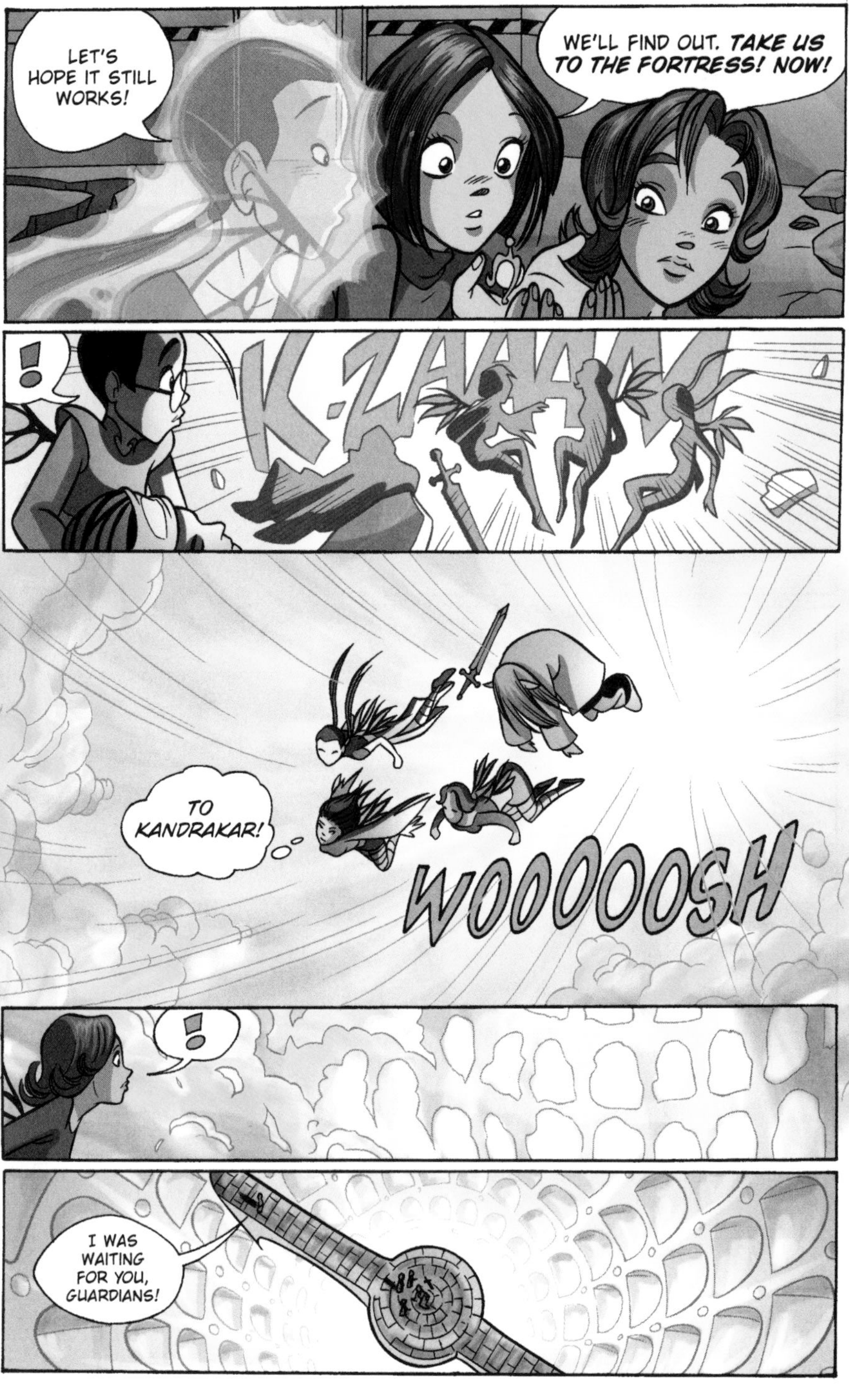
LET'S HOPE IT STILL WORKS!
WE'LL FIND OUT. TAKE US TO THE FORTRESS! NOW!
!
K-ZAAAM
TO KANDRAKAR!
WOOOOOSH
!
I WAS WAITING FOR YOU, GUARDIANS!

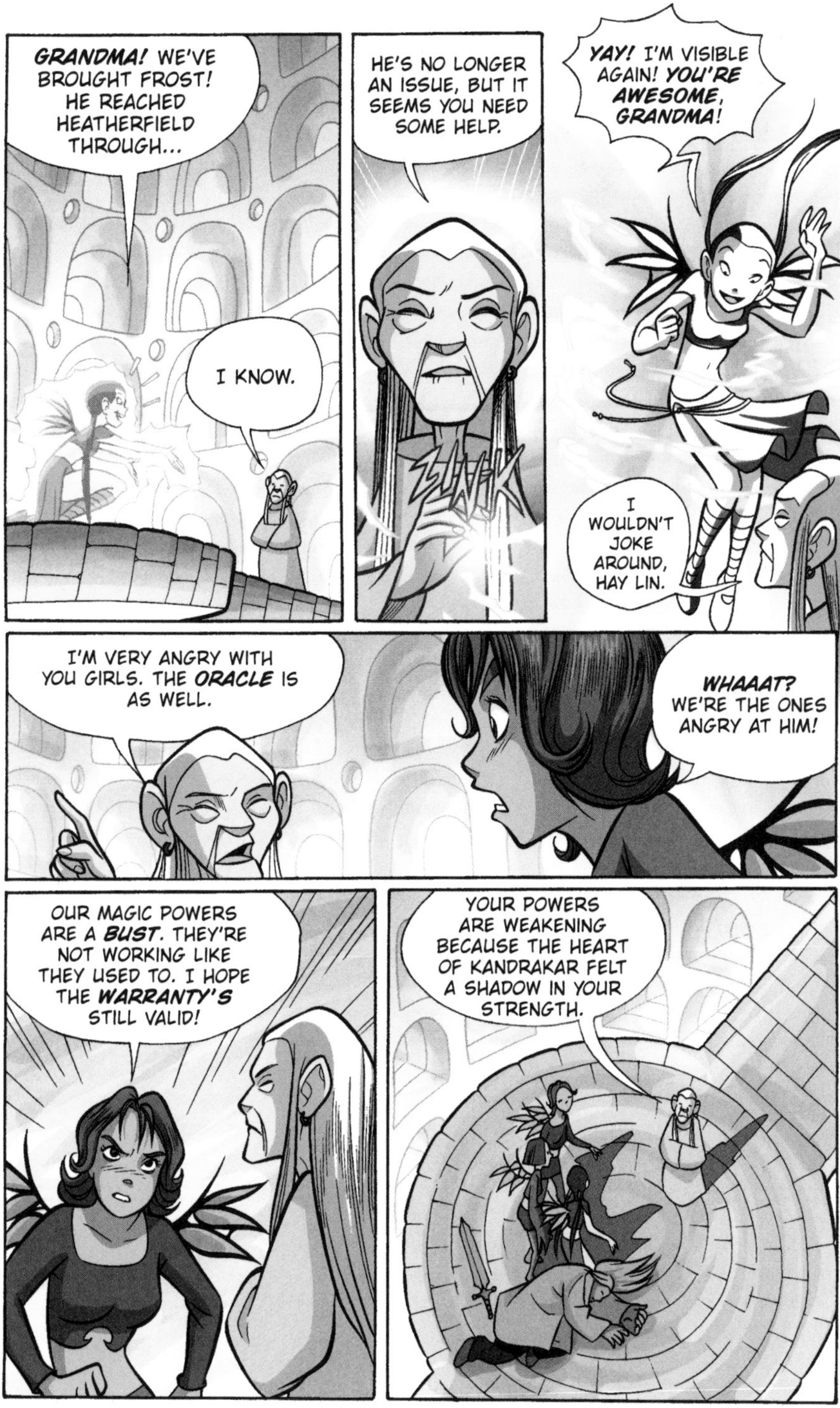
GRANDMA! WE'VE BROUGHT FROST! HE REACHED HEATHERFIELD THROUGH...
I KNOW.
HE'S NO LONGER AN ISSUE, BUT IT SEEMS YOU NEED SOME HELP.
YAY! I'M VISIBLE AGAIN! YOU'RE AWESOME, GRANDMA!
I WOULDN'T JOKE AROUND, HAY LIN.
I'M VERY ANGRY WITH YOU GIRLS. THE ORACLE IS AS WELL.
WHAAAT? WE'RE THE ONES ANGRY AT HIM!
OUR MAGIC POWERS ARE A BUST. THEY'RE NOT WORKING LIKE THEY USED TO. I HOPE THE WARRANTY'S STILL VALID!
YOUR POWERS ARE WEAKENING BECAUSE THE HEART OF KANDRAKAR FELT A SHADOW IN YOUR STRENGTH.

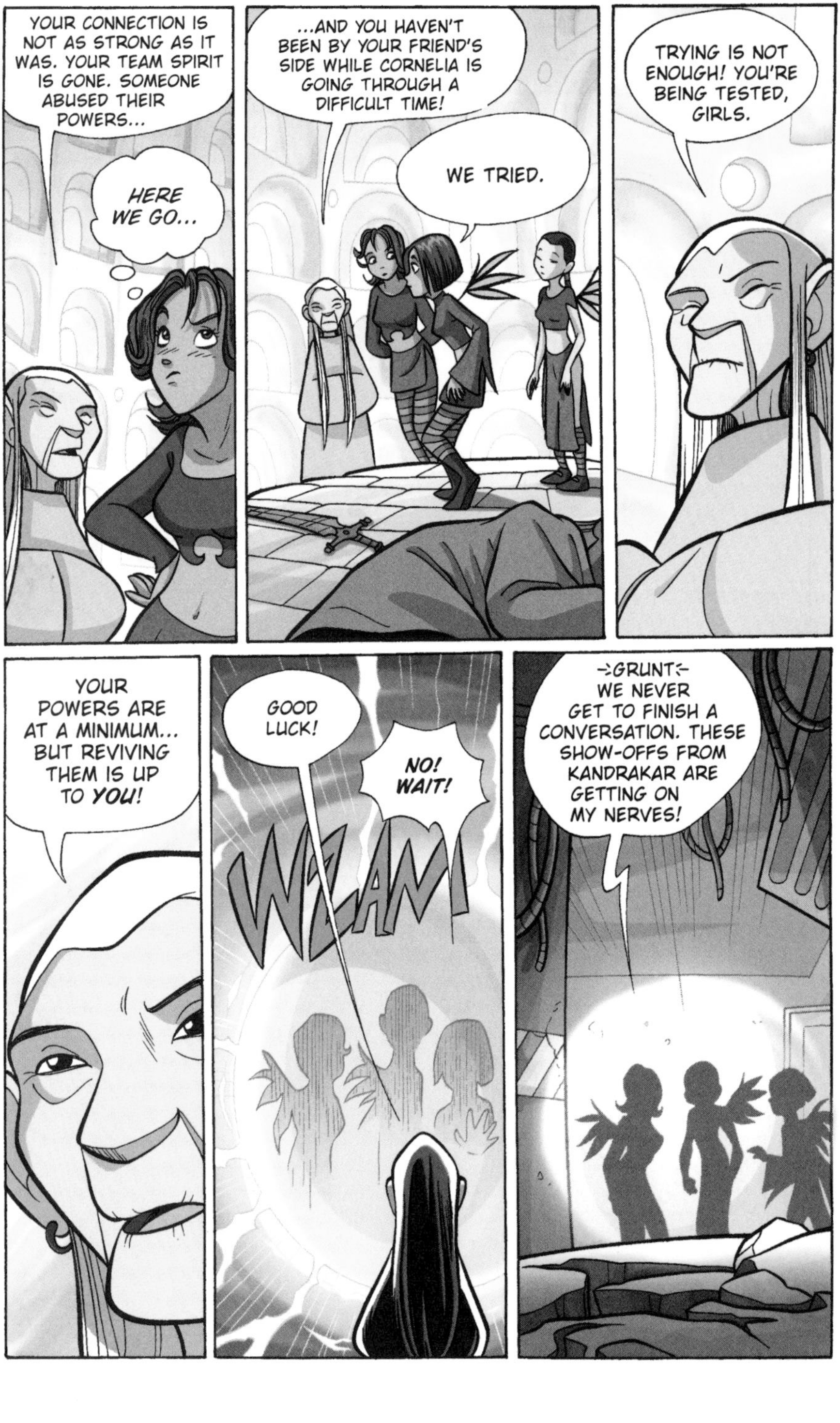

YOUR CONNECTION IS NOT AS STRONG AS IT WAS. YOUR TEAM SPIRIT IS GONE. SOMEONE ABUSED THEIR POWERS...
HERE WE GO...
...AND YOU HAVEN'T BEEN BY YOUR FRIEND'S SIDE WHILE CORNELIA IS GOING THROUGH A DIFFICULT TIME!
WE TRIED.
TRYING IS NOT ENOUGH! YOU'RE BEING TESTED, GIRLS.
YOUR POWERS ARE AT A MINIMUM... BUT REVIVING THEM IS UP TO YOU!
GOOD LUCK!
NO! WAIT!
WZAM
GRUNT
WE NEVER GET TO FINISH A CONVERSATION. THESE SHOW-OFFS FROM KANDRAKAR ARE GETTING ON MY NERVES!

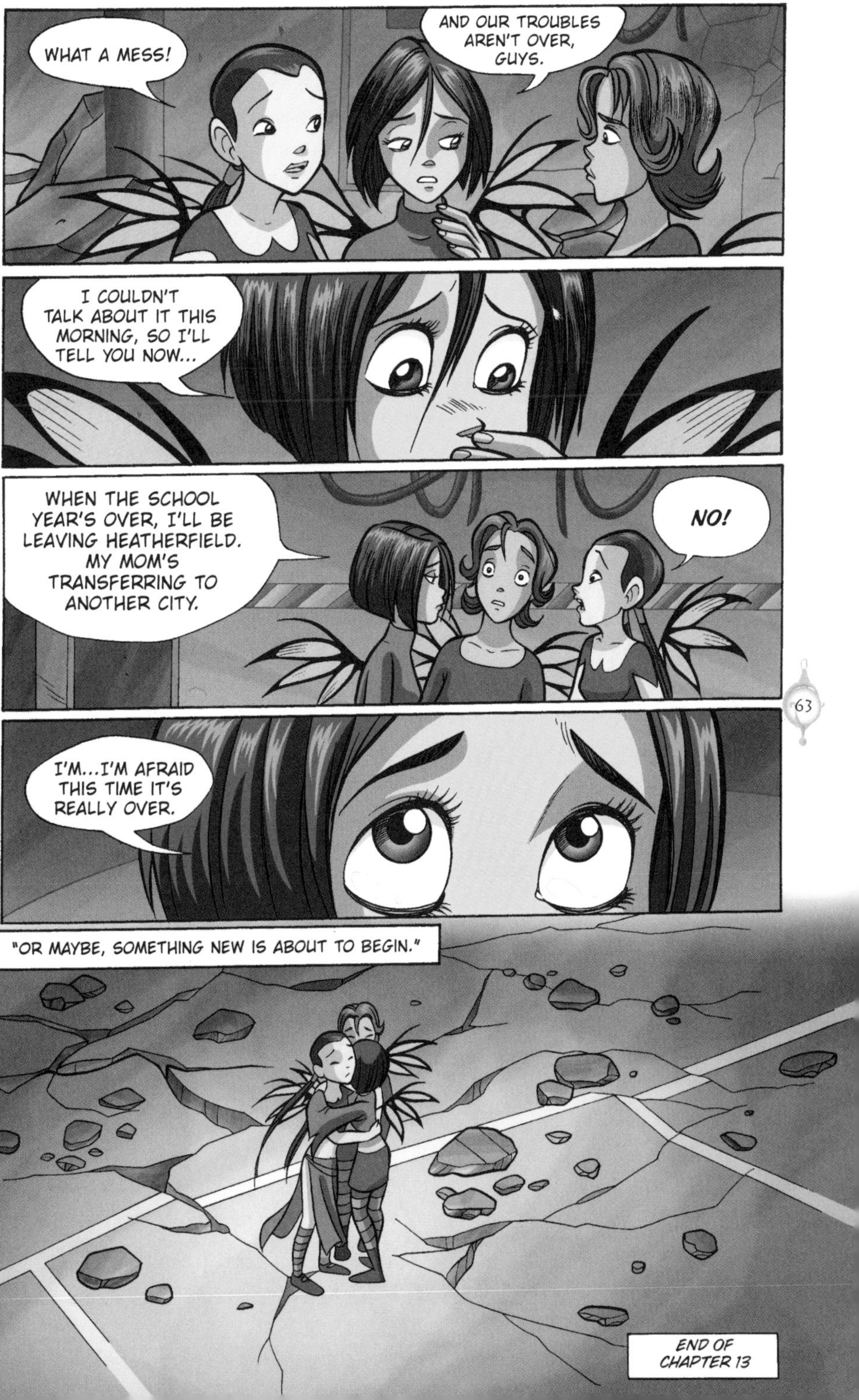
WHAT A MESS!
AND OUR TROUBLES AREN'T OVER, GUYS.
I COULDN'T TALK ABOUT IT THIS MORNING, SO I'LL TELL YOU NOW...
WHEN THE SCHOOL YEAR'S OVER, I'LL BE LEAVING HEATHERFIELD. MY MOM'S TRANSFERRING TO ANOTHER CITY.
NO!
I'M...I'M AFRAID THIS TIME IT'S REALLY OVER.
"OR MAYBE, SOMETHING NEW IS ABOUT TO BEGIN."
END OF CHAPTER 13

"Friendship needs to be fought for."

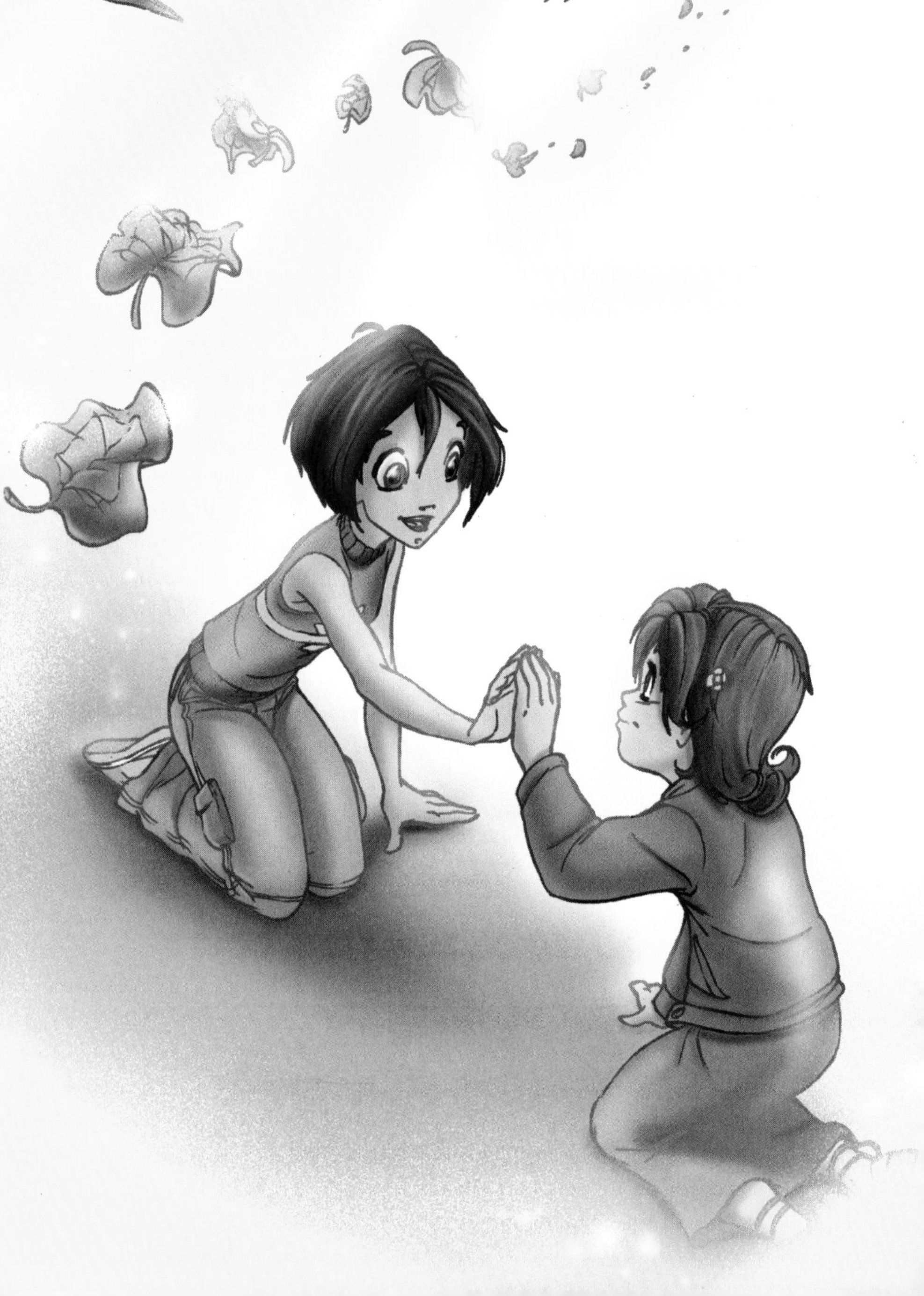

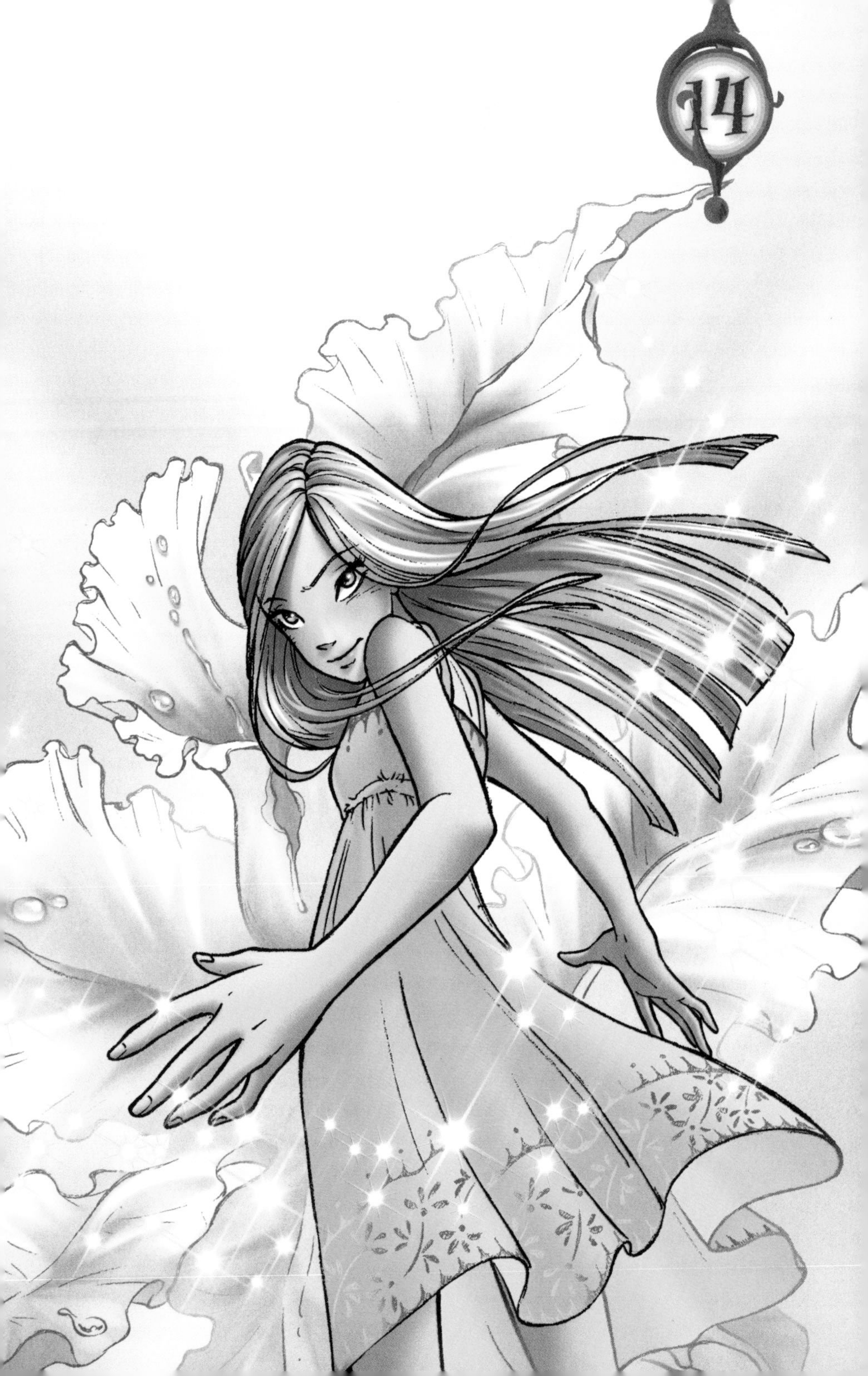

END OF A DREAM

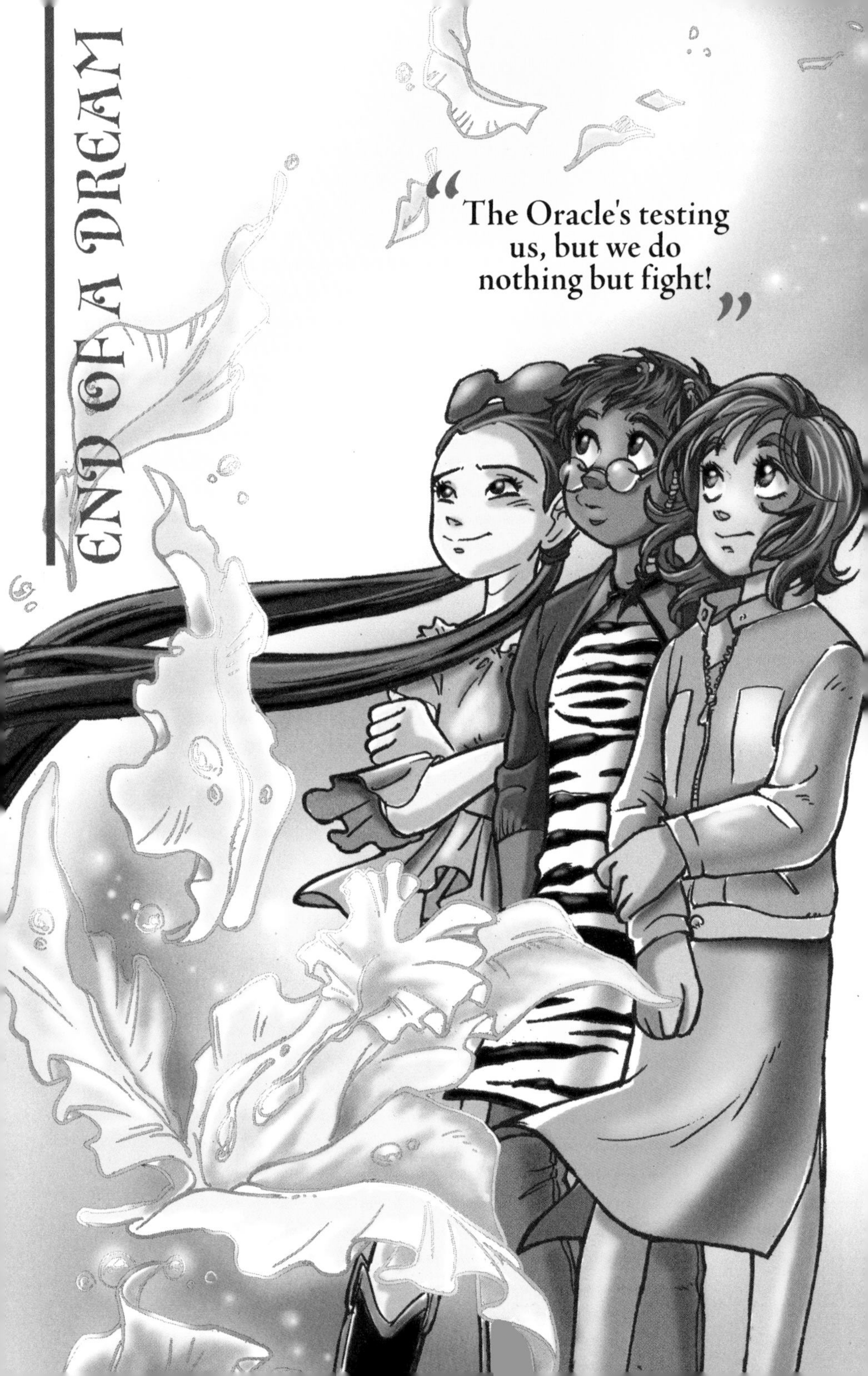
"The Oracle's testing us, but we do nothing but fight!"

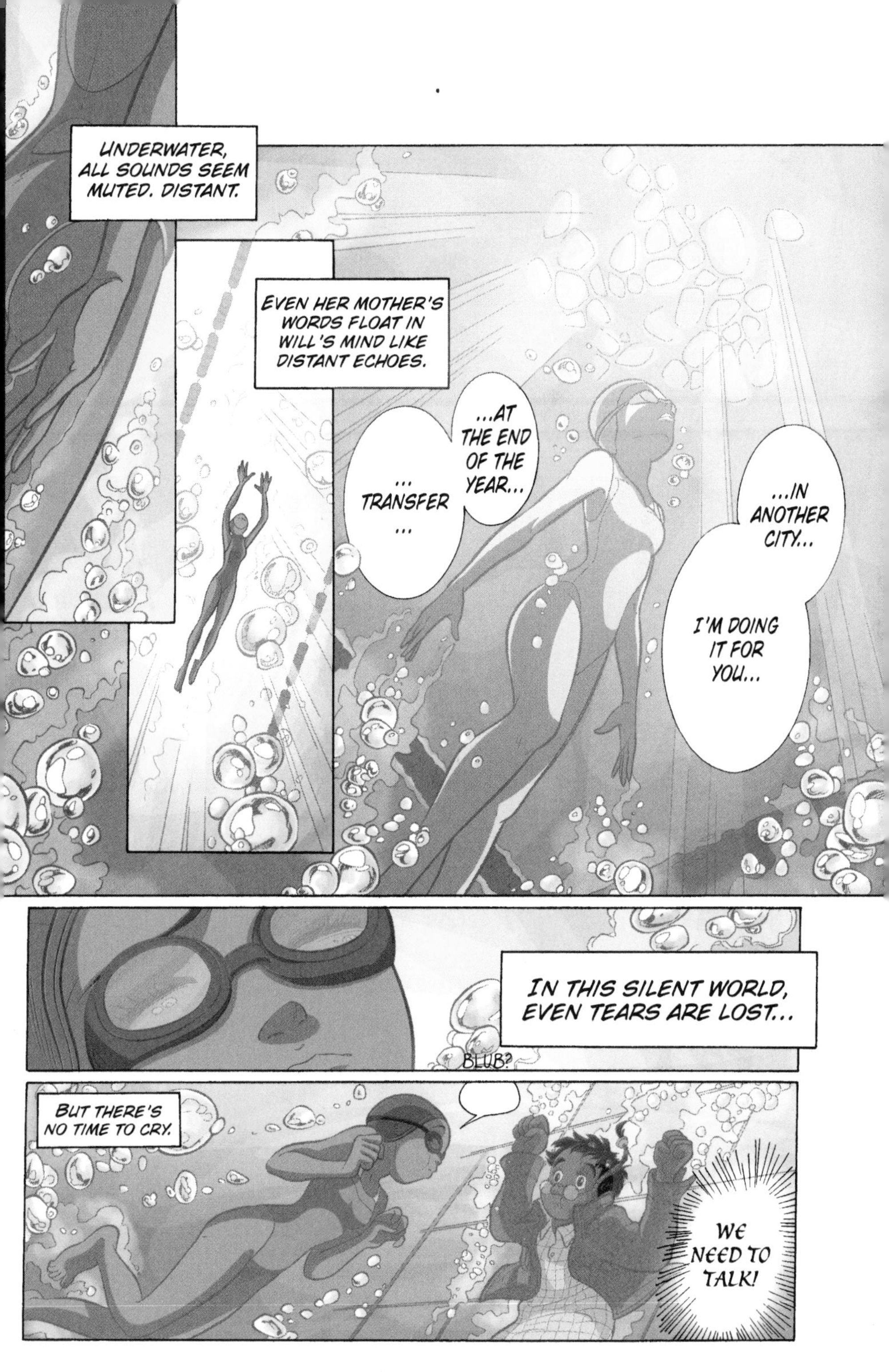
UNDERWATER, ALL SOUNDS SEEM MUTED. DISTANT.
EVEN HER MOTHER'S WORDS FLOAT IN WILL'S MIND LIKE DISTANT ECHOES.
...TRANSFER...
...AT THE END OF THE YEAR...
...IN ANOTHER CITY...
I'M DOING IT FOR YOU...
IN THIS SILENT WORLD, EVEN TEARS ARE LOST...
BLUB?
BUT THERE'S NO TIME TO CRY.
WE NEED TO TALK!

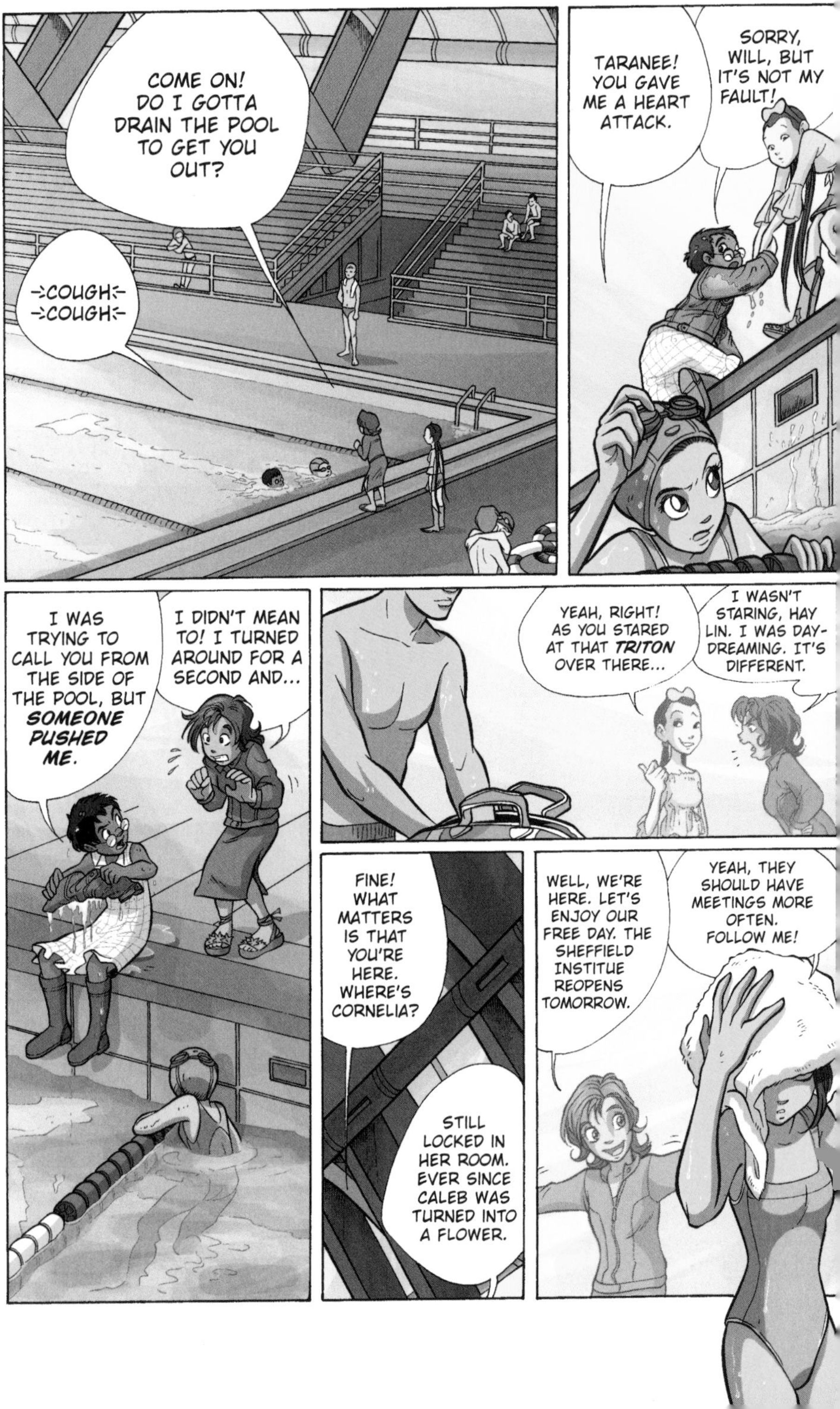
COME ON! DO I GOTTA DRAIN THE POOL TO GET YOU OUT?
COUGH COUGH
TARANEE! YOU GAVE ME A HEART ATTACK.
SORRY, WILL, BUT IT'S NOT MY FAULT!
I WAS TRYING TO CALL YOU FROM THE SIDE OF THE POOL, BUT **SOMEONE PUSHED ME**.
I DIDN'T MEAN TO! I TURNED AROUND FOR A SECOND AND...
YEAH, RIGHT! AS YOU STARED AT THAT ***TRITON*** OVER THERE...
I WASN'T STARING, HAY LIN. I WAS DAY-DREAMING. IT'S DIFFERENT.
FINE! WHAT MATTERS IS THAT YOU'RE HERE. WHERE'S CORNELIA?
STILL LOCKED IN HER ROOM. EVER SINCE CALEB WAS TURNED INTO A FLOWER.
WELL, WE'RE HERE. LET'S ENJOY OUR FREE DAY. THE SHEFFIELD INSTITUE REOPENS TOMORROW.
YEAH, THEY SHOULD HAVE MEETINGS MORE OFTEN. FOLLOW ME!

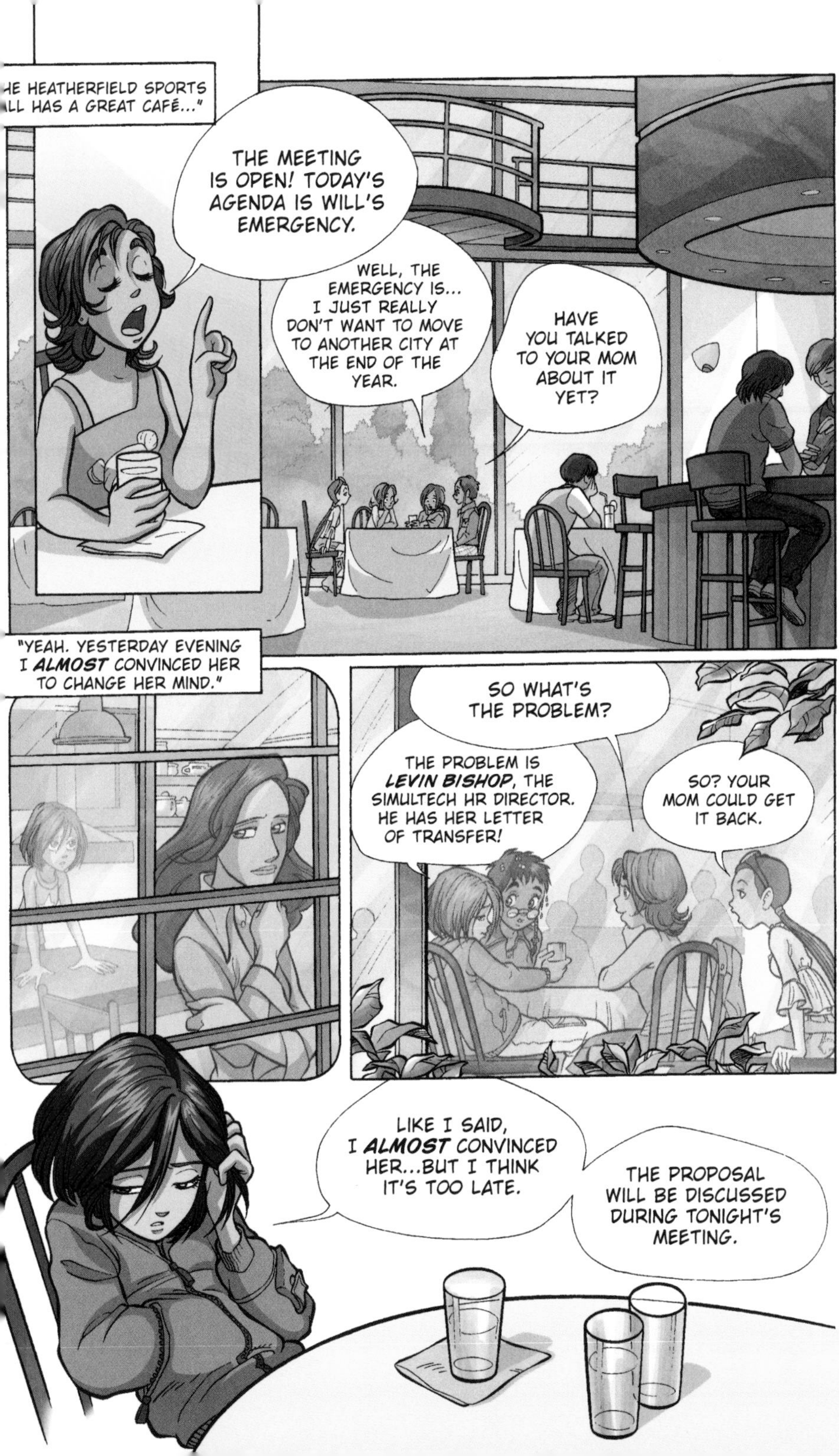

HE HEATHERFIELD SPORTS
LL HAS A GREAT CAFÉ..."
THE MEETING IS OPEN! TODAY'S AGENDA IS WILL'S EMERGENCY.
WELL, THE EMERGENCY IS... I JUST REALLY DON'T WANT TO MOVE TO ANOTHER CITY AT THE END OF THE YEAR.
HAVE YOU TALKED TO YOUR MOM ABOUT IT YET?
"YEAH. YESTERDAY EVENING I ALMOST CONVINCED HER TO CHANGE HER MIND."
SO WHAT'S THE PROBLEM?
THE PROBLEM IS LEVIN BISHOP, THE SIMULTECH HR DIRECTOR. HE HAS HER LETTER OF TRANSFER!
SO? YOUR MOM COULD GET IT BACK.
LIKE I SAID, I ALMOST CONVINCED HER...BUT I THINK IT'S TOO LATE.
THE PROPOSAL WILL BE DISCUSSED DURING TONIGHT'S MEETING.

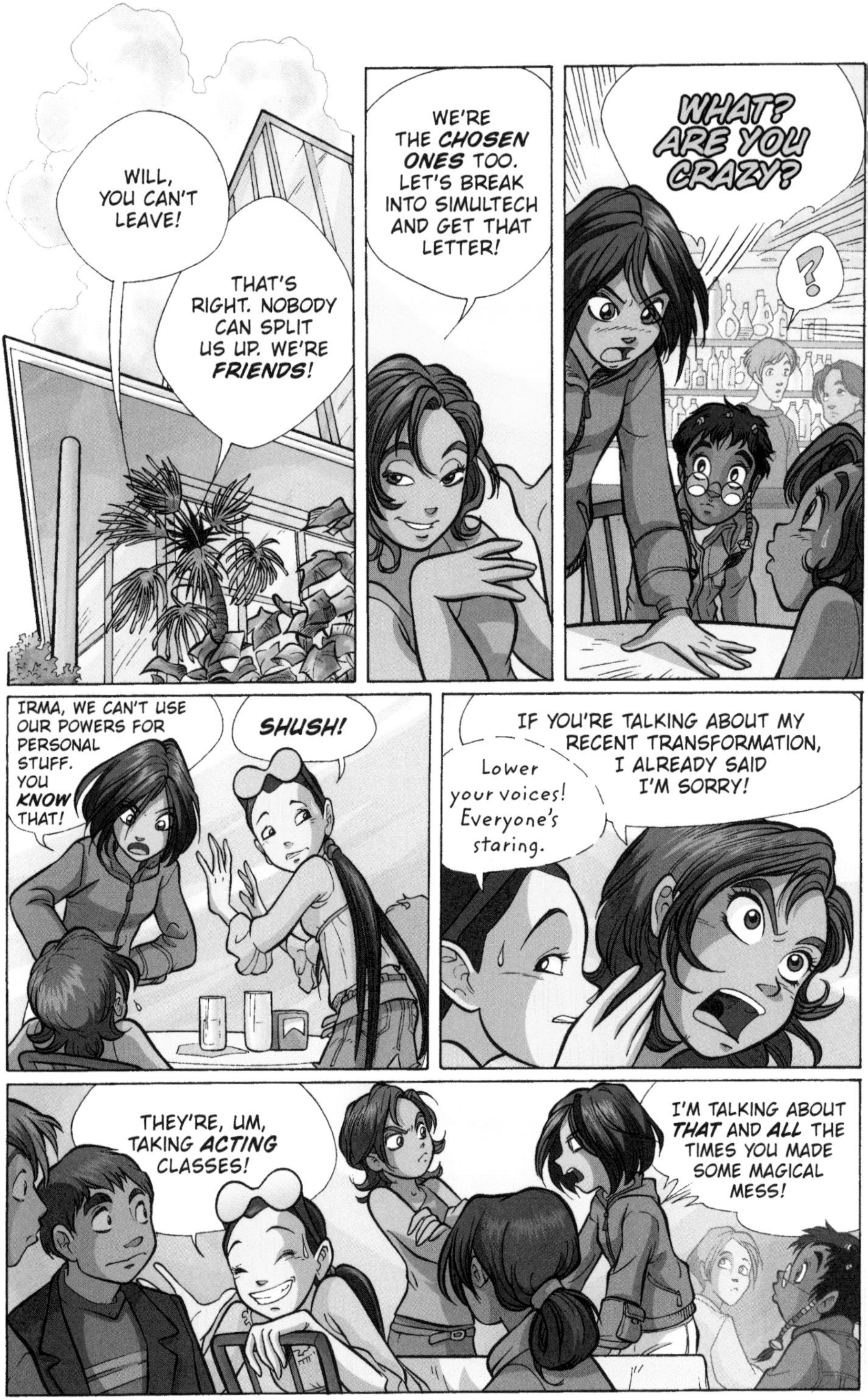
WILL, YOU CAN'T LEAVE!
THAT'S RIGHT. NOBODY CAN SPLIT US UP. WE'RE FRIENDS!
WE'RE THE CHOSEN ONES TOO. LET'S BREAK INTO SIMULTECH AND GET THAT LETTER!
WHAT? ARE YOU CRAZY?
?
IRMA, WE CAN'T USE OUR POWERS FOR PERSONAL STUFF. YOU KNOW THAT!
SHUSH!
IF YOU'RE TALKING ABOUT MY RECENT TRANSFORMATION, I ALREADY SAID I'M SORRY!
Lower your voices! Everyone's staring.
THEY'RE, UM, TAKING ACTING CLASSES!
I'M TALKING ABOUT THAT AND ALL THE TIMES YOU MADE SOME MAGICAL MESS!

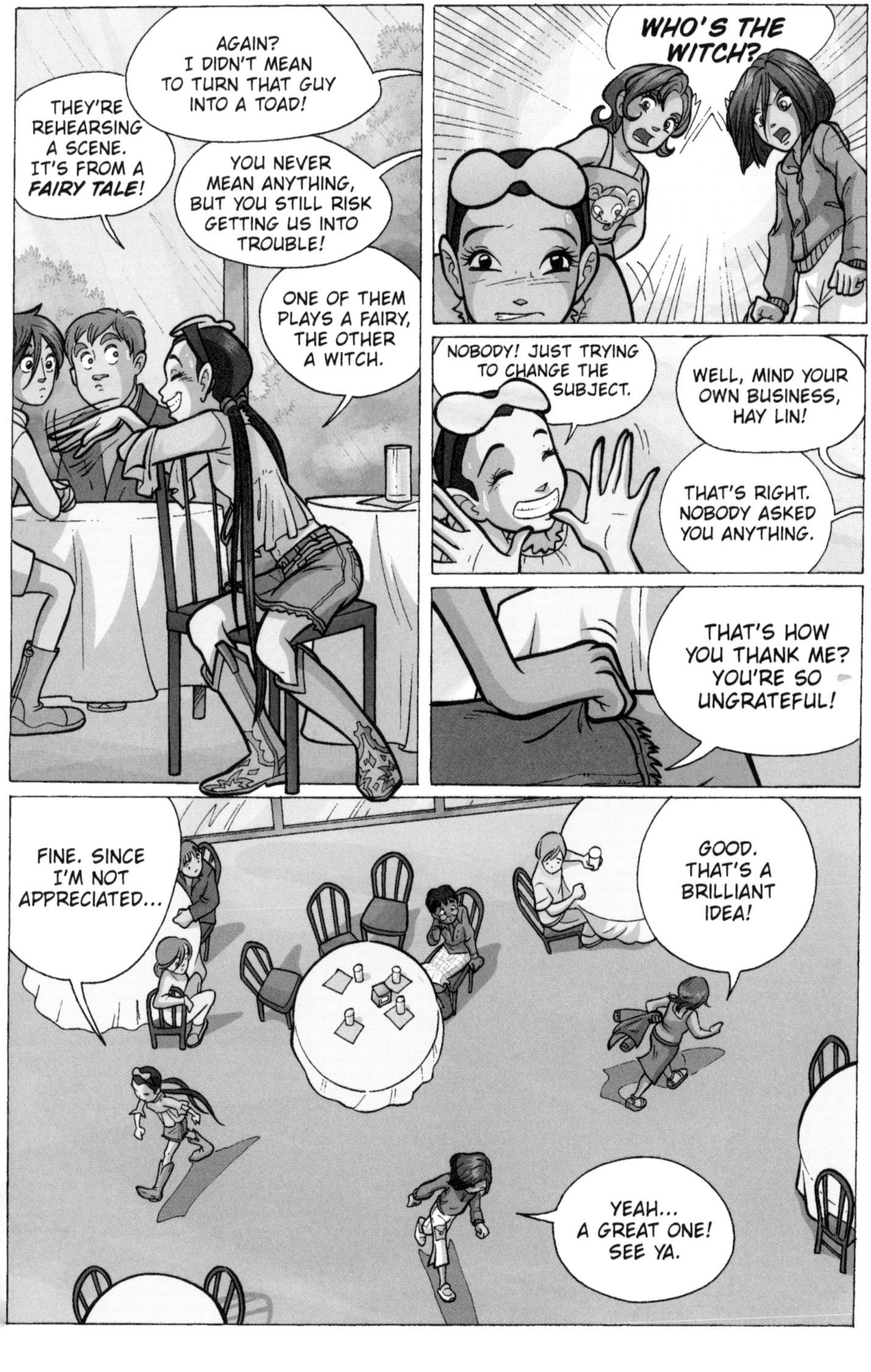

THEY'RE REHEARSING A SCENE. IT'S FROM A FAIRY TALE!
AGAIN? I DIDN'T MEAN TO TURN THAT GUY INTO A TOAD!
YOU NEVER MEAN ANYTHING, BUT YOU STILL RISK GETTING US INTO TROUBLE!
ONE OF THEM PLAYS A FAIRY, THE OTHER A WITCH.
WHO'S THE WITCH?
NOBODY! JUST TRYING TO CHANGE THE SUBJECT.
WELL, MIND YOUR OWN BUSINESS, HAY LIN!
THAT'S RIGHT. NOBODY ASKED YOU ANYTHING.
THAT'S HOW YOU THANK ME? YOU'RE SO UNGRATEFUL!
FINE. SINCE I'M NOT APPRECIATED...
GOOD. THAT'S A BRILLIANT IDEA!
YEAH... A GREAT ONE! SEE YA.

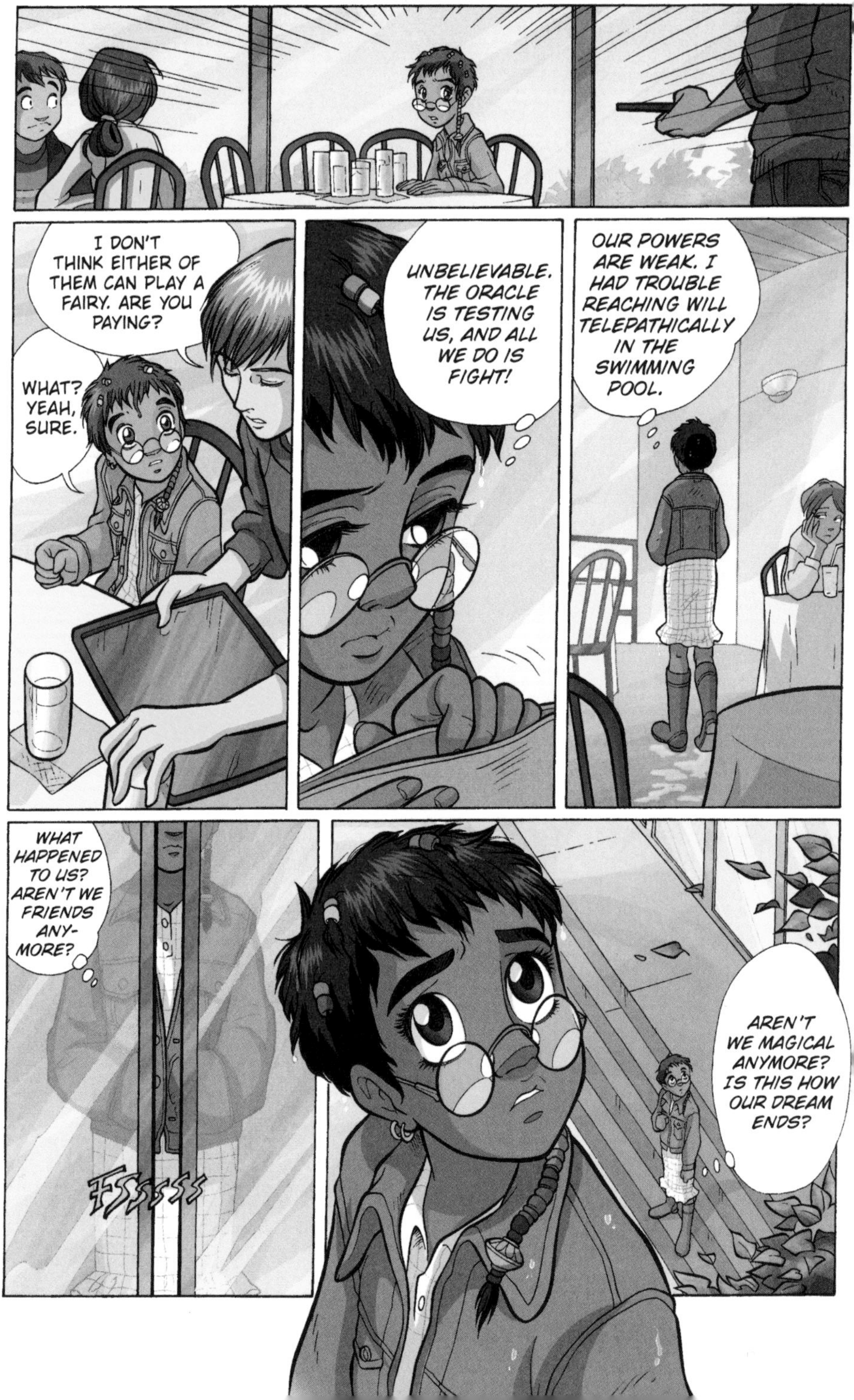
I DON'T THINK EITHER OF THEM CAN PLAY A FAIRY. ARE YOU PAYING?
WHAT? YEAH, SURE.
UNBELIEVABLE. THE ORACLE IS TESTING US, AND ALL WE DO IS FIGHT!
OUR POWERS ARE WEAK. I HAD TROUBLE REACHING WILL TELEPATHICALLY IN THE SWIMMING POOL.
WHAT HAPPENED TO US? AREN'T WE FRIENDS ANY-MORE?
FSSSSS
AREN'T WE MAGICAL ANYMORE? IS THIS HOW OUR DREAM ENDS?

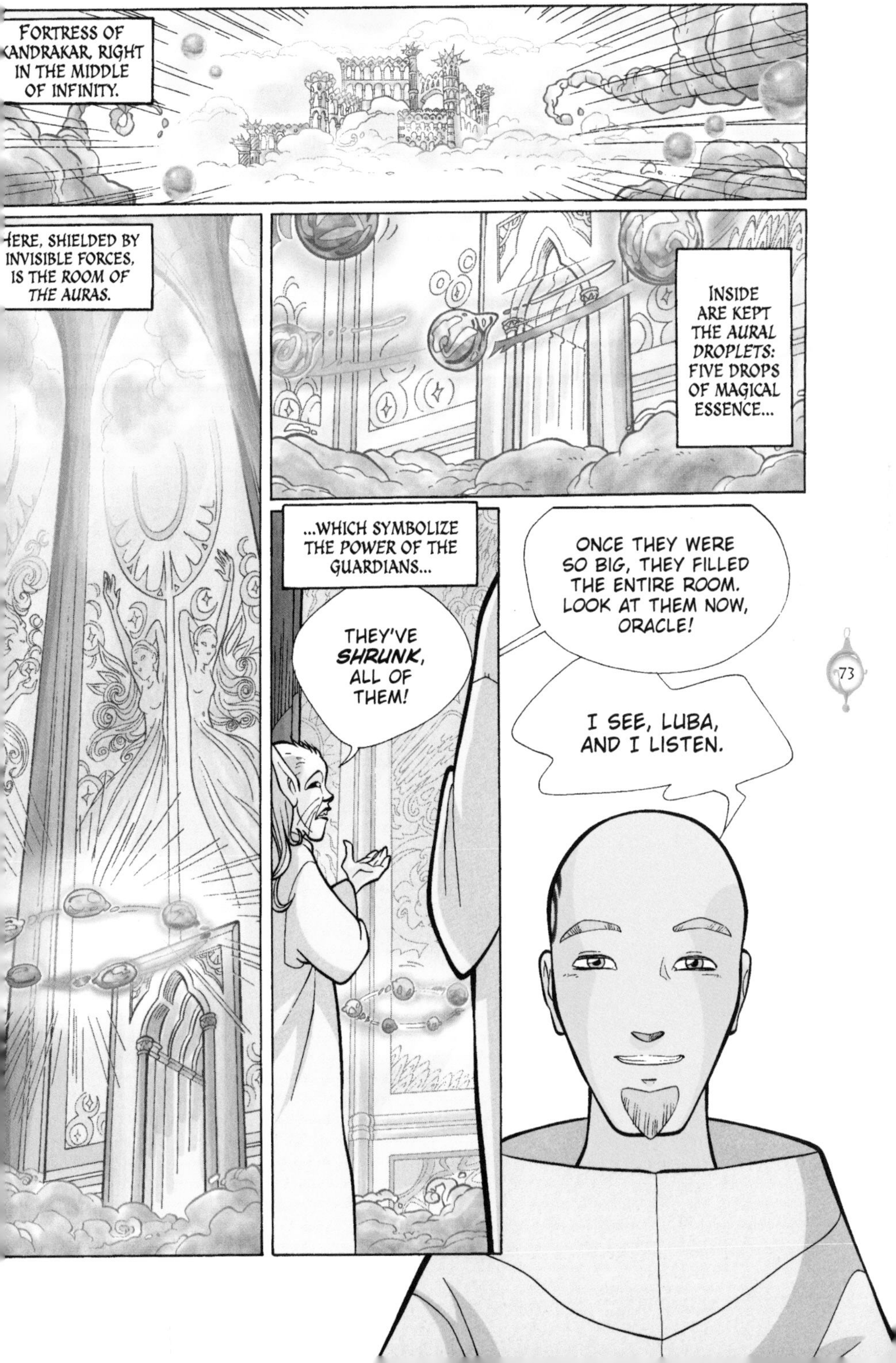

FORTRESS OF KANDRAKAR, RIGHT IN THE MIDDLE OF INFINITY.
HERE, SHIELDED BY INVISIBLE FORCES, IS THE *ROOM OF THE AURAS.*
INSIDE ARE KEPT THE *AURAL DROPLETS:* FIVE DROPS OF MAGICAL ESSENCE...
...WHICH SYMBOLIZE THE *POWER OF THE* GUARDIANS...
ONCE THEY WERE SO BIG, THEY FILLED THE ENTIRE ROOM. LOOK AT THEM NOW, ORACLE!
THEY'VE ***SHRUNK***, ALL OF THEM!
I SEE, LUBA, AND I LISTEN.

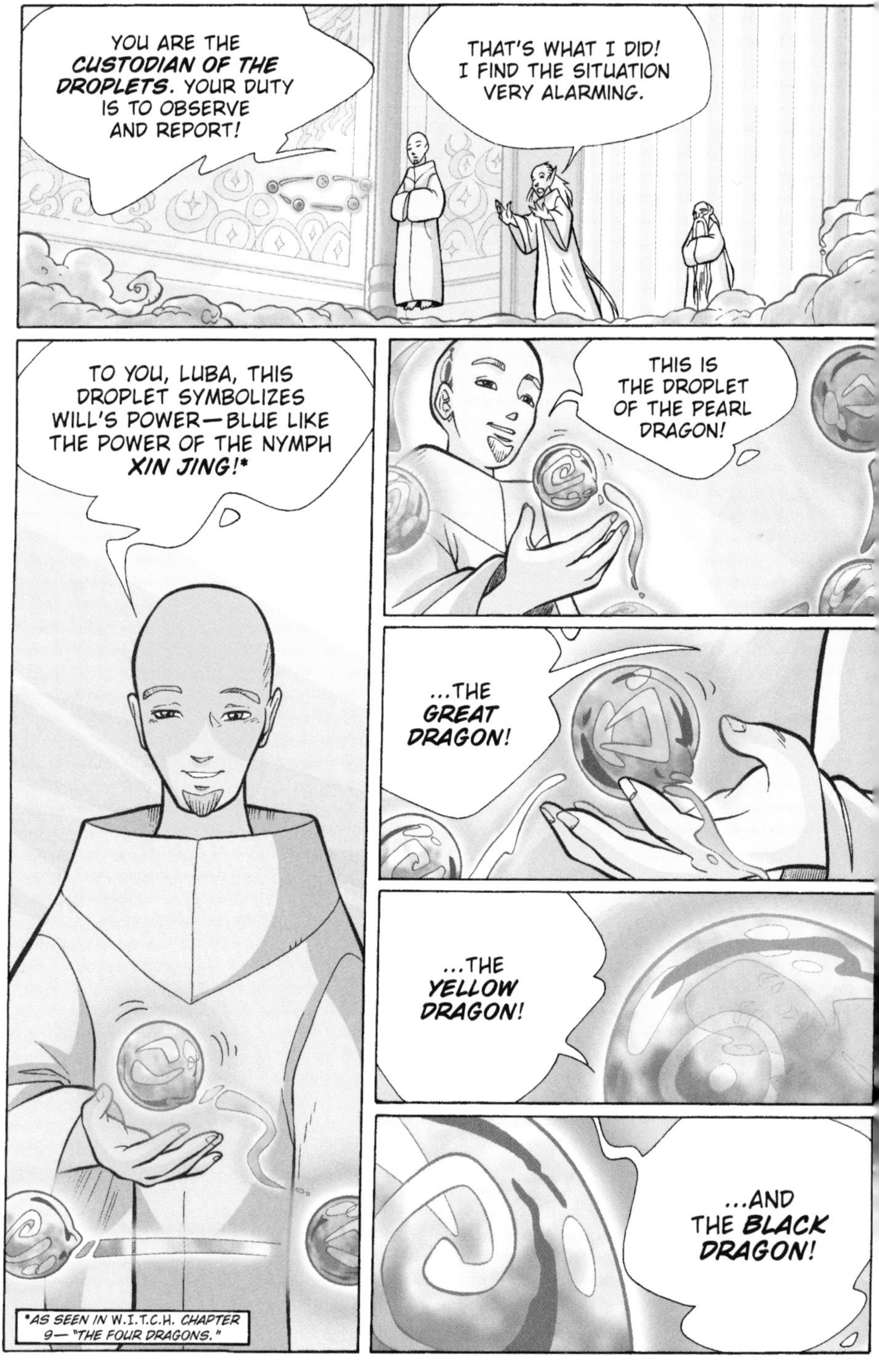
YOU ARE THE CUSTODIAN OF THE DROPLETS. YOUR DUTY IS TO OBSERVE AND REPORT!
THAT'S WHAT I DID! I FIND THE SITUATION VERY ALARMING.
TO YOU, LUBA, THIS DROPLET SYMBOLIZES WILL'S POWER—BLUE LIKE THE POWER OF THE NYMPH XIN JING!*
THIS IS THE DROPLET OF THE PEARL DRAGON!
...THE GREAT DRAGON!
...THE YELLOW DRAGON!
...AND THE BLACK DRAGON!
*AS SEEN IN W.I.T.C.H. CHAPTER 9— "THE FOUR DRAGONS."

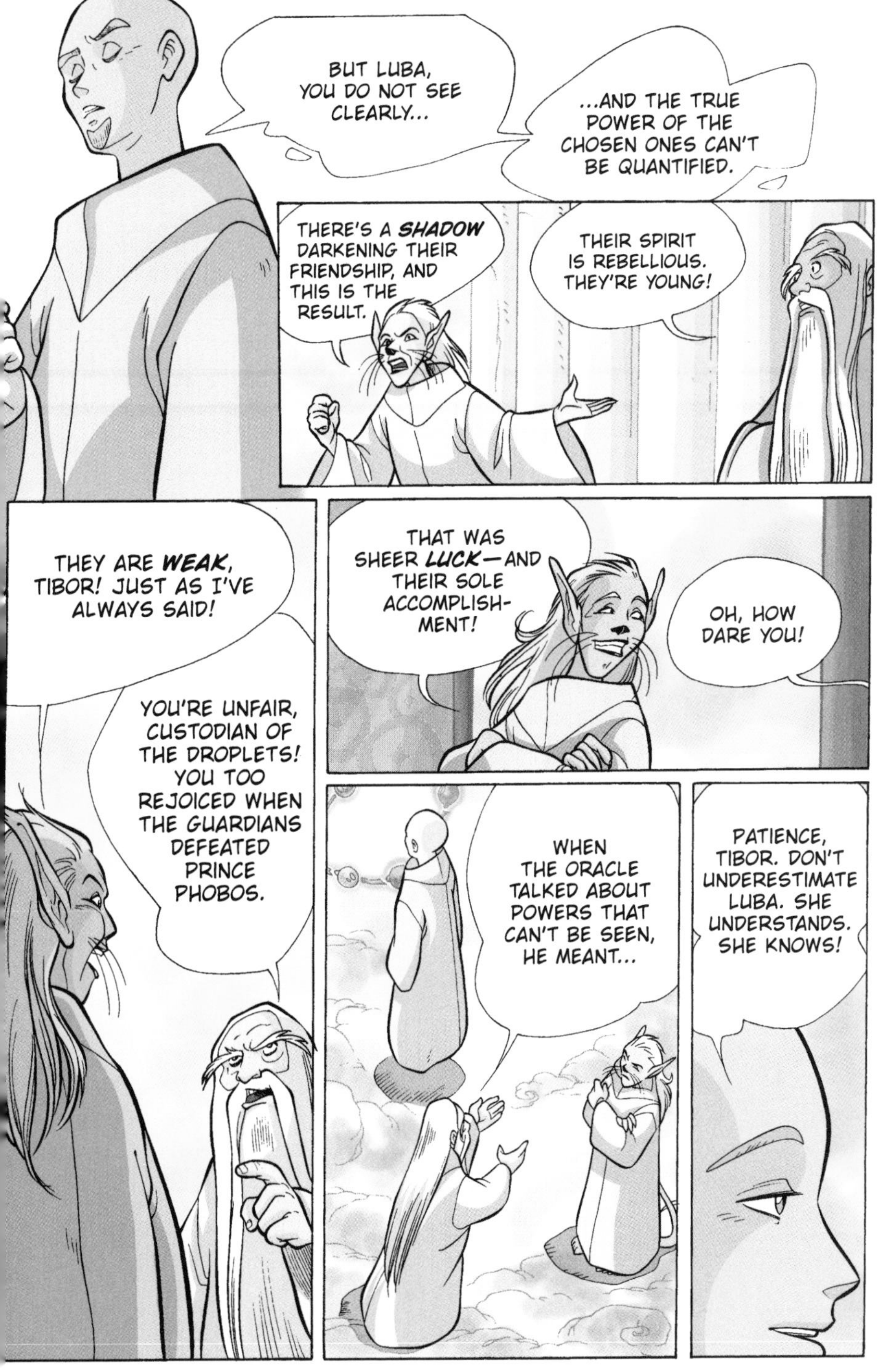
BUT LUBA, YOU DO NOT SEE CLEARLY...
...AND THE TRUE POWER OF THE CHOSEN ONES CAN'T BE QUANTIFIED.
THERE'S A SHADOW DARKENING THEIR FRIENDSHIP, AND THIS IS THE RESULT.
THEIR SPIRIT IS REBELLIOUS. THEY'RE YOUNG!
THEY ARE WEAK, TIBOR! JUST AS I'VE ALWAYS SAID!
YOU'RE UNFAIR, CUSTODIAN OF THE DROPLETS! YOU TOO REJOICED WHEN THE GUARDIANS DEFEATED PRINCE PHOBOS.
THAT WAS SHEER LUCK—AND THEIR SOLE ACCOMPLISHMENT!
OH, HOW DARE YOU!
WHEN THE ORACLE TALKED ABOUT POWERS THAT CAN'T BE SEEN, HE MEANT...
PATIENCE, TIBOR. DON'T UNDERESTIMATE LUBA. SHE UNDERSTANDS. SHE KNOWS!

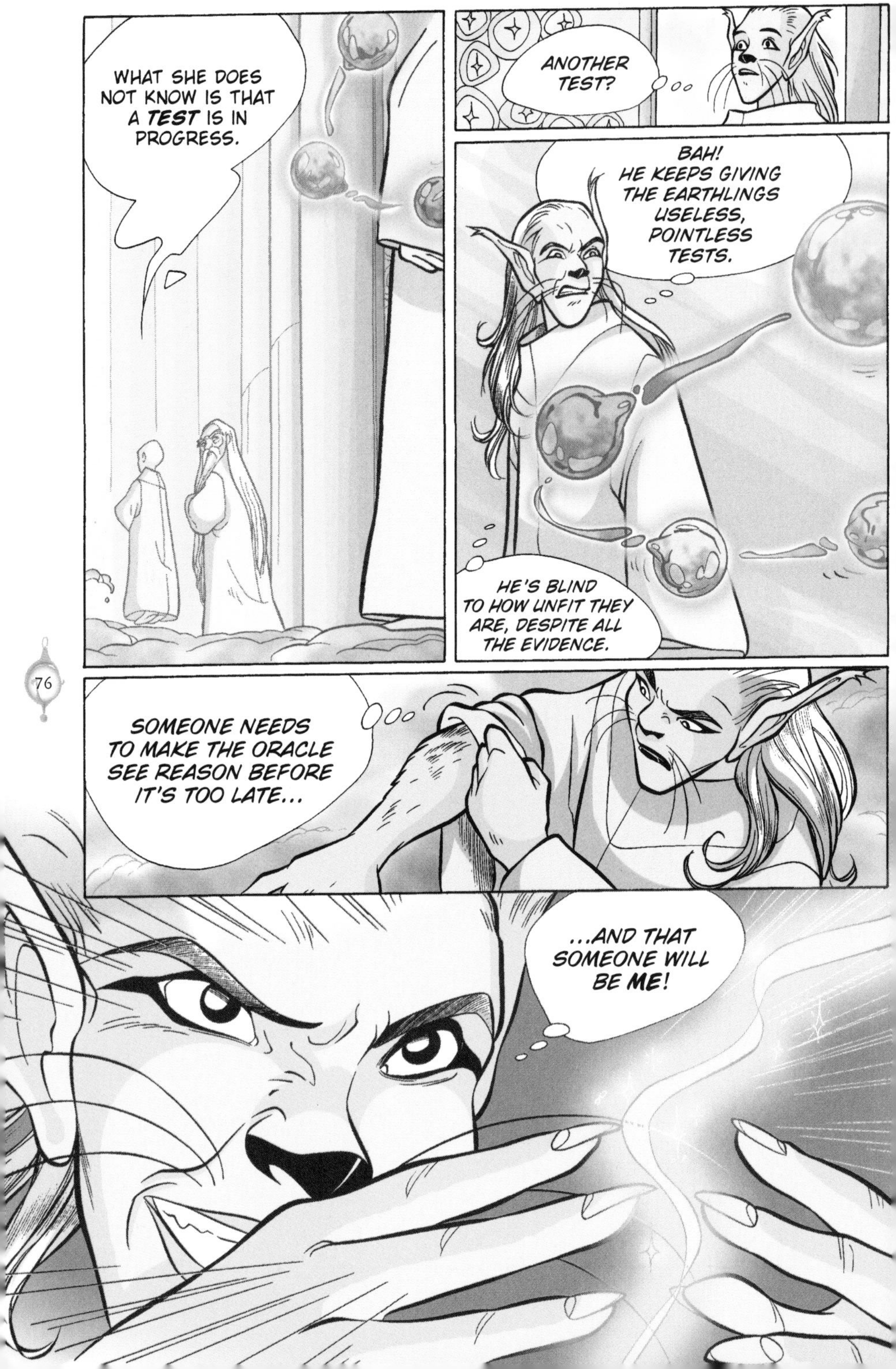
WHAT SHE DOES NOT KNOW IS THAT A TEST IS IN PROGRESS.
ANOTHER TEST?
BAH! HE KEEPS GIVING THE EARTHLINGS USELESS, POINTLESS TESTS.
HE'S BLIND TO HOW UNFIT THEY ARE, DESPITE ALL THE EVIDENCE.
SOMEONE NEEDS TO MAKE THE ORACLE SEE REASON BEFORE IT'S TOO LATE...
...AND THAT SOMEONE WILL BE ME!

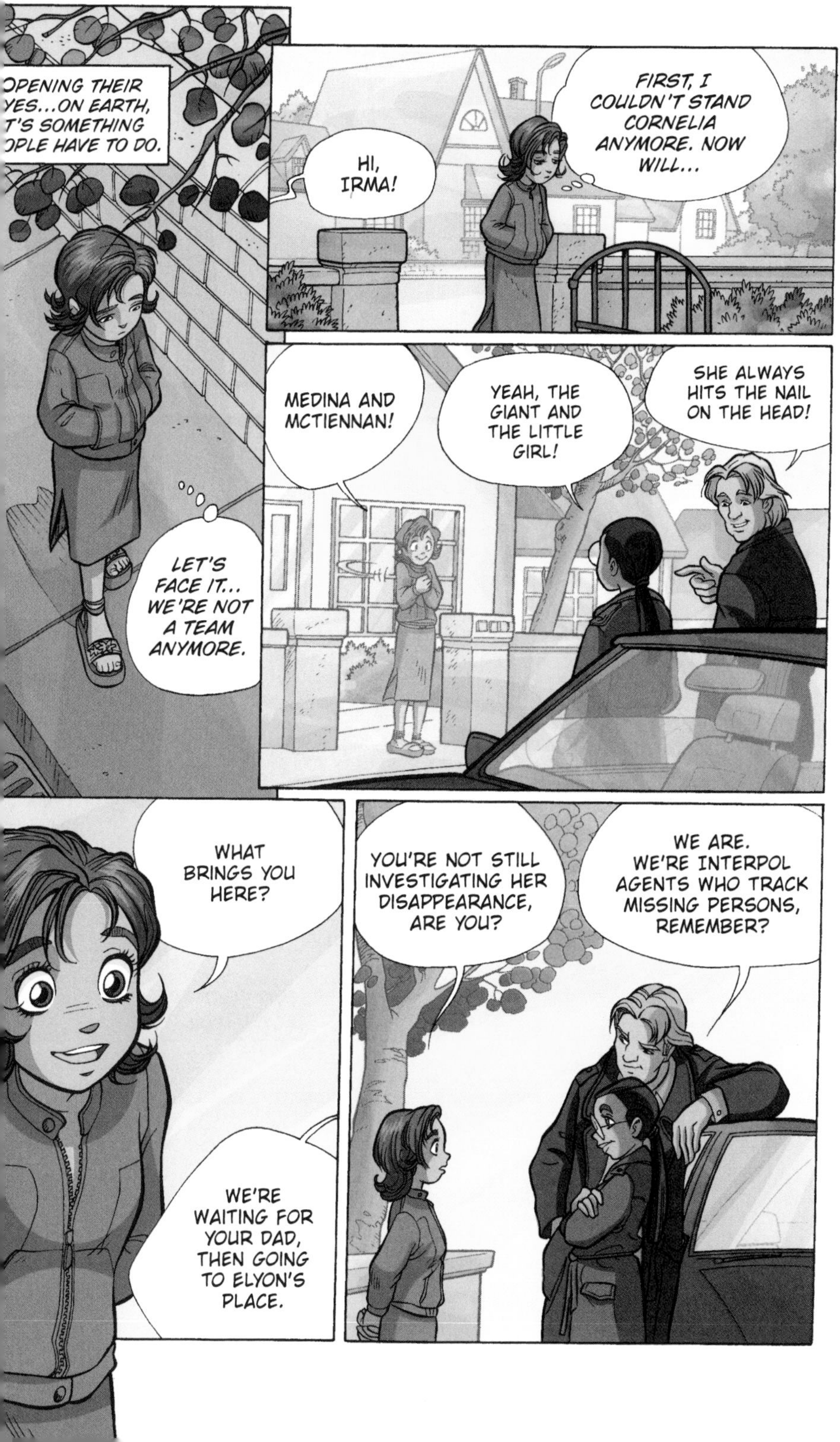
OPENING THEIR
YES...ON EARTH,
T'S SOMETHING
OPLE HAVE TO DO.
HI, IRMA!
FIRST, I COULDN'T STAND CORNELIA ANYMORE. NOW WILL...
LET'S FACE IT... WE'RE NOT A TEAM ANYMORE.
MEDINA AND MCTIENNAN!
YEAH, THE GIANT AND THE LITTLE GIRL!
SHE ALWAYS HITS THE NAIL ON THE HEAD!
WHAT BRINGS YOU HERE?
WE'RE WAITING FOR YOUR DAD, THEN GOING TO ELYON'S PLACE.
YOU'RE NOT STILL INVESTIGATING HER DISAPPEARANCE, ARE YOU?
WE ARE. WE'RE INTERPOL AGENTS WHO TRACK MISSING PERSONS, REMEMBER?

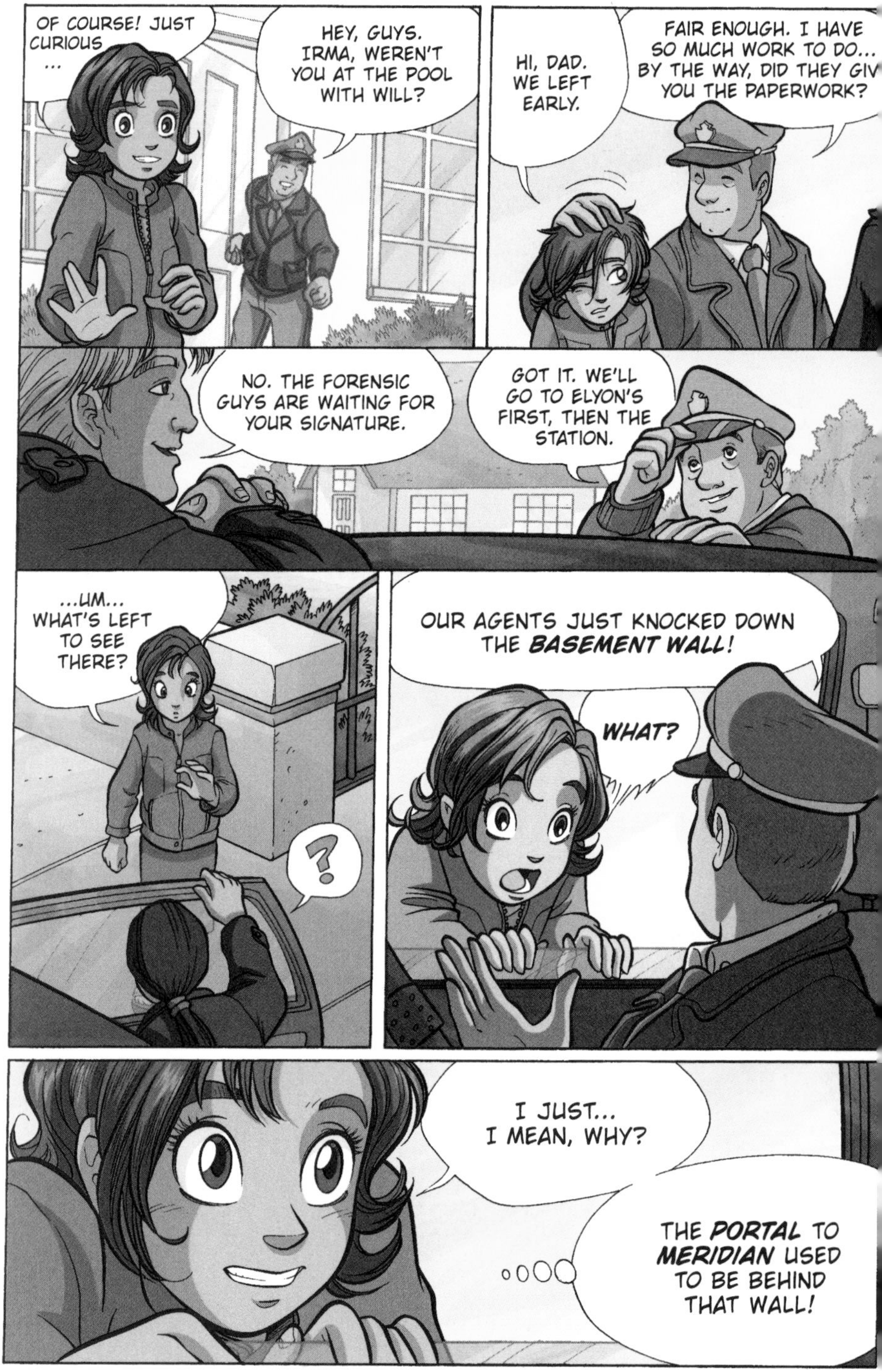

OF COURSE! JUST CURIOUS ...
HEY, GUYS. IRMA, WEREN'T YOU AT THE POOL WITH WILL?
HI, DAD. WE LEFT EARLY.
FAIR ENOUGH. I HAVE SO MUCH WORK TO DO... BY THE WAY, DID THEY GIV YOU THE PAPERWORK?
NO. THE FORENSIC GUYS ARE WAITING FOR YOUR SIGNATURE.
GOT IT. WE'LL GO TO ELYON'S FIRST, THEN THE STATION.
...UM... WHAT'S LEFT TO SEE THERE?
?
OUR AGENTS JUST KNOCKED DOWN THE BASEMENT WALL!
WHAT?
I JUST... I MEAN, WHY?
THE PORTAL TO MERIDIAN USED TO BE BEHIND THAT WALL!

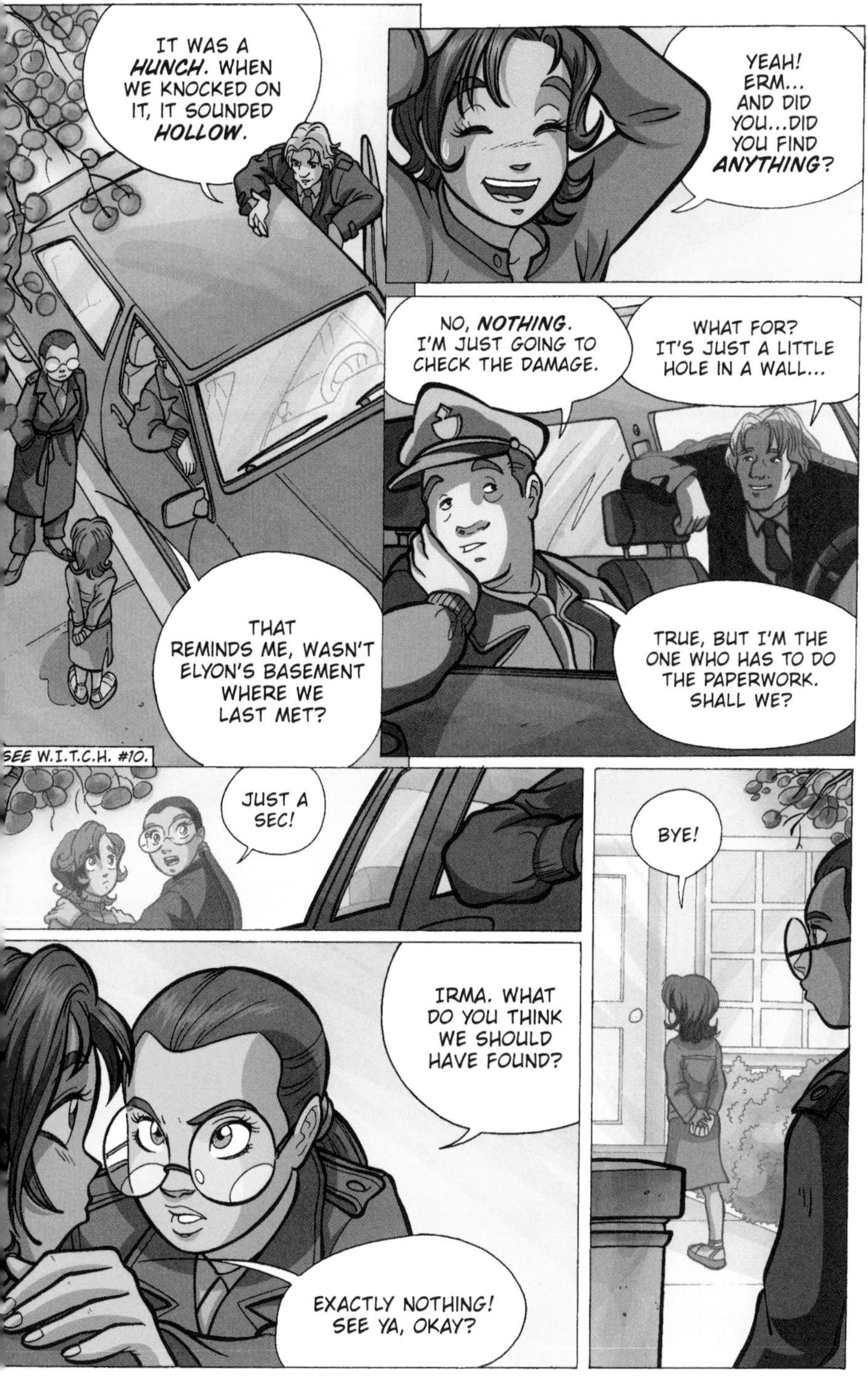
IT WAS A HUNCH. WHEN WE KNOCKED ON IT, IT SOUNDED HOLLOW.
YEAH! ERM... AND DID YOU...DID YOU FIND ANYTHING?
NO, NOTHING. I'M JUST GOING TO CHECK THE DAMAGE.
WHAT FOR? IT'S JUST A LITTLE HOLE IN A WALL...
THAT REMINDS ME, WASN'T ELYON'S BASEMENT WHERE WE LAST MET?
TRUE, BUT I'M THE ONE WHO HAS TO DO THE PAPERWORK. SHALL WE?
SEE W.I.T.C.H. #10.
JUST A SEC!
BYE!
IRMA. WHAT DO YOU THINK WE SHOULD HAVE FOUND?
EXACTLY NOTHING! SEE YA, OKAY?

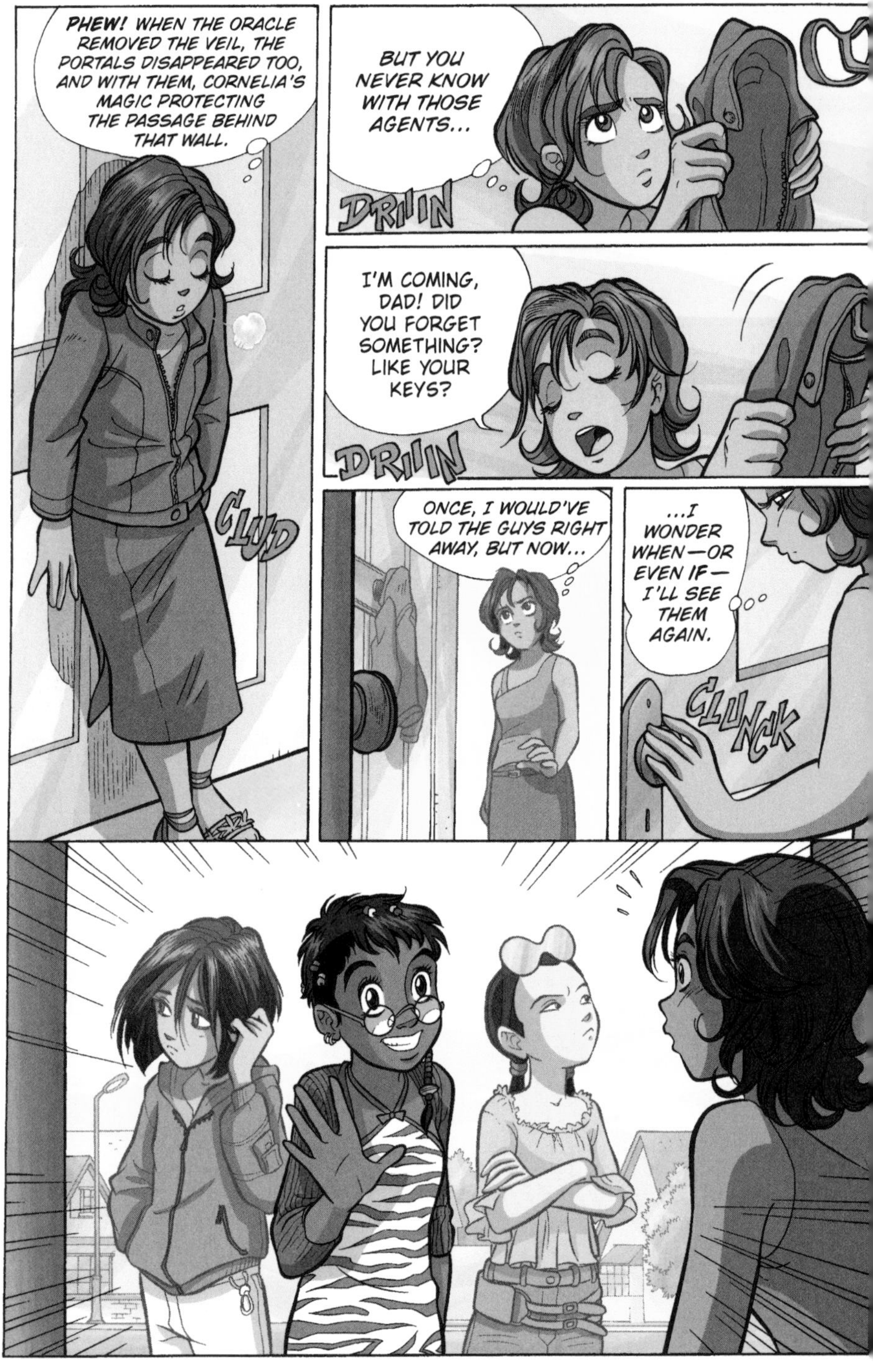
PHEW! WHEN THE ORACLE REMOVED THE VEIL, THE PORTALS DISAPPEARED TOO, AND WITH THEM, CORNELIA'S MAGIC PROTECTING THE PASSAGE BEHIND THAT WALL.
CLUD
BUT YOU NEVER KNOW WITH THOSE AGENTS...
DRIIIN
I'M COMING, DAD! DID YOU FORGET SOMETHING? LIKE YOUR KEYS?
DRIIIN
ONCE, I WOULD'VE TOLD THE GUYS RIGHT AWAY, BUT NOW...
...I WONDER WHEN—OR EVEN IF—I'LL SEE THEM AGAIN.
CLUNCK

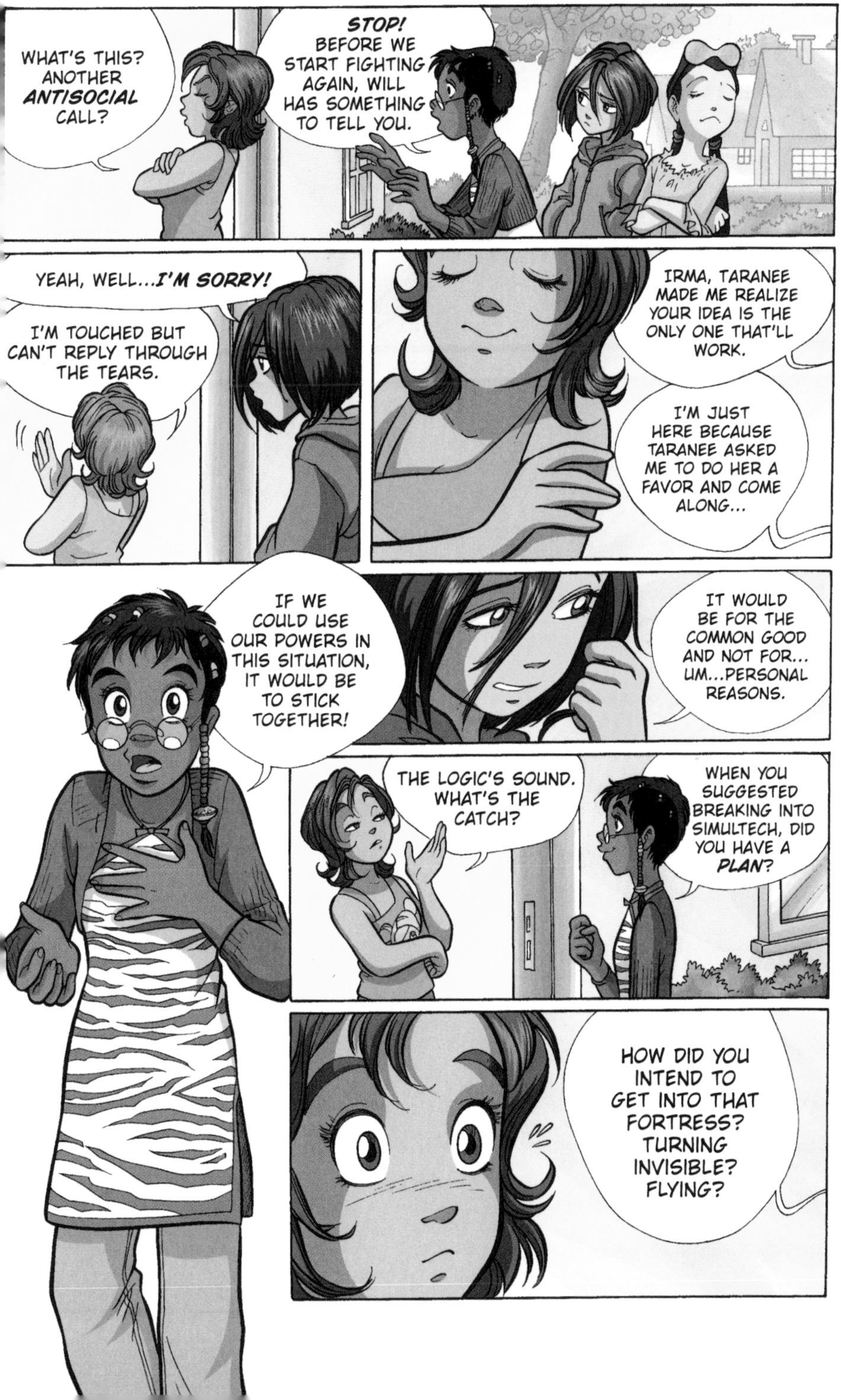

WHAT'S THIS? ANOTHER ANTISOCIAL CALL?
STOP! BEFORE WE START FIGHTING AGAIN, WILL HAS SOMETHING TO TELL YOU.
YEAH, WELL...I'M SORRY!
I'M TOUCHED BUT CAN'T REPLY THROUGH THE TEARS.
IRMA, TARANEE MADE ME REALIZE YOUR IDEA IS THE ONLY ONE THAT'LL WORK.
I'M JUST HERE BECAUSE TARANEE ASKED ME TO DO HER A FAVOR AND COME ALONG...
IF WE COULD USE OUR POWERS IN THIS SITUATION, IT WOULD BE TO STICK TOGETHER!
IT WOULD BE FOR THE COMMON GOOD AND NOT FOR... UM...PERSONAL REASONS.
THE LOGIC'S SOUND. WHAT'S THE CATCH?
WHEN YOU SUGGESTED BREAKING INTO SIMULTECH, DID YOU HAVE A PLAN?
HOW DID YOU INTEND TO GET INTO THAT FORTRESS? TURNING INVISIBLE? FLYING?

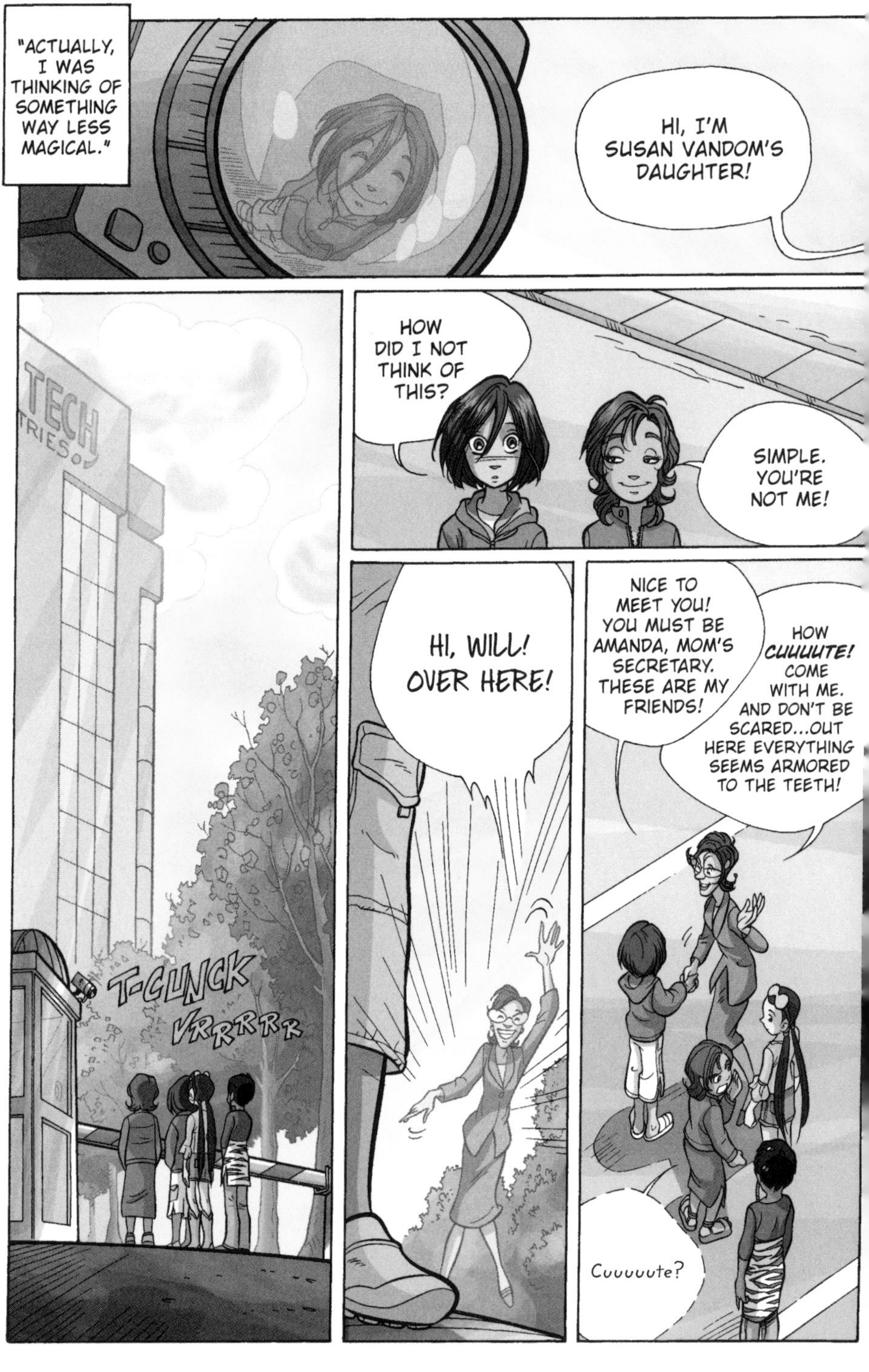
"ACTUALLY, I WAS THINKING OF SOMETHING WAY LESS MAGICAL."
HI, I'M SUSAN VANDOM'S DAUGHTER!
TECH
TRIES
T-CLNCK
VRRRRR
HOW DID I NOT THINK OF THIS?
SIMPLE. YOU'RE NOT ME!
HI, WILL! OVER HERE!
NICE TO MEET YOU! YOU MUST BE AMANDA, MOM'S SECRETARY. THESE ARE MY FRIENDS!
HOW CUUUUTE! COME WITH ME. AND DON'T BE SCARED...OUT HERE EVERYTHING SEEMS ARMORED TO THE TEETH!
Cuuuuute?

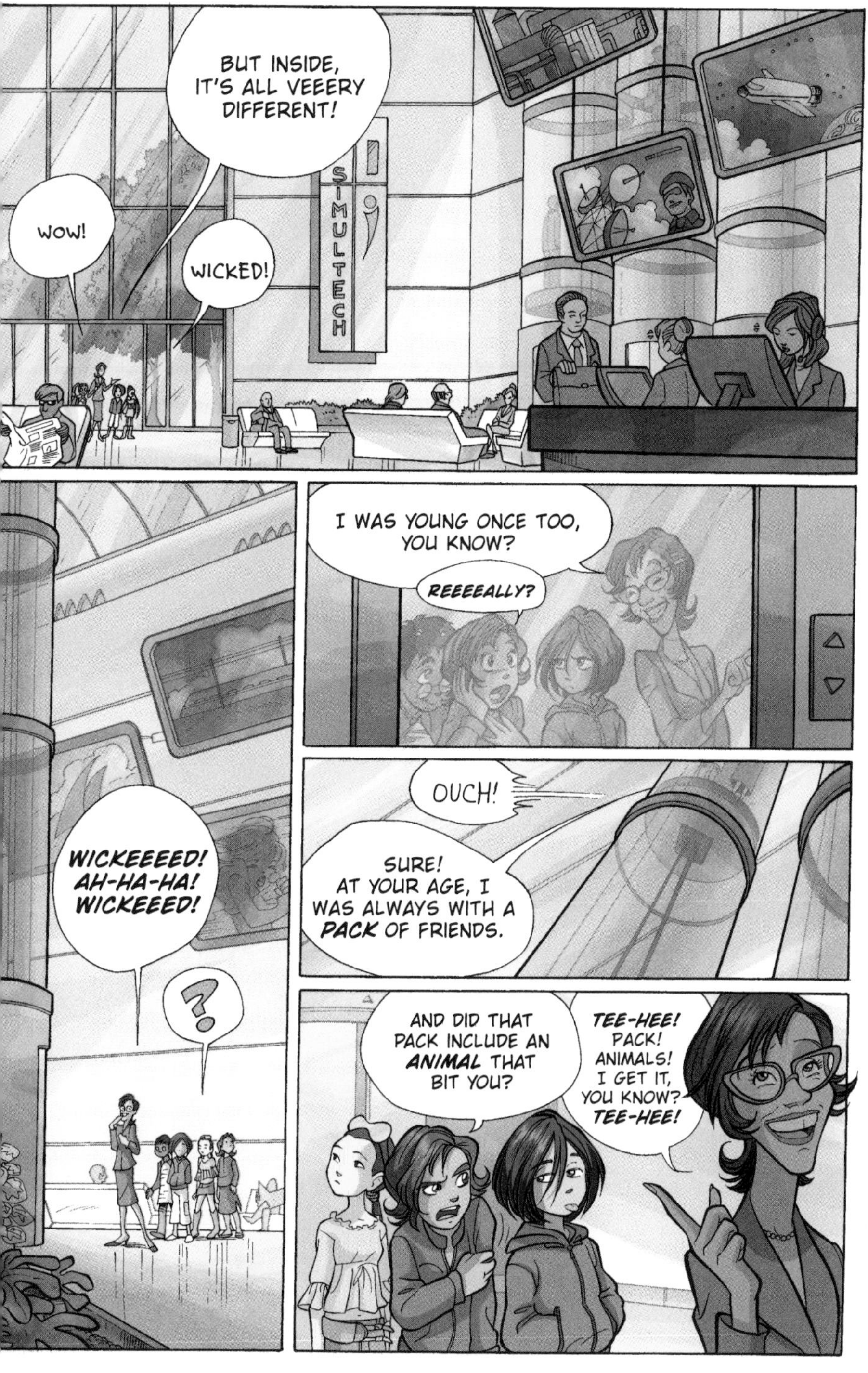
BUT INSIDE, IT'S ALL VEEERY DIFFERENT!
WOW!
WICKED!
SIMULTECH
I WAS YOUNG ONCE TOO, YOU KNOW?
REEEEALLY?
WICKEEEED! AH-HA-HA! WICKEEED!
?
OUCH!
SURE! AT YOUR AGE, I WAS ALWAYS WITH A PACK OF FRIENDS.
AND DID THAT PACK INCLUDE AN ANIMAL THAT BIT YOU?
TEE-HEE! PACK! ANIMALS! I GET IT, YOU KNOW? TEE-HEE!

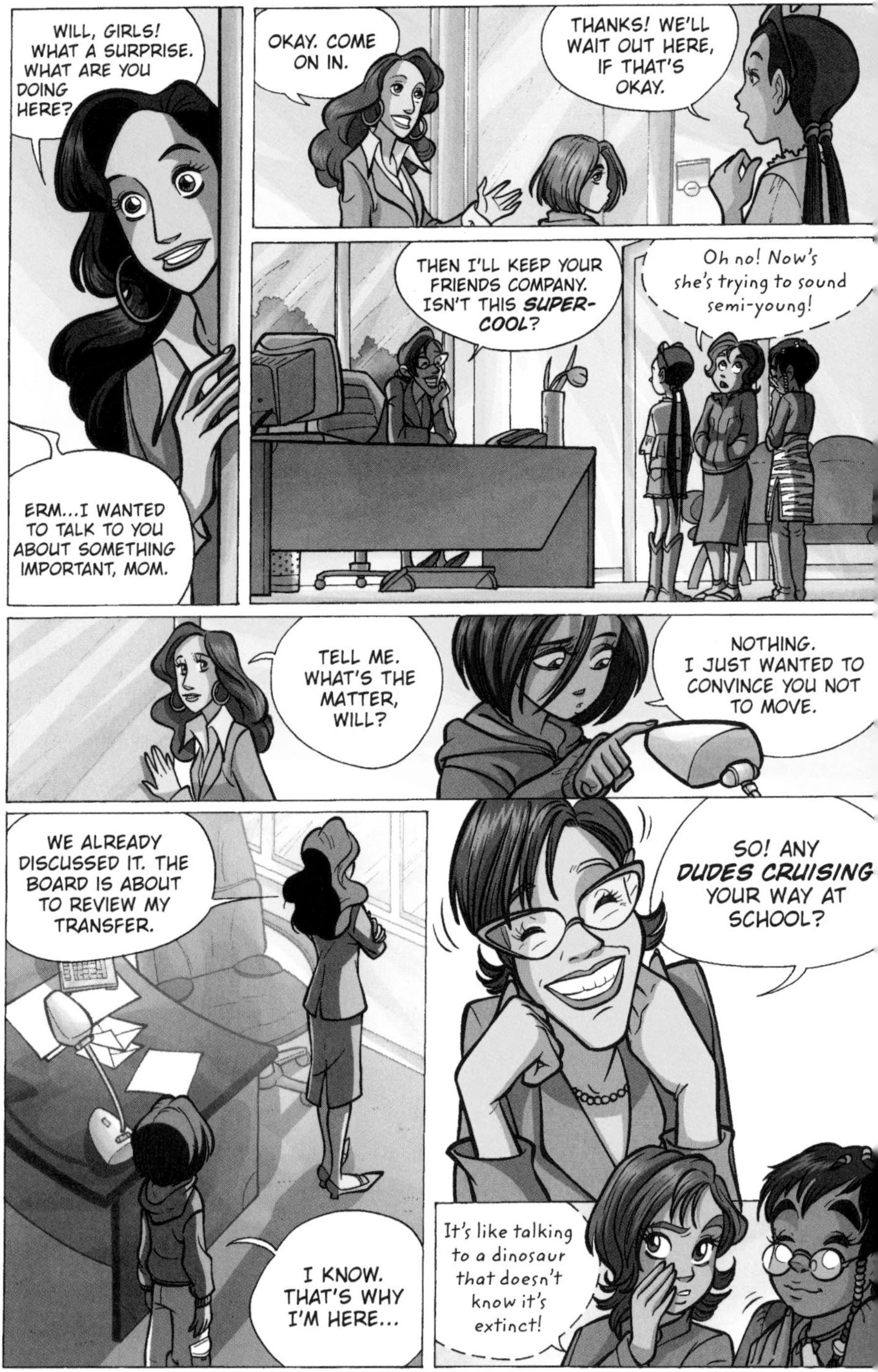
WILL, GIRLS! WHAT A SURPRISE. WHAT ARE YOU DOING HERE?
ERM...I WANTED TO TALK TO YOU ABOUT SOMETHING IMPORTANT, MOM.
OKAY. COME ON IN.
THANKS! WE'LL WAIT OUT HERE, IF THAT'S OKAY.
THEN I'LL KEEP YOUR FRIENDS COMPANY. ISN'T THIS SUPER-COOL?
Oh no! Now's she's trying to sound semi-young!
TELL ME. WHAT'S THE MATTER, WILL?
NOTHING. I JUST WANTED TO CONVINCE YOU NOT TO MOVE.
WE ALREADY DISCUSSED IT. THE BOARD IS ABOUT TO REVIEW MY TRANSFER.
I KNOW. THAT'S WHY I'M HERE...
SO! ANY DUDES CRUISING YOUR WAY AT SCHOOL?
It's like talking to a dinosaur that doesn't know it's extinct!

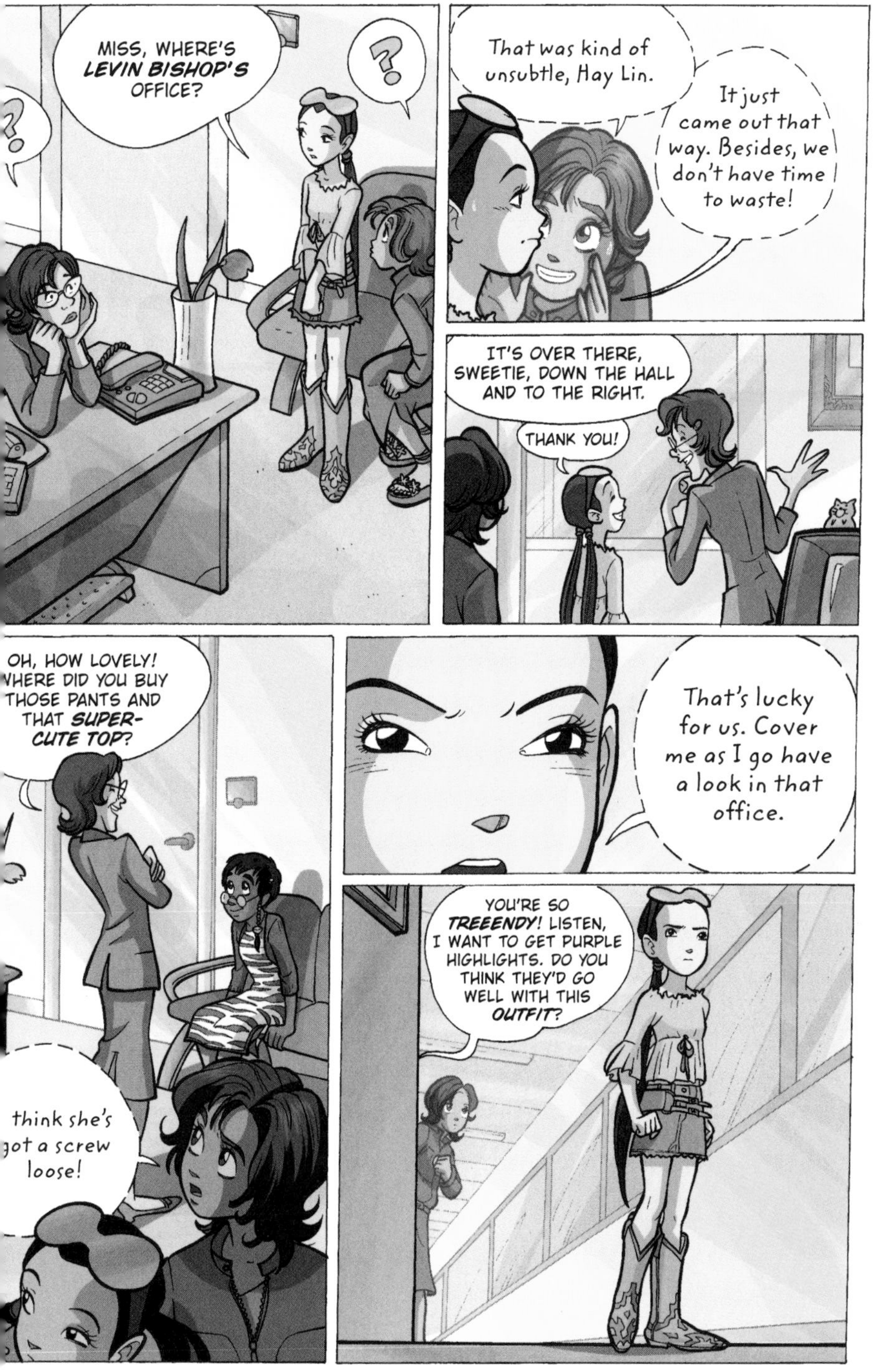
MISS, WHERE'S **LEVIN BISHOP'S** OFFICE?
?
?
That was kind of unsubtle, Hay Lin.
It just came out that way. Besides, we don't have time to waste!
IT'S OVER THERE, SWEETIE, DOWN THE HALL AND TO THE RIGHT.
THANK YOU!
OH, HOW LOVELY! WHERE DID YOU BUY THOSE PANTS AND THAT **SUPER-CUTE TOP**?
think she's got a screw loose!
That's lucky for us. Cover me as I go have a look in that office.
YOU'RE SO **TREEENDY!** LISTEN, I WANT TO GET PURPLE HIGHLIGHTS. DO YOU THINK THEY'D GO WELL WITH THIS **OUTFIT**?

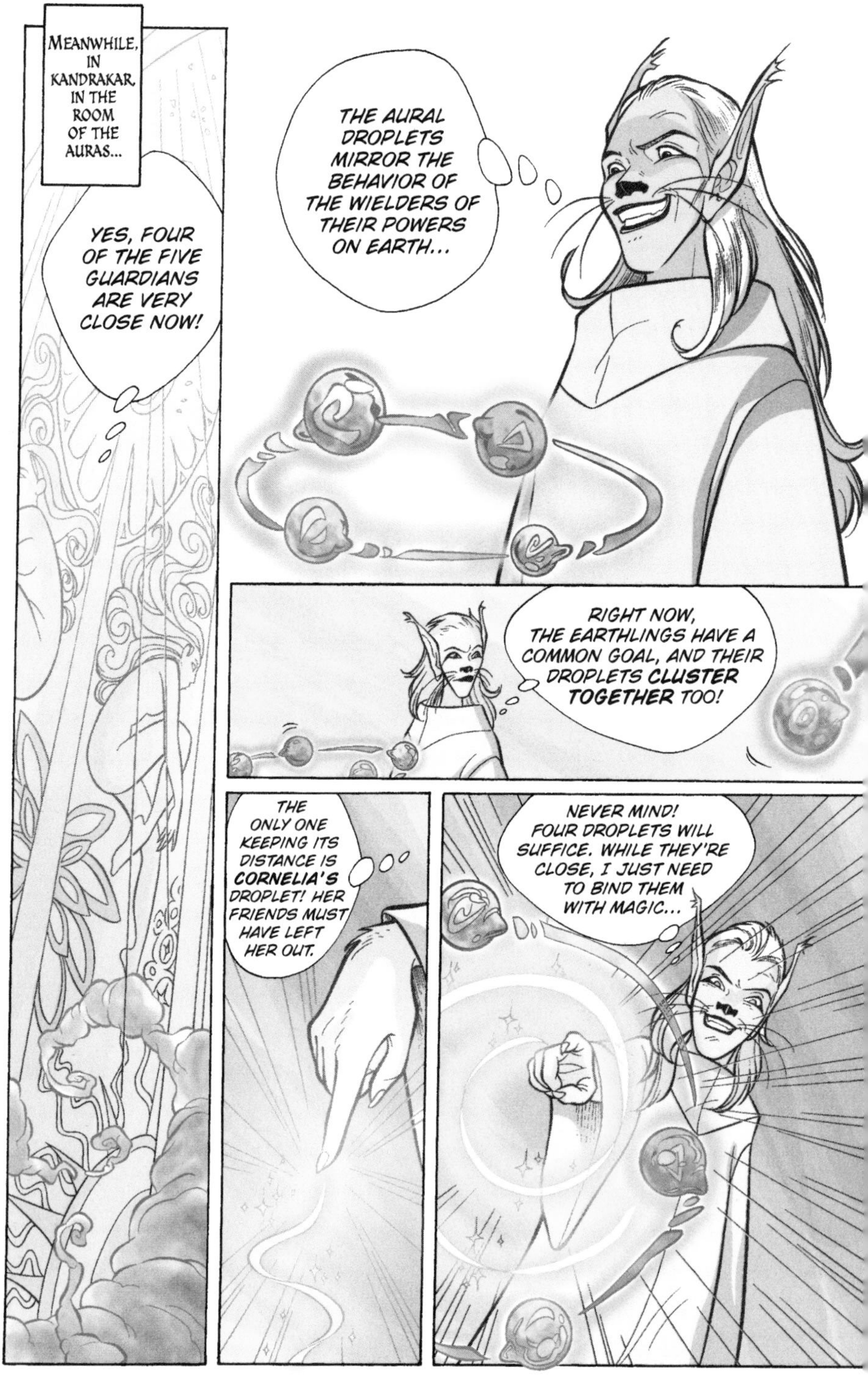
MEANWHILE, IN KANDRAKAR, IN THE ROOM OF THE AURAS...
YES, FOUR OF THE FIVE GUARDIANS ARE VERY CLOSE NOW!
THE AURAL DROPLETS MIRROR THE BEHAVIOR OF THE WIELDERS OF THEIR POWERS ON EARTH...
RIGHT NOW, THE EARTHLINGS HAVE A COMMON GOAL, AND THEIR DROPLETS **CLUSTER TOGETHER** TOO!
THE ONLY ONE KEEPING ITS DISTANCE IS **CORNELIA'S** DROPLET! HER FRIENDS MUST HAVE LEFT HER OUT.
NEVER MIND! FOUR DROPLETS WILL SUFFICE. WHILE THEY'RE CLOSE, I JUST NEED TO BIND THEM WITH MAGIC...

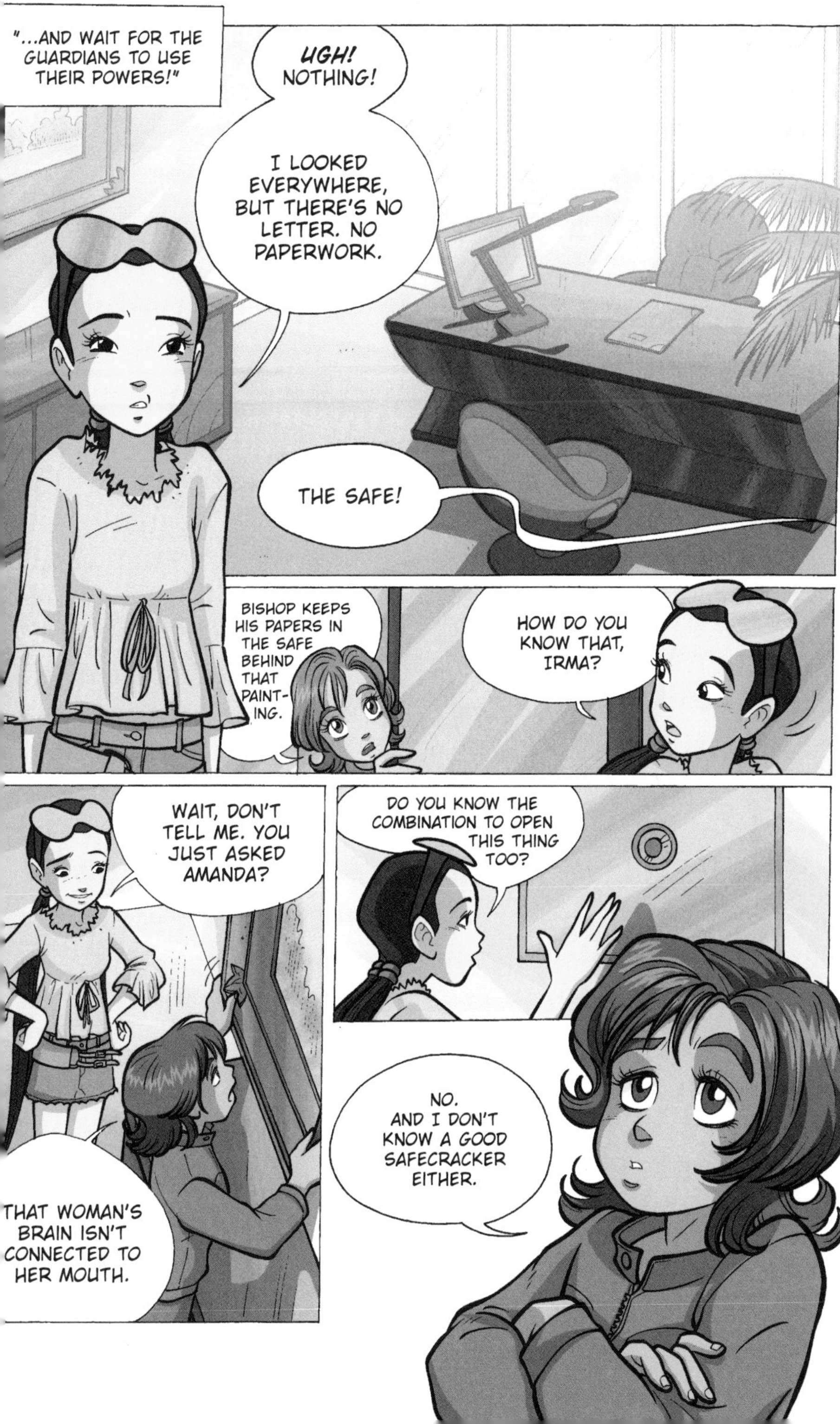
"...AND WAIT FOR THE GUARDIANS TO USE THEIR POWERS!"
UGH! NOTHING!
I LOOKED EVERYWHERE, BUT THERE'S NO LETTER. NO PAPERWORK.
THE SAFE!
BISHOP KEEPS HIS PAPERS IN THE SAFE BEHIND THAT PAINT-ING.
HOW DO YOU KNOW THAT, IRMA?
WAIT, DON'T TELL ME. YOU JUST ASKED AMANDA?
THAT WOMAN'S BRAIN ISN'T CONNECTED TO HER MOUTH.
DO YOU KNOW THE COMBINATION TO OPEN THIS THING TOO?
NO. AND I DON'T KNOW A GOOD SAFECRACKER EITHER.

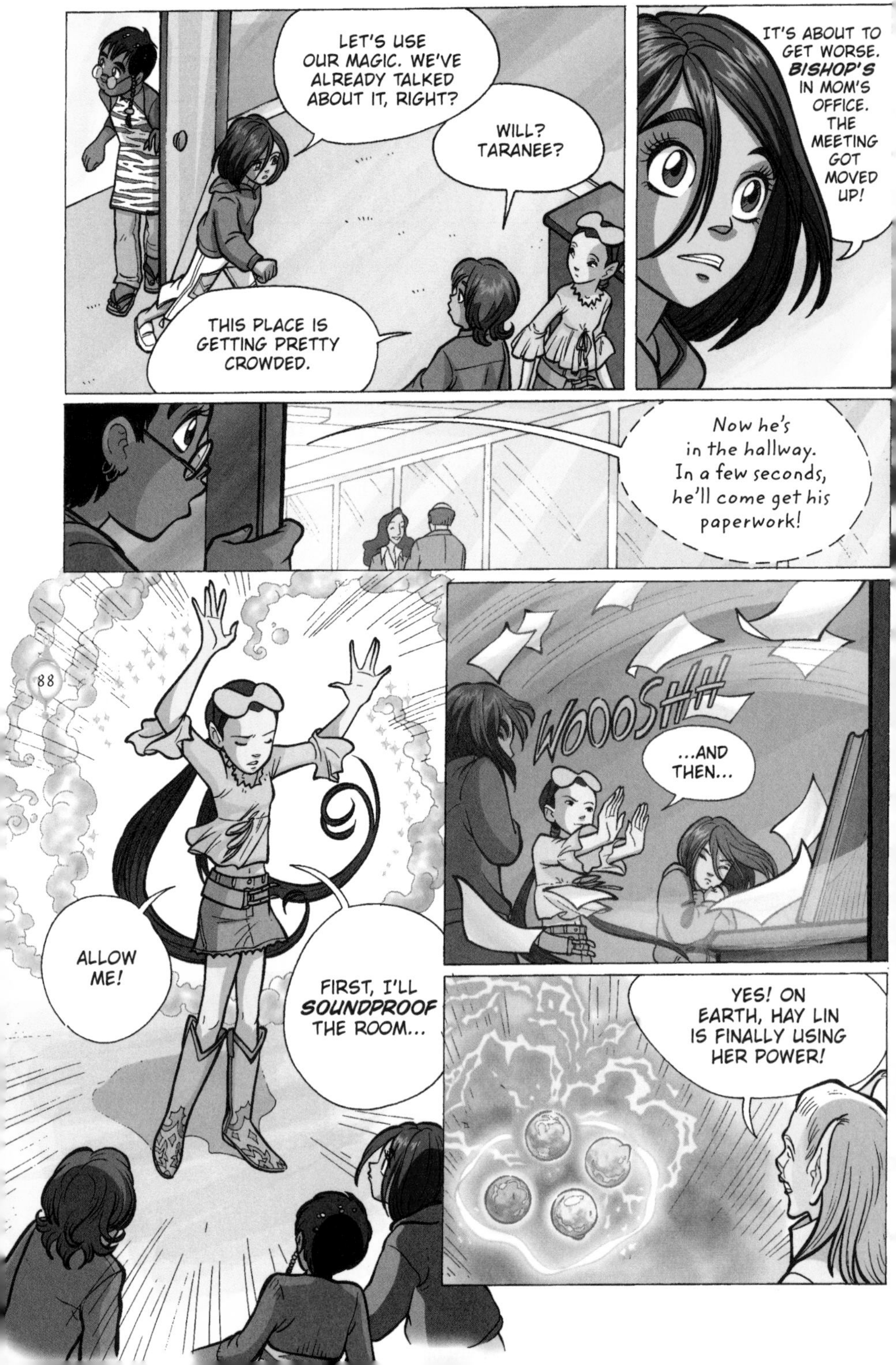
LET'S USE OUR MAGIC. WE'VE ALREADY TALKED ABOUT IT, RIGHT?
WILL? TARANEE?
THIS PLACE IS GETTING PRETTY CROWDED.
IT'S ABOUT TO GET WORSE. BISHOP'S IN MOM'S OFFICE. THE MEETING GOT MOVED UP!
Now he's in the hallway. In a few seconds, he'll come get his paperwork!
ALLOW ME!
FIRST, I'LL SOUNDPROOF THE ROOM...
WOOOSHH
...AND THEN...
YES! ON EARTH, HAY LIN IS FINALLY USING HER POWER!

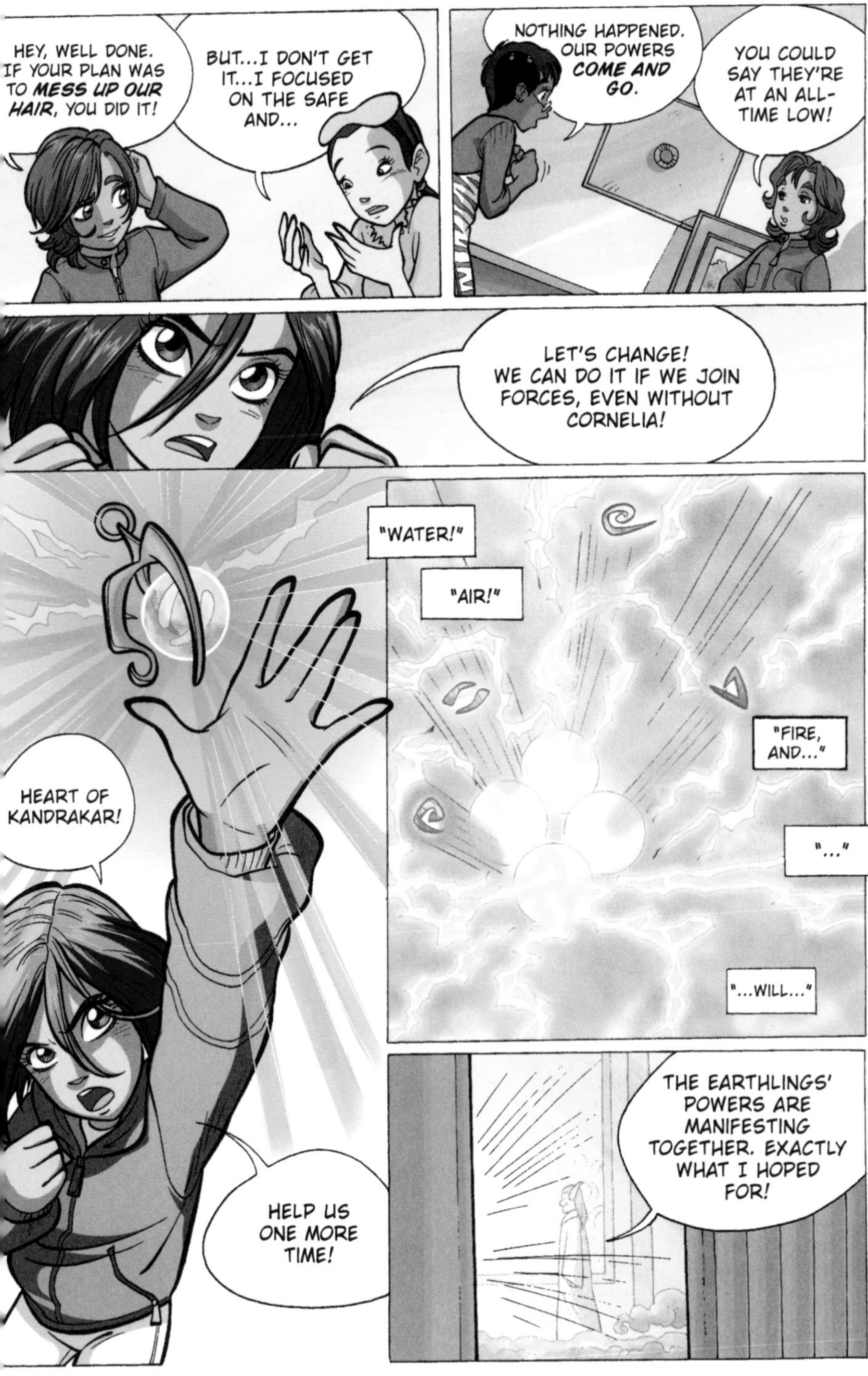

HEY, WELL DONE. IF YOUR PLAN WAS TO MESS UP OUR HAIR, YOU DID IT!
BUT...I DON'T GET IT...I FOCUSED ON THE SAFE AND...
NOTHING HAPPENED. OUR POWERS COME AND GO.
YOU COULD SAY THEY'RE AT AN ALL-TIME LOW!
LET'S CHANGE! WE CAN DO IT IF WE JOIN FORCES, EVEN WITHOUT CORNELIA!
HEART OF KANDRAKAR!
HELP US ONE MORE TIME!
"WATER!"
"AIR!"
"FIRE, AND..."
"..."
"...WILL..."
THE EARTHLINGS' POWERS ARE MANIFESTING TOGETHER. EXACTLY WHAT I HOPED FOR!

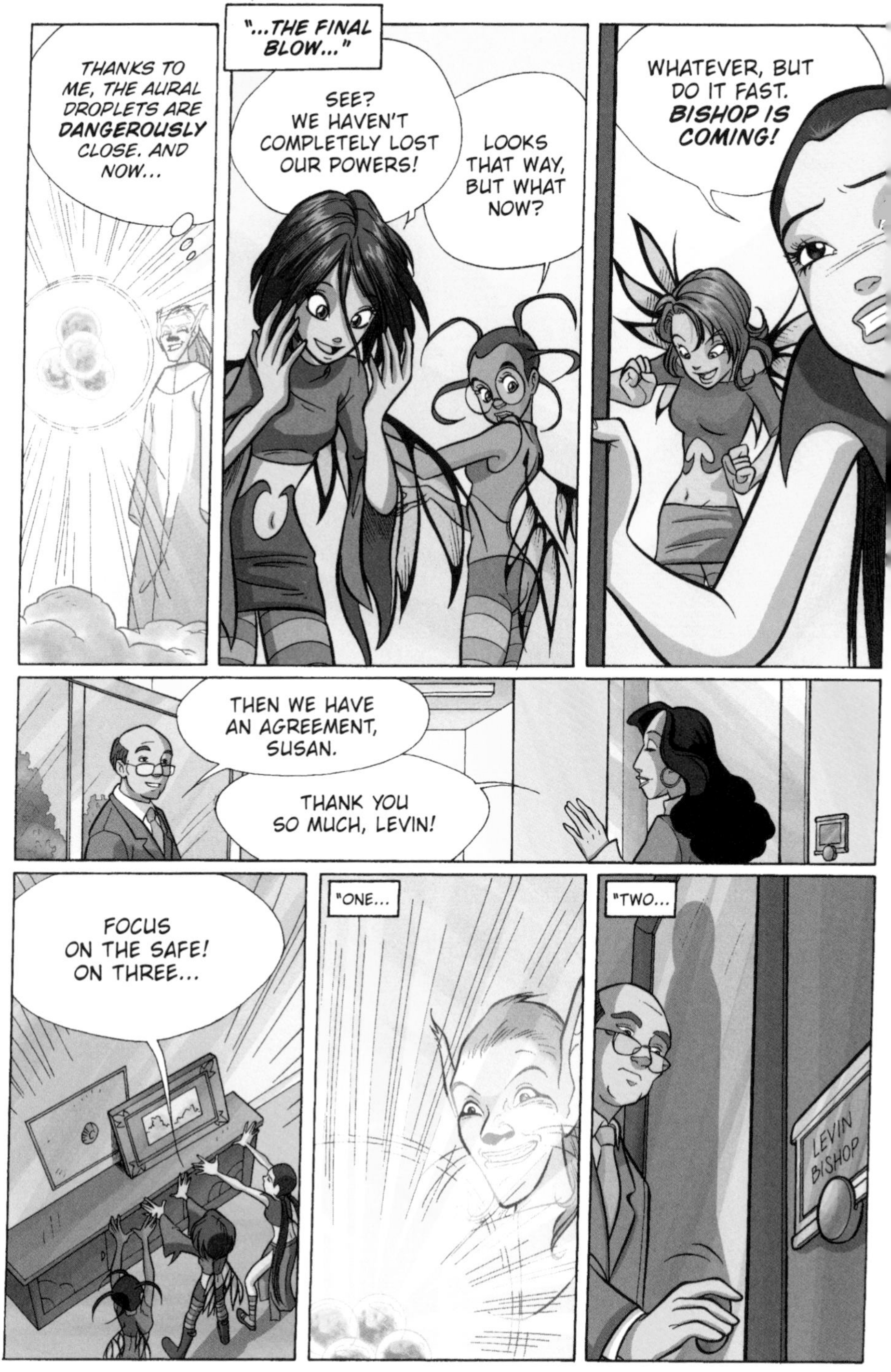

THANKS TO ME, THE AURAL DROPLETS ARE DANGEROUSLY CLOSE. AND NOW...
"...THE FINAL BLOW..."
SEE? WE HAVEN'T COMPLETELY LOST OUR POWERS!
LOOKS THAT WAY, BUT WHAT NOW?
WHATEVER, BUT DO IT FAST. BISHOP IS COMING!
THEN WE HAVE AN AGREEMENT, SUSAN.
THANK YOU SO MUCH, LEVIN!
FOCUS ON THE SAFE! ON THREE...
"ONE...
"TWO...
LEVIN BISHOP

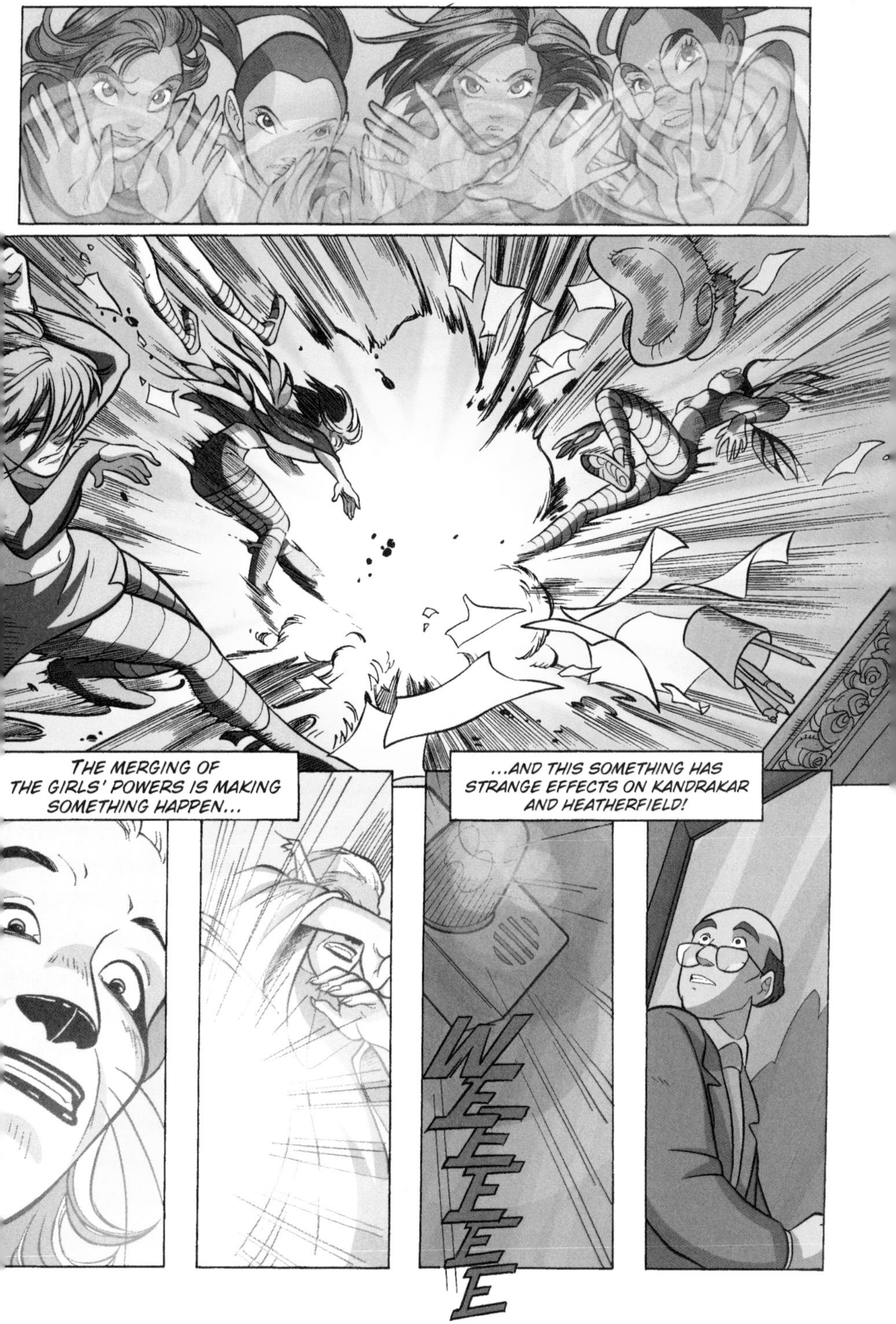
THE MERGING OF THE GIRLS' POWERS IS MAKING SOMETHING HAPPEN...
...AND THIS SOMETHING HAS STRANGE EFFECTS ON KANDRAKAR AND HEATHERFIELD!
WEEEEE

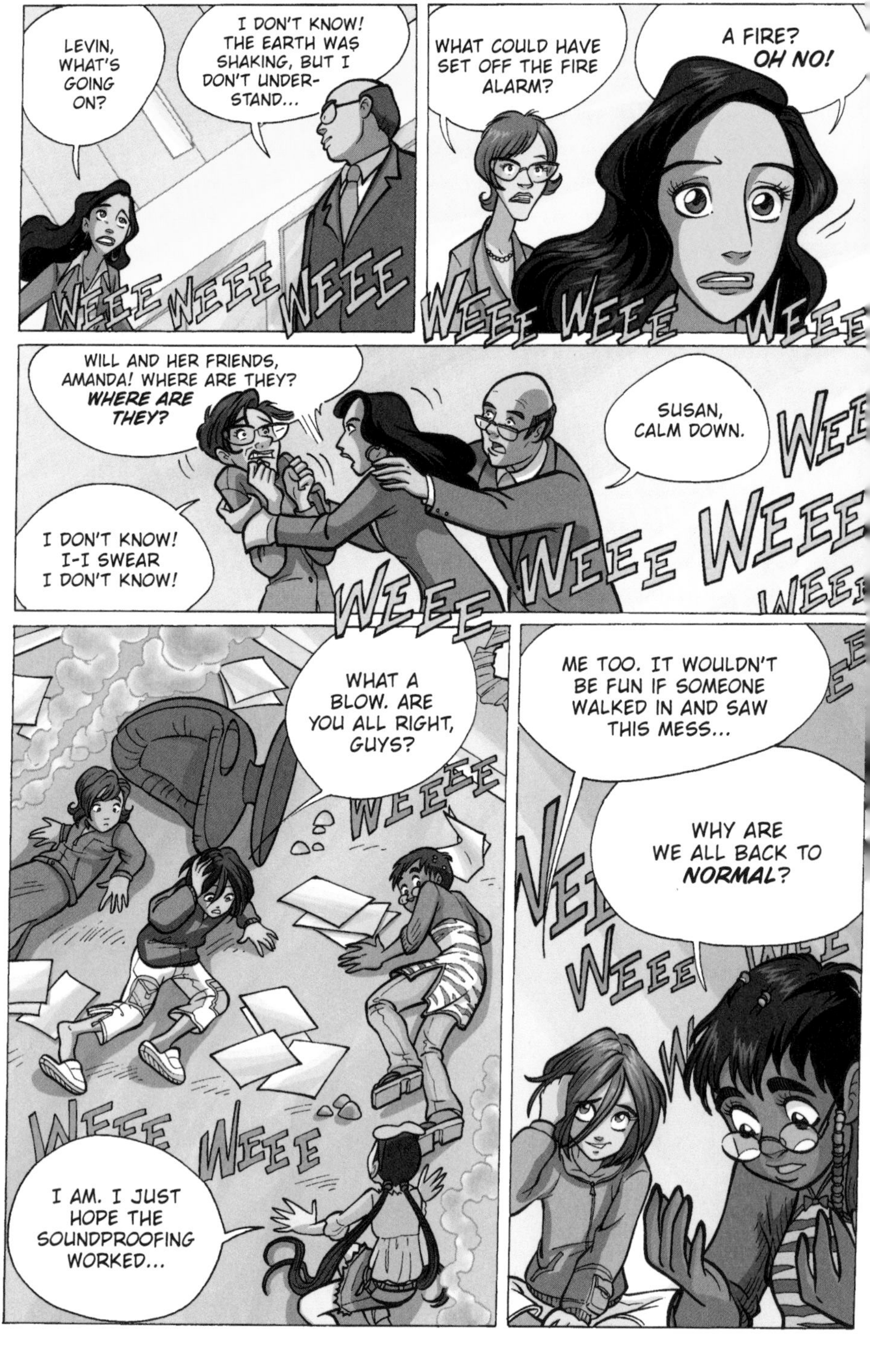
LEVIN, WHAT'S GOING ON?
I DON'T KNOW! THE EARTH WAS SHAKING, BUT I DON'T UNDERSTAND...
WEEE WEEE WEEE
WHAT COULD HAVE SET OFF THE FIRE ALARM?
A FIRE? OH NO!
WEEE WEEE WEEE
WILL AND HER FRIENDS, AMANDA! WHERE ARE THEY? WHERE ARE THEY?
SUSAN, CALM DOWN.
I DON'T KNOW! I-I SWEAR I DON'T KNOW!
WEEE WEEE WEEE
WHAT A BLOW. ARE YOU ALL RIGHT, GUYS?
WEEE
WEEE WEEE
I AM. I JUST HOPE THE SOUNDPROOFING WORKED...
ME TOO. IT WOULDN'T BE FUN IF SOMEONE WALKED IN AND SAW THIS MESS...
WHY ARE WE ALL BACK TO NORMAL?
WEEE

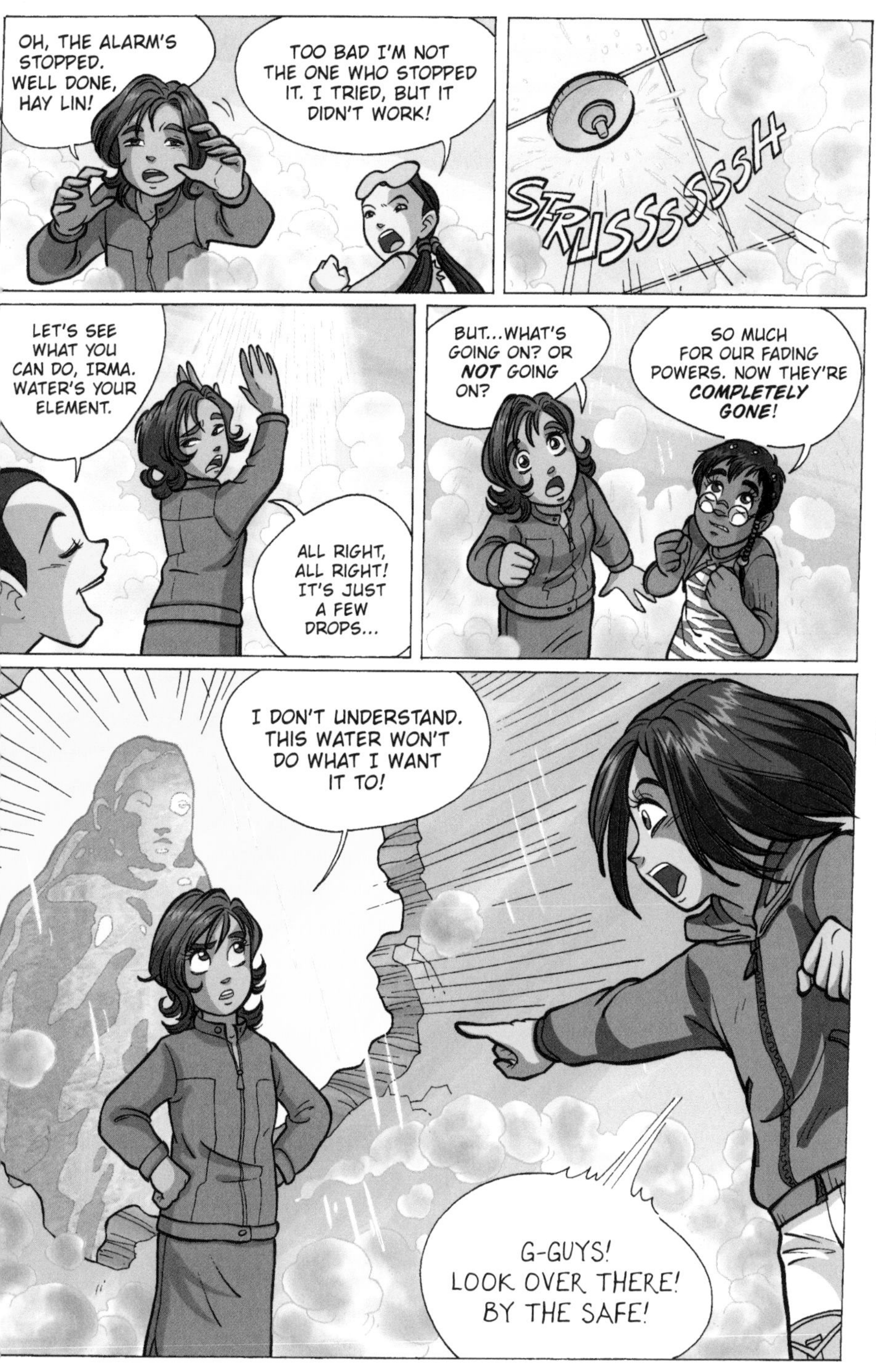
OH, THE ALARM'S STOPPED. WELL DONE, HAY LIN!
TOO BAD I'M NOT THE ONE WHO STOPPED IT. I TRIED, BUT IT DIDN'T WORK!
SFRUSSSSSSH
LET'S SEE WHAT YOU CAN DO, IRMA. WATER'S YOUR ELEMENT.
ALL RIGHT, ALL RIGHT! IT'S JUST A FEW DROPS...
BUT...WHAT'S GOING ON? OR **NOT** GOING ON?
SO MUCH FOR OUR FADING POWERS. NOW THEY'RE ***COMPLETELY GONE!***
I DON'T UNDERSTAND. THIS WATER WON'T DO WHAT I WANT IT TO!
G-GUYS! LOOK OVER THERE! BY THE SAFE!

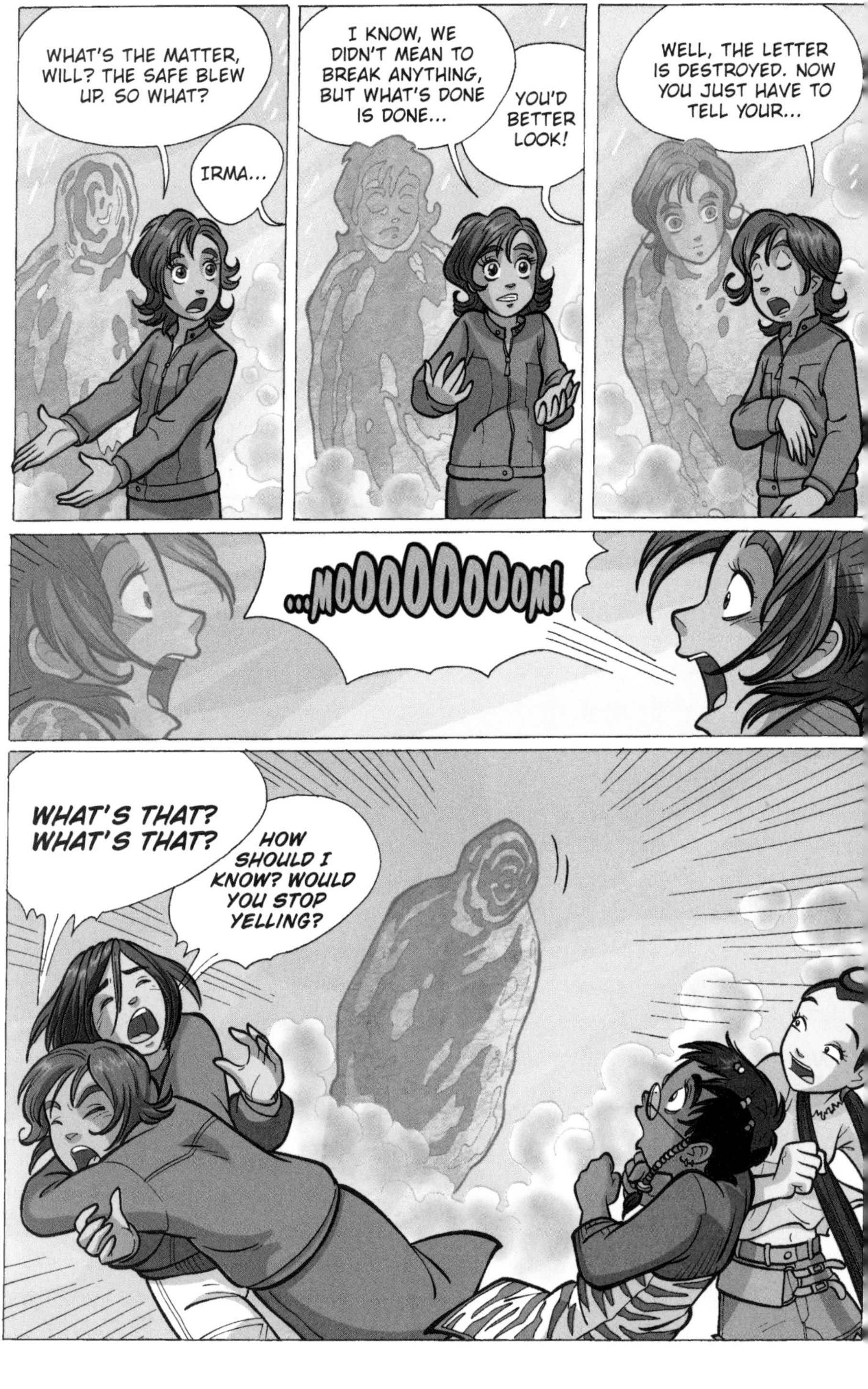
WHAT'S THE MATTER, WILL? THE SAFE BLEW UP. SO WHAT?
IRMA...
I KNOW, WE DIDN'T MEAN TO BREAK ANYTHING, BUT WHAT'S DONE IS DONE...
YOU'D BETTER LOOK!
WELL, THE LETTER IS DESTROYED. NOW YOU JUST HAVE TO TELL YOUR...
...MOOOOOOOOM!
WHAT'S THAT? WHAT'S THAT?
HOW SHOULD I KNOW? WOULD YOU STOP YELLING?

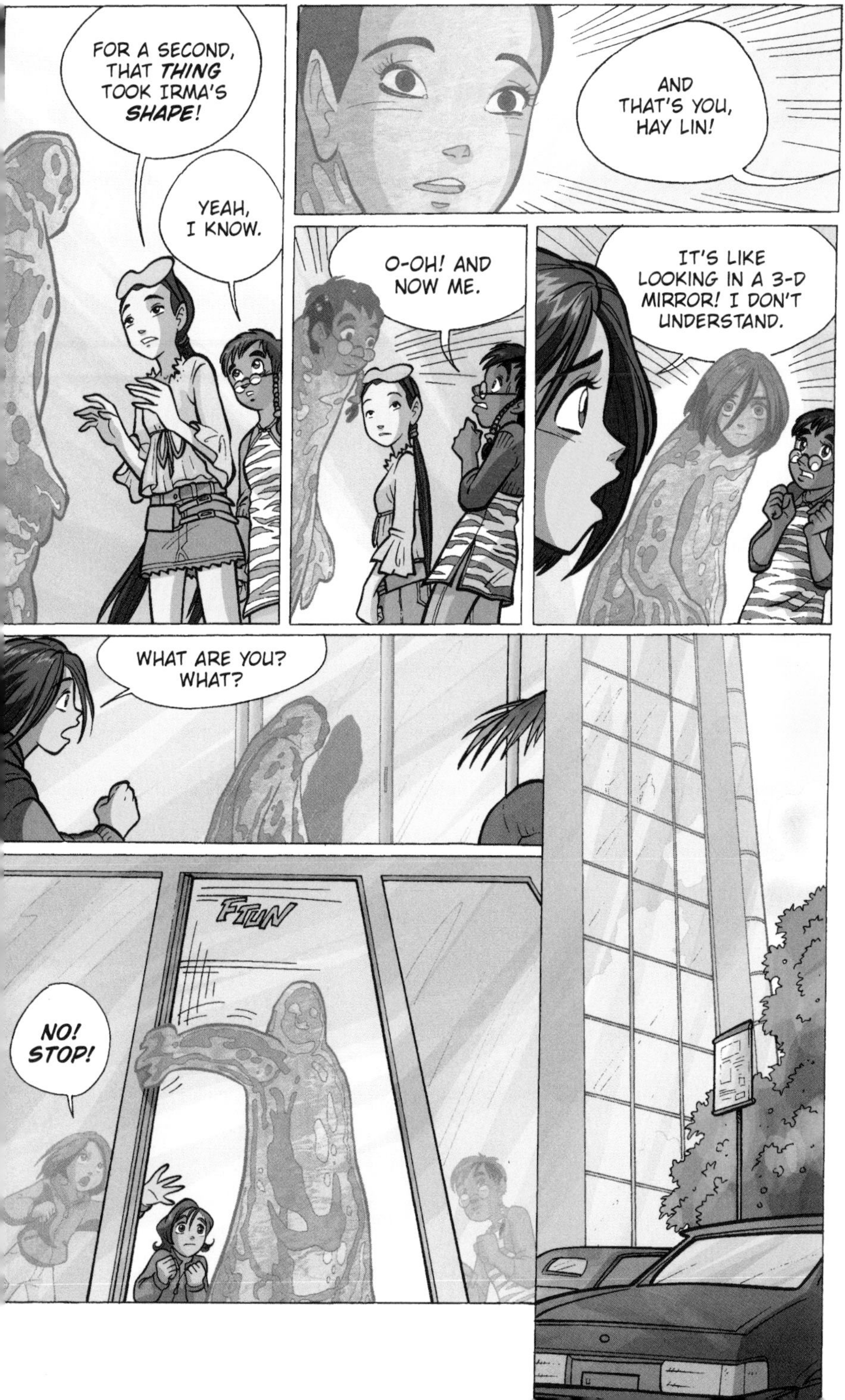
FOR A SECOND, THAT *THING* TOOK IRMA'S *SHAPE*!
YEAH, I KNOW.
AND THAT'S YOU, HAY LIN!
O-OH! AND NOW ME.
IT'S LIKE LOOKING IN A 3-D MIRROR! I DON'T UNDERSTAND.
WHAT ARE YOU? WHAT?
FTUN
NO! STOP!

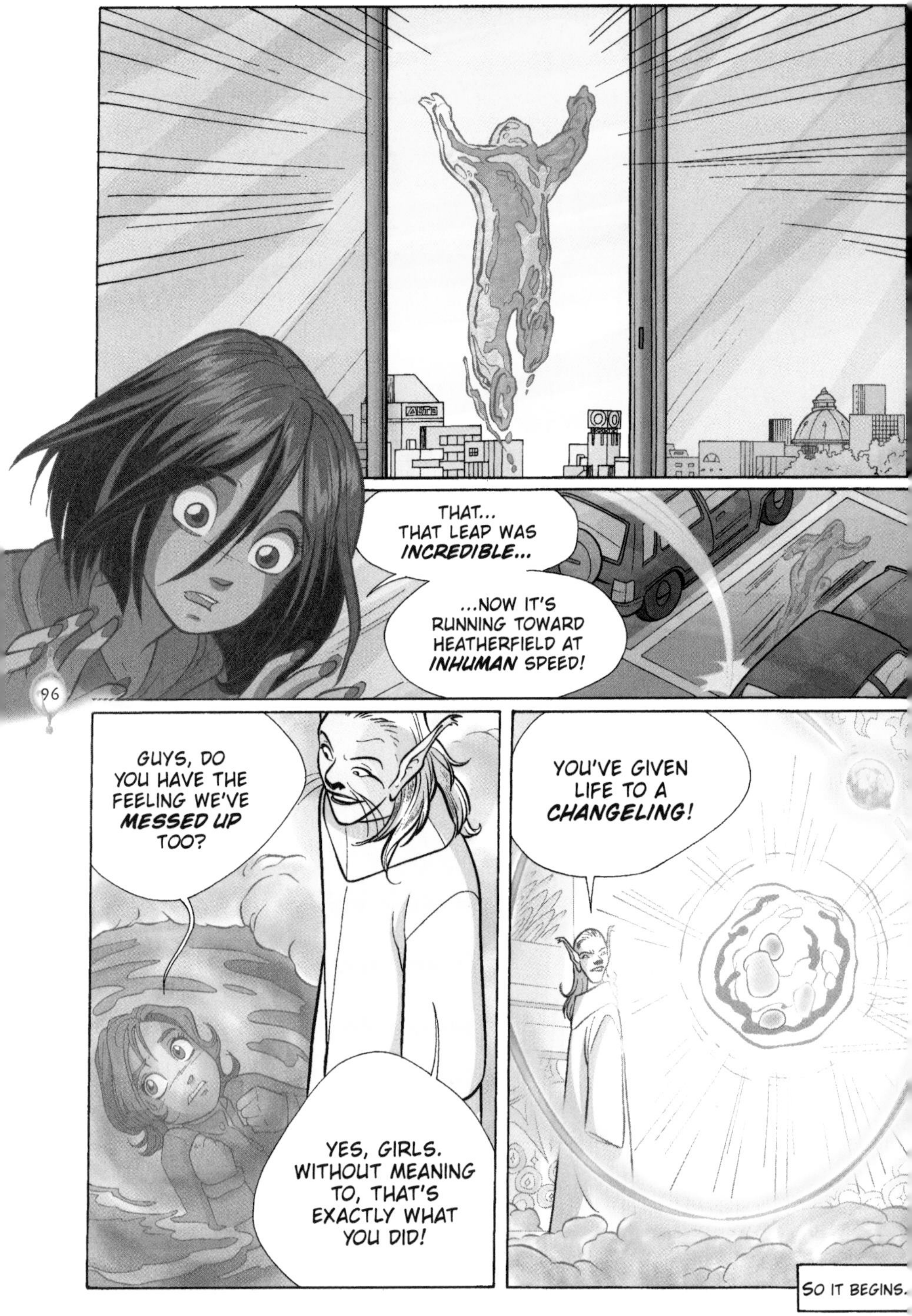
THAT... THAT LEAP WAS INCREDIBLE...
...NOW IT'S RUNNING TOWARD HEATHERFIELD AT INHUMAN SPEED!
GUYS, DO YOU HAVE THE FEELING WE'VE MESSED UP TOO?
YES, GIRLS. WITHOUT MEANING TO, THAT'S EXACTLY WHAT YOU DID!
YOU'VE GIVEN LIFE TO A CHANGELING!
SO IT BEGINS.

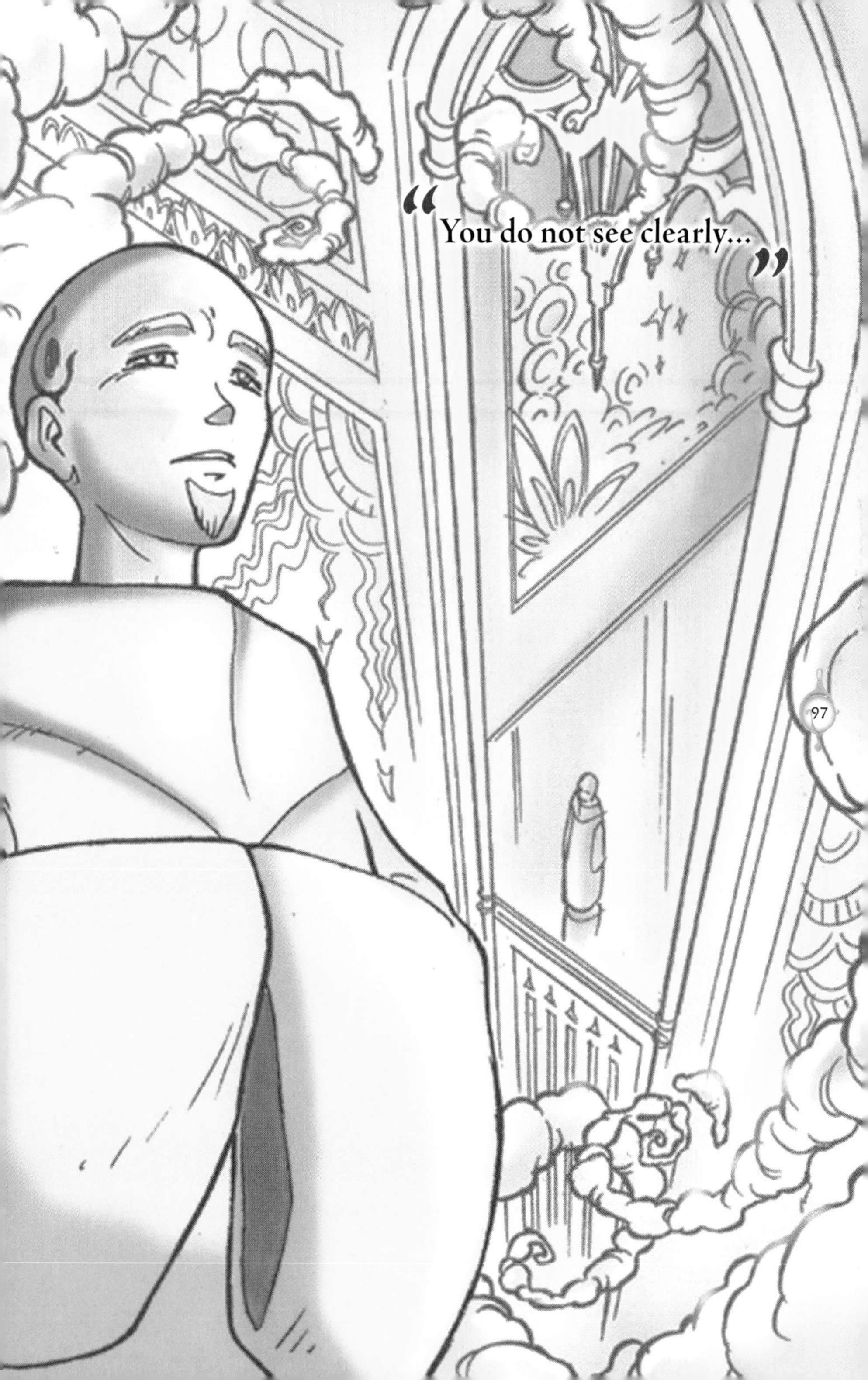
"You do not see clearly..."

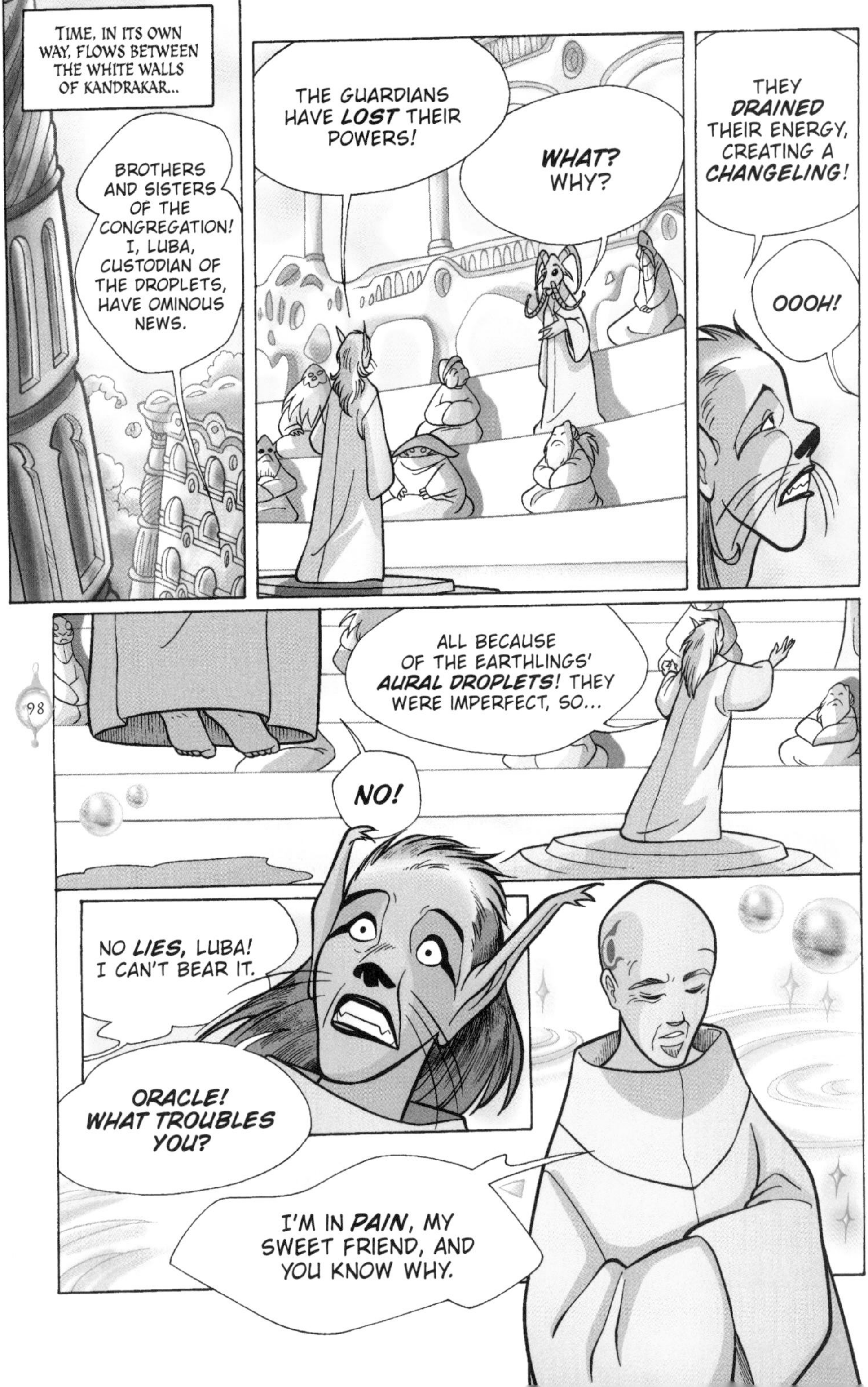

TIME, IN ITS OWN WAY, FLOWS BETWEEN THE WHITE WALLS OF KANDRAKAR...
BROTHERS AND SISTERS OF THE CONGREGATION! I, LUBA, CUSTODIAN OF THE DROPLETS, HAVE OMINOUS NEWS.
THE GUARDIANS HAVE LOST THEIR POWERS!
WHAT? WHY?
THEY DRAINED THEIR ENERGY, CREATING A CHANGELING!
OOOH!
ALL BECAUSE OF THE EARTHLINGS' AURAL DROPLETS! THEY WERE IMPERFECT, SO...
NO!
NO LIES, LUBA! I CAN'T BEAR IT.
ORACLE! WHAT TROUBLES YOU?
I'M IN PAIN, MY SWEET FRIEND, AND YOU KNOW WHY.

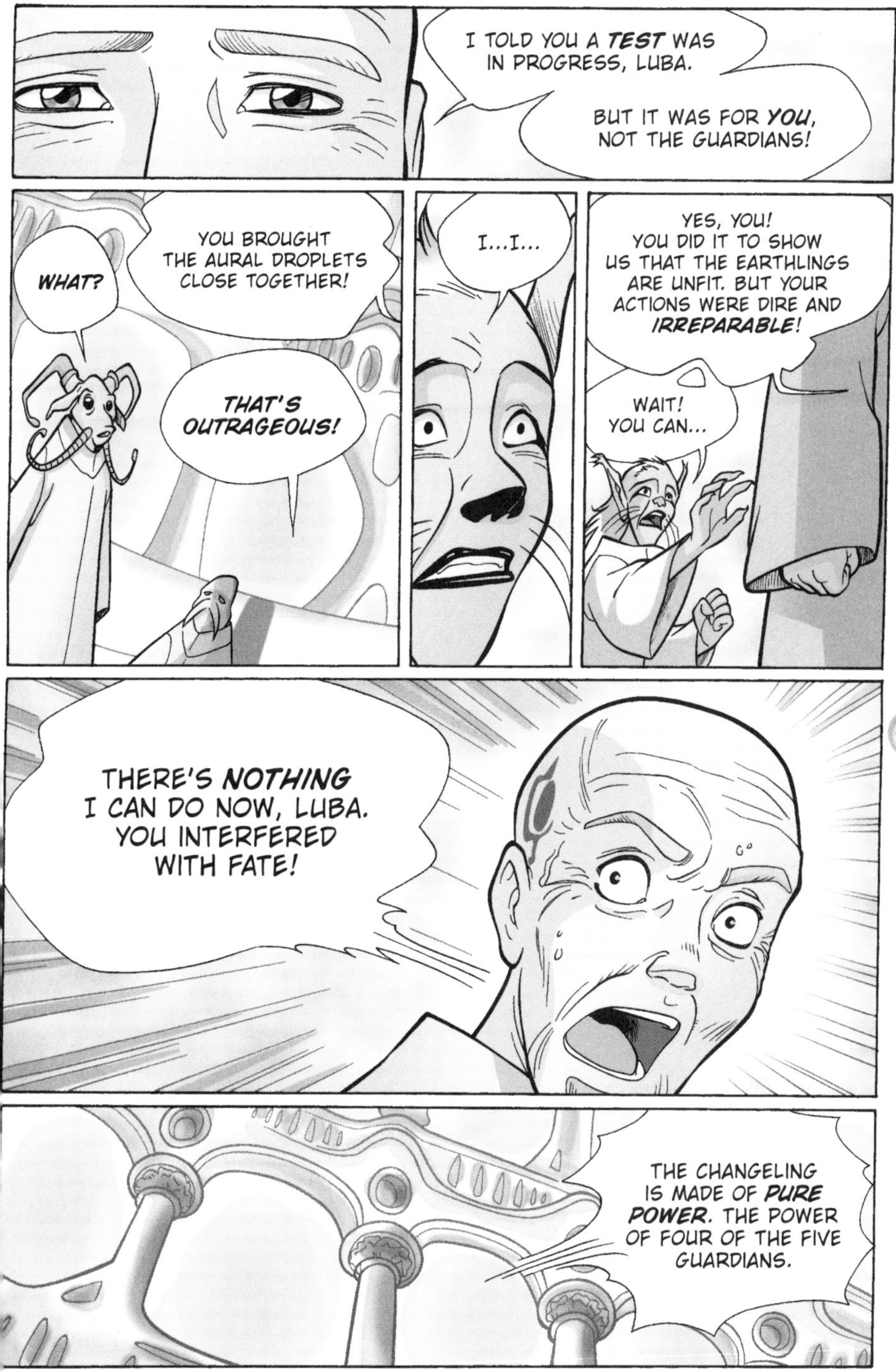
I TOLD YOU A TEST WAS IN PROGRESS, LUBA.
BUT IT WAS FOR YOU, NOT THE GUARDIANS!
WHAT?
YOU BROUGHT THE AURAL DROPLETS CLOSE TOGETHER!
THAT'S OUTRAGEOUS!
I...I...
YES, YOU! YOU DID IT TO SHOW US THAT THE EARTHLINGS ARE UNFIT. BUT YOUR ACTIONS WERE DIRE AND IRREPARABLE!
WAIT! YOU CAN...
THERE'S NOTHING I CAN DO NOW, LUBA. YOU INTERFERED WITH FATE!
THE CHANGELING IS MADE OF PURE POWER. THE POWER OF FOUR OF THE FIVE GUARDIANS.

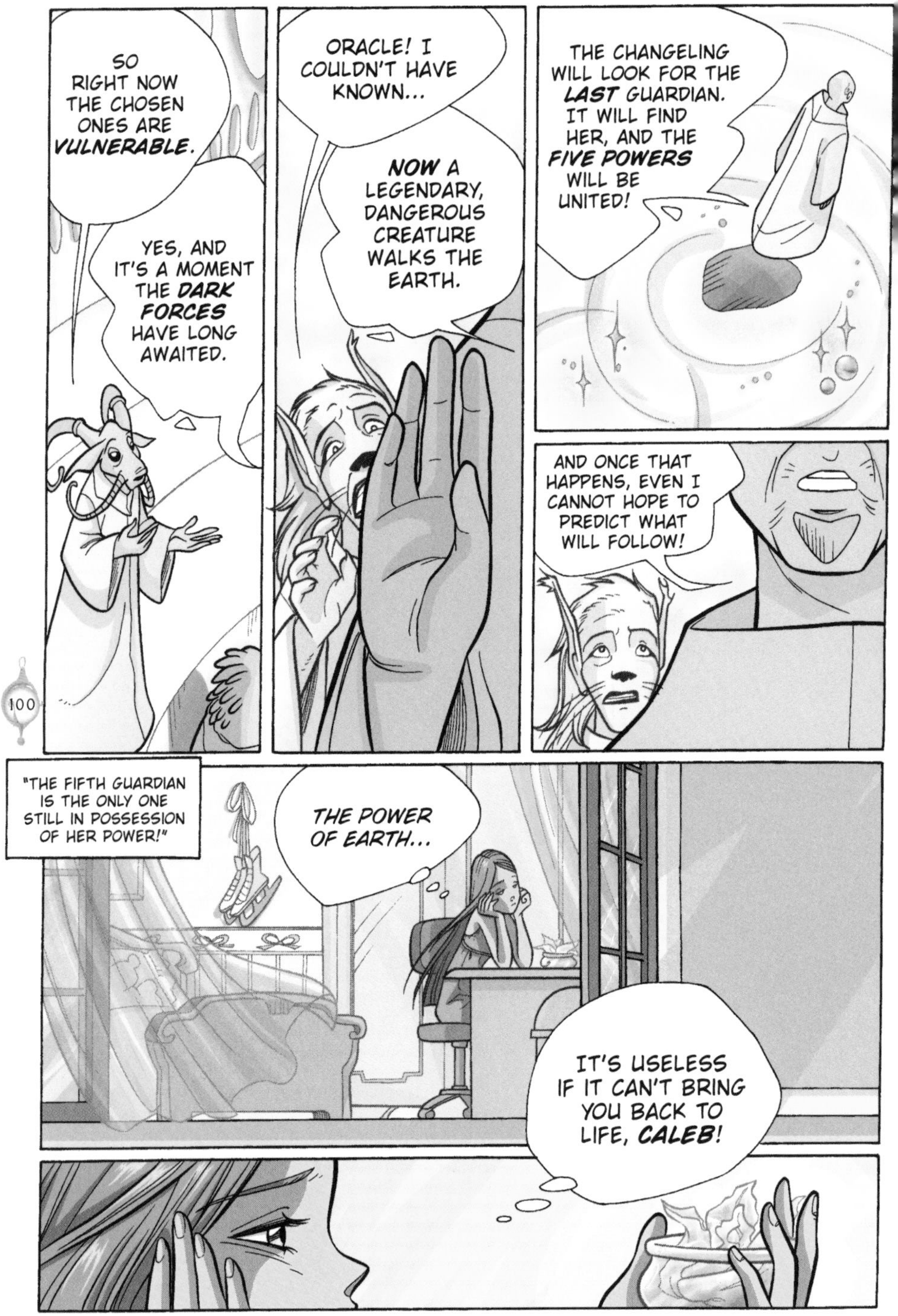
SO RIGHT NOW THE CHOSEN ONES ARE VULNERABLE.
YES, AND IT'S A MOMENT THE DARK FORCES HAVE LONG AWAITED.
ORACLE! I COULDN'T HAVE KNOWN...
NOW A LEGENDARY, DANGEROUS CREATURE WALKS THE EARTH.
THE CHANGELING WILL LOOK FOR THE LAST GUARDIAN. IT WILL FIND HER, AND THE FIVE POWERS WILL BE UNITED!
AND ONCE THAT HAPPENS, EVEN I CANNOT HOPE TO PREDICT WHAT WILL FOLLOW!
"THE FIFTH GUARDIAN IS THE ONLY ONE STILL IN POSSESSION OF HER POWER!"
THE POWER OF EARTH...
IT'S USELESS IF IT CAN'T BRING YOU BACK TO LIFE, CALEB!

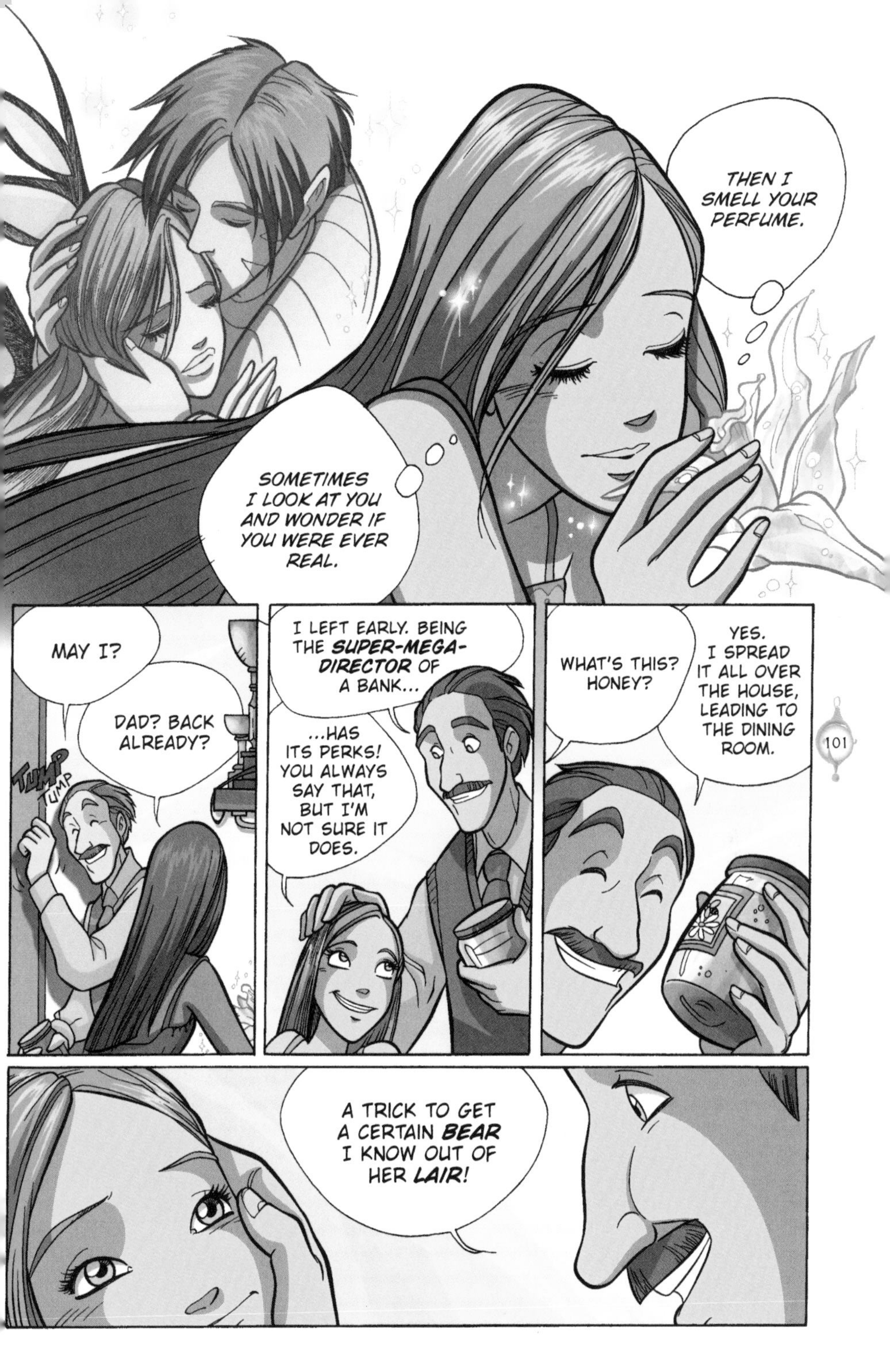
THEN I SMELL YOUR PERFUME.
SOMETIMES I LOOK AT YOU AND WONDER IF YOU WERE EVER REAL.
MAY I?
DAD? BACK ALREADY?
TUMP TUMP
I LEFT EARLY. BEING THE SUPER-MEGA-DIRECTOR OF A BANK...
...HAS ITS PERKS! YOU ALWAYS SAY THAT, BUT I'M NOT SURE IT DOES.
WHAT'S THIS? HONEY?
YES. I SPREAD IT ALL OVER THE HOUSE, LEADING TO THE DINING ROOM.
A TRICK TO GET A CERTAIN BEAR I KNOW OUT OF HER LAIR!

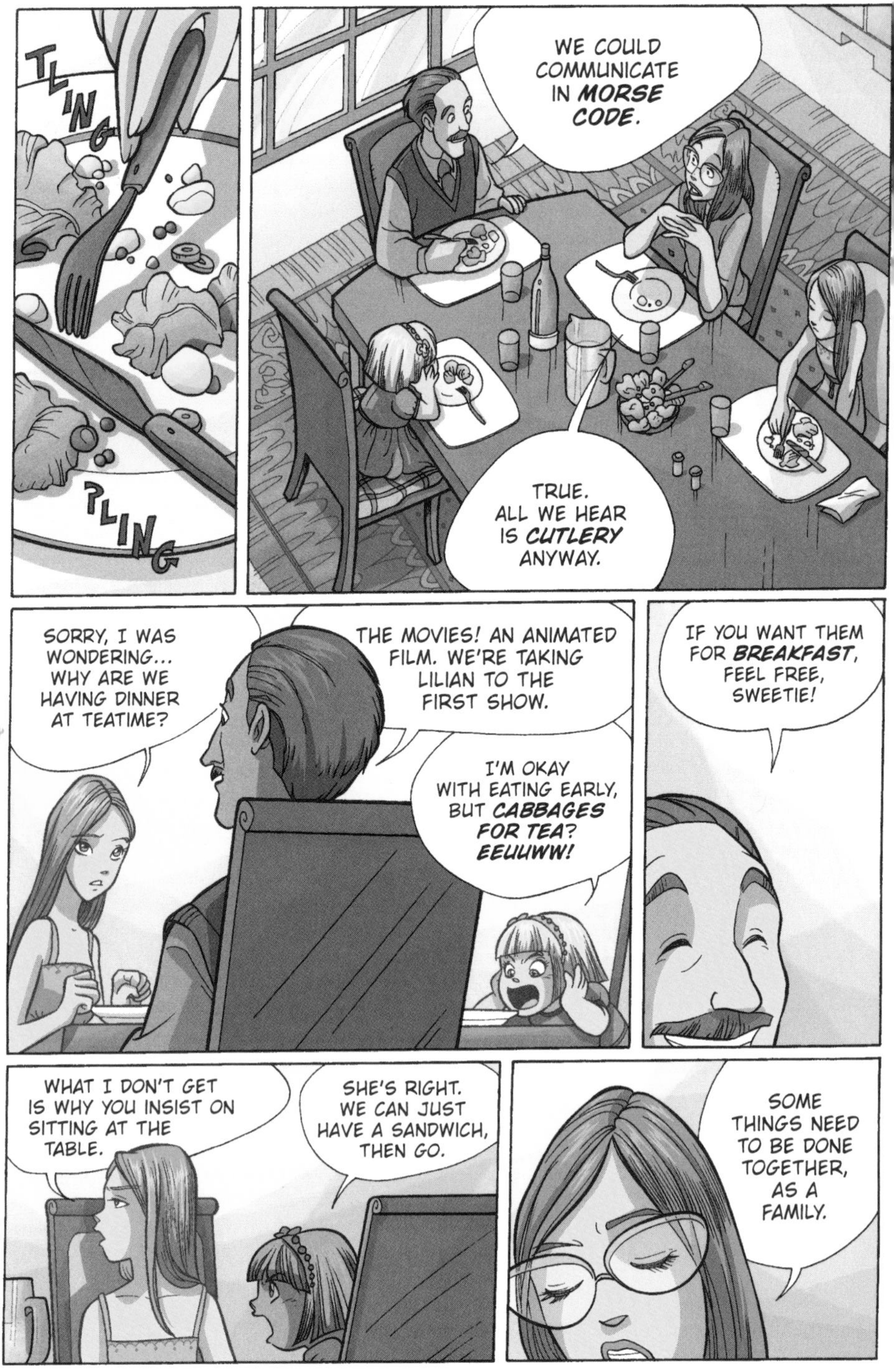
TLING
PLING
WE COULD COMMUNICATE IN MORSE CODE.
TRUE. ALL WE HEAR IS CUTLERY ANYWAY.
SORRY, I WAS WONDERING... WHY ARE WE HAVING DINNER AT TEATIME?
THE MOVIES! AN ANIMATED FILM. WE'RE TAKING LILIAN TO THE FIRST SHOW.
I'M OKAY WITH EATING EARLY, BUT CABBAGES FOR TEA? EEUUWW!
IF YOU WANT THEM FOR BREAKFAST, FEEL FREE, SWEETIE!
WHAT I DON'T GET IS WHY YOU INSIST ON SITTING AT THE TABLE.
SHE'S RIGHT. WE CAN JUST HAVE A SANDWICH, THEN GO.
SOME THINGS NEED TO BE DONE TOGETHER, AS A FAMILY.

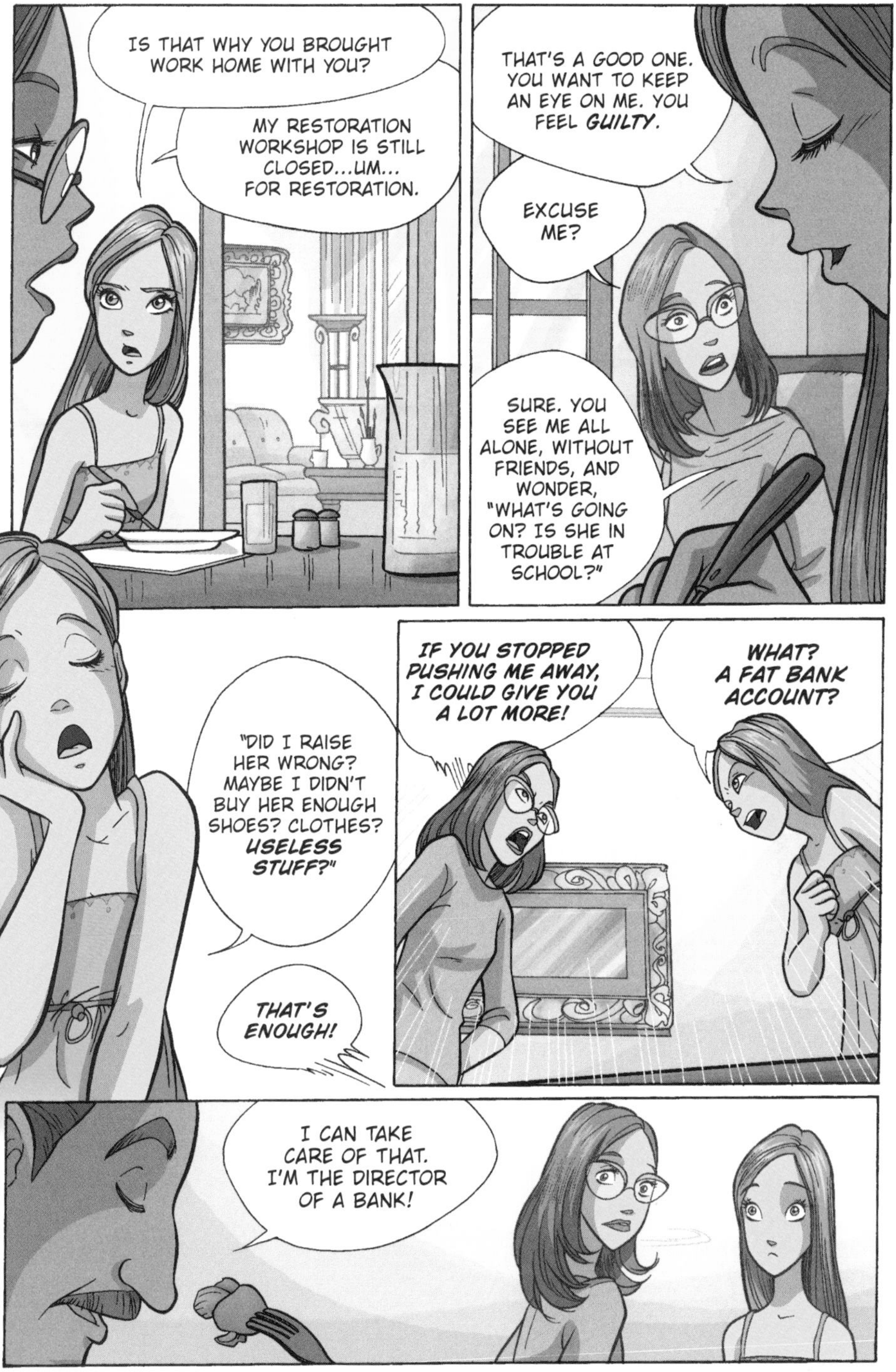
IS THAT WHY YOU BROUGHT WORK HOME WITH YOU?
MY RESTORATION WORKSHOP IS STILL CLOSED...UM... FOR RESTORATION.
THAT'S A GOOD ONE. YOU WANT TO KEEP AN EYE ON ME. YOU FEEL *GUILTY*.
EXCUSE ME?
SURE. YOU SEE ME ALL ALONE, WITHOUT FRIENDS, AND WONDER, "WHAT'S GOING ON? IS SHE IN TROUBLE AT SCHOOL?"
"DID I RAISE HER WRONG? MAYBE I DIDN'T BUY HER ENOUGH SHOES? CLOTHES? *USELESS STUFF?*"
THAT'S ENOUGH!
IF YOU STOPPED PUSHING ME AWAY, I COULD GIVE YOU A LOT MORE!
WHAT? A FAT BANK ACCOUNT?
I CAN TAKE CARE OF THAT. I'M THE DIRECTOR OF A BANK!

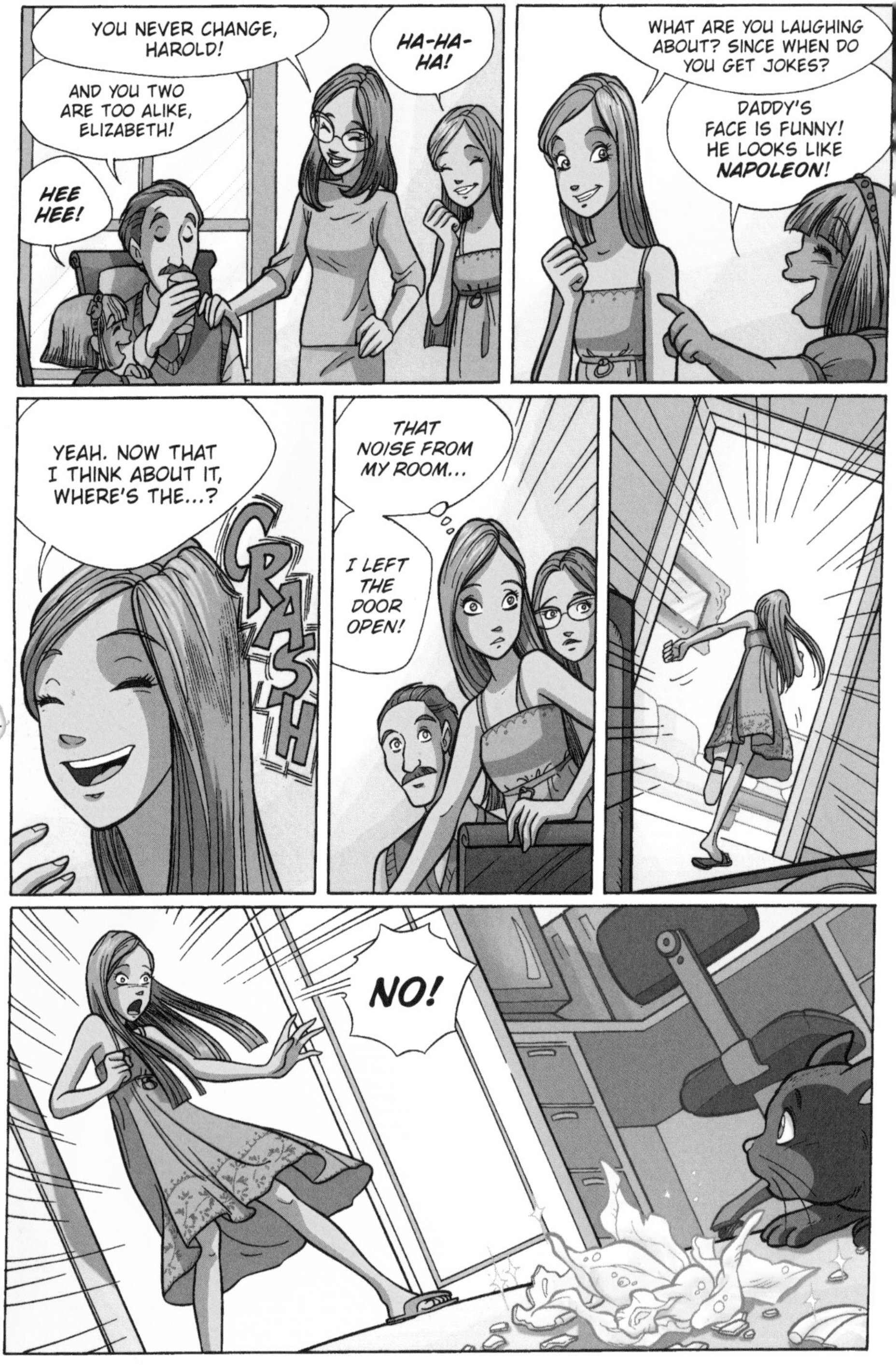
YOU NEVER CHANGE, HAROLD!
AND YOU TWO ARE TOO ALIKE, ELIZABETH!
HEE HEE!
HA-HA-HA!
WHAT ARE YOU LAUGHING ABOUT? SINCE WHEN DO YOU GET JOKES?
DADDY'S FACE IS FUNNY! HE LOOKS LIKE NAPOLEON!
YEAH. NOW THAT I THINK ABOUT IT, WHERE'S THE...?
CRASH
THAT NOISE FROM MY ROOM...
I LEFT THE DOOR OPEN!
NO!

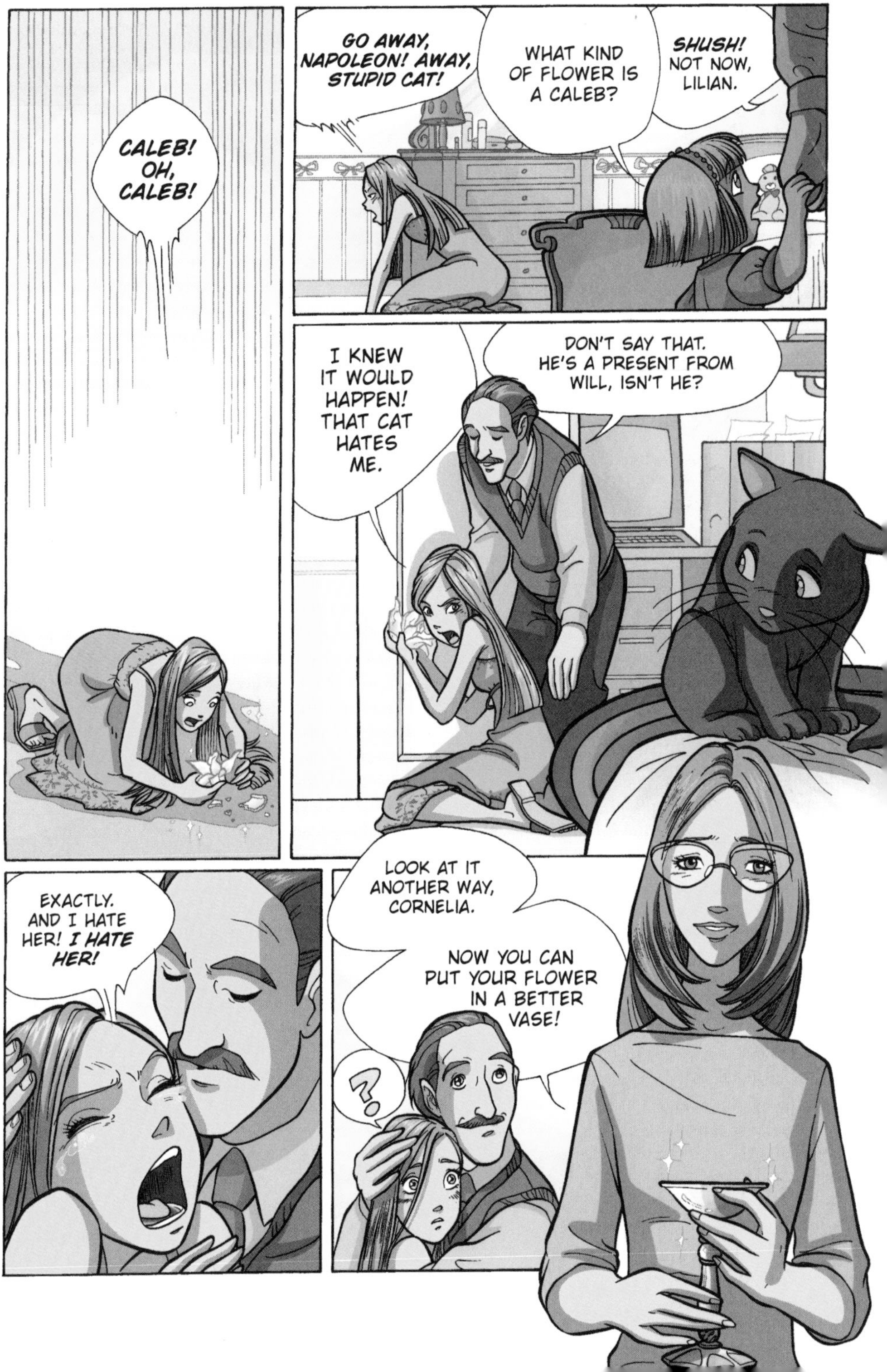
CALEB! OH, CALEB!
GO AWAY, NAPOLEON! AWAY, STUPID CAT!
WHAT KIND OF FLOWER IS A CALEB?
SHUSH! NOT NOW, LILIAN.
I KNEW IT WOULD HAPPEN! THAT CAT HATES ME.
DON'T SAY THAT. HE'S A PRESENT FROM WILL, ISN'T HE?
EXACTLY. AND I HATE HER! I HATE HER!
LOOK AT IT ANOTHER WAY, CORNELIA.
NOW YOU CAN PUT YOUR FLOWER IN A BETTER VASE!
?

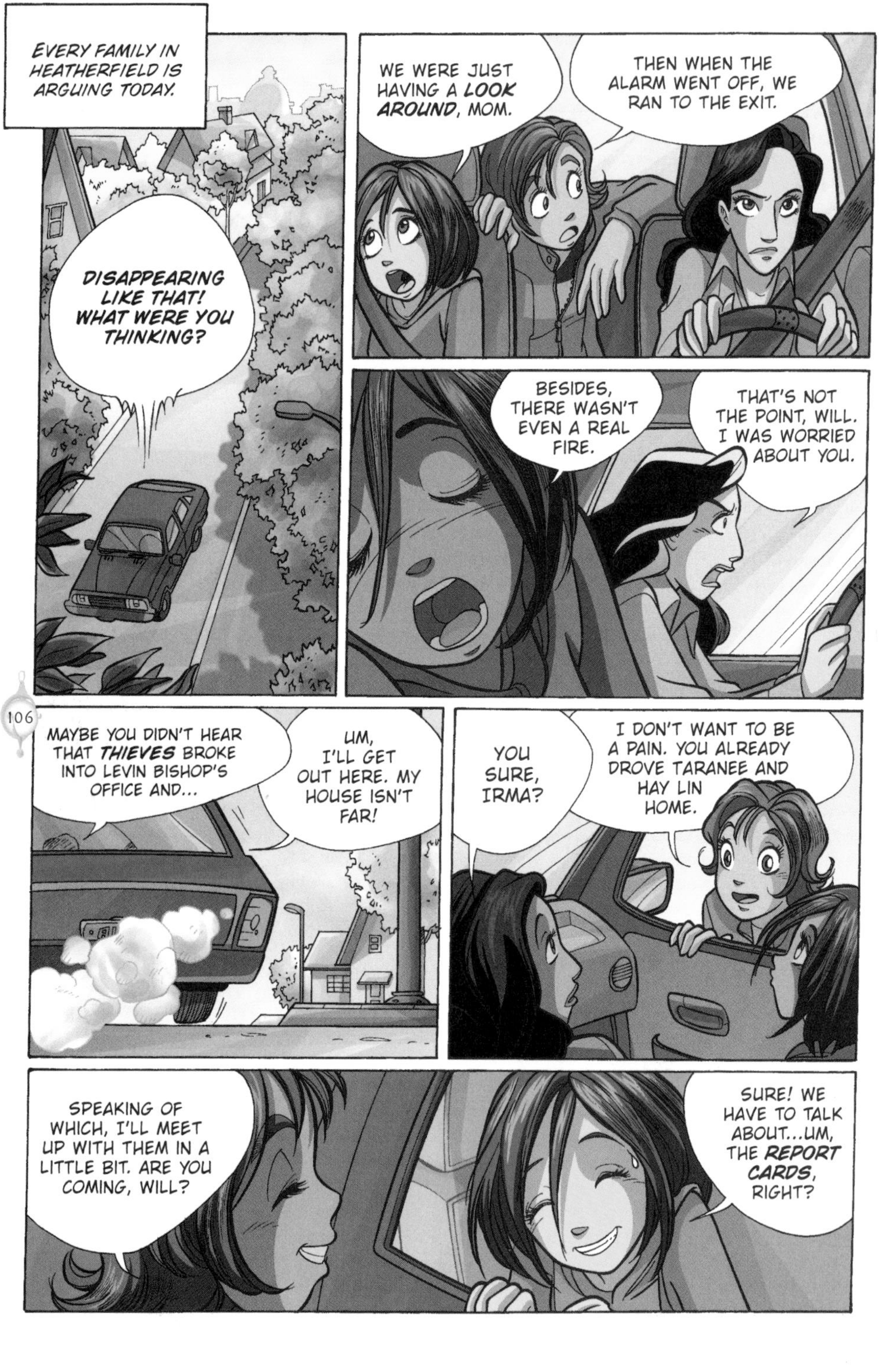
EVERY FAMILY IN HEATHERFIELD IS ARGUING TODAY.
DISAPPEARING LIKE THAT! WHAT WERE YOU THINKING?
WE WERE JUST HAVING A LOOK AROUND, MOM.
THEN WHEN THE ALARM WENT OFF, WE RAN TO THE EXIT.
BESIDES, THERE WASN'T EVEN A REAL FIRE.
THAT'S NOT THE POINT, WILL. I WAS WORRIED ABOUT YOU.
MAYBE YOU DIDN'T HEAR THAT THIEVES BROKE INTO LEVIN BISHOP'S OFFICE AND...
UM, I'LL GET OUT HERE. MY HOUSE ISN'T FAR!
YOU SURE, IRMA?
I DON'T WANT TO BE A PAIN. YOU ALREADY DROVE TARANEE AND HAY LIN HOME.
SPEAKING OF WHICH, I'LL MEET UP WITH THEM IN A LITTLE BIT. ARE YOU COMING, WILL?
SURE! WE HAVE TO TALK ABOUT...UM, THE REPORT CARDS, RIGHT?

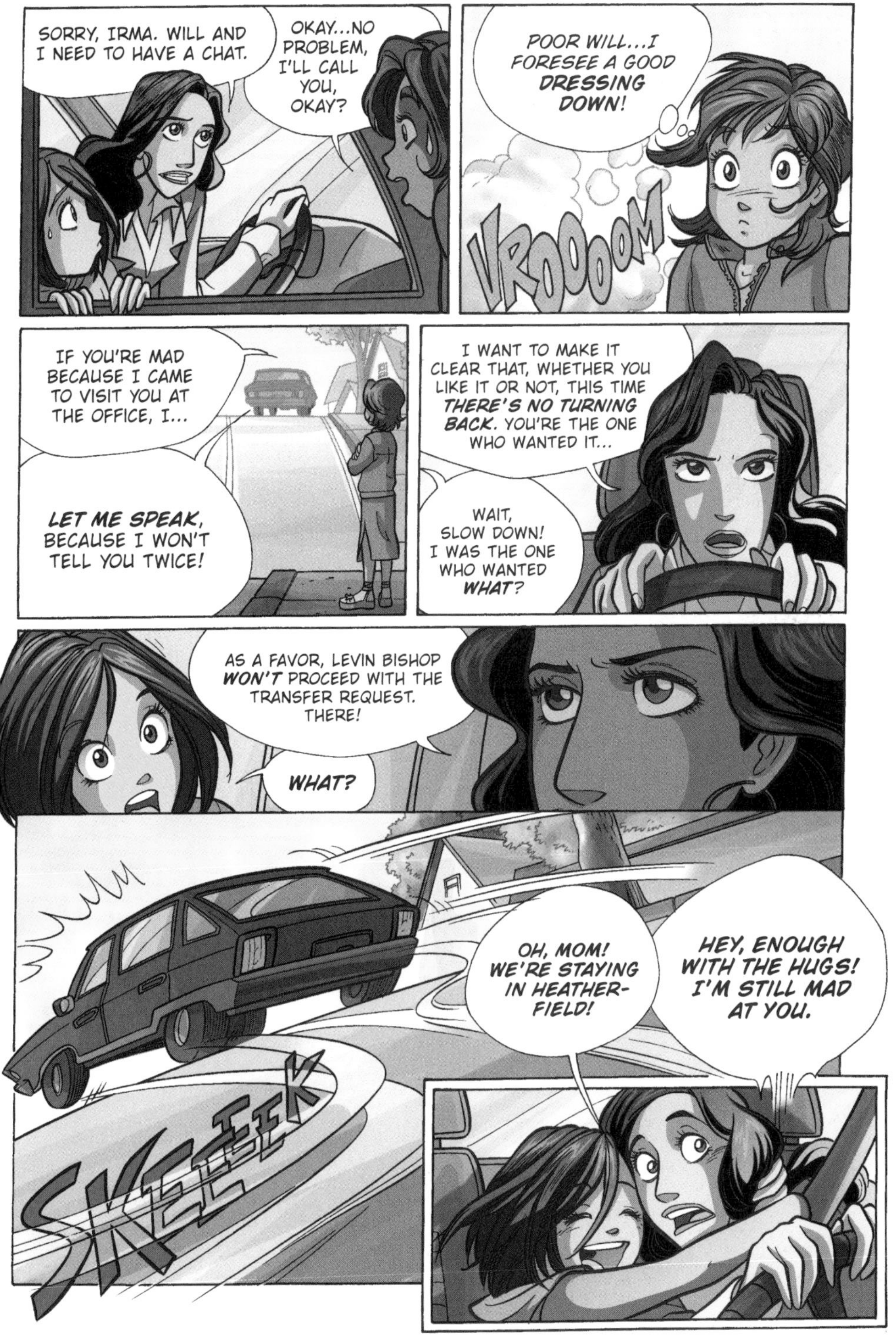
SORRY, IRMA. WILL AND I NEED TO HAVE A CHAT.
OKAY...NO PROBLEM, I'LL CALL YOU, OKAY?
POOR WILL...I FORESEE A GOOD DRESSING DOWN!
VROOOOM
IF YOU'RE MAD BECAUSE I CAME TO VISIT YOU AT THE OFFICE, I...
LET ME SPEAK, BECAUSE I WON'T TELL YOU TWICE!
I WANT TO MAKE IT CLEAR THAT, WHETHER YOU LIKE IT OR NOT, THIS TIME THERE'S NO TURNING BACK. YOU'RE THE ONE WHO WANTED IT...
WAIT, SLOW DOWN! I WAS THE ONE WHO WANTED WHAT?
AS A FAVOR, LEVIN BISHOP WON'T PROCEED WITH THE TRANSFER REQUEST. THERE!
WHAT?
SKREEEK
OH, MOM! WE'RE STAYING IN HEATHER-FIELD!
HEY, ENOUGH WITH THE HUGS! I'M STILL MAD AT YOU.

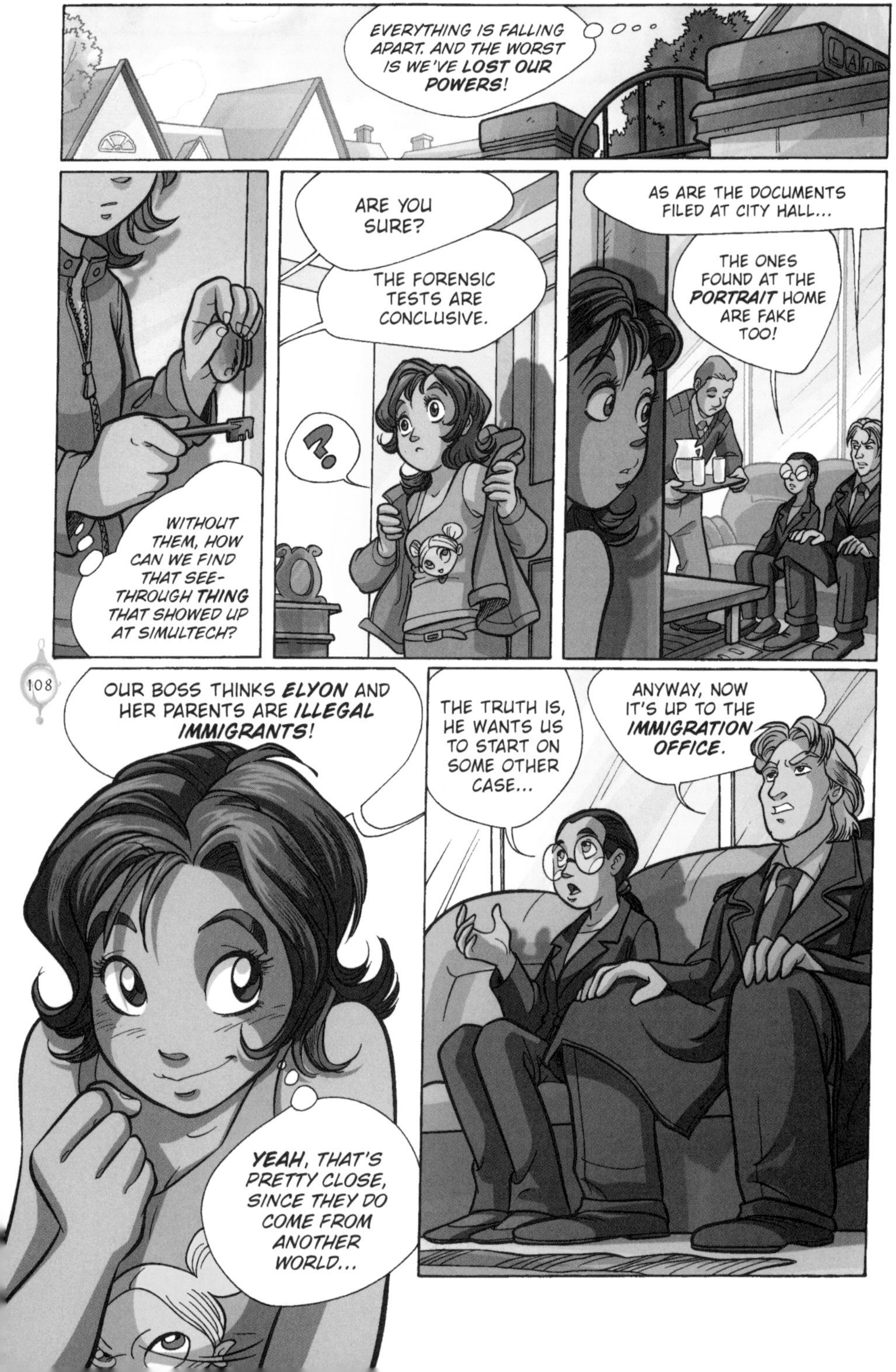

EVERYTHING IS FALLING APART. AND THE WORST IS WE'VE LOST OUR POWERS!
WITHOUT THEM, HOW CAN WE FIND THAT SEE-THROUGH THING THAT SHOWED UP AT SIMULTECH?
ARE YOU SURE?
THE FORENSIC TESTS ARE CONCLUSIVE.
?
AS ARE THE DOCUMENTS FILED AT CITY HALL...
THE ONES FOUND AT THE PORTRAIT HOME ARE FAKE TOO!
OUR BOSS THINKS ELYON AND HER PARENTS ARE ILLEGAL IMMIGRANTS!
YEAH, THAT'S PRETTY CLOSE, SINCE THEY DO COME FROM ANOTHER WORLD...
THE TRUTH IS, HE WANTS US TO START ON SOME OTHER CASE...
ANYWAY, NOW IT'S UP TO THE IMMIGRATION OFFICE.

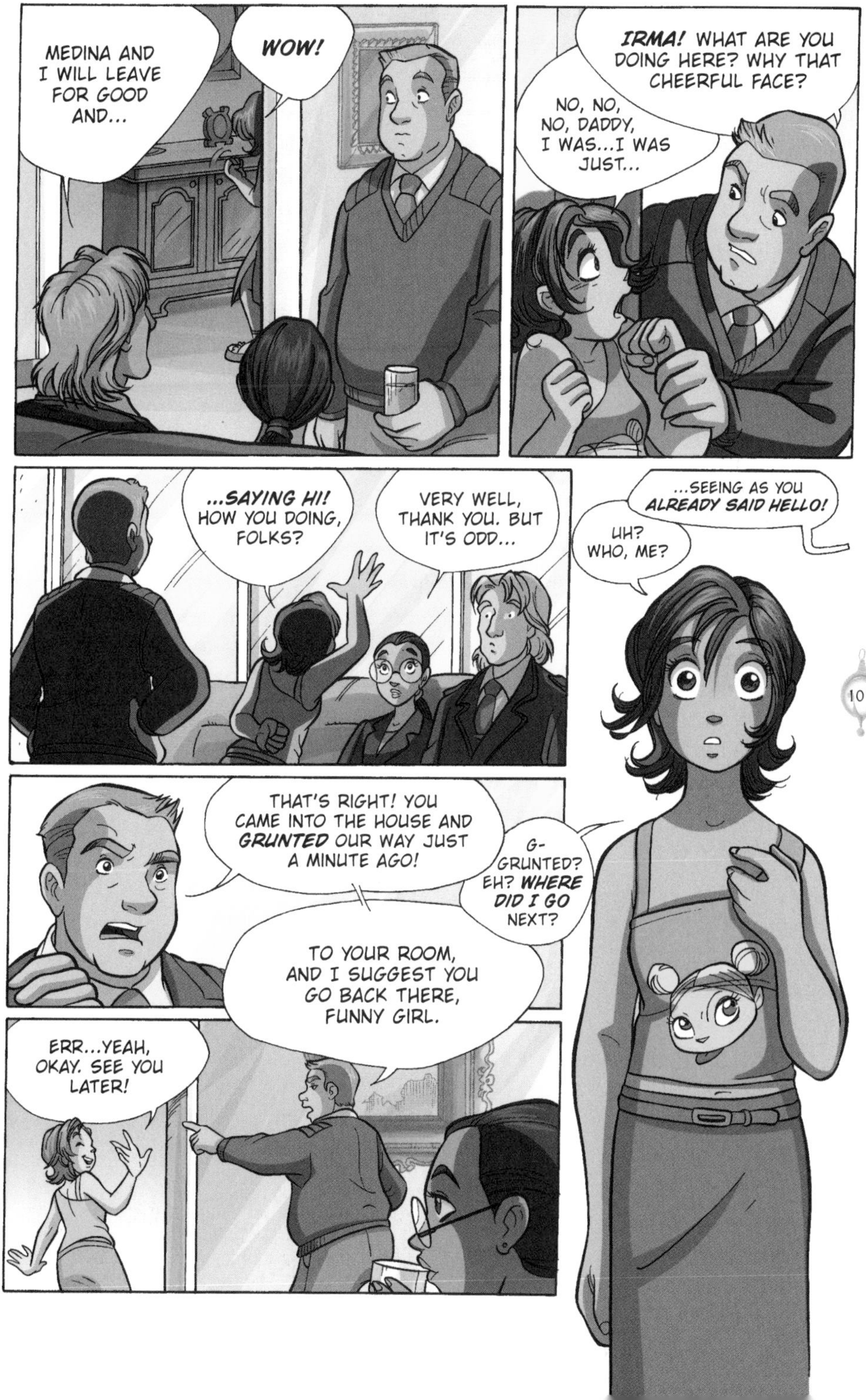

MEDINA AND I WILL LEAVE FOR GOOD AND...
WOW!
IRMA! WHAT ARE YOU DOING HERE? WHY THAT CHEERFUL FACE?
NO, NO, NO, DADDY, I WAS...I WAS JUST...
...SAYING HI! HOW YOU DOING, FOLKS?
VERY WELL, THANK YOU. BUT IT'S ODD...
...SEEING AS YOU ALREADY SAID HELLO!
UH? WHO, ME?
THAT'S RIGHT! YOU CAME INTO THE HOUSE AND GRUNTED OUR WAY JUST A MINUTE AGO!
G-GRUNTED? EH? WHERE DID I GO NEXT?
TO YOUR ROOM, AND I SUGGEST YOU GO BACK THERE, FUNNY GIRL.
ERR...YEAH, OKAY. SEE YOU LATER!

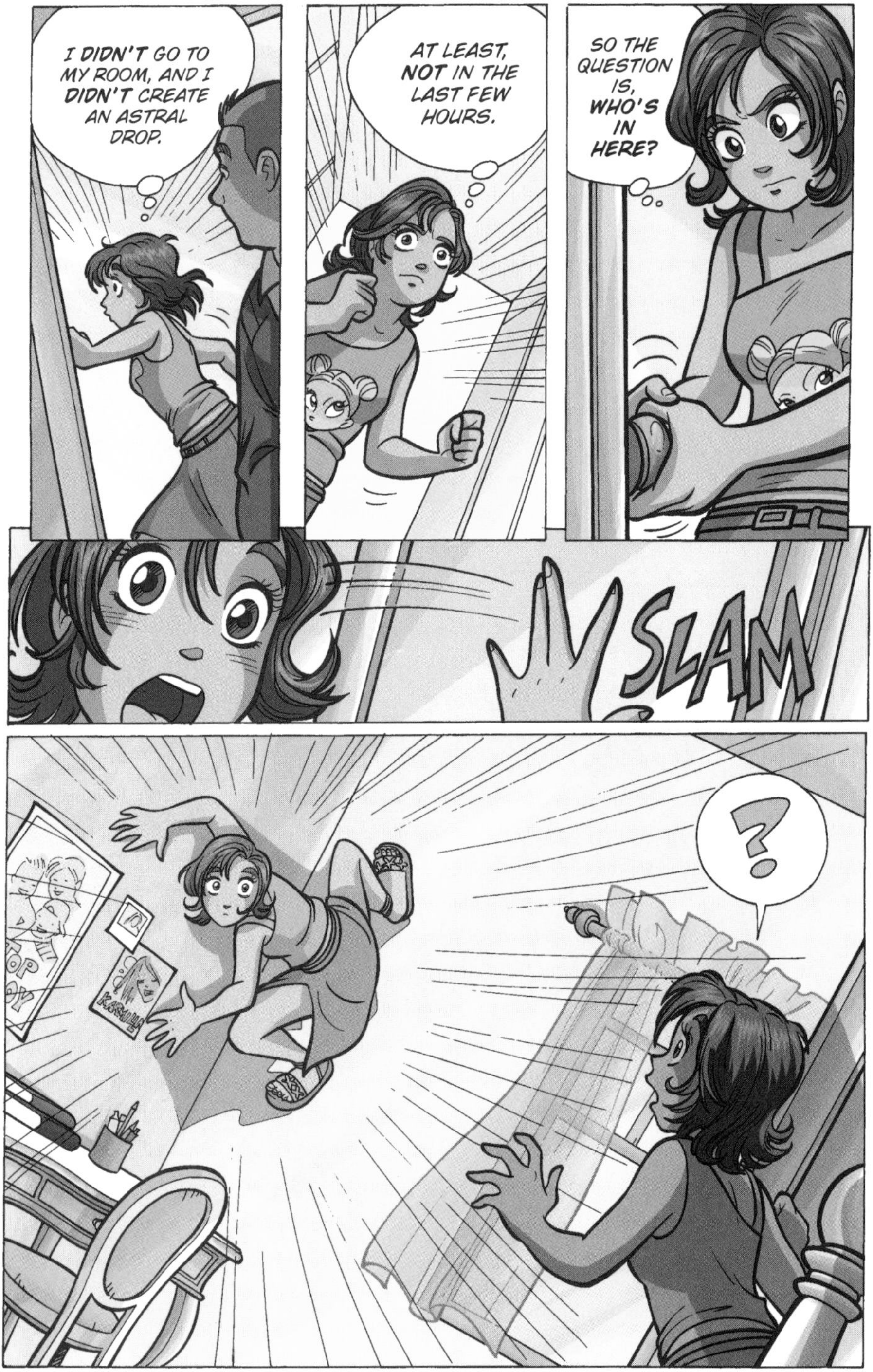

I DIDN'T GO TO MY ROOM, AND I DIDN'T CREATE AN ASTRAL DROP.
AT LEAST, NOT IN THE LAST FEW HOURS.
SO THE QUESTION IS, WHO'S IN HERE?
SLAM
?

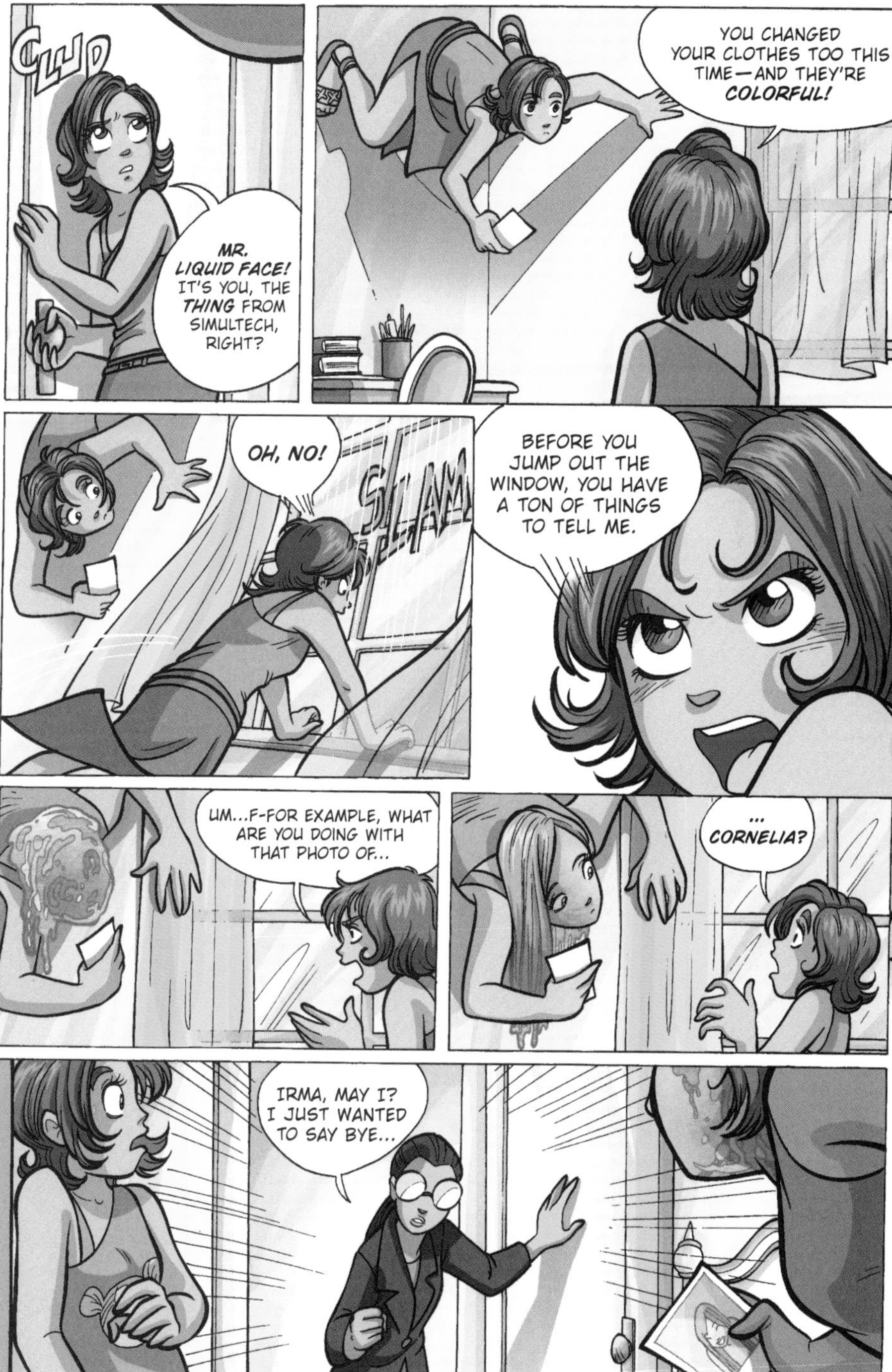
CLUD
MR. LIQUID FACE! IT'S YOU, THE THING FROM SIMULTECH, RIGHT?
YOU CHANGED YOUR CLOTHES TOO THIS TIME—AND THEY'RE COLORFUL!
OH, NO!
SLAM
BEFORE YOU JUMP OUT THE WINDOW, YOU HAVE A TON OF THINGS TO TELL ME.
UM...F-FOR EXAMPLE, WHAT ARE YOU DOING WITH THAT PHOTO OF...
... CORNELIA?
IRMA, MAY I? I JUST WANTED TO SAY BYE...

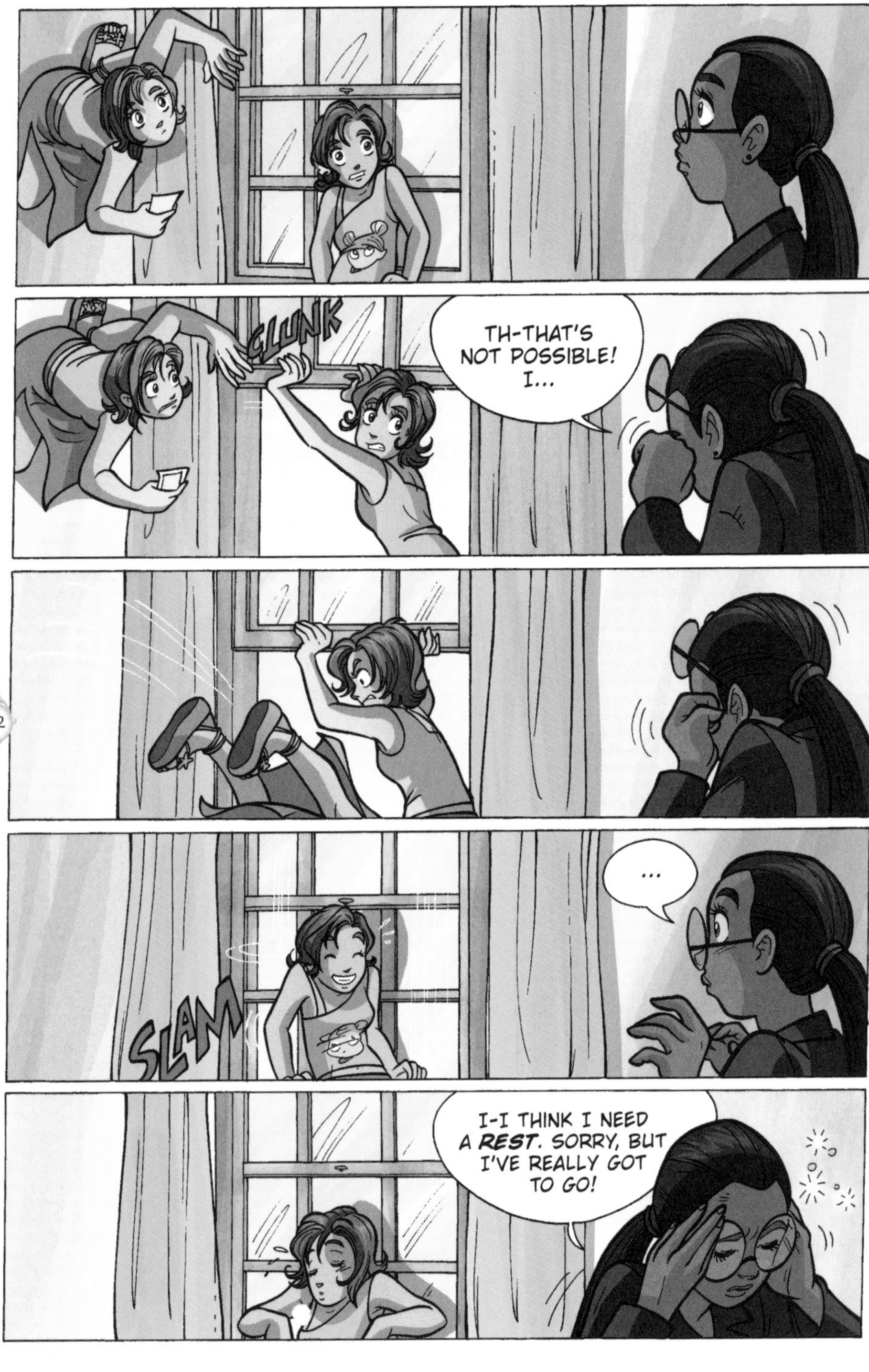
CLUNK
TH-THAT'S NOT POSSIBLE! I...
...
SLAM
I-I THINK I NEED A **REST**. SORRY, BUT I'VE REALLY GOT TO GO!

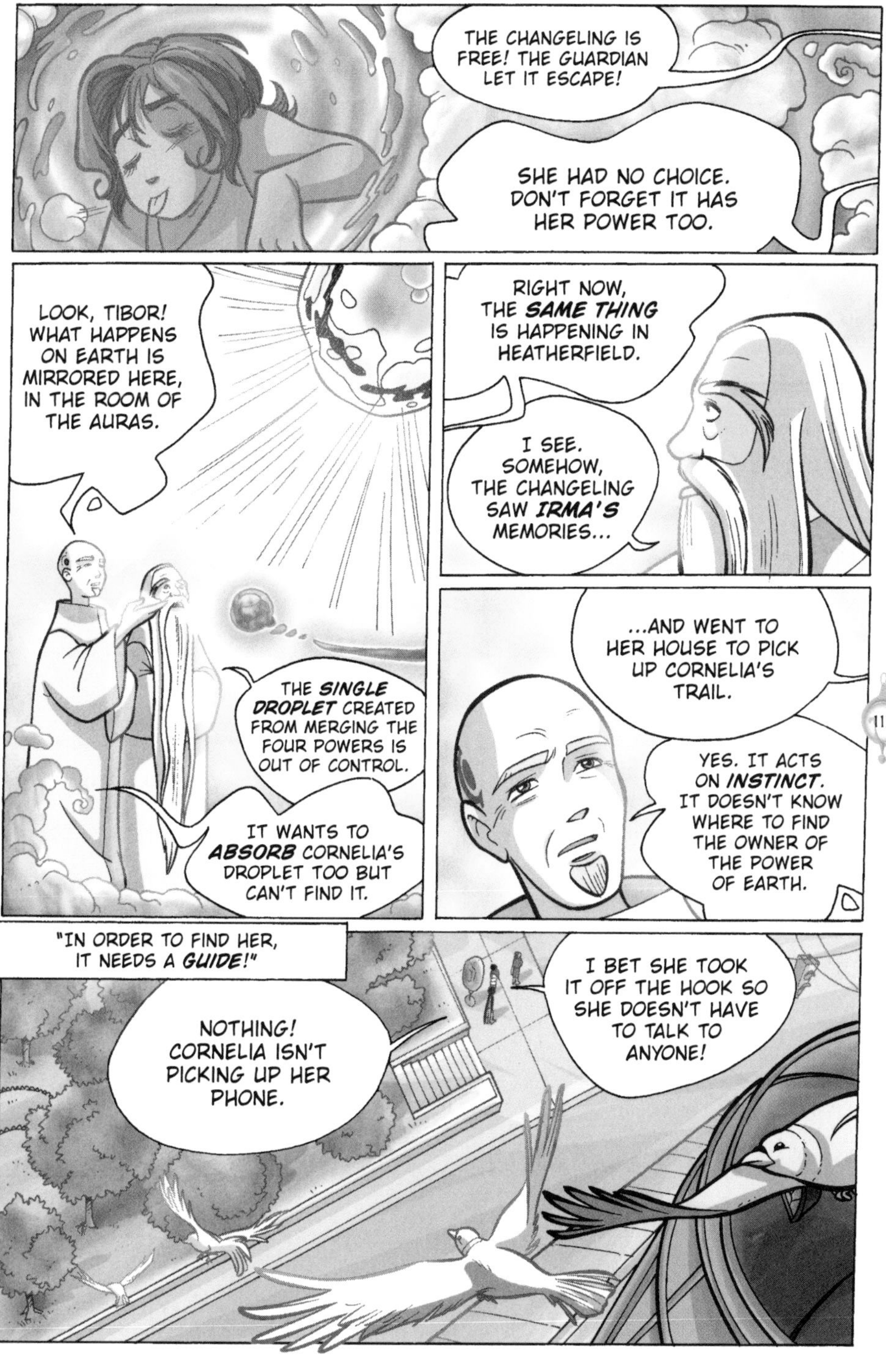
THE CHANGELING IS FREE! THE GUARDIAN LET IT ESCAPE!
SHE HAD NO CHOICE. DON'T FORGET IT HAS HER POWER TOO.
LOOK, TIBOR! WHAT HAPPENS ON EARTH IS MIRRORED HERE, IN THE ROOM OF THE AURAS.
THE SINGLE DROPLET CREATED FROM MERGING THE FOUR POWERS IS OUT OF CONTROL.
IT WANTS TO ABSORB CORNELIA'S DROPLET TOO BUT CAN'T FIND IT.
RIGHT NOW, THE SAME THING IS HAPPENING IN HEATHERFIELD.
I SEE. SOMEHOW, THE CHANGELING SAW IRMA'S MEMORIES...
...AND WENT TO HER HOUSE TO PICK UP CORNELIA'S TRAIL.
YES. IT ACTS ON INSTINCT. IT DOESN'T KNOW WHERE TO FIND THE OWNER OF THE POWER OF EARTH.
"IN ORDER TO FIND HER, IT NEEDS A GUIDE!"
NOTHING! CORNELIA ISN'T PICKING UP HER PHONE.
I BET SHE TOOK IT OFF THE HOOK SO SHE DOESN'T HAVE TO TALK TO ANYONE!

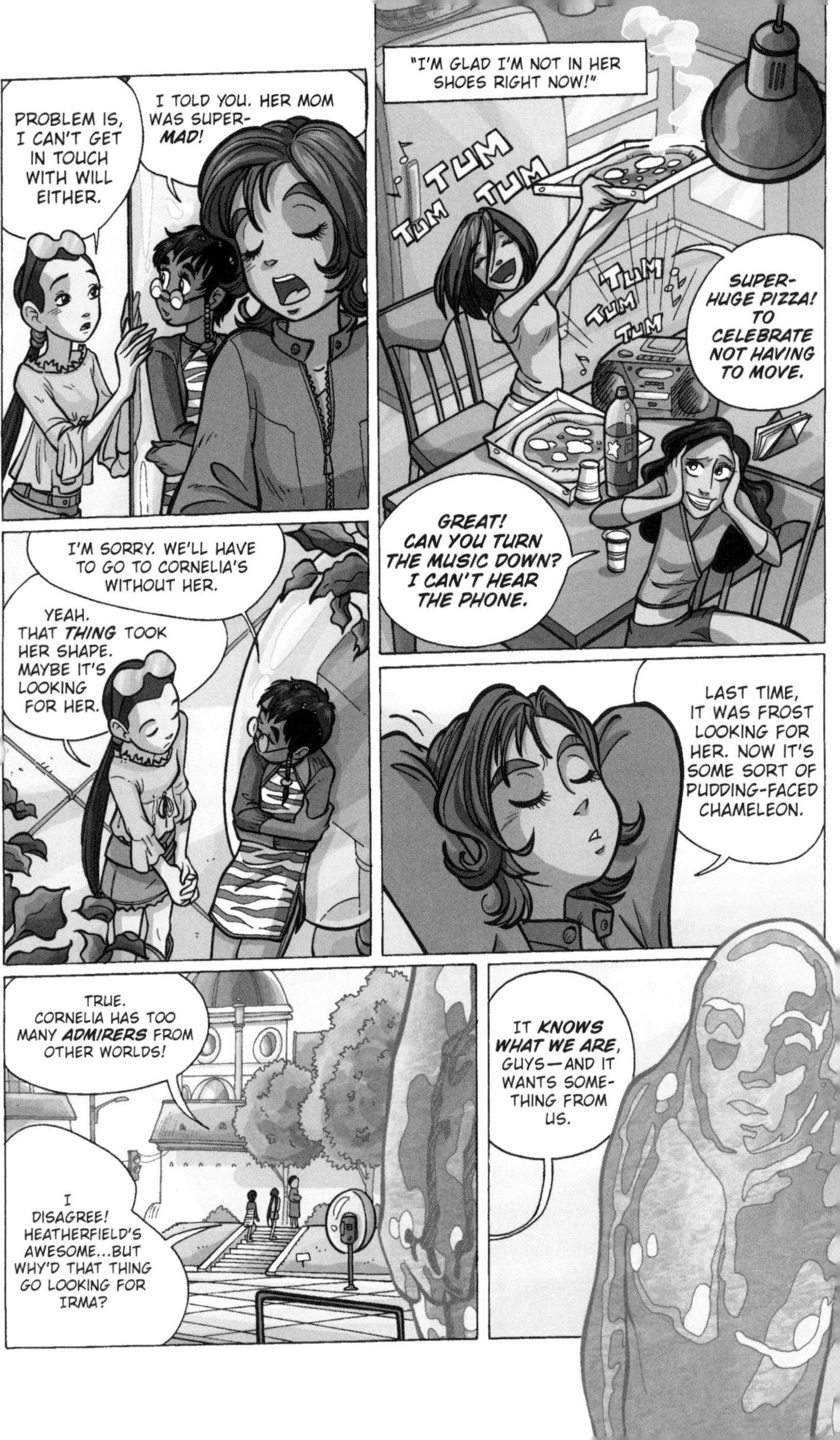
PROBLEM IS, I CAN'T GET IN TOUCH WITH WILL EITHER.
I TOLD YOU. HER MOM WAS SUPER-MAD!
"I'M GLAD I'M NOT IN HER SHOES RIGHT NOW!"
TUM TUM TUM
TUM TUM TUM
SUPER-HUGE PIZZA! TO CELEBRATE NOT HAVING TO MOVE.
GREAT! CAN YOU TURN THE MUSIC DOWN? I CAN'T HEAR THE PHONE.
I'M SORRY. WE'LL HAVE TO GO TO CORNELIA'S WITHOUT HER.
YEAH. THAT THING TOOK HER SHAPE. MAYBE IT'S LOOKING FOR HER.
LAST TIME, IT WAS FROST LOOKING FOR HER. NOW IT'S SOME SORT OF PUDDING-FACED CHAMELEON.
TRUE. CORNELIA HAS TOO MANY ADMIRERS FROM OTHER WORLDS!
I DISAGREE! HEATHERFIELD'S AWESOME...BUT WHY'D THAT THING GO LOOKING FOR IRMA?
IT KNOWS WHAT WE ARE, GUYS—AND IT WANTS SOME-THING FROM US.

114

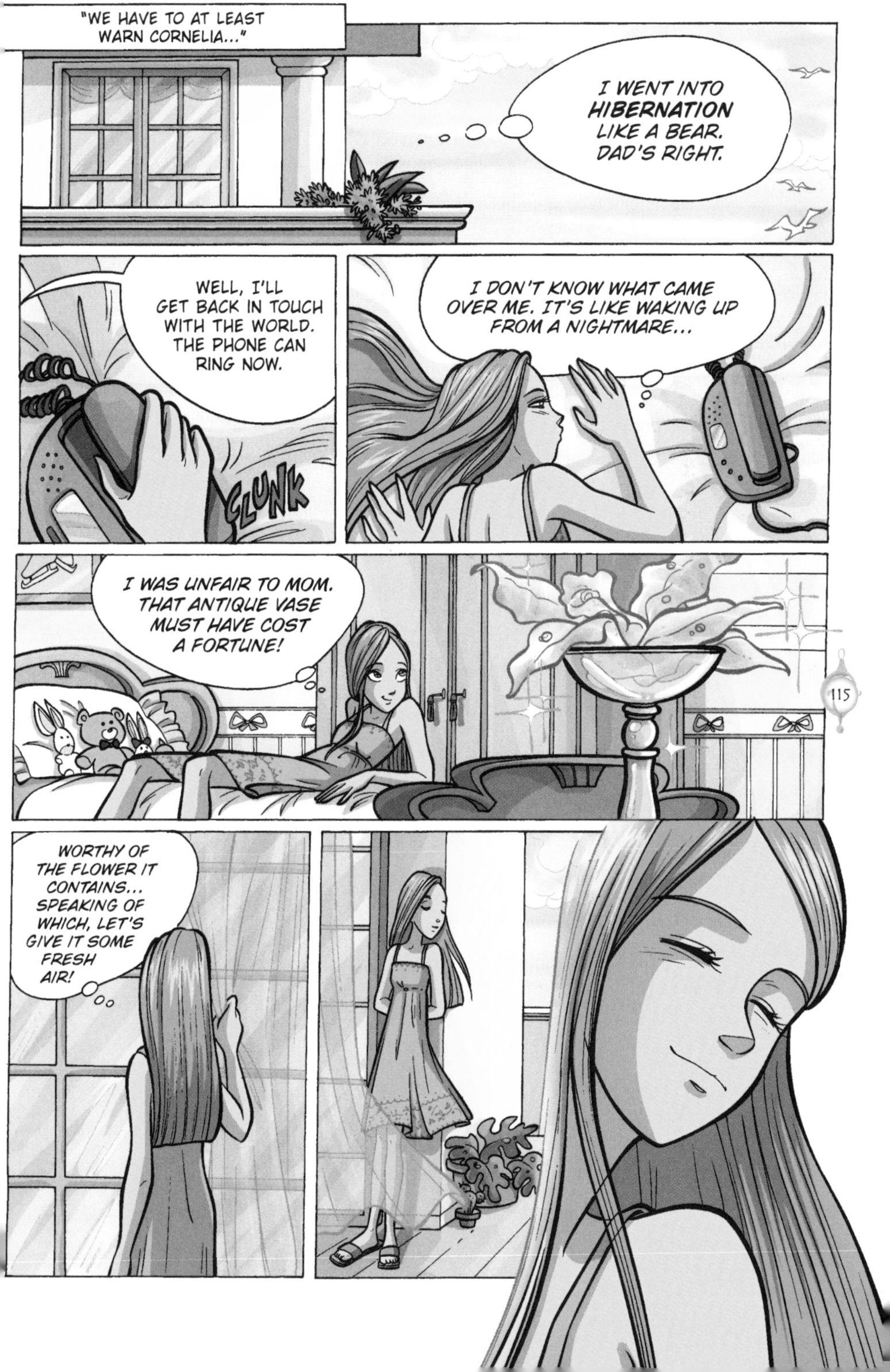
"WE HAVE TO AT LEAST WARN CORNELIA..."
I WENT INTO HIBERNATION LIKE A BEAR. DAD'S RIGHT.
WELL, I'LL GET BACK IN TOUCH WITH THE WORLD. THE PHONE CAN RING NOW.
CLUNK
I DON'T KNOW WHAT CAME OVER ME. IT'S LIKE WAKING UP FROM A NIGHTMARE...
I WAS UNFAIR TO MOM. THAT ANTIQUE VASE MUST HAVE COST A FORTUNE!
WORTHY OF THE FLOWER IT CONTAINS... SPEAKING OF WHICH, LET'S GIVE IT SOME FRESH AIR!

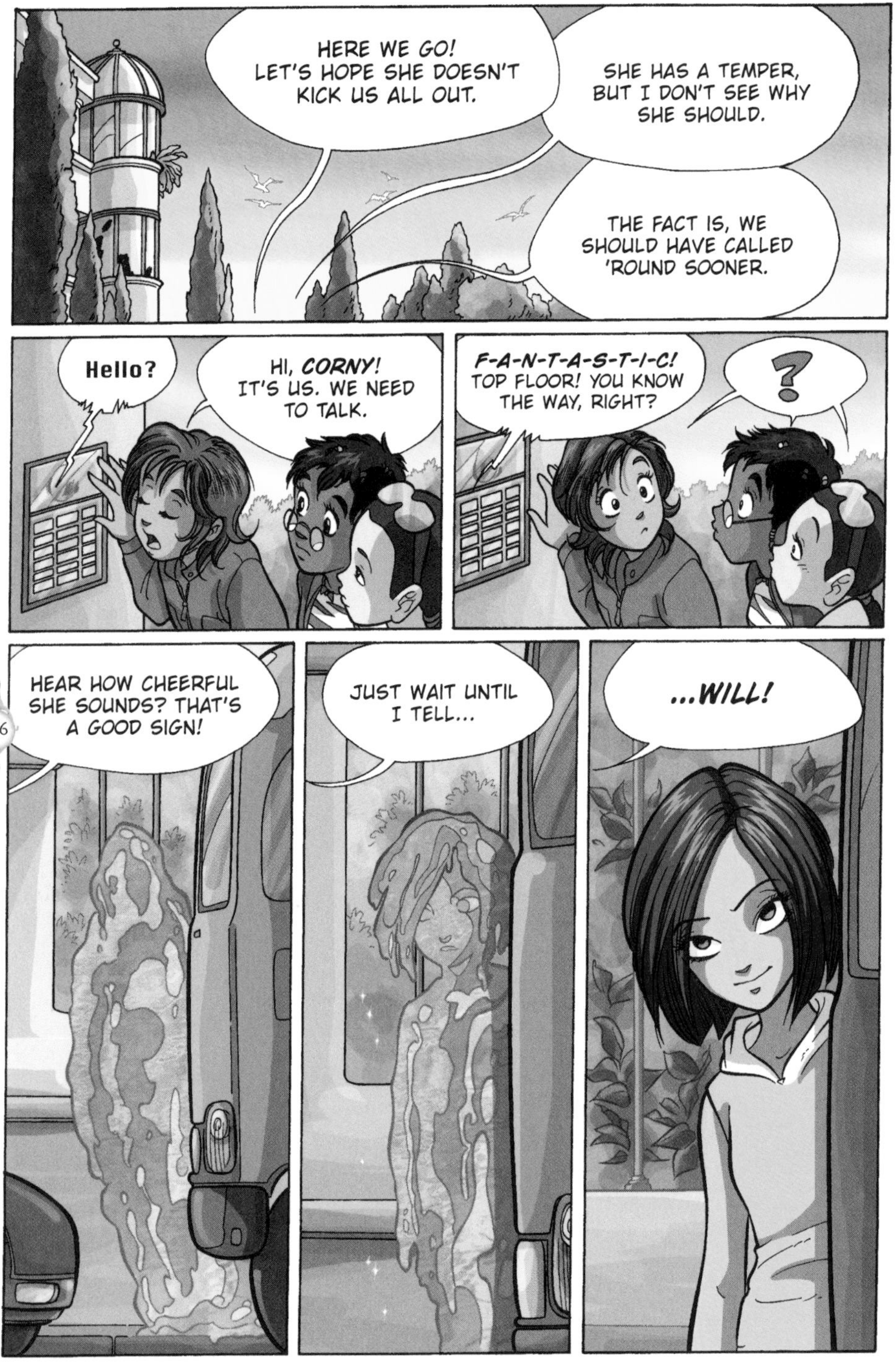
HERE WE GO! LET'S HOPE SHE DOESN'T KICK US ALL OUT.
SHE HAS A TEMPER, BUT I DON'T SEE WHY SHE SHOULD.
THE FACT IS, WE SHOULD HAVE CALLED 'ROUND SOONER.
Hello?
HI, CORNY! IT'S US. WE NEED TO TALK.
F-A-N-T-A-S-T-I-C! TOP FLOOR! YOU KNOW THE WAY, RIGHT?
?
HEAR HOW CHEERFUL SHE SOUNDS? THAT'S A GOOD SIGN!
JUST WAIT UNTIL I TELL...
...WILL!

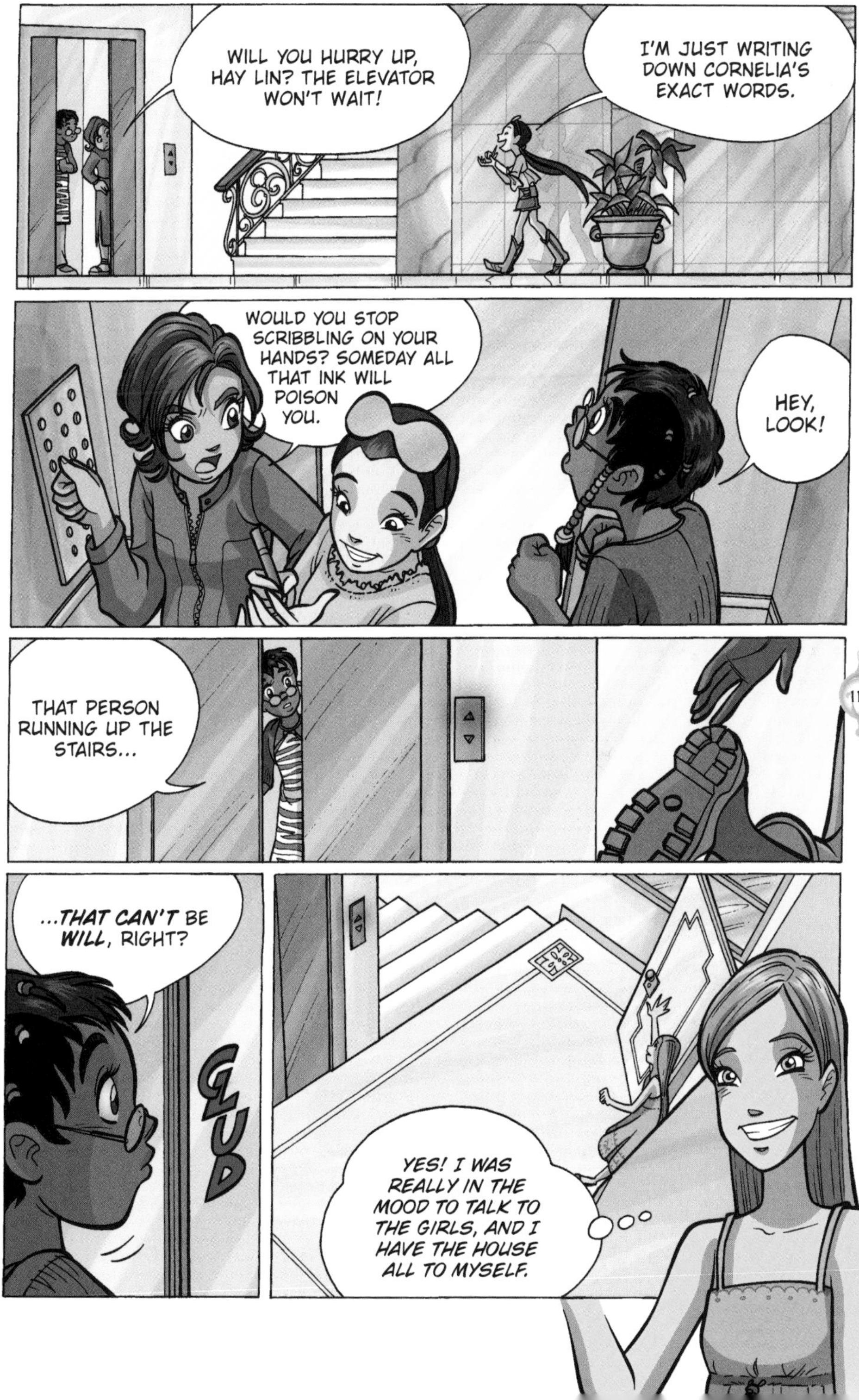

WILL YOU HURRY UP, HAY LIN? THE ELEVATOR WON'T WAIT!
I'M JUST WRITING DOWN CORNELIA'S EXACT WORDS.
WOULD YOU STOP SCRIBBLING ON YOUR HANDS? SOMEDAY ALL THAT INK WILL POISON YOU.
HEY, LOOK!
THAT PERSON RUNNING UP THE STAIRS...
...*THAT CAN'T* BE *WILL*, RIGHT?
GLUD
YES! I WAS REALLY IN THE MOOD TO TALK TO THE GIRLS, AND I HAVE THE HOUSE ALL TO MYSELF.

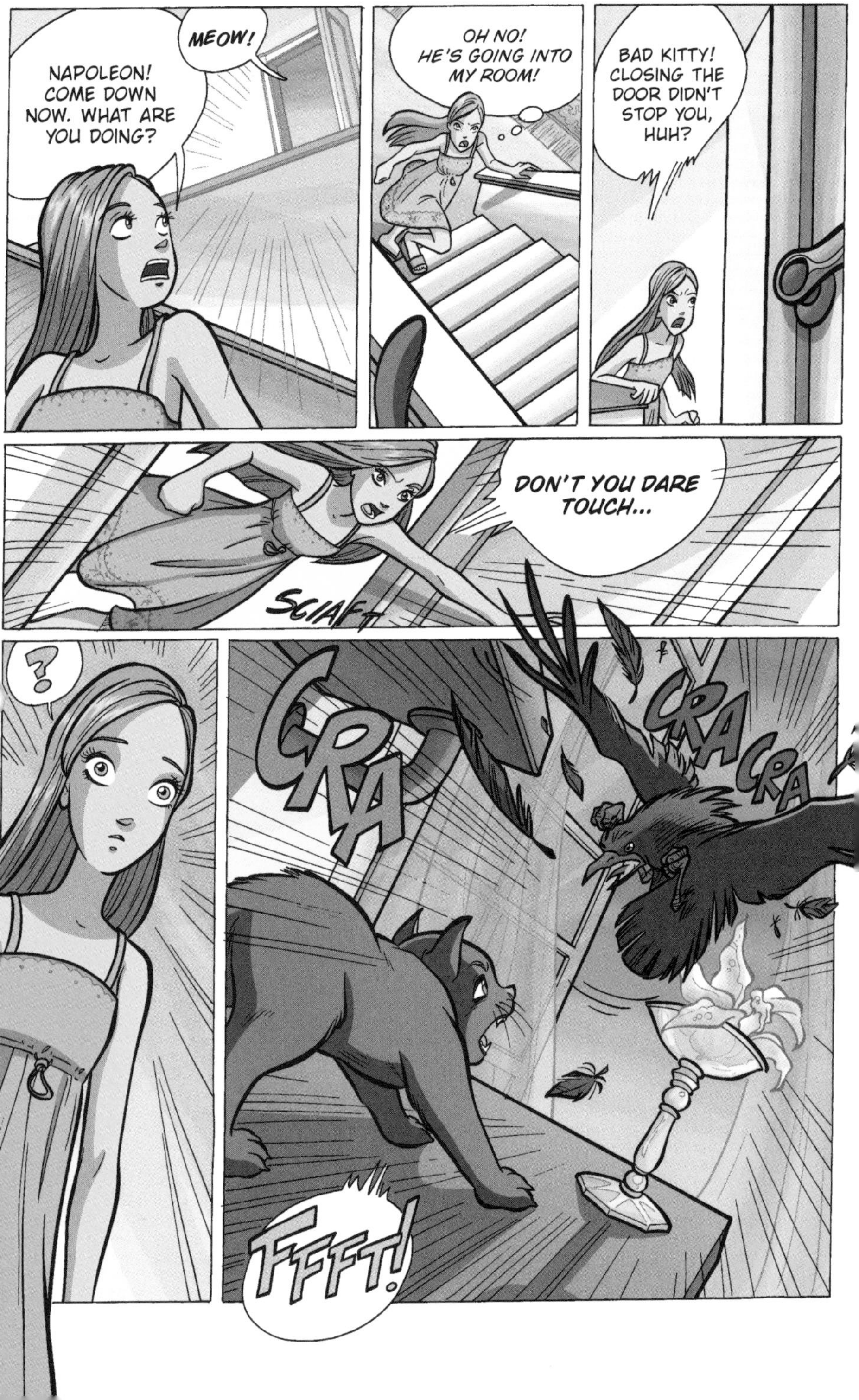
NAPOLEON! COME DOWN NOW. WHAT ARE YOU DOING?
MEOW!
OH NO! HE'S GOING INTO MY ROOM!
BAD KITTY! CLOSING THE DOOR DIDN'T STOP YOU, HUH?
DON'T YOU DARE TOUCH...
SCIAFT
?
CRA
CRA CRA CRA
FFFT!

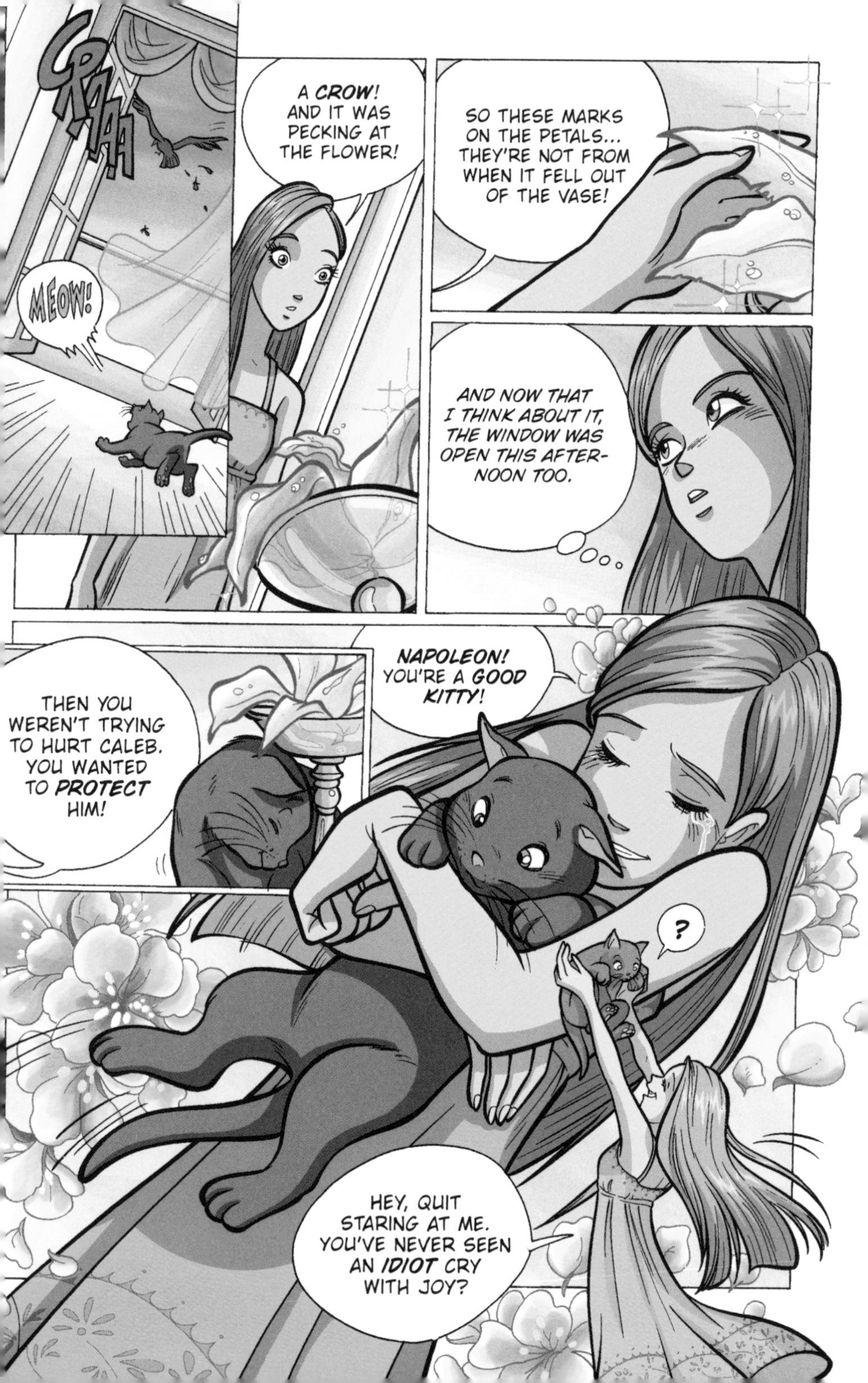
CRAAA
MEOW!
A CROW! AND IT WAS PECKING AT THE FLOWER!
SO THESE MARKS ON THE PETALS... THEY'RE NOT FROM WHEN IT FELL OUT OF THE VASE!
AND NOW THAT I THINK ABOUT IT, THE WINDOW WAS OPEN THIS AFTER-NOON TOO.
THEN YOU WEREN'T TRYING TO HURT CALEB. YOU WANTED TO PROTECT HIM!
NAPOLEON! YOU'RE A GOOD KITTY!
?
HEY, QUIT STARING AT ME. YOU'VE NEVER SEEN AN IDIOT CRY WITH JOY?

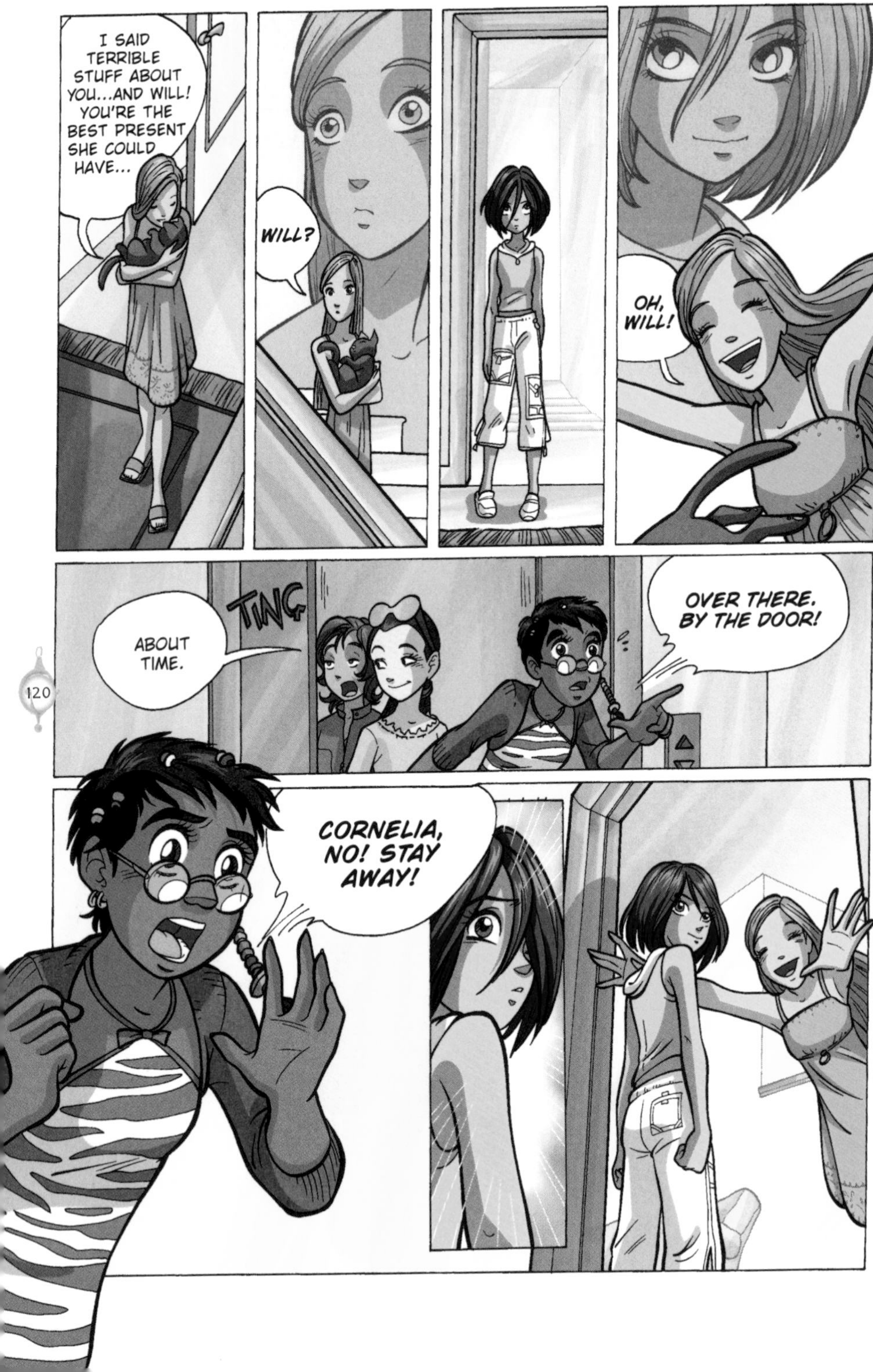
I SAID TERRIBLE STUFF ABOUT YOU...AND WILL! YOU'RE THE BEST PRESENT SHE COULD HAVE...
WILL?
OH, WILL!
TING
ABOUT TIME.
OVER THERE. BY THE DOOR!
CORNELIA, NO! STAY AWAY!

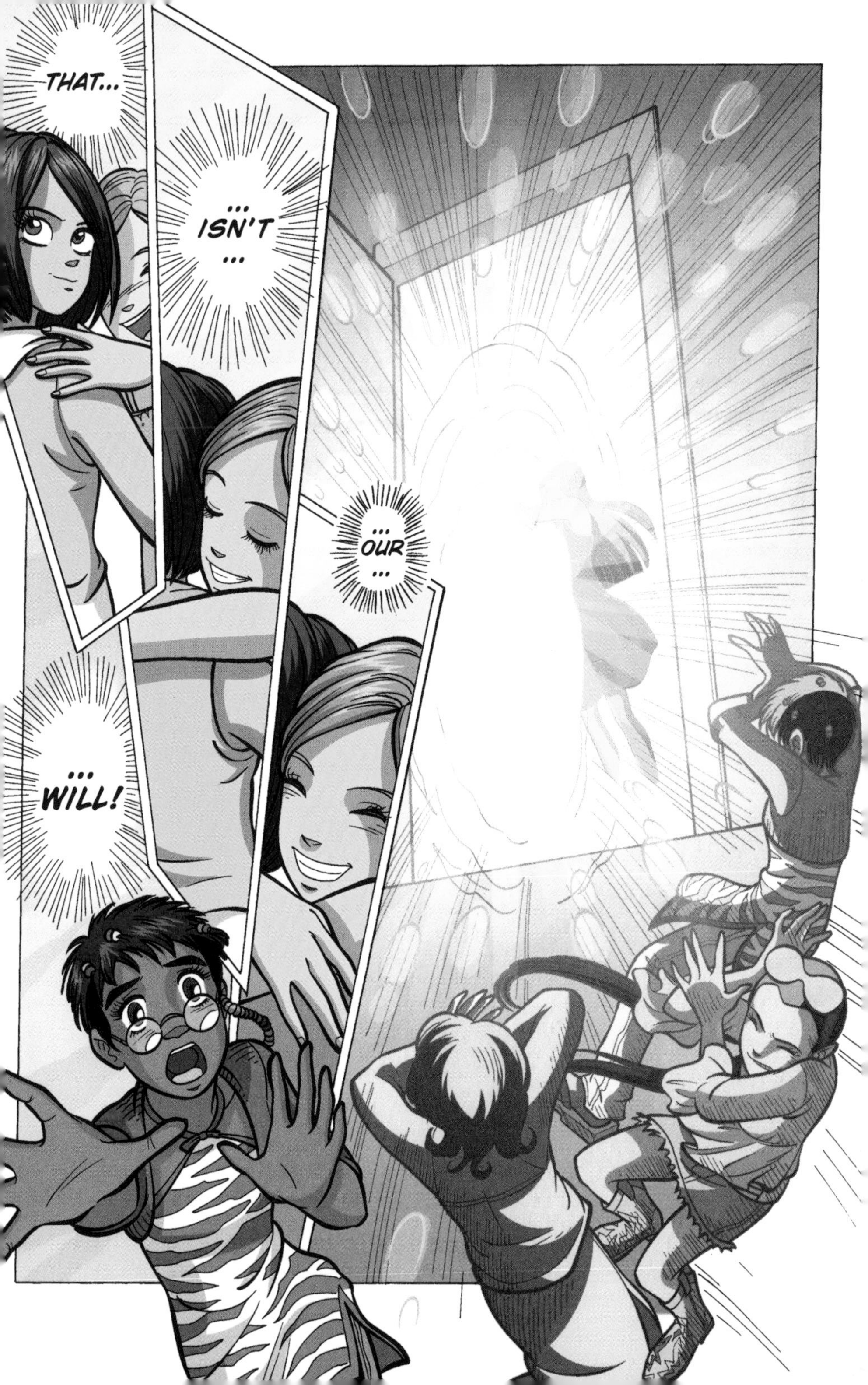
THAT...
... ISN'T ...
... OUR ...
... WILL!

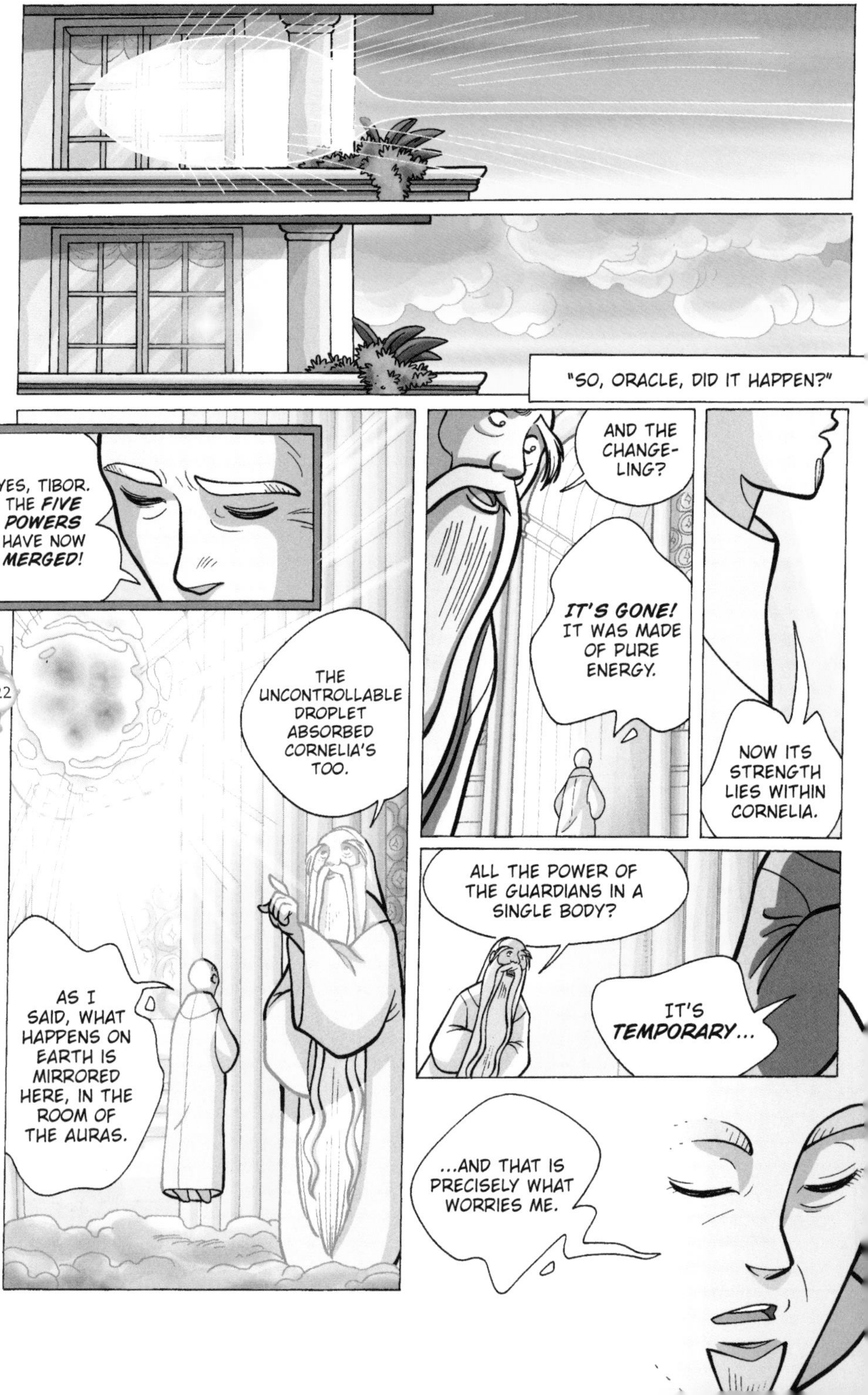

"SO, ORACLE, DID IT HAPPEN?"
YES, TIBOR. THE FIVE POWERS HAVE NOW MERGED!
THE UNCONTROLLABLE DROPLET ABSORBED CORNELIA'S TOO.
AS I SAID, WHAT HAPPENS ON EARTH IS MIRRORED HERE, IN THE ROOM OF THE AURAS.
AND THE CHANGE-LING?
IT'S GONE! IT WAS MADE OF PURE ENERGY.
NOW ITS STRENGTH LIES WITHIN CORNELIA.
ALL THE POWER OF THE GUARDIANS IN A SINGLE BODY?
IT'S TEMPORARY...
...AND THAT IS PRECISELY WHAT WORRIES ME.

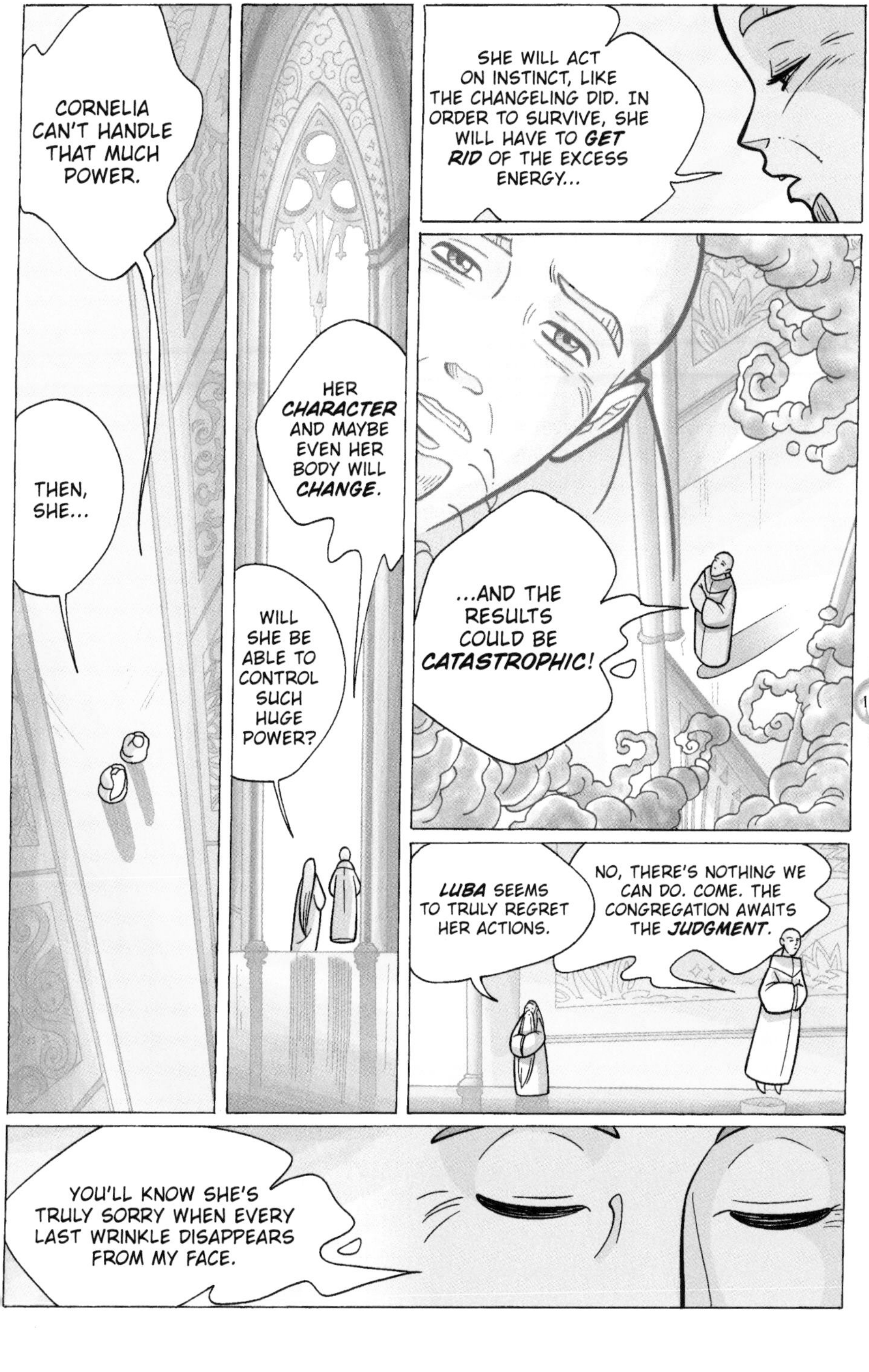
CORNELIA CAN'T HANDLE THAT MUCH POWER.
THEN, SHE...
HER CHARACTER AND MAYBE EVEN HER BODY WILL CHANGE.
WILL SHE BE ABLE TO CONTROL SUCH HUGE POWER?
SHE WILL ACT ON INSTINCT, LIKE THE CHANGELING DID. IN ORDER TO SURVIVE, SHE WILL HAVE TO GET RID OF THE EXCESS ENERGY...
...AND THE RESULTS COULD BE CATASTROPHIC!
LUBA SEEMS TO TRULY REGRET HER ACTIONS.
NO, THERE'S NOTHING WE CAN DO. COME. THE CONGREGATION AWAITS THE JUDGMENT.
YOU'LL KNOW SHE'S TRULY SORRY WHEN EVERY LAST WRINKLE DISAPPEARS FROM MY FACE.

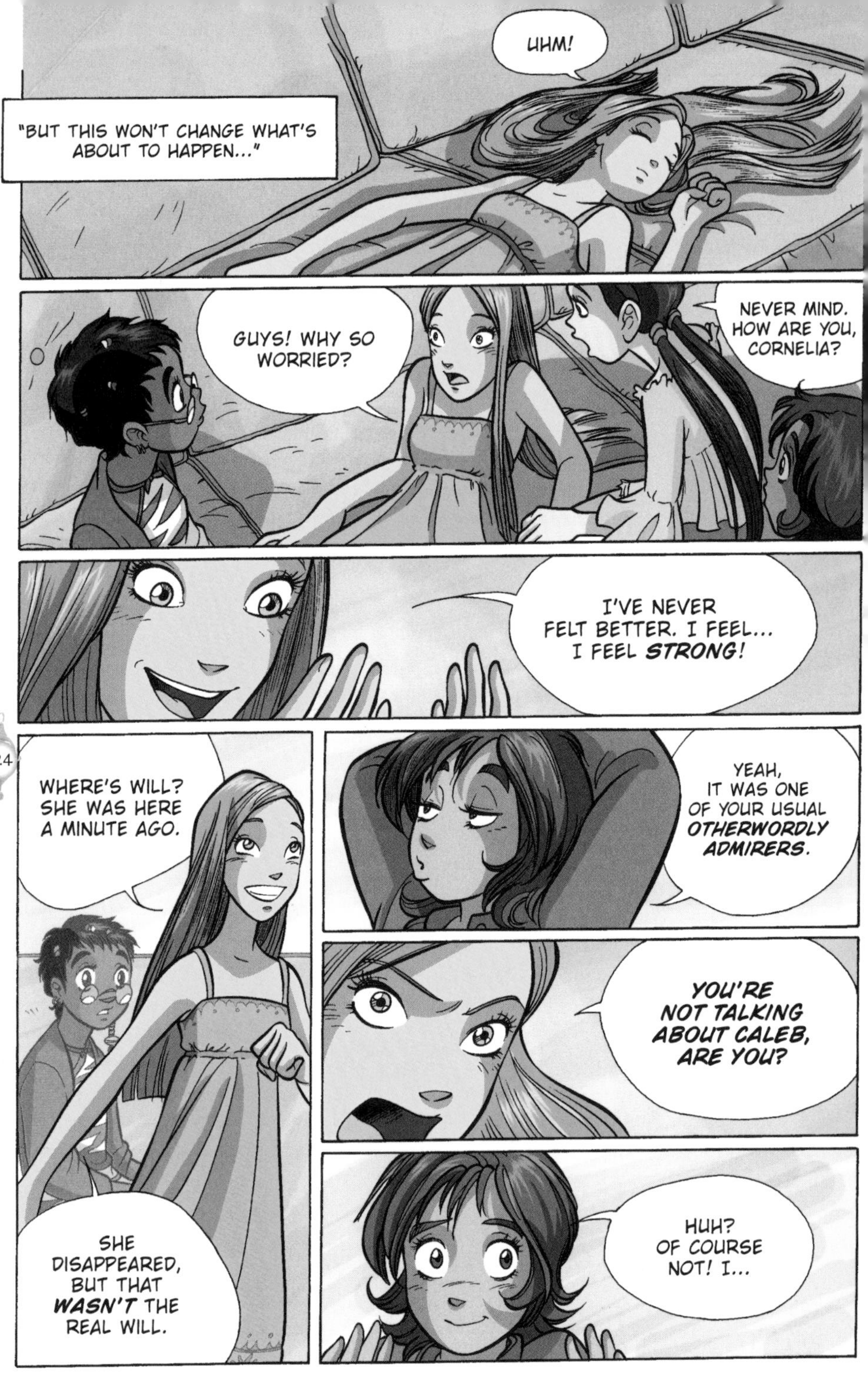
UHM!
"BUT THIS WON'T CHANGE WHAT'S ABOUT TO HAPPEN..."
GUYS! WHY SO WORRIED?
NEVER MIND. HOW ARE YOU, CORNELIA?
I'VE NEVER FELT BETTER. I FEEL... I FEEL **STRONG**!
WHERE'S WILL? SHE WAS HERE A MINUTE AGO.
SHE DISAPPEARED, BUT THAT **WASN'T** THE REAL WILL.
YEAH, IT WAS ONE OF YOUR USUAL ***OTHERWORDLY ADMIRERS***.
YOU'RE NOT TALKING ABOUT CALEB, ARE YOU?
HUH? OF COURSE NOT! I...

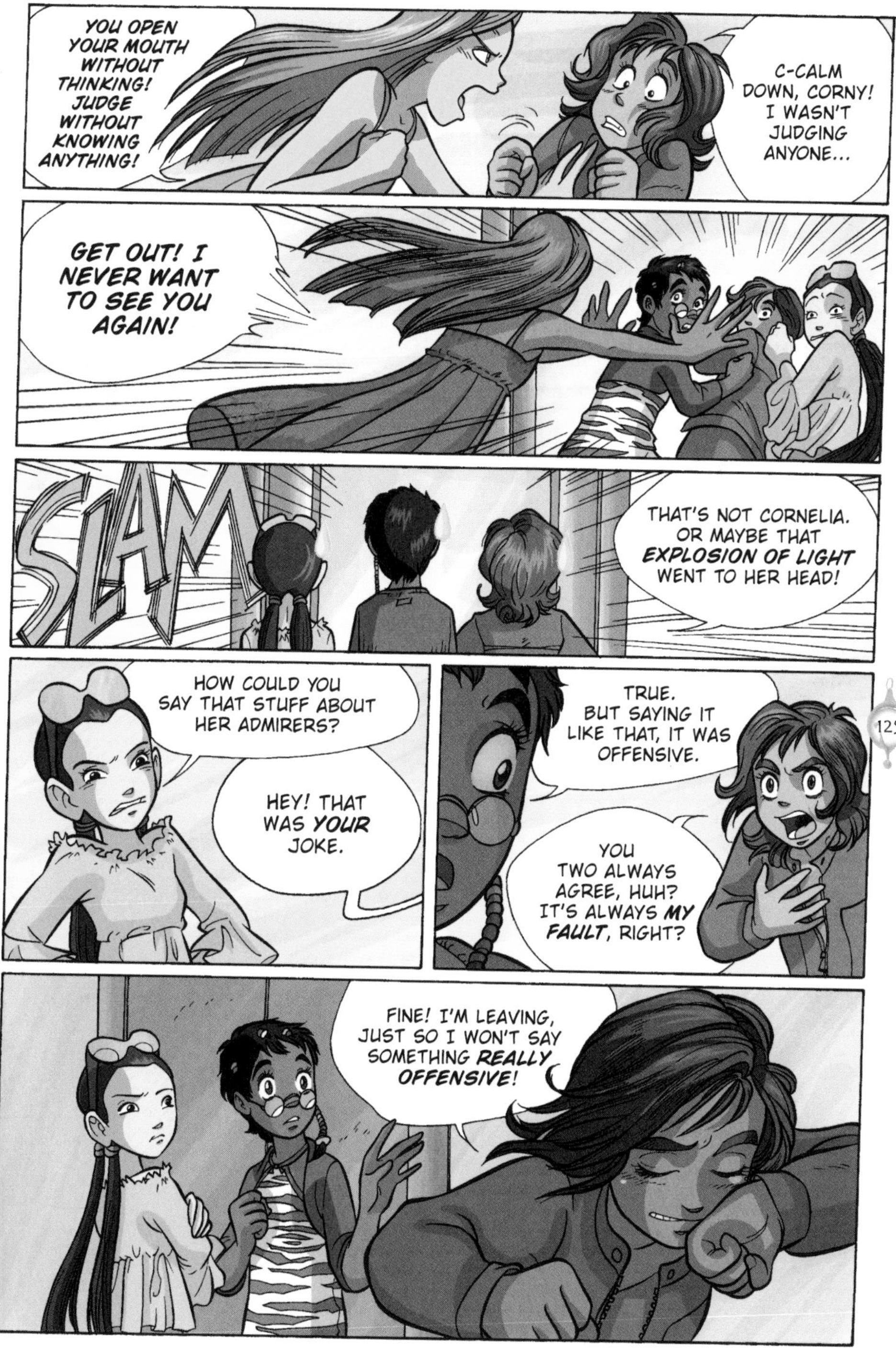
YOU OPEN YOUR MOUTH WITHOUT THINKING! JUDGE WITHOUT KNOWING ANYTHING!
C-CALM DOWN, CORNY! I WASN'T JUDGING ANYONE...
GET OUT! I NEVER WANT TO SEE YOU AGAIN!
SLAM
THAT'S NOT CORNELIA. OR MAYBE THAT EXPLOSION OF LIGHT WENT TO HER HEAD!
HOW COULD YOU SAY THAT STUFF ABOUT HER ADMIRERS?
HEY! THAT WAS YOUR JOKE.
TRUE. BUT SAYING IT LIKE THAT, IT WAS OFFENSIVE.
YOU TWO ALWAYS AGREE, HUH? IT'S ALWAYS MY FAULT, RIGHT?
FINE! I'M LEAVING, JUST SO I WON'T SAY SOMETHING REALLY OFFENSIVE!

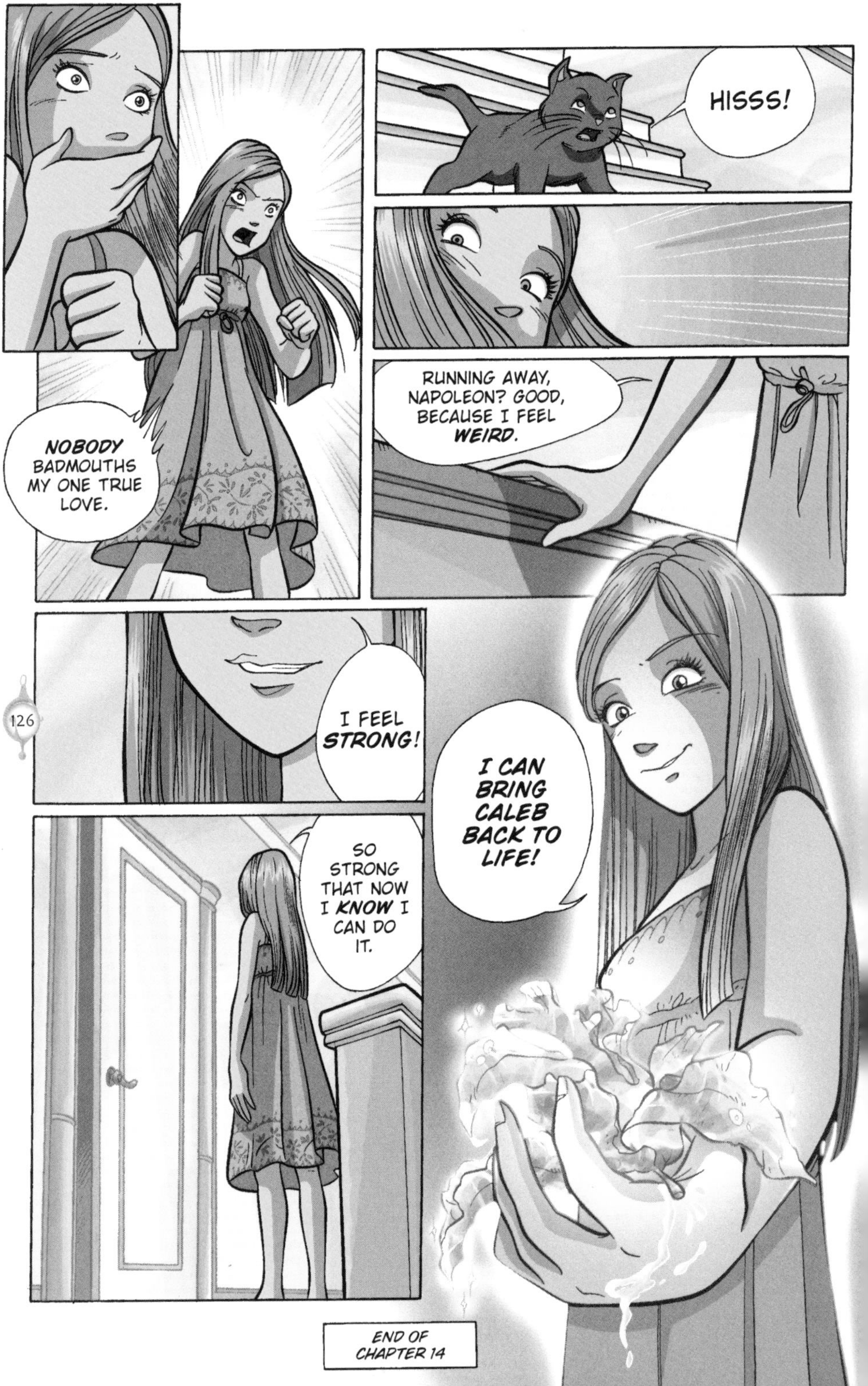
HISSS!
NOBODY BADMOUTHS MY ONE TRUE LOVE.
RUNNING AWAY, NAPOLEON? GOOD, BECAUSE I FEEL WEIRD.
I FEEL STRONG!
SO STRONG THAT NOW I KNOW I CAN DO IT.
I CAN BRING CALEB BACK TO LIFE!
END OF CHAPTER 14

15

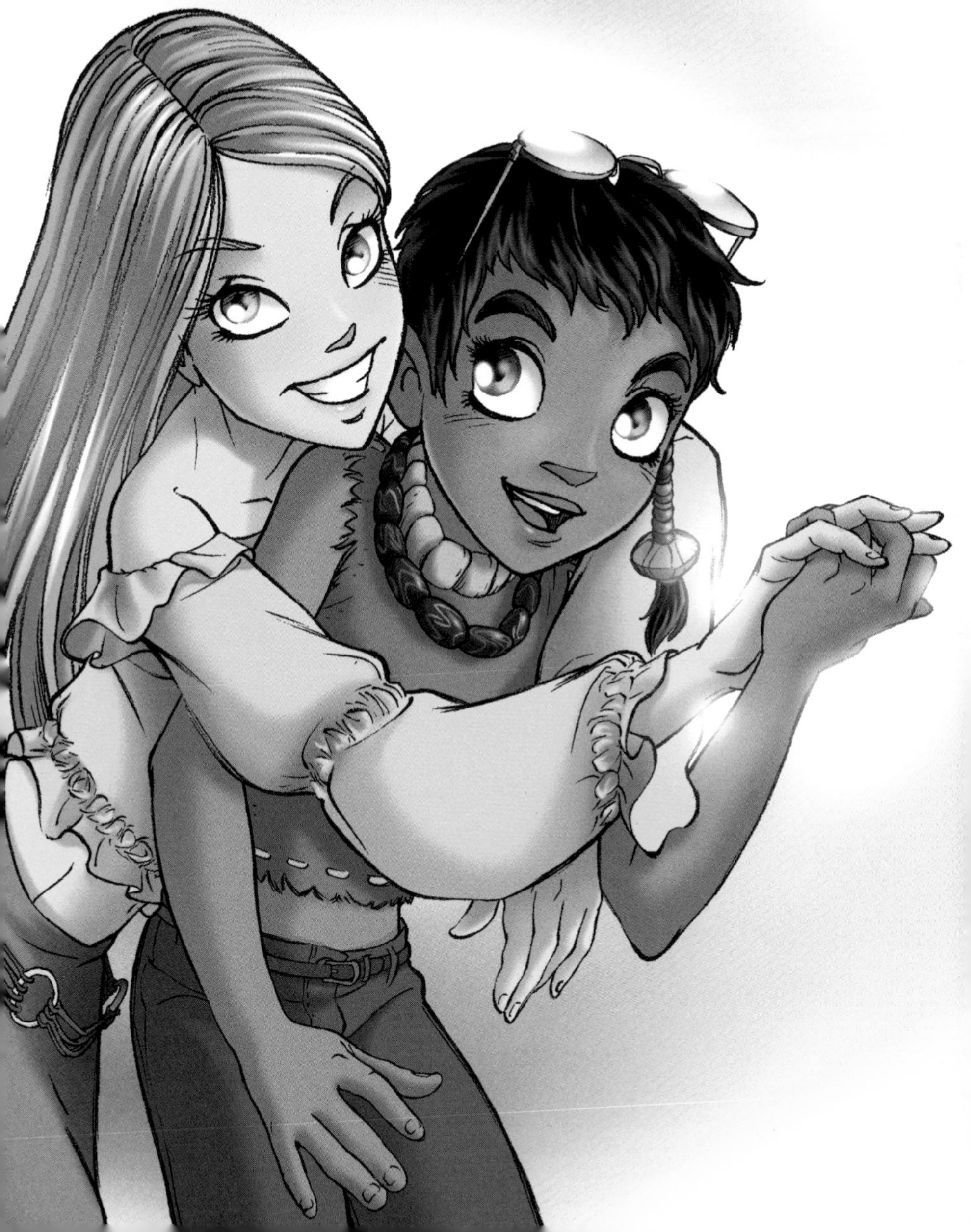

THE COURAGE TO CHOOSE

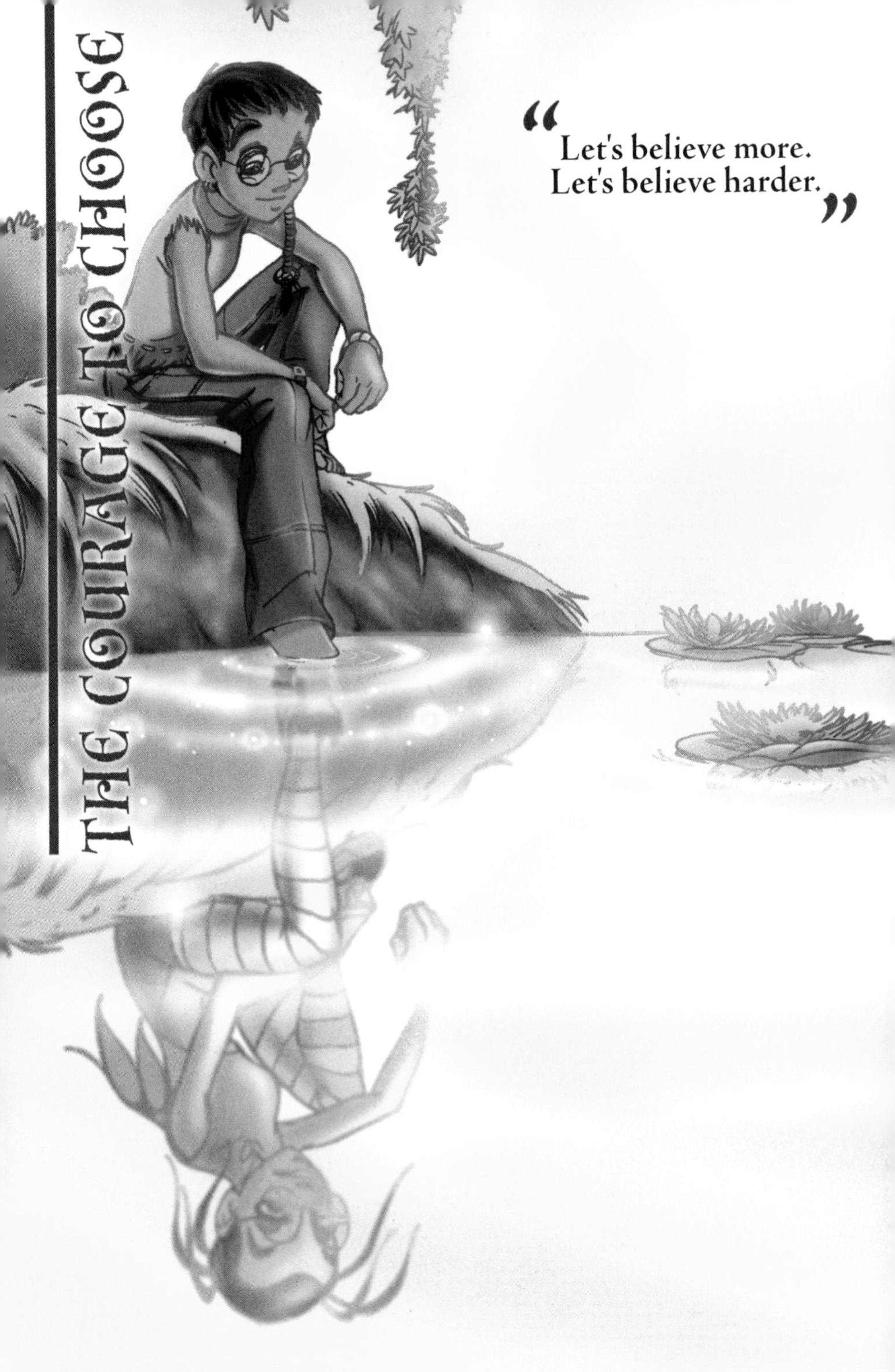

"Let's believe more.
Let's believe harder."

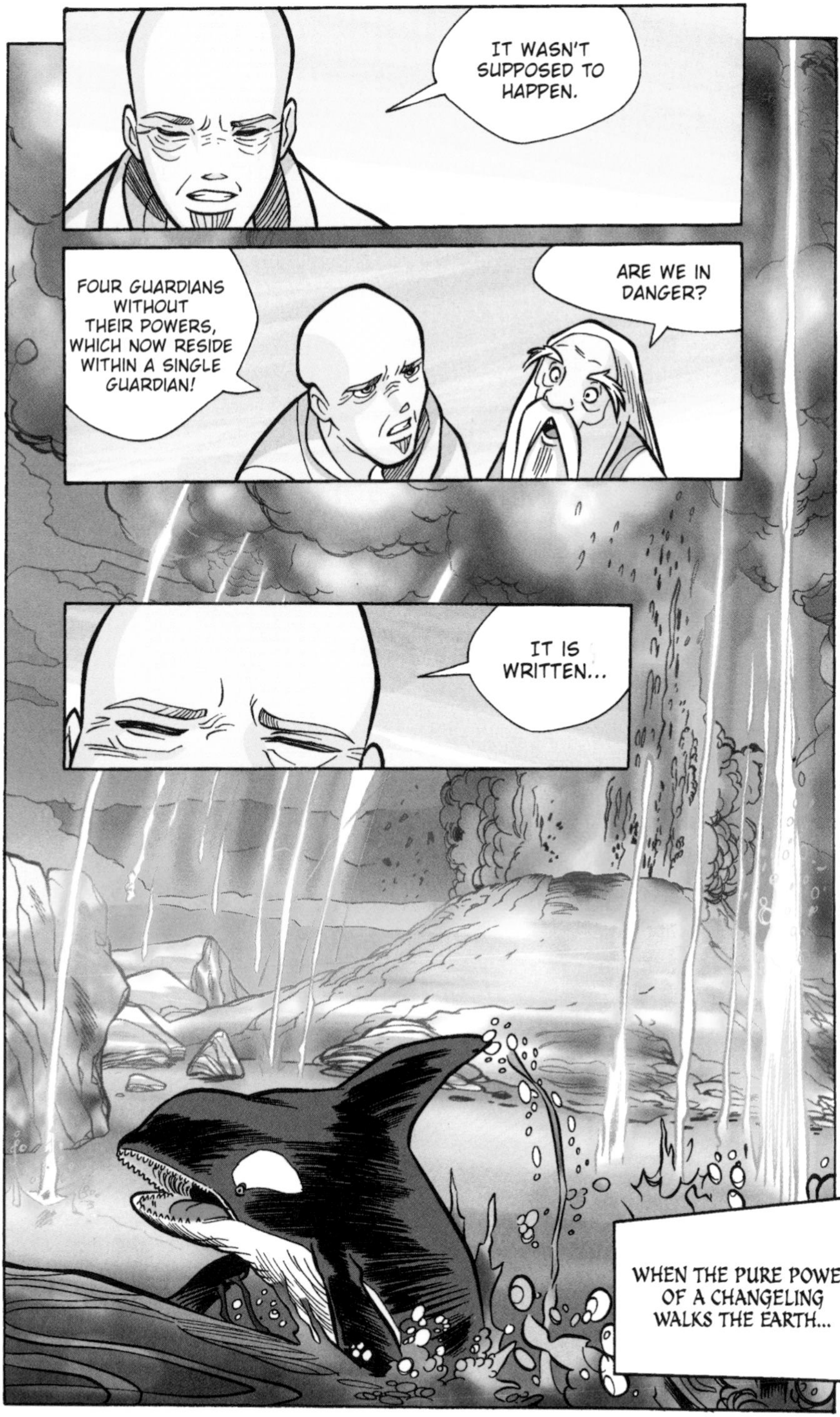
IT WASN'T SUPPOSED TO HAPPEN.
FOUR GUARDIANS WITHOUT THEIR POWERS, WHICH NOW RESIDE WITHIN A SINGLE GUARDIAN!
ARE WE IN DANGER?
IT IS WRITTEN...
WHEN THE PURE POWER OF A CHANGELING WALKS THE EARTH...

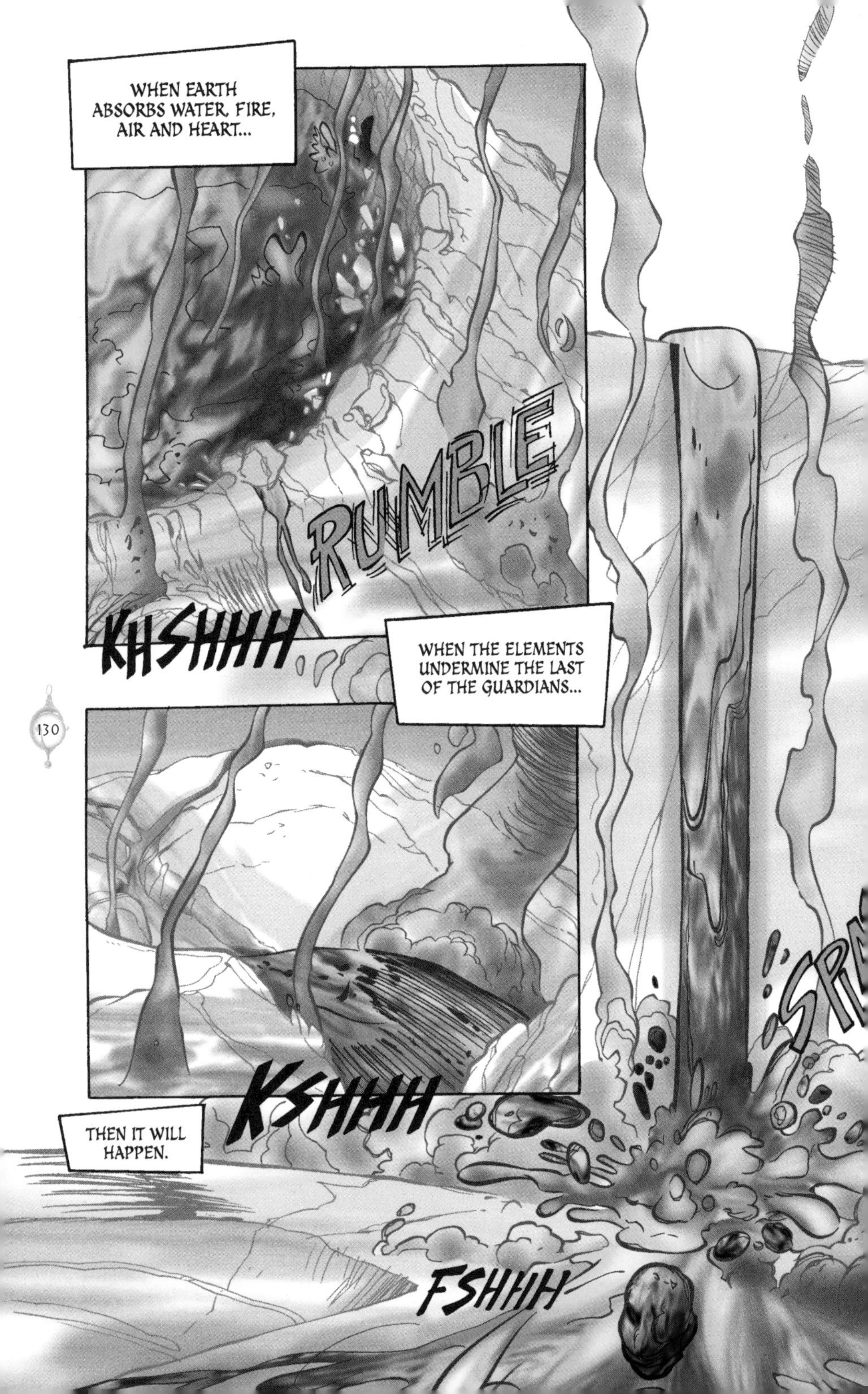
WHEN EARTH ABSORBS WATER, FIRE, AIR AND HEART...
RUMBLE
KHSHHH
WHEN THE ELEMENTS UNDERMINE THE LAST OF THE GUARDIANS...
KSHHH
THEN IT WILL HAPPEN.
FSHHH

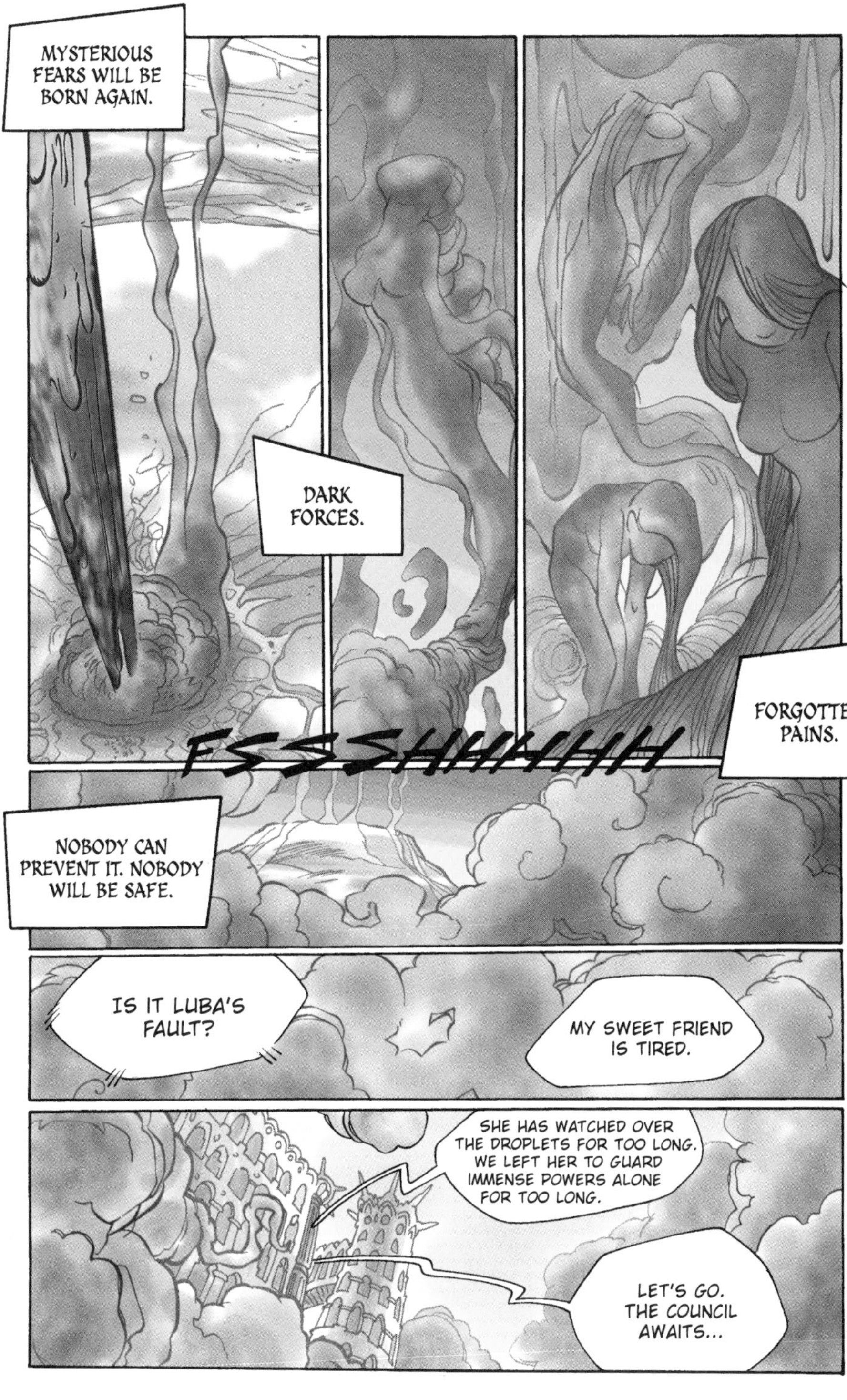
MYSTERIOUS FEARS WILL BE BORN AGAIN.
DARK FORCES.
FORGOTTEN PAINS.
FSSSHHHHHH
NOBODY CAN PREVENT IT. NOBODY WILL BE SAFE.
IS IT LUBA'S FAULT?
MY SWEET FRIEND IS TIRED.
SHE HAS WATCHED OVER THE DROPLETS FOR TOO LONG. WE LEFT HER TO GUARD IMMENSE POWERS ALONE FOR TOO LONG.
LET'S GO. THE COUNCIL AWAITS...

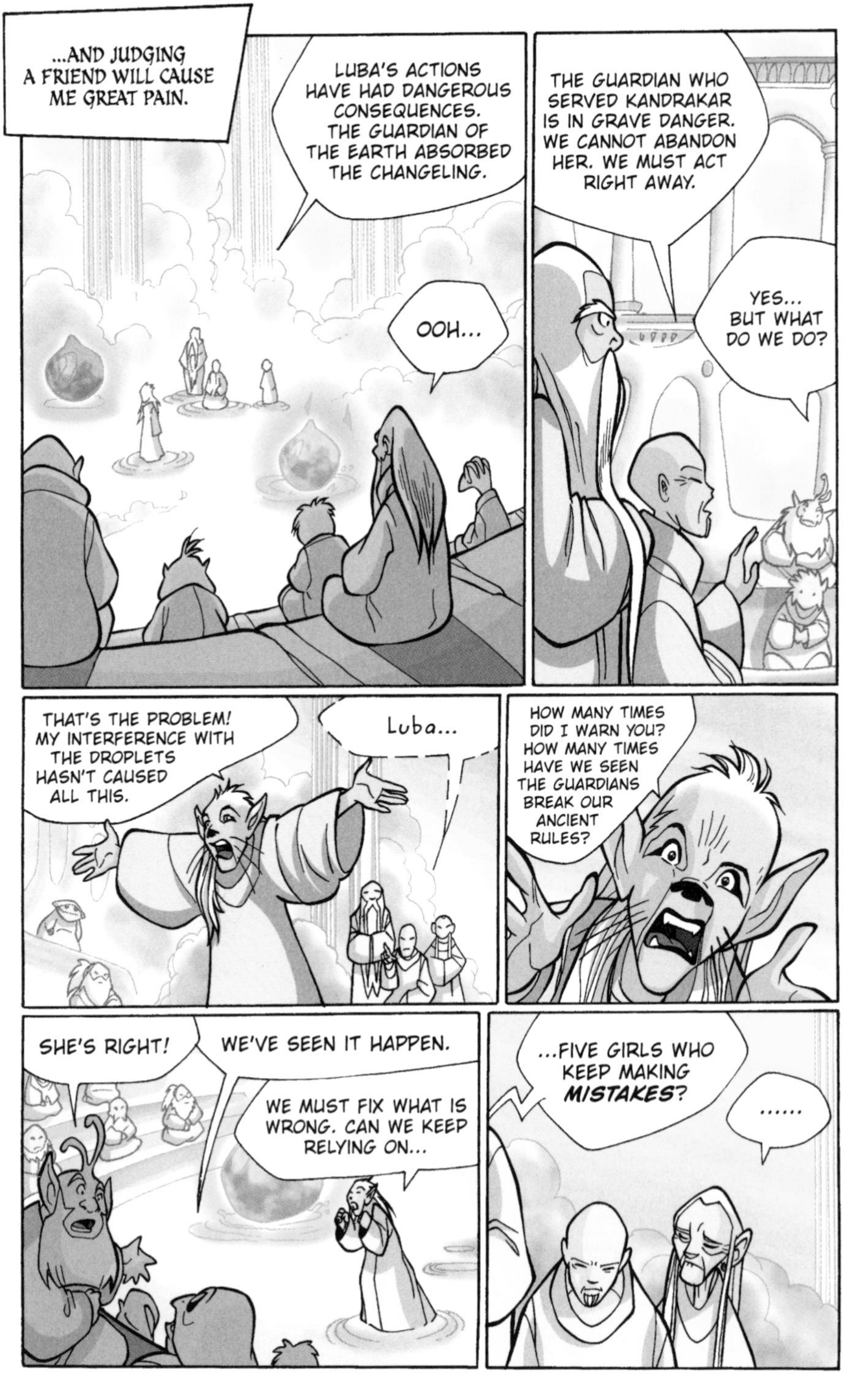
...AND JUDGING A FRIEND WILL CAUSE ME GREAT PAIN.
LUBA'S ACTIONS HAVE HAD DANGEROUS CONSEQUENCES. THE GUARDIAN OF THE EARTH ABSORBED THE CHANGELING.
OOH...
THE GUARDIAN WHO SERVED KANDRAKAR IS IN GRAVE DANGER. WE CANNOT ABANDON HER. WE MUST ACT RIGHT AWAY.
YES... BUT WHAT DO WE DO?
THAT'S THE PROBLEM! MY INTERFERENCE WITH THE DROPLETS HASN'T CAUSED ALL THIS.
Luba...
HOW MANY TIMES DID I WARN YOU? HOW MANY TIMES HAVE WE SEEN THE GUARDIANS BREAK OUR ANCIENT RULES?
SHE'S RIGHT!
WE'VE SEEN IT HAPPEN.
WE MUST FIX WHAT IS WRONG. CAN WE KEEP RELYING ON...
...FIVE GIRLS WHO KEEP MAKING *MISTAKES*?
......

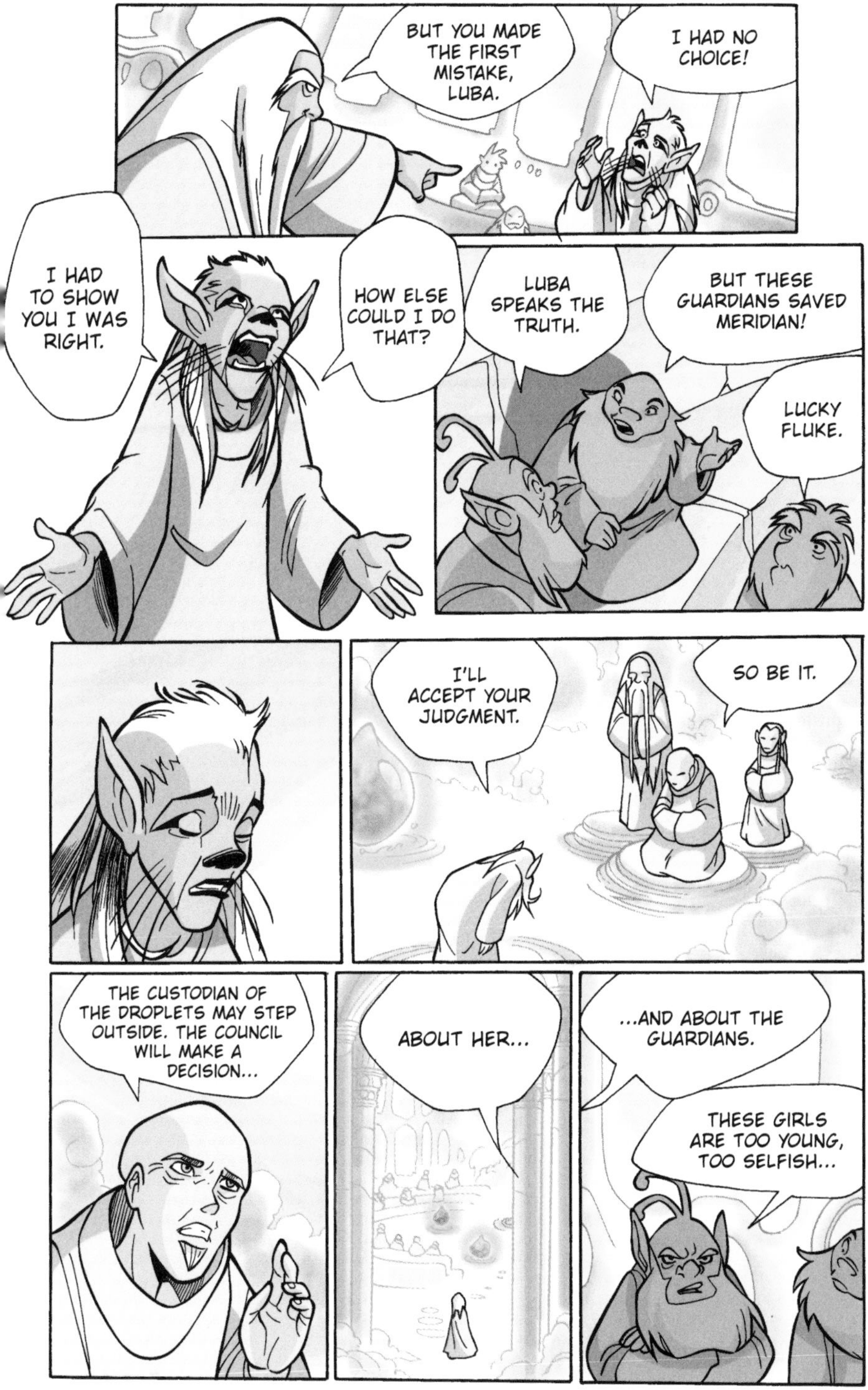
BUT YOU MADE THE FIRST MISTAKE, LUBA.
I HAD NO CHOICE!
I HAD TO SHOW YOU I WAS RIGHT.
HOW ELSE COULD I DO THAT?
LUBA SPEAKS THE TRUTH.
BUT THESE GUARDIANS SAVED MERIDIAN!
LUCKY FLUKE.
I'LL ACCEPT YOUR JUDGMENT.
SO BE IT.
THE CUSTODIAN OF THE DROPLETS MAY STEP OUTSIDE. THE COUNCIL WILL MAKE A DECISION...
ABOUT HER...
...AND ABOUT THE GUARDIANS.
THESE GIRLS ARE TOO YOUNG, TOO SELFISH...

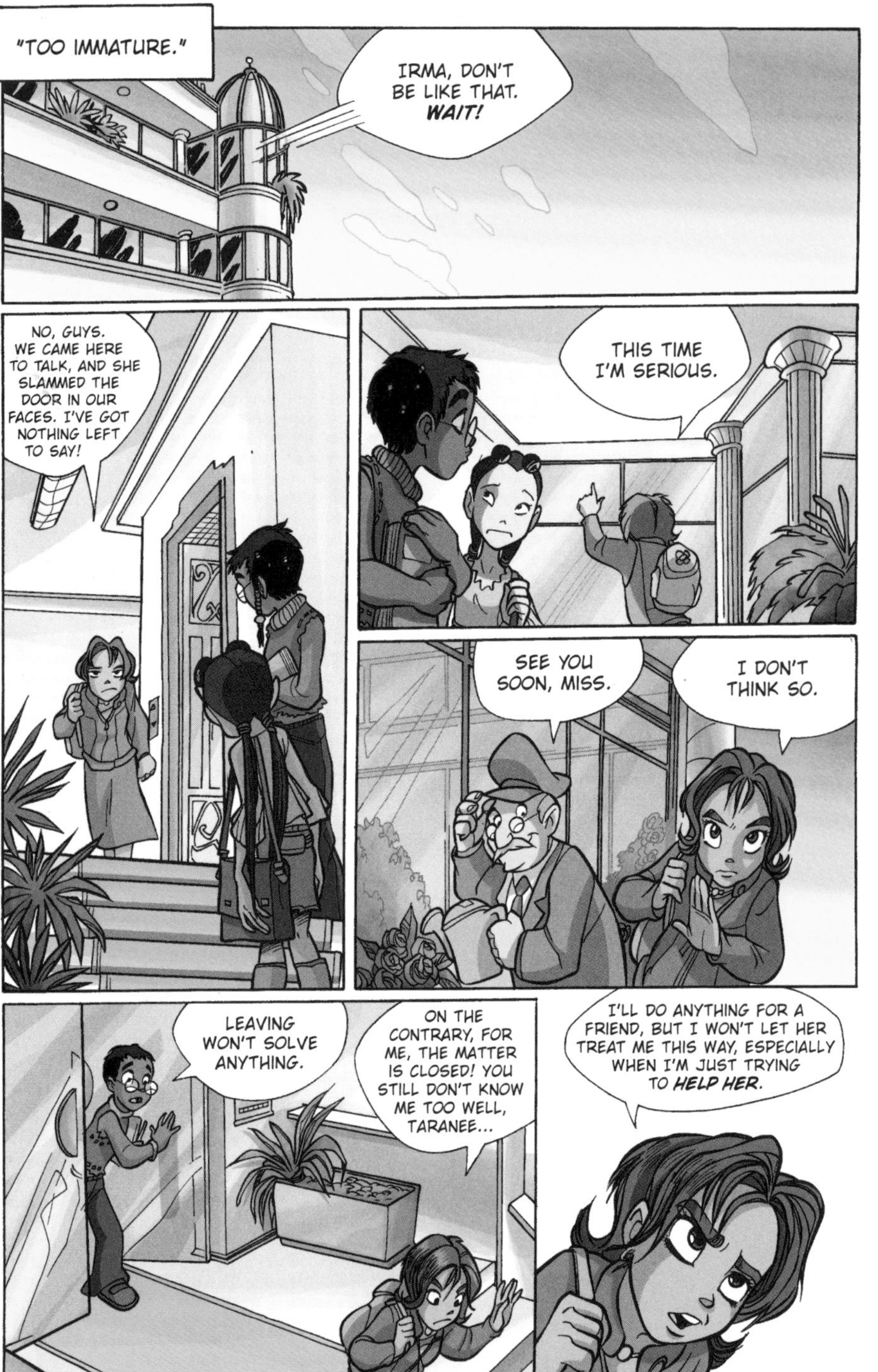
"TOO IMMATURE."
IRMA, DON'T BE LIKE THAT. *WAIT!*
NO, GUYS. WE CAME HERE TO TALK, AND SHE SLAMMED THE DOOR IN OUR FACES. I'VE GOT NOTHING LEFT TO SAY!
THIS TIME I'M SERIOUS.
SEE YOU SOON, MISS.
I DON'T THINK SO.
LEAVING WON'T SOLVE ANYTHING.
ON THE CONTRARY, FOR ME, THE MATTER IS CLOSED! YOU STILL DON'T KNOW ME TOO WELL, TARANEE...
I'LL DO ANYTHING FOR A FRIEND, BUT I WON'T LET HER TREAT ME THIS WAY, ESPECIALLY WHEN I'M JUST TRYING TO *HELP HER*.

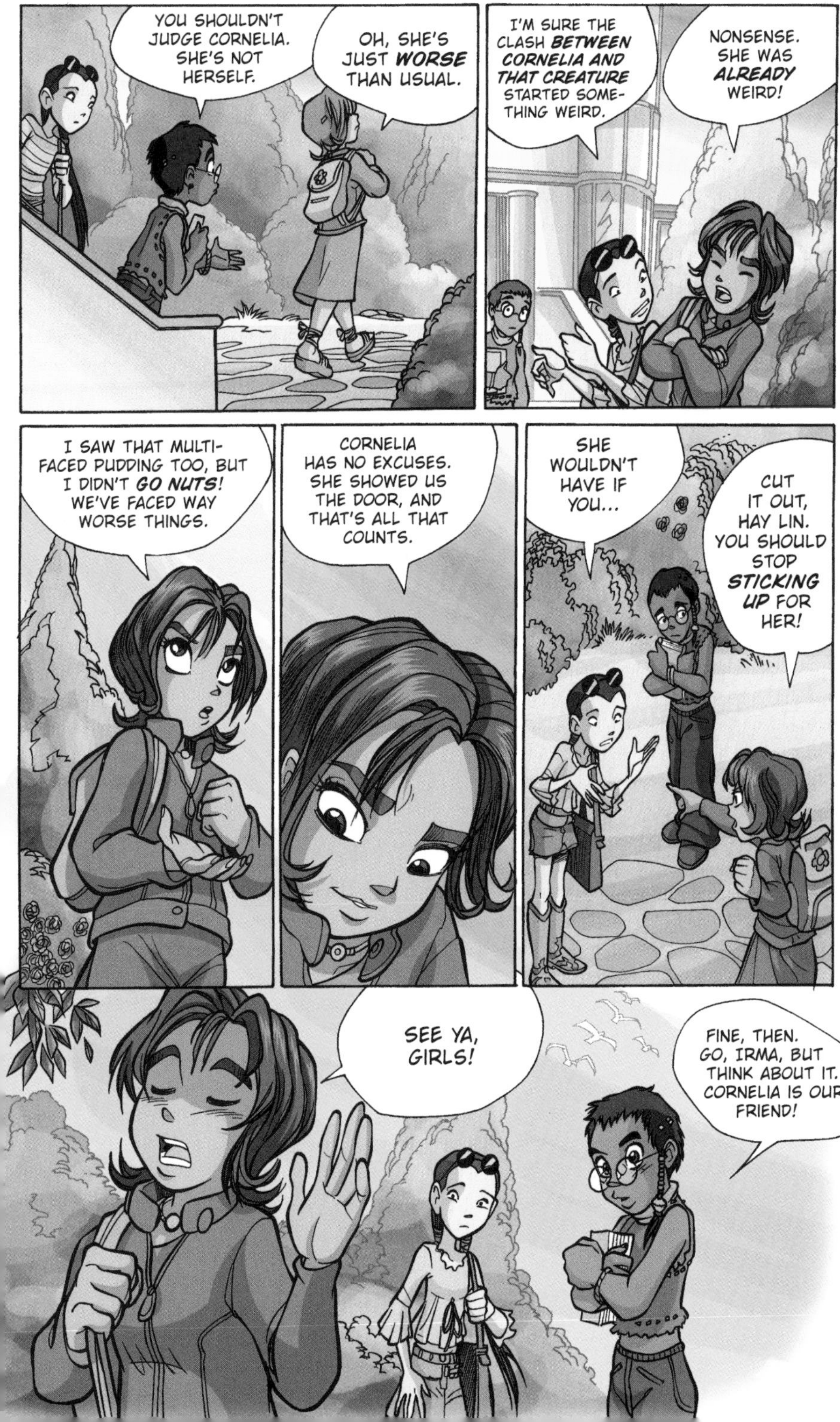
YOU SHOULDN'T JUDGE CORNELIA. SHE'S NOT HERSELF.
OH, SHE'S JUST **WORSE** THAN USUAL.
I'M SURE THE CLASH **BETWEEN CORNELIA AND THAT CREATURE** STARTED SOMETHING WEIRD.
NONSENSE. SHE WAS **ALREADY** WEIRD!
I SAW THAT MULTI-FACED PUDDING TOO, BUT I DIDN'T **GO NUTS**! WE'VE FACED WAY WORSE THINGS.
CORNELIA HAS NO EXCUSES. SHE SHOWED US THE DOOR, AND THAT'S ALL THAT COUNTS.
SHE WOULDN'T HAVE IF YOU...
CUT IT OUT, HAY LIN. YOU SHOULD STOP **STICKING UP** FOR HER!
SEE YA, GIRLS!
FINE, THEN. GO, IRMA, BUT THINK ABOUT IT. CORNELIA IS OUR FRIEND!

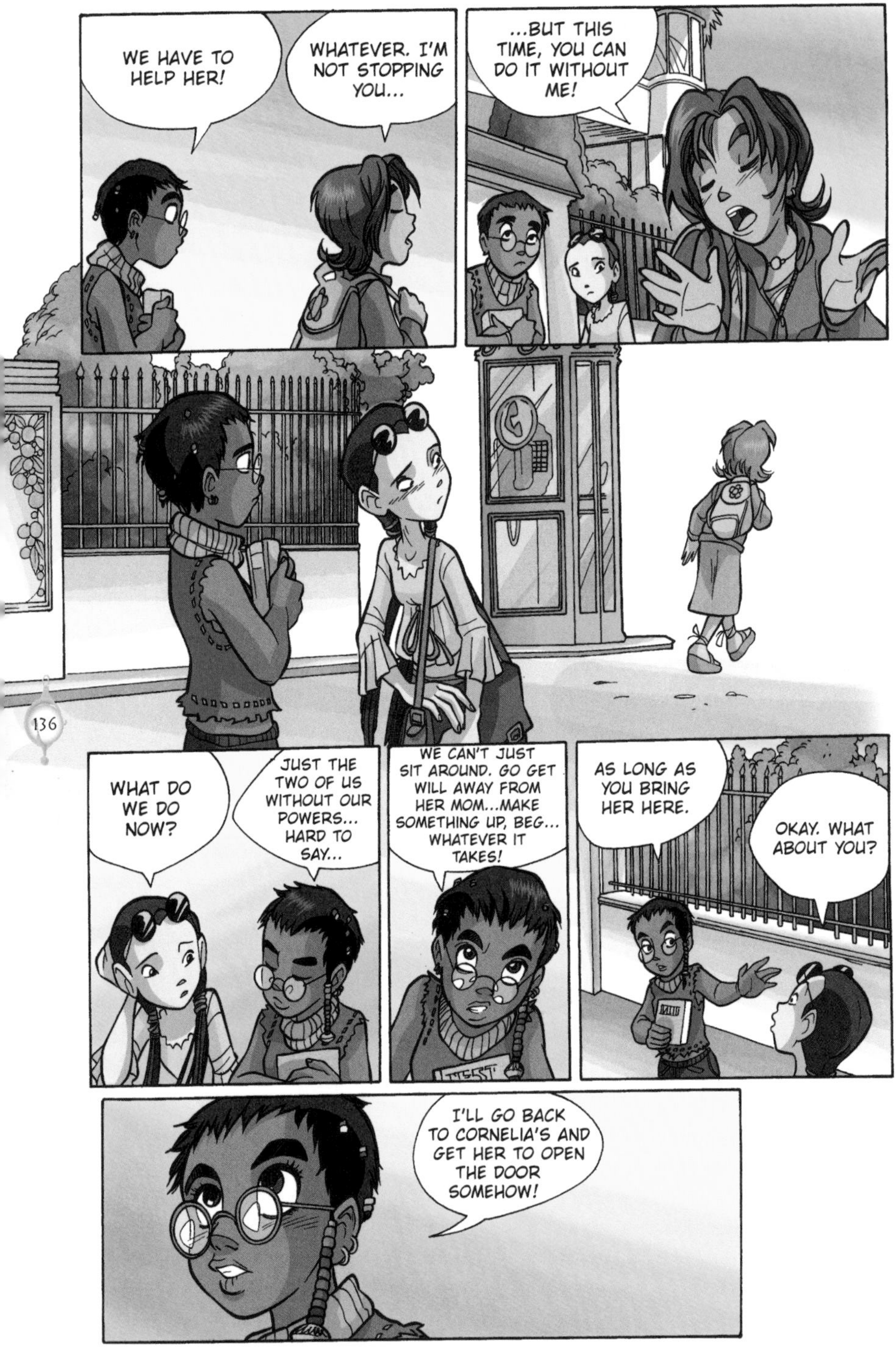
WE HAVE TO HELP HER!
WHATEVER. I'M NOT STOPPING YOU...
...BUT THIS TIME, YOU CAN DO IT WITHOUT ME!
WHAT DO WE DO NOW?
JUST THE TWO OF US WITHOUT OUR POWERS... HARD TO SAY...
WE CAN'T JUST SIT AROUND. GO GET WILL AWAY FROM HER MOM...MAKE SOMETHING UP, BEG... WHATEVER IT TAKES!
AS LONG AS YOU BRING HER HERE.
OKAY. WHAT ABOUT YOU?
I'LL GO BACK TO CORNELIA'S AND GET HER TO OPEN THE DOOR SOMEHOW!

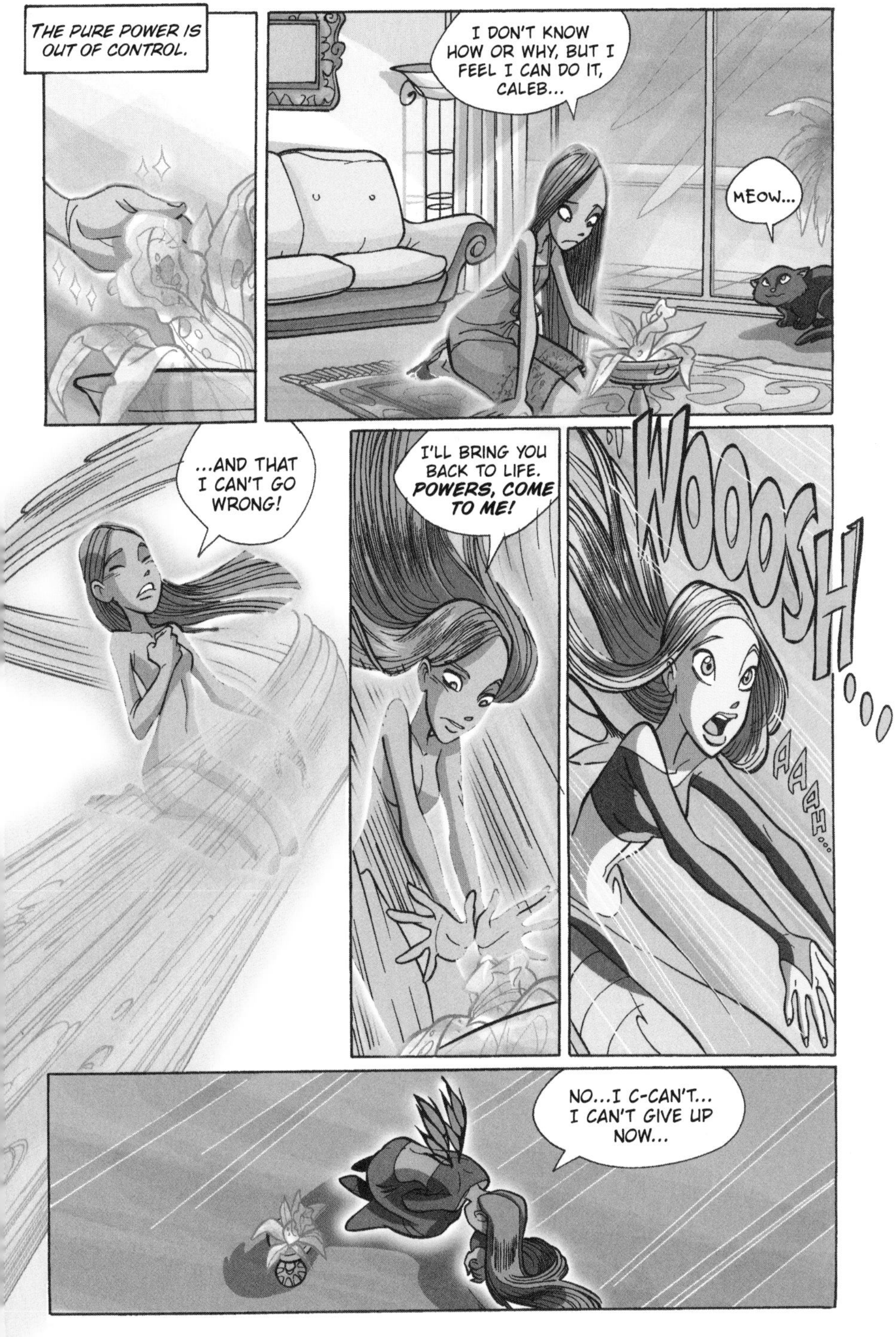
THE PURE POWER IS OUT OF CONTROL.
I DON'T KNOW HOW OR WHY, BUT I FEEL I CAN DO IT, CALEB...
MEOW...
...AND THAT I CAN'T GO WRONG!
I'LL BRING YOU BACK TO LIFE. POWERS, COME TO ME!
WOOOSH...
AAAH...
NO...I C-CAN'T... I CAN'T GIVE UP NOW...

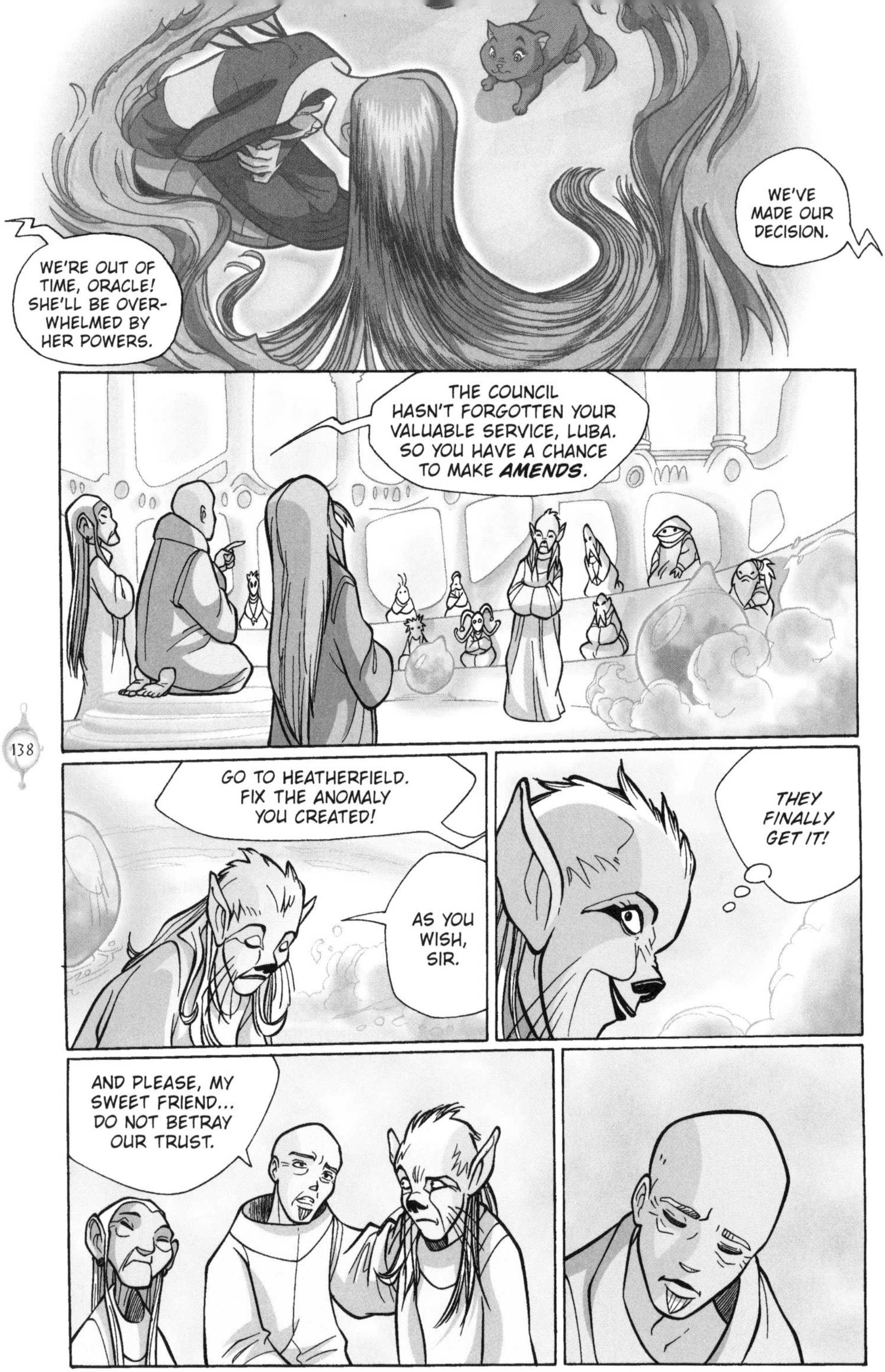
WE'RE OUT OF TIME, ORACLE! SHE'LL BE OVER-WHELMED BY HER POWERS.
WE'VE MADE OUR DECISION.
THE COUNCIL HASN'T FORGOTTEN YOUR VALUABLE SERVICE, LUBA. SO YOU HAVE A CHANCE TO MAKE AMENDS.
GO TO HEATHERFIELD. FIX THE ANOMALY YOU CREATED!
AS YOU WISH, SIR.
THEY FINALLY GET IT!
AND PLEASE, MY SWEET FRIEND... DO NOT BETRAY OUR TRUST.

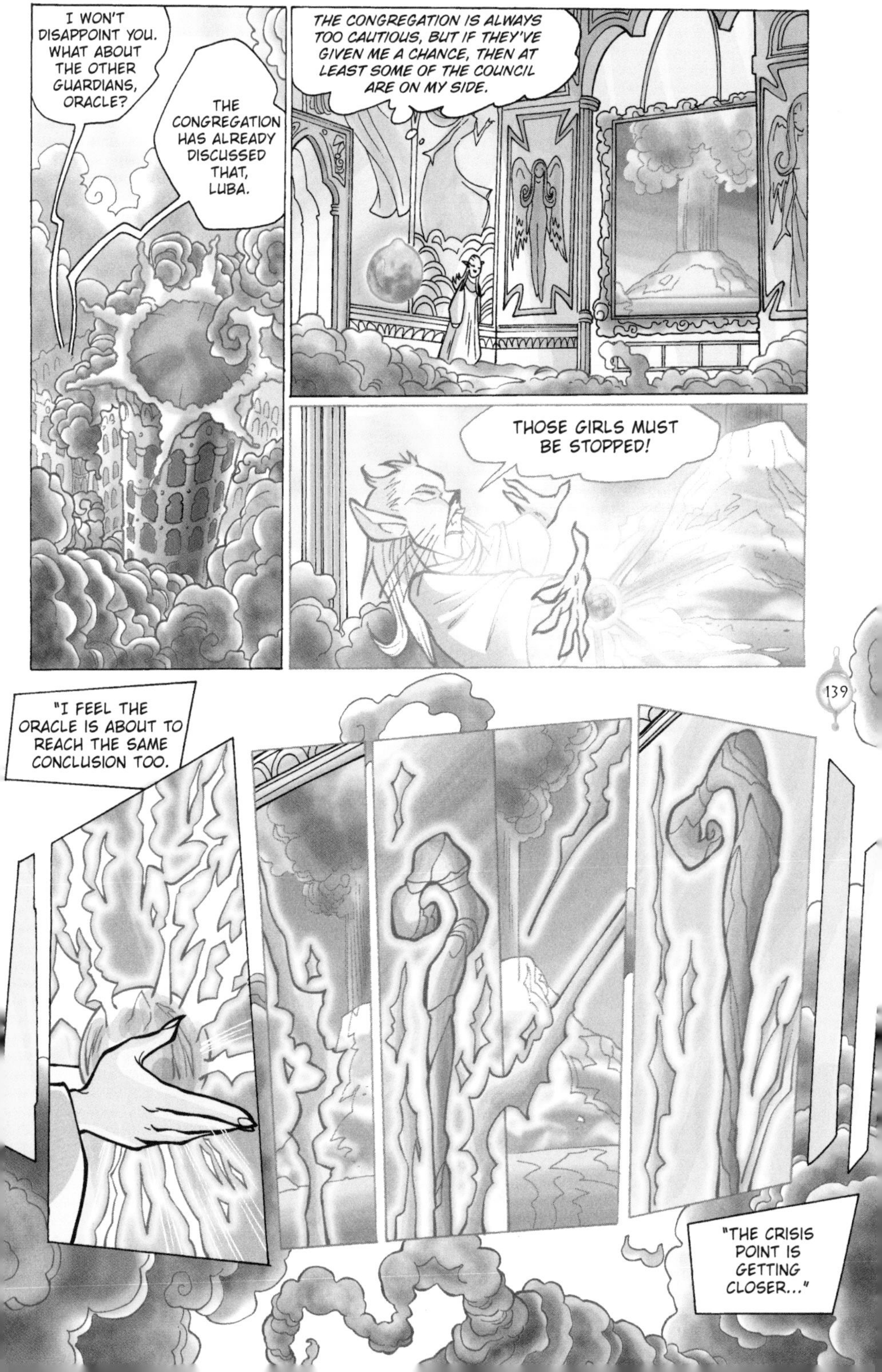
I WON'T DISAPPOINT YOU. WHAT ABOUT THE OTHER GUARDIANS, ORACLE?
THE CONGREGATION HAS ALREADY DISCUSSED THAT, LUBA.
THE CONGREGATION IS ALWAYS TOO CAUTIOUS, BUT IF THEY'VE GIVEN ME A CHANCE, THEN AT LEAST SOME OF THE COUNCIL ARE ON MY SIDE.
THOSE GIRLS MUST BE STOPPED!
"I FEEL THE ORACLE IS ABOUT TO REACH THE SAME CONCLUSION TOO.
"THE CRISIS POINT IS GETTING CLOSER..."

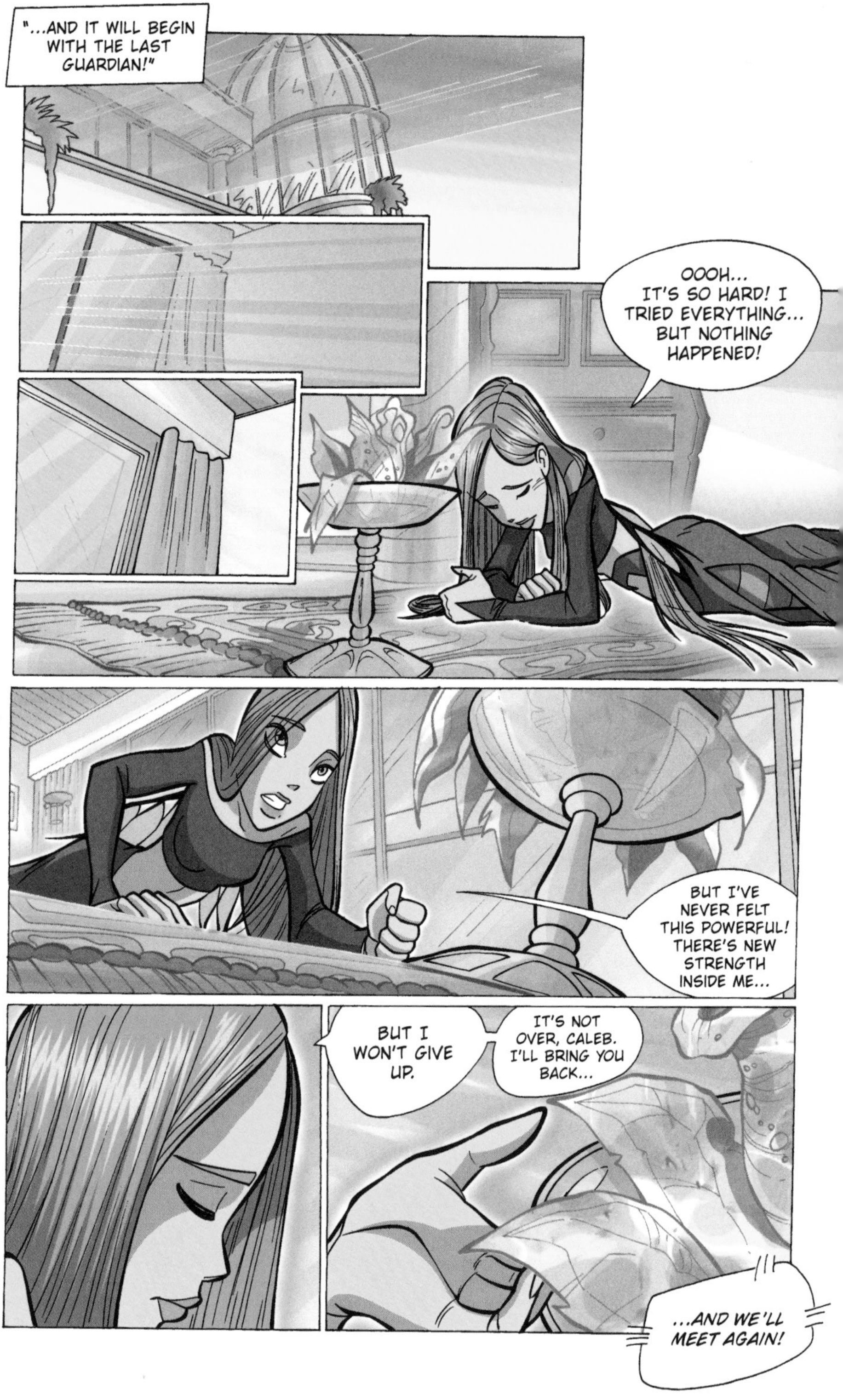
"...AND IT WILL BEGIN WITH THE LAST GUARDIAN!"
OOOH... IT'S SO HARD! I TRIED EVERYTHING... BUT NOTHING HAPPENED!
BUT I'VE NEVER FELT THIS POWERFUL! THERE'S NEW STRENGTH INSIDE ME...
BUT I WON'T GIVE UP.
IT'S NOT OVER, CALEB. I'LL BRING YOU BACK...
...AND WE'LL MEET AGAIN!

140

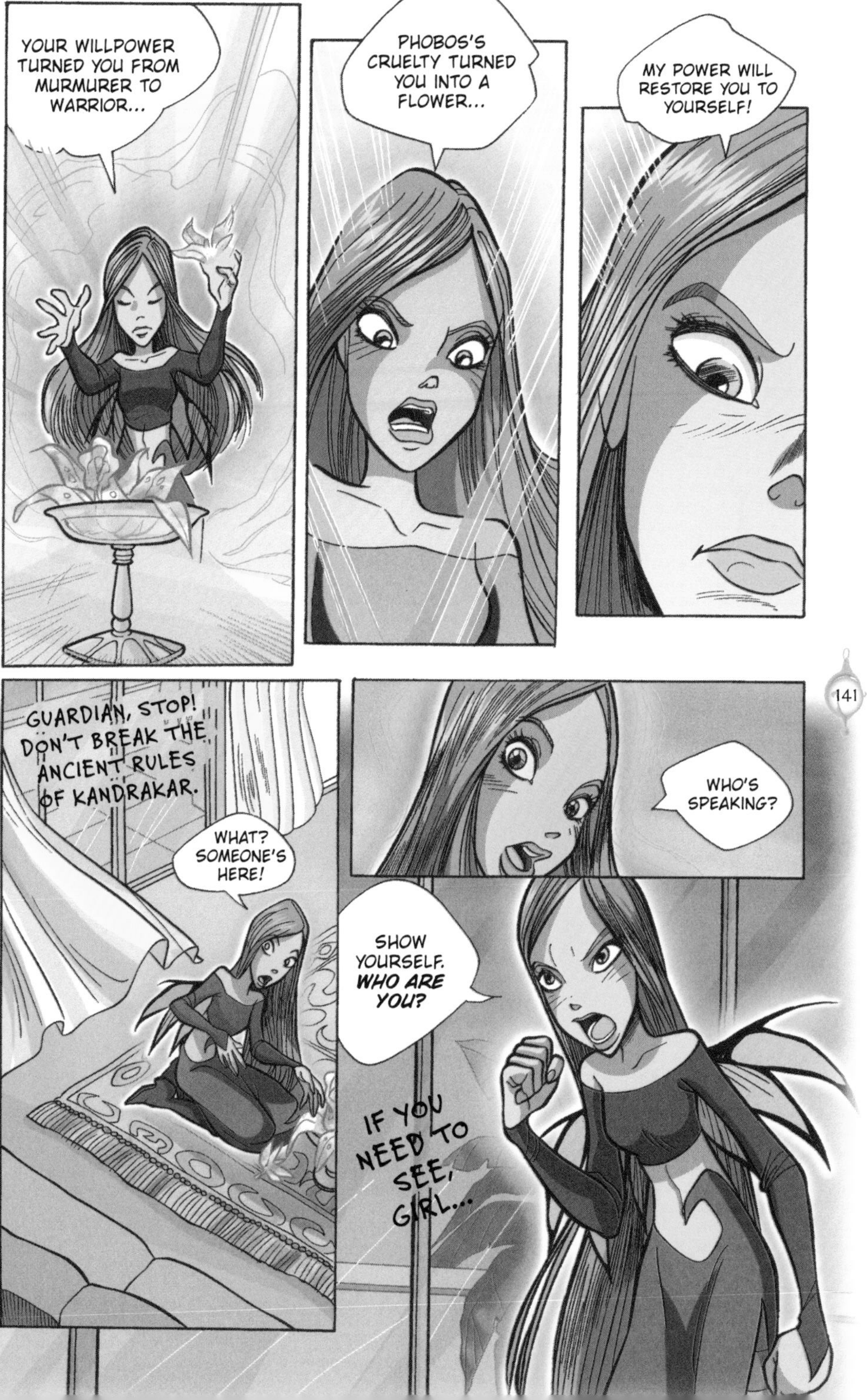
YOUR WILLPOWER TURNED YOU FROM MURMURER TO WARRIOR...
PHOBOS'S CRUELTY TURNED YOU INTO A FLOWER...
MY POWER WILL RESTORE YOU TO YOURSELF!
GUARDIAN, STOP! DON'T BREAK THE ANCIENT RULES OF KANDRAKAR.
WHAT? SOMEONE'S HERE!
WHO'S SPEAKING?
SHOW YOURSELF. WHO ARE YOU?
IF YOU NEED TO SEE, GIRL...

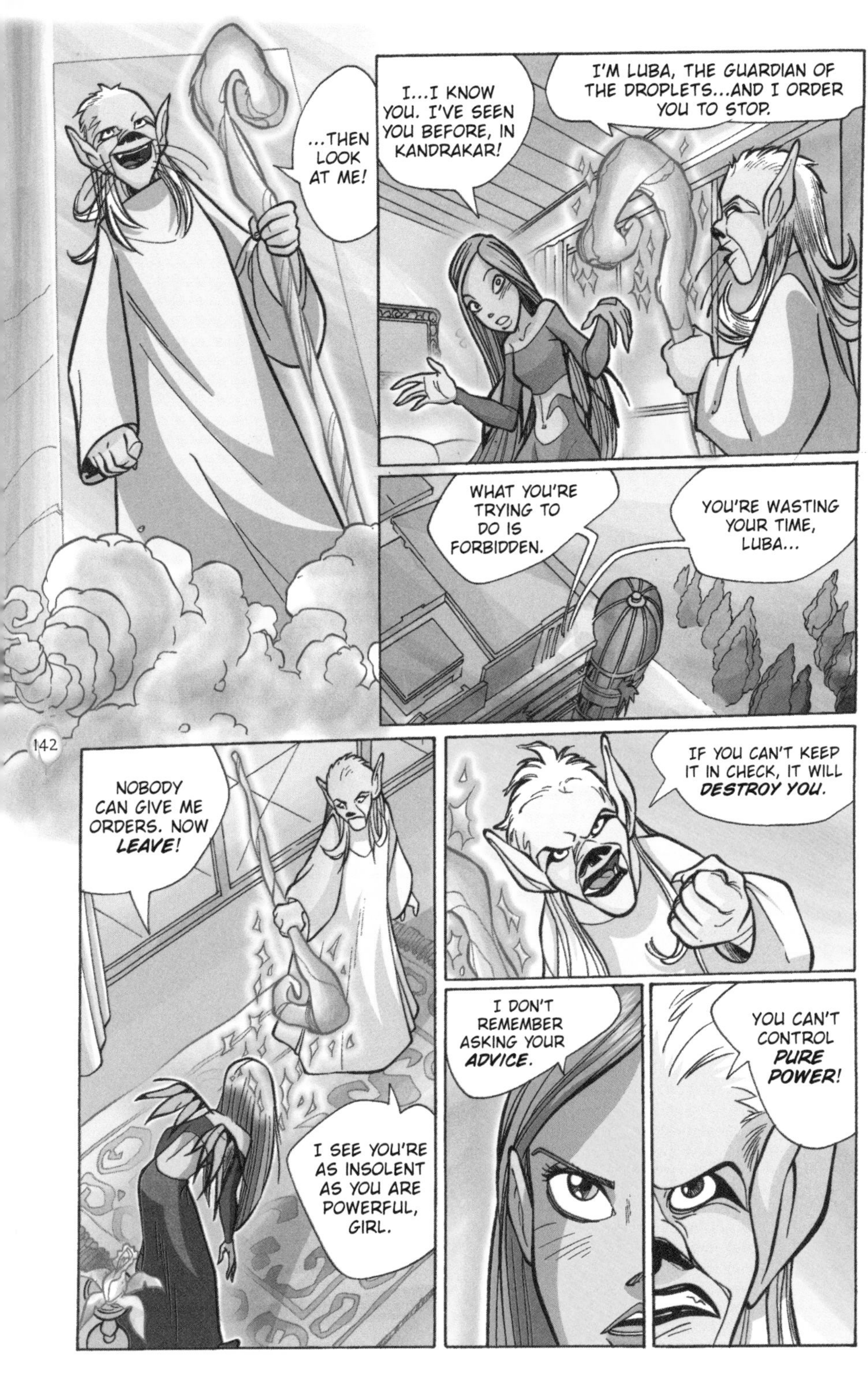
...THEN LOOK AT ME!
I...I KNOW YOU. I'VE SEEN YOU BEFORE, IN KANDRAKAR!
I'M LUBA, THE GUARDIAN OF THE DROPLETS...AND I ORDER YOU TO STOP.
WHAT YOU'RE TRYING TO DO IS FORBIDDEN.
YOU'RE WASTING YOUR TIME, LUBA...
NOBODY CAN GIVE ME ORDERS. NOW LEAVE!
I SEE YOU'RE AS INSOLENT AS YOU ARE POWERFUL, GIRL.
IF YOU CAN'T KEEP IT IN CHECK, IT WILL DESTROY YOU.
I DON'T REMEMBER ASKING YOUR ADVICE.
YOU CAN'T CONTROL PURE POWER!

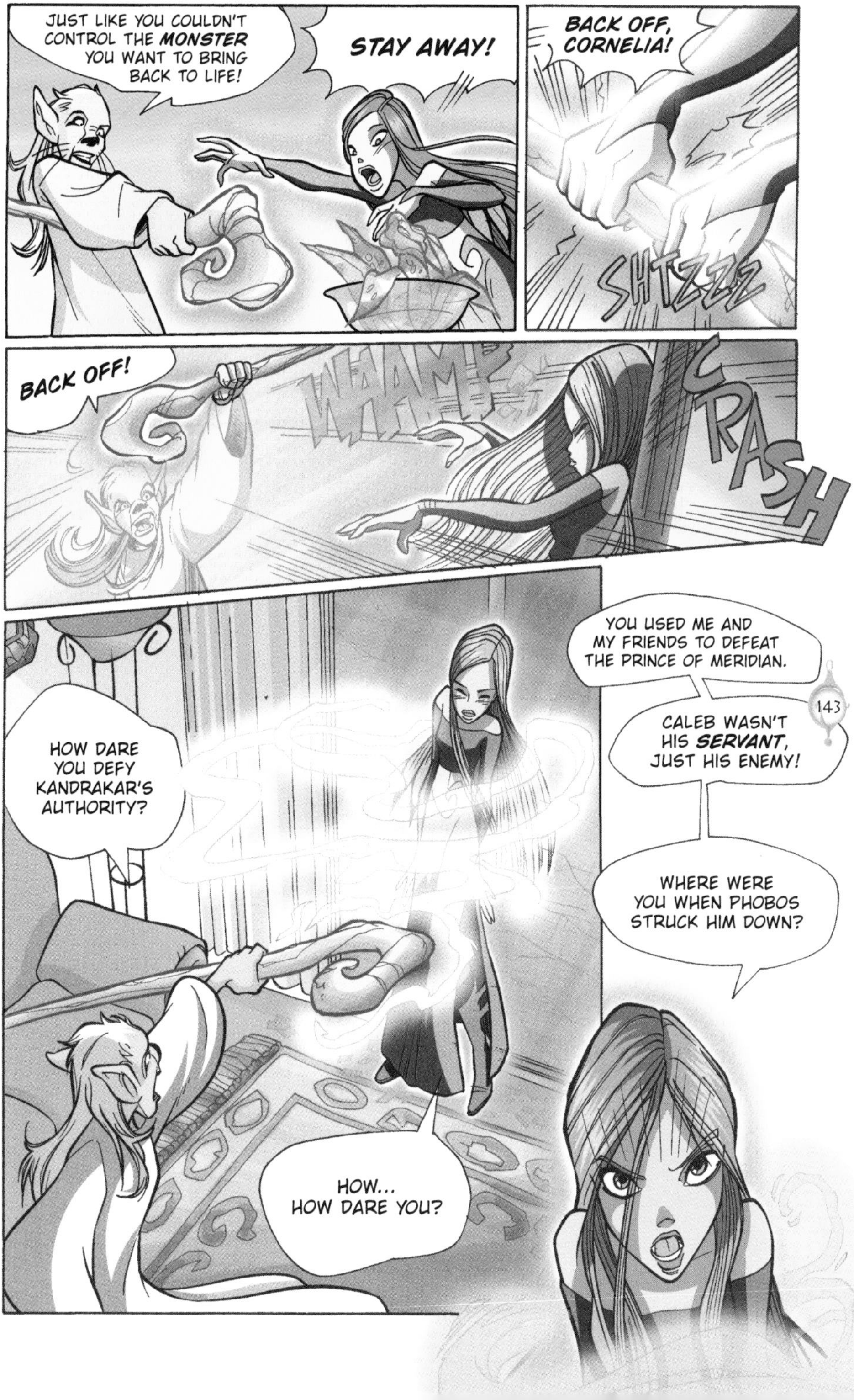
JUST LIKE YOU COULDN'T CONTROL THE MONSTER YOU WANT TO BRING BACK TO LIFE!
STAY AWAY!
BACK OFF, CORNELIA!
SHTZZZ
BACK OFF!
WHAMP
CRASH
HOW DARE YOU DEFY KANDRAKAR'S AUTHORITY?
HOW... HOW DARE YOU?
YOU USED ME AND MY FRIENDS TO DEFEAT THE PRINCE OF MERIDIAN.
CALEB WASN'T HIS SERVANT, JUST HIS ENEMY!
WHERE WERE YOU WHEN PHOBOS STRUCK HIM DOWN?

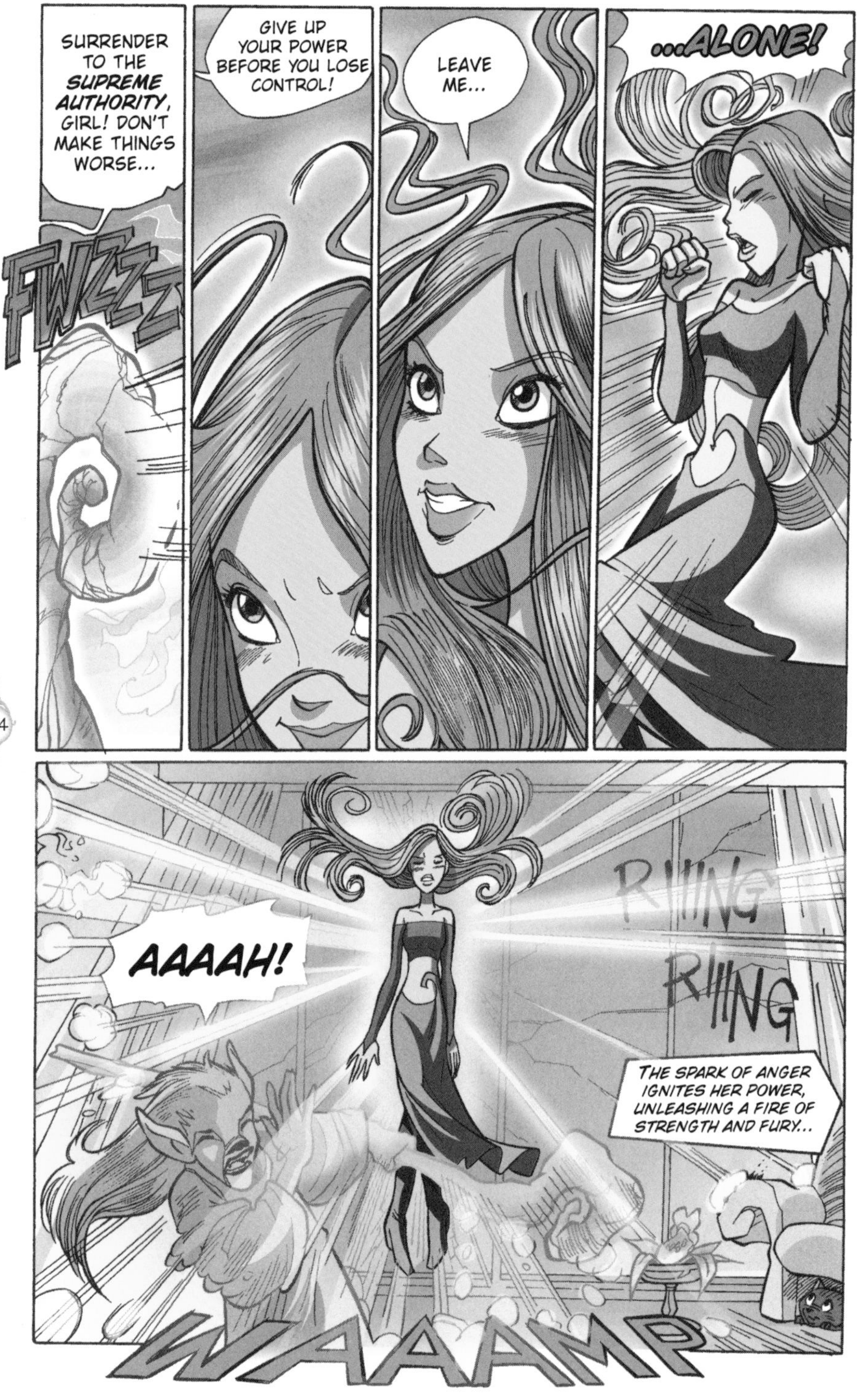
SURRENDER TO THE SUPREME AUTHORITY, GIRL! DON'T MAKE THINGS WORSE...
FWZZZ
GIVE UP YOUR POWER BEFORE YOU LOSE CONTROL!
LEAVE ME...
...ALONE!
AAAAH!
RIIING
RIIING
THE SPARK OF ANGER IGNITES HER POWER, UNLEASHING A FIRE OF STRENGTH AND FURY...
WAAAMP

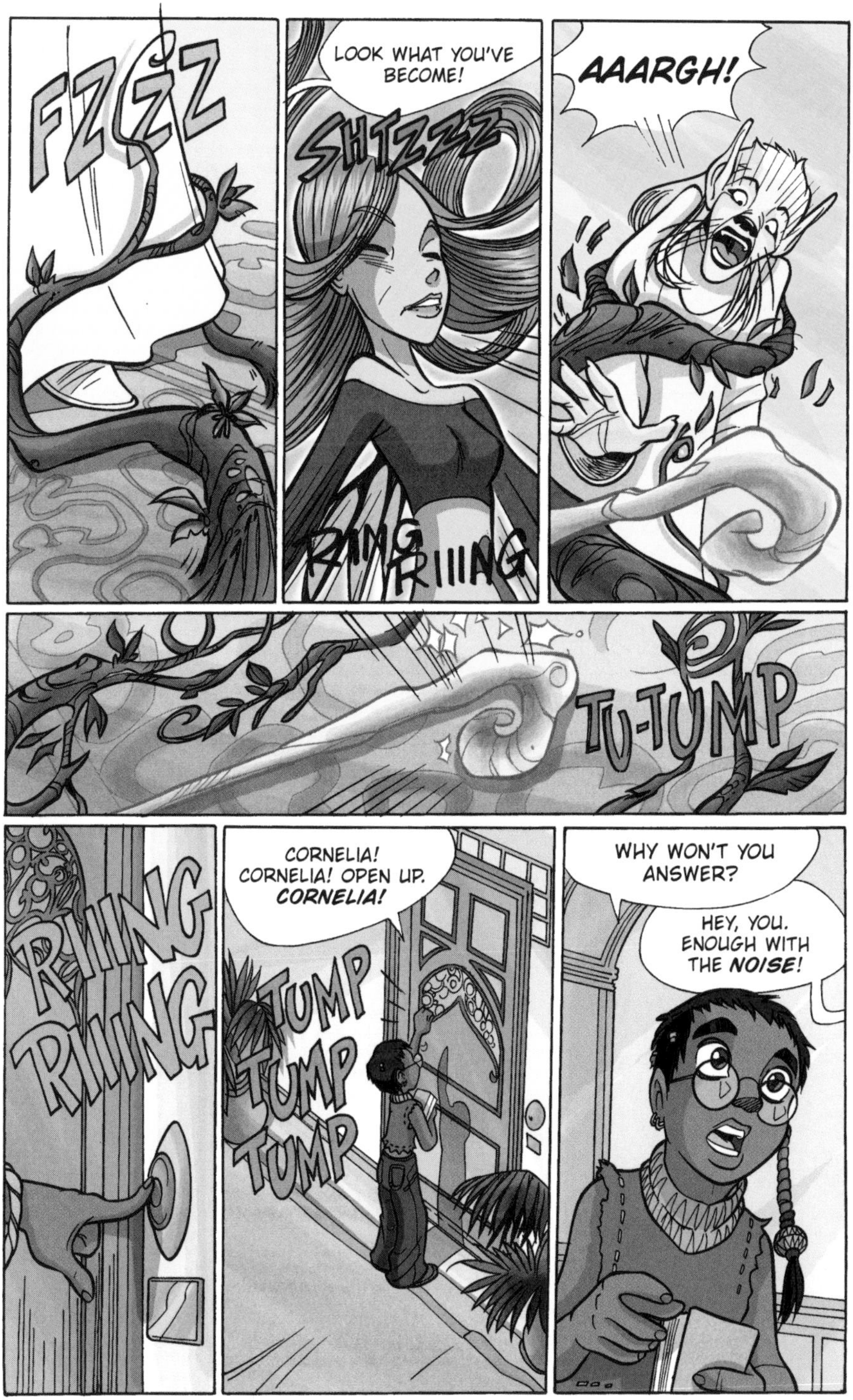
FZZZZ
LOOK WHAT YOU'VE BECOME!
SHIZZZ
RING RIIING
AAARGH!
TU-TUMP
RIIING RIIING
CORNELIA! CORNELIA! OPEN UP. ***CORNELIA!***
TUMP TUMP TUMP TUMP
WHY WON'T YOU ANSWER?
HEY, YOU. ENOUGH WITH THE ***NOISE!***

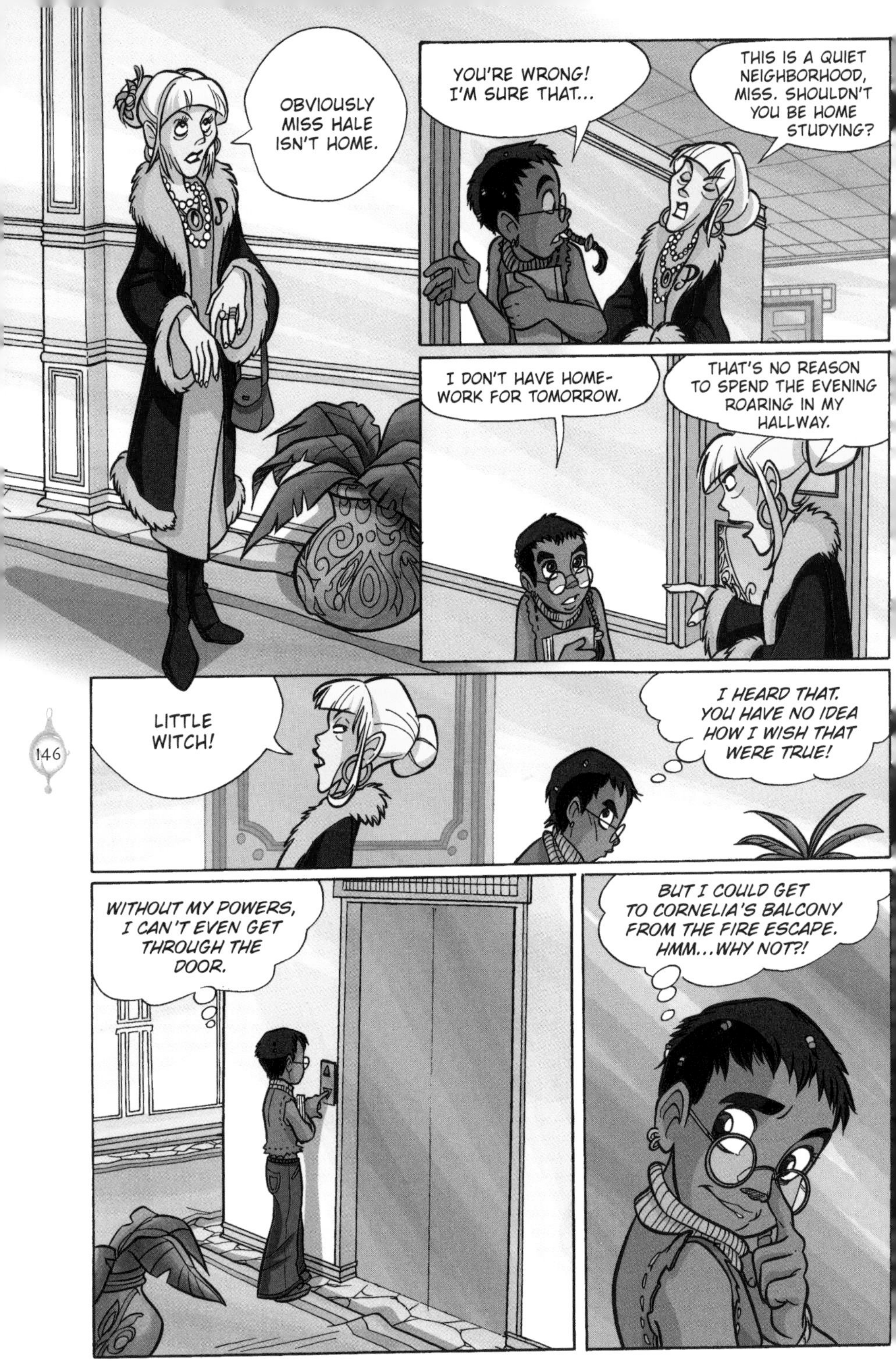
OBVIOUSLY MISS HALE ISN'T HOME.
YOU'RE WRONG! I'M SURE THAT...
THIS IS A QUIET NEIGHBORHOOD, MISS. SHOULDN'T YOU BE HOME STUDYING?
I DON'T HAVE HOME-WORK FOR TOMORROW.
THAT'S NO REASON TO SPEND THE EVENING ROARING IN MY HALLWAY.
LITTLE WITCH!
I HEARD THAT. YOU HAVE NO IDEA HOW I WISH THAT WERE TRUE!
WITHOUT MY POWERS, I CAN'T EVEN GET THROUGH THE DOOR.
BUT I COULD GET TO CORNELIA'S BALCONY FROM THE FIRE ESCAPE. HMM...WHY NOT?!

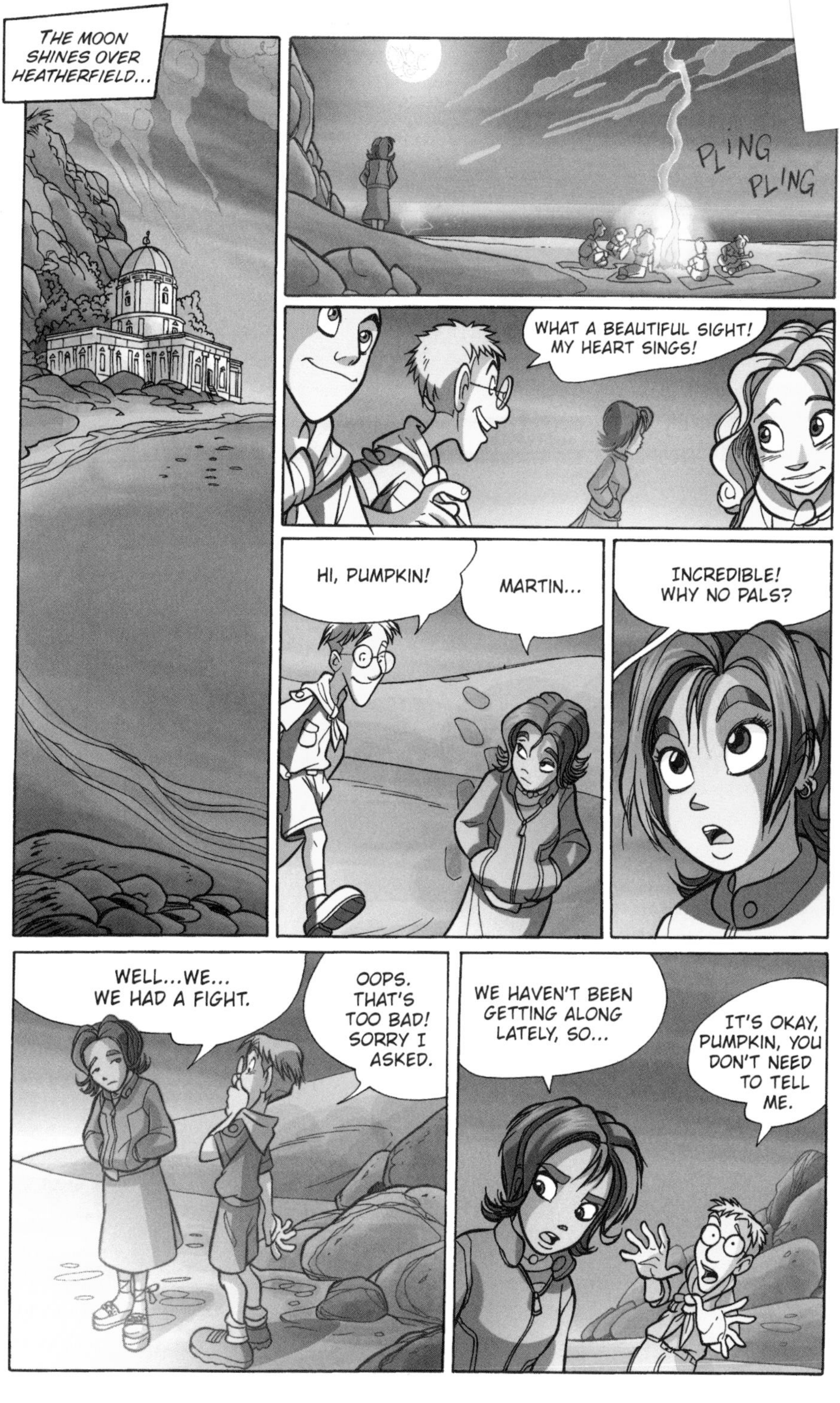

THE MOON SHINES OVER HEATHERFIELD...
PLING PLING
WHAT A BEAUTIFUL SIGHT! MY HEART SINGS!
HI, PUMPKIN!
MARTIN...
INCREDIBLE! WHY NO PALS?
WELL...WE... WE HAD A FIGHT.
OOPS. THAT'S TOO BAD! SORRY I ASKED.
WE HAVEN'T BEEN GETTING ALONG LATELY, SO...
IT'S OKAY, PUMPKIN, YOU DON'T NEED TO TELL ME.

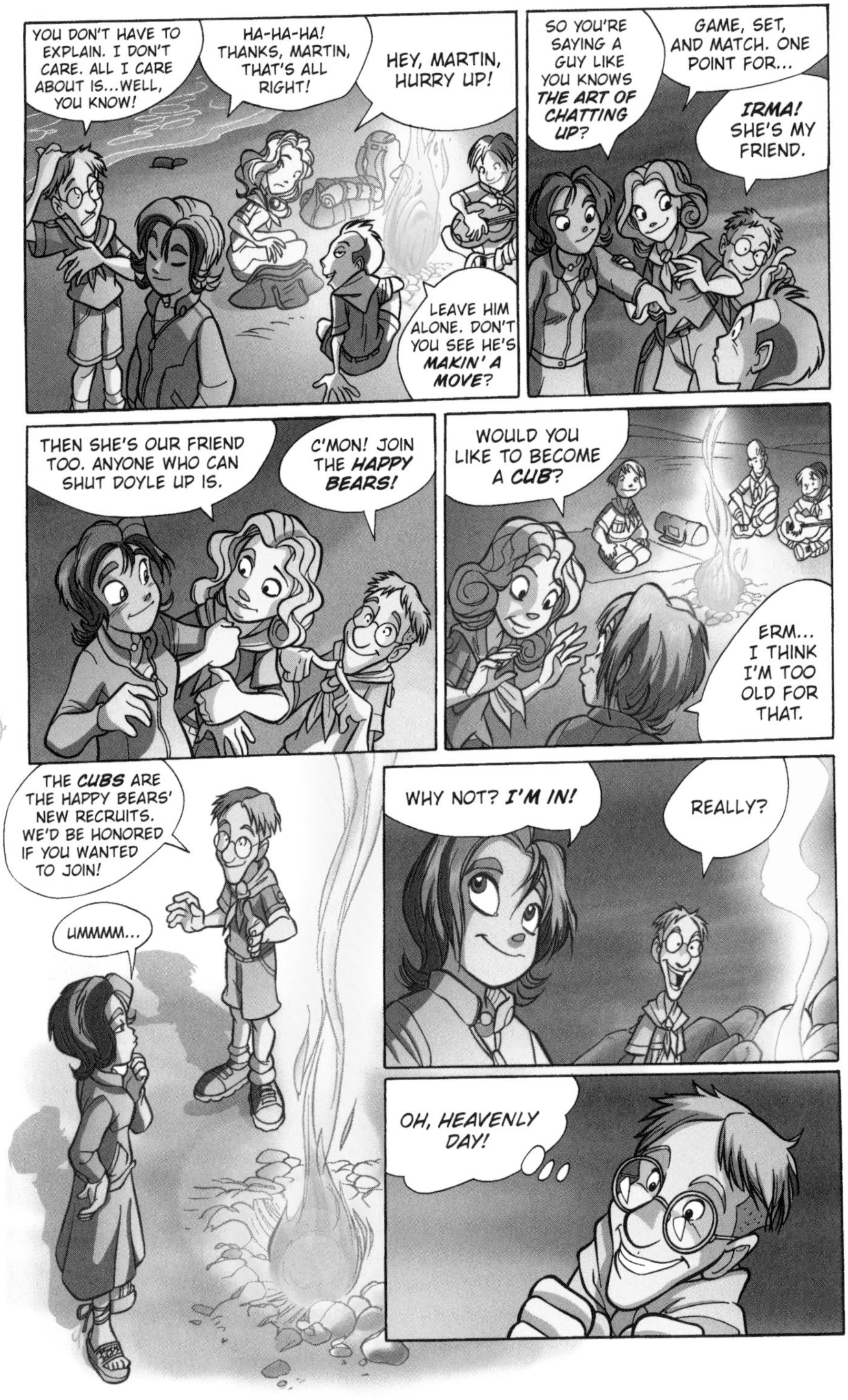
YOU DON'T HAVE TO EXPLAIN. I DON'T CARE. ALL I CARE ABOUT IS...WELL, YOU KNOW!
HA-HA-HA! THANKS, MARTIN, THAT'S ALL RIGHT!
HEY, MARTIN, HURRY UP!
LEAVE HIM ALONE. DON'T YOU SEE HE'S MAKIN' A MOVE?
SO YOU'RE SAYING A GUY LIKE YOU KNOWS THE ART OF CHATTING UP?
GAME, SET, AND MATCH. ONE POINT FOR...
IRMA! SHE'S MY FRIEND.
THEN SHE'S OUR FRIEND TOO. ANYONE WHO CAN SHUT DOYLE UP IS.
C'MON! JOIN THE HAPPY BEARS!
WOULD YOU LIKE TO BECOME A CUB?
ERM... I THINK I'M TOO OLD FOR THAT.
THE CUBS ARE THE HAPPY BEARS' NEW RECRUITS. WE'D BE HONORED IF YOU WANTED TO JOIN!
UMMMM...
WHY NOT? I'M IN!
REALLY?
OH, HEAVENLY DAY!

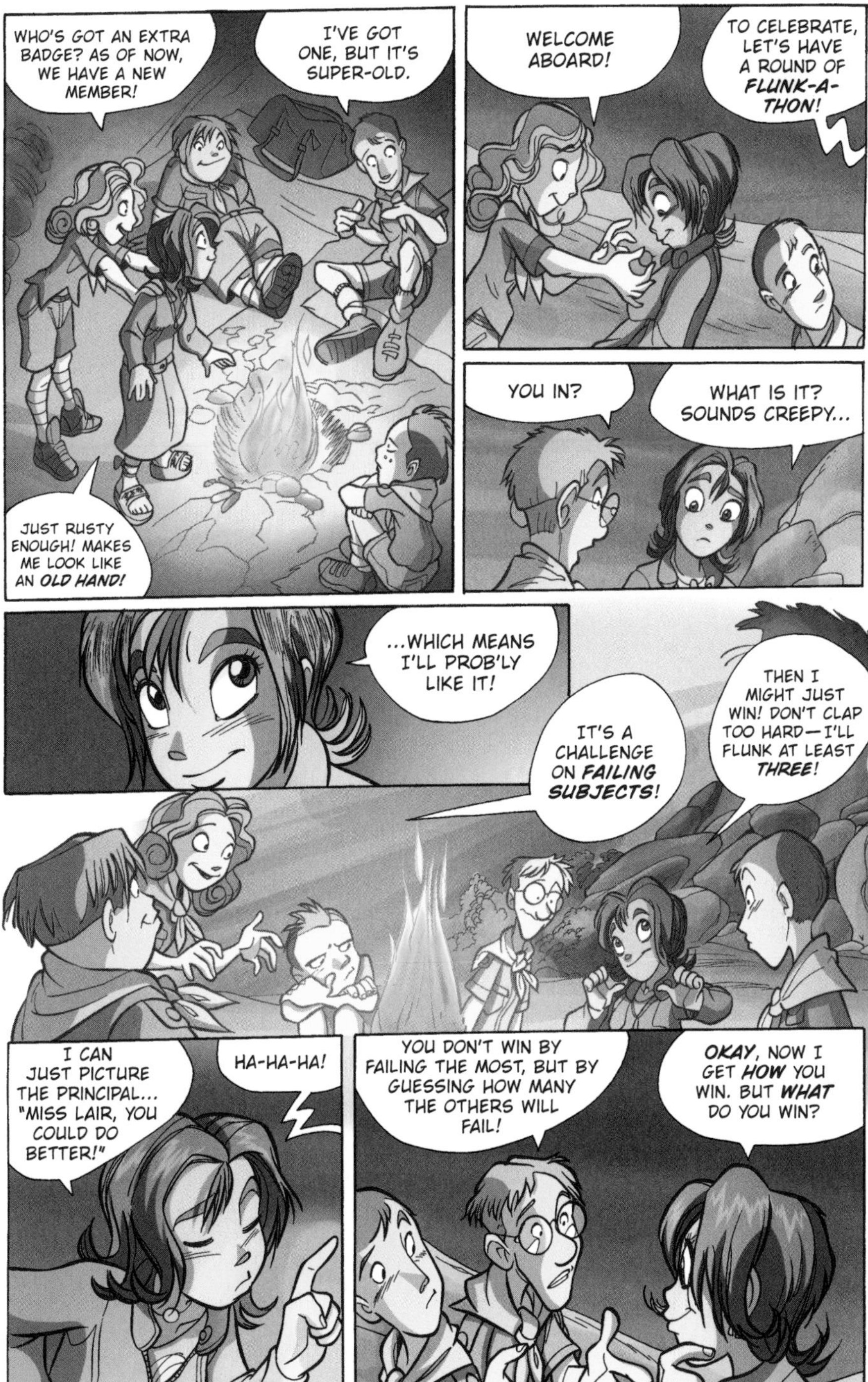
WHO'S GOT AN EXTRA BADGE? AS OF NOW, WE HAVE A NEW MEMBER!
I'VE GOT ONE, BUT IT'S SUPER-OLD.
JUST RUSTY ENOUGH! MAKES ME LOOK LIKE AN OLD HAND!
WELCOME ABOARD!
TO CELEBRATE, LET'S HAVE A ROUND OF FLUNK-A-THON!
YOU IN?
WHAT IS IT? SOUNDS CREEPY...
...WHICH MEANS I'LL PROB'LY LIKE IT!
IT'S A CHALLENGE ON FAILING SUBJECTS!
THEN I MIGHT JUST WIN! DON'T CLAP TOO HARD—I'LL FLUNK AT LEAST THREE!
I CAN JUST PICTURE THE PRINCIPAL... "MISS LAIR, YOU COULD DO BETTER!"
HA-HA-HA!
YOU DON'T WIN BY FAILING THE MOST, BUT BY GUESSING HOW MANY THE OTHERS WILL FAIL!
OKAY, NOW I GET HOW YOU WIN. BUT WHAT DO YOU WIN?

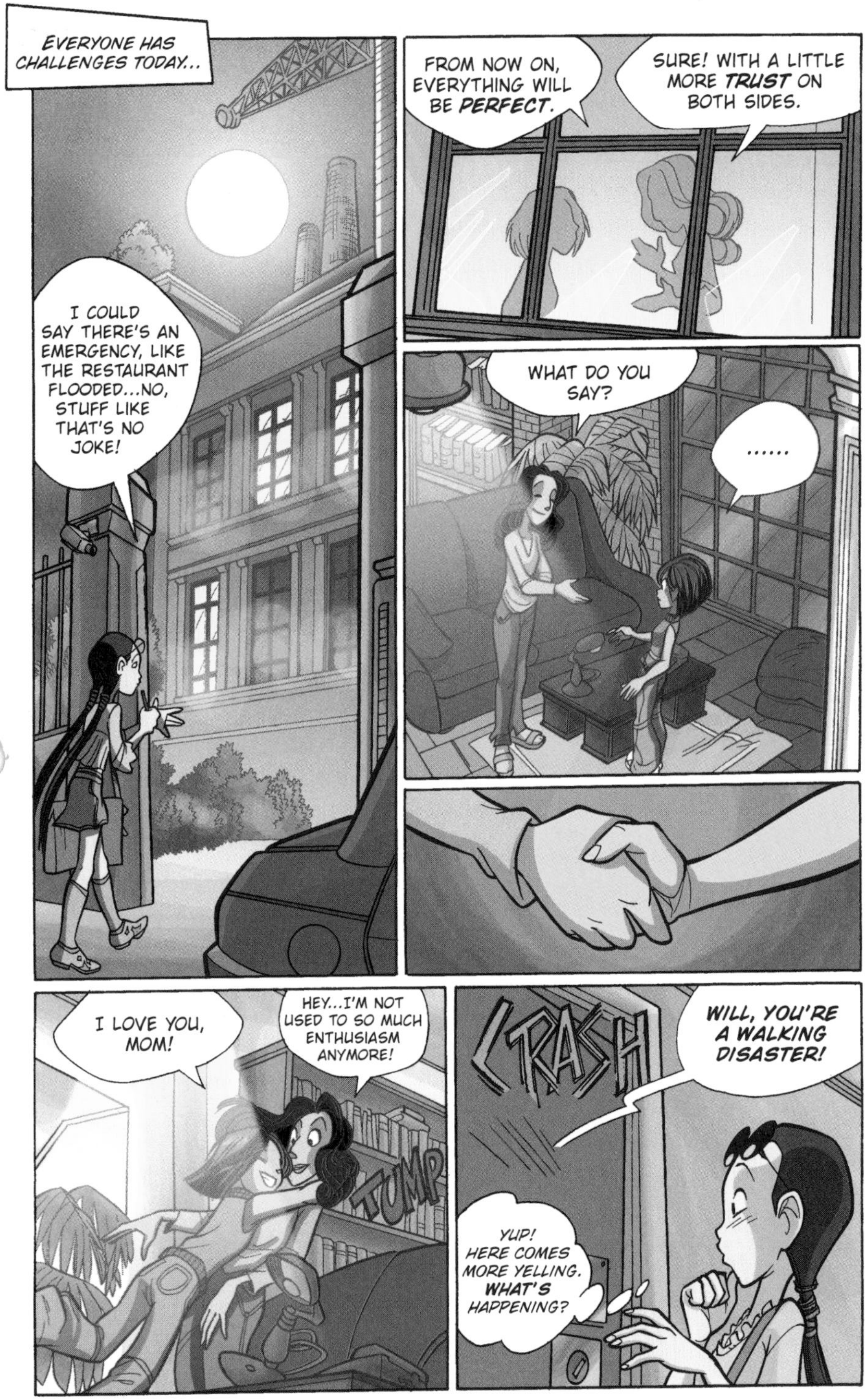
EVERYONE HAS CHALLENGES TODAY...
I COULD SAY THERE'S AN EMERGENCY, LIKE THE RESTAURANT FLOODED...NO, STUFF LIKE THAT'S NO JOKE!
FROM NOW ON, EVERYTHING WILL BE **PERFECT**.
SURE! WITH A LITTLE MORE **TRUST** ON BOTH SIDES.
WHAT DO YOU SAY?
......
I LOVE YOU, MOM!
HEY...I'M NOT USED TO SO MUCH ENTHUSIASM ANYMORE!
TUMP
CRASH
WILL, YOU'RE A WALKING DISASTER!
YUP! HERE COMES MORE YELLING. **WHAT'S** HAPPENING?

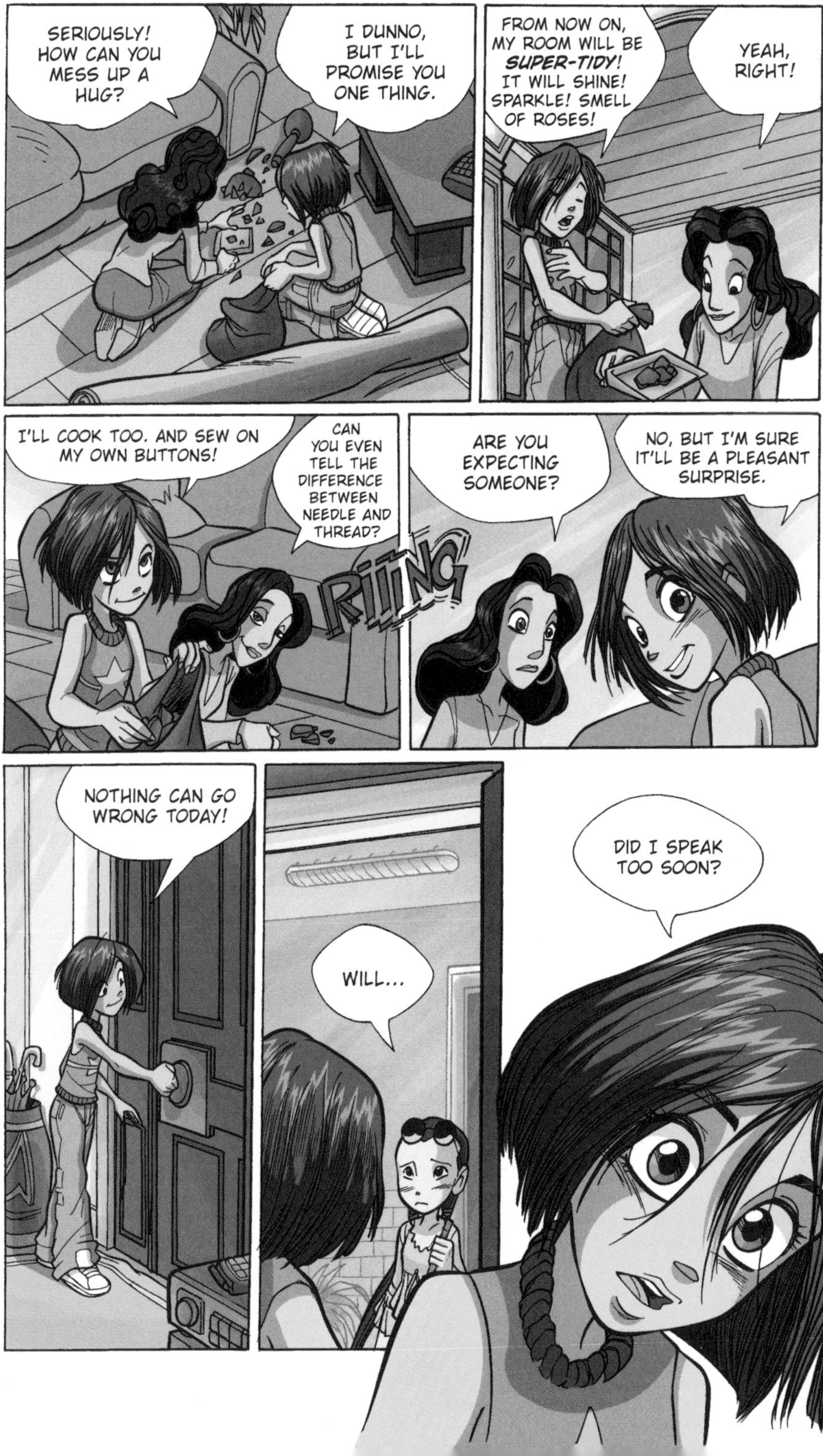
SERIOUSLY! HOW CAN YOU MESS UP A HUG?
I DUNNO, BUT I'LL PROMISE YOU ONE THING.
FROM NOW ON, MY ROOM WILL BE ***SUPER-TIDY***! IT WILL SHINE! SPARKLE! SMELL OF ROSES!
YEAH, RIGHT!
I'LL COOK TOO. AND SEW ON MY OWN BUTTONS!
CAN YOU EVEN TELL THE DIFFERENCE BETWEEN NEEDLE AND THREAD?
RIIING
ARE YOU EXPECTING SOMEONE?
NO, BUT I'M SURE IT'LL BE A PLEASANT SURPRISE.
NOTHING CAN GO WRONG TODAY!
WILL...
DID I SPEAK TOO SOON?

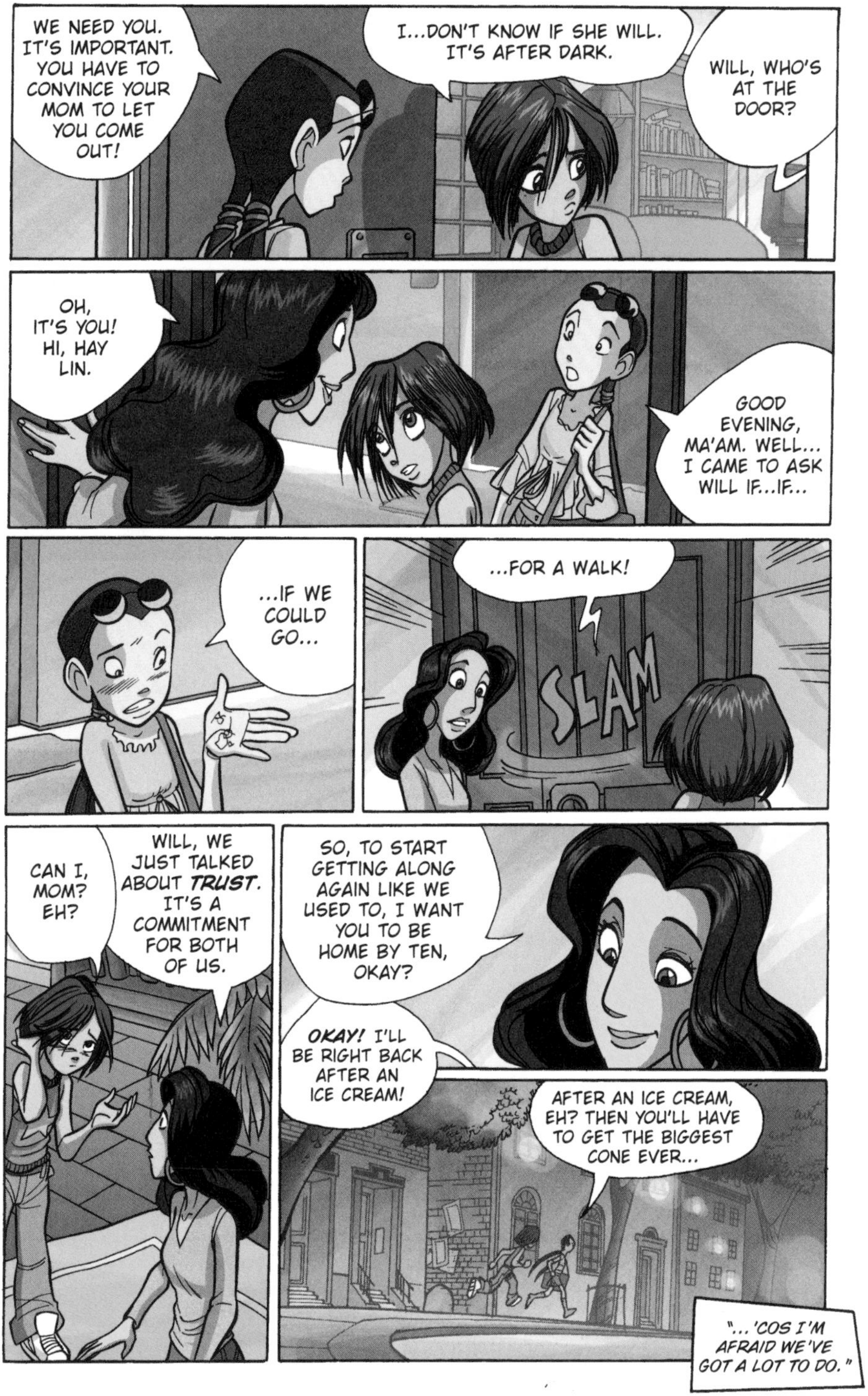

WE NEED YOU. IT'S IMPORTANT. YOU HAVE TO CONVINCE YOUR MOM TO LET YOU COME OUT!
I...DON'T KNOW IF SHE WILL. IT'S AFTER DARK.
WILL, WHO'S AT THE DOOR?
OH, IT'S YOU! HI, HAY LIN.
GOOD EVENING, MA'AM. WELL... I CAME TO ASK WILL IF...IF...
...IF WE COULD GO...
...FOR A WALK!
SLAM
CAN I, MOM? EH?
WILL, WE JUST TALKED ABOUT *TRUST*. IT'S A COMMITMENT FOR BOTH OF US.
SO, TO START GETTING ALONG AGAIN LIKE WE USED TO, I WANT YOU TO BE HOME BY TEN, OKAY?
OKAY! I'LL BE RIGHT BACK AFTER AN ICE CREAM!
AFTER AN ICE CREAM, EH? THEN YOU'LL HAVE TO GET THE BIGGEST CONE EVER...
"...'COS I'M AFRAID WE'VE GOT A LOT TO DO."

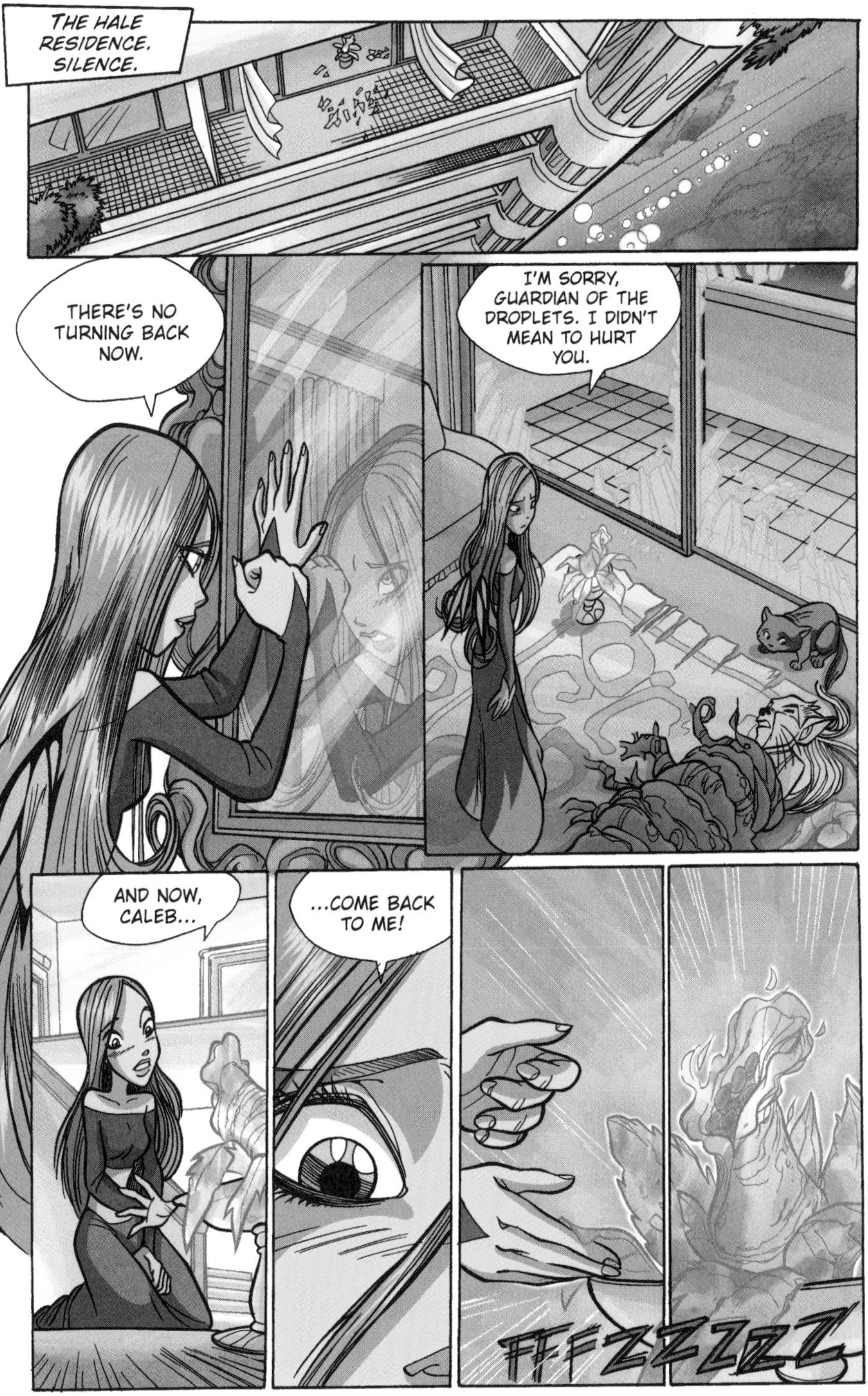
THE HALE RESIDENCE. SILENCE.
THERE'S NO TURNING BACK NOW.
I'M SORRY, GUARDIAN OF THE DROPLETS. I DIDN'T MEAN TO HURT YOU.
AND NOW, CALEB...
...COME BACK TO ME!
FFFZZZZZZ

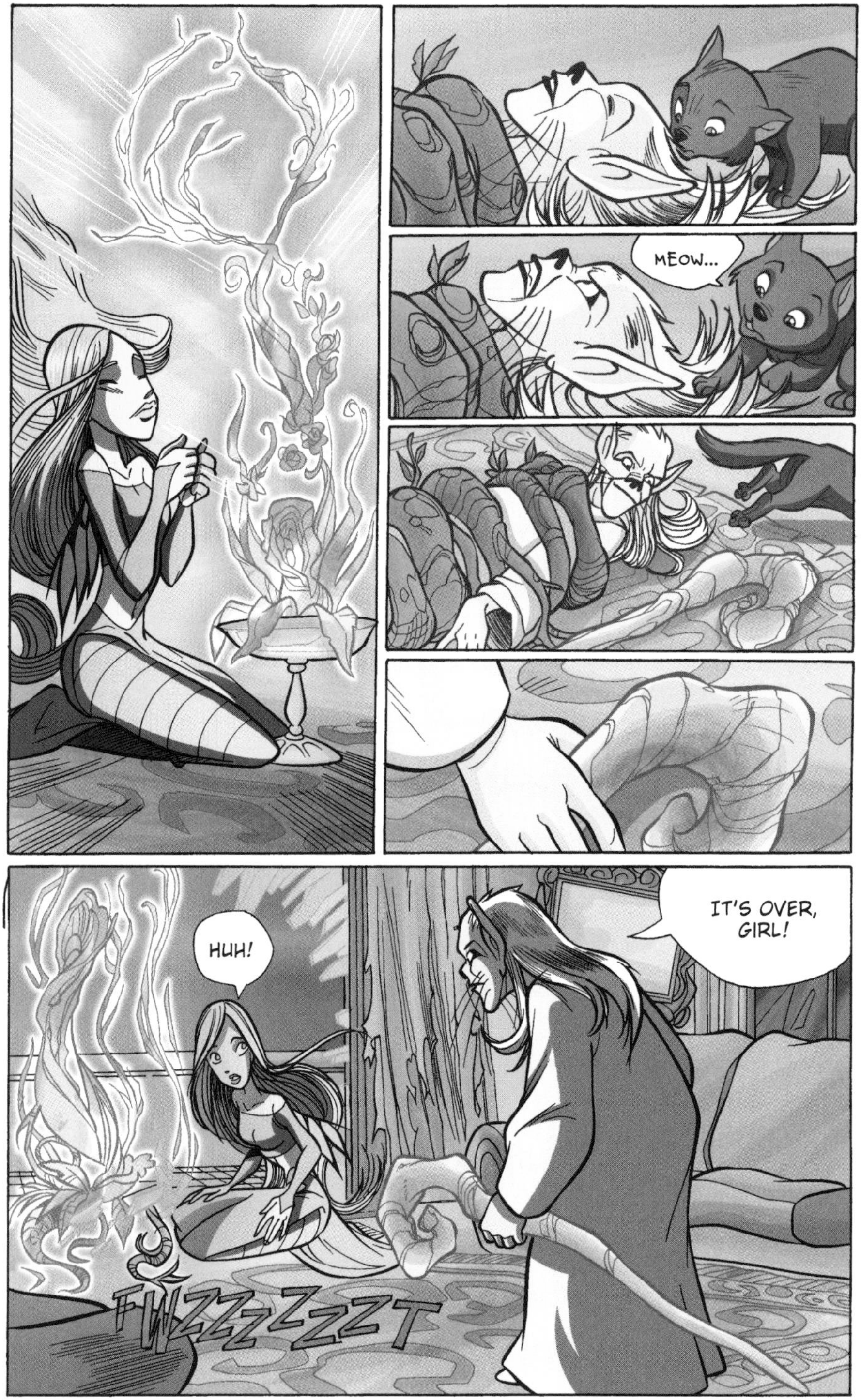
MEOW...
HUH!
IT'S OVER, GIRL!
FWZZZZZZT

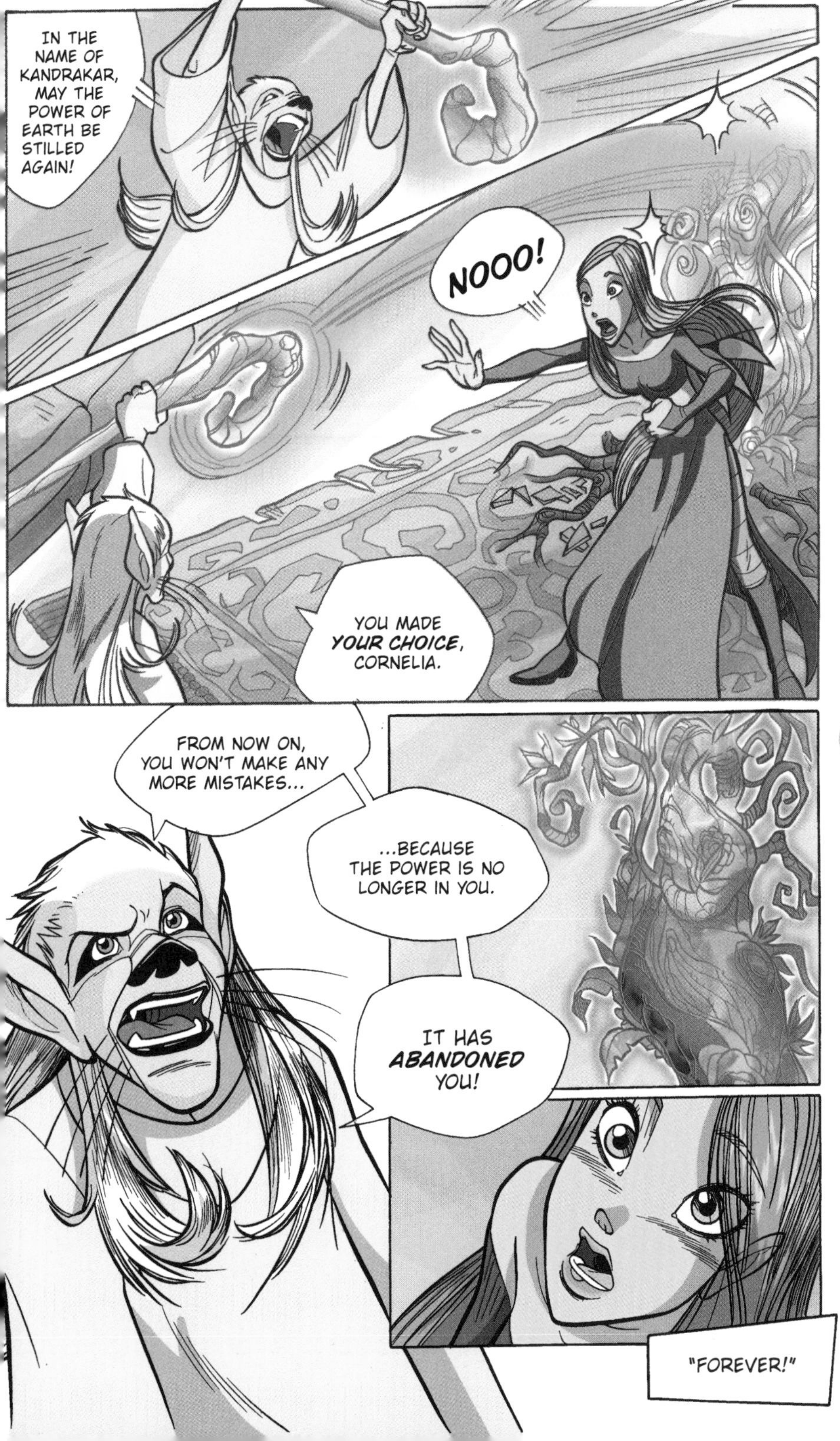
IN THE NAME OF KANDRAKAR, MAY THE POWER OF EARTH BE STILLED AGAIN!
NOOO!
YOU MADE YOUR CHOICE, CORNELIA.
FROM NOW ON, YOU WON'T MAKE ANY MORE MISTAKES...
...BECAUSE THE POWER IS NO LONGER IN YOU.
IT HAS ABANDONED YOU!
"FOREVER!"

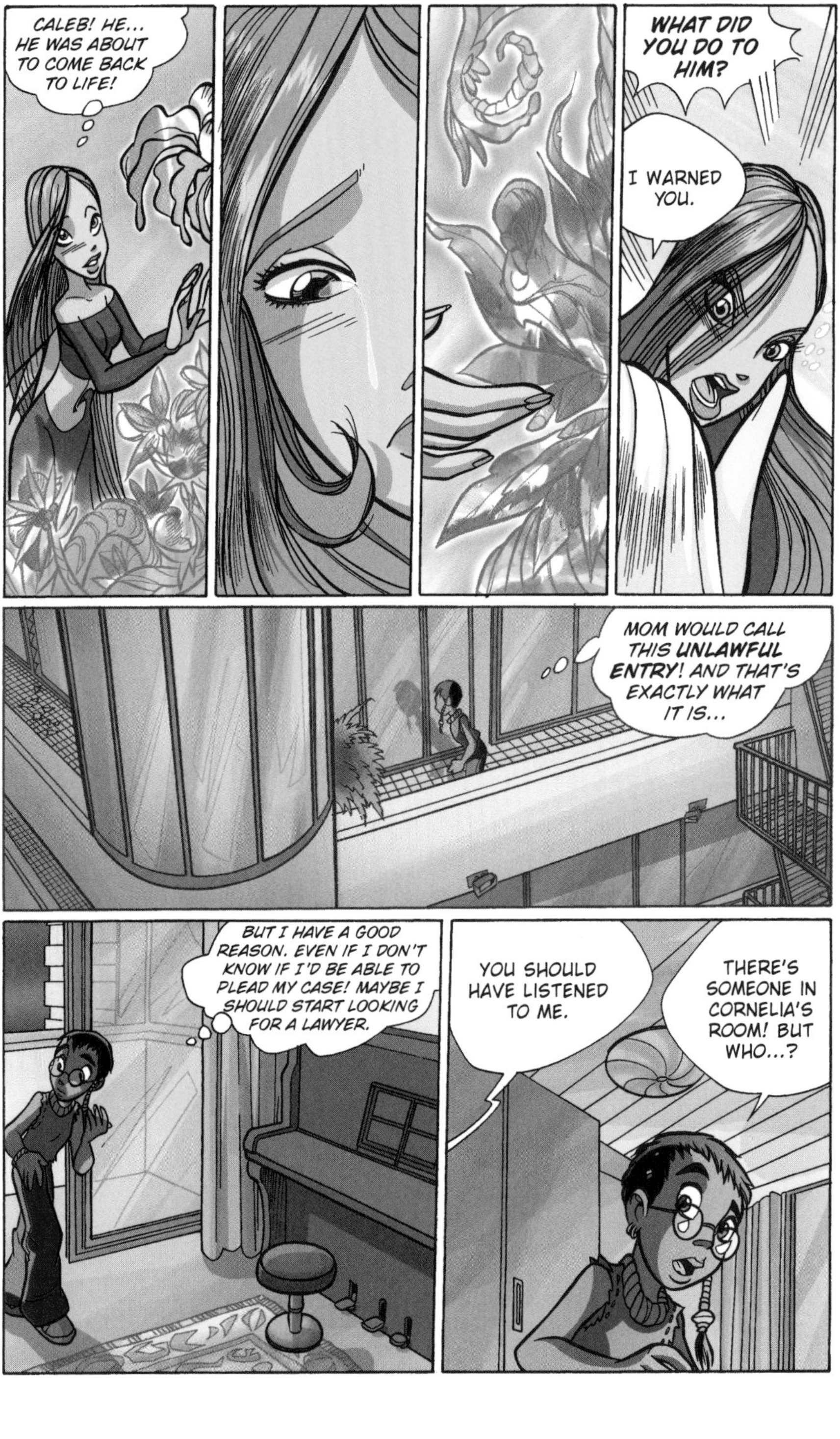
CALEB! HE... HE WAS ABOUT TO COME BACK TO LIFE!
WHAT DID YOU DO TO HIM?
I WARNED YOU.
MOM WOULD CALL THIS UNLAWFUL ENTRY! AND THAT'S EXACTLY WHAT IT IS...
BUT I HAVE A GOOD REASON. EVEN IF I DON'T KNOW IF I'D BE ABLE TO PLEAD MY CASE! MAYBE I SHOULD START LOOKING FOR A LAWYER.
YOU SHOULD HAVE LISTENED TO ME.
THERE'S SOMEONE IN CORNELIA'S ROOM! BUT WHO...?

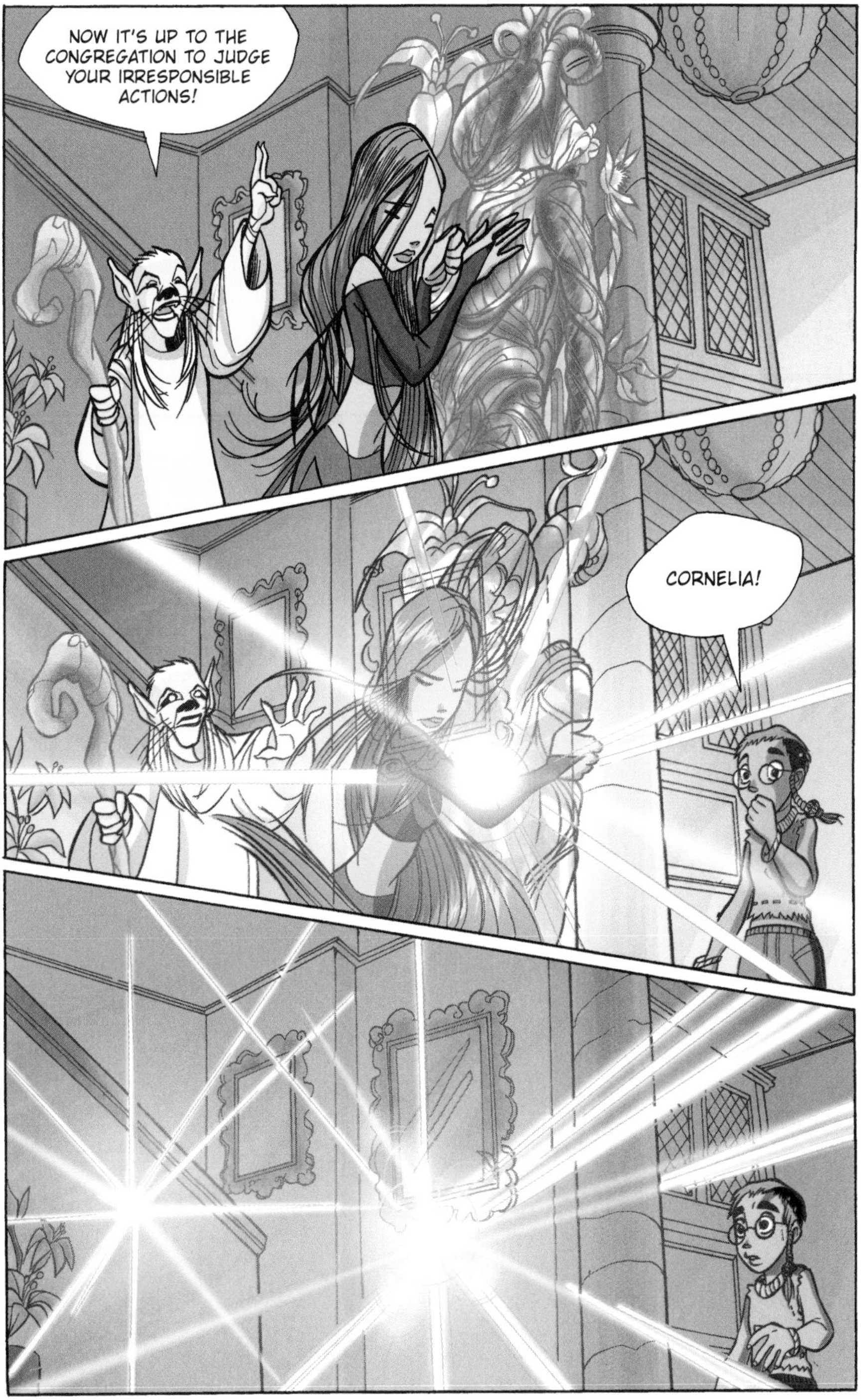
NOW IT'S UP TO THE CONGREGATION TO JUDGE YOUR IRRESPONSIBLE ACTIONS!
CORNELIA!

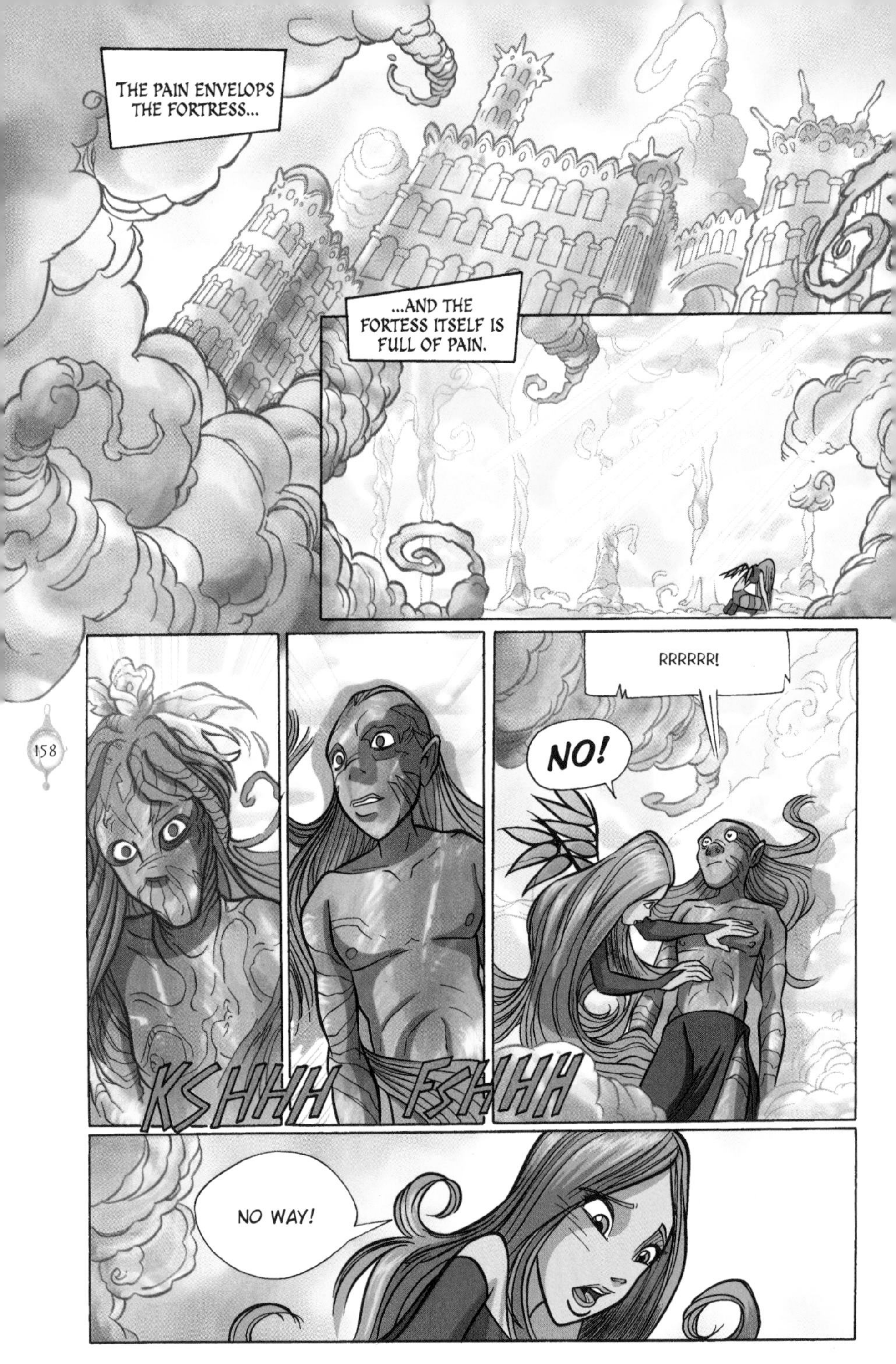

THE PAIN ENVELOPS THE FORTRESS...
...AND THE FORTESS ITSELF IS FULL OF PAIN.
KSHHH FSHHH
RRRRRR!
NO!
NO WAY!

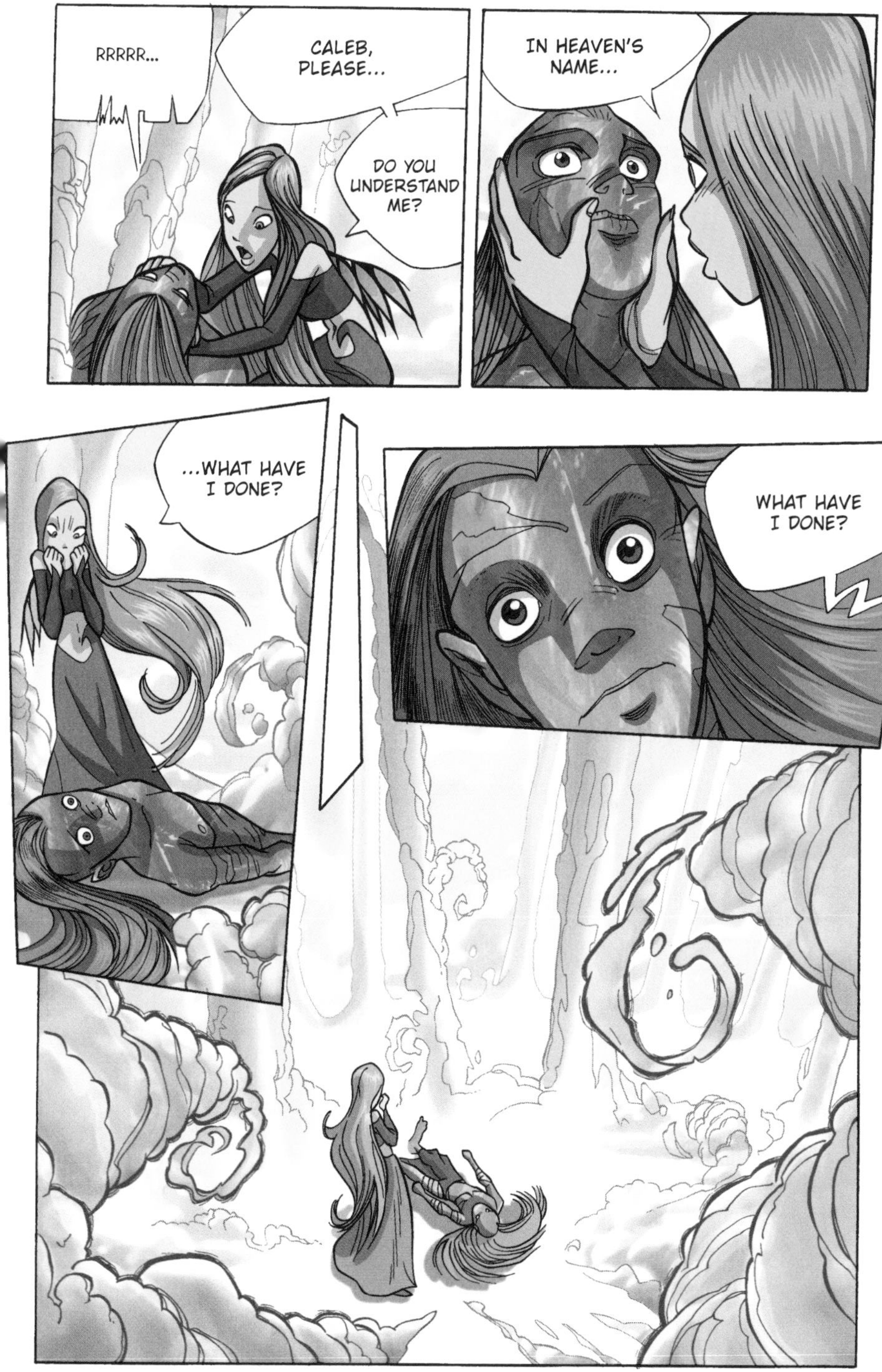
RRRRR...
CALEB, PLEASE...
DO YOU UNDERSTAND ME?
IN HEAVEN'S NAME...
...WHAT HAVE I DONE?
WHAT HAVE I DONE?

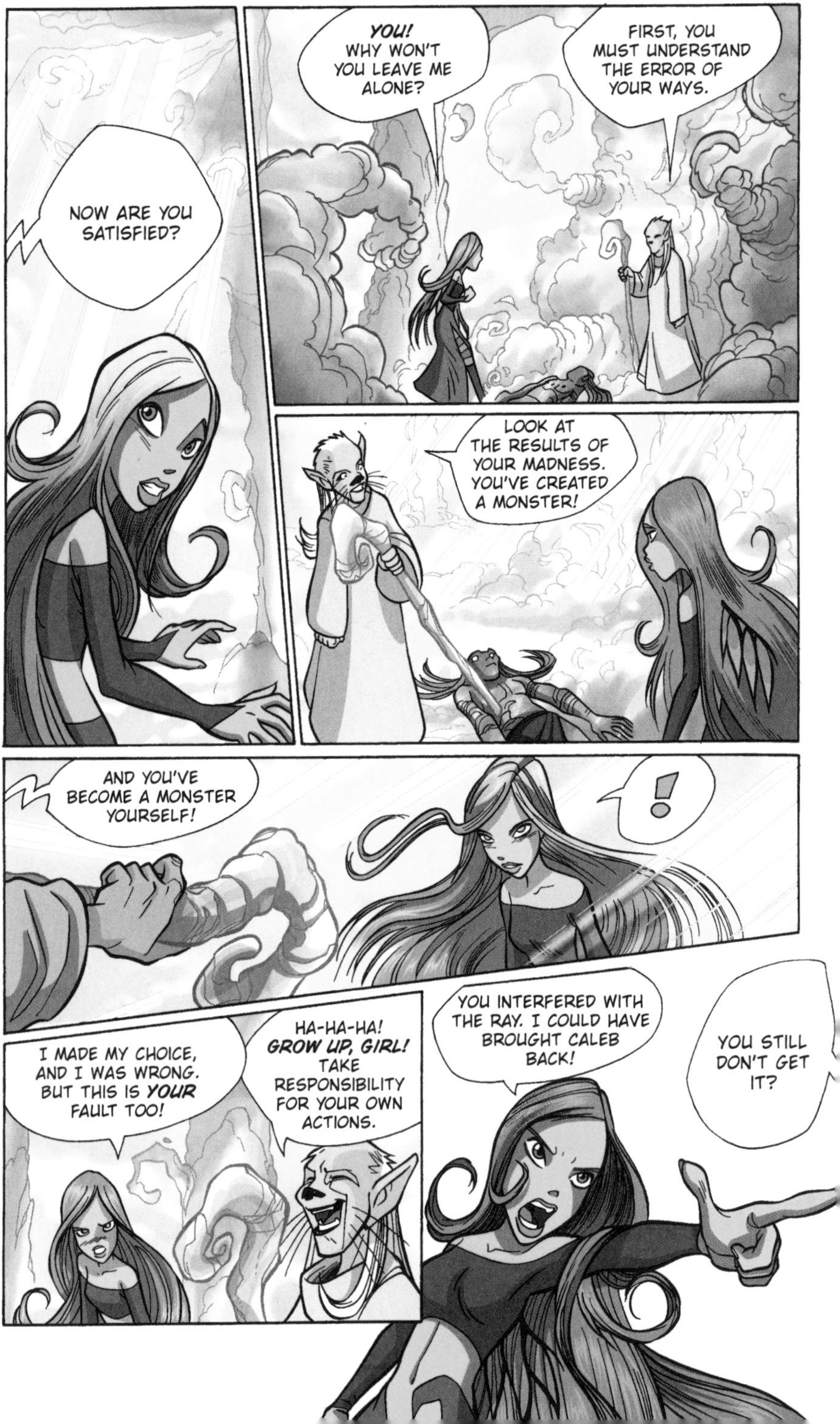
NOW ARE YOU SATISFIED?
YOU! WHY WON'T YOU LEAVE ME ALONE?
FIRST, YOU MUST UNDERSTAND THE ERROR OF YOUR WAYS.
LOOK AT THE RESULTS OF YOUR MADNESS. YOU'VE CREATED A MONSTER!
AND YOU'VE BECOME A MONSTER YOURSELF!
!
I MADE MY CHOICE, AND I WAS WRONG. BUT THIS IS YOUR FAULT TOO!
HA-HA-HA! GROW UP, GIRL! TAKE RESPONSIBILITY FOR YOUR OWN ACTIONS.
YOU INTERFERED WITH THE RAY. I COULD HAVE BROUGHT CALEB BACK!
YOU STILL DON'T GET IT?

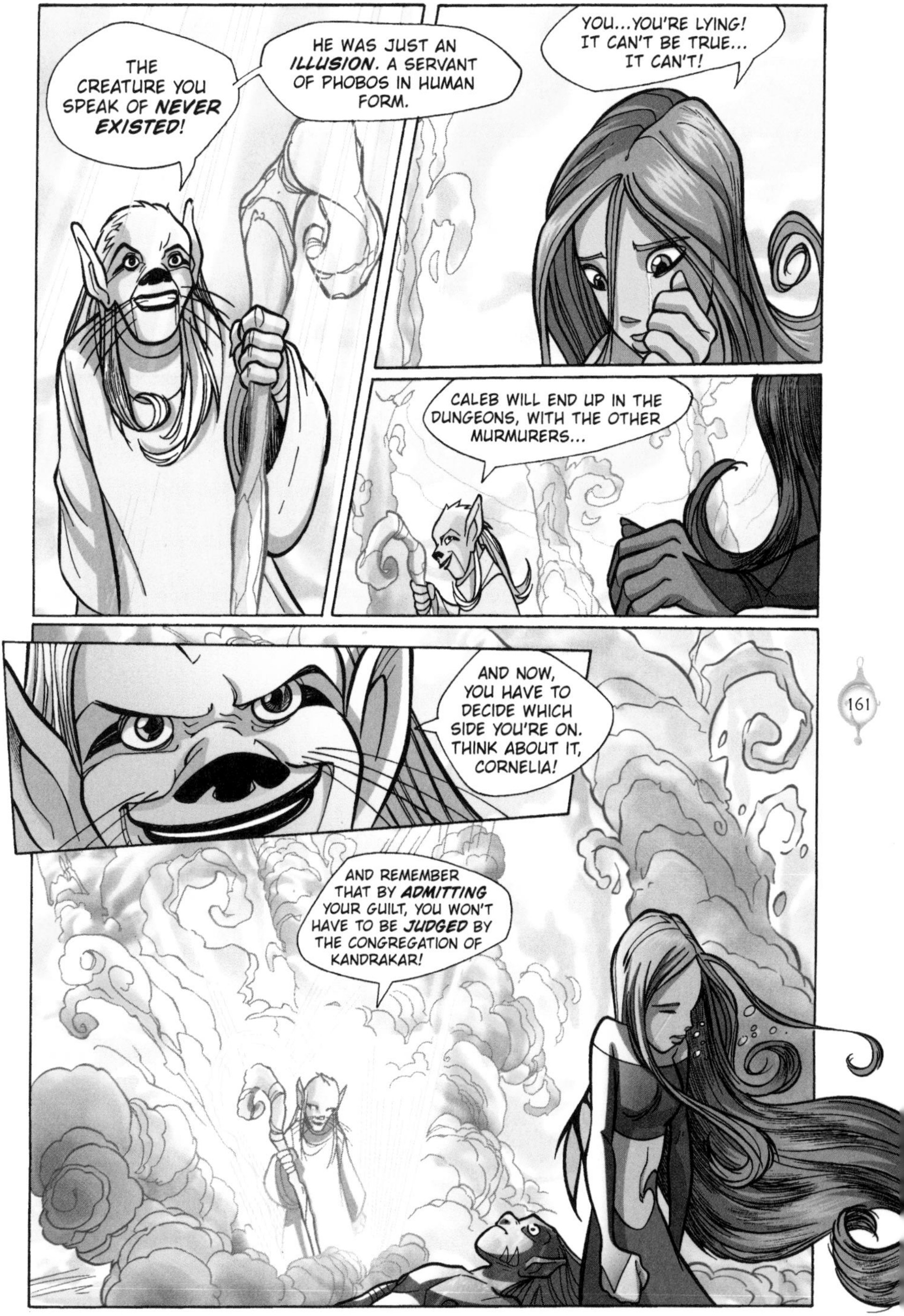
THE CREATURE YOU SPEAK OF NEVER EXISTED!
HE WAS JUST AN ILLUSION. A SERVANT OF PHOBOS IN HUMAN FORM.
YOU...YOU'RE LYING! IT CAN'T BE TRUE... IT CAN'T!
CALEB WILL END UP IN THE DUNGEONS, WITH THE OTHER MURMURERS...
AND NOW, YOU HAVE TO DECIDE WHICH SIDE YOU'RE ON. THINK ABOUT IT, CORNELIA!
AND REMEMBER THAT BY ADMITTING YOUR GUILT, YOU WON'T HAVE TO BE JUDGED BY THE CONGREGATION OF KANDRAKAR!

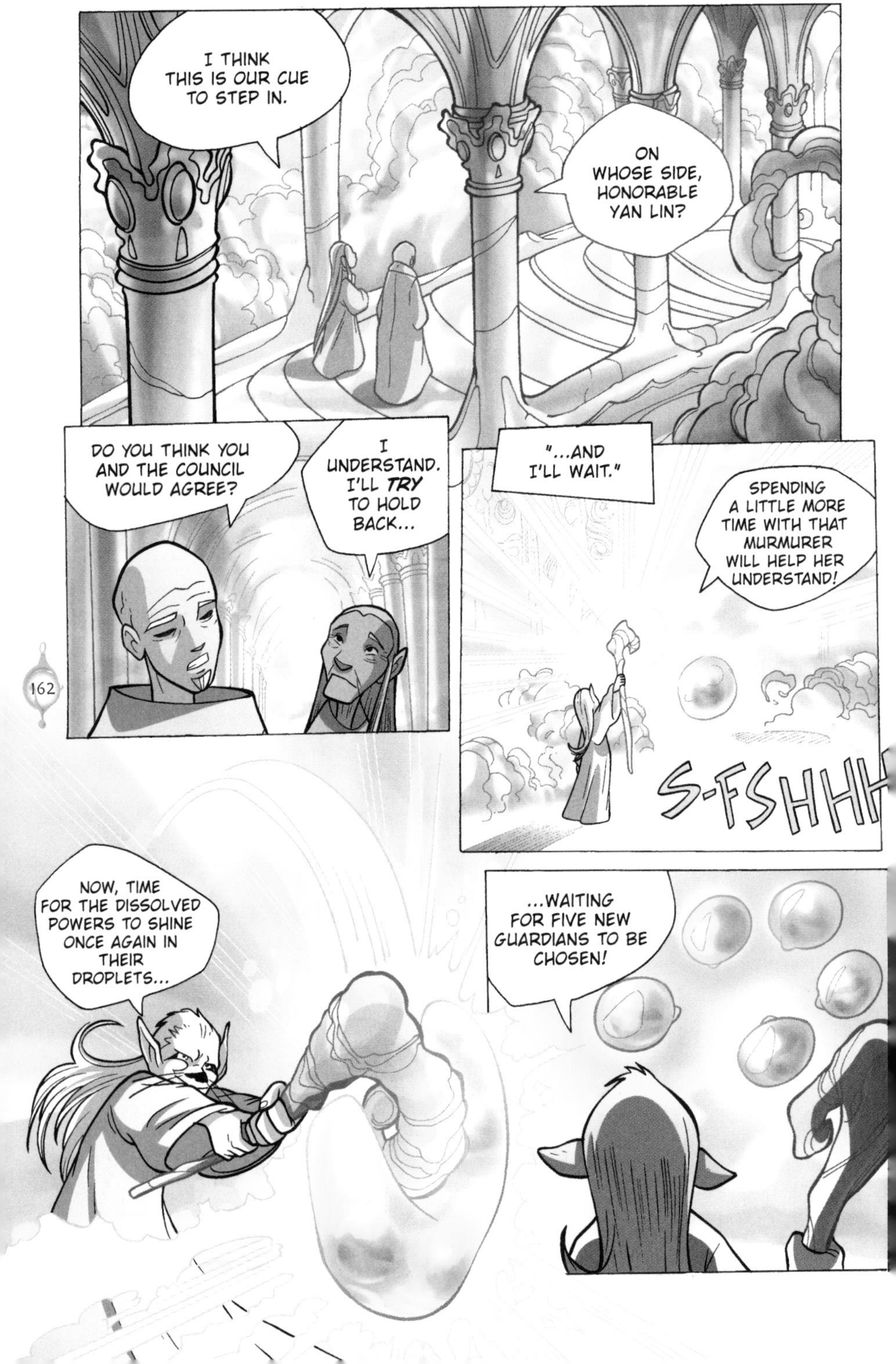

I THINK THIS IS OUR CUE TO STEP IN.
ON WHOSE SIDE, HONORABLE YAN LIN?
DO YOU THINK YOU AND THE COUNCIL WOULD AGREE?
I UNDERSTAND. I'LL *TRY* TO HOLD BACK...
"...AND I'LL WAIT."
SPENDING A LITTLE MORE TIME WITH THAT MURMURER WILL HELP HER UNDERSTAND!
S-FSHHH
NOW, TIME FOR THE DISSOLVED POWERS TO SHINE ONCE AGAIN IN THEIR DROPLETS...
...WAITING FOR FIVE NEW GUARDIANS TO BE CHOSEN!

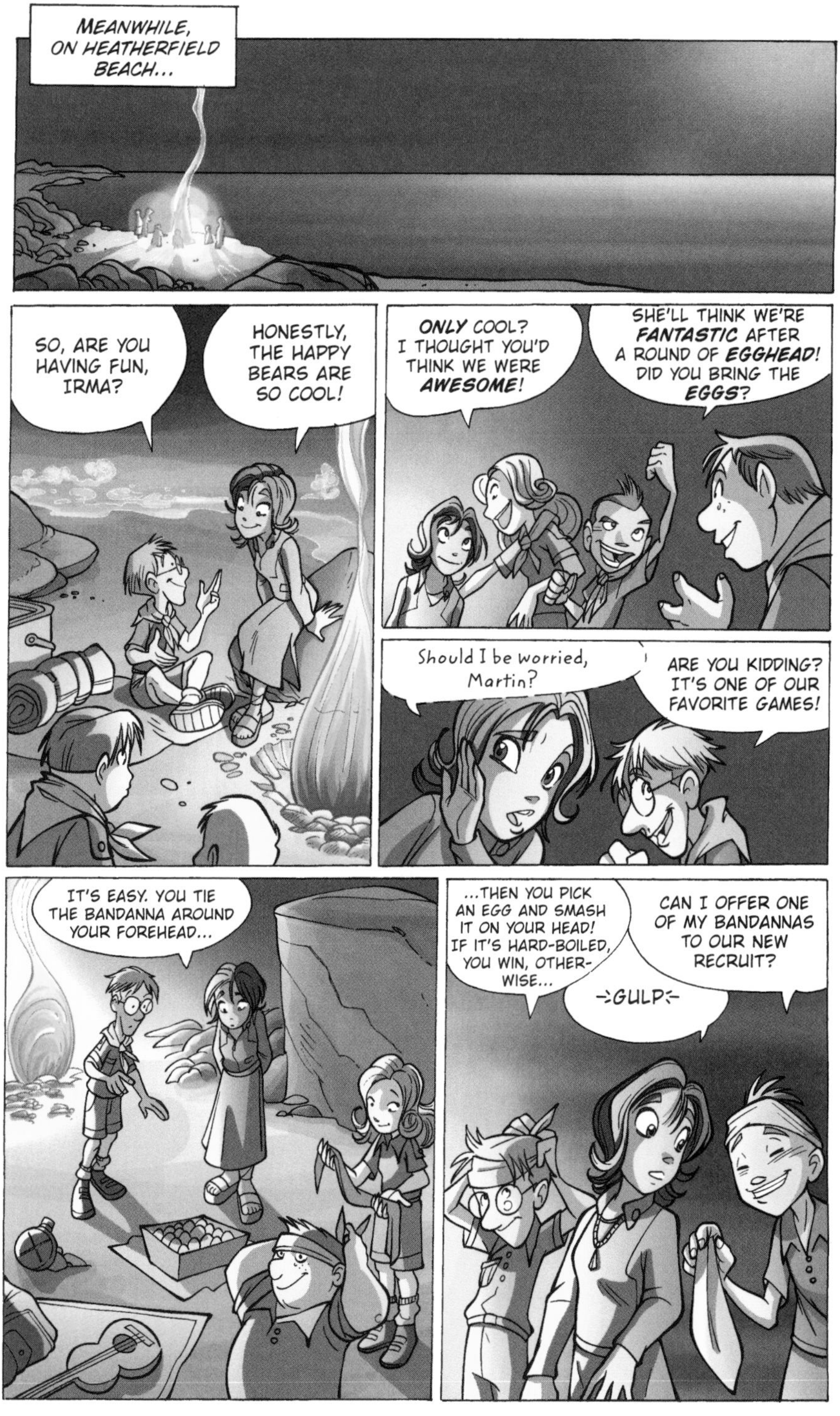
MEANWHILE, ON HEATHERFIELD BEACH...
SO, ARE YOU HAVING FUN, IRMA?
HONESTLY, THE HAPPY BEARS ARE SO COOL!
ONLY COOL? I THOUGHT YOU'D THINK WE WERE AWESOME!
SHE'LL THINK WE'RE FANTASTIC AFTER A ROUND OF EGGHEAD! DID YOU BRING THE EGGS?
Should I be worried, Martin?
ARE YOU KIDDING? IT'S ONE OF OUR FAVORITE GAMES!
IT'S EASY. YOU TIE THE BANDANNA AROUND YOUR FOREHEAD...
...THEN YOU PICK AN EGG AND SMASH IT ON YOUR HEAD! IF IT'S HARD-BOILED, YOU WIN, OTHERWISE...
GULP
CAN I OFFER ONE OF MY BANDANNAS TO OUR NEW RECRUIT?

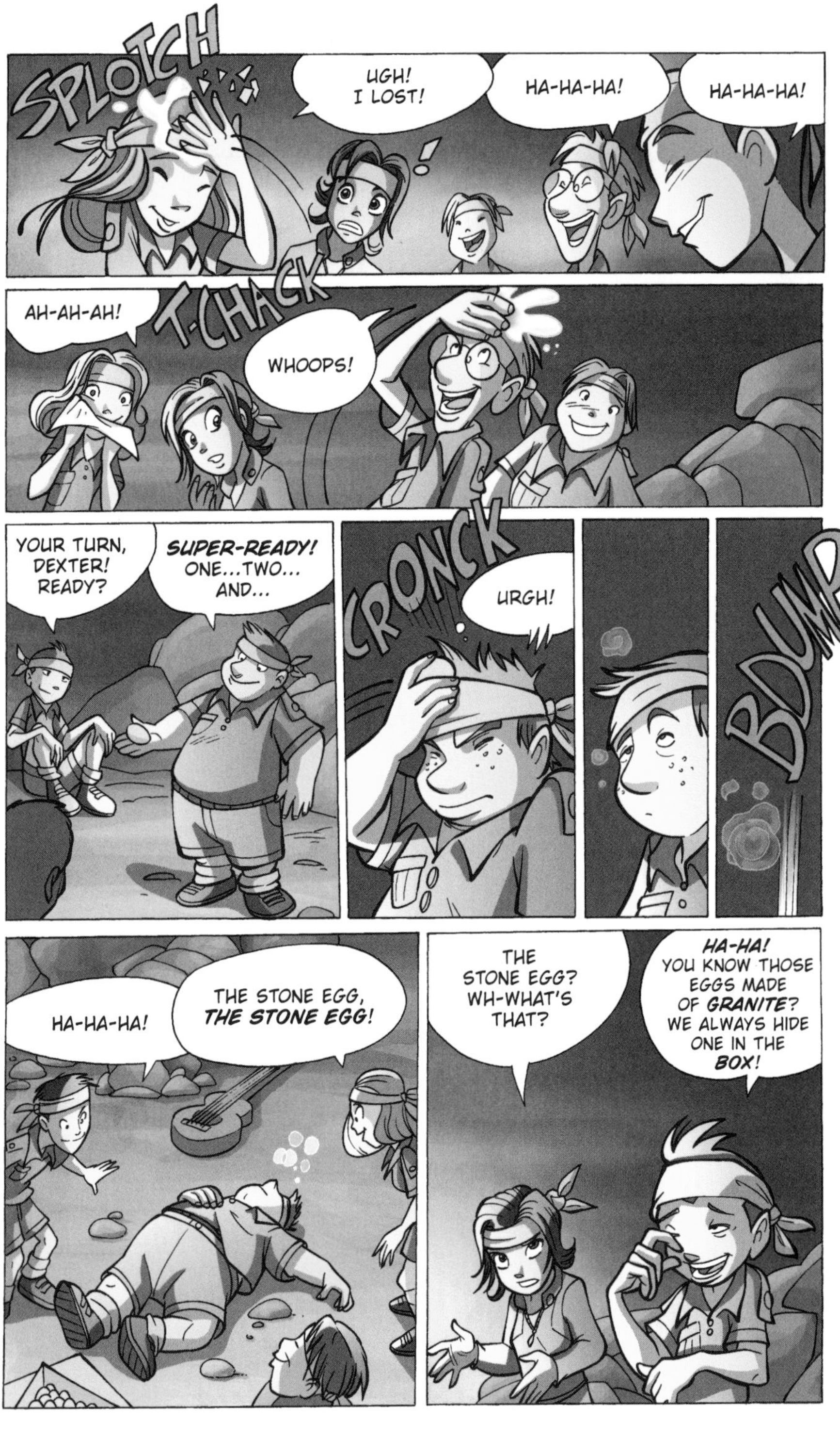
SPLOTCH
UGH! I LOST!
HA-HA-HA!
HA-HA-HA!
AH-AH-AH!
T-CHACK
WHOOPS!
YOUR TURN, DEXTER! READY?
SUPER-READY! ONE...TWO... AND...
CRONCK
URGH!
BDUMP
HA-HA-HA!
THE STONE EGG, THE STONE EGG!
THE STONE EGG? WH-WHAT'S THAT?
HA-HA! YOU KNOW THOSE EGGS MADE OF GRANITE? WE ALWAYS HIDE ONE IN THE BOX!

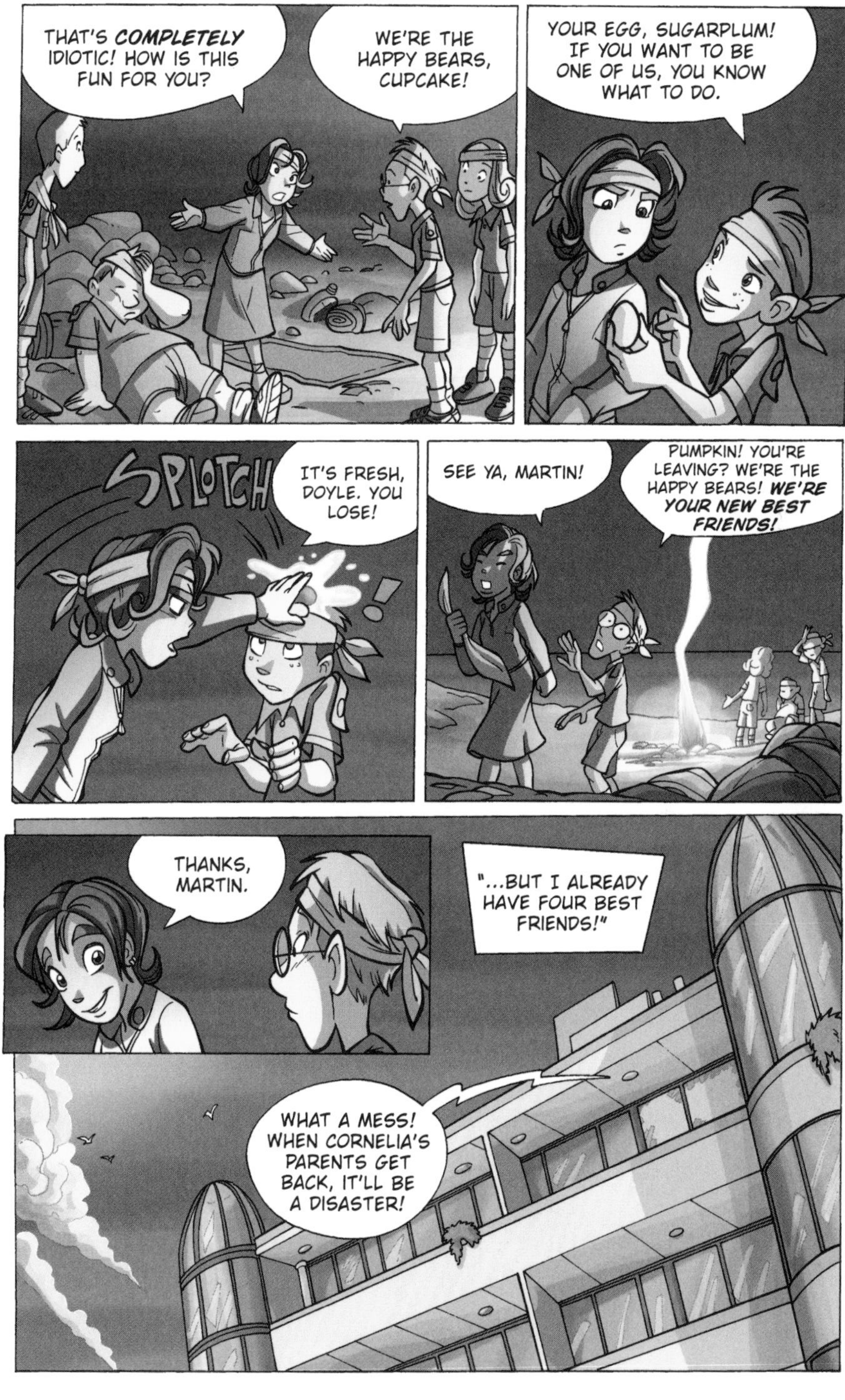
THAT'S COMPLETELY IDIOTIC! HOW IS THIS FUN FOR YOU?
WE'RE THE HAPPY BEARS, CUPCAKE!
YOUR EGG, SUGARPLUM! IF YOU WANT TO BE ONE OF US, YOU KNOW WHAT TO DO.
SPLOTCH
IT'S FRESH, DOYLE. YOU LOSE!
SEE YA, MARTIN!
PUMPKIN! YOU'RE LEAVING? WE'RE THE HAPPY BEARS! WE'RE YOUR NEW BEST FRIENDS!
THANKS, MARTIN.
"...BUT I ALREADY HAVE FOUR BEST FRIENDS!"
WHAT A MESS! WHEN CORNELIA'S PARENTS GET BACK, IT'LL BE A DISASTER!

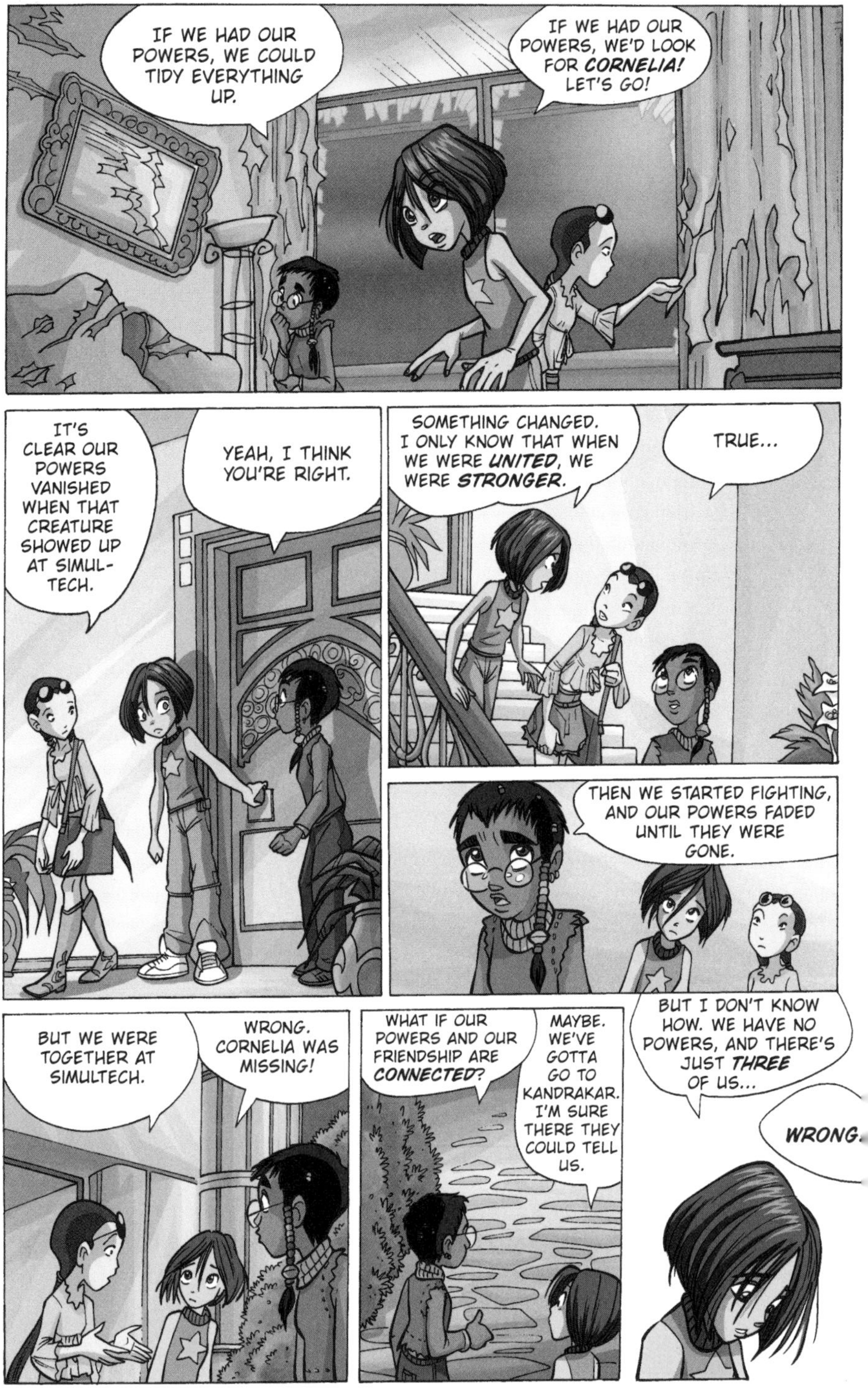

IF WE HAD OUR POWERS, WE COULD TIDY EVERYTHING UP.
IF WE HAD OUR POWERS, WE'D LOOK FOR CORNELIA! LET'S GO!
IT'S CLEAR OUR POWERS VANISHED WHEN THAT CREATURE SHOWED UP AT SIMUL-TECH.
YEAH, I THINK YOU'RE RIGHT.
SOMETHING CHANGED. I ONLY KNOW THAT WHEN WE WERE UNITED, WE WERE STRONGER.
TRUE...
THEN WE STARTED FIGHTING, AND OUR POWERS FADED UNTIL THEY WERE GONE.
BUT WE WERE TOGETHER AT SIMULTECH.
WRONG. CORNELIA WAS MISSING!
WHAT IF OUR POWERS AND OUR FRIENDSHIP ARE CONNECTED?
MAYBE. WE'VE GOTTA GO TO KANDRAKAR. I'M SURE THERE THEY COULD TELL US.
BUT I DON'T KNOW HOW. WE HAVE NO POWERS, AND THERE'S JUST THREE OF US...
WRONG.

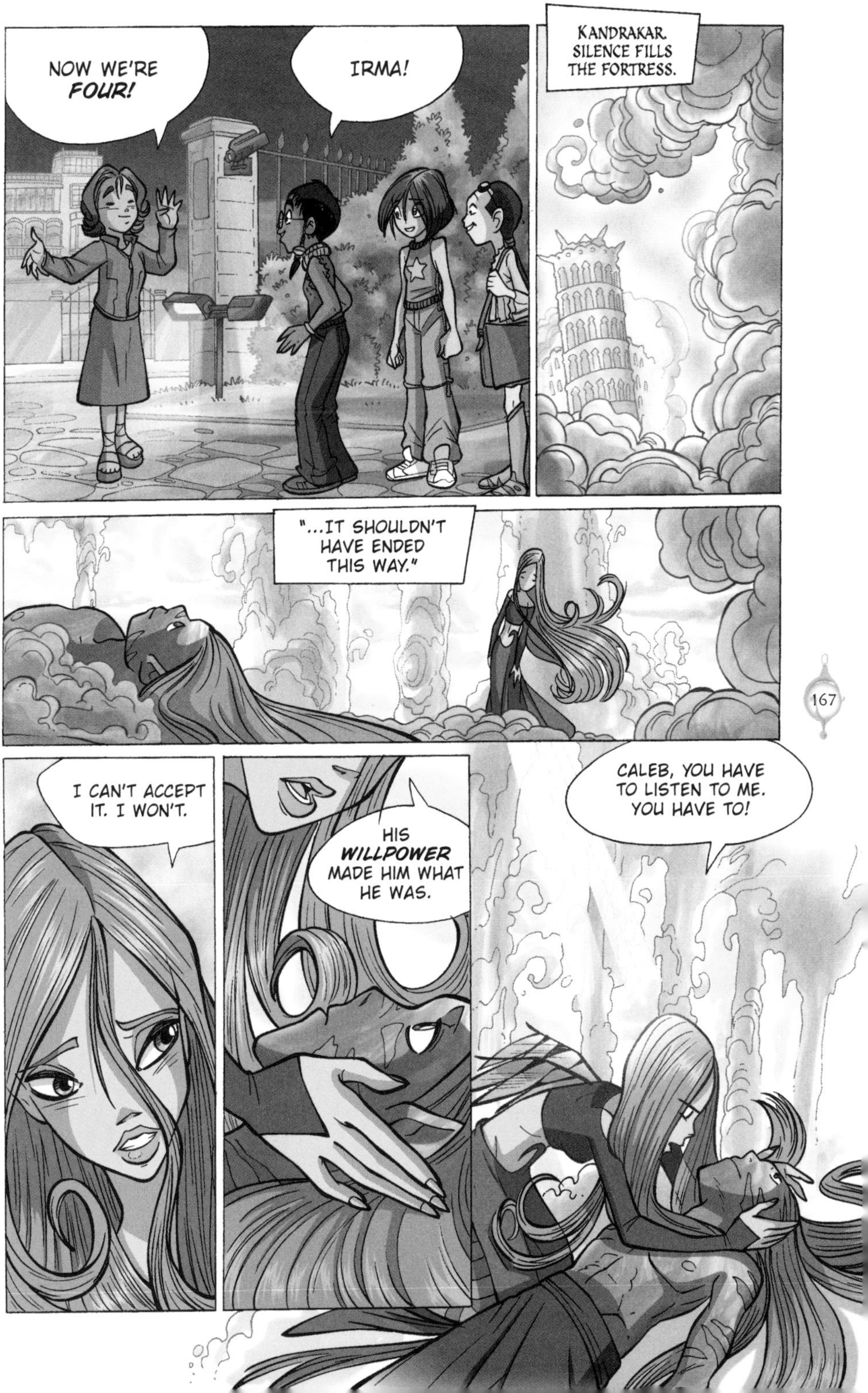

NOW WE'RE FOUR!
IRMA!
KANDRAKAR. SILENCE FILLS THE FORTRESS.
"...IT SHOULDN'T HAVE ENDED THIS WAY."
I CAN'T ACCEPT IT. I WON'T.
HIS WILLPOWER MADE HIM WHAT HE WAS.
CALEB, YOU HAVE TO LISTEN TO ME. YOU HAVE TO!

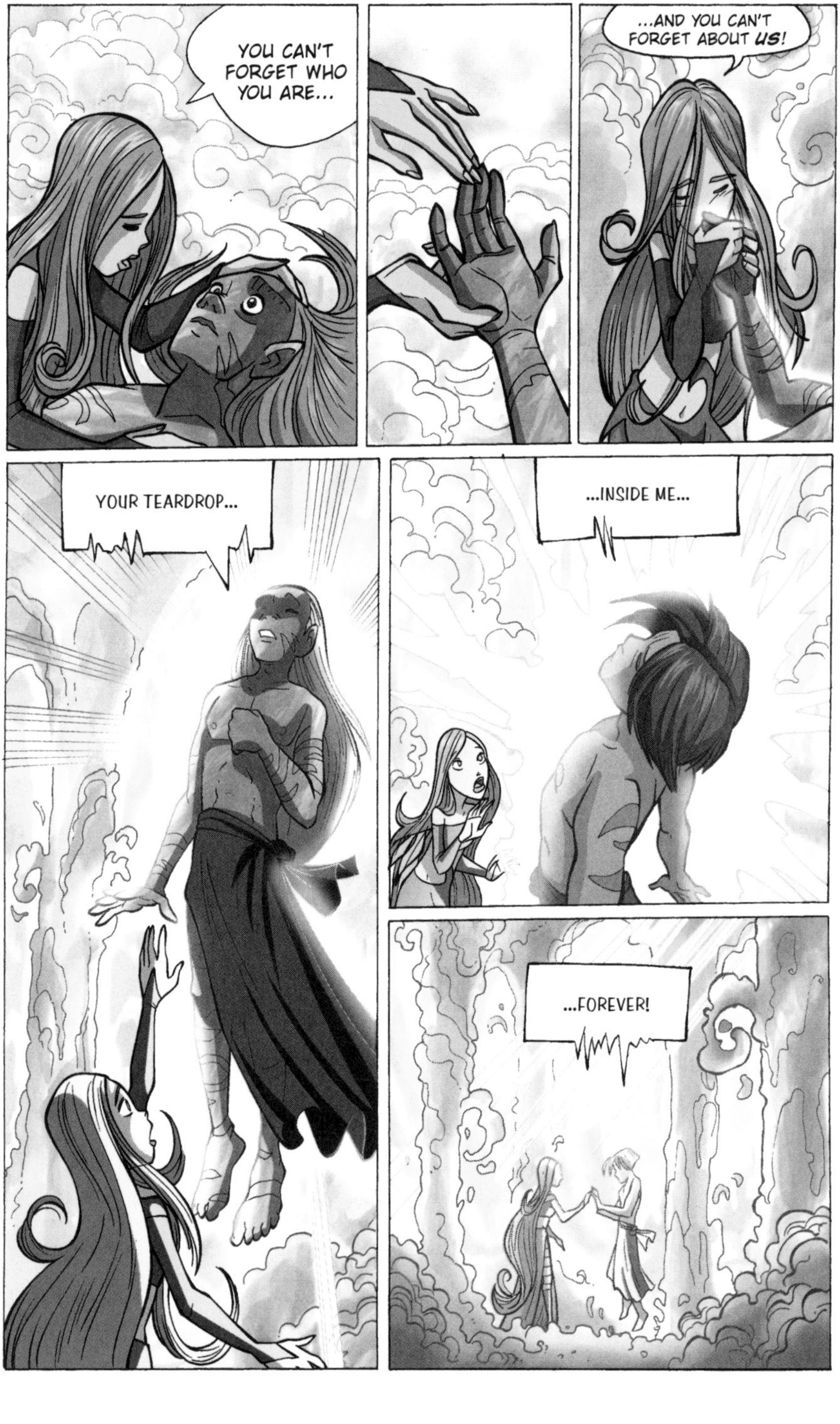

YOU CAN'T FORGET WHO YOU ARE...
...AND YOU CAN'T FORGET ABOUT US!
YOUR TEARDROP...
...INSIDE ME...
...FOREVER!

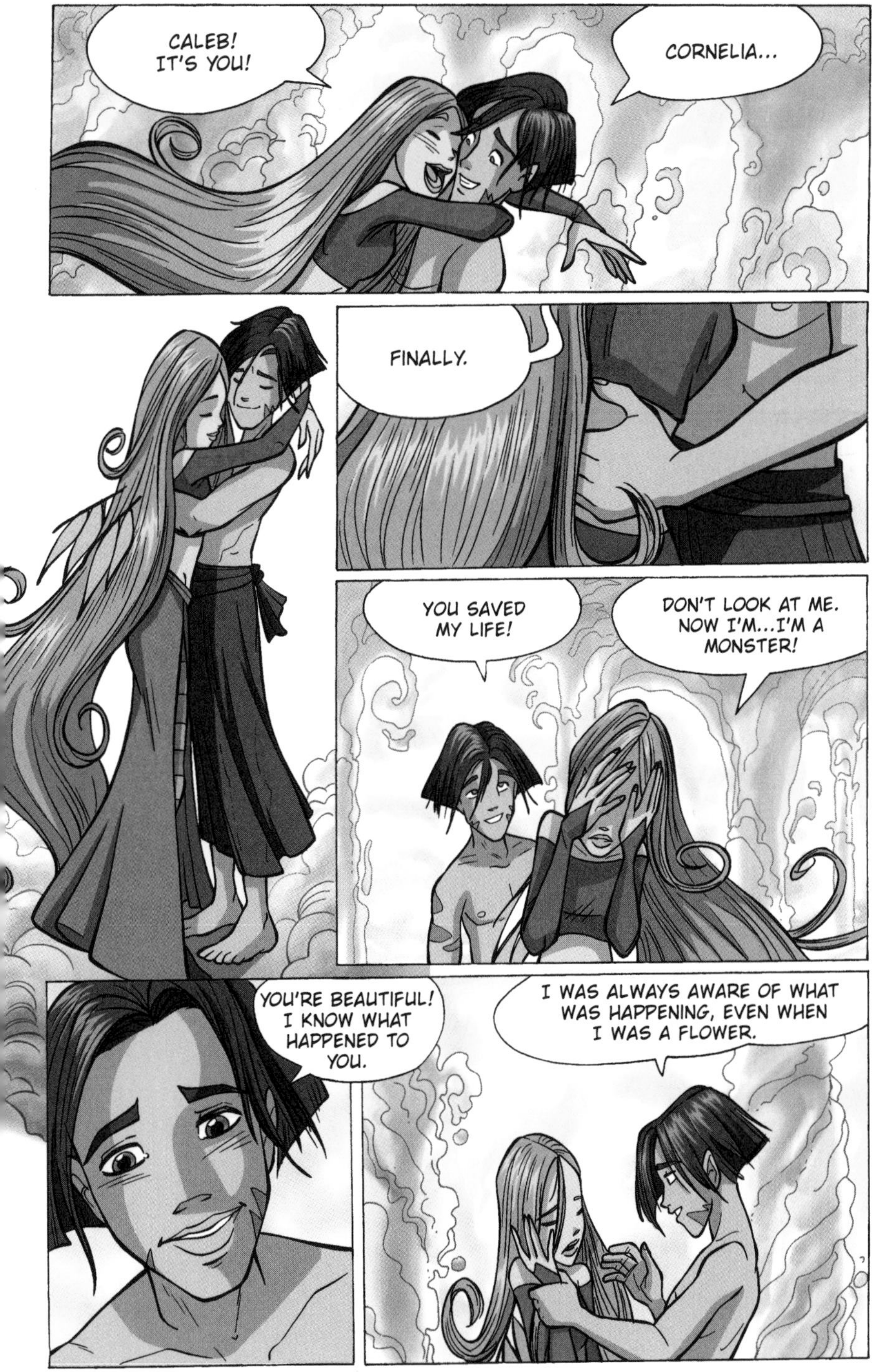

CALEB! IT'S YOU!
CORNELIA...
FINALLY.
YOU SAVED MY LIFE!
DON'T LOOK AT ME. NOW I'M...I'M A MONSTER!
YOU'RE BEAUTIFUL! I KNOW WHAT HAPPENED TO YOU.
I WAS ALWAYS AWARE OF WHAT WAS HAPPENING, EVEN WHEN I WAS A FLOWER.

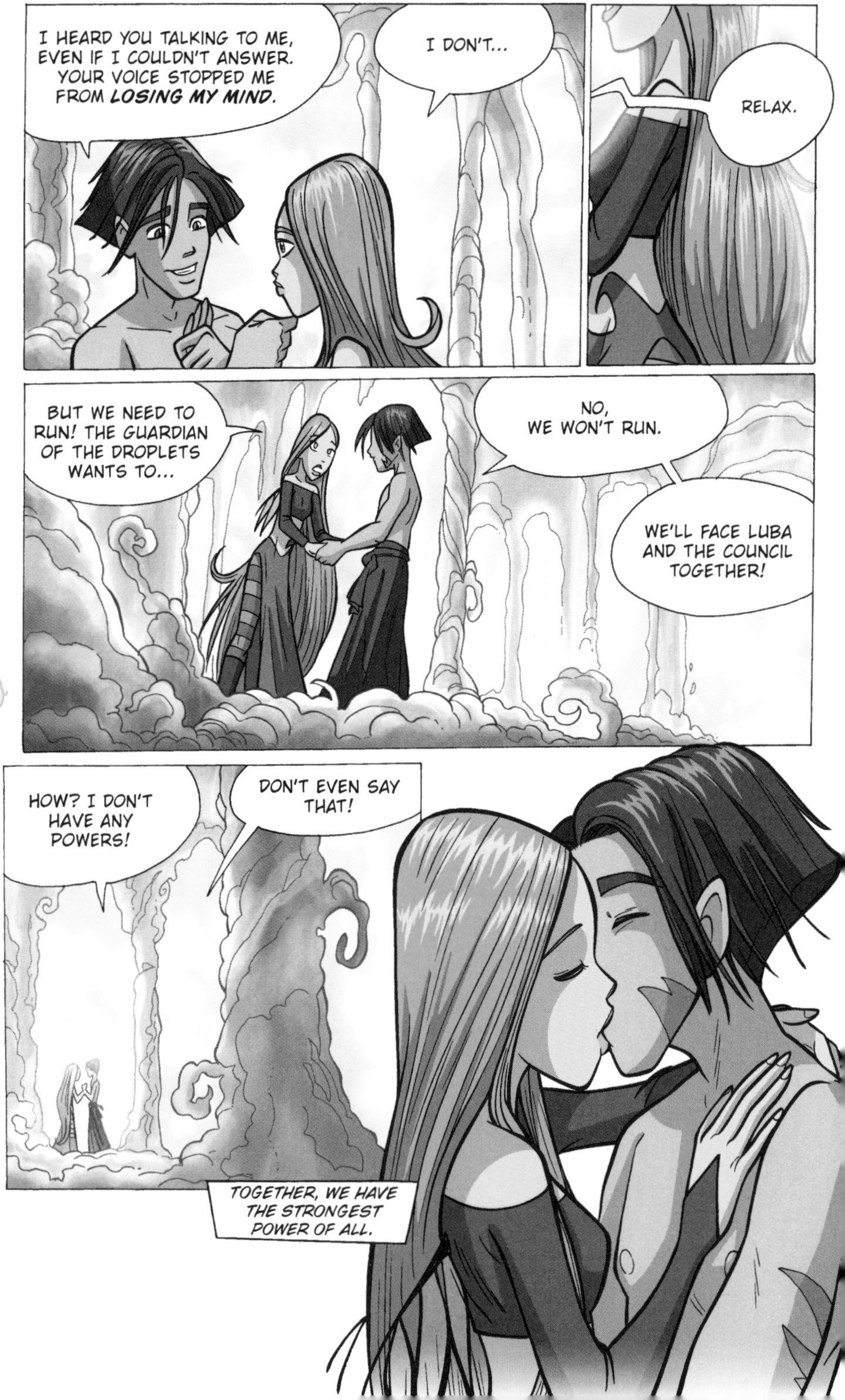
I HEARD YOU TALKING TO ME, EVEN IF I COULDN'T ANSWER. YOUR VOICE STOPPED ME FROM *LOSING MY MIND.*
I DON'T...
RELAX.
BUT WE NEED TO RUN! THE GUARDIAN OF THE DROPLETS WANTS TO...
NO, WE WON'T RUN.
WE'LL FACE LUBA AND THE COUNCIL TOGETHER!
HOW? I DON'T HAVE ANY POWERS!
DON'T EVEN SAY THAT!
TOGETHER, WE HAVE THE STRONGEST POWER OF ALL.

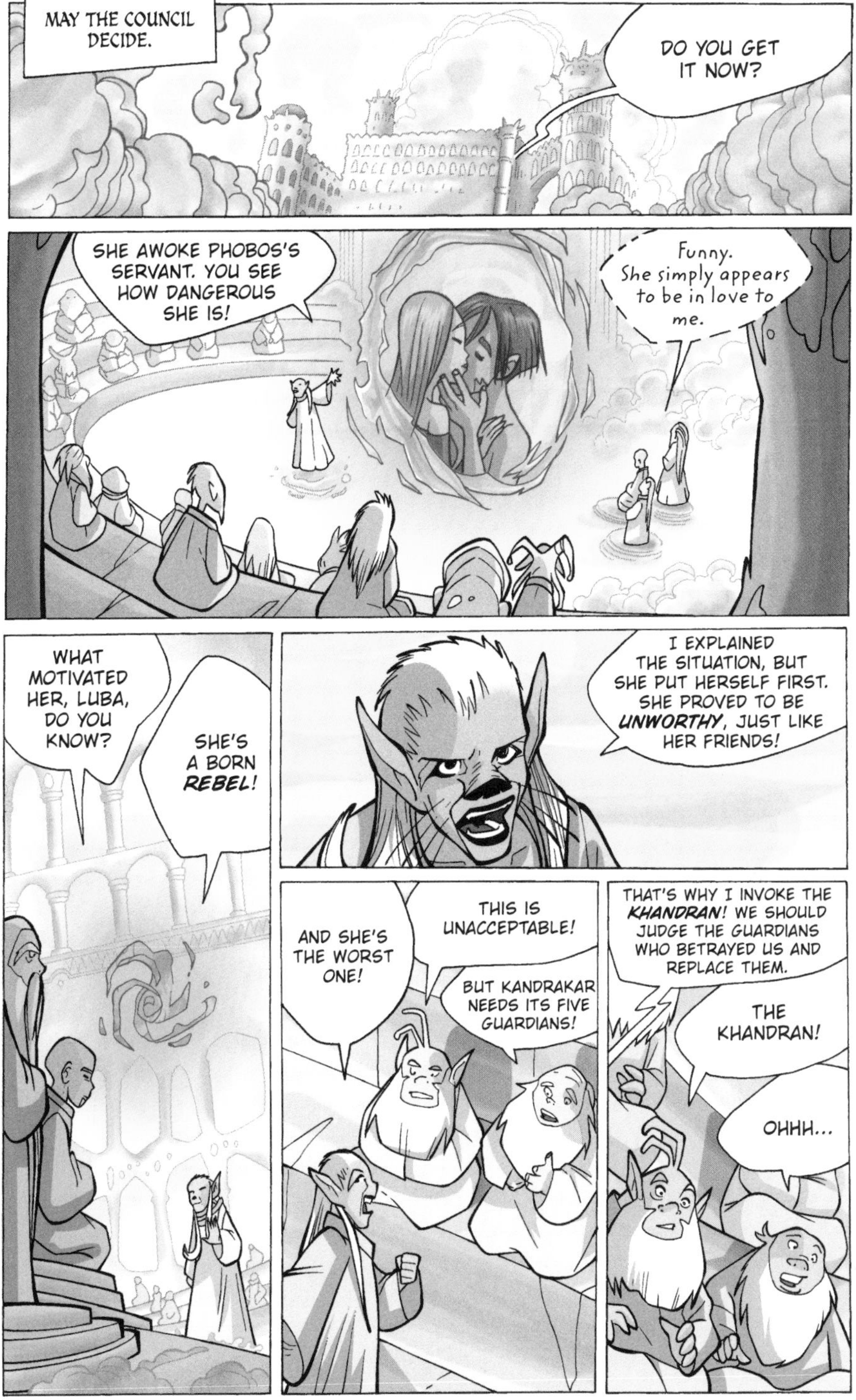
MAY THE COUNCIL DECIDE.
DO YOU GET IT NOW?
SHE AWOKE PHOBOS'S SERVANT. YOU SEE HOW DANGEROUS SHE IS!
Funny. She simply appears to be in love to me.
WHAT MOTIVATED HER, LUBA, DO YOU KNOW?
SHE'S A BORN *REBEL*!
I EXPLAINED THE SITUATION, BUT SHE PUT HERSELF FIRST. SHE PROVED TO BE *UNWORTHY*, JUST LIKE HER FRIENDS!
AND SHE'S THE WORST ONE!
THIS IS UNACCEPTABLE!
BUT KANDRAKAR NEEDS ITS FIVE GUARDIANS!
THAT'S WHY I INVOKE THE *KHANDRAN*! WE SHOULD JUDGE THE GUARDIANS WHO BETRAYED US AND REPLACE THEM.
THE KHANDRAN!
OHHH...

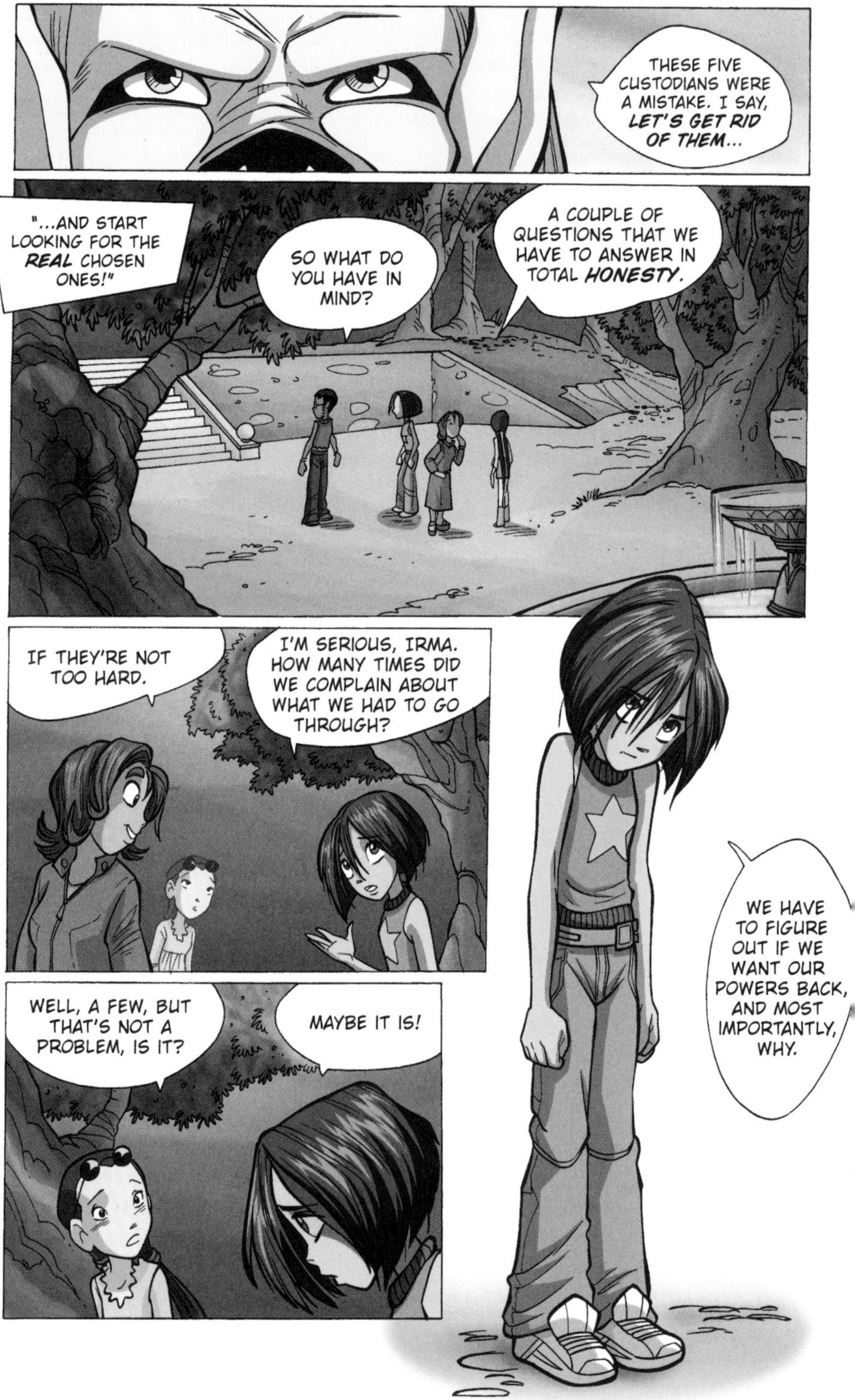
THESE FIVE CUSTODIANS WERE A MISTAKE. I SAY, LET'S GET RID OF THEM...
"...AND START LOOKING FOR THE REAL CHOSEN ONES!"
SO WHAT DO YOU HAVE IN MIND?
A COUPLE OF QUESTIONS THAT WE HAVE TO ANSWER IN TOTAL HONESTY.
IF THEY'RE NOT TOO HARD.
I'M SERIOUS, IRMA. HOW MANY TIMES DID WE COMPLAIN ABOUT WHAT WE HAD TO GO THROUGH?
WELL, A FEW, BUT THAT'S NOT A PROBLEM, IS IT?
MAYBE IT IS!
WE HAVE TO FIGURE OUT IF WE WANT OUR POWERS BACK, AND MOST IMPORTANTLY, WHY.

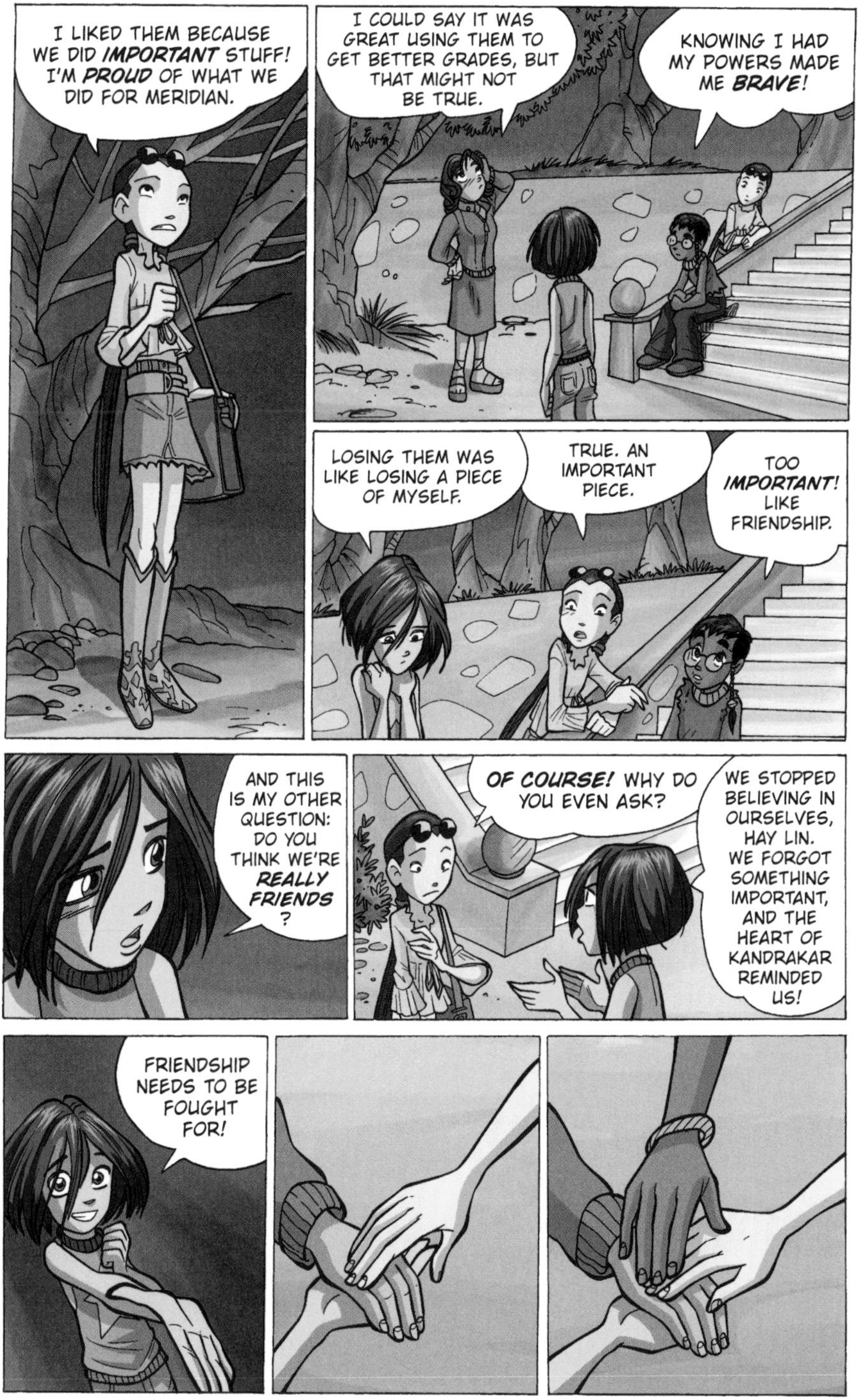
I LIKED THEM BECAUSE WE DID IMPORTANT STUFF! I'M PROUD OF WHAT WE DID FOR MERIDIAN.
I COULD SAY IT WAS GREAT USING THEM TO GET BETTER GRADES, BUT THAT MIGHT NOT BE TRUE.
KNOWING I HAD MY POWERS MADE ME BRAVE!
LOSING THEM WAS LIKE LOSING A PIECE OF MYSELF.
TRUE. AN IMPORTANT PIECE.
TOO IMPORTANT! LIKE FRIENDSHIP.
AND THIS IS MY OTHER QUESTION: DO YOU THINK WE'RE REALLY FRIENDS ?
OF COURSE! WHY DO YOU EVEN ASK?
WE STOPPED BELIEVING IN OURSELVES, HAY LIN. WE FORGOT SOMETHING IMPORTANT, AND THE HEART OF KANDRAKAR REMINDED US!
FRIENDSHIP NEEDS TO BE FOUGHT FOR!

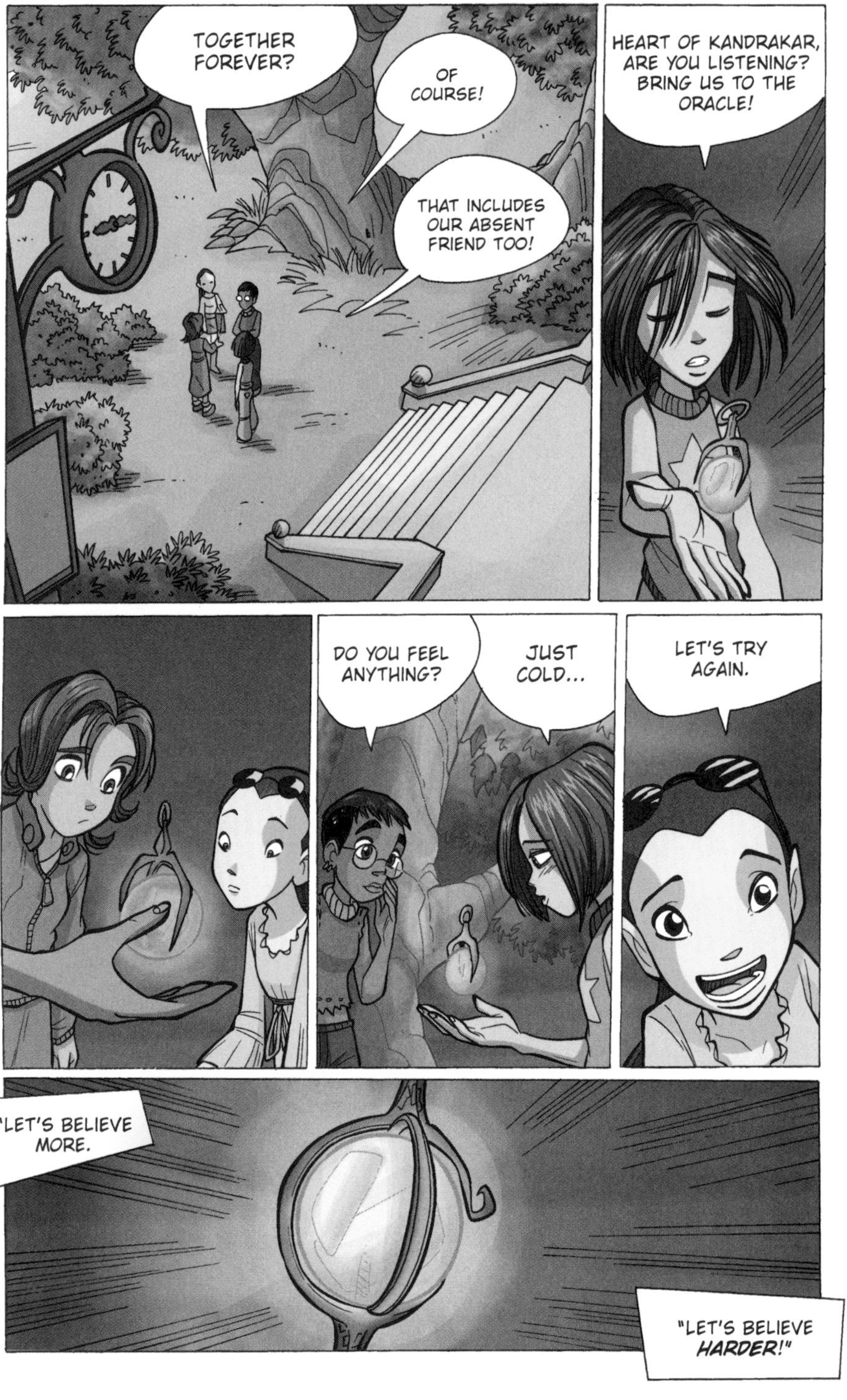
TOGETHER FOREVER?
OF COURSE!
THAT INCLUDES OUR ABSENT FRIEND TOO!
HEART OF KANDRAKAR, ARE YOU LISTENING? BRING US TO THE ORACLE!
DO YOU FEEL ANYTHING?
JUST COLD...
LET'S TRY AGAIN.
"LET'S BELIEVE MORE.
"LET'S BELIEVE *HARDER!*"

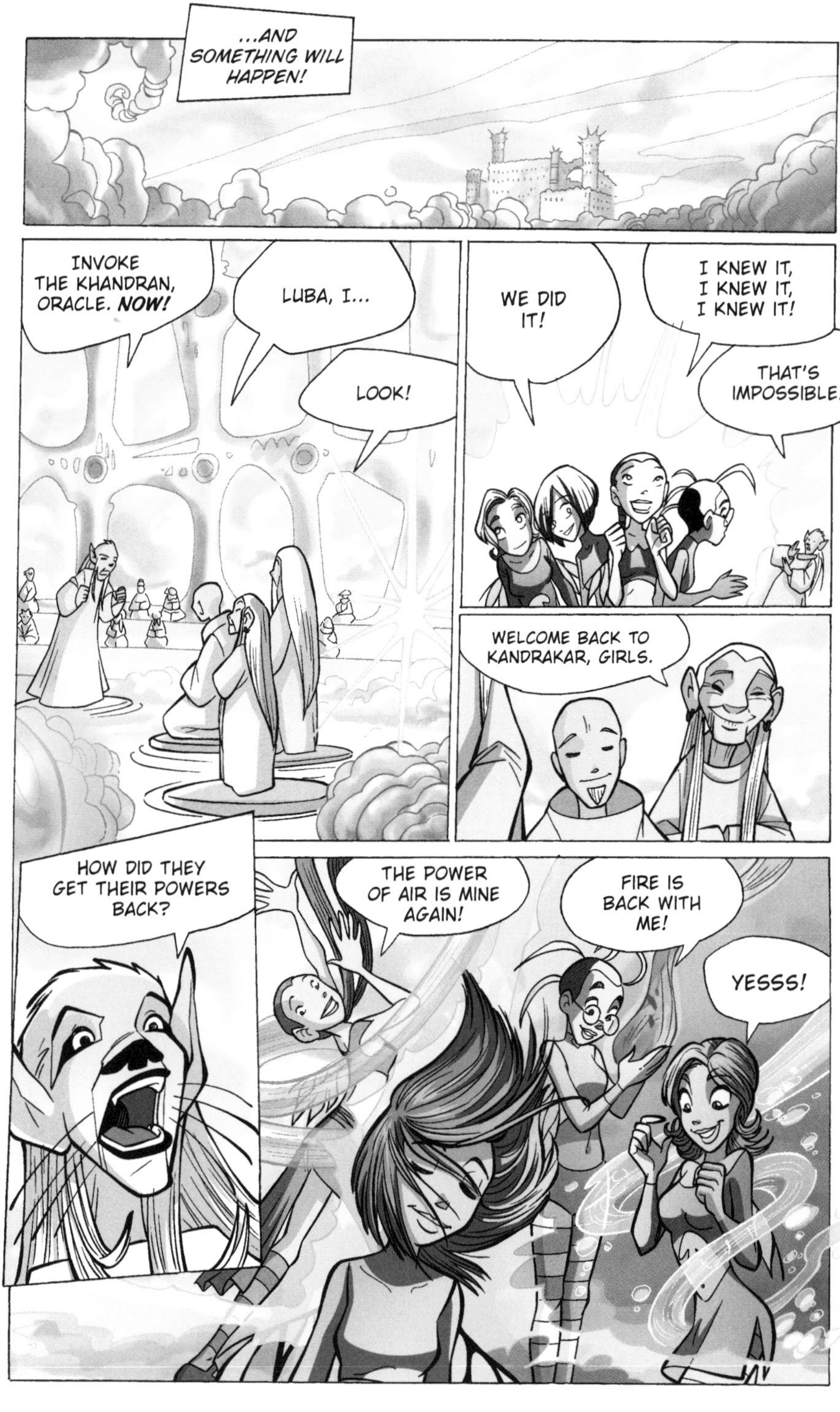
...AND SOMETHING WILL HAPPEN!
INVOKE THE KHANDRAN, ORACLE. NOW!
LUBA, I...
LOOK!
WE DID IT!
I KNEW IT, I KNEW IT, I KNEW IT!
THAT'S IMPOSSIBLE!
WELCOME BACK TO KANDRAKAR, GIRLS.
HOW DID THEY GET THEIR POWERS BACK?
THE POWER OF AIR IS MINE AGAIN!
FIRE IS BACK WITH ME!
YESSS!

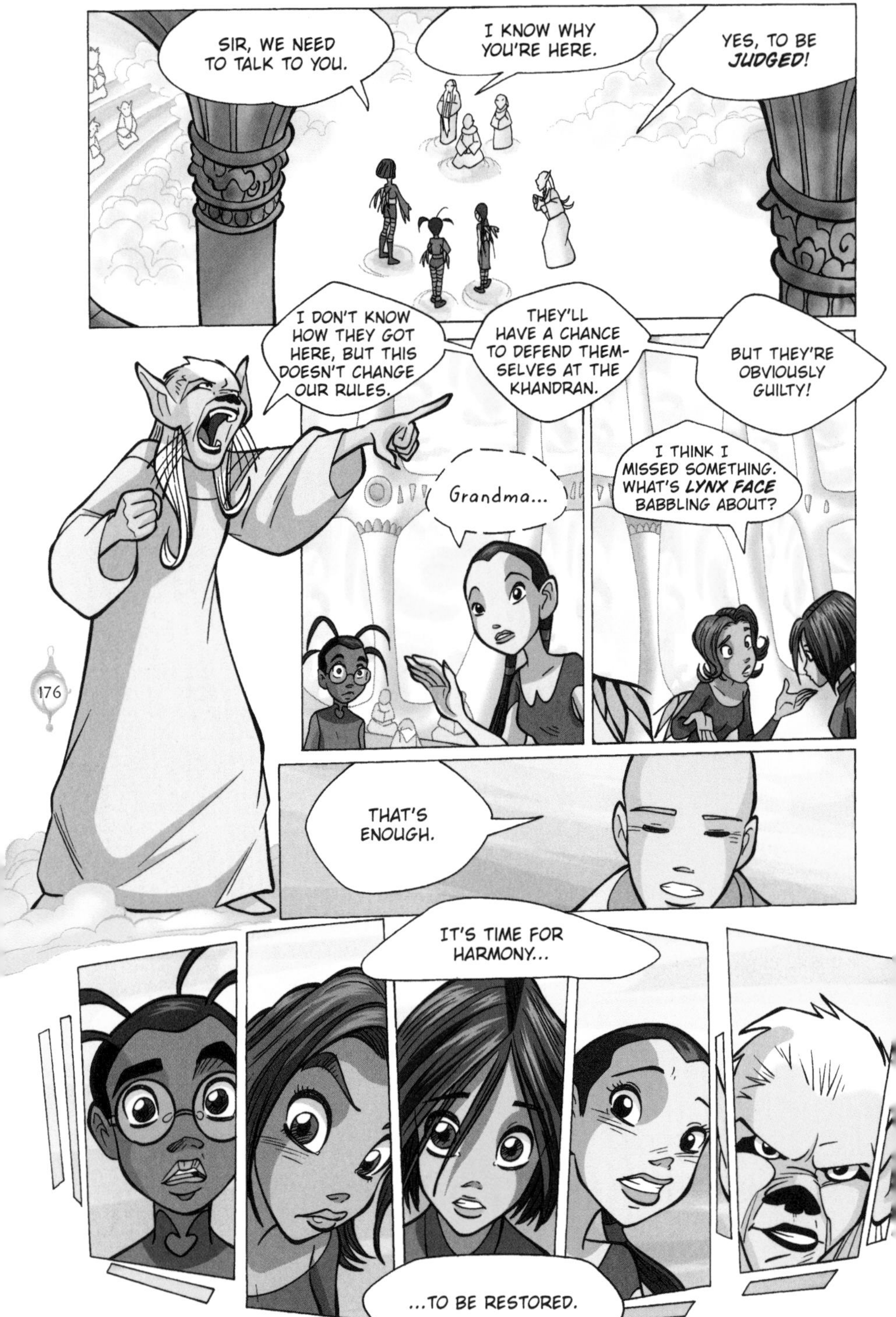
SIR, WE NEED TO TALK TO YOU.
I KNOW WHY YOU'RE HERE.
YES, TO BE JUDGED!
I DON'T KNOW HOW THEY GOT HERE, BUT THIS DOESN'T CHANGE OUR RULES.
THEY'LL HAVE A CHANCE TO DEFEND THEMSELVES AT THE KHANDRAN.
BUT THEY'RE OBVIOUSLY GUILTY!
Grandma...
I THINK I MISSED SOMETHING. WHAT'S LYNX FACE BABBLING ABOUT?
THAT'S ENOUGH.
IT'S TIME FOR HARMONY...
...TO BE RESTORED.

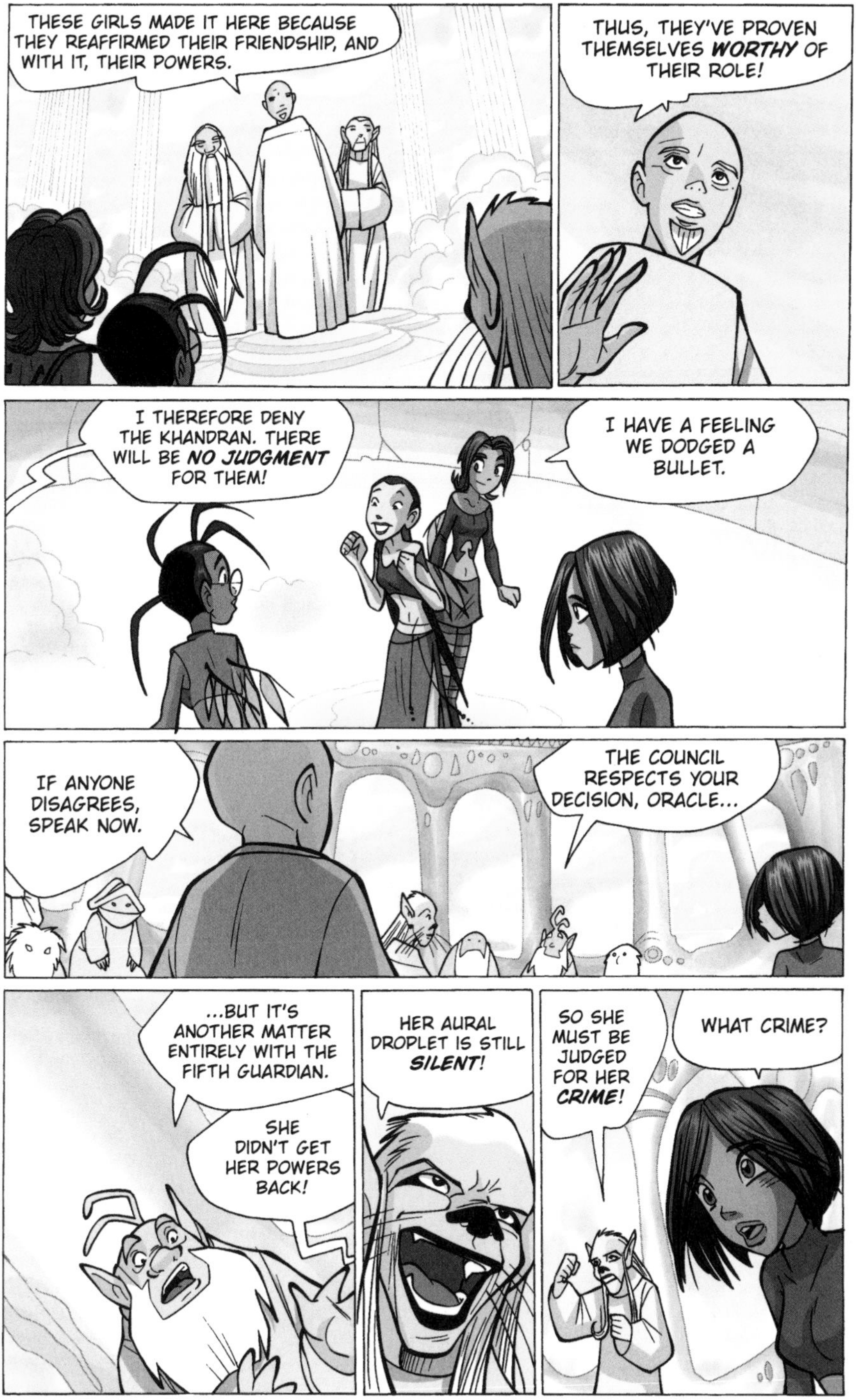

THESE GIRLS MADE IT HERE BECAUSE THEY REAFFIRMED THEIR FRIENDSHIP, AND WITH IT, THEIR POWERS.
THUS, THEY'VE PROVEN THEMSELVES WORTHY OF THEIR ROLE!
I THEREFORE DENY THE KHANDRAN. THERE WILL BE NO JUDGMENT FOR THEM!
I HAVE A FEELING WE DODGED A BULLET.
IF ANYONE DISAGREES, SPEAK NOW.
THE COUNCIL RESPECTS YOUR DECISION, ORACLE...
...BUT IT'S ANOTHER MATTER ENTIRELY WITH THE FIFTH GUARDIAN.
SHE DIDN'T GET HER POWERS BACK!
HER AURAL DROPLET IS STILL SILENT!
SO SHE MUST BE JUDGED FOR HER CRIME!
WHAT CRIME?

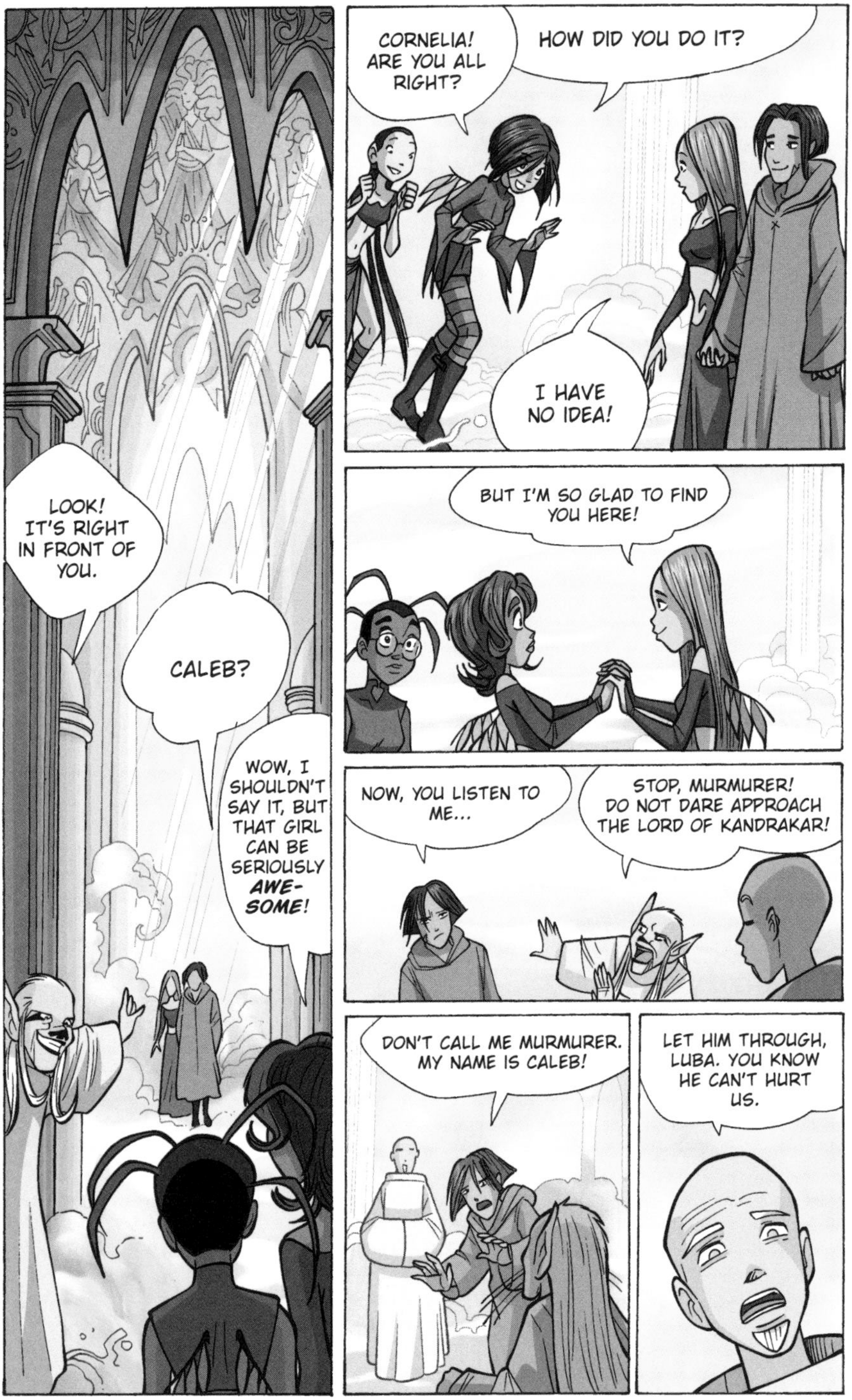
LOOK! IT'S RIGHT IN FRONT OF YOU.
CALEB?
WOW, I SHOULDN'T SAY IT, BUT THAT GIRL CAN BE SERIOUSLY **AWE-SOME**!
CORNELIA! ARE YOU ALL RIGHT?
HOW DID YOU DO IT?
I HAVE NO IDEA!
BUT I'M SO GLAD TO FIND YOU HERE!
NOW, YOU LISTEN TO ME...
STOP, MURMURER! DO NOT DARE APPROACH THE LORD OF KANDRAKAR!
DON'T CALL ME MURMURER. MY NAME IS CALEB!
LET HIM THROUGH, LUBA. YOU KNOW HE CAN'T HURT US.

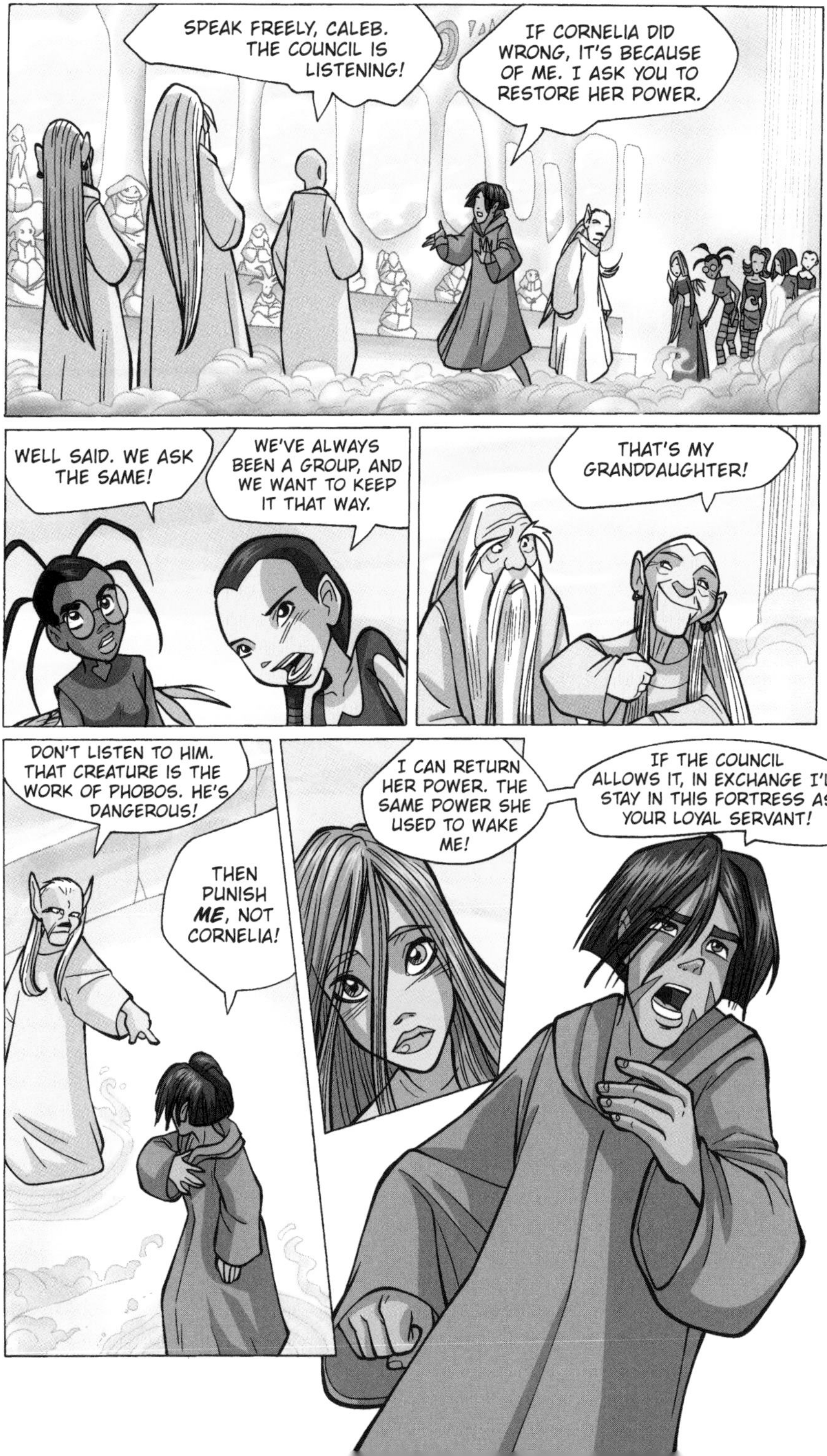
SPEAK FREELY, CALEB. THE COUNCIL IS LISTENING!
IF CORNELIA DID WRONG, IT'S BECAUSE OF ME. I ASK YOU TO RESTORE HER POWER.
WELL SAID. WE ASK THE SAME!
WE'VE ALWAYS BEEN A GROUP, AND WE WANT TO KEEP IT THAT WAY.
THAT'S MY GRANDDAUGHTER!
DON'T LISTEN TO HIM. THAT CREATURE IS THE WORK OF PHOBOS. HE'S DANGEROUS!
THEN PUNISH **ME**, NOT CORNELIA!
I CAN RETURN HER POWER. THE SAME POWER SHE USED TO WAKE ME!
IF THE COUNCIL ALLOWS IT, IN EXCHANGE I'LL STAY IN THIS FORTRESS AS YOUR LOYAL SERVANT!

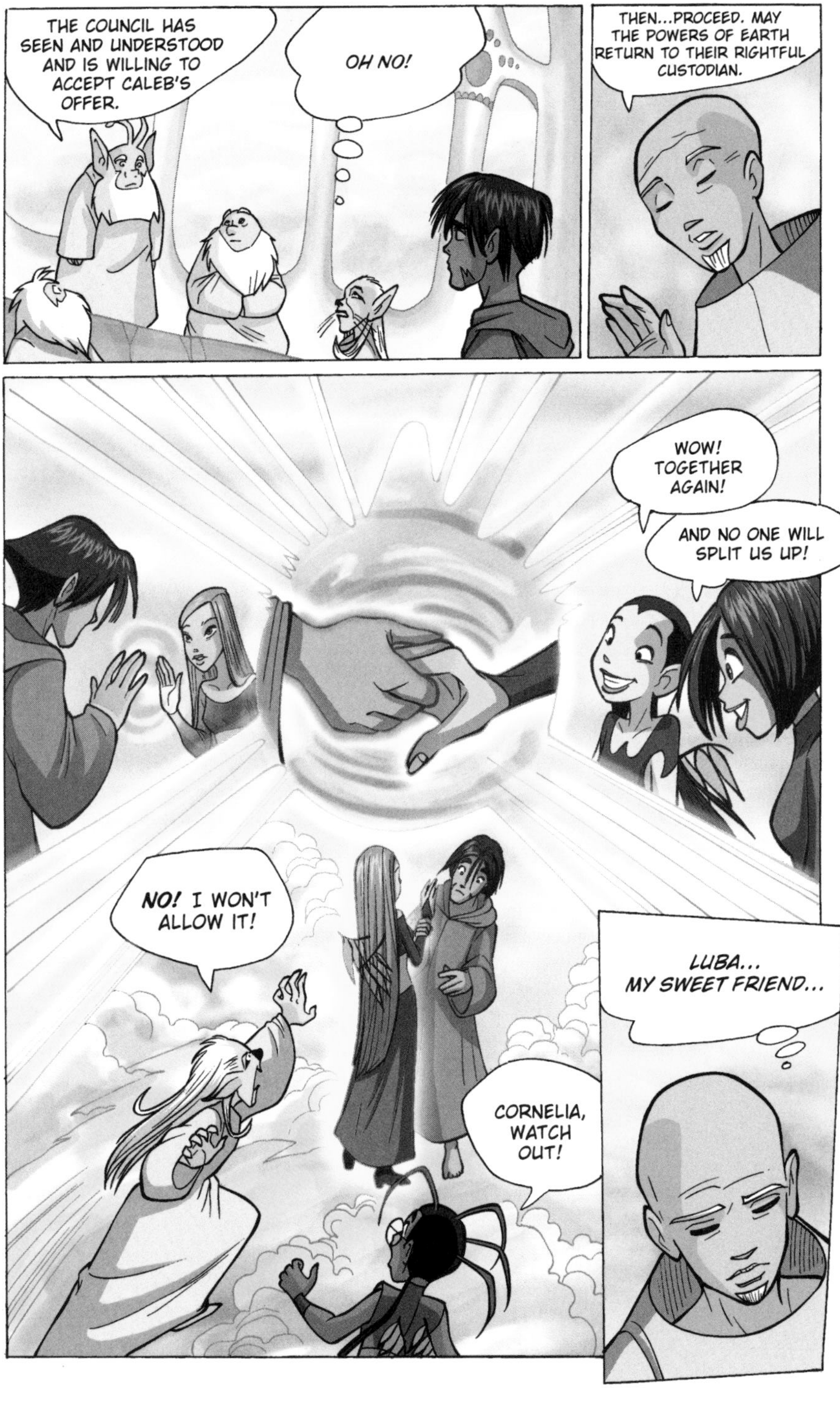

THE COUNCIL HAS SEEN AND UNDERSTOOD AND IS WILLING TO ACCEPT CALEB'S OFFER.
OH NO!
THEN...PROCEED. MAY THE POWERS OF EARTH RETURN TO THEIR RIGHTFUL CUSTODIAN.
WOW! TOGETHER AGAIN!
AND NO ONE WILL SPLIT US UP!
NO! I WON'T ALLOW IT!
CORNELIA, WATCH OUT!
LUBA... MY SWEET FRIEND...

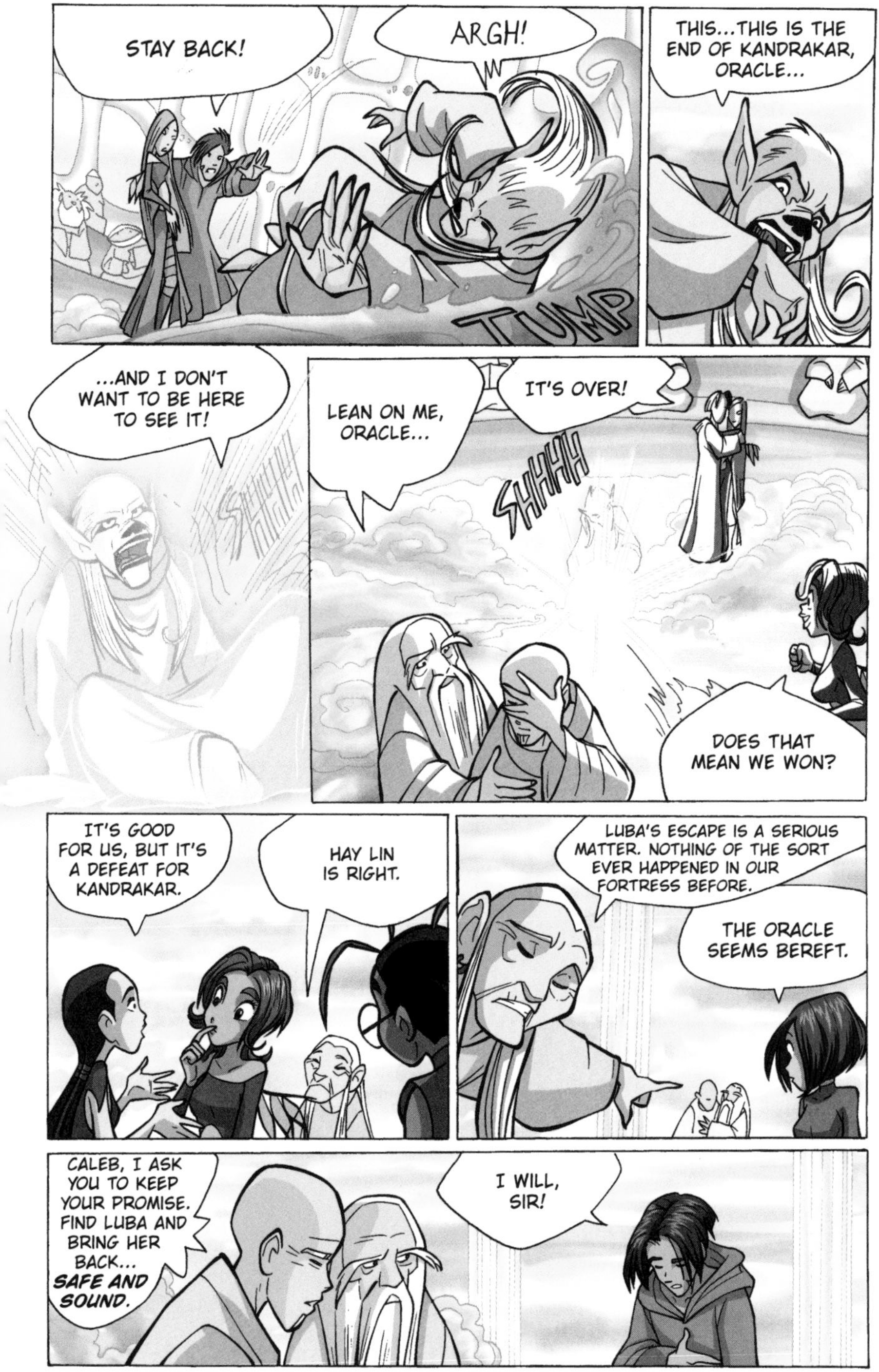
STAY BACK!
ARGH!
TUMP
THIS...THIS IS THE END OF KANDRAKAR, ORACLE...
...AND I DON'T WANT TO BE HERE TO SEE IT!
LEAN ON ME, ORACLE...
IT'S OVER!
SHHHH
DOES THAT MEAN WE WON?
IT'S GOOD FOR US, BUT IT'S A DEFEAT FOR KANDRAKAR.
HAY LIN IS RIGHT.
LUBA'S ESCAPE IS A SERIOUS MATTER. NOTHING OF THE SORT EVER HAPPENED IN OUR FORTRESS BEFORE.
THE ORACLE SEEMS BEREFT.
CALEB, I ASK YOU TO KEEP YOUR PROMISE. FIND LUBA AND BRING HER BACK... SAFE AND SOUND.
I WILL, SIR!

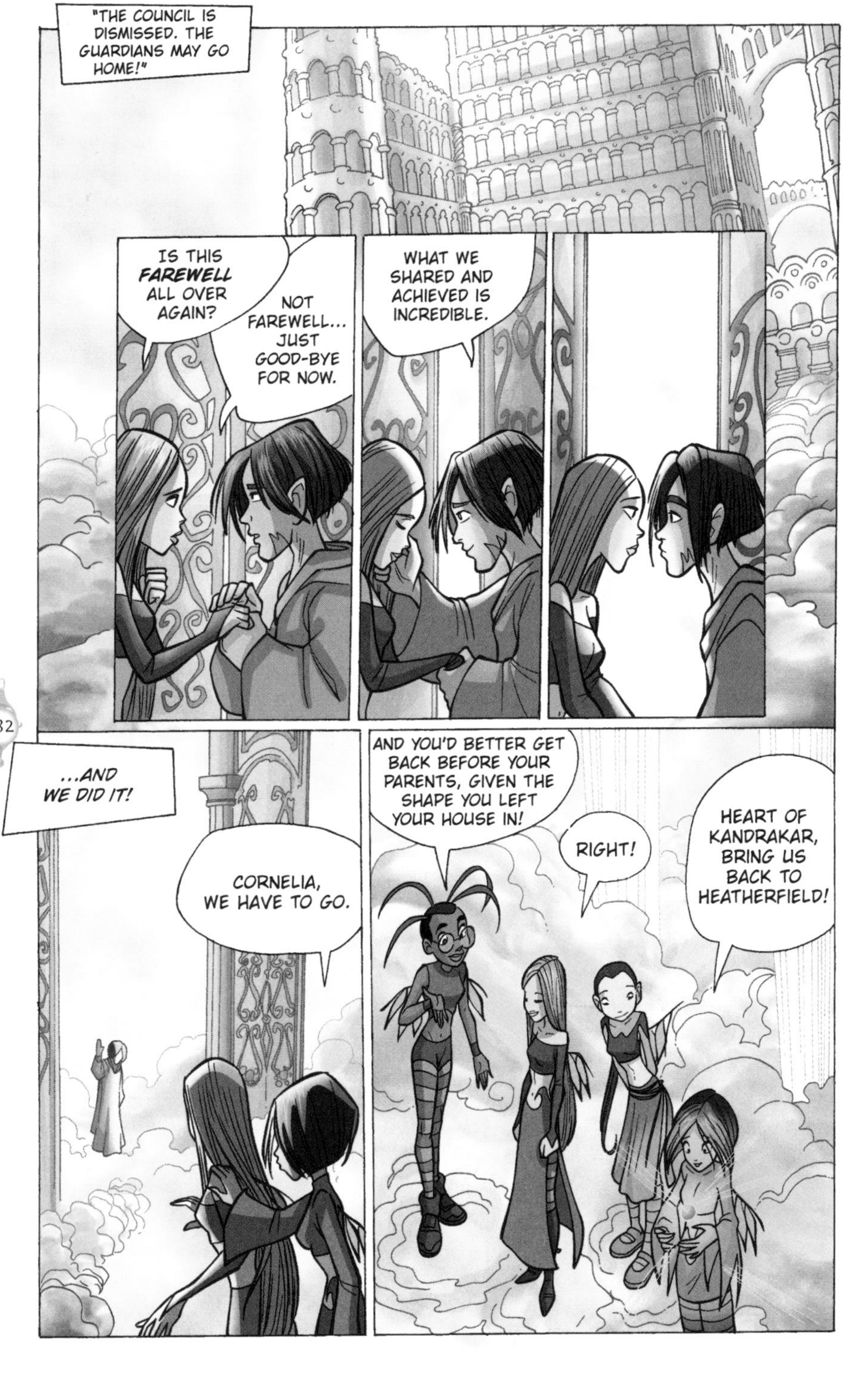
"THE COUNCIL IS DISMISSED. THE GUARDIANS MAY GO HOME!"
IS THIS **FAREWELL** ALL OVER AGAIN?
NOT FAREWELL... JUST GOOD-BYE FOR NOW.
WHAT WE SHARED AND ACHIEVED IS INCREDIBLE.
...AND WE DID IT!
CORNELIA, WE HAVE TO GO.
AND YOU'D BETTER GET BACK BEFORE YOUR PARENTS, GIVEN THE SHAPE YOU LEFT YOUR HOUSE IN!
RIGHT!
HEART OF KANDRAKAR, BRING US BACK TO HEATHERFIELD!

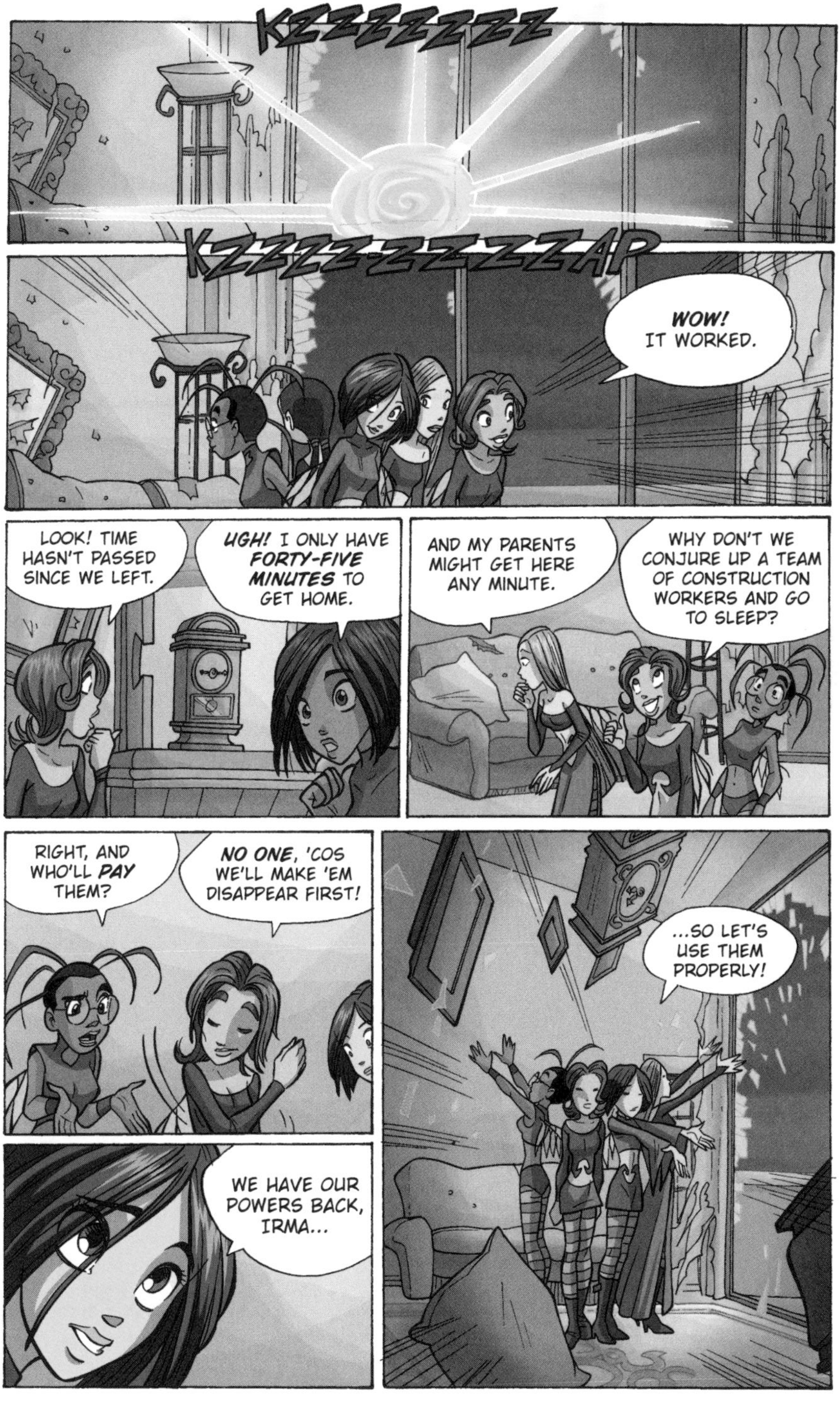
KZZZZZZZZ
KZZZZZZZZZZZZAP
WOW! IT WORKED.
LOOK! TIME HASN'T PASSED SINCE WE LEFT.
UGH! I ONLY HAVE FORTY-FIVE MINUTES TO GET HOME.
AND MY PARENTS MIGHT GET HERE ANY MINUTE.
WHY DON'T WE CONJURE UP A TEAM OF CONSTRUCTION WORKERS AND GO TO SLEEP?
RIGHT, AND WHO'LL PAY THEM?
NO ONE, 'COS WE'LL MAKE 'EM DISAPPEAR FIRST!
WE HAVE OUR POWERS BACK, IRMA...
...SO LET'S USE THEM PROPERLY!

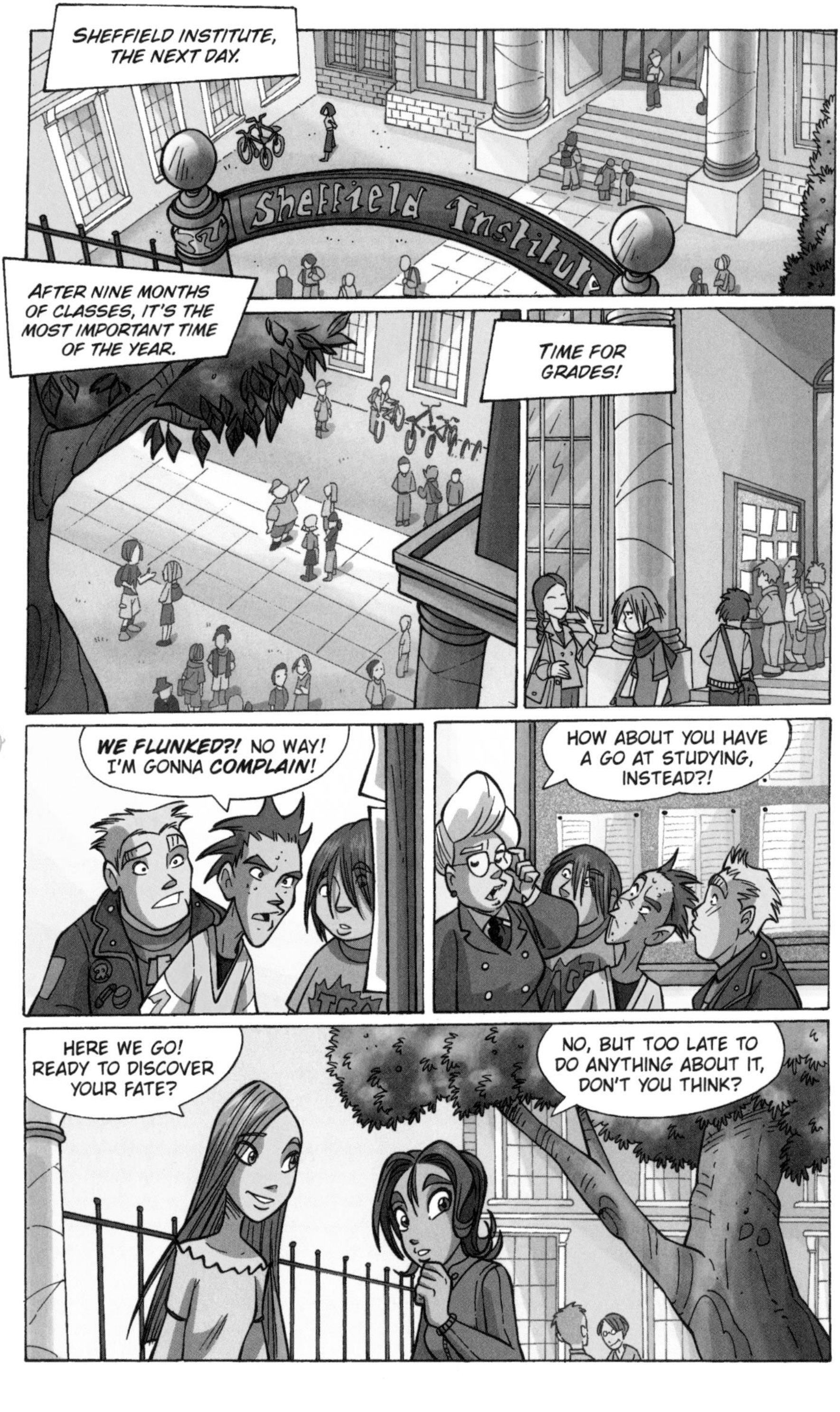
SHEFFIELD INSTITUTE, THE NEXT DAY.
Sheffield Institute
AFTER NINE MONTHS OF CLASSES, IT'S THE MOST IMPORTANT TIME OF THE YEAR.
TIME FOR GRADES!
WE FLUNKED?! NO WAY! I'M GONNA COMPLAIN!
HOW ABOUT YOU HAVE A GO AT STUDYING, INSTEAD?!
HERE WE GO! READY TO DISCOVER YOUR FATE?
NO, BUT TOO LATE TO DO ANYTHING ABOUT IT, DON'T YOU THINK?

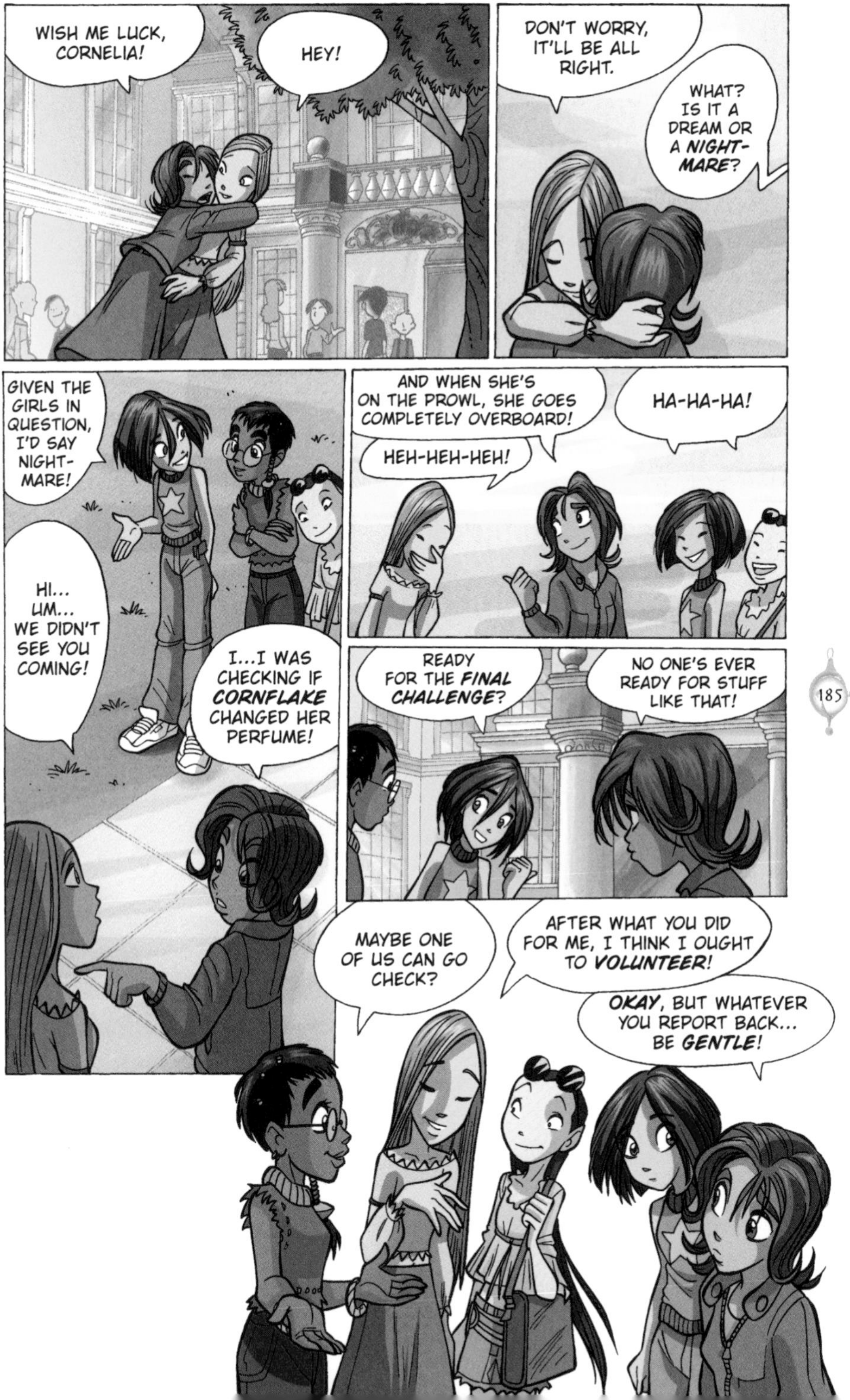
WISH ME LUCK, CORNELIA!
HEY!
DON'T WORRY, IT'LL BE ALL RIGHT.
WHAT? IS IT A DREAM OR A NIGHT-MARE?
GIVEN THE GIRLS IN QUESTION, I'D SAY NIGHT-MARE!
AND WHEN SHE'S ON THE PROWL, SHE GOES COMPLETELY OVERBOARD!
HA-HA-HA!
HEH-HEH-HEH!
HI... UM... WE DIDN'T SEE YOU COMING!
I...I WAS CHECKING IF CORNFLAKE CHANGED HER PERFUME!
READY FOR THE FINAL CHALLENGE?
NO ONE'S EVER READY FOR STUFF LIKE THAT!
MAYBE ONE OF US CAN GO CHECK?
AFTER WHAT YOU DID FOR ME, I THINK I OUGHT TO VOLUNTEER!
OKAY, BUT WHATEVER YOU REPORT BACK... BE GENTLE!

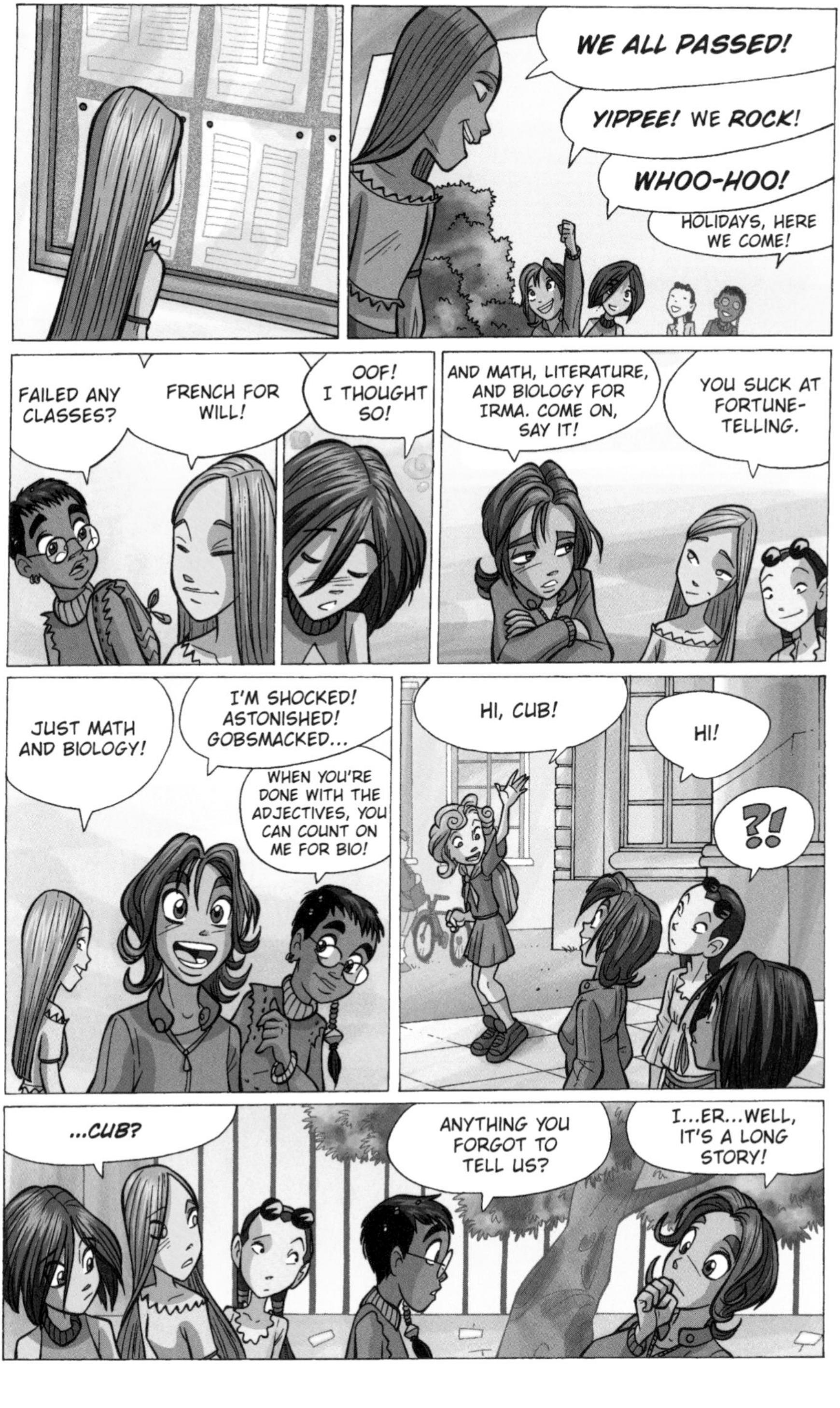
WE ALL PASSED!
YIPPEE! WE ROCK!
WHOO-HOO!
HOLIDAYS, HERE WE COME!
FAILED ANY CLASSES?
FRENCH FOR WILL!
OOF! I THOUGHT SO!
AND MATH, LITERATURE, AND BIOLOGY FOR IRMA. COME ON, SAY IT!
YOU SUCK AT FORTUNE-TELLING.
JUST MATH AND BIOLOGY!
I'M SHOCKED! ASTONISHED! GOBSMACKED...
WHEN YOU'RE DONE WITH THE ADJECTIVES, YOU CAN COUNT ON ME FOR BIO!
HI, CUB!
HI!
?!
...CUB?
ANYTHING YOU FORGOT TO TELL US?
I...ER...WELL, IT'S A LONG STORY!

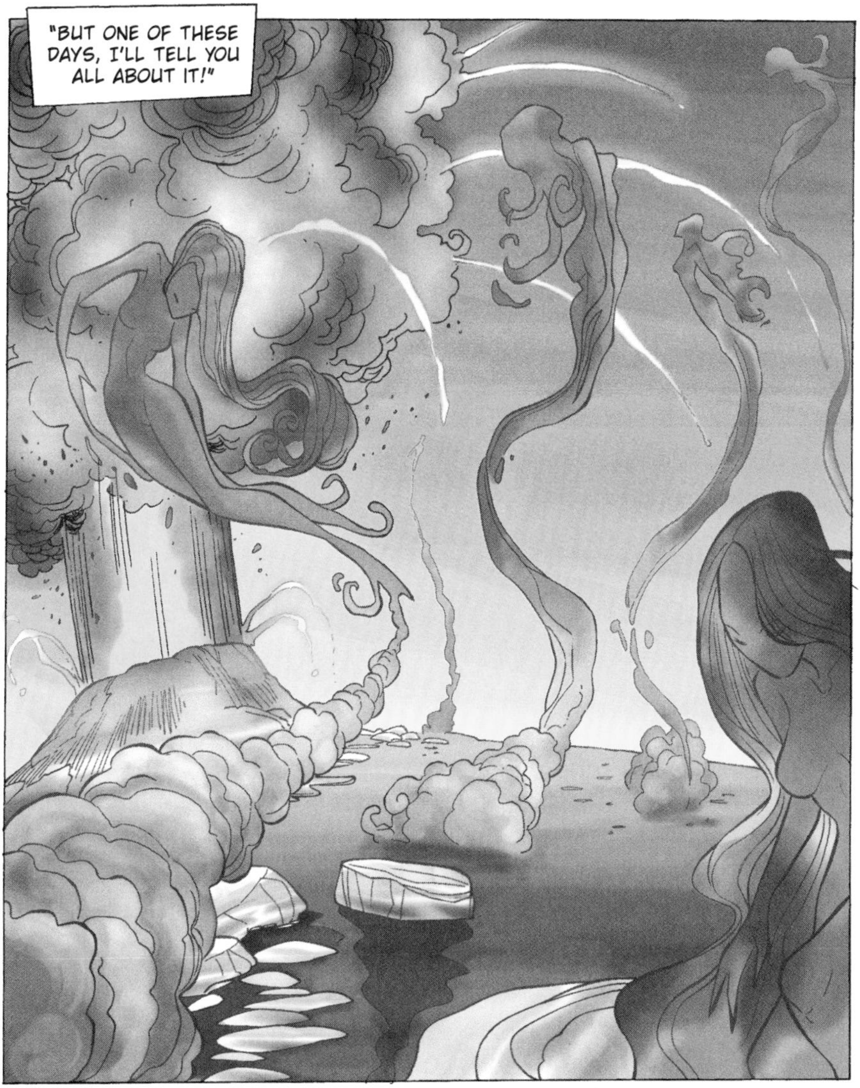
"BUT ONE OF THESE DAYS, I'LL TELL YOU ALL ABOUT IT!"

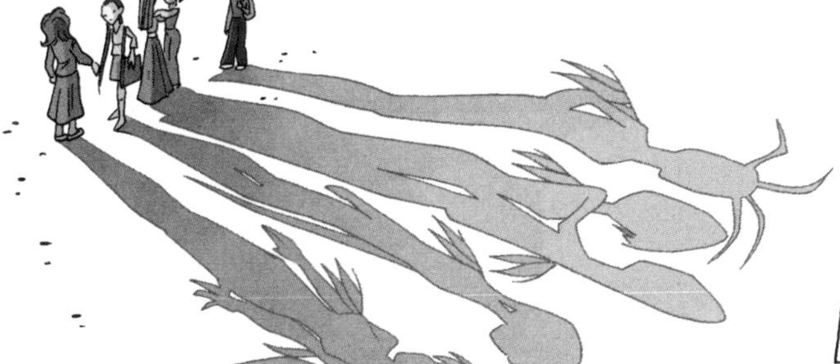

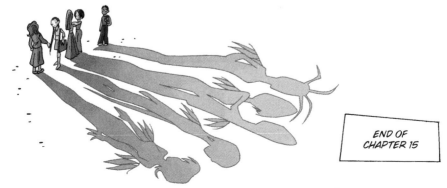

END OF CHAPTER 15

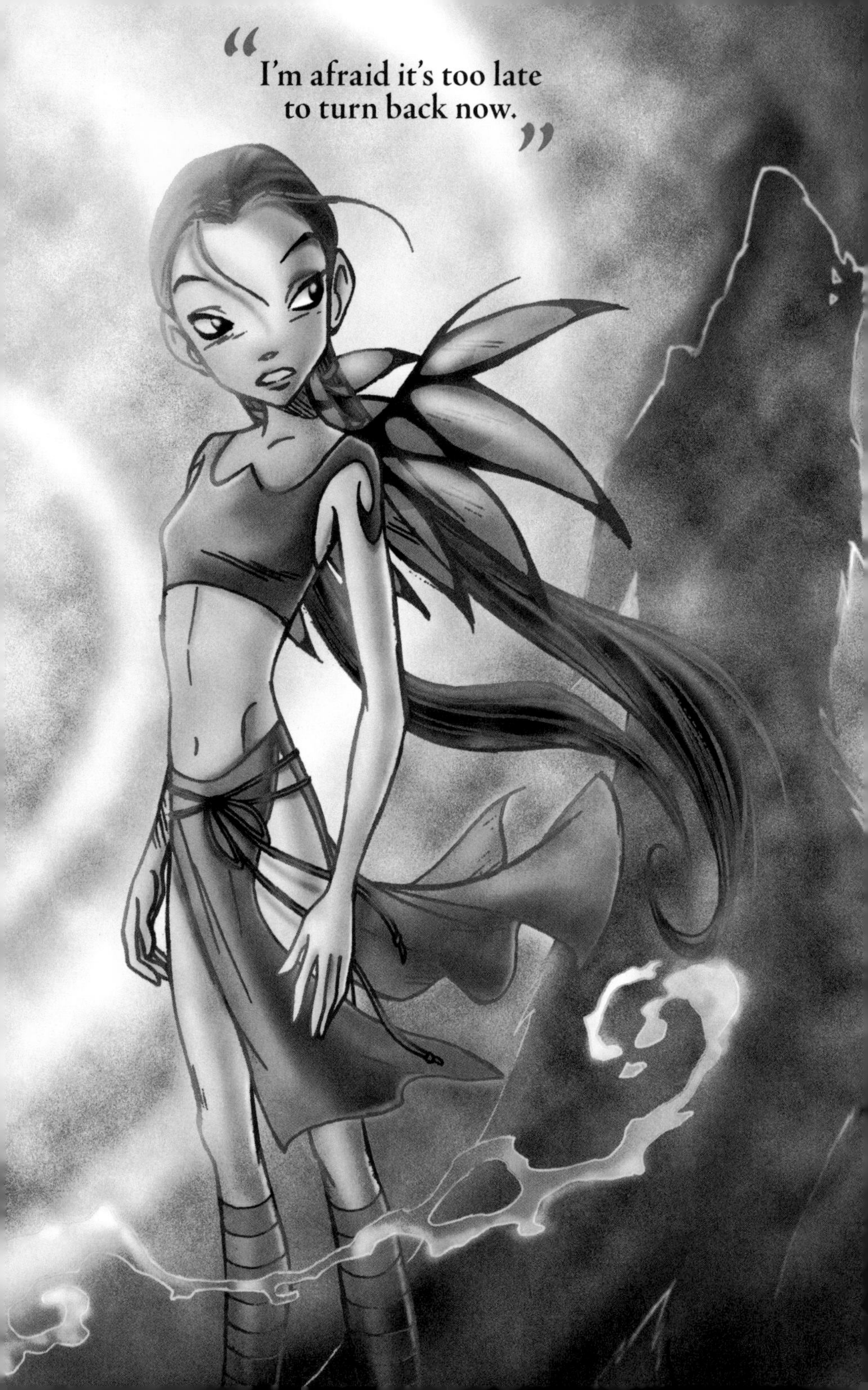
"I'm afraid it's too late to turn back now."

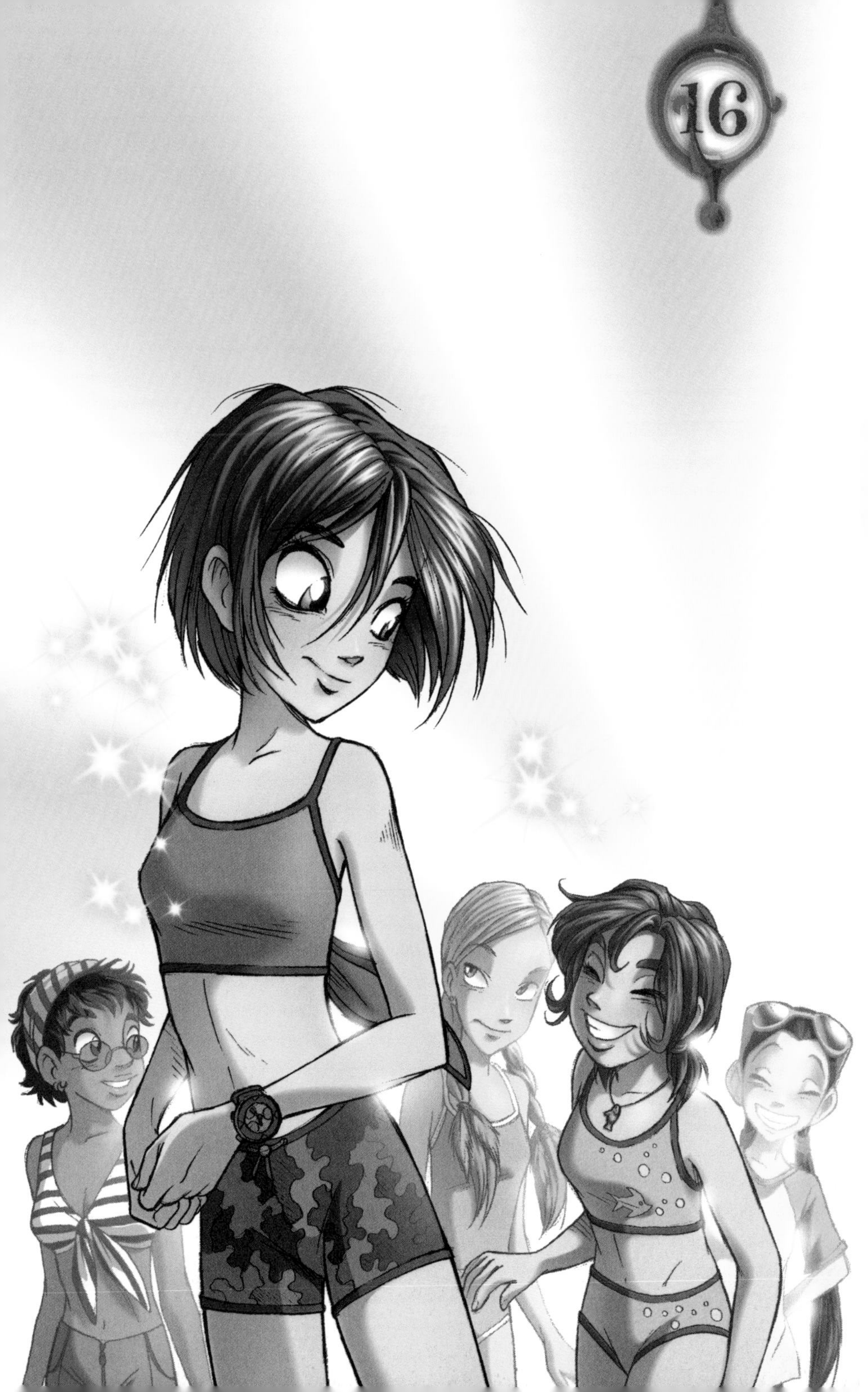
16

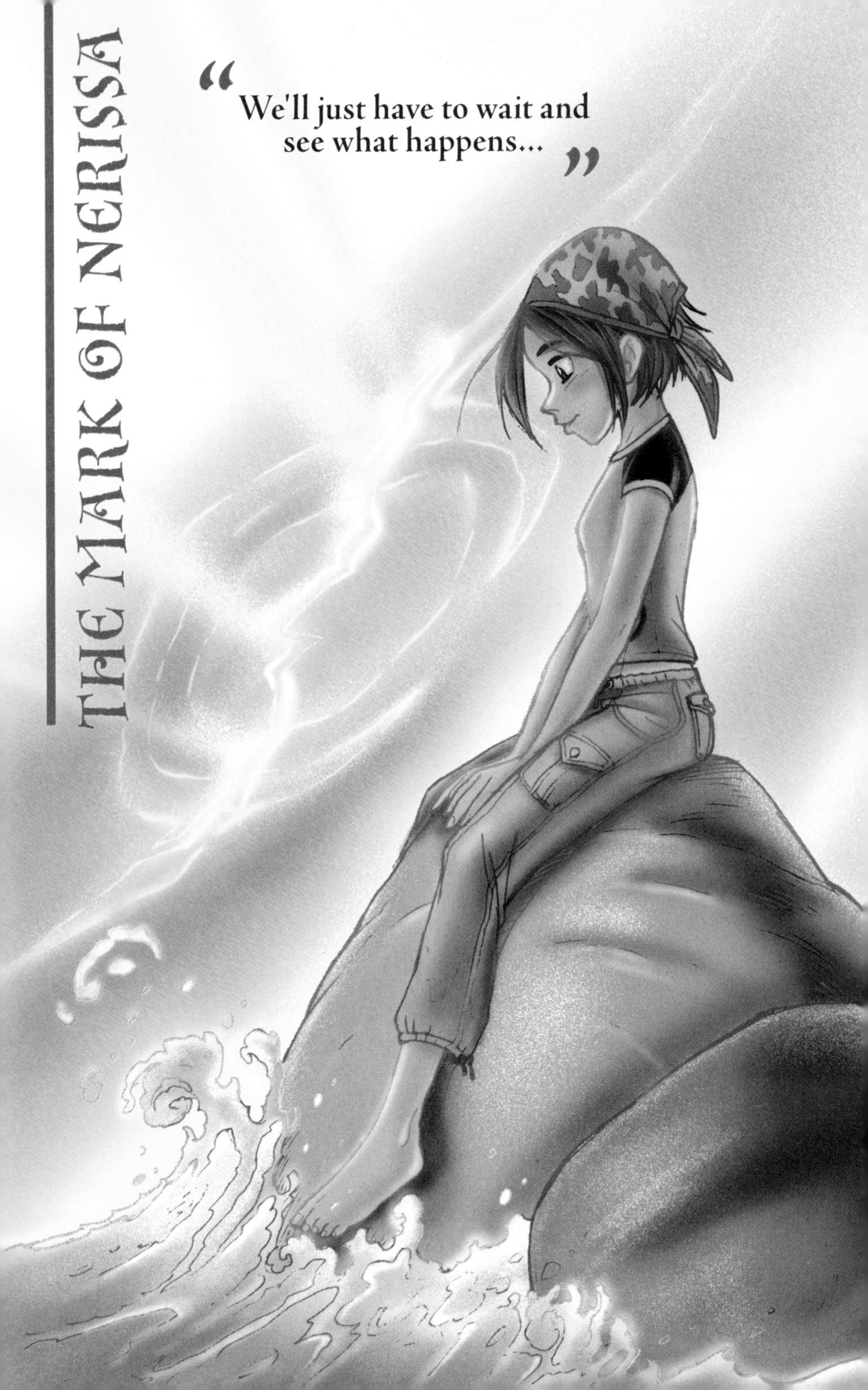
THE MARK OF NERISSA
"We'll just have to wait and see what happens..."

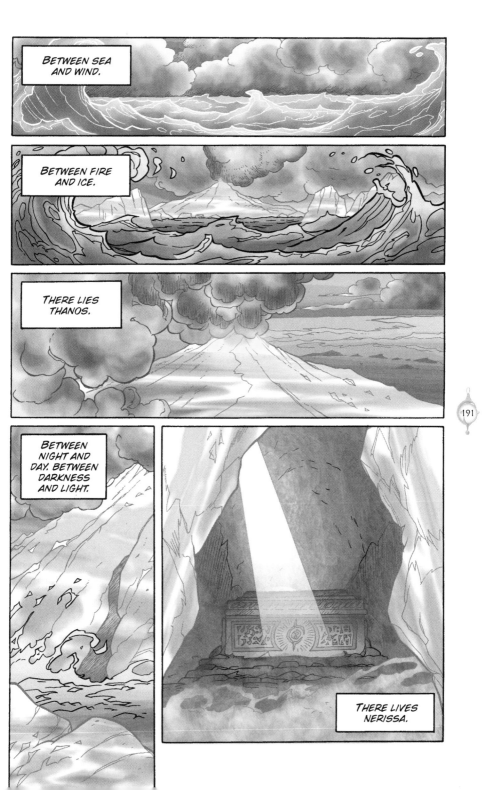

BETWEEN SEA AND WIND.

BETWEEN FIRE AND ICE.

THERE LIES THANOS.

BETWEEN NIGHT AND DAY. BETWEEN DARKNESS AND LIGHT.

THERE LIVES NERISSA.

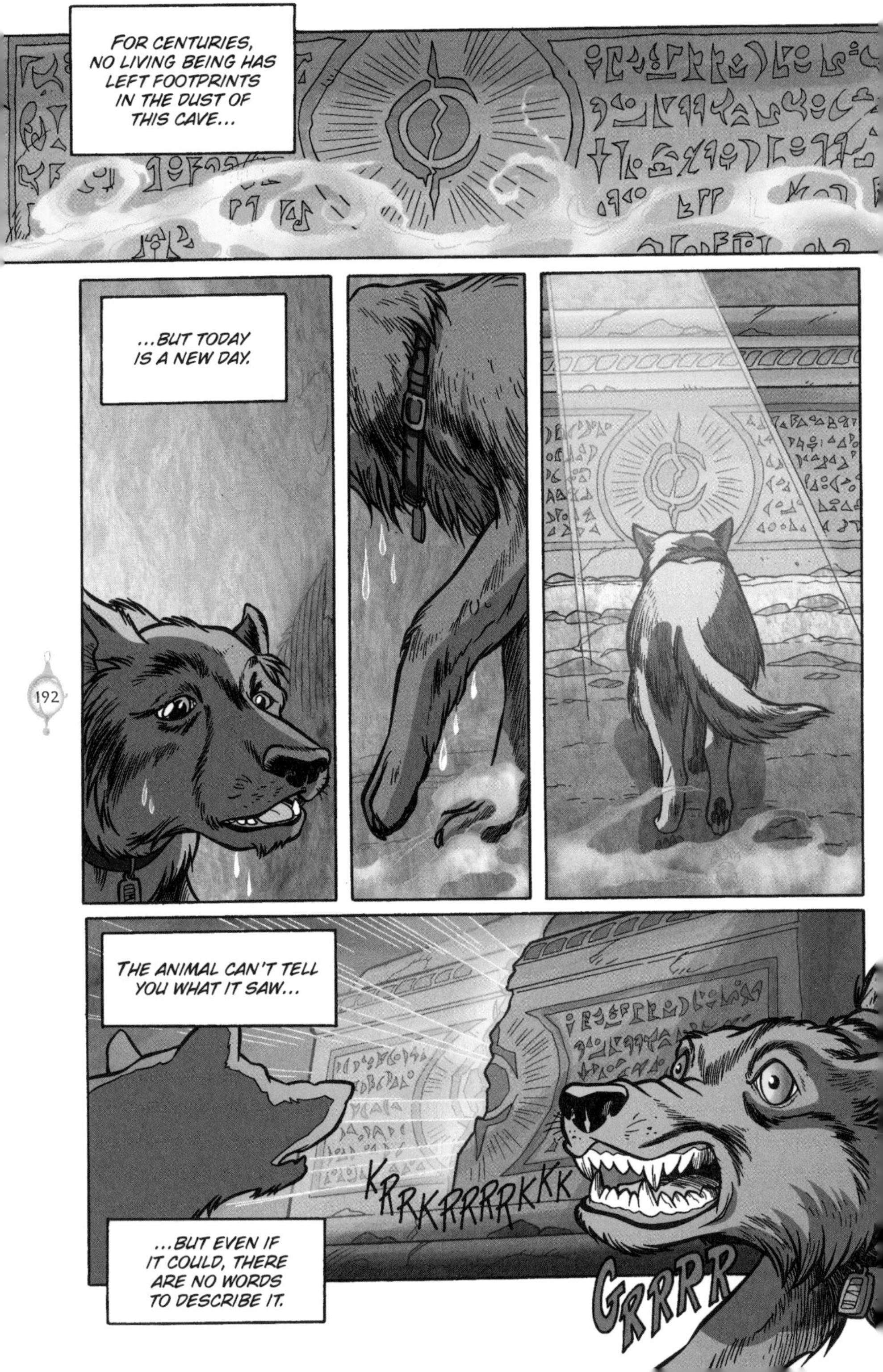
FOR CENTURIES, NO LIVING BEING HAS LEFT FOOTPRINTS IN THE DUST OF THIS CAVE...
...BUT TODAY IS A NEW DAY.
THE ANIMAL CAN'T TELL YOU WHAT IT SAW...
KRRKRRRRRKKK
...BUT EVEN IF IT COULD, THERE ARE NO WORDS TO DESCRIBE IT.
GRRRR

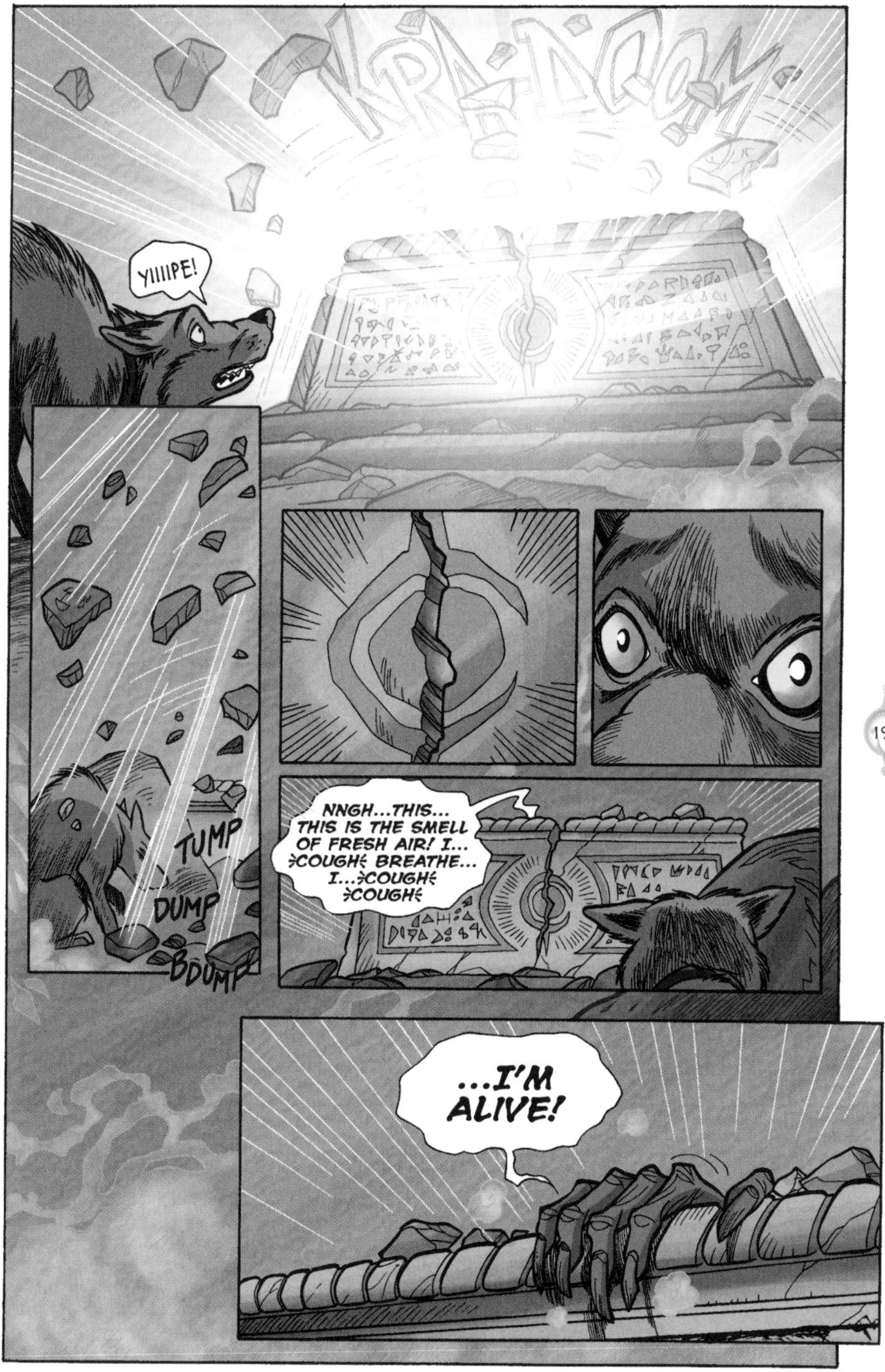
KRA-DOOM
YIIIIPE!
TUMP
DUMP
BDUMP
NNGH...THIS... THIS IS THE SMELL OF FRESH AIR! I... ≯COUGH≮ BREATHE... I...≯COUGH≮ ≯COUGH≮
...I'M ALIVE!

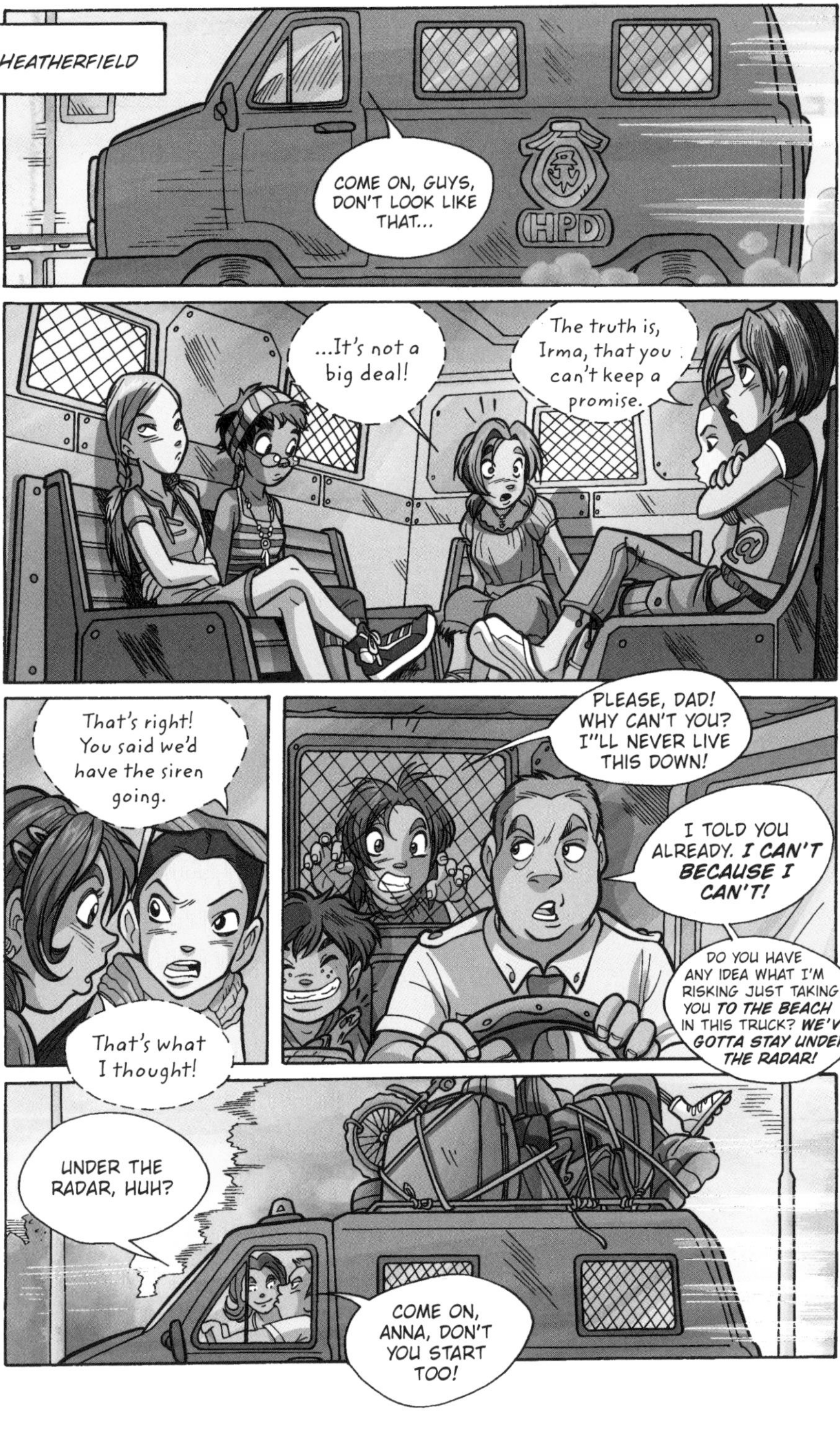
HEATHERFIELD
COME ON, GUYS, DON'T LOOK LIKE THAT...
...It's not a big deal!
The truth is, Irma, that you can't keep a promise.
That's right! You said we'd have the siren going.
That's what I thought!
PLEASE, DAD! WHY CAN'T YOU? I'LL NEVER LIVE THIS DOWN!
I TOLD YOU ALREADY. I CAN'T BECAUSE I CAN'T!
DO YOU HAVE ANY IDEA WHAT I'M RISKING JUST TAKING YOU TO THE BEACH IN THIS TRUCK? WE'VE GOTTA STAY UNDER THE RADAR!
UNDER THE RADAR, HUH?
COME ON, ANNA, DON'T YOU START TOO!

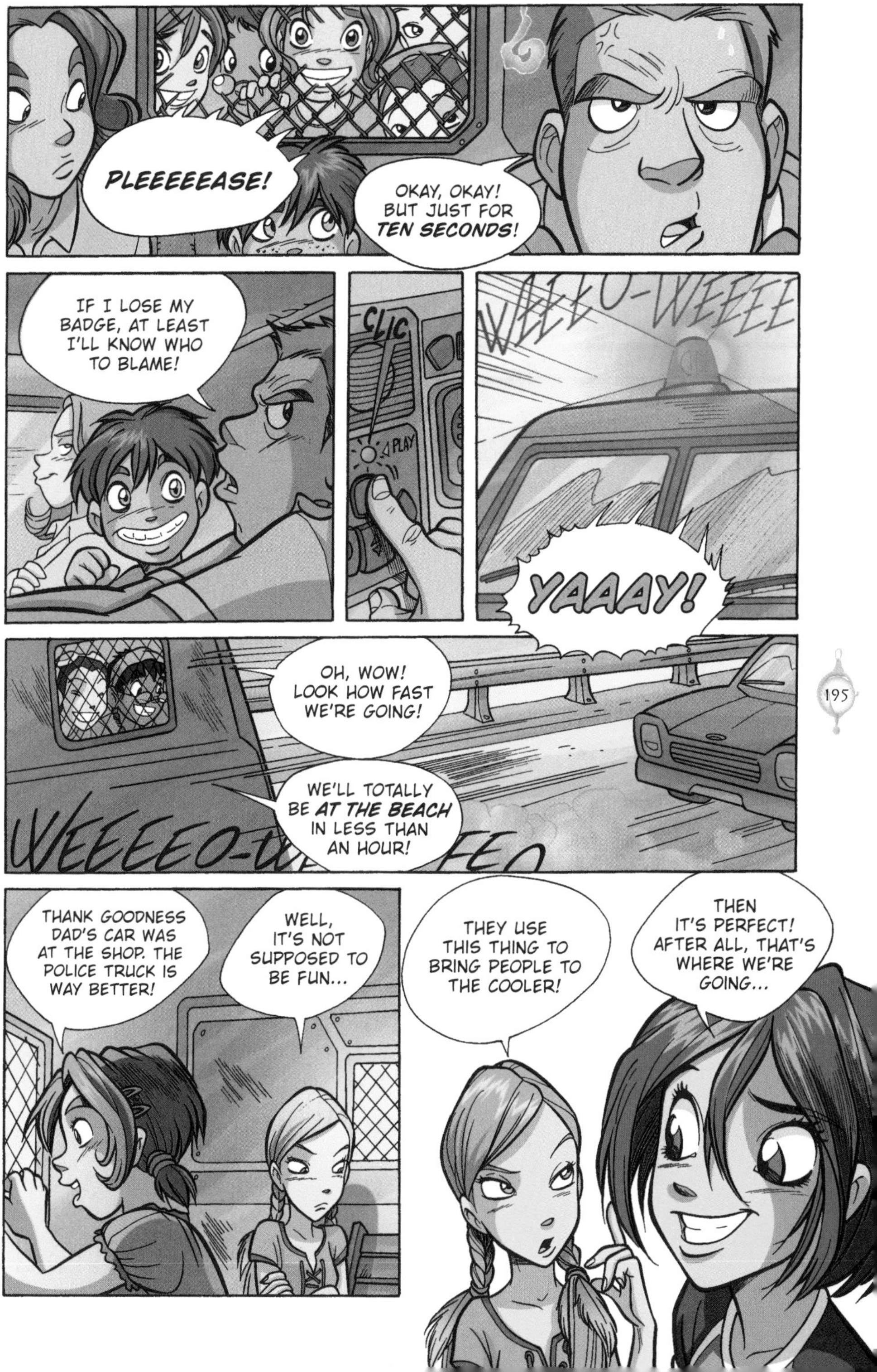
PLEEEEEASE!
OKAY, OKAY! BUT JUST FOR TEN SECONDS!
IF I LOSE MY BADGE, AT LEAST I'LL KNOW WHO TO BLAME!
CLIC
PLAY
WEEEO-WEEEE
YAAAY!
OH, WOW! LOOK HOW FAST WE'RE GOING!
WE'LL TOTALLY BE AT THE BEACH IN LESS THAN AN HOUR!
THANK GOODNESS DAD'S CAR WAS AT THE SHOP. THE POLICE TRUCK IS WAY BETTER!
WELL, IT'S NOT SUPPOSED TO BE FUN...
THEY USE THIS THING TO BRING PEOPLE TO THE COOLER!
THEN IT'S PERFECT! AFTER ALL, THAT'S WHERE WE'RE GOING...

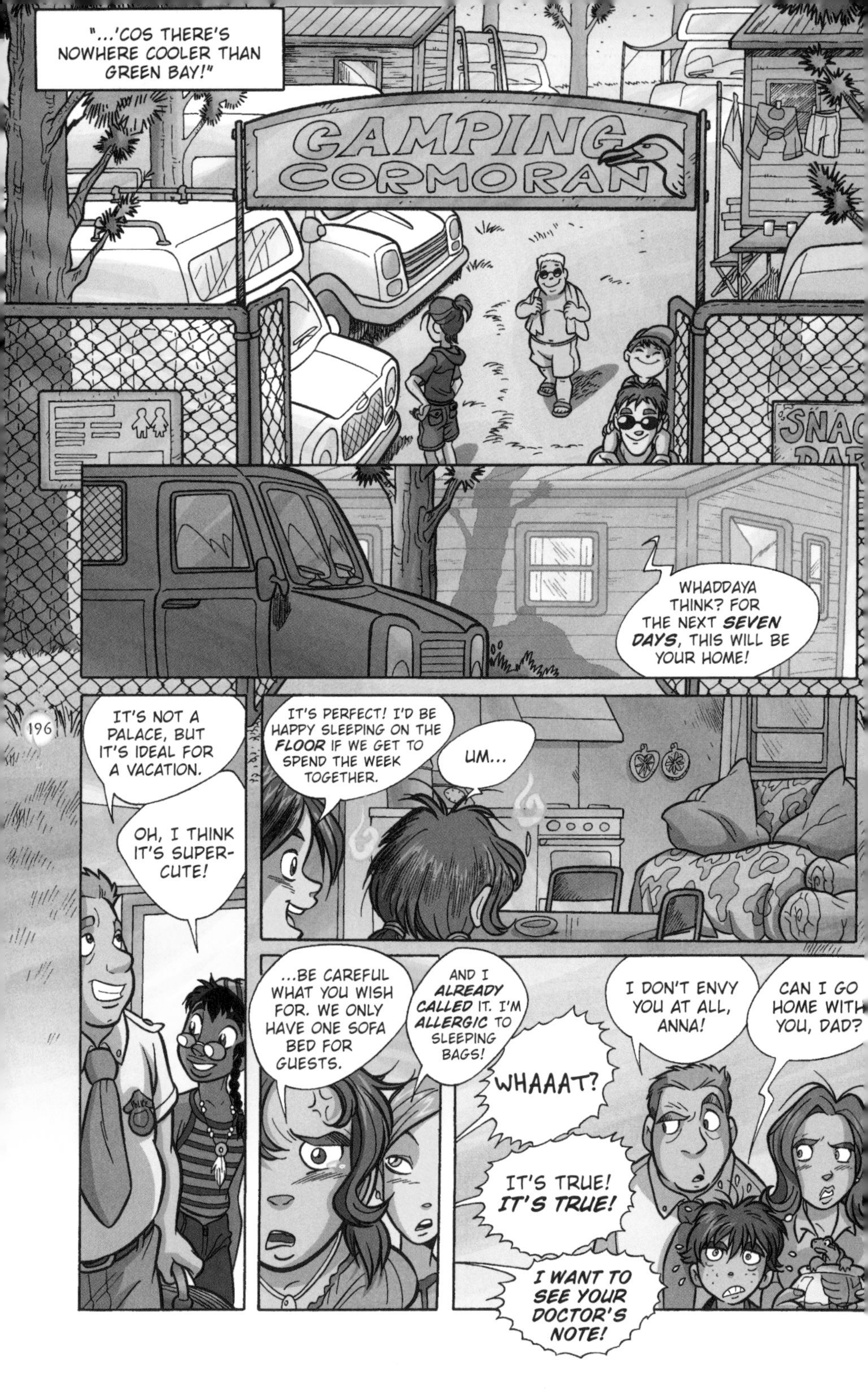
"...'COS THERE'S NOWHERE COOLER THAN GREEN BAY!"
CAMPING CORMORAN
WHADDAYA THINK? FOR THE NEXT SEVEN DAYS, THIS WILL BE YOUR HOME!
IT'S NOT A PALACE, BUT IT'S IDEAL FOR A VACATION.
OH, I THINK IT'S SUPER-CUTE!
IT'S PERFECT! I'D BE HAPPY SLEEPING ON THE FLOOR IF WE GET TO SPEND THE WEEK TOGETHER.
UM...
...BE CAREFUL WHAT YOU WISH FOR. WE ONLY HAVE ONE SOFA BED FOR GUESTS.
AND I ALREADY CALLED IT. I'M ALLERGIC TO SLEEPING BAGS!
WHAAAT?
IT'S TRUE! IT'S TRUE!
I WANT TO SEE YOUR DOCTOR'S NOTE!
I DON'T ENVY YOU AT ALL, ANNA!
CAN I GO HOME WITH YOU, DAD?
196

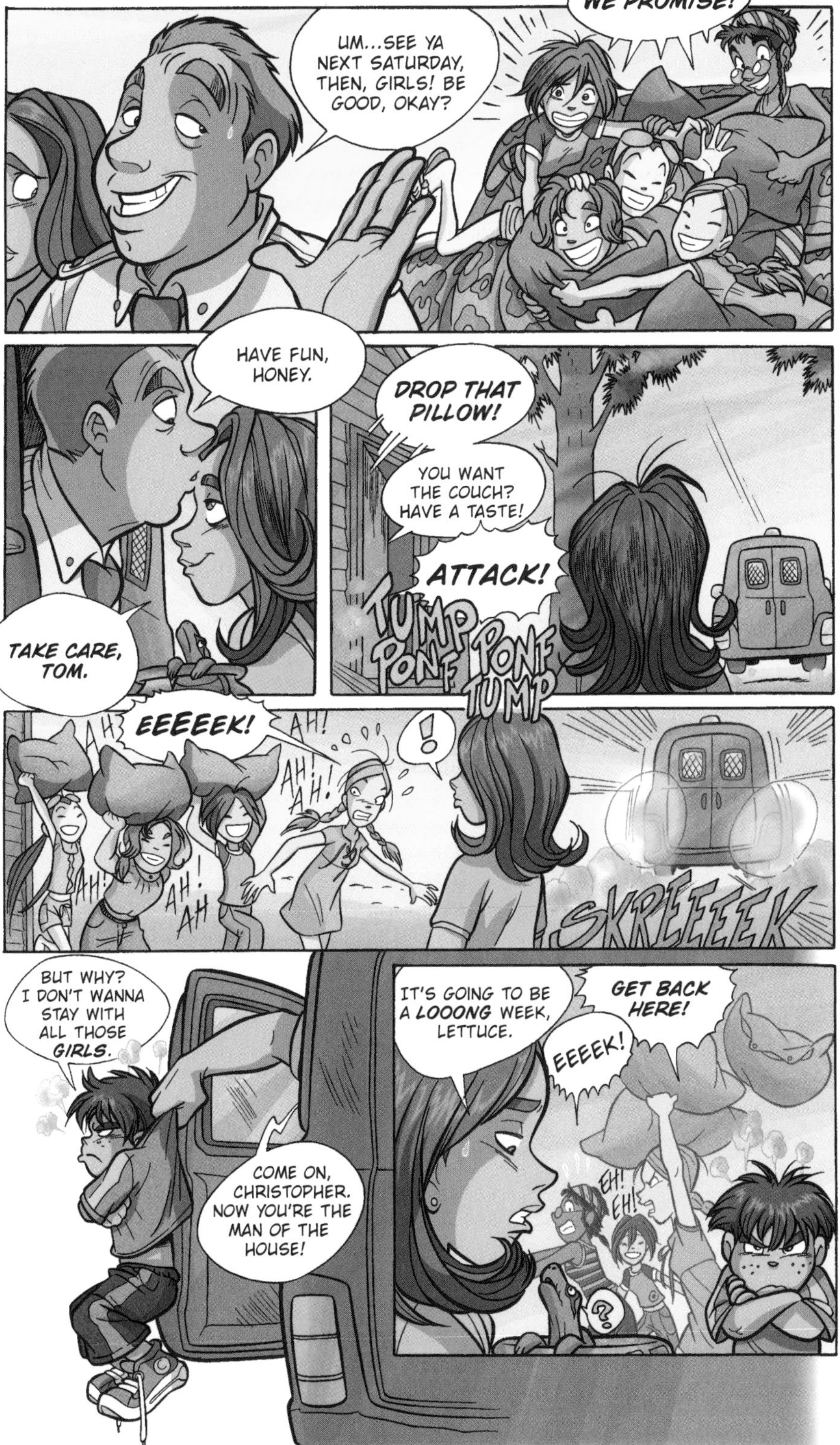
UM...SEE YA NEXT SATURDAY, THEN, GIRLS! BE GOOD, OKAY?
WE PROMISE!
HAVE FUN, HONEY.
TAKE CARE, TOM.
DROP THAT PILLOW!
YOU WANT THE COUCH? HAVE A TASTE!
ATTACK!
TUMP PONF PONF TUMP
AH!
EEEEEK!
AH!
AH! AH!
!
AH! AH AH
SKREEEEK
BUT WHY? I DON'T WANNA STAY WITH ALL THOSE GIRLS.
COME ON, CHRISTOPHER. NOW YOU'RE THE MAN OF THE HOUSE!
IT'S GOING TO BE A LOOOONG WEEK, LETTUCE.
GET BACK HERE!
EEEEK!
EH! EH!
?

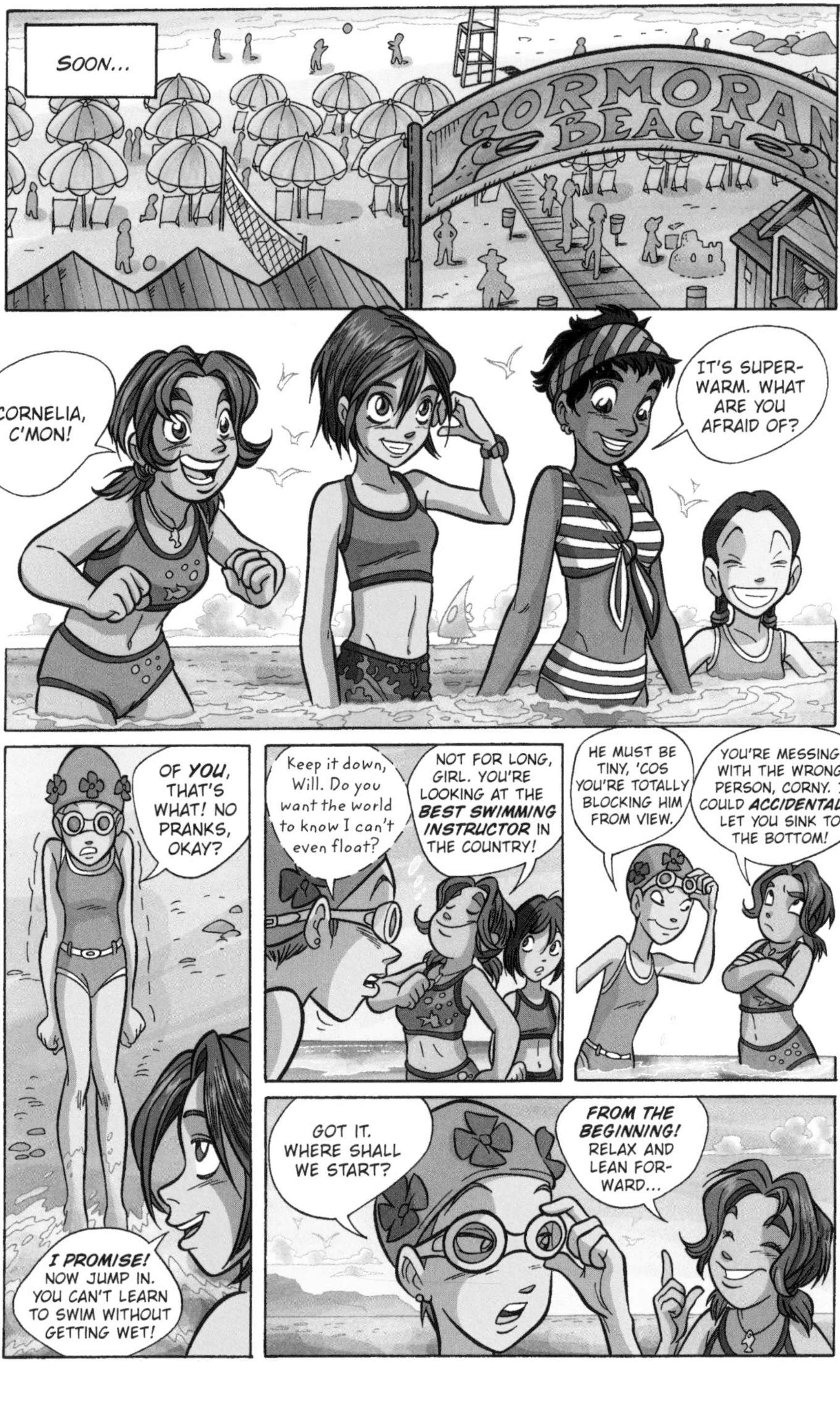
SOON...
CORMORAN BEACH
CORNELIA, C'MON!
IT'S SUPER-WARM. WHAT ARE YOU AFRAID OF?
OF *YOU*, THAT'S WHAT! NO PRANKS, OKAY?
I PROMISE! NOW JUMP IN. YOU CAN'T LEARN TO SWIM WITHOUT GETTING WET!
Keep it down, Will. Do you want the world to know I can't even float?
NOT FOR LONG, GIRL. YOU'RE LOOKING AT THE *BEST SWIMMING INSTRUCTOR* IN THE COUNTRY!
HE MUST BE TINY, 'COS YOU'RE TOTALLY BLOCKING HIM FROM VIEW.
YOU'RE MESSING WITH THE WRONG PERSON, CORNY. I COULD *ACCIDENTALLY* LET YOU SINK TO THE BOTTOM!
GOT IT. WHERE SHALL WE START?
FROM THE BEGINNING! RELAX AND LEAN FOR-WARD...

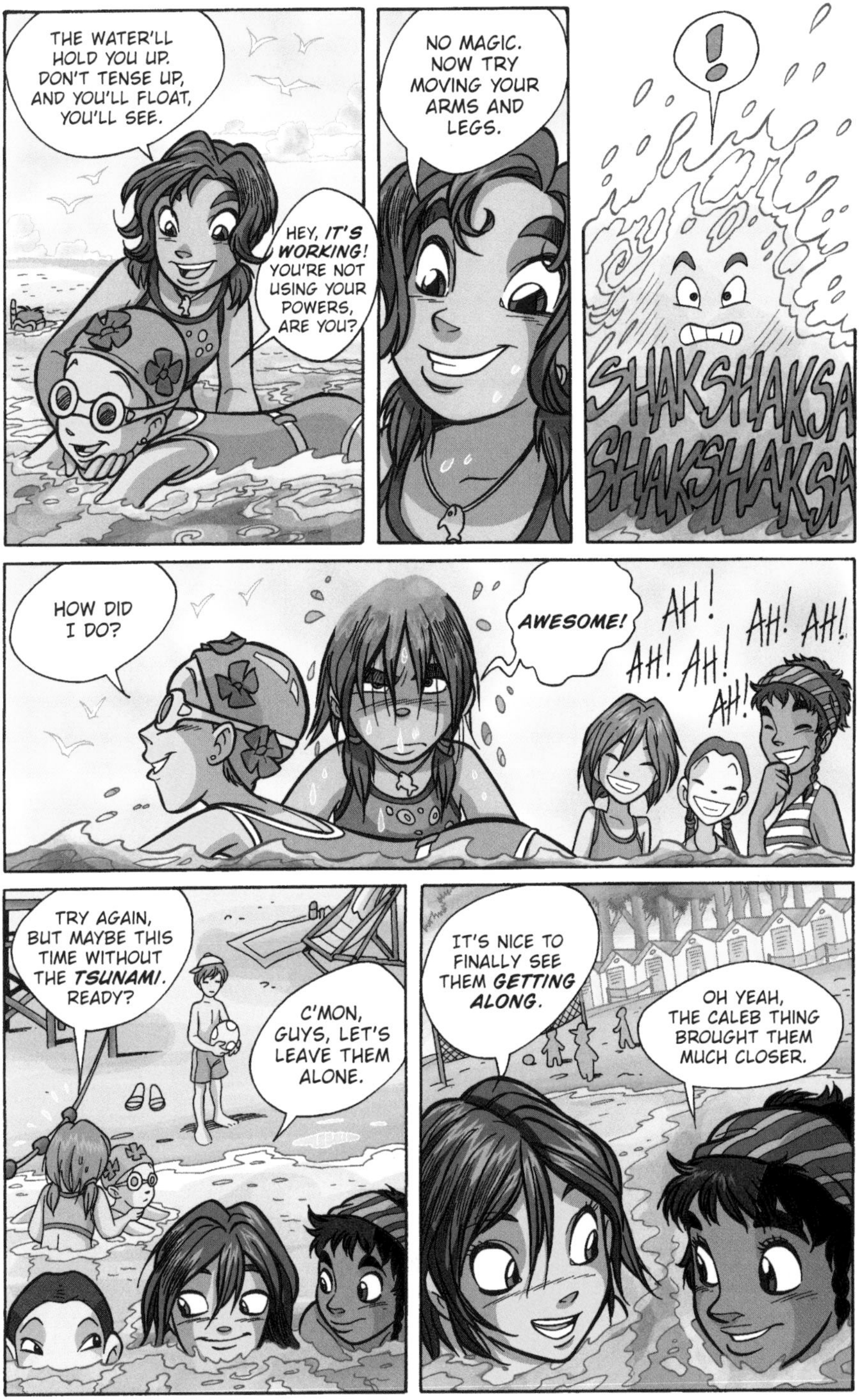

THE WATER'LL HOLD YOU UP. DON'T TENSE UP, AND YOU'LL FLOAT, YOU'LL SEE.
HEY, IT'S WORKING! YOU'RE NOT USING YOUR POWERS, ARE YOU?
NO MAGIC. NOW TRY MOVING YOUR ARMS AND LEGS.
!
SHAKSHAKSA SHAKSHAKSA
HOW DID I DO?
AWESOME!
AH! AH! AH! AH! AH! AH!
TRY AGAIN, BUT MAYBE THIS TIME WITHOUT THE TSUNAMI. READY?
C'MON, GUYS, LET'S LEAVE THEM ALONE.
IT'S NICE TO FINALLY SEE THEM GETTING ALONG.
OH YEAH, THE CALEB THING BROUGHT THEM MUCH CLOSER.

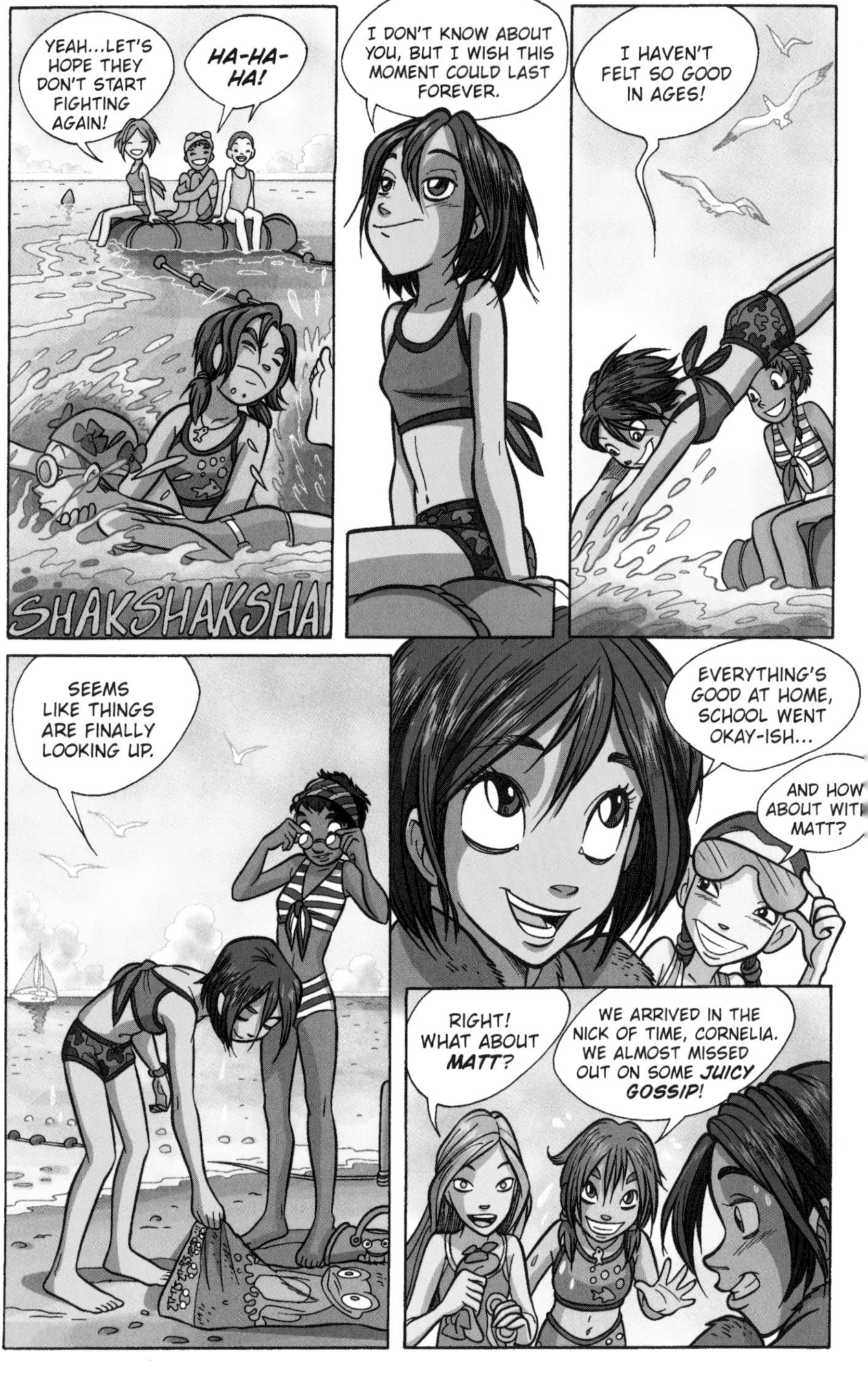

YEAH...LET'S HOPE THEY DON'T START FIGHTING AGAIN!
HA-HA-HA!
SHAKSHAKSHA
I DON'T KNOW ABOUT YOU, BUT I WISH THIS MOMENT COULD LAST FOREVER.
I HAVEN'T FELT SO GOOD IN AGES!
SEEMS LIKE THINGS ARE FINALLY LOOKING UP.
EVERYTHING'S GOOD AT HOME, SCHOOL WENT OKAY-ISH...
AND HOW ABOUT WIT MATT?
RIGHT! WHAT ABOUT MATT?
WE ARRIVED IN THE NICK OF TIME, CORNELIA. WE ALMOST MISSED OUT ON SOME JUICY GOSSIP!

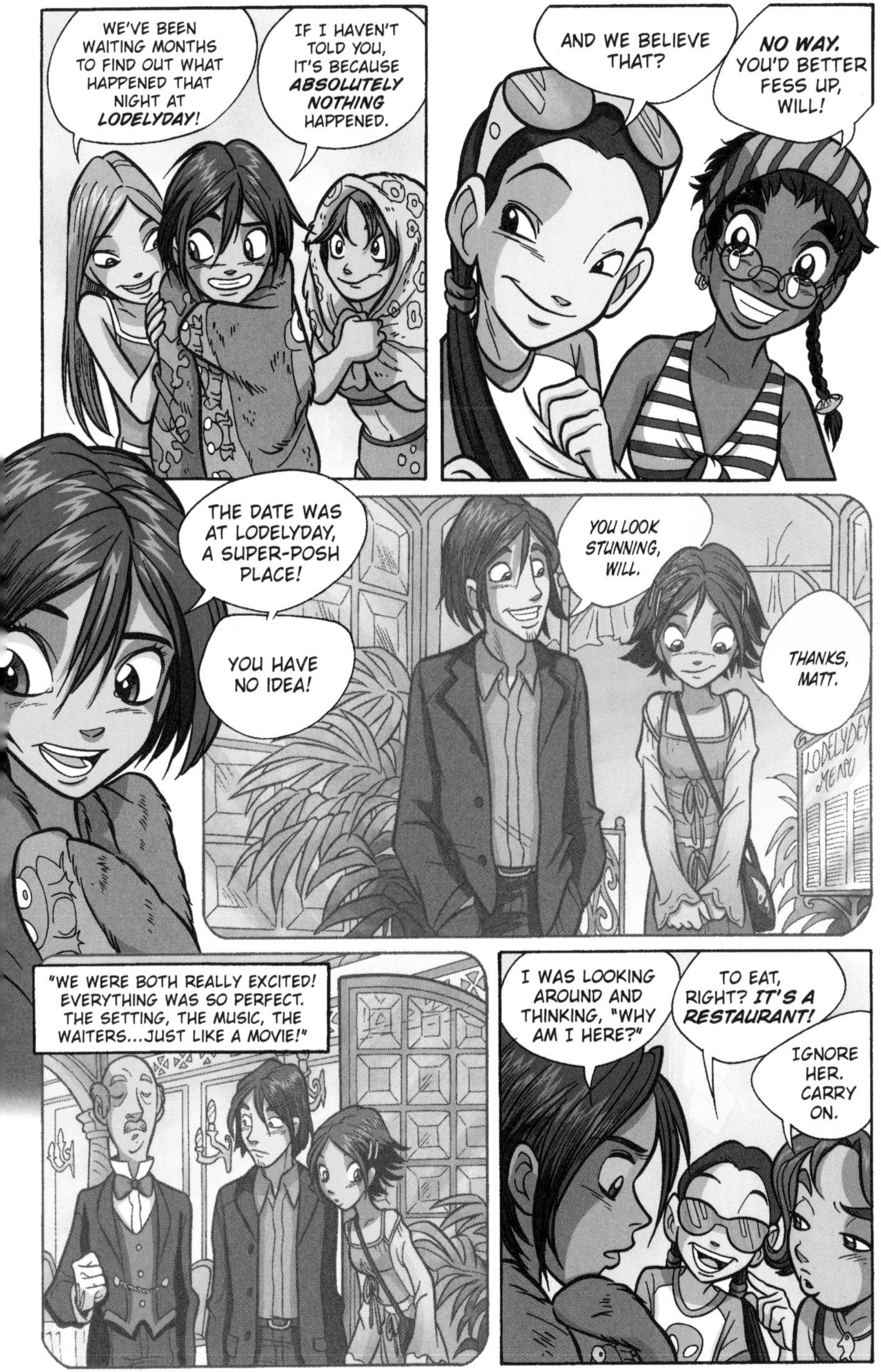
WE'VE BEEN WAITING MONTHS TO FIND OUT WHAT HAPPENED THAT NIGHT AT LODELYDAY!
IF I HAVEN'T TOLD YOU, IT'S BECAUSE ABSOLUTELY NOTHING HAPPENED.
AND WE BELIEVE THAT?
NO WAY. YOU'D BETTER FESS UP, WILL!
THE DATE WAS AT LODELYDAY, A SUPER-POSH PLACE!
YOU HAVE NO IDEA!
YOU LOOK STUNNING, WILL.
THANKS, MATT.
LODELYDEY MENU
"WE WERE BOTH REALLY EXCITED! EVERYTHING WAS SO PERFECT. THE SETTING, THE MUSIC, THE WAITERS...JUST LIKE A MOVIE!"
I WAS LOOKING AROUND AND THINKING, "WHY AM I HERE?"
TO EAT, RIGHT? IT'S A RESTAURANT!
IGNORE HER. CARRY ON.

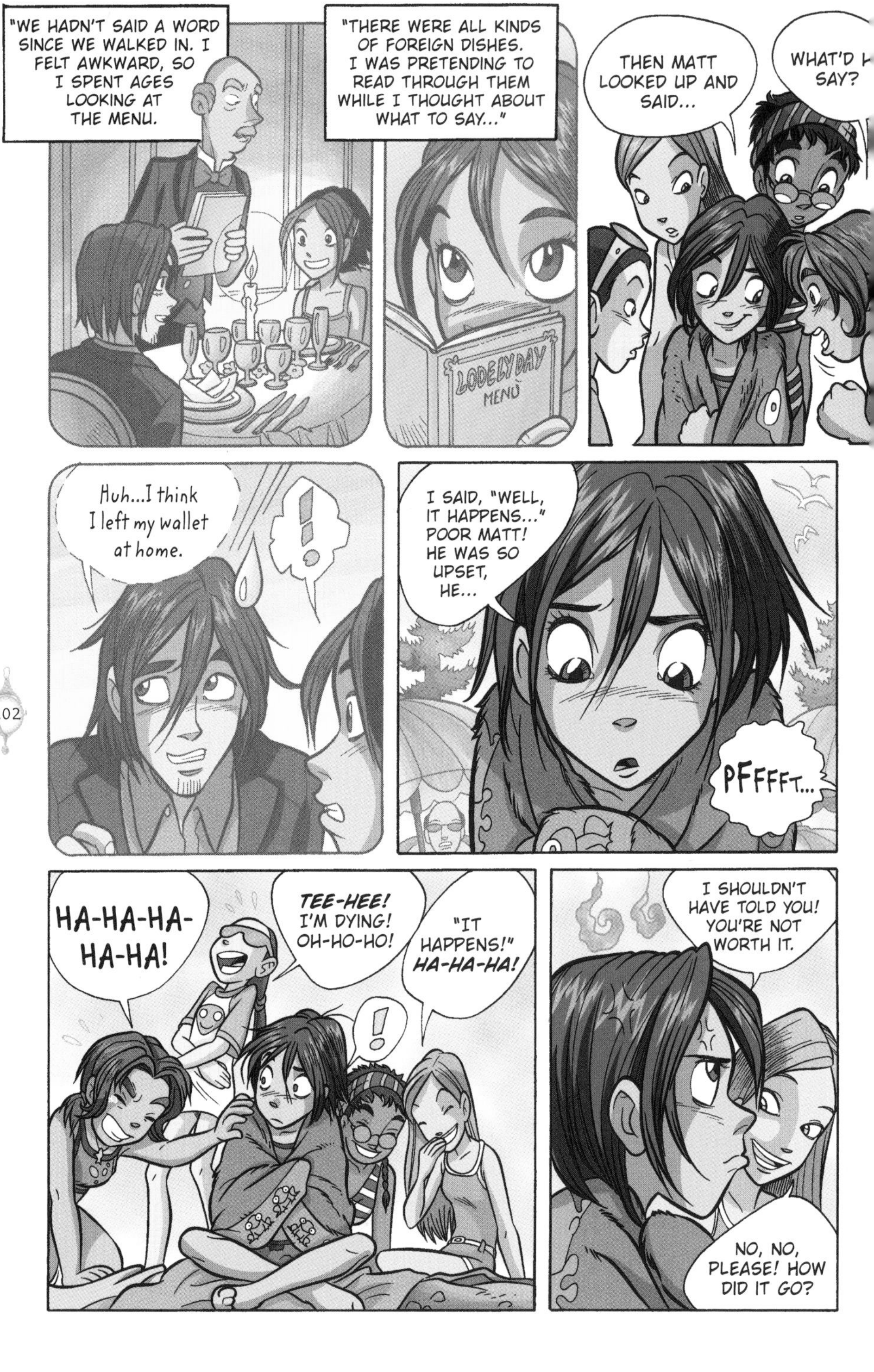
"WE HADN'T SAID A WORD SINCE WE WALKED IN. I FELT AWKWARD, SO I SPENT AGES LOOKING AT THE MENU.
"THERE WERE ALL KINDS OF FOREIGN DISHES. I WAS PRETENDING TO READ THROUGH THEM WHILE I THOUGHT ABOUT WHAT TO SAY..."
LODELY DAY MENU
THEN MATT LOOKED UP AND SAID...
WHAT'D H SAY?
Huh...I think I left my wallet at home.
!
I SAID, "WELL, IT HAPPENS..." POOR MATT! HE WAS SO UPSET, HE...
PFFFFT...
HA-HA-HA-HA-HA!
TEE-HEE! I'M DYING! OH-HO-HO!
"IT HAPPENS!" HA-HA-HA!
!
I SHOULDN'T HAVE TOLD YOU! YOU'RE NOT WORTH IT.
NO, NO, PLEASE! HOW DID IT GO?

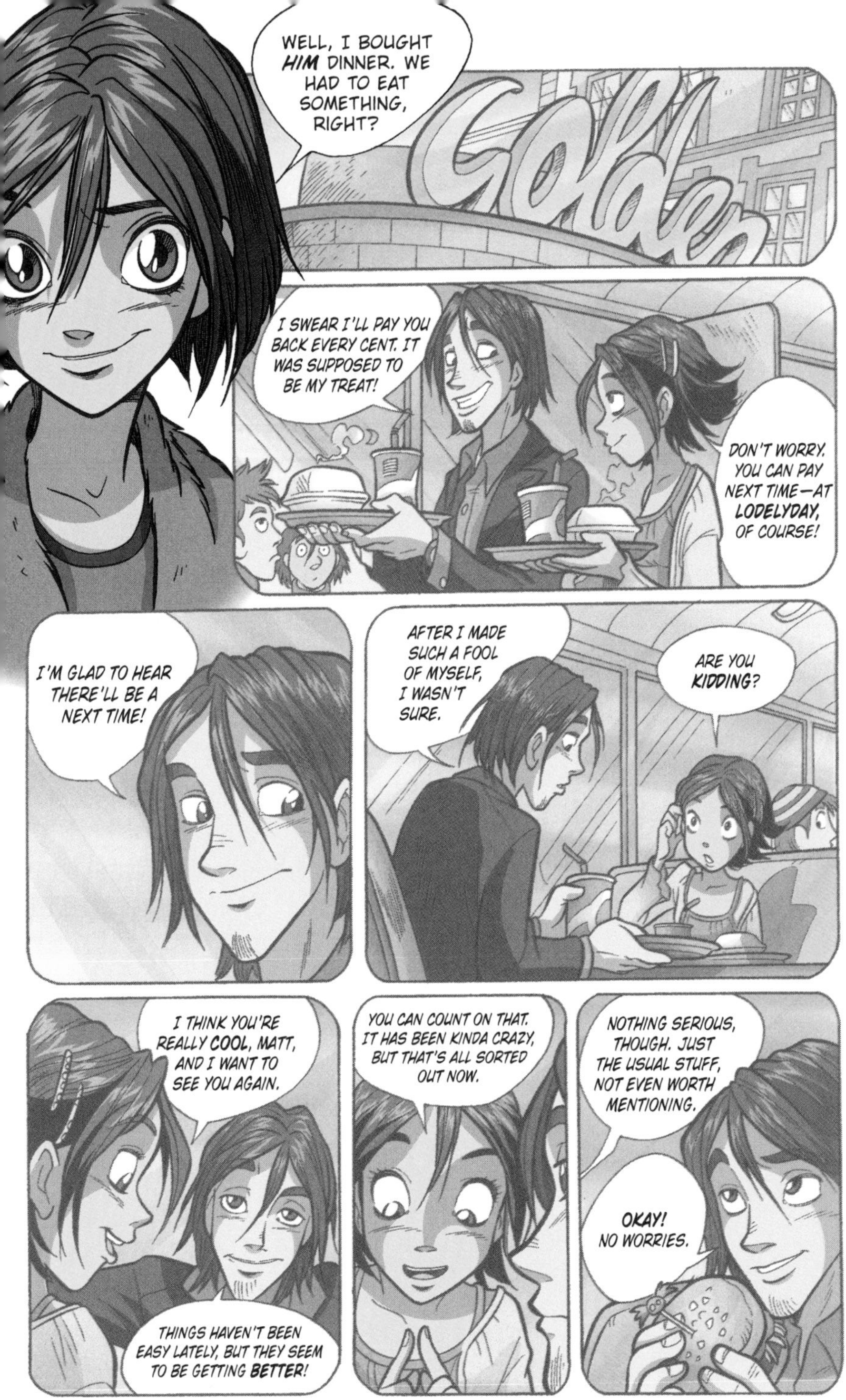

WELL, I BOUGHT HIM DINNER. WE HAD TO EAT SOMETHING, RIGHT?
I SWEAR I'LL PAY YOU BACK EVERY CENT. IT WAS SUPPOSED TO BE MY TREAT!
DON'T WORRY. YOU CAN PAY NEXT TIME—AT LODELYDAY, OF COURSE!
I'M GLAD TO HEAR THERE'LL BE A NEXT TIME!
AFTER I MADE SUCH A FOOL OF MYSELF, I WASN'T SURE.
ARE YOU KIDDING?
I THINK YOU'RE REALLY COOL, MATT, AND I WANT TO SEE YOU AGAIN.
THINGS HAVEN'T BEEN EASY LATELY, BUT THEY SEEM TO BE GETTING BETTER!
YOU CAN COUNT ON THAT. IT HAS BEEN KINDA CRAZY, BUT THAT'S ALL SORTED OUT NOW.
NOTHING SERIOUS, THOUGH. JUST THE USUAL STUFF, NOT EVEN WORTH MENTIONING.
OKAY! NO WORRIES.

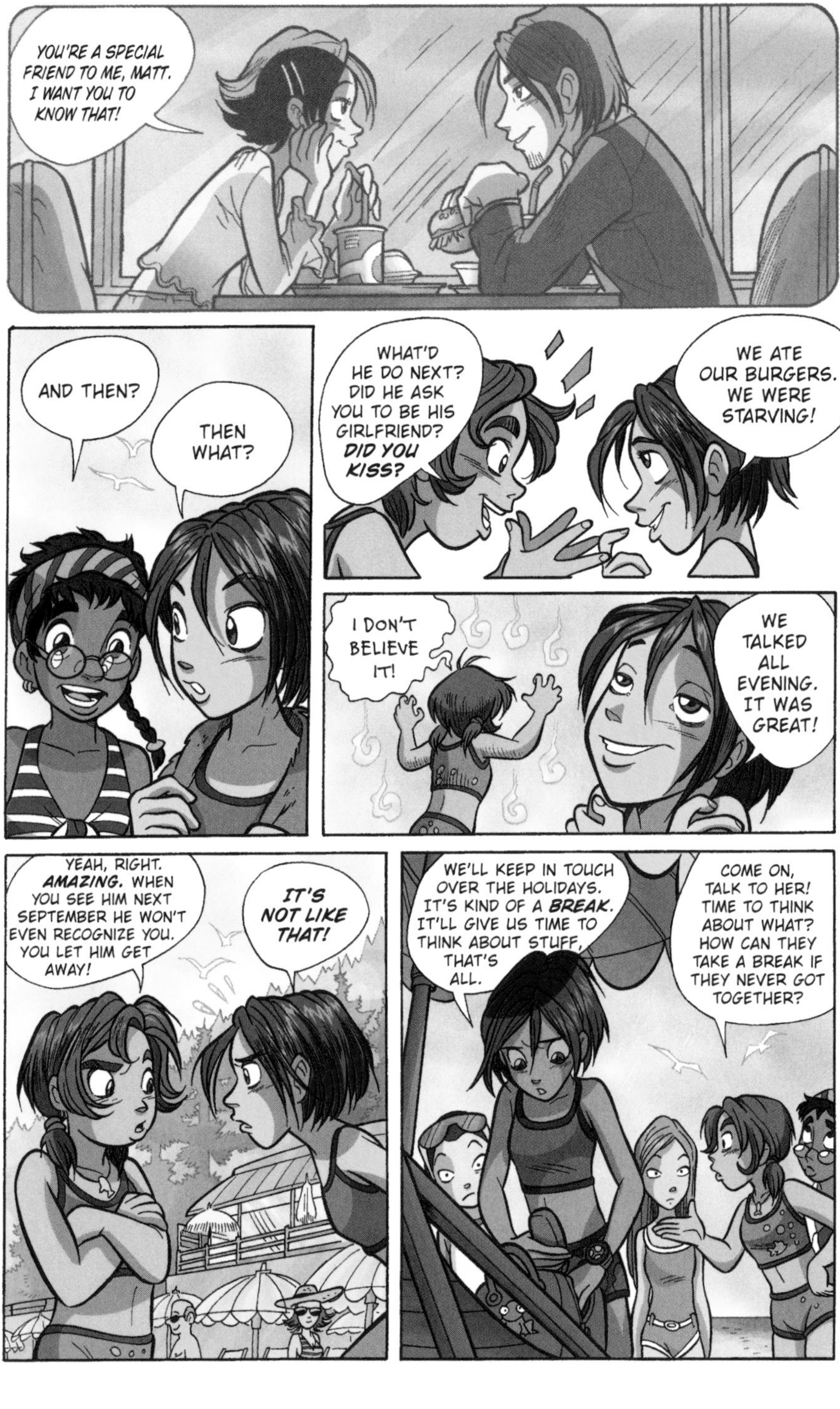
YOU'RE A SPECIAL FRIEND TO ME, MATT. I WANT YOU TO KNOW THAT!
AND THEN?
THEN WHAT?
WHAT'D HE DO NEXT? DID HE ASK YOU TO BE HIS GIRLFRIEND? DID YOU KISS?
WE ATE OUR BURGERS. WE WERE STARVING!
I DON'T BELIEVE IT!
WE TALKED ALL EVENING. IT WAS GREAT!
YEAH, RIGHT. AMAZING. WHEN YOU SEE HIM NEXT SEPTEMBER HE WON'T EVEN RECOGNIZE YOU. YOU LET HIM GET AWAY!
IT'S NOT LIKE THAT!
WE'LL KEEP IN TOUCH OVER THE HOLIDAYS. IT'S KIND OF A BREAK. IT'LL GIVE US TIME TO THINK ABOUT STUFF, THAT'S ALL.
COME ON, TALK TO HER! TIME TO THINK ABOUT WHAT? HOW CAN THEY TAKE A BREAK IF THEY NEVER GOT TOGETHER?

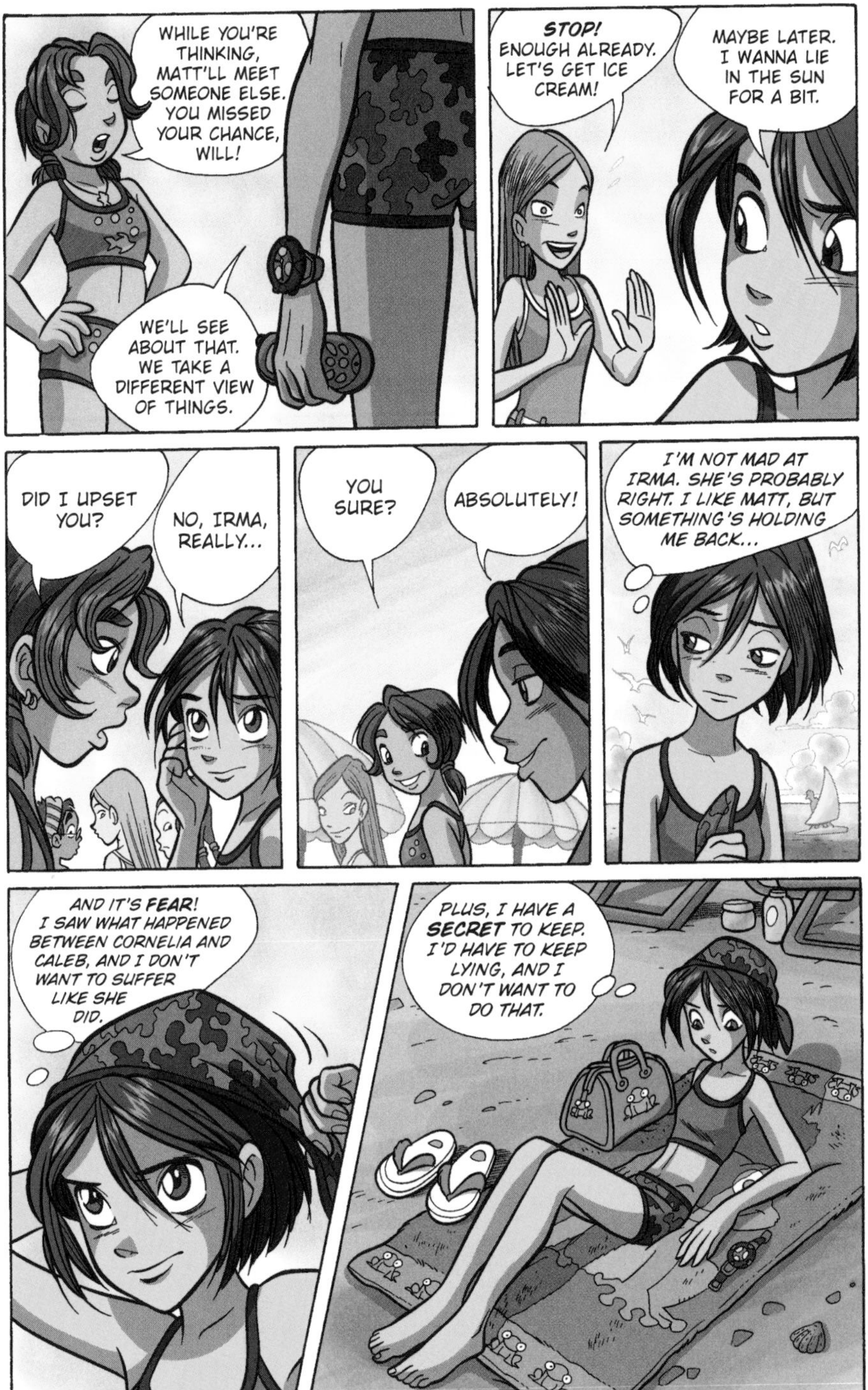
WHILE YOU'RE THINKING, MATT'LL MEET SOMEONE ELSE. YOU MISSED YOUR CHANCE, WILL!
WE'LL SEE ABOUT THAT. WE TAKE A DIFFERENT VIEW OF THINGS.
STOP! ENOUGH ALREADY. LET'S GET ICE CREAM!
MAYBE LATER. I WANNA LIE IN THE SUN FOR A BIT.
DID I UPSET YOU?
NO, IRMA, REALLY...
YOU SURE?
ABSOLUTELY!
I'M NOT MAD AT IRMA. SHE'S PROBABLY RIGHT. I LIKE MATT, BUT SOMETHING'S HOLDING ME BACK...
AND IT'S FEAR! I SAW WHAT HAPPENED BETWEEN CORNELIA AND CALEB, AND I DON'T WANT TO SUFFER LIKE SHE DID.
PLUS, I HAVE A SECRET TO KEEP. I'D HAVE TO KEEP LYING, AND I DON'T WANT TO DO THAT.

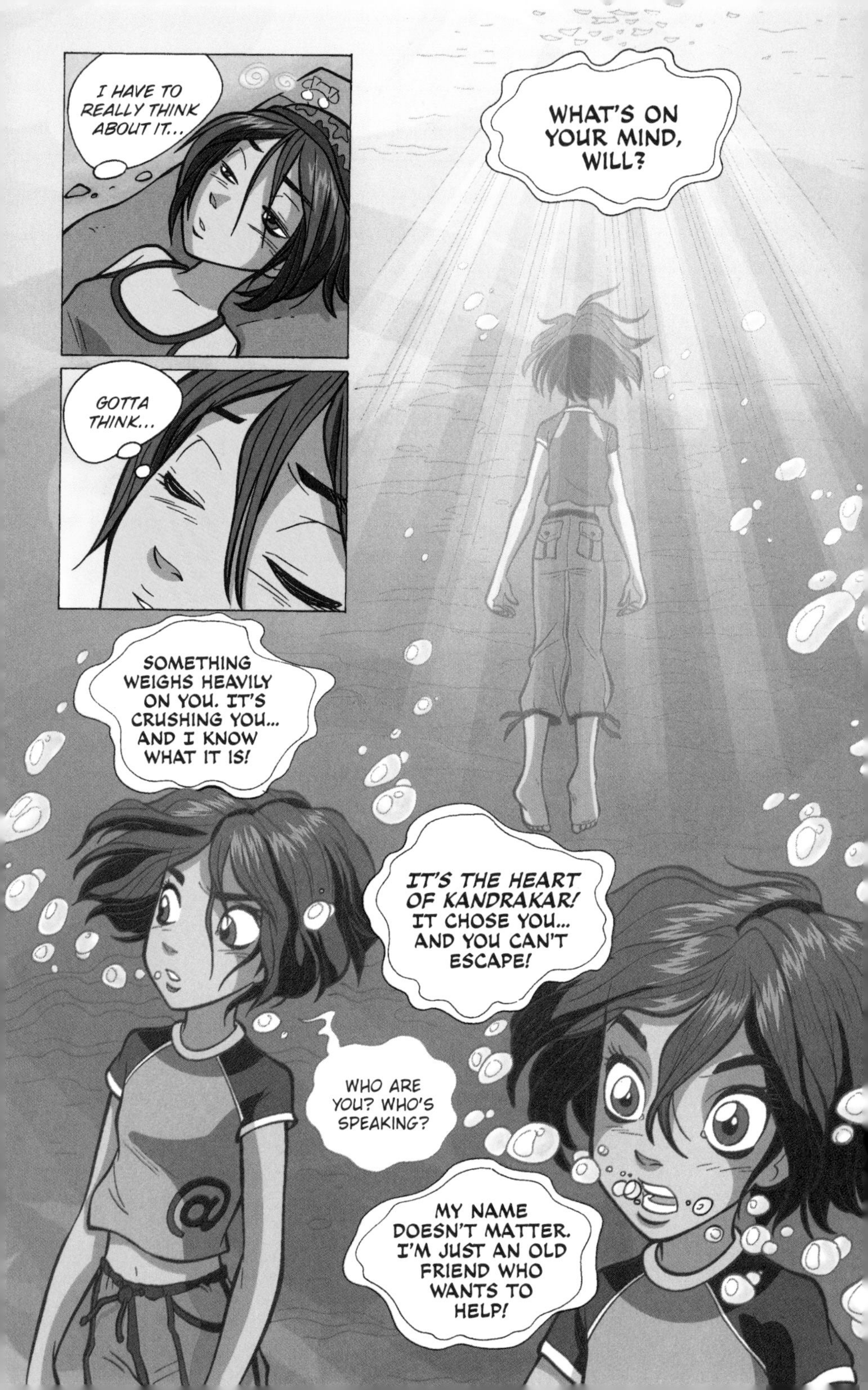
I HAVE TO REALLY THINK ABOUT IT...
WHAT'S ON YOUR MIND, WILL?
GOTTA THINK...
SOMETHING WEIGHS HEAVILY ON YOU. IT'S CRUSHING YOU... AND I KNOW WHAT IT IS!
IT'S THE HEART OF KANDRAKAR! IT CHOSE YOU... AND YOU CAN'T ESCAPE!
WHO ARE YOU? WHO'S SPEAKING?
MY NAME DOESN'T MATTER. I'M JUST AN OLD FRIEND WHO WANTS TO HELP!

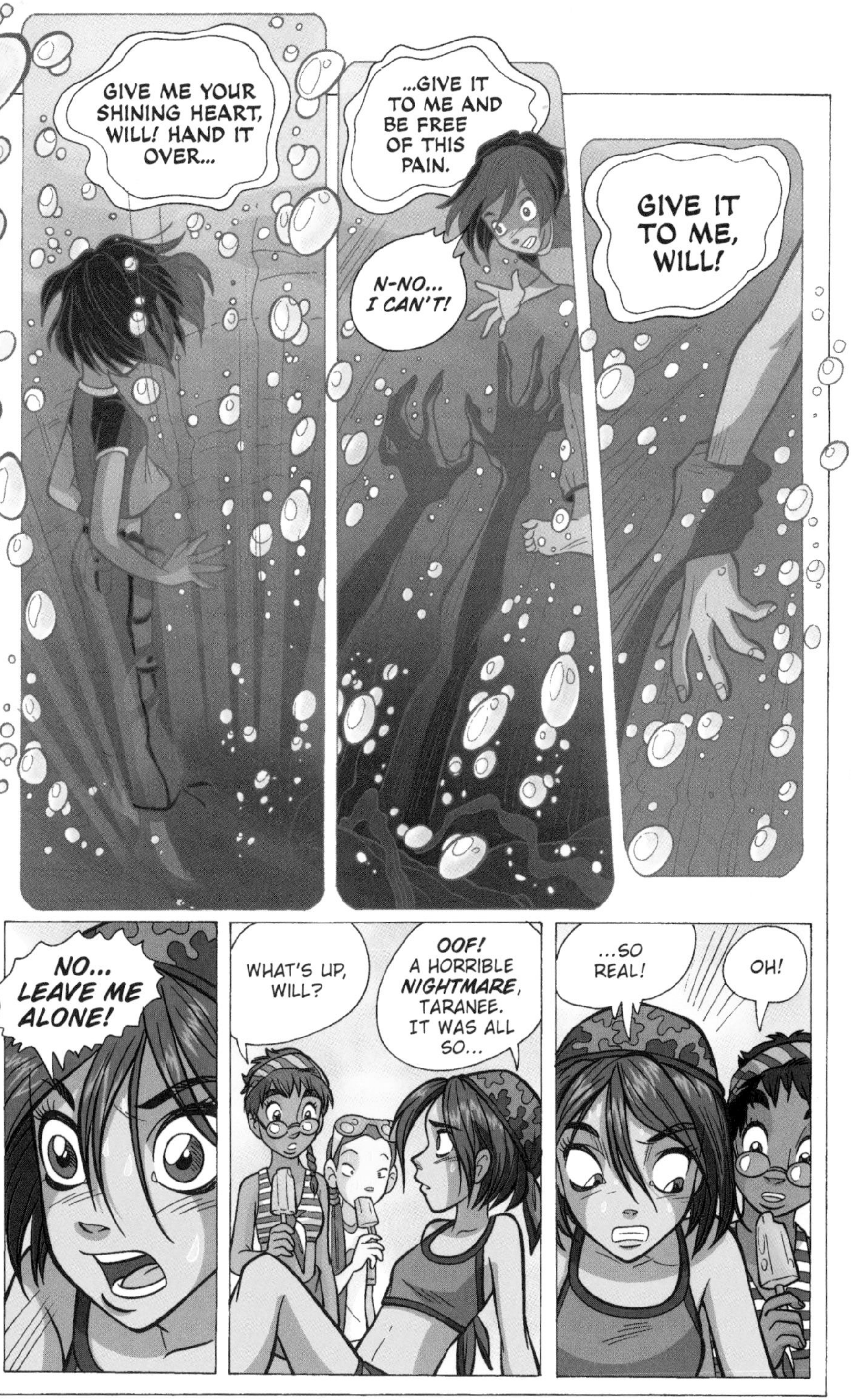
GIVE ME YOUR SHINING HEART, WILL! HAND IT OVER...
...GIVE IT TO ME AND BE FREE OF THIS PAIN.
N-NO... I CAN'T!
GIVE IT TO ME, WILL!
NO... LEAVE ME ALONE!
WHAT'S UP, WILL?
OOF! A HORRIBLE NIGHTMARE, TARANEE. IT WAS ALL SO...
...SO REAL!
OH!

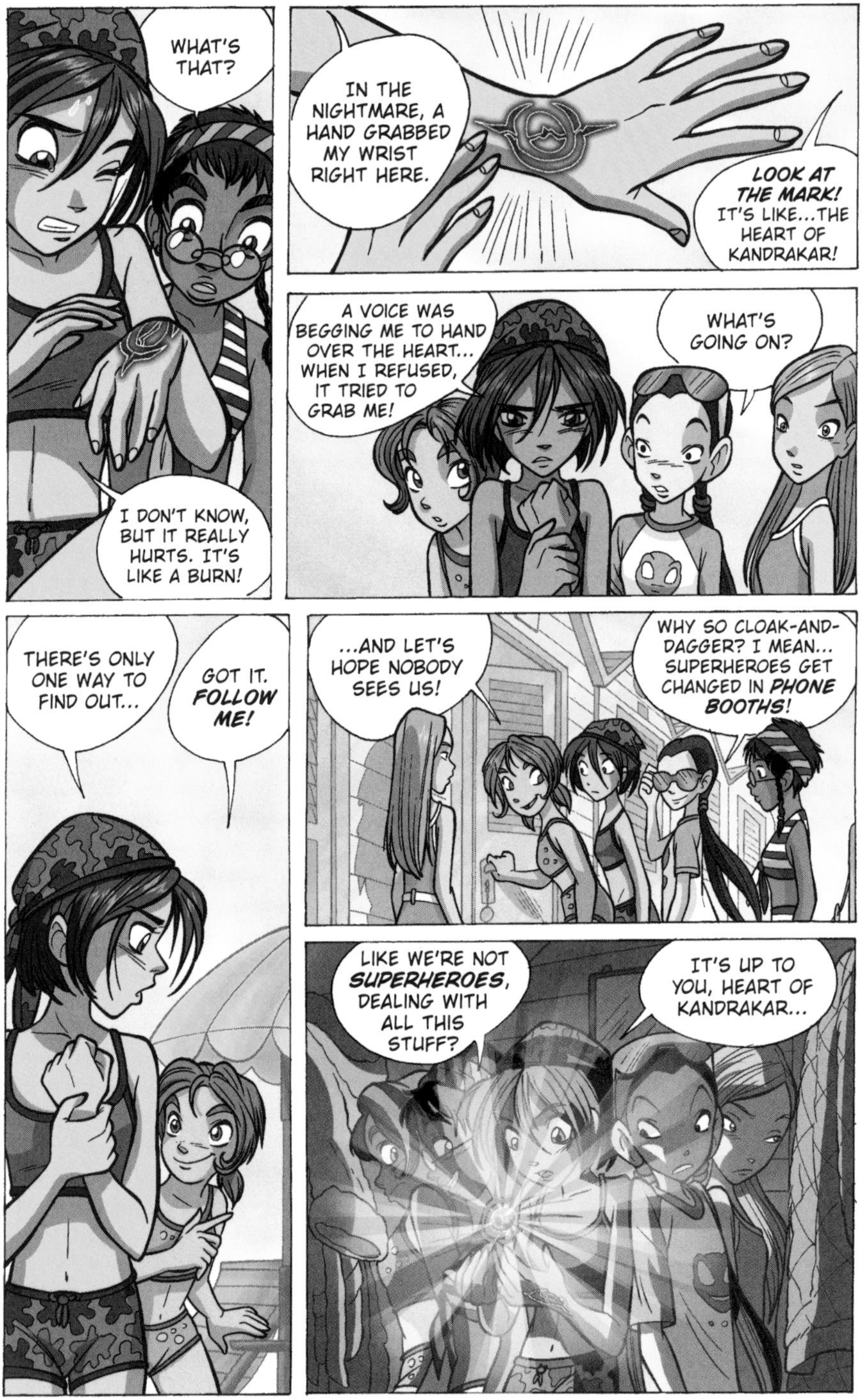
WHAT'S THAT?
I DON'T KNOW, BUT IT REALLY HURTS. IT'S LIKE A BURN!
IN THE NIGHTMARE, A HAND GRABBED MY WRIST RIGHT HERE.
LOOK AT THE MARK! IT'S LIKE...THE HEART OF KANDRAKAR!
A VOICE WAS BEGGING ME TO HAND OVER THE HEART... WHEN I REFUSED, IT TRIED TO GRAB ME!
WHAT'S GOING ON?
THERE'S ONLY ONE WAY TO FIND OUT...
GOT IT. FOLLOW ME!
...AND LET'S HOPE NOBODY SEES US!
WHY SO CLOAK-AND-DAGGER? I MEAN... SUPERHEROES GET CHANGED IN PHONE BOOTHS!
LIKE WE'RE NOT SUPERHEROES, DEALING WITH ALL THIS STUFF?
IT'S UP TO YOU, HEART OF KANDRAKAR...

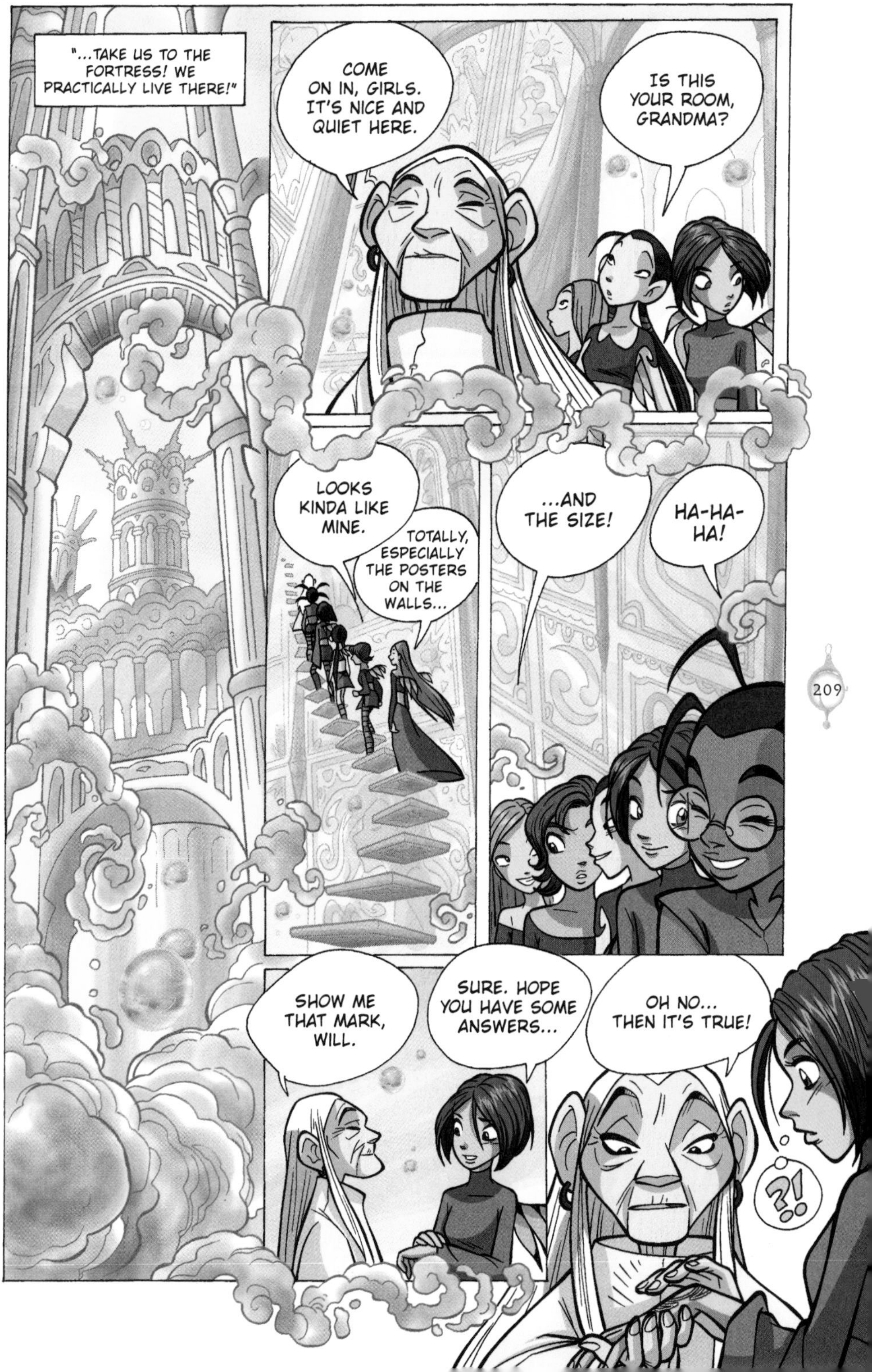
"...TAKE US TO THE FORTRESS! WE PRACTICALLY LIVE THERE!"
COME ON IN, GIRLS. IT'S NICE AND QUIET HERE.
IS THIS YOUR ROOM, GRANDMA?
LOOKS KINDA LIKE MINE.
TOTALLY, ESPECIALLY THE POSTERS ON THE WALLS...
...AND THE SIZE!
HA-HA-HA!
SHOW ME THAT MARK, WILL.
SURE. HOPE YOU HAVE SOME ANSWERS...
OH NO... THEN IT'S TRUE!
?!

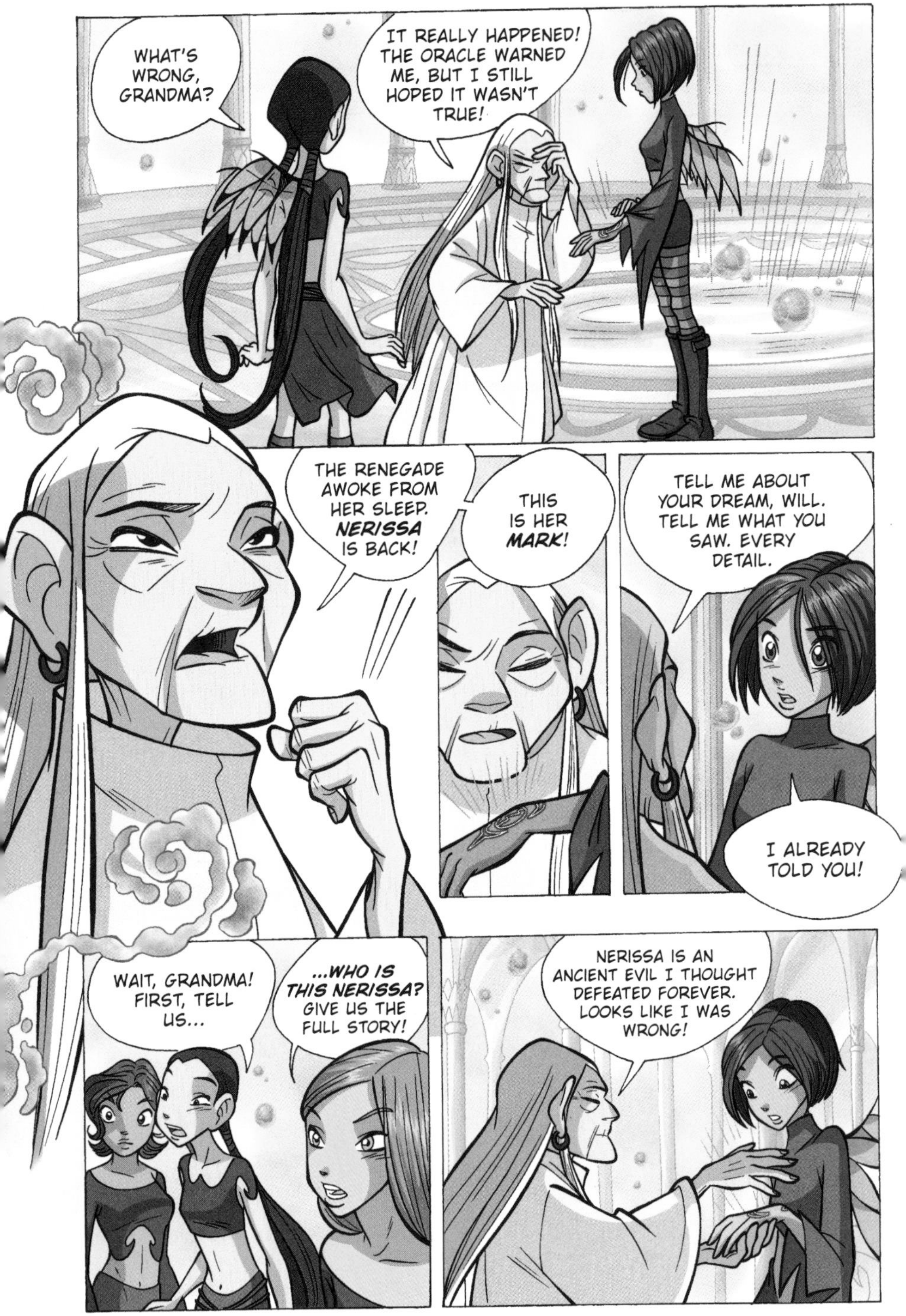

WHAT'S WRONG, GRANDMA?
IT REALLY HAPPENED! THE ORACLE WARNED ME, BUT I STILL HOPED IT WASN'T TRUE!
THE RENEGADE AWOKE FROM HER SLEEP. NERISSA IS BACK!
THIS IS HER MARK!
TELL ME ABOUT YOUR DREAM, WILL. TELL ME WHAT YOU SAW. EVERY DETAIL.
I ALREADY TOLD YOU!
WAIT, GRANDMA! FIRST, TELL US...
...WHO IS THIS NERISSA? GIVE US THE FULL STORY!
NERISSA IS AN ANCIENT EVIL I THOUGHT DEFEATED FOREVER. LOOKS LIKE I WAS WRONG!

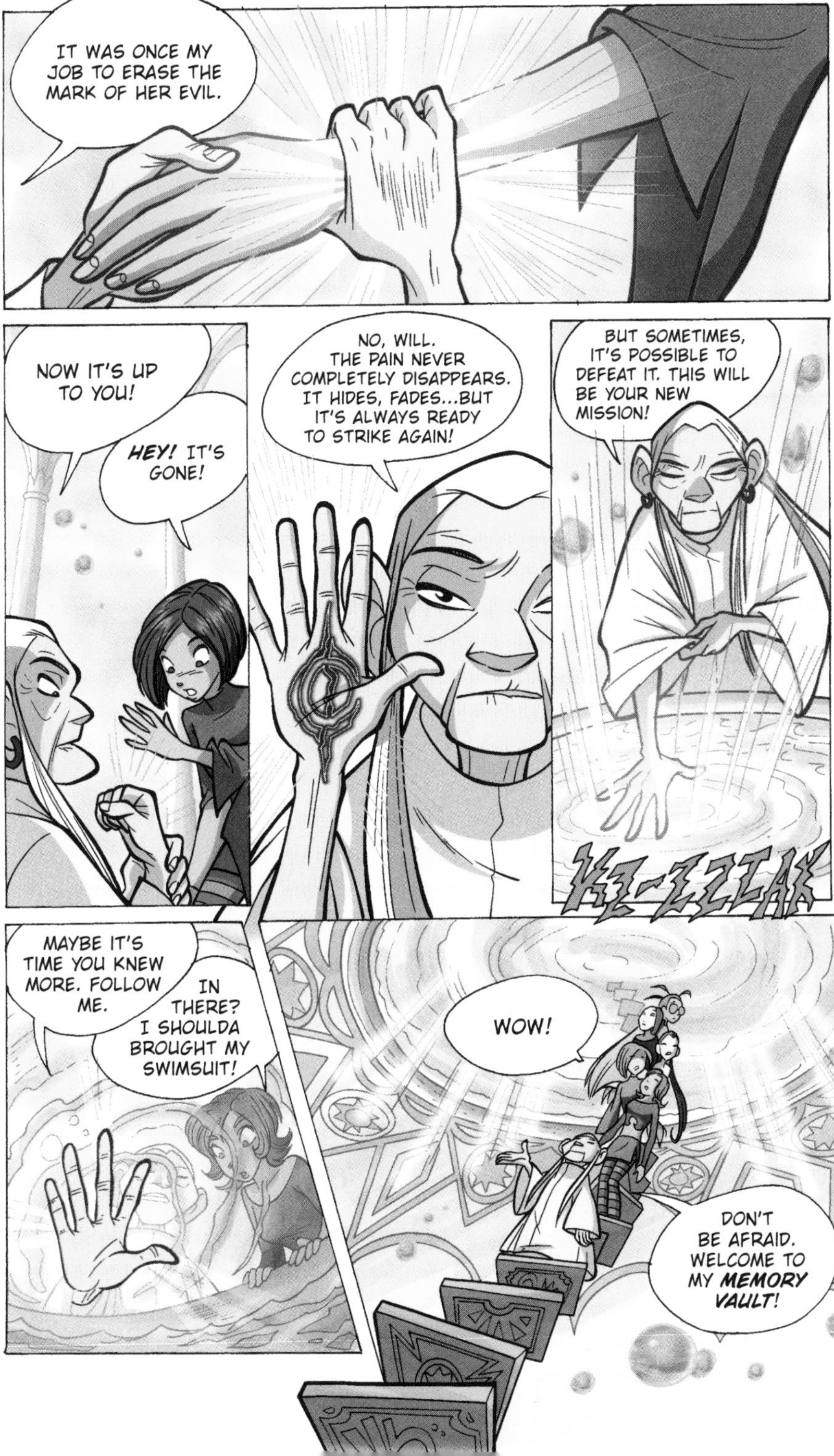
IT WAS ONCE MY JOB TO ERASE THE MARK OF HER EVIL.
NOW IT'S UP TO YOU!
HEY! IT'S GONE!
NO, WILL. THE PAIN NEVER COMPLETELY DISAPPEARS. IT HIDES, FADES...BUT IT'S ALWAYS READY TO STRIKE AGAIN!
BUT SOMETIMES, IT'S POSSIBLE TO DEFEAT IT. THIS WILL BE YOUR NEW MISSION!
KZ-ZZZAK
MAYBE IT'S TIME YOU KNEW MORE. FOLLOW ME.
IN THERE? I SHOULDA BROUGHT MY SWIMSUIT!
WOW!
DON'T BE AFRAID. WELCOME TO MY **MEMORY VAULT**!

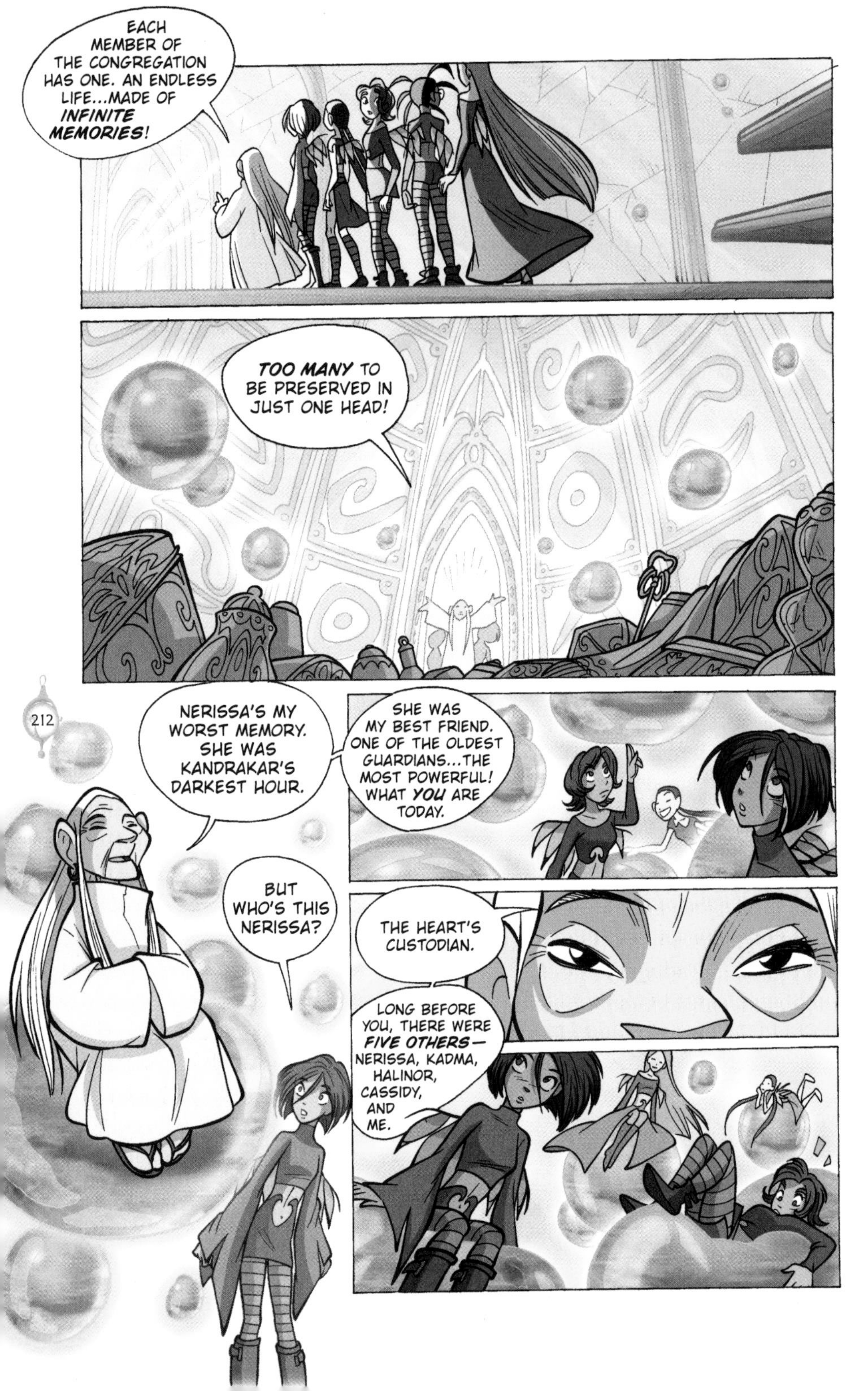
EACH MEMBER OF THE CONGREGATION HAS ONE. AN ENDLESS LIFE...MADE OF INFINITE MEMORIES!
TOO MANY TO BE PRESERVED IN JUST ONE HEAD!
NERISSA'S MY WORST MEMORY. SHE WAS KANDRAKAR'S DARKEST HOUR.
SHE WAS MY BEST FRIEND. ONE OF THE OLDEST GUARDIANS...THE MOST POWERFUL! WHAT YOU ARE TODAY.
BUT WHO'S THIS NERISSA?
THE HEART'S CUSTODIAN.
LONG BEFORE YOU, THERE WERE FIVE OTHERS— NERISSA, KADMA, HALINOR, CASSIDY, AND ME.

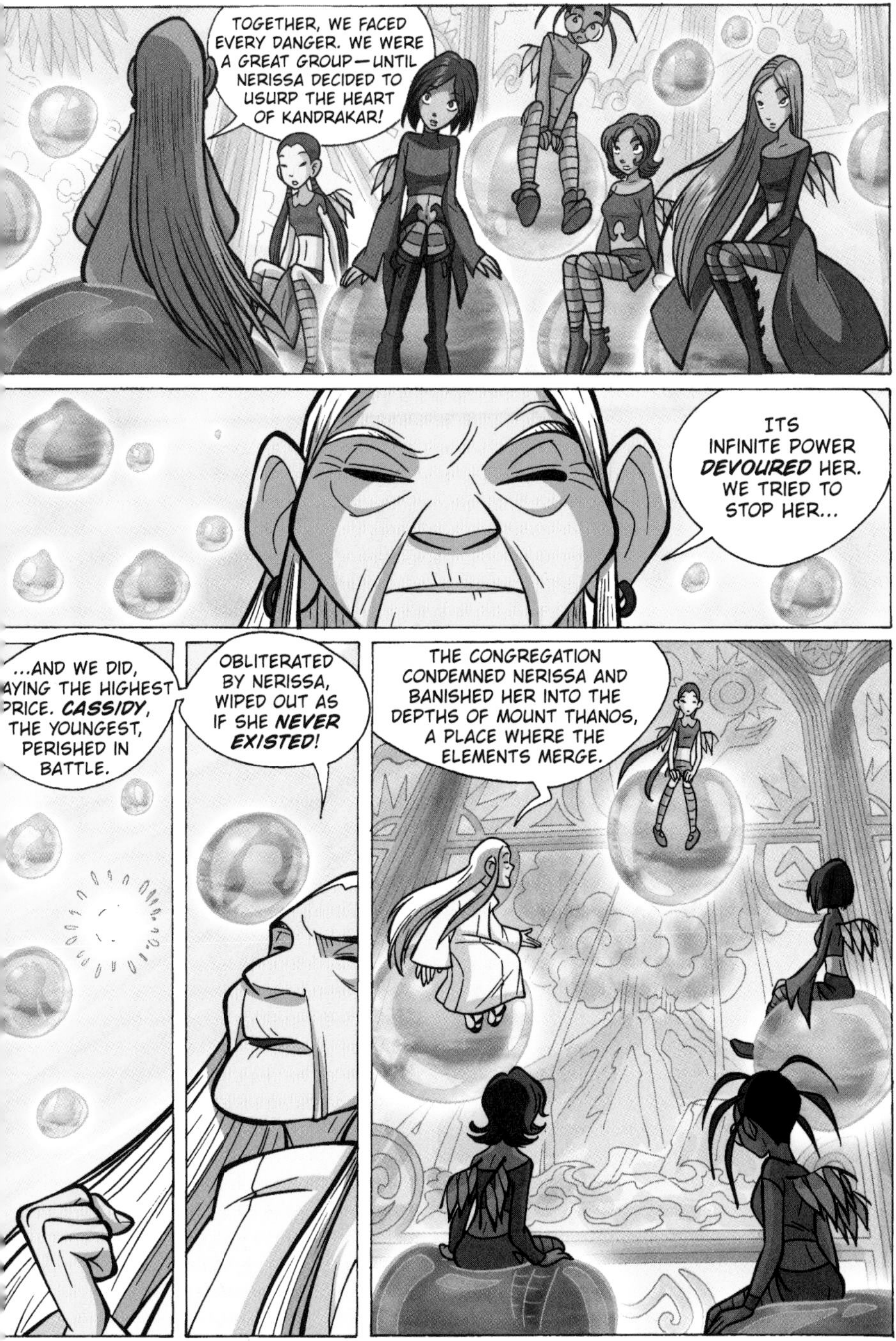
TOGETHER, WE FACED EVERY DANGER. WE WERE A GREAT GROUP—UNTIL NERISSA DECIDED TO USURP THE HEART OF KANDRAKAR!
ITS INFINITE POWER DEVOURED HER. WE TRIED TO STOP HER...
...AND WE DID, AYING THE HIGHEST RICE. CASSIDY, THE YOUNGEST, PERISHED IN BATTLE.
OBLITERATED BY NERISSA, WIPED OUT AS IF SHE NEVER EXISTED!
THE CONGREGATION CONDEMNED NERISSA AND BANISHED HER INTO THE DEPTHS OF MOUNT THANOS, A PLACE WHERE THE ELEMENTS MERGE.

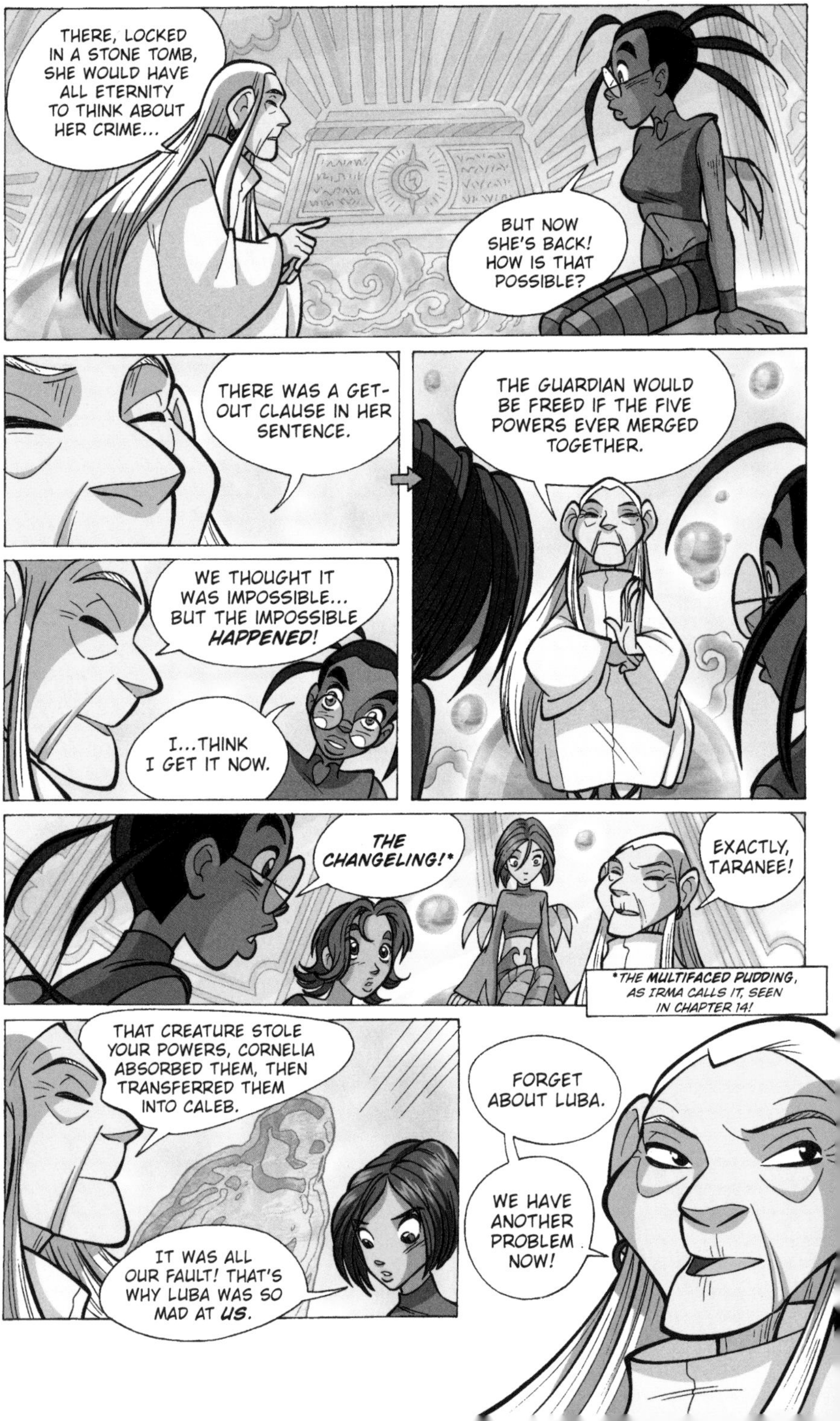

THERE, LOCKED IN A STONE TOMB, SHE WOULD HAVE ALL ETERNITY TO THINK ABOUT HER CRIME...
BUT NOW SHE'S BACK! HOW IS THAT POSSIBLE?
THERE WAS A GET-OUT CLAUSE IN HER SENTENCE.
THE GUARDIAN WOULD BE FREED IF THE FIVE POWERS EVER MERGED TOGETHER.
WE THOUGHT IT WAS IMPOSSIBLE... BUT THE IMPOSSIBLE HAPPENED!
I...THINK I GET IT NOW.
THE CHANGELING!*
EXACTLY, TARANEE!
*THE MULTIFACED PUDDING, AS IRMA CALLS IT, SEEN IN CHAPTER 14!
THAT CREATURE STOLE YOUR POWERS, CORNELIA ABSORBED THEM, THEN TRANSFERRED THEM INTO CALEB.
IT WAS ALL OUR FAULT! THAT'S WHY LUBA WAS SO MAD AT US.
FORGET ABOUT LUBA.
WE HAVE ANOTHER PROBLEM NOW!

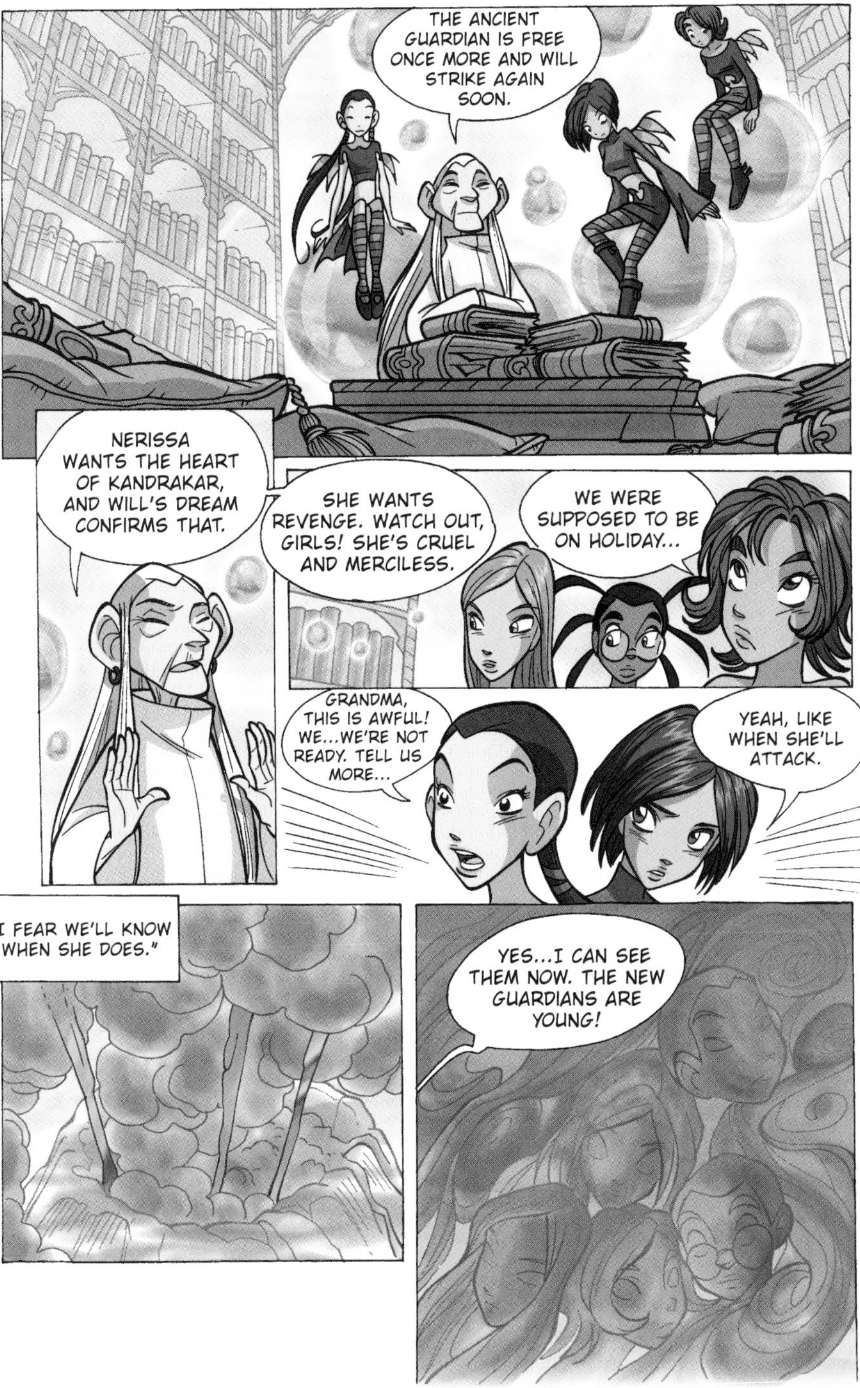
THE ANCIENT GUARDIAN IS FREE ONCE MORE AND WILL STRIKE AGAIN SOON.
NERISSA WANTS THE HEART OF KANDRAKAR, AND WILL'S DREAM CONFIRMS THAT.
SHE WANTS REVENGE. WATCH OUT, GIRLS! SHE'S CRUEL AND MERCILESS.
WE WERE SUPPOSED TO BE ON HOLIDAY...
GRANDMA, THIS IS AWFUL! WE...WE'RE NOT READY. TELL US MORE...
YEAH, LIKE WHEN SHE'LL ATTACK.
"I FEAR WE'LL KNOW WHEN SHE DOES."
YES...I CAN SEE THEM NOW. THE NEW GUARDIANS ARE YOUNG!

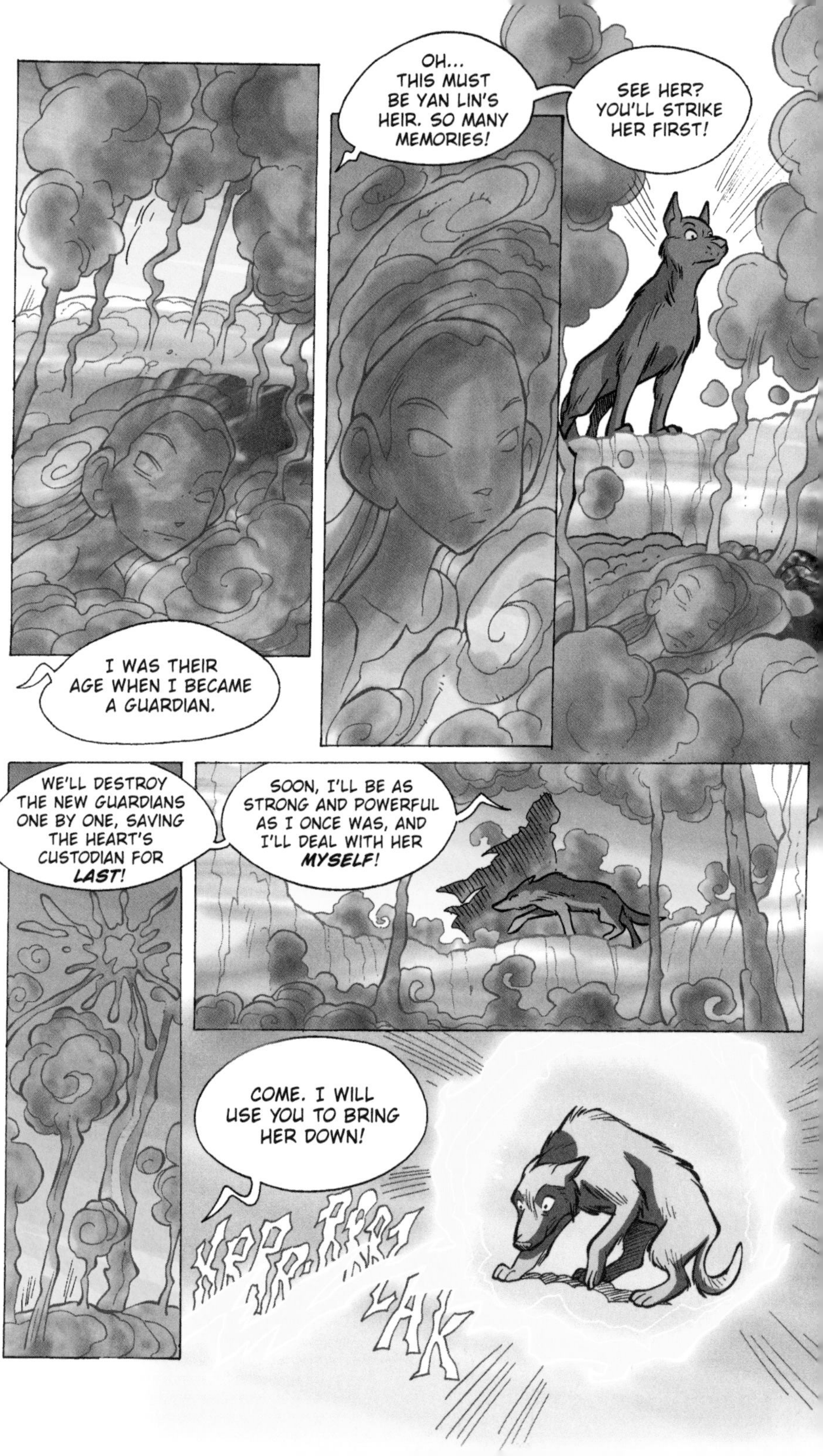
OH... THIS MUST BE YAN LIN'S HEIR. SO MANY MEMORIES!
SEE HER? YOU'LL STRIKE HER FIRST!
I WAS THEIR AGE WHEN I BECAME A GUARDIAN.
WE'LL DESTROY THE NEW GUARDIANS ONE BY ONE, SAVING THE HEART'S CUSTODIAN FOR LAST!
SOON, I'LL BE AS STRONG AND POWERFUL AS I ONCE WAS, AND I'LL DEAL WITH HER MYSELF!
COME. I WILL USE YOU TO BRING HER DOWN!

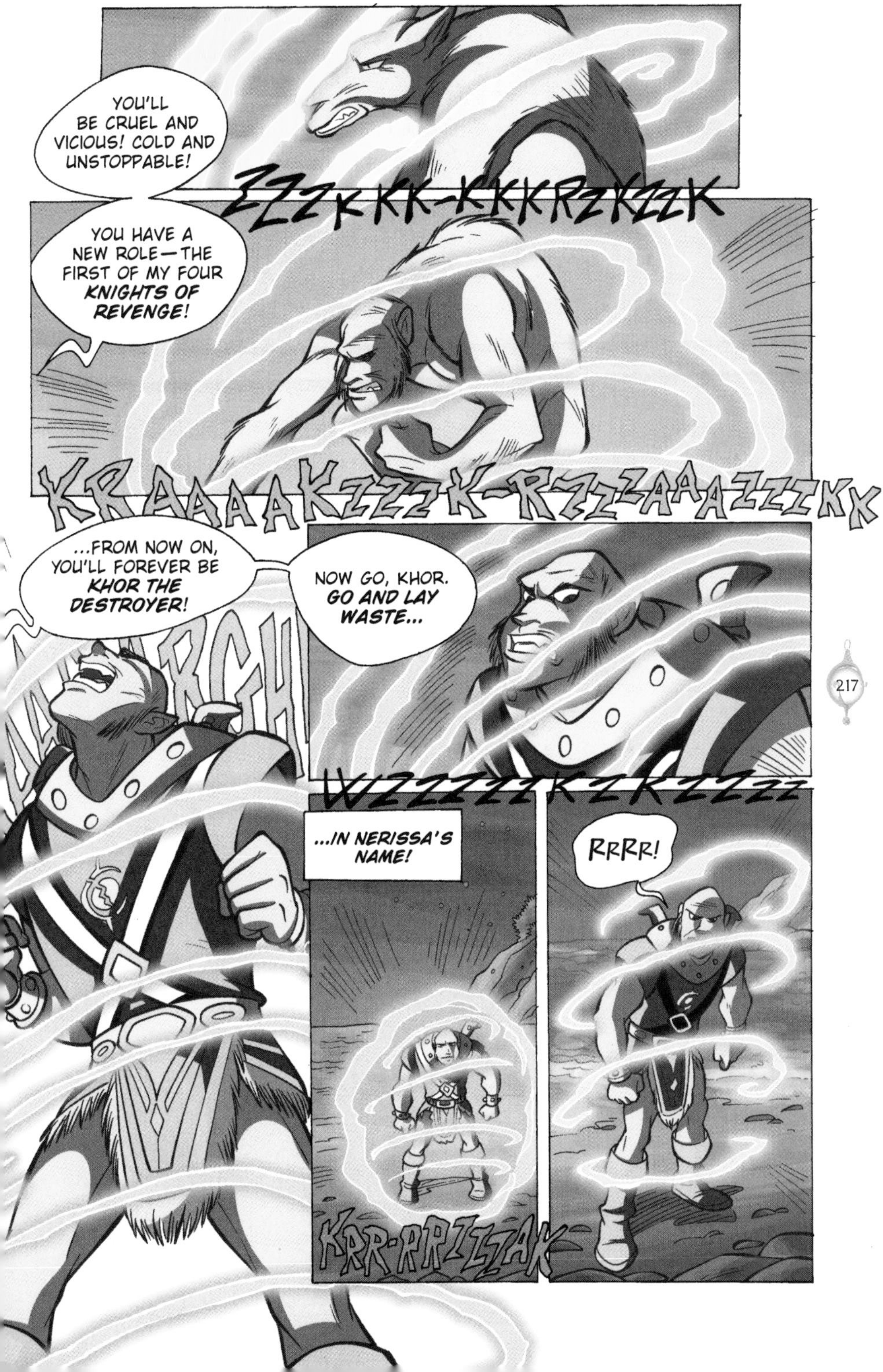
YOU'LL BE CRUEL AND VICIOUS! COLD AND UNSTOPPABLE!
YOU HAVE A NEW ROLE—THE FIRST OF MY FOUR **KNIGHTS OF REVENGE!**
...FROM NOW ON, YOU'LL FOREVER BE **KHOR THE DESTROYER!**
NOW GO, KHOR. **GO AND LAY WASTE...**
...IN NERISSA'S NAME!
RRRR!

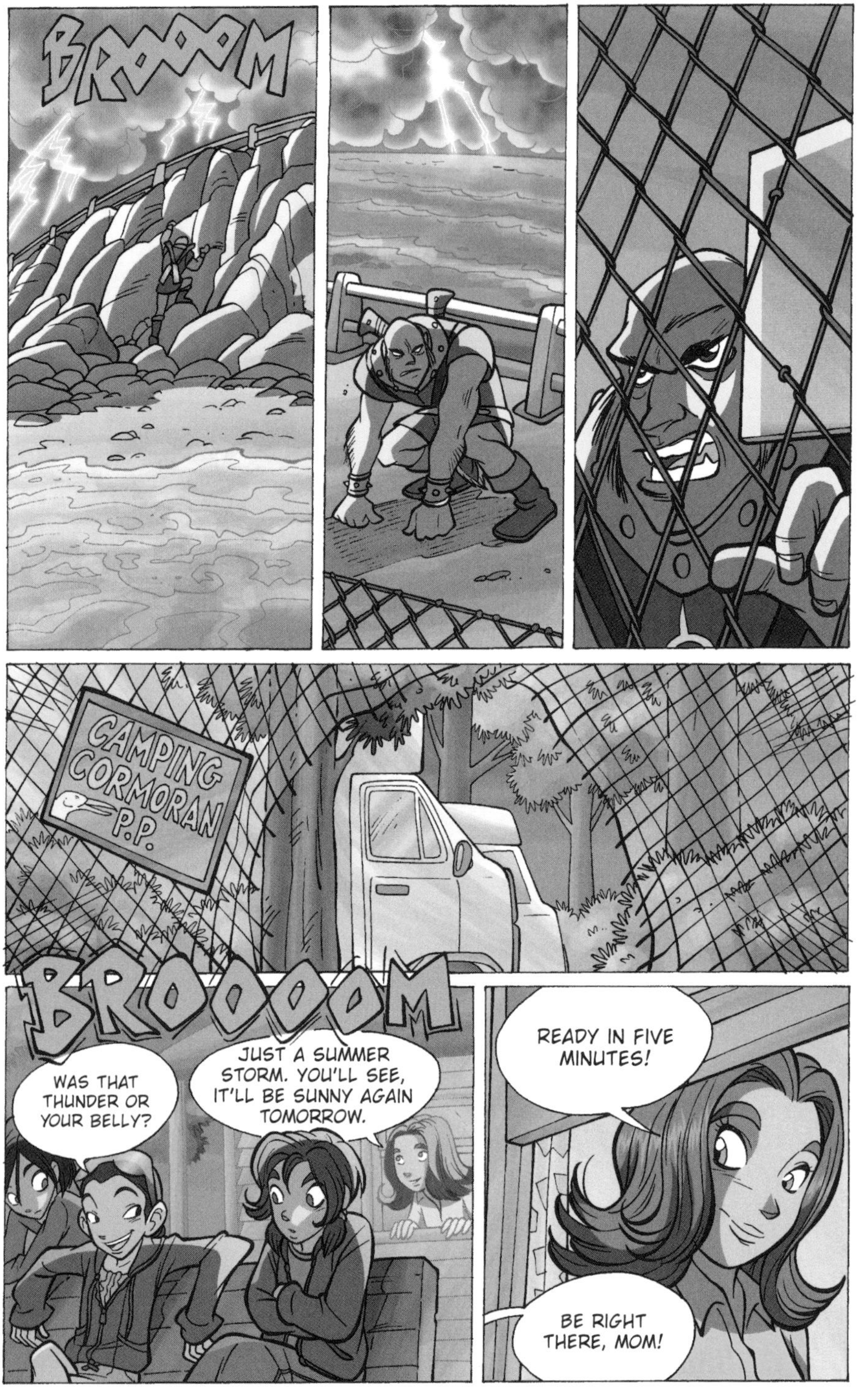
BROOOM
CAMPING CORMORAN P.P.
BROOOOM
WAS THAT THUNDER OR YOUR BELLY?
JUST A SUMMER STORM. YOU'LL SEE, IT'LL BE SUNNY AGAIN TOMORROW.
READY IN FIVE MINUTES!
BE RIGHT THERE, MOM!

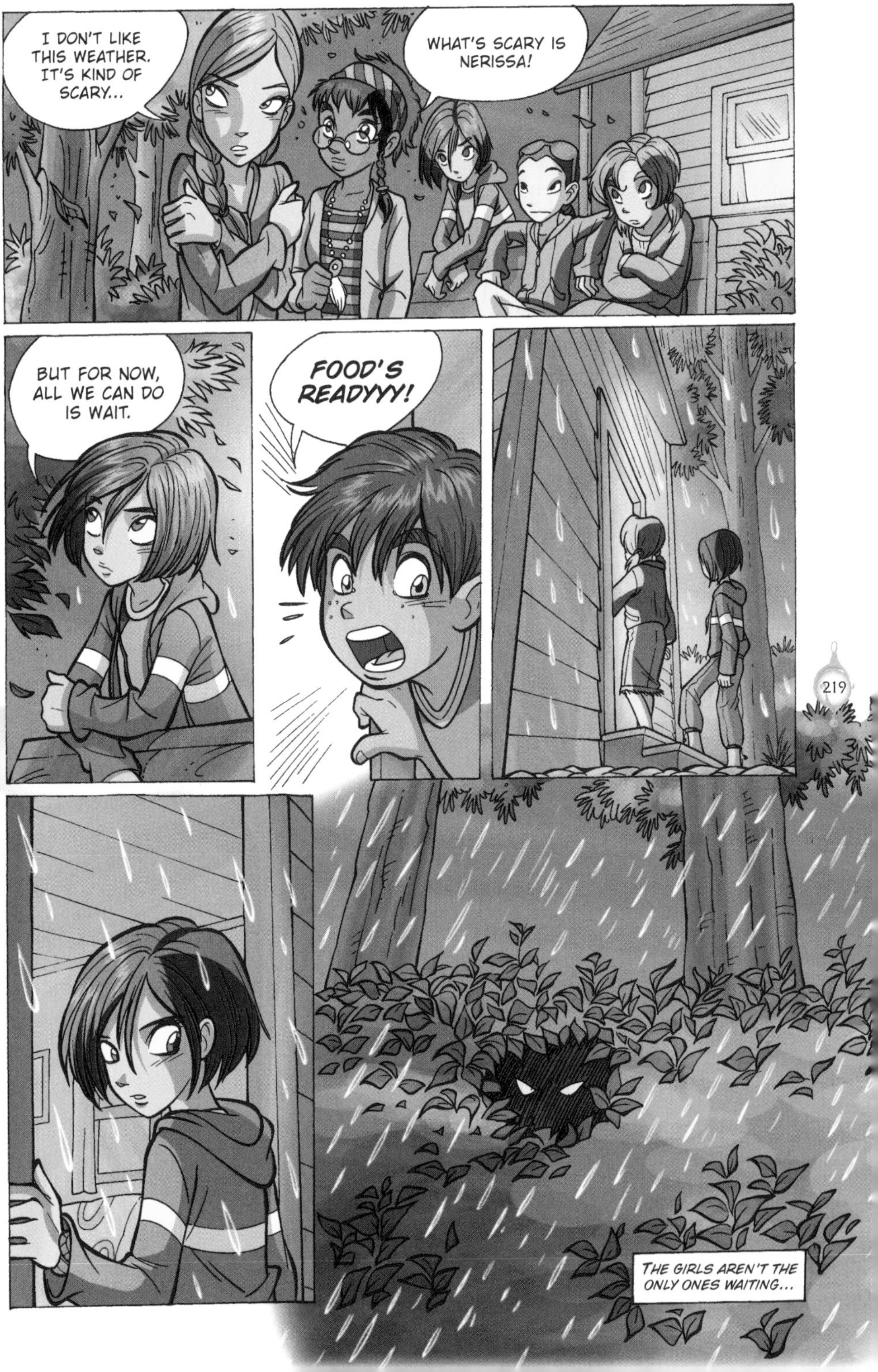
I DON'T LIKE THIS WEATHER. IT'S KIND OF SCARY...
WHAT'S SCARY IS NERISSA!
BUT FOR NOW, ALL WE CAN DO IS WAIT.
FOOD'S READYYY!
THE GIRLS AREN'T THE ONLY ONES WAITING...

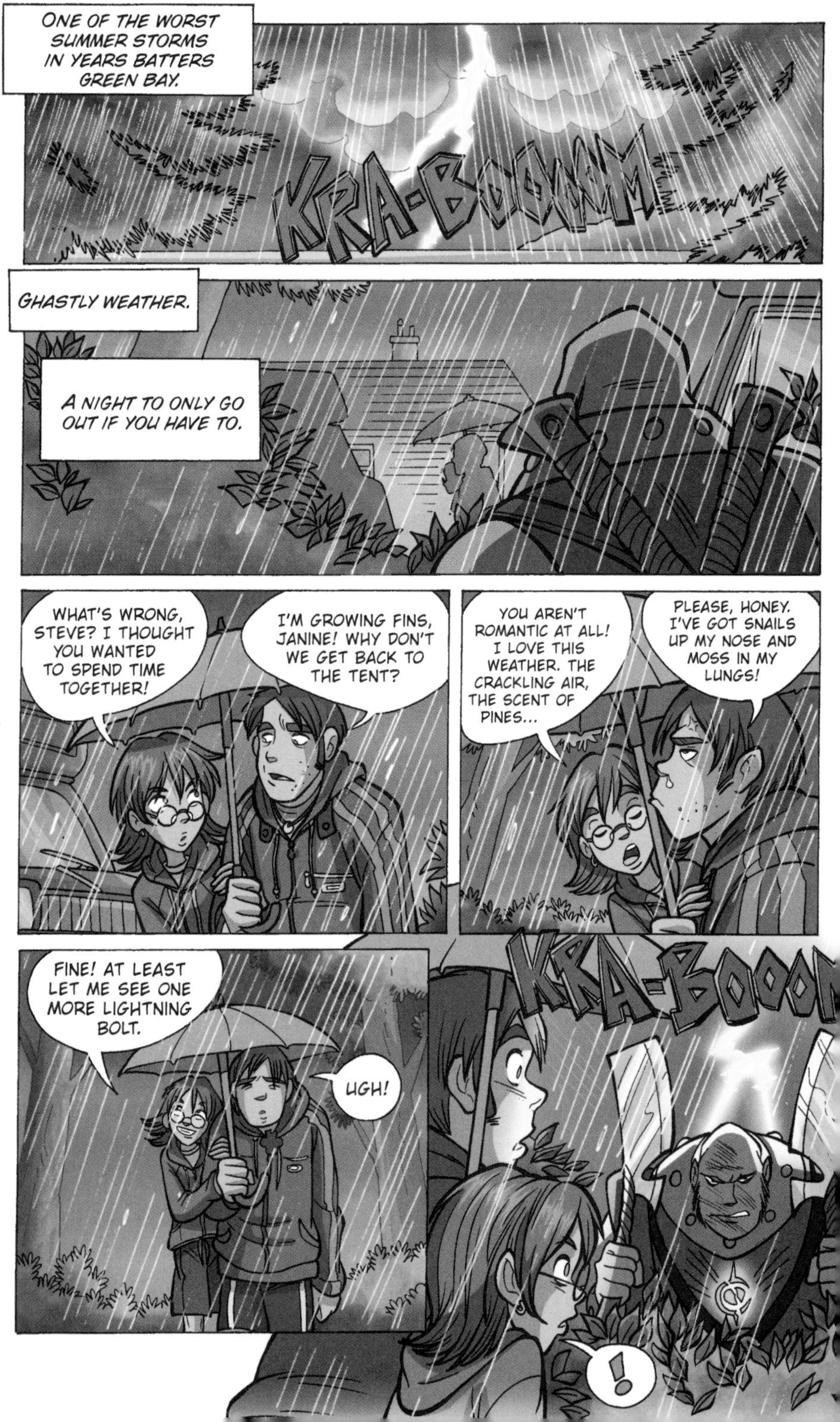
ONE OF THE WORST SUMMER STORMS IN YEARS BATTERS GREEN BAY.
KRA-BOOWM
GHASTLY WEATHER.
A NIGHT TO ONLY GO OUT IF YOU HAVE TO.
WHAT'S WRONG, STEVE? I THOUGHT YOU WANTED TO SPEND TIME TOGETHER!
I'M GROWING FINS, JANINE! WHY DON'T WE GET BACK TO THE TENT?
YOU AREN'T ROMANTIC AT ALL! I LOVE THIS WEATHER. THE CRACKLING AIR, THE SCENT OF PINES...
PLEASE, HONEY. I'VE GOT SNAILS UP MY NOSE AND MOSS IN MY LUNGS!
FINE! AT LEAST LET ME SEE ONE MORE LIGHTNING BOLT.
UGH!
KRA-BOOO
!

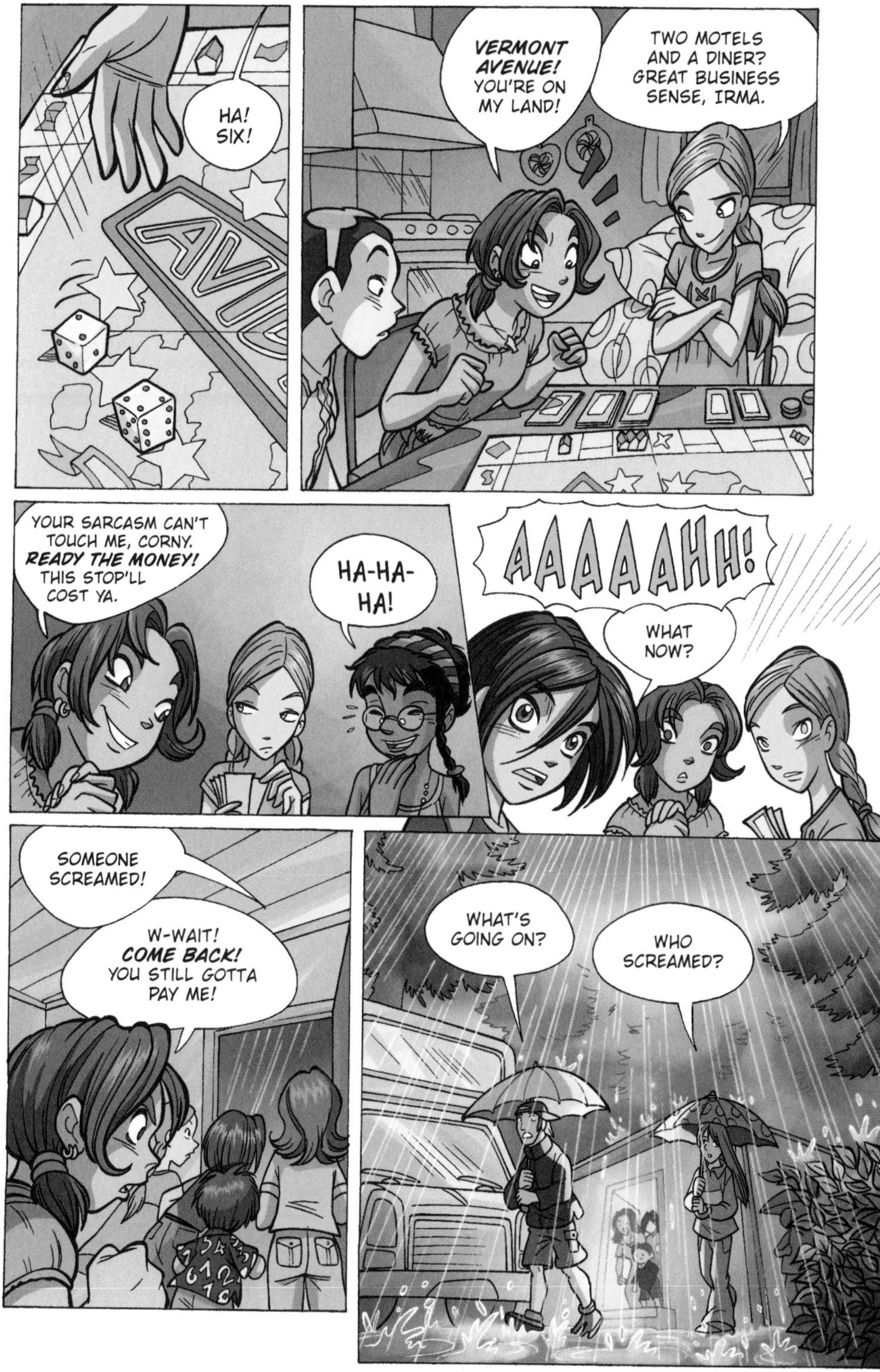
HA!
SIX!
VERMONT AVENUE! YOU'RE ON MY LAND!
TWO MOTELS AND A DINER? GREAT BUSINESS SENSE, IRMA.
YOUR SARCASM CAN'T TOUCH ME, CORNY. READY THE MONEY! THIS STOP'LL COST YA.
HA-HA-HA!
AAAAAHH!
WHAT NOW?
SOMEONE SCREAMED!
W-WAIT! COME BACK! YOU STILL GOTTA PAY ME!
WHAT'S GOING ON?
WHO SCREAMED?

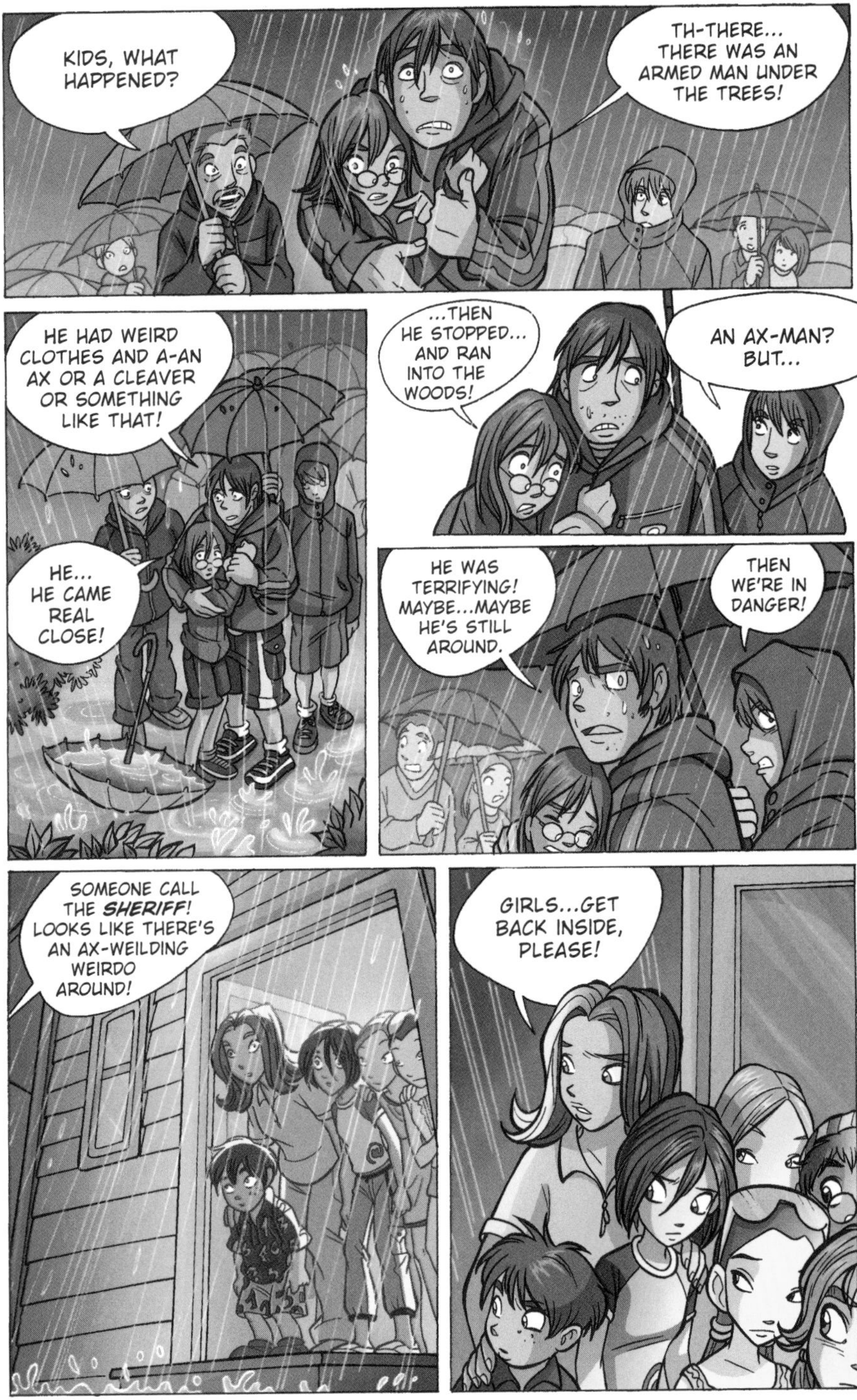
KIDS, WHAT HAPPENED?
TH-THERE... THERE WAS AN ARMED MAN UNDER THE TREES!
HE HAD WEIRD CLOTHES AND A-AN AX OR A CLEAVER OR SOMETHING LIKE THAT!
HE... HE CAME REAL CLOSE!
...THEN HE STOPPED... AND RAN INTO THE WOODS!
AN AX-MAN? BUT...
HE WAS TERRIFYING! MAYBE...MAYBE HE'S STILL AROUND.
THEN WE'RE IN DANGER!
SOMEONE CALL THE SHERIFF! LOOKS LIKE THERE'S AN AX-WEILDING WEIRDO AROUND!
GIRLS...GET BACK INSIDE, PLEASE!

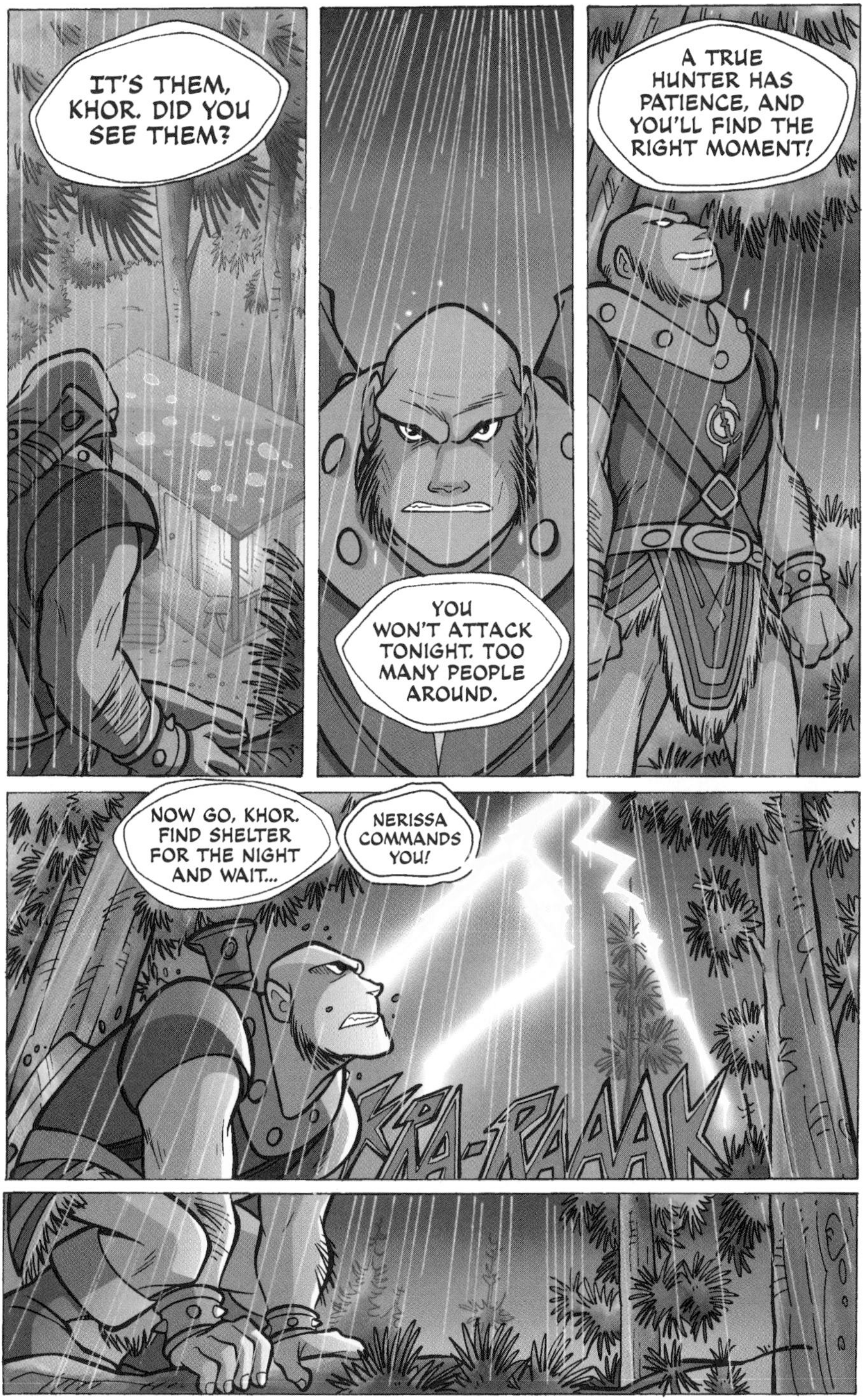
IT'S THEM, KHOR. DID YOU SEE THEM?
YOU WON'T ATTACK TONIGHT. TOO MANY PEOPLE AROUND.
A TRUE HUNTER HAS PATIENCE, AND YOU'LL FIND THE RIGHT MOMENT!
NOW GO, KHOR. FIND SHELTER FOR THE NIGHT AND WAIT...
NERISSA COMMANDS YOU!
KRA-RAAAK

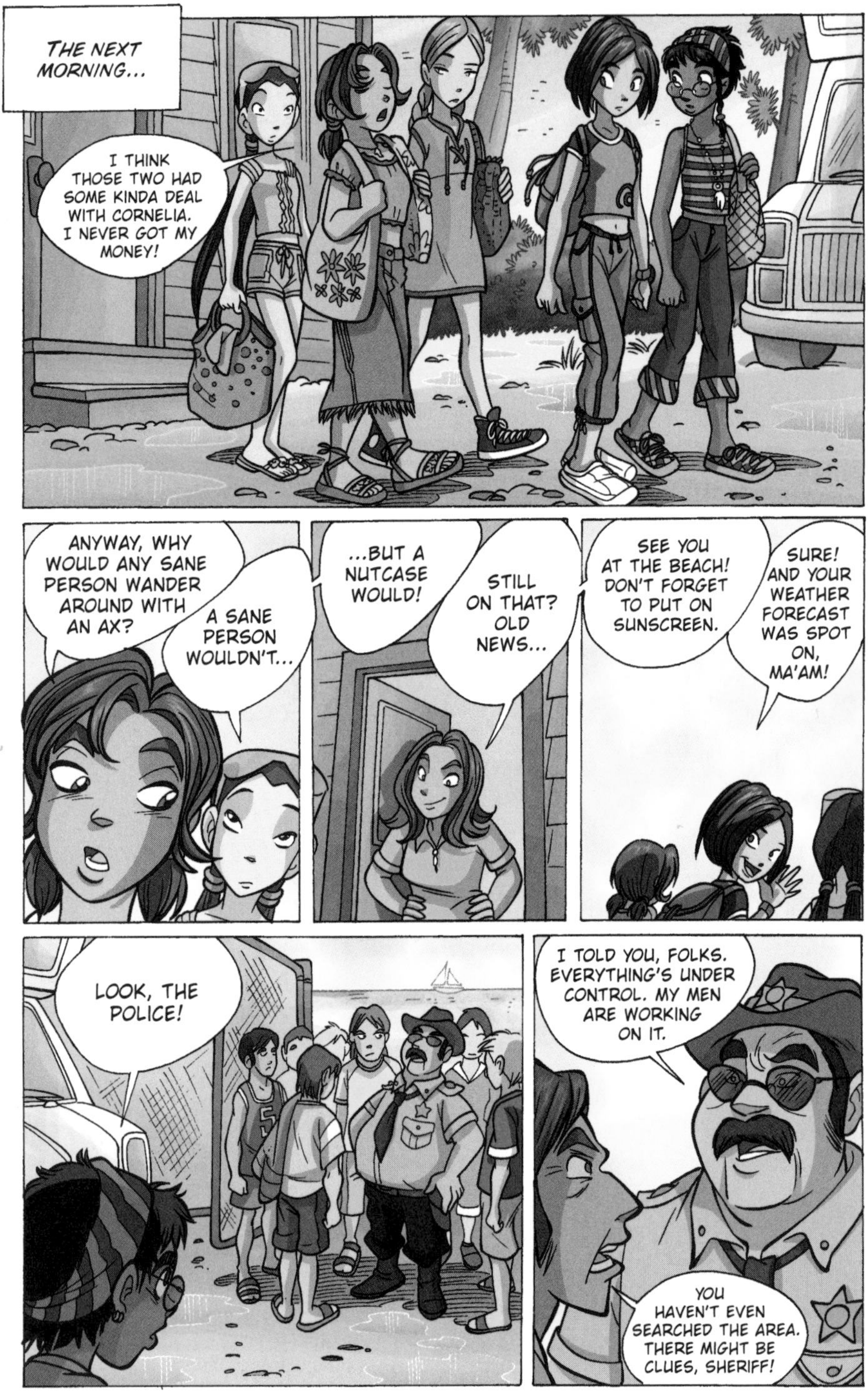
THE NEXT MORNING...
I THINK THOSE TWO HAD SOME KINDA DEAL WITH CORNELIA. I NEVER GOT MY MONEY!
ANYWAY, WHY WOULD ANY SANE PERSON WANDER AROUND WITH AN AX?
A SANE PERSON WOULDN'T...
...BUT A NUTCASE WOULD!
STILL ON THAT? OLD NEWS...
SEE YOU AT THE BEACH! DON'T FORGET TO PUT ON SUNSCREEN.
SURE! AND YOUR WEATHER FORECAST WAS SPOT ON, MA'AM!
LOOK, THE POLICE!
I TOLD YOU, FOLKS. EVERYTHING'S UNDER CONTROL. MY MEN ARE WORKING ON IT.
YOU HAVEN'T EVEN SEARCHED THE AREA. THERE MIGHT BE CLUES, SHERIFF!

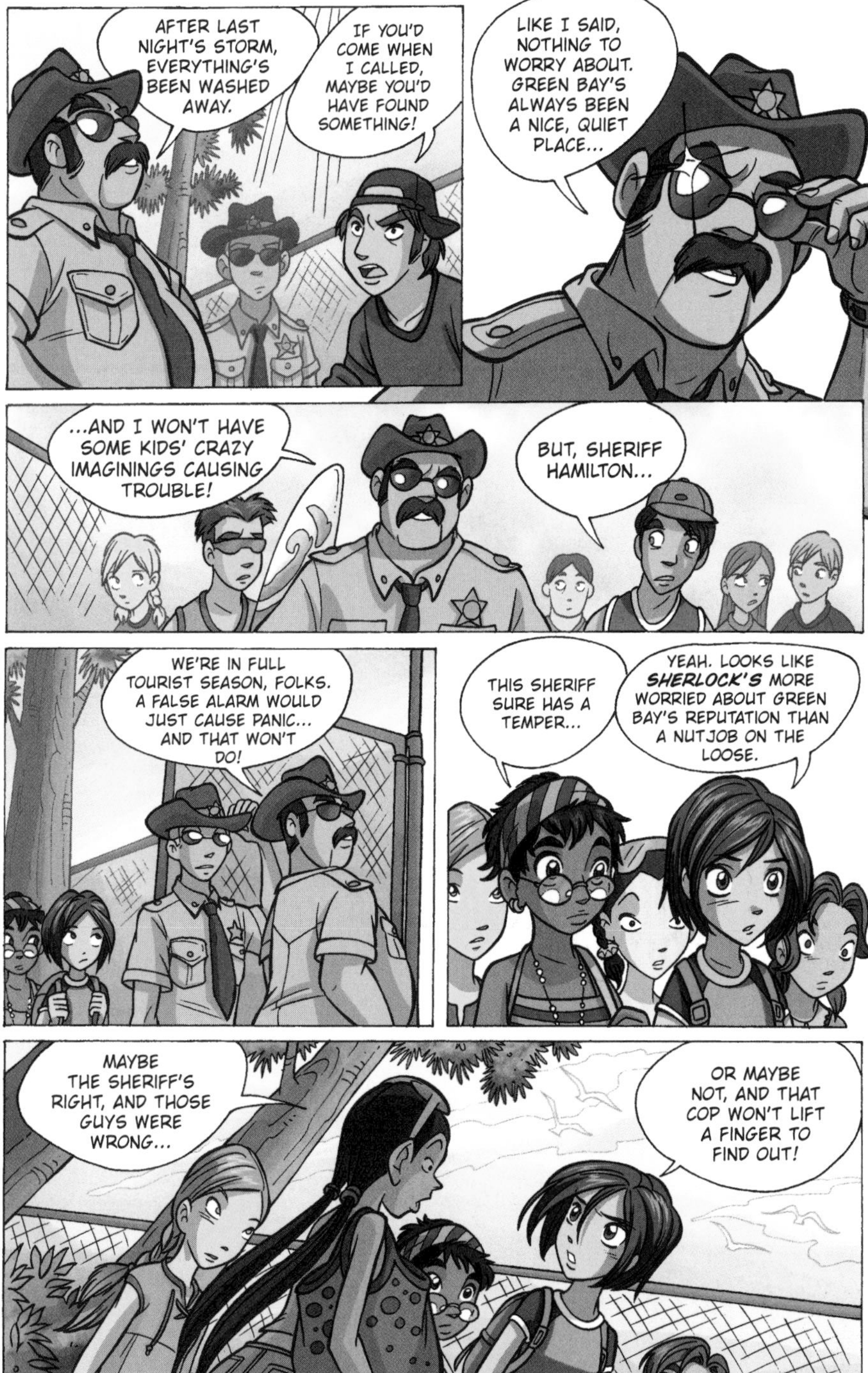
AFTER LAST NIGHT'S STORM, EVERYTHING'S BEEN WASHED AWAY.
IF YOU'D COME WHEN I CALLED, MAYBE YOU'D HAVE FOUND SOMETHING!
LIKE I SAID, NOTHING TO WORRY ABOUT. GREEN BAY'S ALWAYS BEEN A NICE, QUIET PLACE...
...AND I WON'T HAVE SOME KIDS' CRAZY IMAGININGS CAUSING TROUBLE!
BUT, SHERIFF HAMILTON...
WE'RE IN FULL TOURIST SEASON, FOLKS. A FALSE ALARM WOULD JUST CAUSE PANIC... AND THAT WON'T DO!
THIS SHERIFF SURE HAS A TEMPER...
YEAH. LOOKS LIKE ***SHERLOCK'S*** MORE WORRIED ABOUT GREEN BAY'S REPUTATION THAN A NUTJOB ON THE LOOSE.
MAYBE THE SHERIFF'S RIGHT, AND THOSE GUYS WERE WRONG...
OR MAYBE NOT, AND THAT COP WON'T LIFT A FINGER TO FIND OUT!

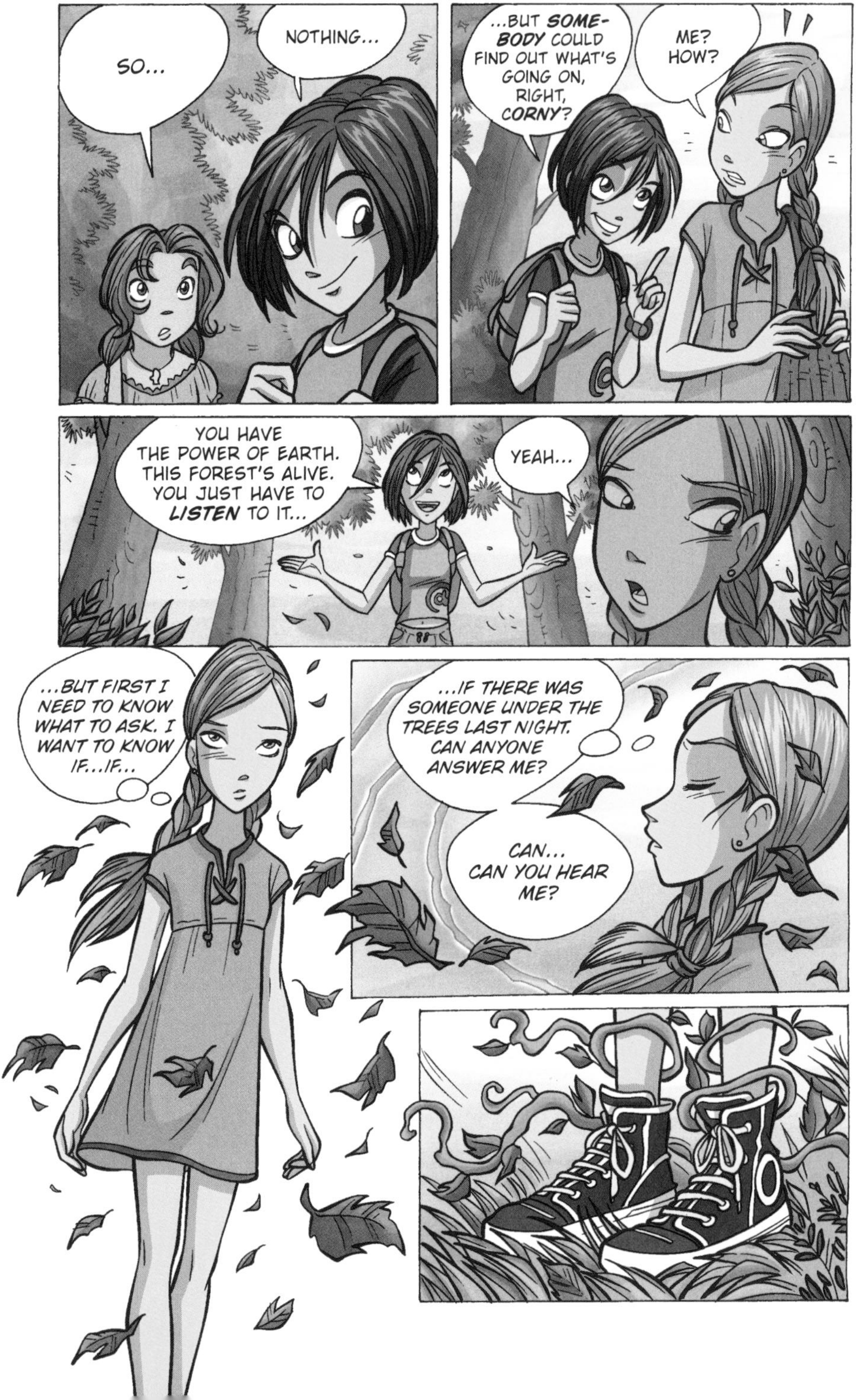
SO...
NOTHING...
...BUT **SOME-BODY** COULD FIND OUT WHAT'S GOING ON, RIGHT, **CORNY**?
ME? HOW?
YOU HAVE THE POWER OF EARTH. THIS FOREST'S ALIVE. YOU JUST HAVE TO **LISTEN** TO IT...
YEAH...
...BUT FIRST I NEED TO KNOW WHAT TO ASK. I WANT TO KNOW IF...IF...
...IF THERE WAS SOMEONE UNDER THE TREES LAST NIGHT. CAN ANYONE ANSWER ME?
CAN... CAN YOU HEAR ME?

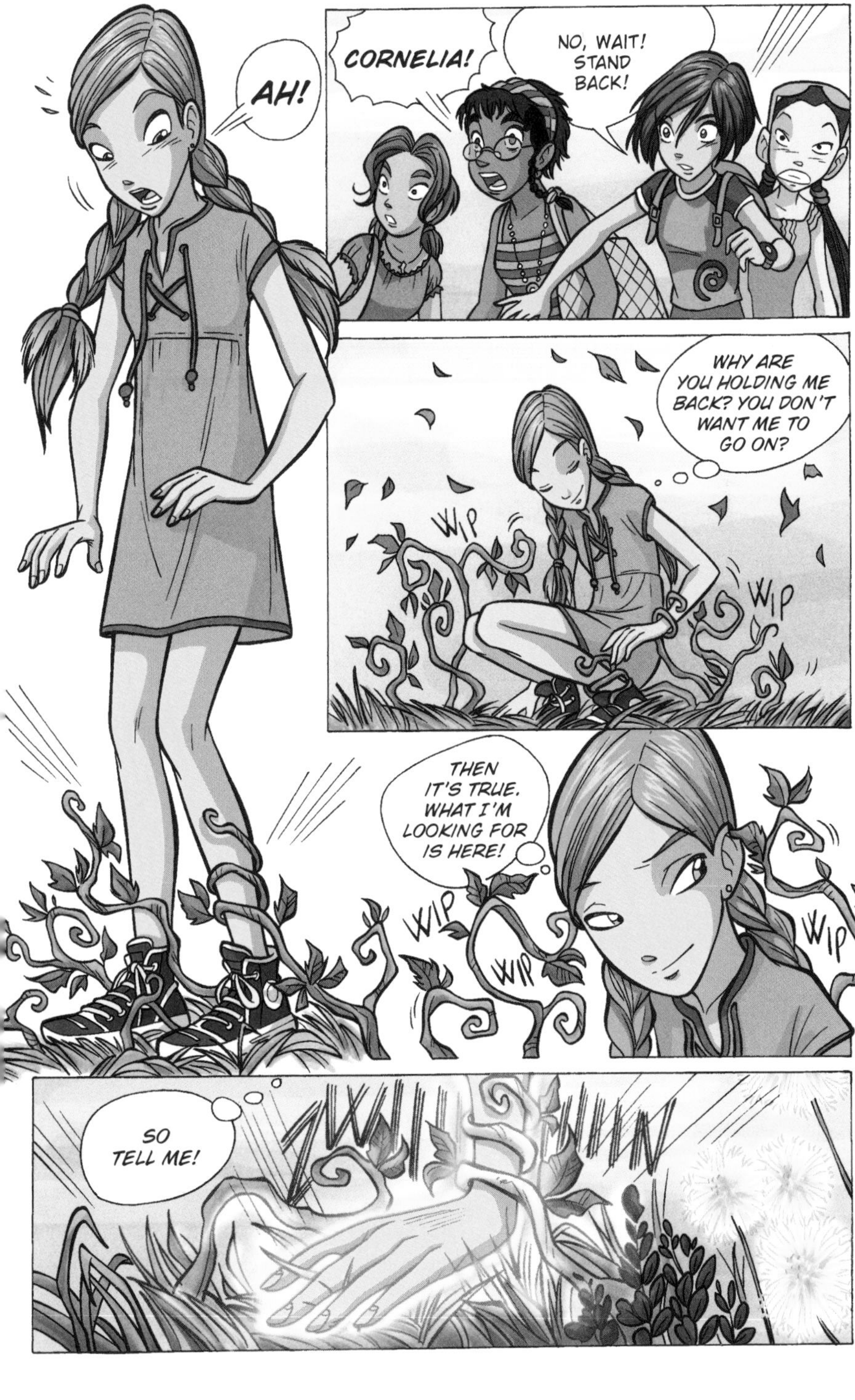
AH!
CORNELIA!
NO, WAIT! STAND BACK!
WHY ARE YOU HOLDING ME BACK? YOU DON'T WANT ME TO GO ON?
WIP
WIP
THEN IT'S TRUE. WHAT I'M LOOKING FOR IS HERE!
WIP
WIP
WIP
SO TELL ME!
ZWIIISHHHN

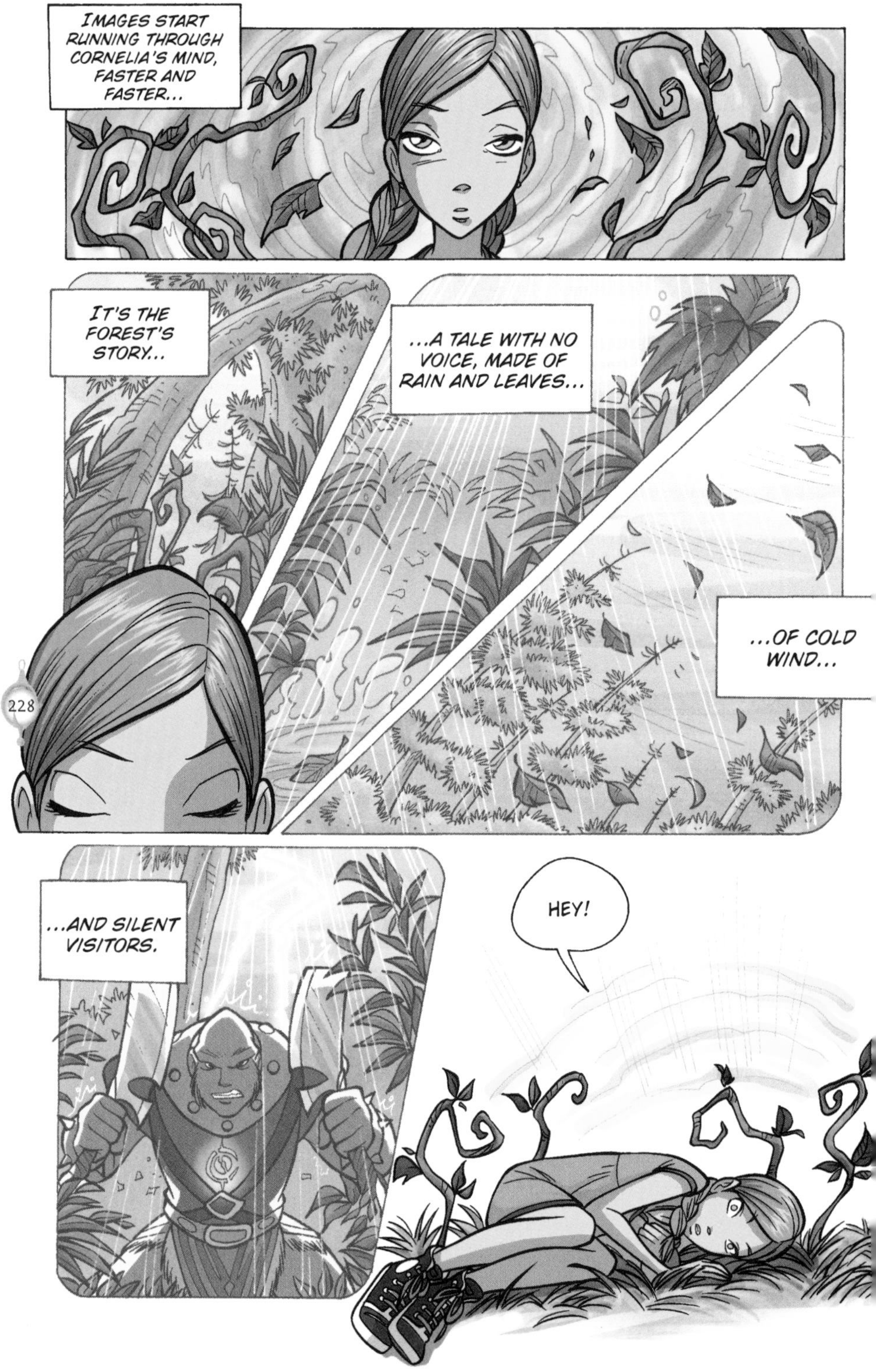
IMAGES START RUNNING THROUGH CORNELIA'S MIND, FASTER AND FASTER...
IT'S THE FOREST'S STORY...
...A TALE WITH NO VOICE, MADE OF RAIN AND LEAVES...
...OF COLD WIND...
...AND SILENT VISITORS.
HEY!

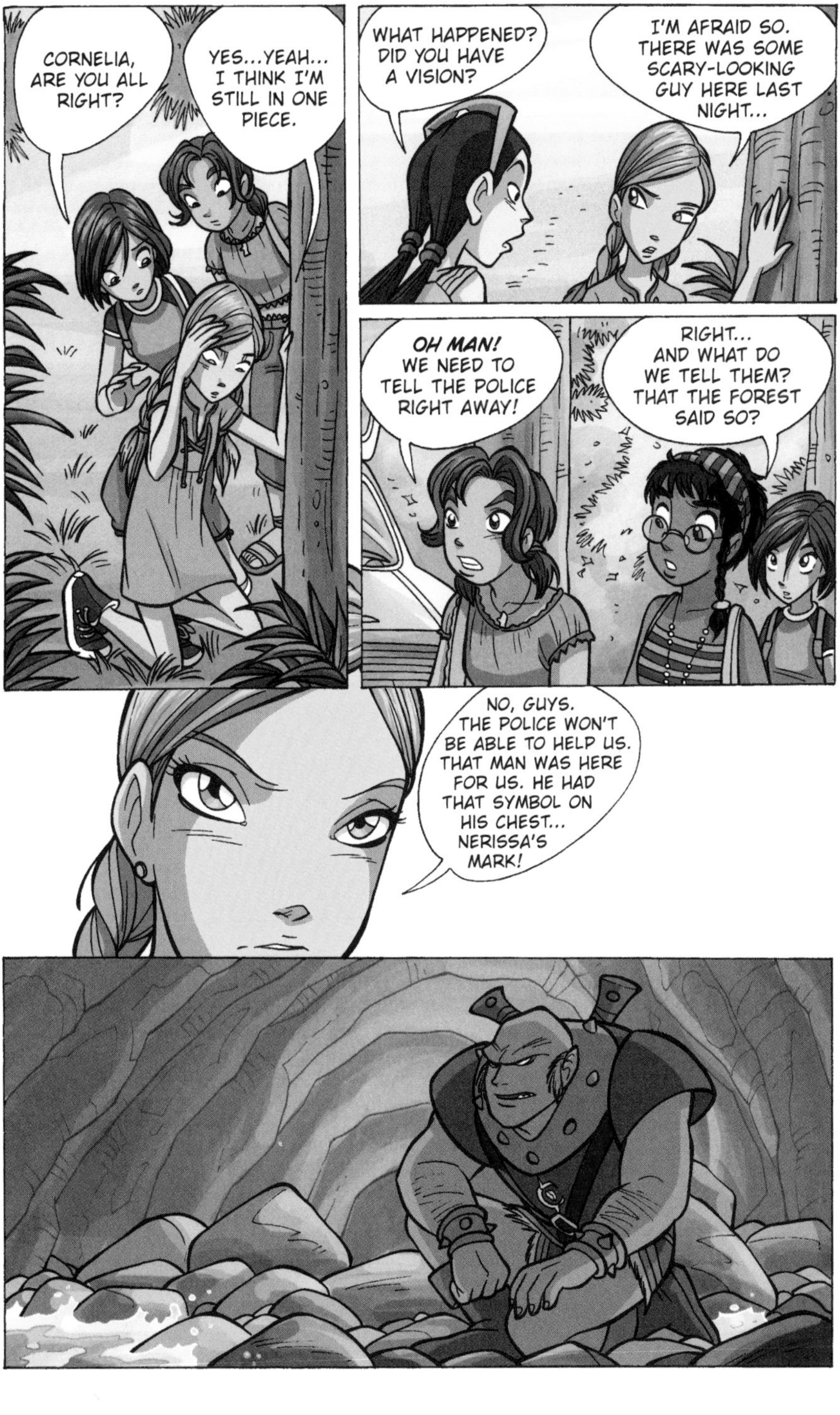
CORNELIA, ARE YOU ALL RIGHT?
YES...YEAH... I THINK I'M STILL IN ONE PIECE.
WHAT HAPPENED? DID YOU HAVE A VISION?
I'M AFRAID SO. THERE WAS SOME SCARY-LOOKING GUY HERE LAST NIGHT...
OH MAN! WE NEED TO TELL THE POLICE RIGHT AWAY!
RIGHT... AND WHAT DO WE TELL THEM? THAT THE FOREST SAID SO?
NO, GUYS. THE POLICE WON'T BE ABLE TO HELP US. THAT MAN WAS HERE FOR US. HE HAD THAT SYMBOL ON HIS CHEST... NERISSA'S MARK!

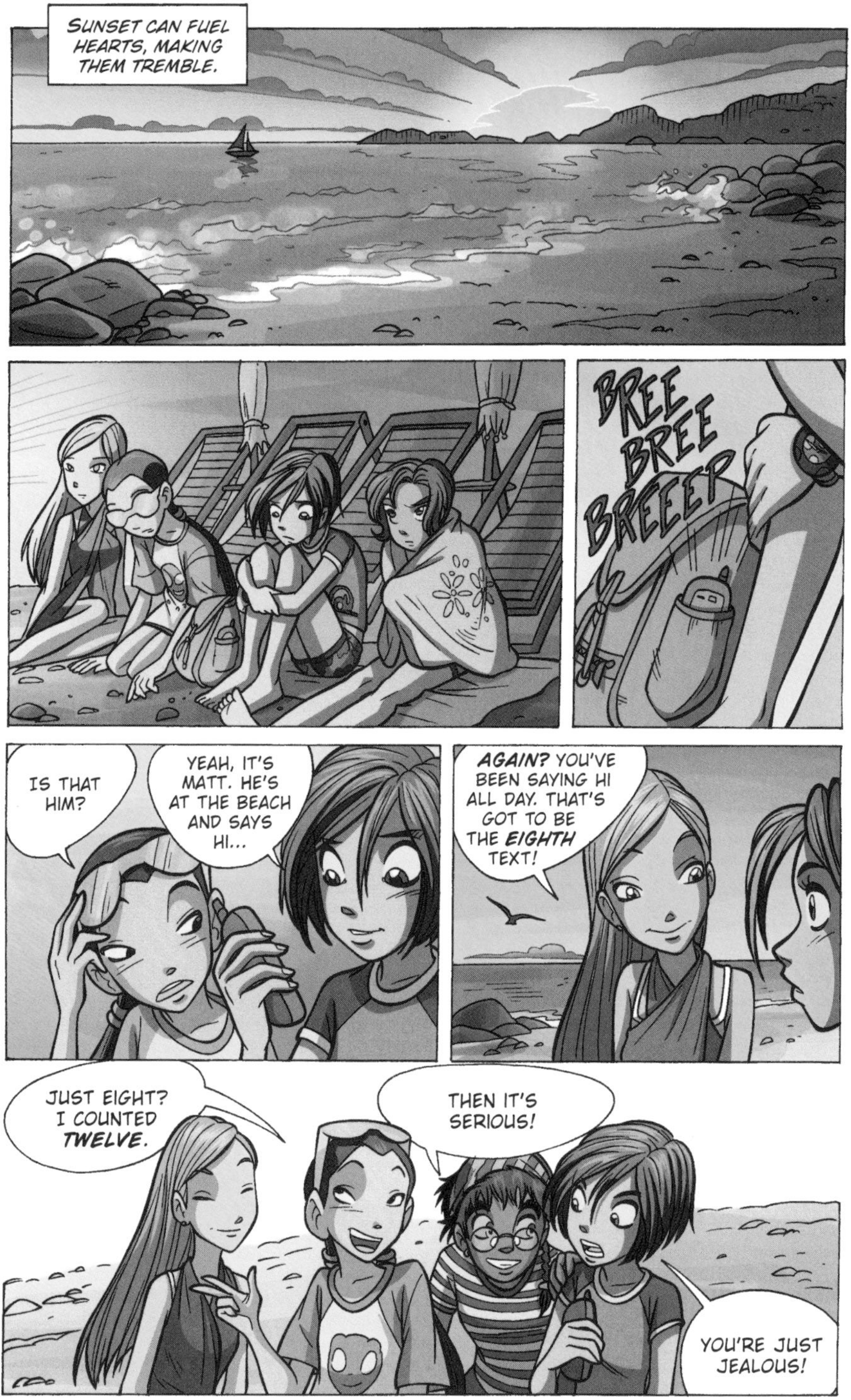
SUNSET CAN FUEL HEARTS, MAKING THEM TREMBLE.
BREE BREE BREEEP
IS THAT HIM?
YEAH, IT'S MATT. HE'S AT THE BEACH AND SAYS HI...
AGAIN? YOU'VE BEEN SAYING HI ALL DAY. THAT'S GOT TO BE THE EIGHTH TEXT!
JUST EIGHT? I COUNTED TWELVE.
THEN IT'S SERIOUS!
YOU'RE JUST JEALOUS!

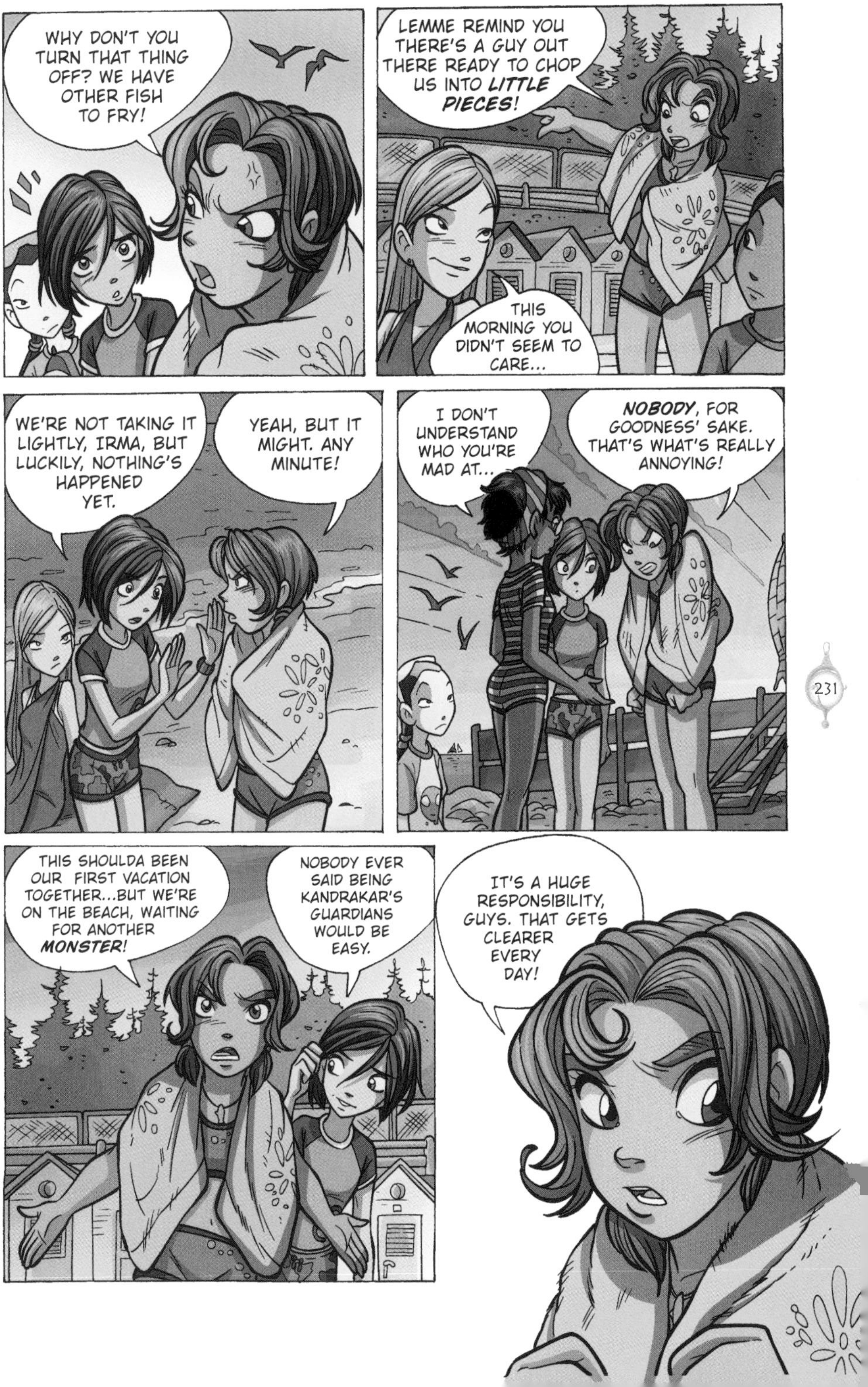
WHY DON'T YOU TURN THAT THING OFF? WE HAVE OTHER FISH TO FRY!
LEMME REMIND YOU THERE'S A GUY OUT THERE READY TO CHOP US INTO LITTLE PIECES!
THIS MORNING YOU DIDN'T SEEM TO CARE...
WE'RE NOT TAKING IT LIGHTLY, IRMA, BUT LUCKILY, NOTHING'S HAPPENED YET.
YEAH, BUT IT MIGHT. ANY MINUTE!
I DON'T UNDERSTAND WHO YOU'RE MAD AT...
NOBODY, FOR GOODNESS' SAKE. THAT'S WHAT'S REALLY ANNOYING!
THIS SHOULDA BEEN OUR FIRST VACATION TOGETHER...BUT WE'RE ON THE BEACH, WAITING FOR ANOTHER MONSTER!
NOBODY EVER SAID BEING KANDRAKAR'S GUARDIANS WOULD BE EASY.
IT'S A HUGE RESPONSIBILITY, GUYS. THAT GETS CLEARER EVERY DAY!

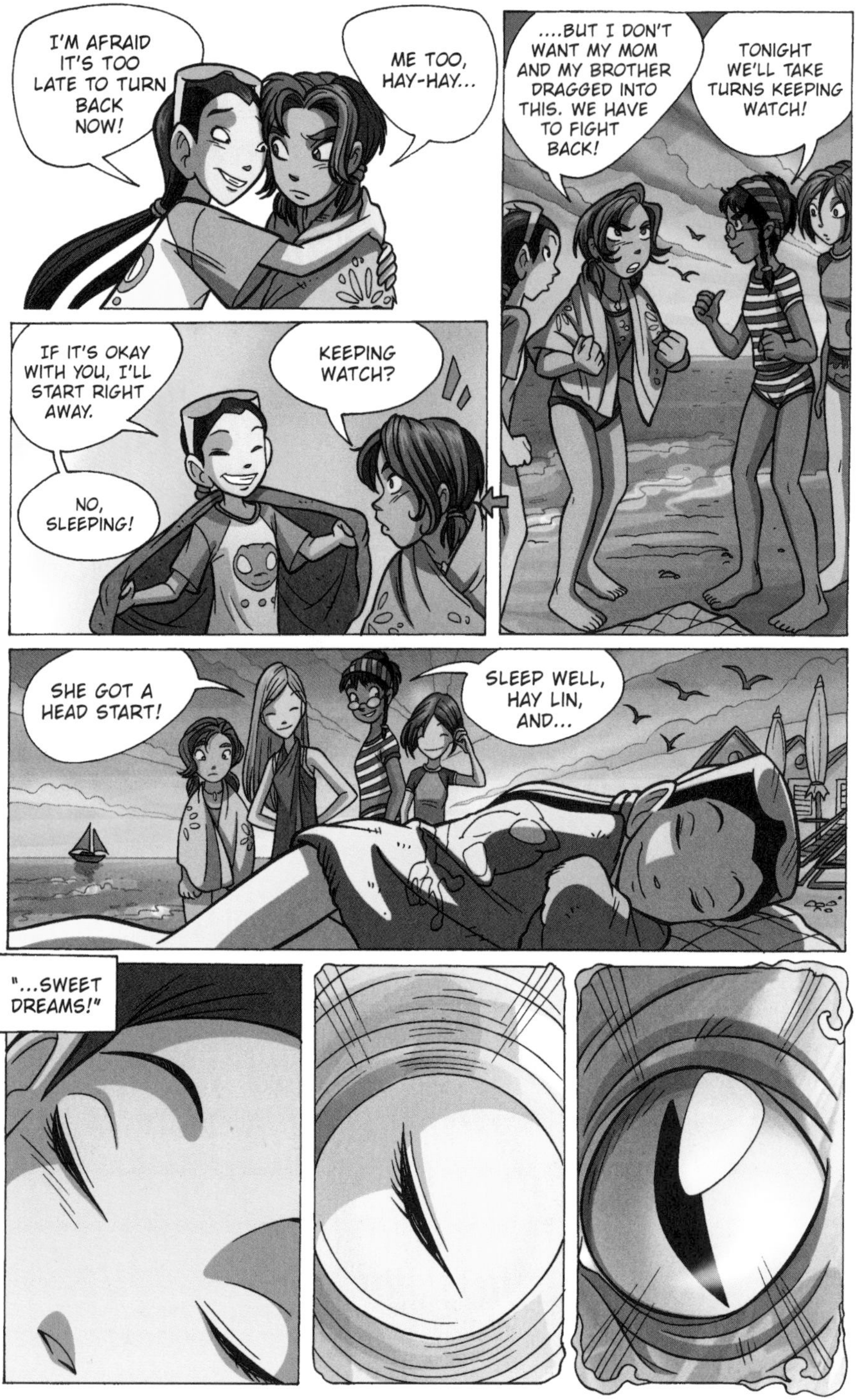
I'M AFRAID IT'S TOO LATE TO TURN BACK NOW!
ME TOO, HAY-HAY...
....BUT I DON'T WANT MY MOM AND MY BROTHER DRAGGED INTO THIS. WE HAVE TO FIGHT BACK!
TONIGHT WE'LL TAKE TURNS KEEPING WATCH!
IF IT'S OKAY WITH YOU, I'LL START RIGHT AWAY.
KEEPING WATCH?
NO, SLEEPING!
SHE GOT A HEAD START!
SLEEP WELL, HAY LIN, AND...
"...SWEET DREAMS!"

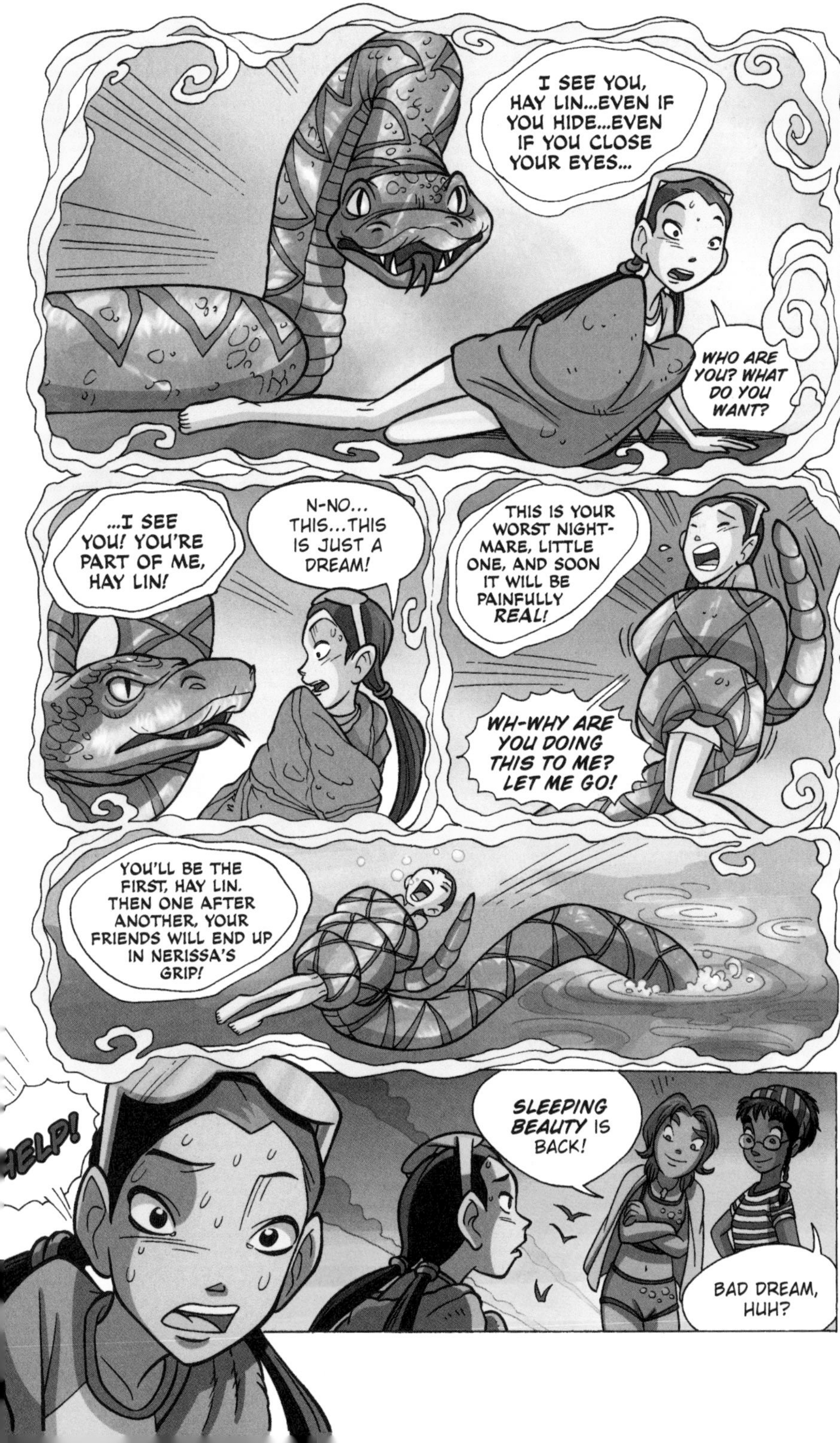
I SEE YOU, HAY LIN...EVEN IF YOU HIDE...EVEN IF YOU CLOSE YOUR EYES...
WHO ARE YOU? WHAT DO YOU WANT?
...I SEE YOU! YOU'RE PART OF ME, HAY LIN!
N-NO... THIS...THIS IS JUST A DREAM!
THIS IS YOUR WORST NIGHT-MARE, LITTLE ONE, AND SOON IT WILL BE PAINFULLY REAL!
WH-WHY ARE YOU DOING THIS TO ME? LET ME GO!
YOU'LL BE THE FIRST, HAY LIN. THEN ONE AFTER ANOTHER, YOUR FRIENDS WILL END UP IN NERISSA'S GRIP!
HELP!
SLEEPING BEAUTY IS BACK!
BAD DREAM, HUH?

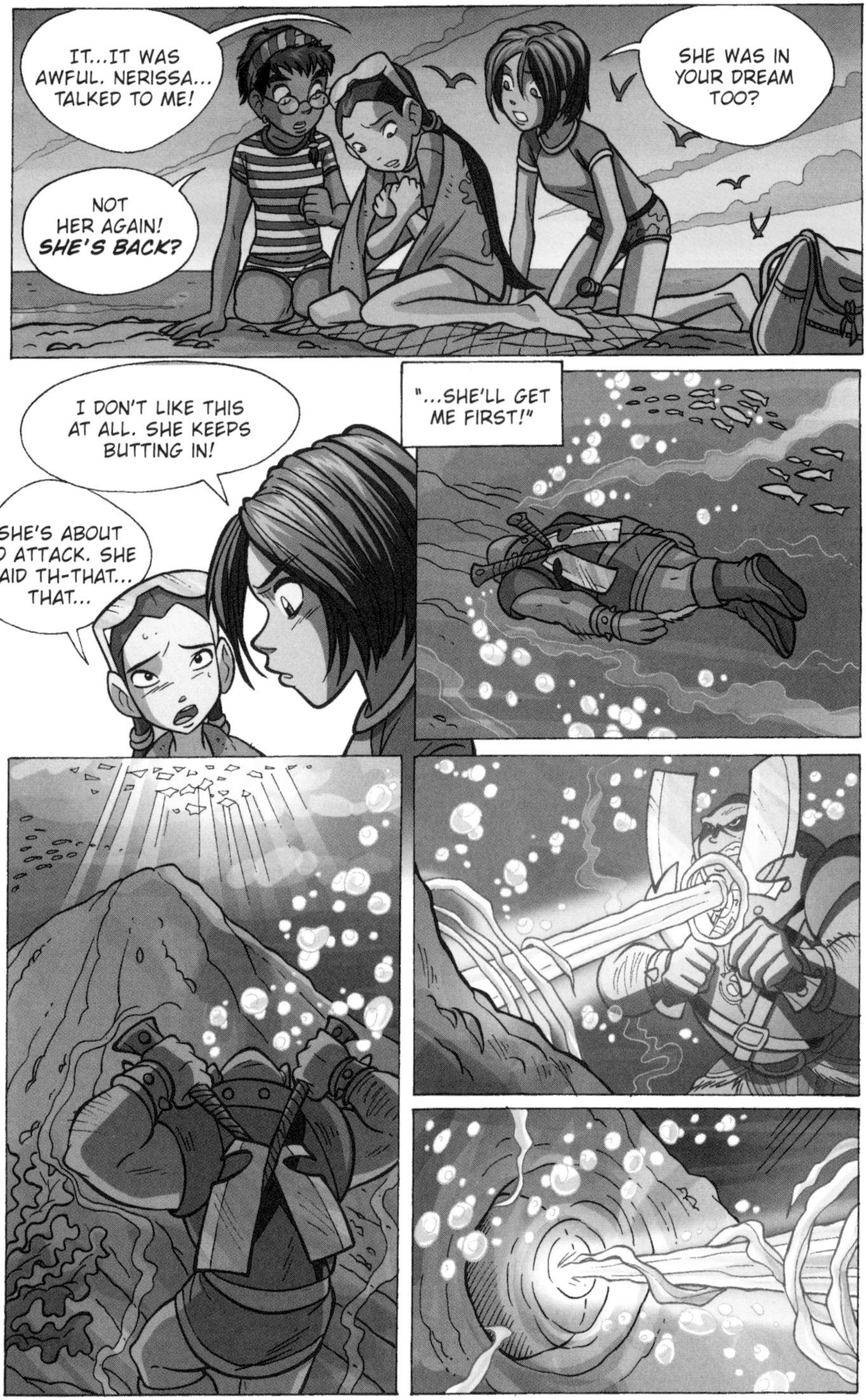
IT...IT WAS AWFUL. NERISSA... TALKED TO ME!
SHE WAS IN YOUR DREAM TOO?
NOT HER AGAIN! SHE'S BACK?
I DON'T LIKE THIS AT ALL. SHE KEEPS BUTTING IN!
SHE'S ABOUT TO ATTACK. SHE SAID TH-THAT... THAT...
"...SHE'LL GET ME FIRST!"

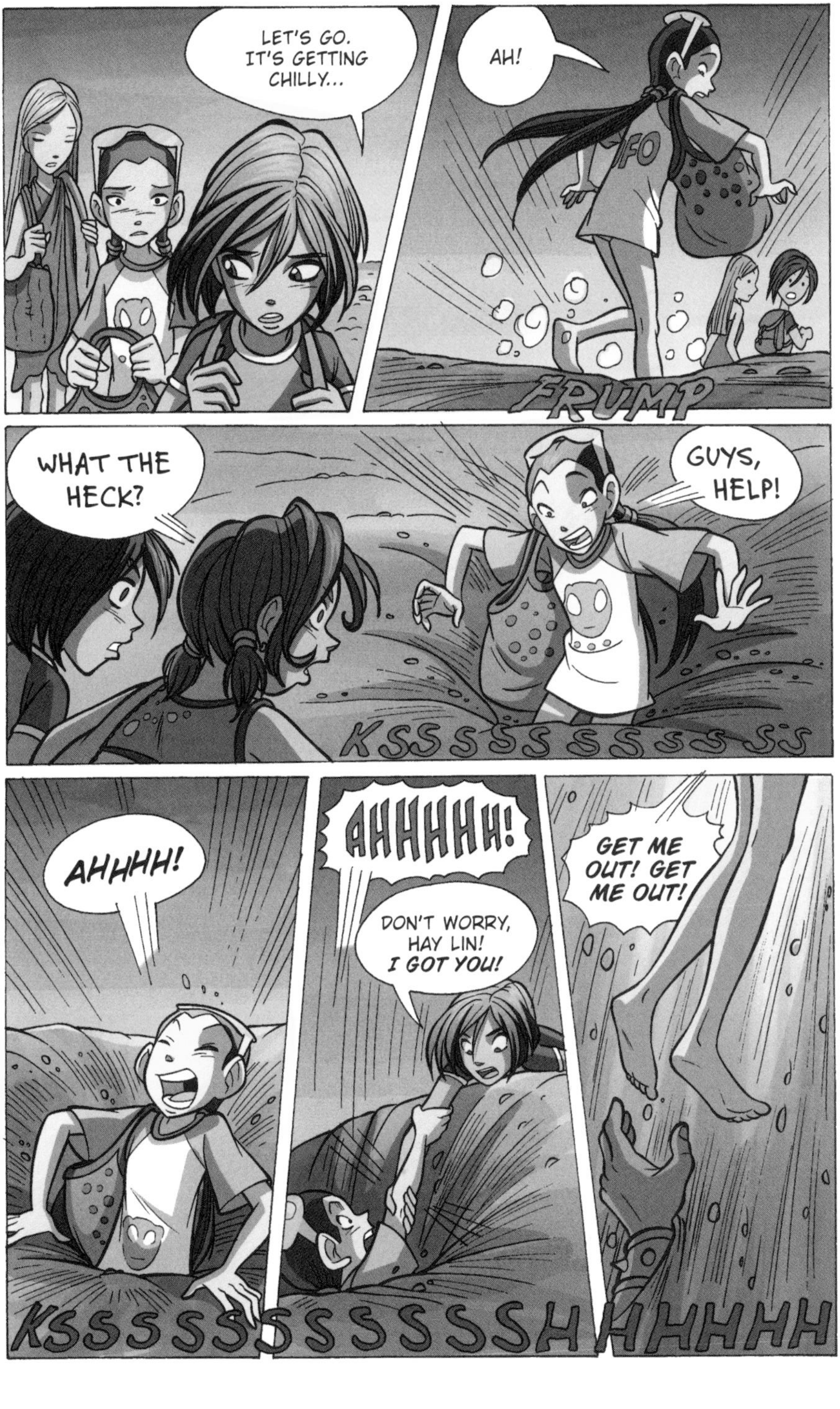
LET'S GO. IT'S GETTING CHILLY...
AH!
FRUMP
WHAT THE HECK?
GUYS, HELP!
KSSSSSSSSSSS
AHHHH!
AHHHHH!
DON'T WORRY, HAY LIN! I GOT YOU!
GET ME OUT! GET ME OUT!
KSSSSSSSSSSSHHHHHH

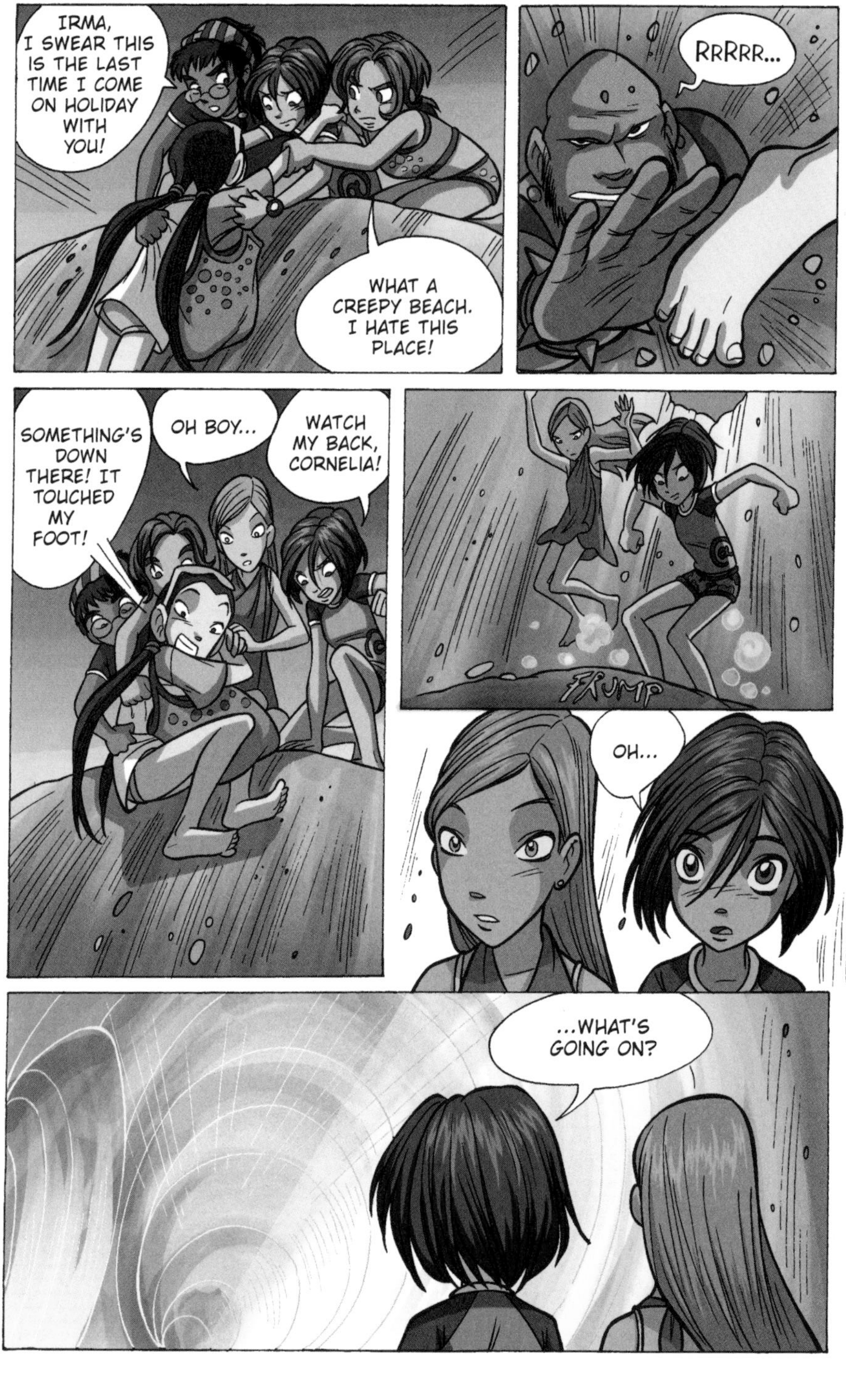
IRMA, I SWEAR THIS IS THE LAST TIME I COME ON HOLIDAY WITH YOU!
WHAT A CREEPY BEACH. I HATE THIS PLACE!
RRRRR...
SOMETHING'S DOWN THERE! IT TOUCHED MY FOOT!
OH BOY...
WATCH MY BACK, CORNELIA!
FRUMP
OH...
...WHAT'S GOING ON?

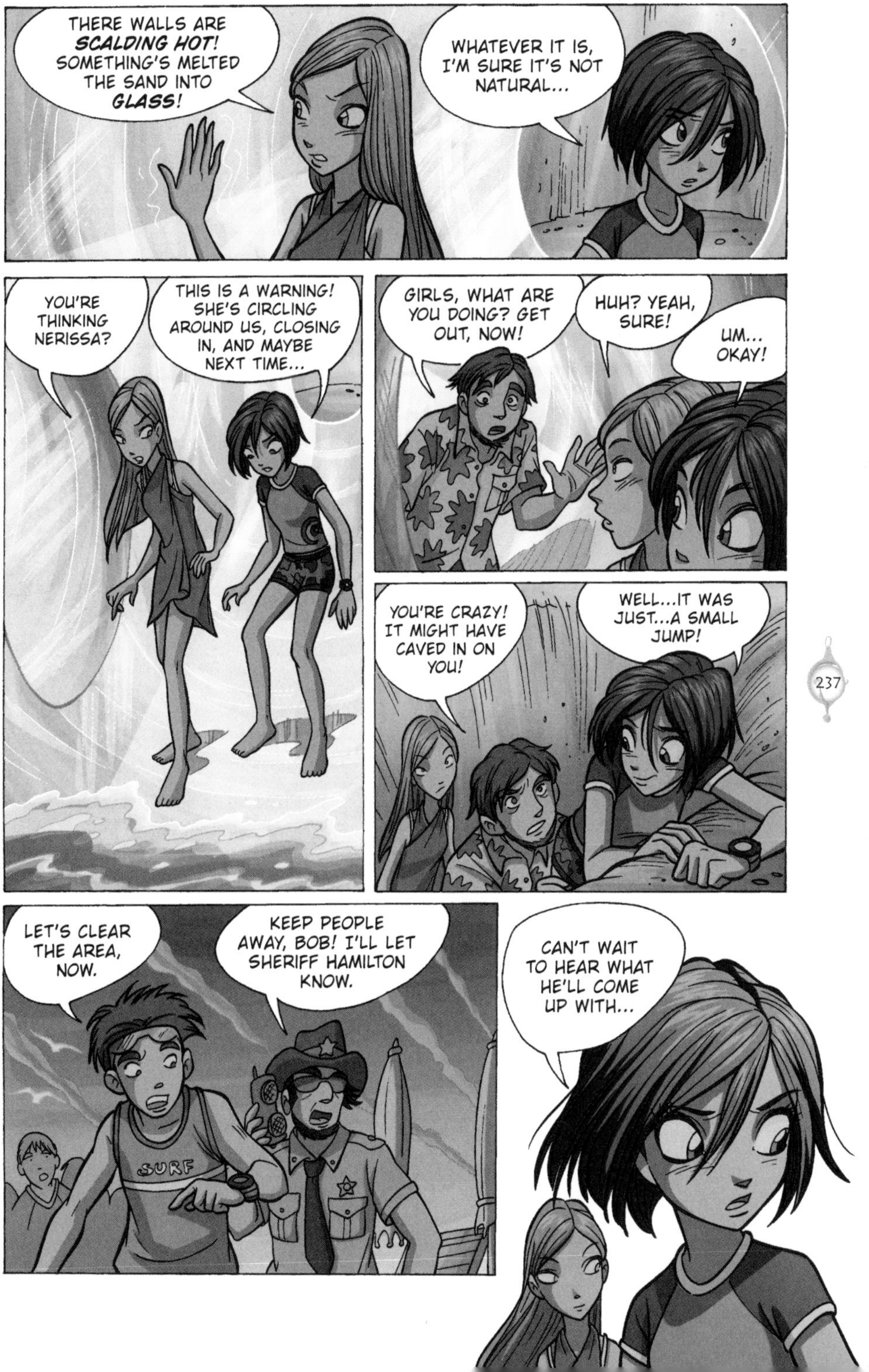
THERE WALLS ARE SCALDING HOT! SOMETHING'S MELTED THE SAND INTO GLASS!
WHATEVER IT IS, I'M SURE IT'S NOT NATURAL...
YOU'RE THINKING NERISSA?
THIS IS A WARNING! SHE'S CIRCLING AROUND US, CLOSING IN, AND MAYBE NEXT TIME...
GIRLS, WHAT ARE YOU DOING? GET OUT, NOW!
HUH? YEAH, SURE!
UM... OKAY!
YOU'RE CRAZY! IT MIGHT HAVE CAVED IN ON YOU!
WELL...IT WAS JUST...A SMALL JUMP!
LET'S CLEAR THE AREA, NOW.
KEEP PEOPLE AWAY, BOB! I'LL LET SHERIFF HAMILTON KNOW.
CAN'T WAIT TO HEAR WHAT HE'LL COME UP WITH...
SURF

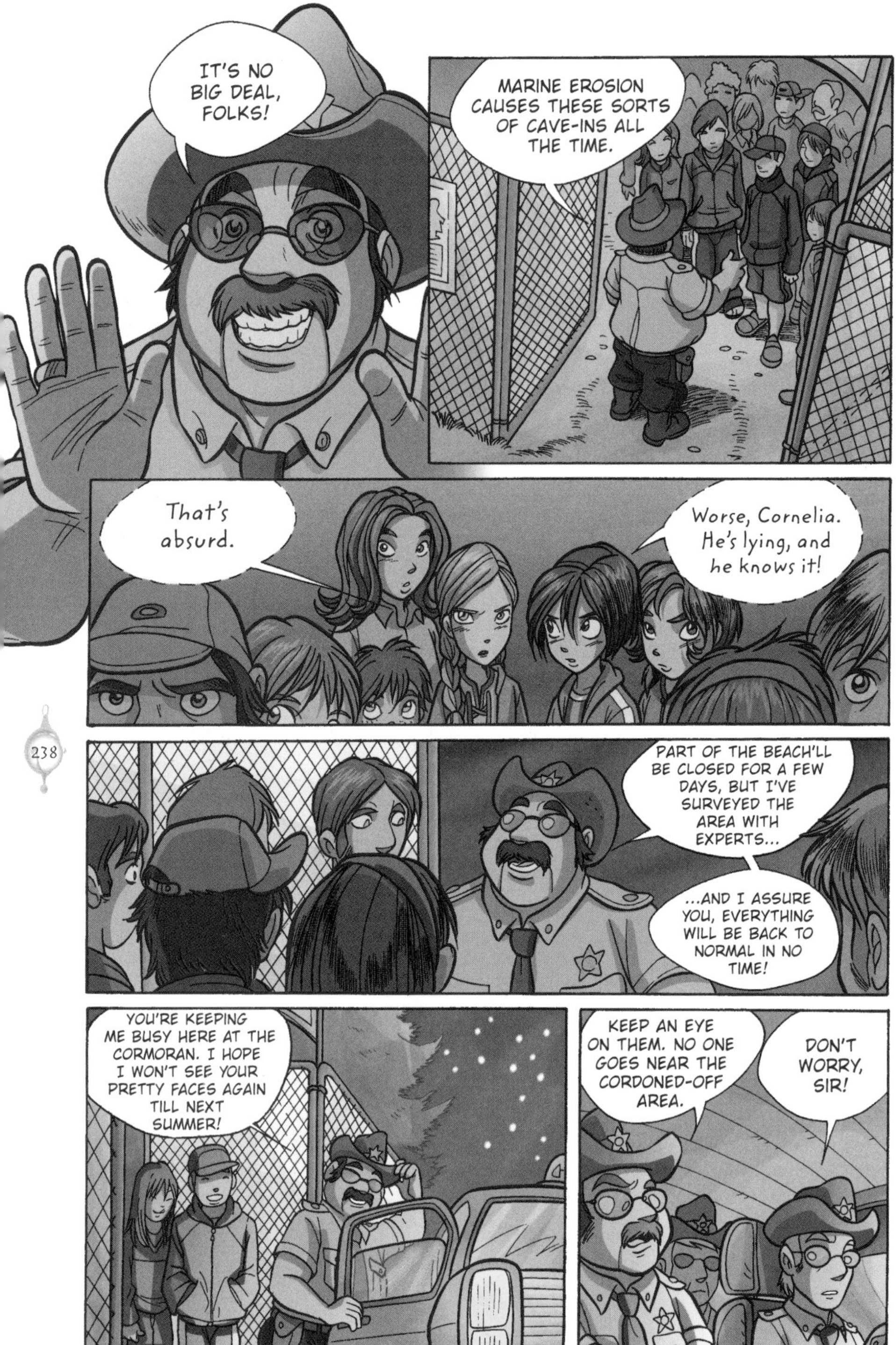
IT'S NO BIG DEAL, FOLKS!
MARINE EROSION CAUSES THESE SORTS OF CAVE-INS ALL THE TIME.
That's absurd.
Worse, Cornelia. He's lying, and he knows it!
PART OF THE BEACH'LL BE CLOSED FOR A FEW DAYS, BUT I'VE SURVEYED THE AREA WITH EXPERTS...
...AND I ASSURE YOU, EVERYTHING WILL BE BACK TO NORMAL IN NO TIME!
YOU'RE KEEPING ME BUSY HERE AT THE CORMORAN. I HOPE I WON'T SEE YOUR PRETTY FACES AGAIN TILL NEXT SUMMER!
KEEP AN EYE ON THEM. NO ONE GOES NEAR THE CORDONED-OFF AREA.
DON'T WORRY, SIR!

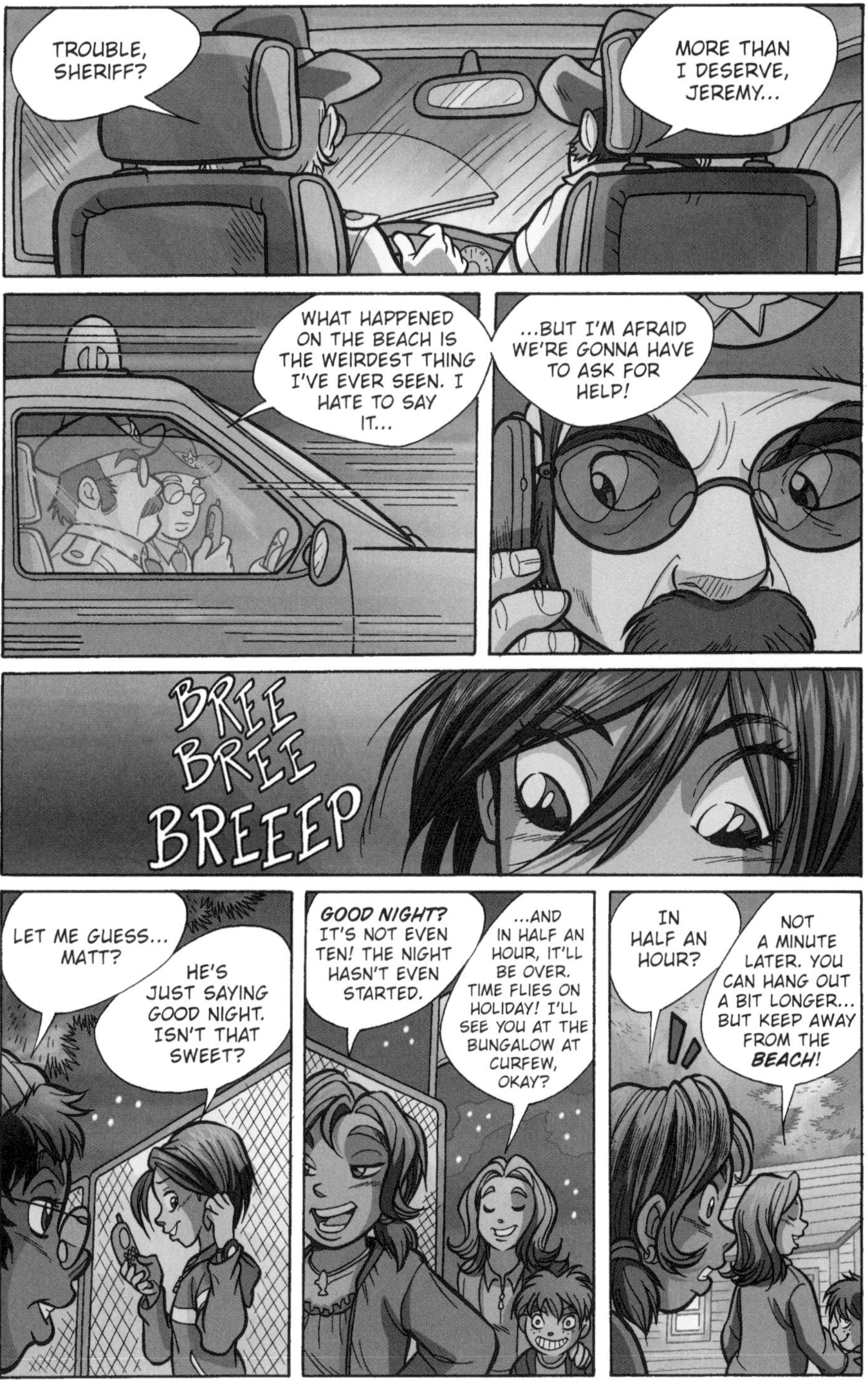
TROUBLE, SHERIFF?
MORE THAN I DESERVE, JEREMY...
WHAT HAPPENED ON THE BEACH IS THE WEIRDEST THING I'VE EVER SEEN. I HATE TO SAY IT...
...BUT I'M AFRAID WE'RE GONNA HAVE TO ASK FOR HELP!
BREE BREE BREEEP
LET ME GUESS... MATT?
HE'S JUST SAYING GOOD NIGHT. ISN'T THAT SWEET?
GOOD NIGHT? IT'S NOT EVEN TEN! THE NIGHT HASN'T EVEN STARTED.
...AND IN HALF AN HOUR, IT'LL BE OVER. TIME FLIES ON HOLIDAY! I'LL SEE YOU AT THE BUNGALOW AT CURFEW, OKAY?
IN HALF AN HOUR?
NOT A MINUTE LATER. YOU CAN HANG OUT A BIT LONGER... BUT KEEP AWAY FROM THE BEACH!

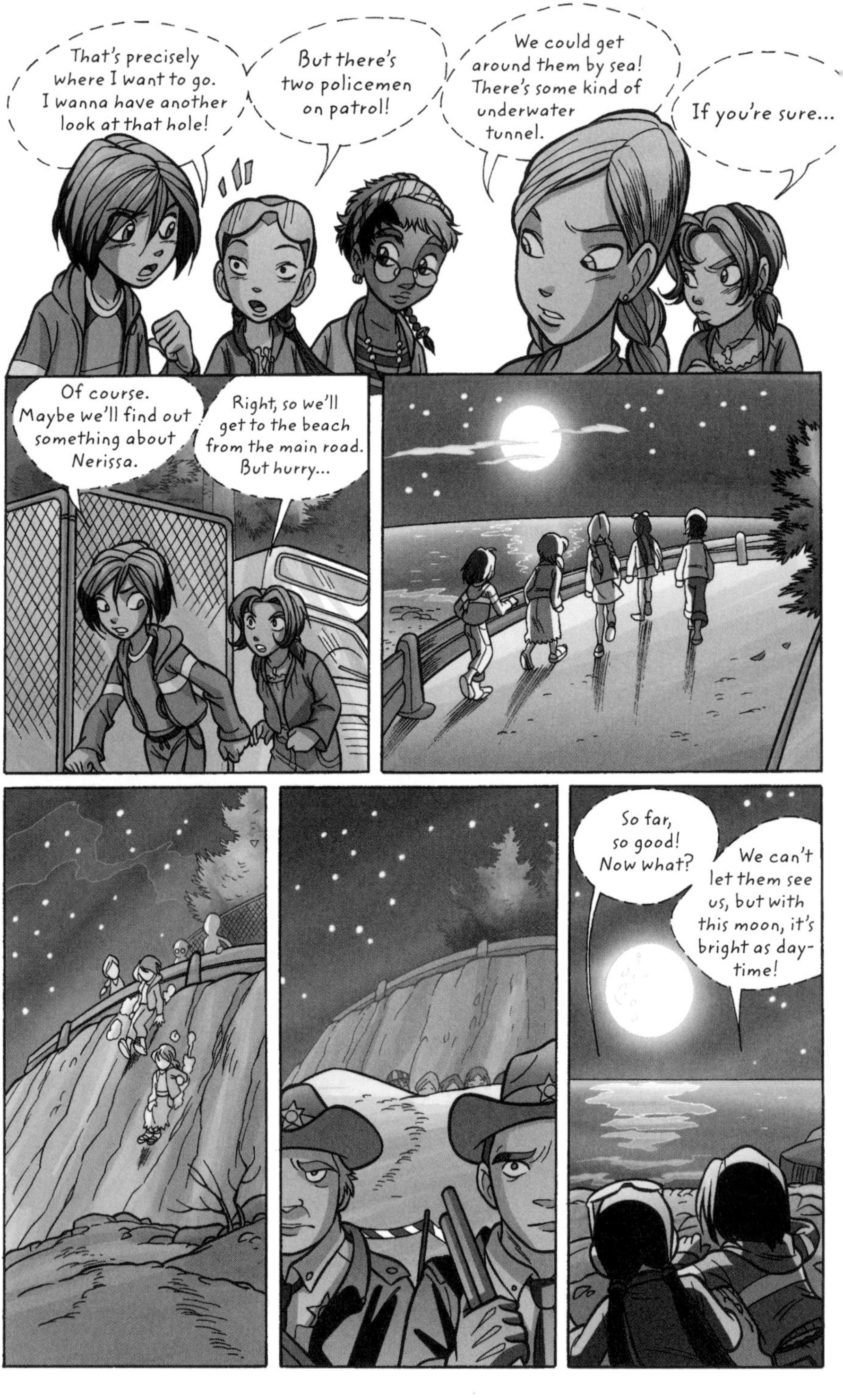

That's precisely where I want to go. I wanna have another look at that hole!
But there's two policemen on patrol!
We could get around them by sea! There's some kind of underwater tunnel.
If you're sure...
Of course. Maybe we'll find out something about Nerissa.
Right, so we'll get to the beach from the main road. But hurry...
So far, so good! Now what?
We can't let them see us, but with this moon, it's bright as day-time!

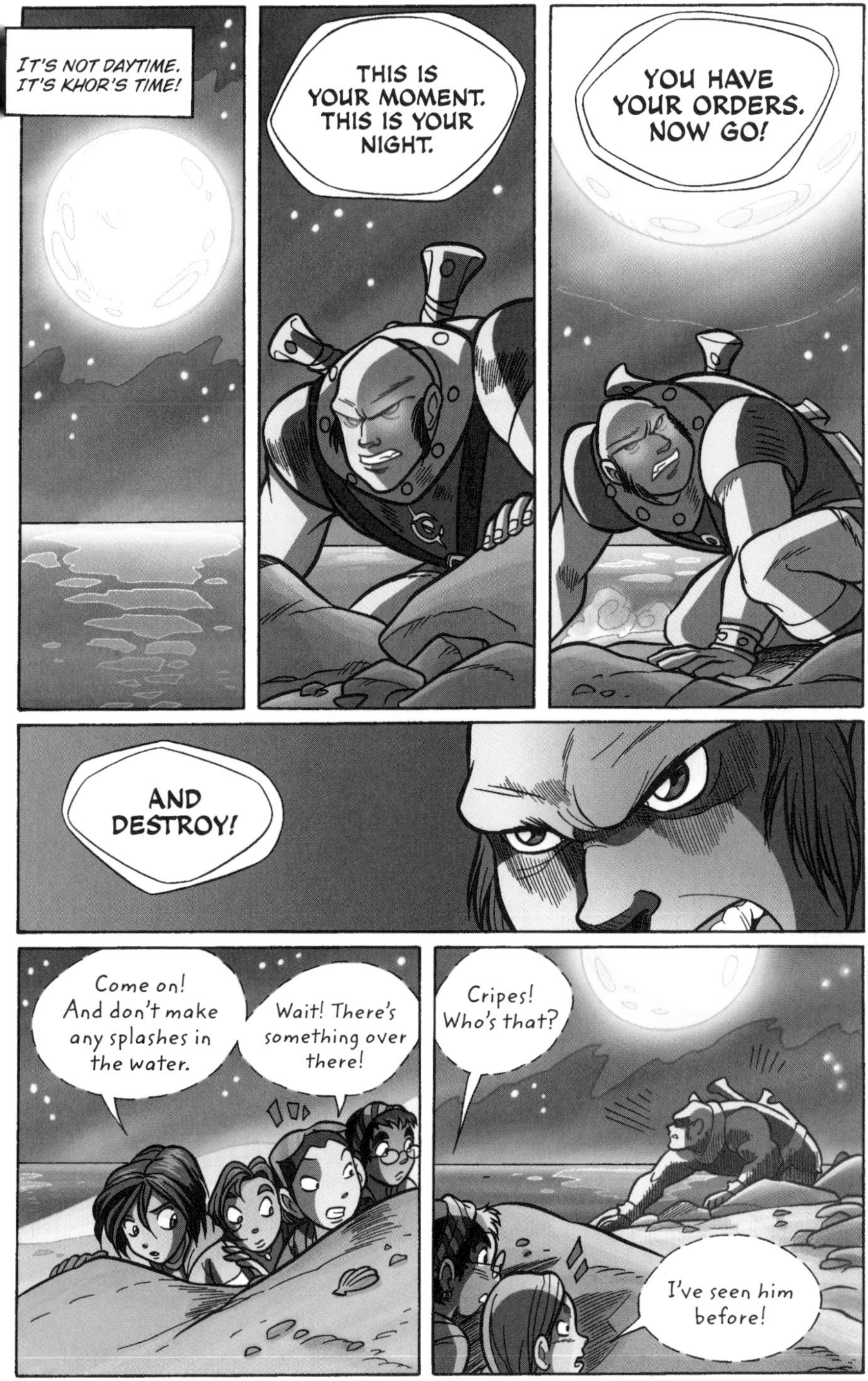
IT'S NOT DAYTIME. IT'S KHOR'S TIME!
THIS IS YOUR MOMENT. THIS IS YOUR NIGHT.
YOU HAVE YOUR ORDERS. NOW GO!
AND DESTROY!
Come on! And don't make any splashes in the water.
Wait! There's something over there!
Cripes! Who's that?
I've seen him before!

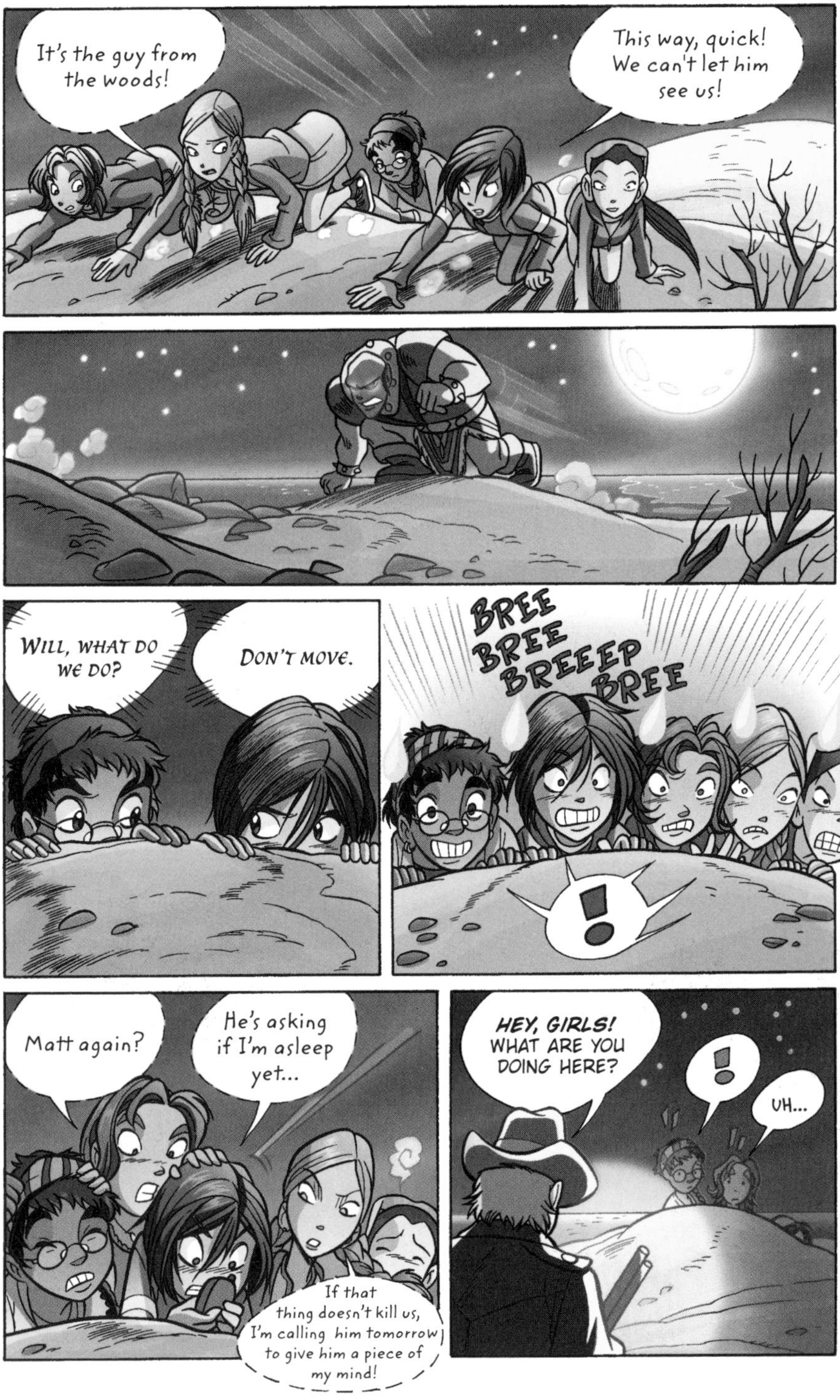
It's the guy from the woods!
This way, quick! We can't let him see us!
WILL, WHAT DO WE DO?
DON'T MOVE.
BREE BREE BREEEP BREE
!
Matt again?
He's asking if I'm asleep yet...
If that thing doesn't kill us, I'm calling him tomorrow to give him a piece of my mind!
HEY, GIRLS! WHAT ARE YOU DOING HERE?
!
UH...

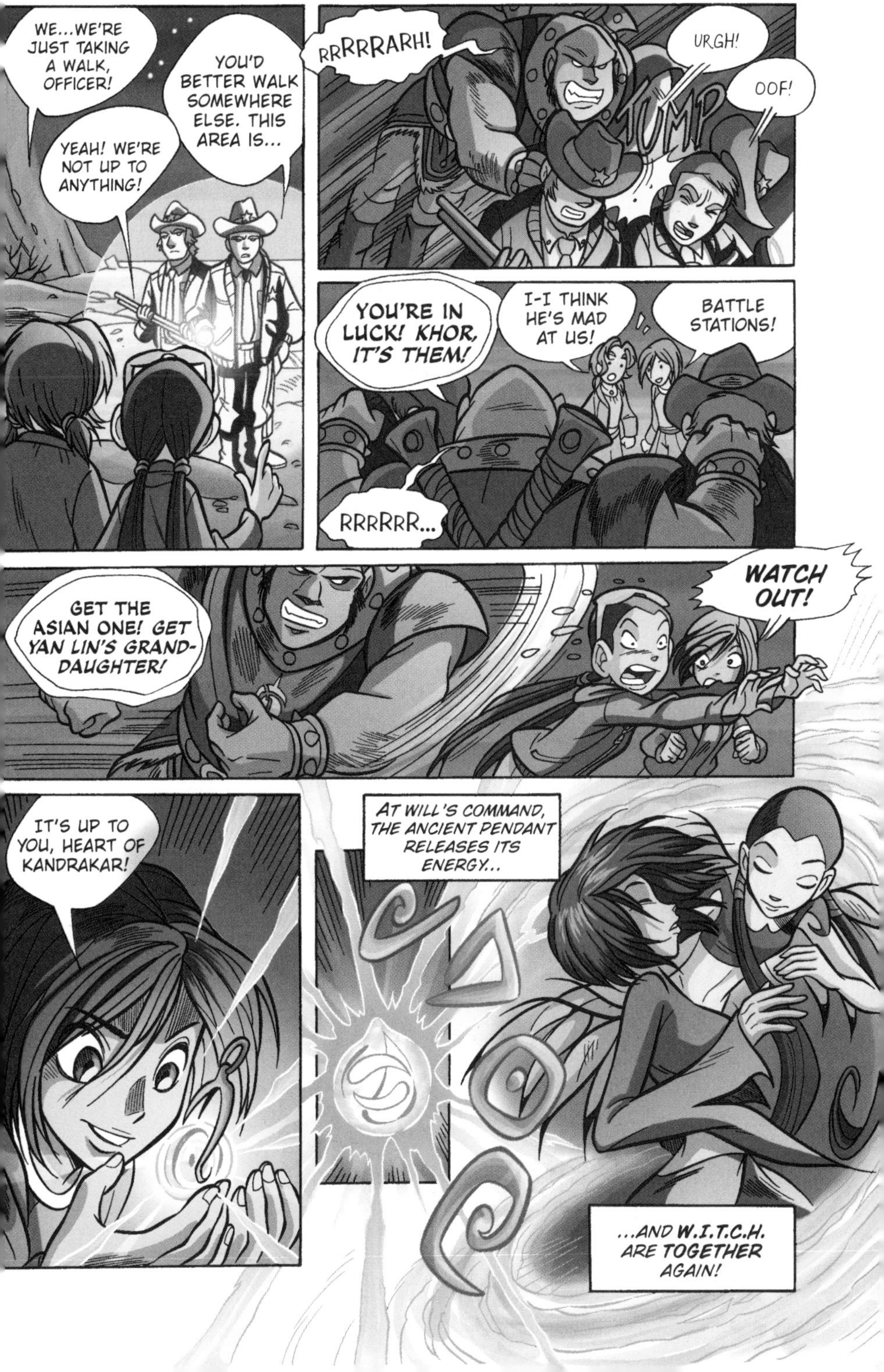
WE...WE'RE JUST TAKING A WALK, OFFICER!
YEAH! WE'RE NOT UP TO ANYTHING!
YOU'D BETTER WALK SOMEWHERE ELSE. THIS AREA IS...
RRRRRARH!
THUMP
URGH!
OOF!
YOU'RE IN LUCK! KHOR, IT'S THEM!
RRRRRR...
I-I THINK HE'S MAD AT US!
BATTLE STATIONS!
GET THE ASIAN ONE! GET YAN LIN'S GRAND-DAUGHTER!
WATCH OUT!
IT'S UP TO YOU, HEART OF KANDRAKAR!
AT WILL'S COMMAND, THE ANCIENT PENDANT RELEASES ITS ENERGY...
...AND W.I.T.C.H. ARE TOGETHER AGAIN!

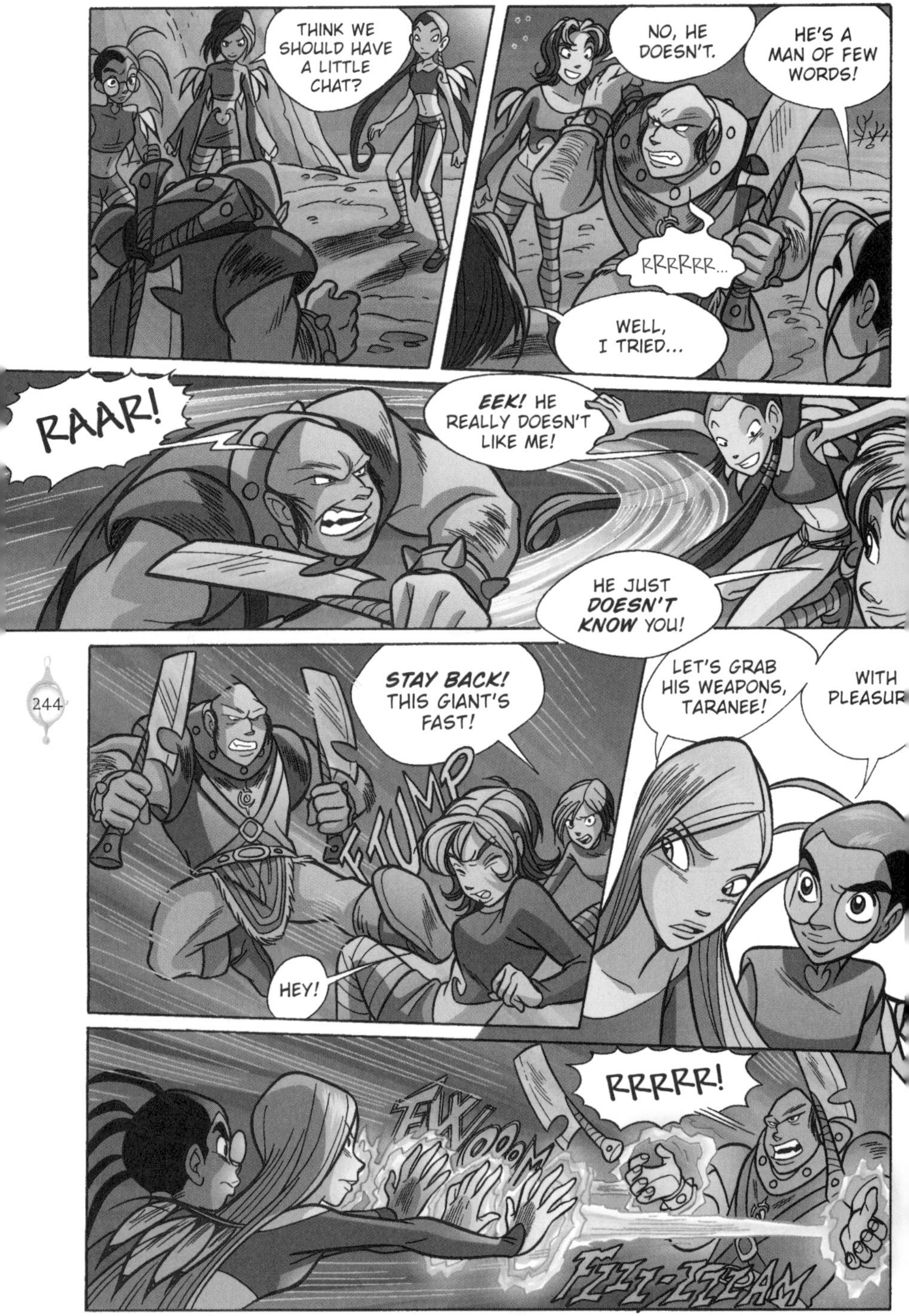
THINK WE SHOULD HAVE A LITTLE CHAT?
NO, HE DOESN'T.
HE'S A MAN OF FEW WORDS!
RRRRRR...
WELL, I TRIED...
RAAR!
EEK! HE REALLY DOESN'T LIKE ME!
HE JUST DOESN'T KNOW YOU!
STAY BACK! THIS GIANT'S FAST!
CLUMP
HEY!
LET'S GRAB HIS WEAPONS, TARANEE!
WITH PLEASUR
RRRRR!
FWOOOM
FIZZ-ZZZAM

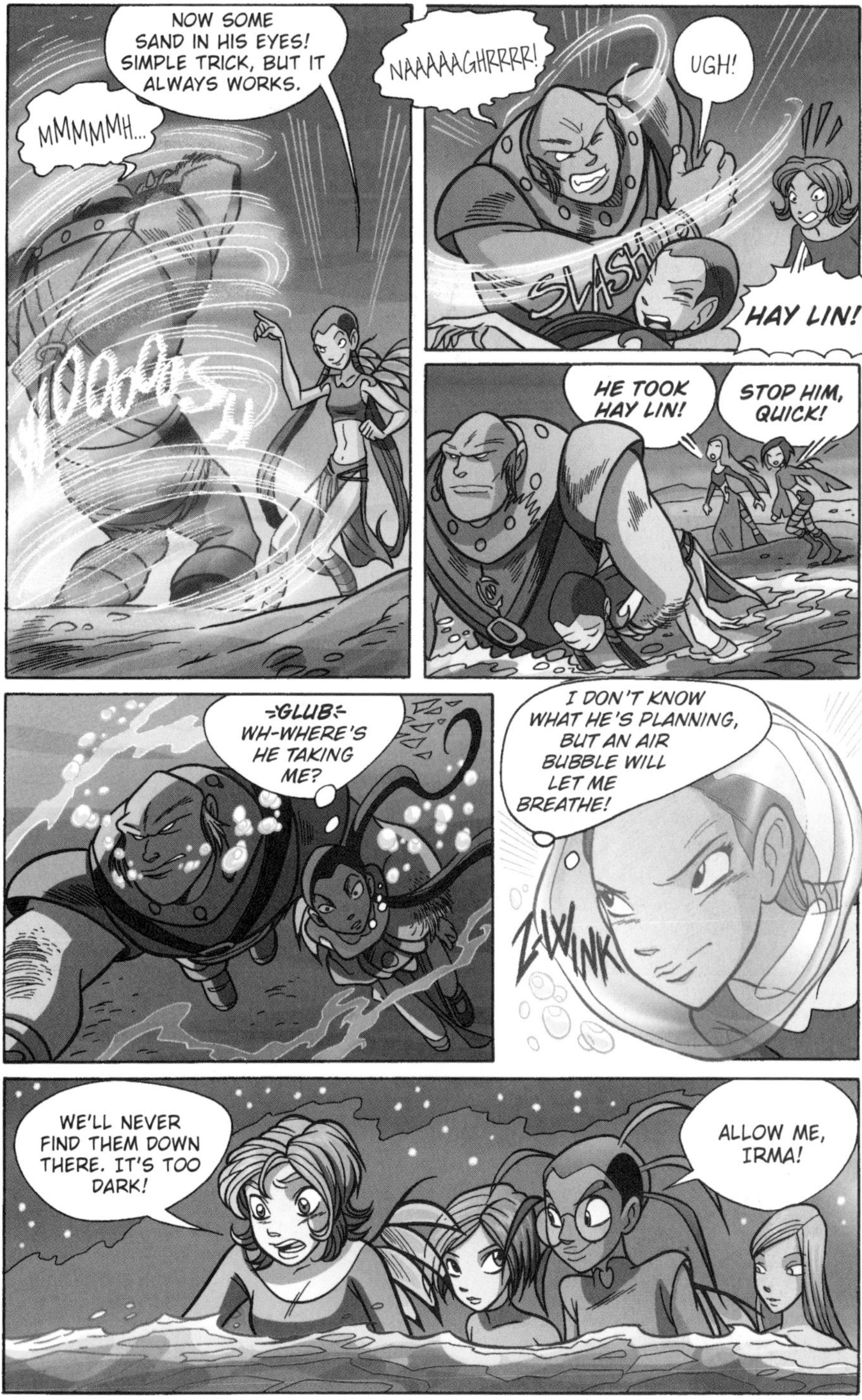
NOW SOME SAND IN HIS EYES! SIMPLE TRICK, BUT IT ALWAYS WORKS.
MMMMMH...
WHOOOOSH
NAAAAAGHRRRR!
UGH!
SLASH
HAY LIN!
HE TOOK HAY LIN!
STOP HIM, QUICK!
GLUB WH-WHERE'S HE TAKING ME?
I DON'T KNOW WHAT HE'S PLANNING, BUT AN AIR BUBBLE WILL LET ME BREATHE!
ZWINK
WE'LL NEVER FIND THEM DOWN THERE. IT'S TOO DARK!
ALLOW ME, IRMA!

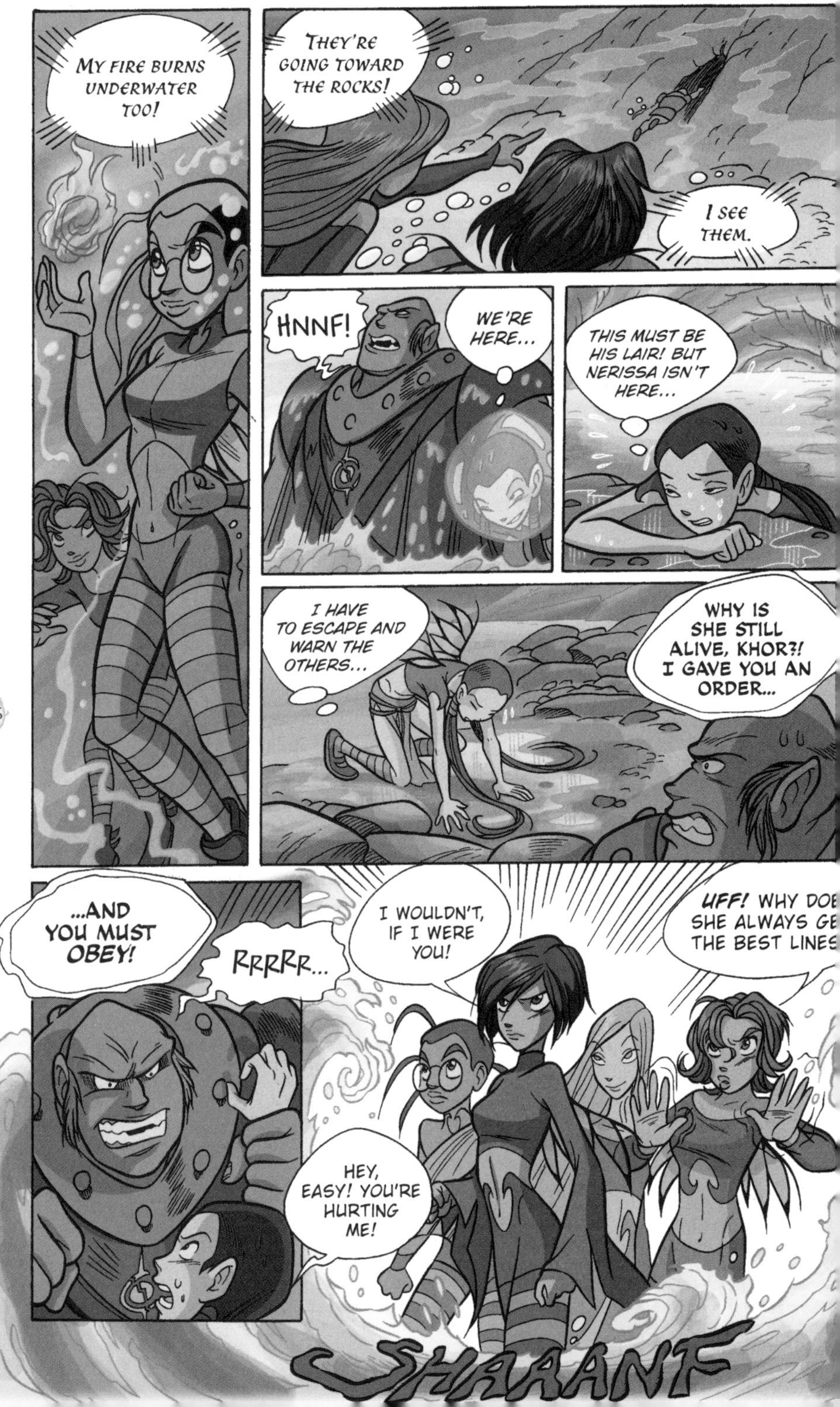

My fire burns underwater too!
They're going toward the rocks!
I see them.
HNNF!
We're here...
This must be his lair! But Nerissa isn't here...
I have to escape and warn the others...
Why is she still alive, Khor?! I gave you an order...
...And you must obey!
RRRRR...
Hey, easy! You're hurting me!
I wouldn't, if I were you!
UFF! Why doe she always ge the best lines
SHAAANF

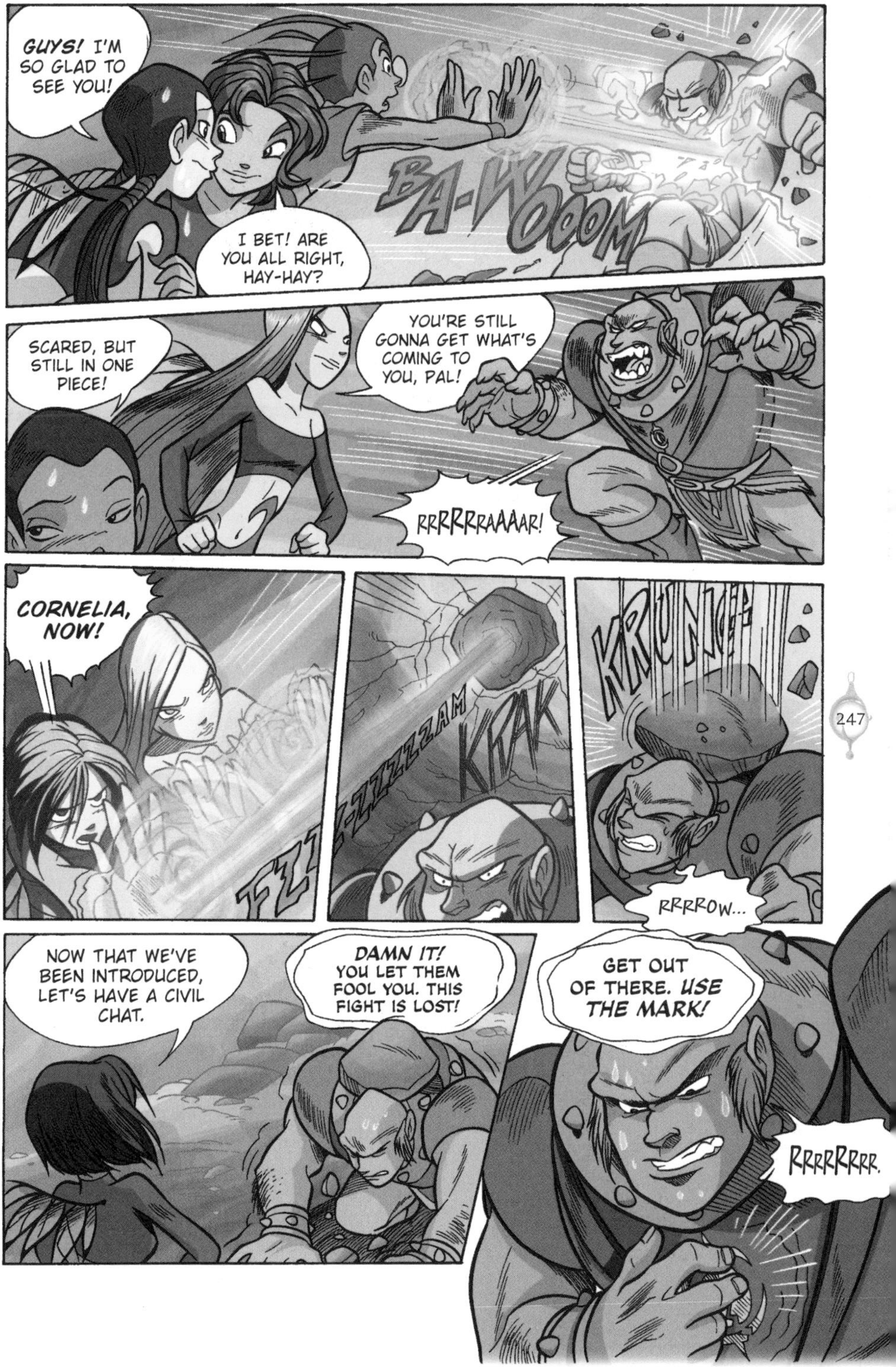
GUYS! I'M SO GLAD TO SEE YOU!
BA-WOOOM
I BET! ARE YOU ALL RIGHT, HAY-HAY?
SCARED, BUT STILL IN ONE PIECE!
YOU'RE STILL GONNA GET WHAT'S COMING TO YOU, PAL!
RRRRRRAAAAR!
CORNELIA, NOW!
FZZ-ZZZZZZAM
KRAK
KRUNCH
RRRROW...
NOW THAT WE'VE BEEN INTRODUCED, LET'S HAVE A CIVIL CHAT.
DAMN IT! YOU LET THEM FOOL YOU. THIS FIGHT IS LOST!
GET OUT OF THERE. USE THE MARK!
RRRRRRRR.

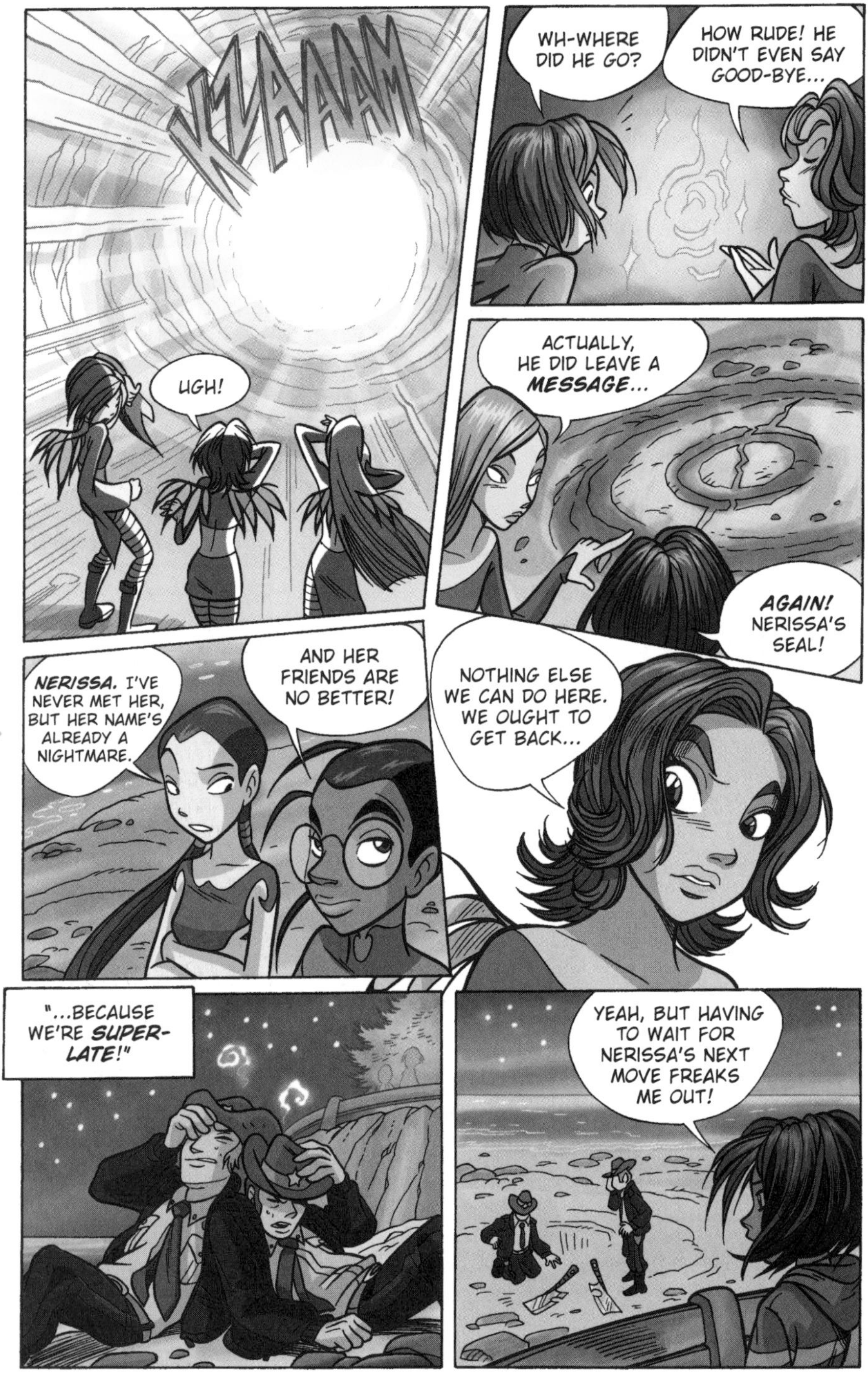
KZZAAAM
UGH!
WH-WHERE DID HE GO?
HOW RUDE! HE DIDN'T EVEN SAY GOOD-BYE...
ACTUALLY, HE DID LEAVE A MESSAGE...
AGAIN! NERISSA'S SEAL!
NERISSA. I'VE NEVER MET HER, BUT HER NAME'S ALREADY A NIGHTMARE.
AND HER FRIENDS ARE NO BETTER!
NOTHING ELSE WE CAN DO HERE. WE OUGHT TO GET BACK...
"...BECAUSE WE'RE SUPER-LATE!"
YEAH, BUT HAVING TO WAIT FOR NERISSA'S NEXT MOVE FREAKS ME OUT!

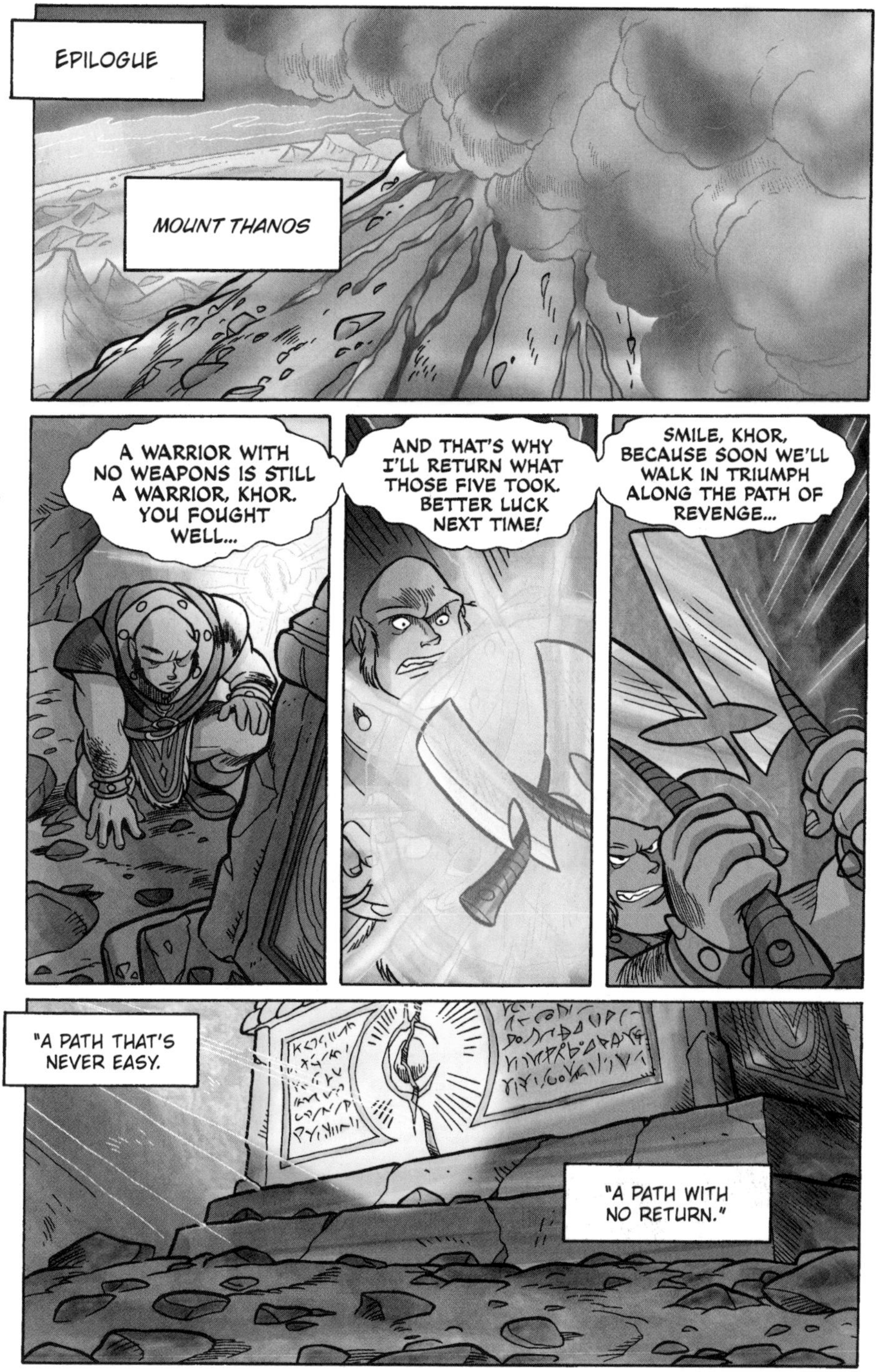
EPILOGUE
MOUNT THANOS
A WARRIOR WITH NO WEAPONS IS STILL A WARRIOR, KHOR. YOU FOUGHT WELL...
AND THAT'S WHY I'LL RETURN WHAT THOSE FIVE TOOK. BETTER LUCK NEXT TIME!
SMILE, KHOR, BECAUSE SOON WE'LL WALK IN TRIUMPH ALONG THE PATH OF REVENGE...
"A PATH THAT'S NEVER EASY.
"A PATH WITH NO RETURN."

END OF CHAPTER 16

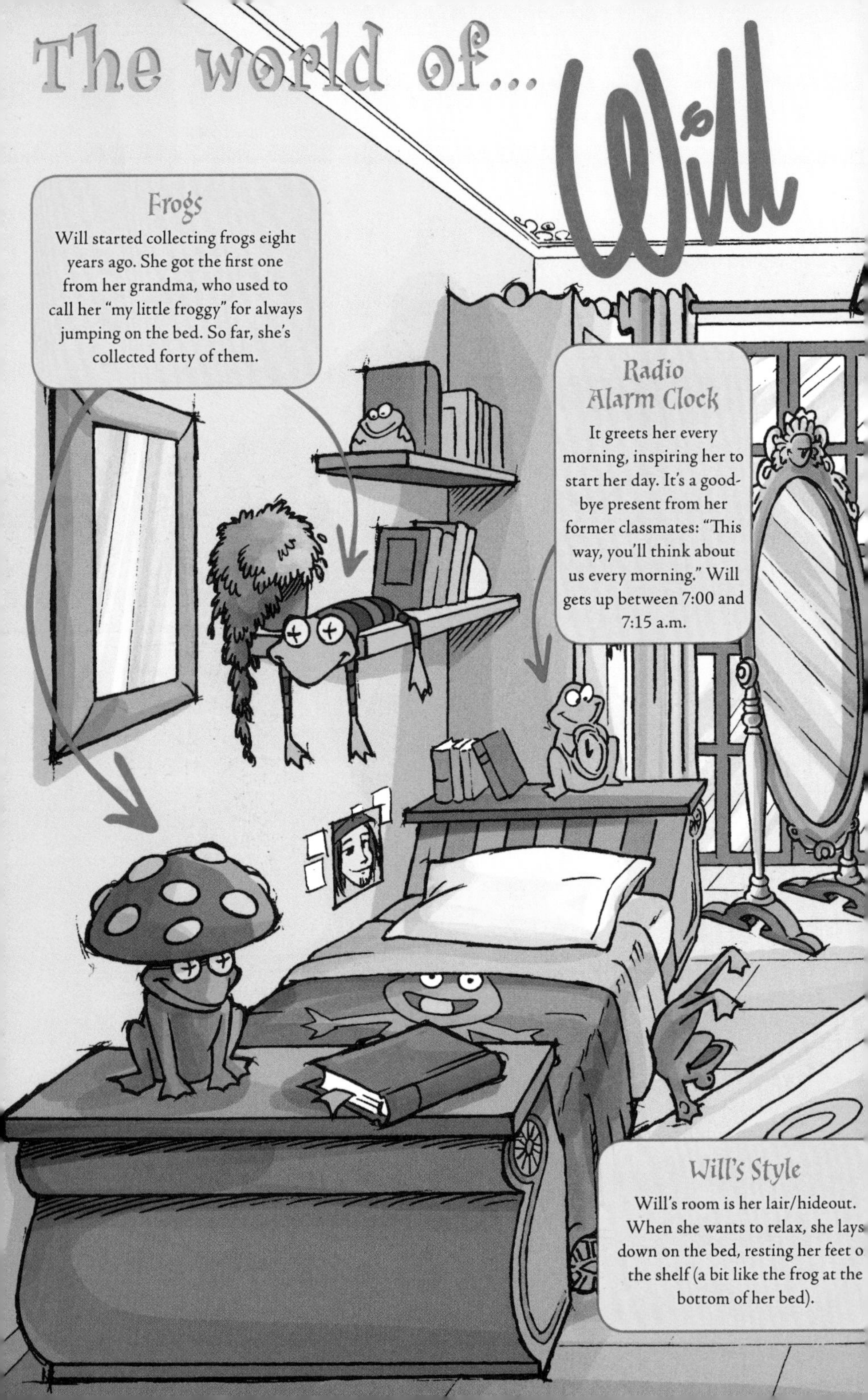
The world of... Will
Frogs
Will started collecting frogs eight years ago. She got the first one from her grandma, who used to call her "my little froggy" for always jumping on the bed. So far, she's collected forty of them.
Radio Alarm Clock
It greets her every morning, inspiring her to start her day. It's a good-bye present from her former classmates: "This way, you'll think about us every morning." Will gets up between 7:00 and 7:15 a.m.
Will's Style
Will's room is her lair/hideout. When she wants to relax, she lays down on the bed, resting her feet o the shelf (a bit like the frog at the bottom of her bed).

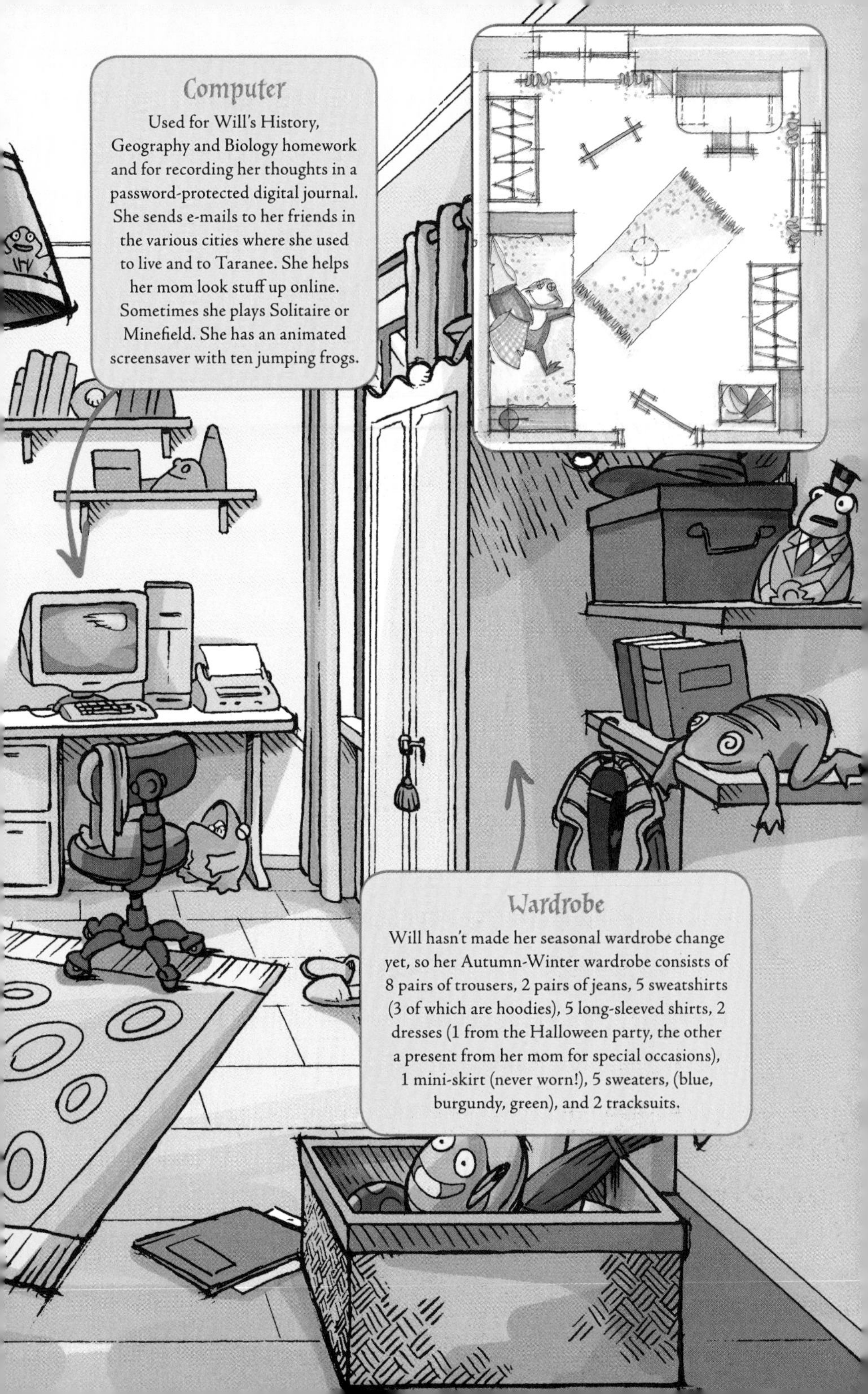

Computer

Used for Will's History, Geography and Biology homework and for recording her thoughts in a password-protected digital journal. She sends e-mails to her friends in the various cities where she used to live and to Taranee. She helps her mom look stuff up online. Sometimes she plays Solitaire or Minefield. She has an animated screensaver with ten jumping frogs.

Wardrobe

Will hasn't made her seasonal wardrobe change yet, so her Autumn-Winter wardrobe consists of 8 pairs of trousers, 2 pairs of jeans, 5 sweatshirts (3 of which are hoodies), 5 long-sleeved shirts, 2 dresses (1 from the Halloween party, the other a present from her mom for special occasions), 1 mini-skirt (never worn!), 5 sweaters, (blue, burgundy, green), and 2 tracksuits.

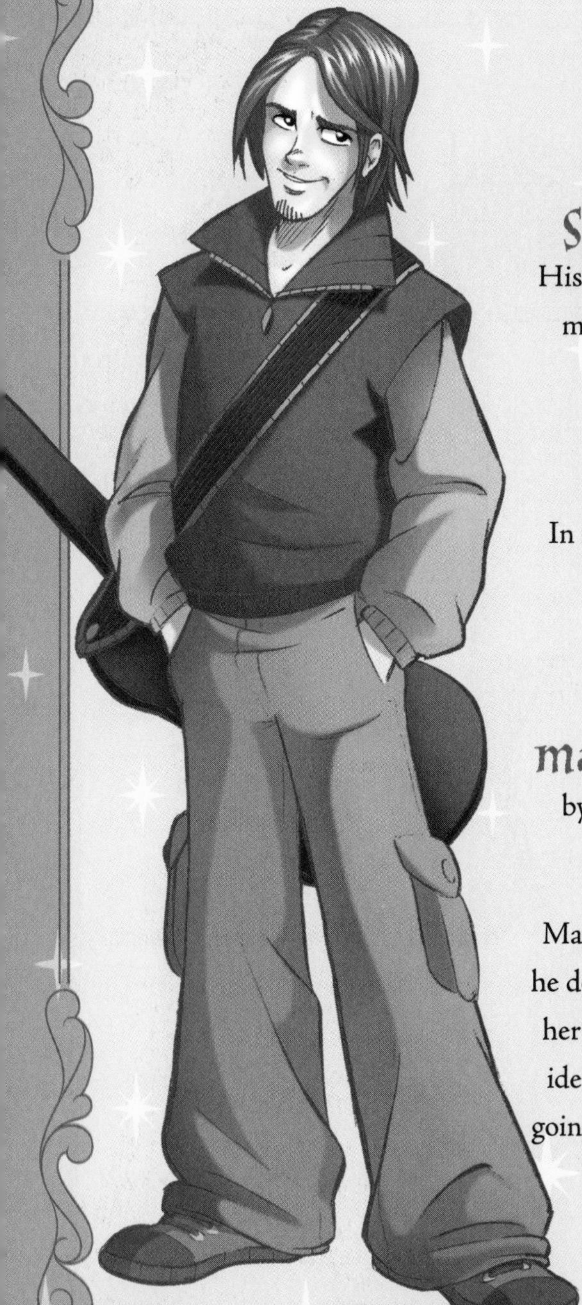

ASTONISHED BY...

Matt

He's in his fourth year at **Sheffield Institute.** His grades are fine, but he devotes most of his free time to music.

Is part of the band **Cobalt Blue.**

In his spare time, he helps out at his grandfather's pet store (He loves it a lot.)

Has a weakness for the **massive** Saint Bernard owned by his friend Jackie Gilligan, a special customer.

Matt is fascinated by Will even if he doesn't understand why. He met her **astral drop** and had no idea. Are Will's mysterious ways going to end up breaking his heart?

ASTONISHED BY...

Peter

Taranee's **older brother.**
His full name is Peter Lancelot.

A fifth-year student at Heatherfield's **Art Institute**, Peter splits his time between the studio, his friends, and sports.

Passionate about **basketball, surfing,** and extreme sports, he's always looking for new activities.

Doesn't have a girlfriend, but he has a special friendship with **Cornelia**.

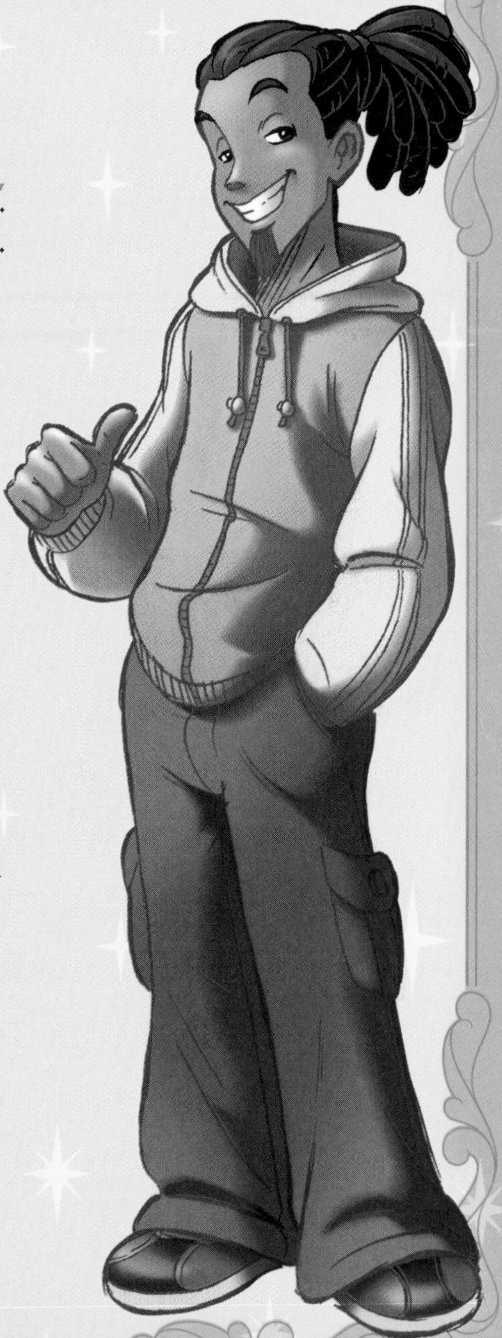

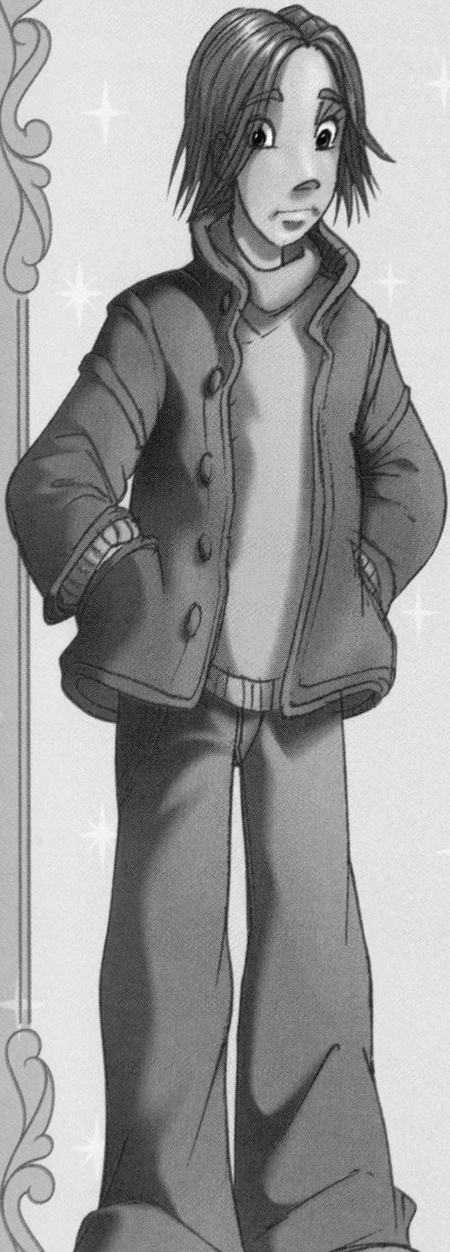

ASTONISHED BY...

Nigel

Nigel Ascroft is classmates with Uriah and his crew and is in his **fourth year** at the Sheffield Institute. School has never been more beautiful since he cut ties with his former "friends."

Quiet and thoughtful, Nigel hid his sensitive side for far too long.

Meeting **Taranee** changed him, but this new friendship also brought new challenges. Nigel isn't particularly well-liked by Taranee's mother, **Judge Cook**.

In the aftermath of the infamous incident at the Heatherfield Museum, Judge Cook was the one who sentenced Nigel (along with Uriah and his **crew**) to three months of community service at the museum.

W.I.T.C.H.

Will Irma Taranee Cornelia Hay Lin

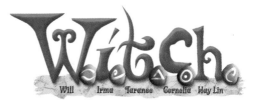

Read on in Volume 5!

Part II. Nerissa's Revenge • Volume I

Series Created by Elisabetta Gnone
Comic Art Direction: Alessandro Barbucci, Barbara Canepa

W.I.T.C.H.: The Graphic Novel, Part II: Nerissa's Revenge © Disney Enterprises, Inc.

English translation © 2018 by Disney Enterprises, Inc.

JY
1290 Avenue of the Americas
New York, NY 10104

Visit us at yenpress.com
facebook.com/yenpress
twitter.com/yenpress
yenpress.tumblr.com
instagram.com/yenpress

First JY Edition: January 2018

JY is an imprint of Yen Press, LLC.
The JY name and logo are trademarks of Yen Press, LLC.

The publisher is not responsible for websites (or their content) that are not owned by the publisher.

Library of Congress Control Number: 2017950917

ISBNs:
978-0-316-51834-5 (paperback)
978-0-316-41510-1 (ebook)

10 9 8 7 6 5 4 3 2 1

LSC-C

Printed in the United States of America

Cover Art by Daniela Vetro
Colors by Andrea Cagol

Translation by Linda Ghio and Stephanie Dagg at Editing Zone
Lettering by Katie Blakeslee

I KNOW WHO YOU ARE

Concept and Script by Francesco Artibani
Layout by Claudio Sciarrone
Art by Federico Bertolucci and Gianluca Panniello
Inks by Marina Baggio and Roberta Zanotta
Color Direction by Francesco Legramandi
Title Page Art by Federico Bertolucci with Colors by Andrea Cagol

END OF A DREAM

Concept and Script by Bruno Enna
Art by Daniela Vetro
Inks by Marina Baggio and Roberta Zanotta
Title Page Art by Daniela Vetro with Colors by Marco Collett

THE COURAGE TO CHOOSE

Concept and Script by Paola Mulazzi
Layout by Giovanni Rigano
Pencils by Graziano Barbaro
Inks by Marina Baggio and Roberta Zanotta
Color and Light Direction by Francesco Legramandi
Title Page Art by Giovanni Rigano with Colors by Marco Colletti

THE MARK OF NERISSA

Concept and Script by Francesco Artibani
Layout and Pencils by Alessia Martusciello
Inks by Marina Baggio and Roberta Zanotta
Color and Light Direction by Francesco Legramandi
Title Page Art by Alessia Martusciello with Colors by Marco Colletti